THE NOVEL OF FERRARA

GIORGIO BASSANI

THE NOVEL OF FERRARA

TRANSLATED BY

Jamie McKendrick

FOREWORD BY

André Aciman

W. W. Norton & Company

INDEPENDENT PUBLISHERS SINCE 1923

NEW YORK / LONDON

For information about special discounts for bulk purchases, please contact
W. W. Norton Special Sales at specialsales@wwnorton.com or 800-233-4830

Manufacturing by LSC Communications Harrisonburg
Book design by Brooke Koven
Production manager: Julia Druskin

ISBN: 978-0-393-08015-5

W. W. Norton & Company, Inc., 500 Fifth Avenue, New York, N.Y. 10110
www.wwnorton.com

W. W. Norton & Company Ltd., 15 Carlisle Street, London W1D 3BS

1 2 3 4 5 6 7 8 9 0

For Niccolò Gallo
To his memory

Certo, il cuore, chi gli dà retta, ha sempre qualche cosa da dire su quello che sarà. Ma che sa il cuore? Appena un poco di quello che è già accaduto.

Of course, for whoever pays heed to it, the heart always has something to say about what's to come. But what does the heart know? Just the least bit about what has happened already.

—ALESSANDRO MANZONI,
I promessi sposi (The Betrothed),
CHAPTER VIII

CONTENTS

FOREWORD

André Aciman

DISCOVERED Giorgio Bassani a year after leaving Rome and settling in New York. I was seventeen that year and totally transfixed by a city the likes of which I'd never seen before. Yet within two or three months, I found myself increasingly, almost desperately, homesick for Italy. The only way to quell the crippling nostalgia for what seemed a world I'd left behind was to lay my hands on every Italian writer whose books I could find at Rizzoli, located in those years on 56th Street, off Fifth Avenue. While living in Rome, I had always been reluctant to read Italian authors—now I devoured them: Alberto Moravia, Carlo Levi, Primo Levi, Vasco Pratolini, Carlo Cassola, Elio Vittorini, Elsa Morante, Cesare Pavese, Natalia Ginzburg, Curzio Malaparte, Ignazio Silone, and, of course, Giuseppe Tomasi di Lampedusa. Lampedusa was already a classic, and in a category all his own. But most all the other writers, with the exception of Pirandello, Svevo, and D'Annunzio, whom I also read that year, had started to publish under Mussolini and established themselves after the fall of Fascism and the end of the Second World War. They were still alive and writing in a contemporary, almost spoken, idiom. In their words I found inflections of the Italy I missed and feared I wouldn't revisit in a long time.

Of all of these writers, the only one whose sensibility struck an immediate chord in me was Giorgio Bassani. He wrote with an intimate understanding of how devastating it can be for some to witness the end of an era, while the experience almost rolls off the shoulders of others. He understood both the helplessness of those who've suffered irreparable horrors and the shrug of others who watched these crimes committed but chose to turn a blind eye. It is hardly surprising to learn that, while Elio Vittorini refused to publish *The Leopard*, by his fellow-Sicilian Giuseppe Tomasi di Lampedusa, it was Bassani, a Jewish northerner who had lived through the virtual end of Ferrara's Jewry, who upheld its publication. Perhaps the two authors shared a vivid sense of how tragic and ultimately ugly and destructive the end of a way of life can be, whether of Lampedusa's declining nineteenth-century Sicilian aristocracy or, more violently, of Bassani's deported Jews of Ferrara. Bassani could never undo the haunting end of Ferrara's Jewish life, the way I too, as an expelled Jew born and raised in Alexandria, Egypt, am still unable to forget—or forgive—the rapid extinction of Jewish and cosmopolitan life in what was once my homeland.

Bassani had lived through Fascism and under Mussolini's racial laws of 1938. These laws prevented Italian Jews from practicing several professions or from hiring help or attending university. Mussolini's alliance with Hitler eventually sent many Italian Jews either into voluntary exile or into hiding, or ultimately to death camps. Some, as Bassani himself records, were shot dead by Mussolini's *squadristi*; others, however, had been fervent Fascists before the advent of the racial laws and didn't quite know now how to navigate a world that was changing faster than they could reckon. They never found their bearings again.

Carlo Levi, Primo Levi, and Natalia (herself née Levi) Ginzburg, as well as Alberto Moravia and Elsa Morante, were also Jewish or partly Jewish, though most were indeed totally secularized; Natalia's husband was killed by the Fascists, and as for Primo Levi, he survived Auschwitz and left perhaps the most clear-eyed portrait of life in the German camps.

Still, Bassani's world is different; it is about people who for one reason or another find themselves suddenly pushed to the margins of a world where, until intolerance became the norm in the late 1930s, they had thrived and led secure, highly respected lives in Ferrara. But things don't last and, for all their stature and position, they don't fight back, or don't know how. The dazzling, wealthy heartbreaker Micòl Finzi-Contini becomes an easy victim of the Shoah; the prestigious Dr. Athos Fadigati turns into a hapless homosexual who loses everything from his wealth to his reputation because of a thuggish slap in public; the camp survivor Geo Josz can never undo the memory of what he saw; and the syphilitic, reclusive, frightened Pino Basilari won't even testify to a crime he witnessed from his very window. Some of Bassani's characters are what the Portuguese call *retornados*, people who return after years, sometimes after generations, to their place of origin, to feel no less uprooted in their own homes than in the places left behind. In Bassani, however, they return to live among those who robbed them of everything.

Bassani left Ferrara, moved to Rome, and made Rome his home. But his prose teems with the names of Ferrara's streets and piazzas, its buildings, movie theaters, restaurants, even brothels. In Bassani, one will always watch a young man riding a bicycle and parking it against a wall somewhere to feel one with a city he still loves but probably foretells won't ever be home again. Bassani's world is a cartography of a city that could only be restored with words, restored to what it was before Hitler, before Fascism, before the war shook the ground beneath him and took so many loved ones away, restored to what perhaps it never really was but might have been. In this the imagination of the historian and the memory of the fiction writer are constantly trading places and can no longer be told apart.

INTRODUCTION

Jamie McKendrick

TAKING a break from the 2016 centenary conference on Giorgio Bassani in Ferrara, where scholars, editors, and translators from all over Europe had gathered to celebrate his work, I found myself in Via Vittoria in front of a disused, derelict building. Its sombre facade of ancient brickwork was undistinguished in appearance from the other neighboring houses, except for a white marble plaque next to the arched doorway. Erected by the Jewish Community of Ferrara on 20 November 1992, that, too, was commemorating a centenary: a quincentenary of the same date in 1492, when Duke Ercole I d'Este had welcomed the Jews exiled from Spain to the city. It also recorded how the Sephardic synagogue on this site had been destroyed by the Nazis in 1944. Its twelve lines spanned five hundred years of history, asserted the place of Sephardic culture in Italy, and recorded these acts of welcome and persecution.

Was this then, I wondered, the site of the third synagogue mentioned in Bassani's *The Garden of the Finzi-Continis* as the place of worship for a small section of the Jewish community, the "Fanese," somewhat shadowy and intriguing to the narrator, whose family attended the main temple in nearby Via Mazzini? The inscription immediately recalled the use Bassani makes—throughout his work, but especially in *Within the Walls*—of the city's public memorials, its plaques, statues, and funerary inscriptions, and of his impulse to flesh out the history hidden behind the public print with the story of the complex private lives of those who witnessed the recorded events.

In that book of short stories alone, apart from the commemorative plaque of General Diaz's 1918 victory speech in the school where Clelia Trotti teaches, two other public memorials take center stage in the narrative. "A Memorial Tablet in Via Mazzini" begins with a peasant boy affixing to the temple facade a tablet listing the names of the 183 Jews deported to the camps and murdered by the Nazis. His work is interrupted by the hesitant protest of a certain Geo Josz, a survivor erroneously listed among the dead. The second is a plaque erected on the wall of the Estense Castle moat that commemorates the eleven citizens rounded up by a Blackshirt squad and shot at dawn on November 15, 1943. These are crucial dates in Ferrara's history, and Bassani's stories explore their significance in the most unexpected ways.

Giorgio Bassani and Ferrara are as inseparable as James Joyce and Dublin or Italo Svevo and Trieste. Like Joyce, Bassani spent only a small but crucial portion of his life in the city of his major work. Though he was born—"accidentally," he claimed—in Bologna, his whole youth was spent in Ferrara, and though he studied at the University of Bologna, under the tuition of the eminent art historian Roberto Longhi, he commuted by train. Those journeys in third class are memorably evoked in several chapters of *The Gold-Rimmed Spectacles* as well as in "Verso Ferrara," one of the high points of his first collection of poems:

> *At this hour when through the hot endless grasslands*
> *the last trains make their way toward Ferrara,*
> *their languid whistles fade as sleep engulfs them*
> *along with the lingering red on village towers.*

Despite the Racial Laws, he graduated in 1939 and taught in the city's Jewish school until he was arrested, in May 1943, for the anti-Fascist activities in which he'd been engaged since his student days. He was released in July, the day after Mussolini was removed from power by the Grand Fascist Council and Victor Emmanuel III. Immediately after his release, Bassani married Valeria Sinigallia, whom he had met in Ferrara's Marfisa tennis club—the model for his Eleanora D'Este Tennis Club, which in the early chapters of *The Garden of the Finzi-Continis* excluded Ferrara's Jews. Two months later, as the Allied forces pushed northward through Italy, the Germans reinstalled Mussolini in the puppet Social Republic of Salò, which, with their military assistance, controlled northern and central Italy and, therefore, Ferrara as well. With Mussolini back in power, the couple had to live under assumed names, first in Florence, then in Rome. After the war, Bassani never returned to live in Ferrara but remained in Rome, where among other jobs he worked as the editor of the prominent literary magazine *Botteghe Oscure* and later in the publishing house Feltrinelli, for whom he had the discernment to accept Giuseppe de Lampedusa's *The Leopard* after it had been rejected by all of Italy's other major publishing houses. Bassani died in 2000 and was buried in the Jewish cemetery in Ferrara, which he describes so vividly in the first chapter of *The Garden of the Finzi-Continis.*

Situated in the Po Valley in Emilia-Romagna in the northeast of Italy, Ferrara was a potent and flourishing city during the Renaissance. Since that time, it had gradually declined in power and influence, but it remained relatively prosperous. During Bassani's youth, the city's population grew from around 110,000 to 120,000. A small though civically prominent community of some seven hundred Jews lived mainly in the triangle formed by the streets Via Vignatagliata, Via Vittoria, and Via Mazzini—the last being the site of the Jewish Temple, which included two active synagogues, one referred to as the "German School," the other as the "Italian School." The presence of three distinct places of worship within such a small area already signals how diverse this community was. The diversity is also reflected in Bassani's warmly inclusive diction, which employs words, phrases, and sentences from Greek, Latin, Hebrew, German, French, English, and Ferrarese, Veneto and Hispano-Jewish dialects, not to mention the peculiar family idiolect of Micòl and Alberto, referred to as *"finzi-continico."* During the 1930s, Ferrara was a stronghold of Fascist adhesion; and notorious squads of Blackshirts controlled the city. In its earlier phase, many Jews, like their Catholic neighbors, were supporters of Fascism; by the latter part of the decade, however, with what became known as *"la svolta al razzismo"*—the turn toward racism—the well-integrated Jewish community found itself utterly isolated.

The six books that make up *The Novel of Ferrara* were published separately between 1956 and 1972, and each, with the possible exception of *The Smell of Hay,* is freestanding and self-sufficient. Yet Bassani chose to extensively and rigorously revise them in order to unite them under the title *Il romanzo di Ferrara,* published in Italy in 1974 and republished after further revisions in 1980. That complete *Novel of Ferrara* in its definitive, final revision now appears in English translation for the first time. At some stage in the writing, it became clear to Bassani that the six books shared not only time and place and a cast of characters but also an essential aesthetic unity. The seed of the entire work—its nucleus and donnée—is already present and apparent in *Within the Walls,* first published as *Cinque storie ferraresi (Five Stories of Ferrara).* In the concluding piece of the whole *Romanzo,* the author steps forward *in prima persona* to give an account of the composition of that first book, and its title "Down There, at the End of the Corridor" echoes a phrase stressed in the opening of the very first story, "Lida Mantovani."

The nearest English equivalent for the word *romanzo* is the generic term "novel," but in Italian it also carries the echo of an older meaning, one that goes back to the medieval "romance"—originally a poem that celebrated the chivalric adventures of a hero or group of protagonists. It's likely that for Bassani the term held some of these poetic resonances. After all, as he insisted in an interview, he was as much a poet as a novelist. That may help explain why he designated this gathering of four short novels and two collections of short stories by the *singular* title of *Romanzo.* But it's also important to remember that for Bassani the role of the poet is to "return from the realm of the dead and speak of what he saw there," as he remarked in the same interview—explicitly referring to the character Geo Josz, who becomes a living record of a history that, during the Liberation, was in the process of erasure; Josz is therefore an increasingly uncomfortable reminder of what his Ferrarese neighbors are busily trying to forget.

Bassani's *Romanzo* has unforgettably put his city, and the Jewish community he belonged to, on the map of modern consciousness. While Ferrara is present in all its formidable weight throughout, it still had to be rebuilt in his imagination, and the birth of this imaginary city had a slow gestation. (In his first collection of stories, *A City of the Plain,* published in 1940— with the Racial Laws prohibiting Jewish publications in full effect—under the nom de plume of Giacomo Marchi, Ferrara is referred to merely as "F.") Aspects of the city's history are adumbrated throughout the *Romanzo,* but the central and recurrent historical focus in most of the works is the Fascist era, and most specifically 1938, the year in which the Racial Laws were enacted. These laws followed the German precedent of the Nuremberg Laws and severely curtailed the lives of Italian Jews with regard to employment, education, and intermarriage, making them, hitherto respected citizens, "strangers in their own home," in the telling phrase of the Portuguese poet Tatiana Faia. This theme emerges again and again for the characters in Bassani's fiction. Both *The Garden of the Finzi-Continis* and, even more centrally, *The Gold-Rimmed Spectacles* observe the process of "eviction" through the eyes of Bassani's first-person narrator, an unnamed alter ego, the "I" of both these books and also of *Behind the Door.* Bassani declared that the "I," which he came to realize was such an essential element in the narrative, was a figure who was not exactly himself, although "very like" in numerous respects.

In *The Gold-Rimmed Spectacles,* the fate of marginalization that befalls the Jewish narrator is shared by the homosexual doctor Athos Fadigati, and it's an act of imaginative generosity that allows Bassani to explore the subtle and devastating parallels between the two figures in this compact masterpiece.

On his return from Buchenwald, Geo Josz finds his house occupied by the partisans and is forced to encamp in the attic, awaiting its delayed repossession. But there are various, less explicit forms of estrangement enacted in these novels. The schoolboy narrator of *Behind the Door* ends the novel alienated from his family and his own well-being because of the treachery of a school companion—a unique case that, the narrator himself concedes, has for once little to do with his Jewish identity. The fiercely hierarchical and competitive school, however, foreshadows some of the cruelties and divisions that will soon become evident in the political sphere.

Perhaps the most profound treatment of eviction occurs in *The Garden of the Finzi-Continis,* where the narrator first experiences the increasing ostracism of the Jewish community; but then, in a turn that is even more psychologically devastating, he is expelled from the Edenic garden itself, which had offered a haven from this trauma. The loss of the garden is also linked to the loss of his first love, the radiant, precocious and elusive Micòl. Of the four "novels" within the *Novel, The Heron* is the most atypical, not sharing the same first-person narrator of the other three, and being mainly set *outside* the city walls, in the nearby countryside. Yet it offers a particularly extreme and harrowing study of the corrosive effects of exclusion. Edgardo Limentani has returned from his Swiss exile and, in the compass of single winter day of 1947, comes to know his full estrangement from his time, his city, his family, and finally his own life.

In his concluding essay, "Down There, at the End of the Corridor," Bassani describes how, when composing his stories, he would find a geometric image taking shape in his mind. His account is oddly like the dream of the ouroboros that helped Friedrich August Kekulé resolve the chemical structure of the benzene ring. One such image that presides over "A Memorial Tablet in Via Mazzini" is of two spheres circling one another, the two spheres being the irreconcilable entities: the city of Ferrara and Geo Josz. It's an image that could serve beyond the particular story's parameters for the entire *Romanzo*. If we see one orbiting circle as Bassani, or his various narrators, and the wall-encircled city of Ferrara as the other, we might have a simplified vision of the intricate construction and interlocking of these six books.

The geometrical images that guided Bassani—his visual imagination likely fostered by his study of art history—highlight a significant feature of his fiction. It is an exploration not only of time lost and time preserved but of space—especially architectural and urban spaces: cemeteries, gardens, streets, porticoes, and, foremost among these, the Jewish Temple described with such virtuosity in *The Garden of the Finzi-Continis*. But even domestic interiors in Bassani are laden with significance. The cramped basement flat in "Lida Mantovani," "Professor" Ermanno Finzi-Contini's crowded study, Dr. Fadigati's surgery, with its aspirational elegance, and the storeroom in Dr. Elia Corcos's mansion are just a few examples of the way space shapes and impinges upon the lives of his characters. Perhaps the most intriguing interior description is of the chemist's room in "A Night in '43"—the room from which Pino Barilari witnesses the massacre of Ferrara's citizens by the squad of Blackshirts and which Bassani approaches with an extraordinary circuitous tact. But none of these instances serve a merely decorative purpose; they are, rather, manifestations of time, or magnetic force fields for history.

The city walls—the *"bastioni,"* as Bassani often metonymically refers to them—are both literal and metaphorical, and are not only the traditional place for romantic trysts but offer views out beyond into the flat countryside of the Po Valley; they are also the site of the first real encounter between the narrator and Micòl. The city walls are topped with a broad tree-lined avenue, along which one can walk or cycle almost uninterruptedly the entire nine-kilometer circumference of the city. (And Ferrara is still one of the few Italian cities where bicycles are the main mode of transport.) One frequently mentioned site, just within the walls at the southeast of the city, is Montagnone ("the big mountain"), which is actually a small hill built from the stone left from the construction of the walls and later turned into a garden. These walls, encrusted with history, are the verdant lookouts and the protective but also imprisoning circle for the many lives that Bassani's fiction illuminates, and there are walls within the walls— the inner walls encircle what was once the ghetto, walled in when Ferrara became one of the Papal States, which leads Bassani to describe his community as *"intra muros."*

Time is not only factored into the tenses and structure of the narrative but is integral to the style and syntax. The characteristically long sentences, rich in subclauses and lengthy embedded parentheses—a translator's challenge, or nightmare—have a way of slowing up time, which is moving toward an ineluctable and fatal conclusion, and resembles those tennis matches played in the idyllic garden of the Finzi-Continis deep into dusk when the ball becomes all but invisible yet the play continues. A more declared sense of the passage of time is perceptible in *The Heron,* which begins when Limentani awakens to the insistent but discreet alarm of his Jaeger clock, and continues as on almost every page he anxiously consults his Swiss Vacheron-Constantin wristwatch to check the time as it elapses. The whole story takes a day (and Bassani speculated that the experience of reading it might be of the same duration)—a day we assume to be the last day in the protagonist's life, and so observing an inexorable Aristotelian unity. (The four sections of the novel, each comprising six chapters, amount, aptly enough, to twenty-four.) The only passage where this succession is suspended is during a midafternoon sleep, which disrupts the tedium of clock time with a bright and confusing dream time that accurately tells of the character's psychic disturbance, the way he is utterly out of step with his times. A well-off, land-owning Jew, he has returned from Swiss exile after the defeat of Fascism to find that he is hated by his tenants and effectively estranged from his home and his Christian wife, while the ex-Fascist Bellagamba, a bullying Blackshirt, has adapted perfectly to the new regime and has set up a prospering hotel restaurant in the neighboring small town of Codigoro.

The actual places and factual dates—sometimes, as I've mentioned, the two combine on memorial plaques and monuments—are Bassani's material, and I can think of no other writer of fiction so concerned with factuality. He claimed to be "one of the few, the very few, contemporary writers who places dates in the context of what he writes." When Vittorio de Sica made his cinematic version of *The Garden of the Finzi-Continis* and had the narrator's father in the end transported to the death camps, Bassani indignantly withdrew his name from the film. That "it didn't happen like that" would seem a strange objection from a novelist, but this gives us an idea of how significant historical veracity was to Bassani. Nevertheless—and this is where the overarching title of *Romanzo* needs to be kept in mind—only through the imaginative liberties he learned how to take, with the material he knew so intimately, could the novelist arrive, as he so convincingly does, at such a fierce and truthful evocation of the reality he, his community, and his city lived through.

THE NOVEL OF FERRARA

: | :

Within the Walls

Lida Mantovani

1.

TURNING back to the distant years of her youth, always, for as long as she lived, Lida Mantovani remembered the birth with emotion, and especially the days just before it. Whenever she thought about it, she was deeply moved.

For more than a month she had lived stretched out on a bed, at the end of a corridor, and for all that time she had done nothing but stare through the usually wide-open window opposite at the leaves of the huge, ancient magnolia which surged up right in the middle of the garden below. Then, toward the end, three or four days before her labor pains began, she had suddenly lost interest even in the magnolia's black leaves, which were shiny, as though they'd been oiled. She had even given up eating. A thing, that's what she'd shrunk into being: a kind of very swollen and numbed thing—although it was only April, it was already warm—abandoned down there, at the end of a hospital corridor.

She hardly ate anything. But Professor Bargellesi, then head of the maternity ward, would repeat that it was better that way.

He observed her from the foot of the bed.

"It's really hot," he'd say, with those frail and reddened fingers of his smoothing his big white beard, stained with nicotine around the mouth. "If you want to breathe as you should, it's better to keep your weight down.

And anyway"—he would add, smiling—"anyway, it seems to me you're quite fat enough already . . ."

2.

AFTER THE birth, time began to pass once more.

At first, thinking of David—irritated, unhappy, he hardly ever spoke to her, staying in bed for whole days, his face hidden under a book or else sleeping—Lida Mantovani tried to keep going on her own in the furnished room of the big apartment block in Via Mortara where she had lived with him for the last six months. But then, after a few more weeks, convinced that she'd heard the last of him, and realizing that the few hundred lire he'd left her were about to run out, and since, besides, her milk was beginning to run dry, she decided to return home to her mother. So in the summer of that same year, Lida reappeared in Via Salinguerra, and began once more to occupy the unattractive room, with its dusty wooden floor and its two iron beds arranged side by side, where she had spent her childhood, adolescence and the first years of her young adulthood.

Although it had once been a carpenter's wood store, entering was by no means easy.

When you made your way into the vestibule, huge and dark as a hay-barn, you had to climb up by a little staircase which obliquely cut across the left-hand wall. The staircase led to a low half-door, and having passed the threshold you found your head brushing a ceiling with small beams, and were suddenly faced with a kind of well. God! How sad it all was, Lida said to herself the evening she returned home, lingering for a moment up there to look down . . . and yet, at the same time, what a sense of peace and protection . . . With the baby draped around her neck, she had slowly descended the steps of the inner staircase, and had walked toward her mother, who in the meantime had lifted her eyes from her sewing, and finally leaned down to give her a kiss on the cheek. And the kiss, without a single word, greeting or comment having passed between them, was returned.

Almost immediately the question of the baptism had to be confronted.

As soon as she became aware of the situation, the mother crossed herself.

"Are you mad?" she exclaimed.

While the mother spoke, anxiously declaring that there wasn't a moment to be lost, Lida felt the shriveling of any will to resist. At the maternity ward, when they had crowded around the bed to hold the baby and had excitedly asked what name she meant to give him, she suddenly thought she must do nothing against David, and this made her reply, No, they should hold off for a bit, she wanted to think about it for a while longer. But now, why on earth should she continue to have any scruples? What would she still be waiting for? That very evening the baby was taken to Santa Maria in Vado. It was her mother who had arranged everything, it was she who argued that he should be called Ireneo, in memory of a dead brother of whose existence Lida had never even been aware . . . Mother and daughter had rushed to the church as though pursued. But they returned slowly, as if drained of all energy, along Via Borgo di Sotto, where the municipal lamplighter was doing his rounds, lighting the streetlamps one by one.

The next morning they began working together again.

Seated again as they had once been, as they had always been before, under the rectangular window which opened above them at street level, their foreheads bent over their sewing, rather than speaking of the time they had recently passed through, so bitter for both of them, they preferred, when the occasion arose, to talk of inconsequential things. They felt more closely bound together than before, much better friends. Both of them, all the same, understood that their harmony could only thus be preserved on condition that they avoided any reference to the sole topic on which their closeness depended.

Sometimes, however, unable to resist, Maria Mantovani risked a joke, a veiled allusion.

She might venture with a sigh:

"Ah, all men are the same!"

Or even:

"Men are always on the prowl—that's for sure."

At this, having raised her head, she would stare raptly at her daughter, remembering, at the same time, the blacksmith of Massa Fiscaglia, who, twenty years earlier, had taken her virginity and made her pregnant; remembering the rented farmhouse, hidden among the fields two or three kilometers outside Massa, where she had been born and grown up, and which, with a little girl to raise, she had had to leave forever; the greasy, ruffled hair, the fat sensual lips, the lazy gestures of the only man in her life would become superimposed upon the figure of David, the young gentleman of Ferrara, Jewish, it's true, but belonging to one of the richest and most respected families of the town (those Camaiolis who lived on Corso Giovecca, just imagine, in that big house that they themselves owned), who for a long while had been making love to Lida, but whom she herself had never known, never once seen, even from a distance. She looked, she watched. Thin, sharp, whittled away by suffering and worry, it was as if in Lida she saw herself as a girl. Everything had been repeated, everything. From A to Z.

One evening she suddenly burst out laughing. She grabbed Lida by the hand and dragged her in front of the wardrobe mirror.

"Just look how similar we've become," she said in a stifled voice.

And while nothing was audible in the room except the whisper of the carbide lamp, they remained staring at their faces for a long time, side by side, almost indistinguishable in the misted surface.

That's not to say that their relations always ran smoothly. Lida was not always prepared to listen without fighting back.

One evening, for example, Maria Mantovani had started telling her own story—something that could never have happened before. At the end she came out with a phrase that made Lida jump to her feet.

"If his parents had been in favor," she had said, "we'd have got married."

Lying on the bed, her face hidden in her hands, Lida silently repeated these words, hearing once again the sigh full of resentment which had accompanied them. No, she wouldn't weep. And, to her mother, who had run after her and who had breathlessly leaned over her, she displayed, as she raised herself up, her cheeks dry, a look full of contempt and boredom.

Otherwise her irritations were rare and if they afflicted her, they did so without warning, like tempestuous squalls on a day of fine weather.

"Lida!" the daughter exclaimed once with a spiteful laugh (her mother was calling her by her name). "How important it was for you when I went to school that I wrote it on my exercise book with that fancy 'y.' What on earth did you think I was going to be—a showgirl?"

Maria Mantovani didn't reply. She smiled. Her daughter's tantrum transported her back to distant events, events whose significance she alone was in a position to assess. "*Lyda!*" she kept repeating to herself. She thought about her own youth. She thought of Andrea, Andrea Tardozzi, the Massa Fiscaglia blacksmith who had been her sweetheart, her lover, and would have been her husband. She had come to live in the city with her baby, and every Sunday he travelled sixty kilometers by bicycle, thirty on the way there, and thirty back. He sat there, just where Lida was now sitting. She seemed to see him once again, with his leather jacket, his corduroy trousers, his tousled hair. Until one night, as he was returning to the village, he was taken by surprise by a heavy rain and fell ill with pleurisy. From then on she never saw him again. He had gone to live in Feltre in the Veneto: a small town at the foot of the mountains, where he took a wife and had children. If his parents hadn't been against it, and if, following that, he hadn't got ill, he would have married her. That was for sure. What did Lida know? What could she understand? She alone understood everything. For the two of them.

After supper, Lida was usually the first to go to bed. But the other bed, beside the one where she and the baby were already asleep, often remained untouched until late into the night, while in the center of the table, still to be cleared, the gas lamp shed its blueish glow.

3.

RATHER IRREGULAR in shape, its cobblestones partly overgrown with grass, Via Salinguerra is a small, subsidiary street which begins in an ill-shapen square, the result of an ancient demolition, and ends at the foot of the city's walls quite close to Porta San Giorgio. This places it within the city and not that far from the medieval center: to confirm this impression, you only need to look at the appearance of the houses which flank both its sides, all of them very poor and of modest proportions, and some old and decrepit, undoubtedly among the oldest in Ferrara. And yet, strolling down Via Salinguerra, even today, the kind of silence that surrounds it (heard from here, the city's church bells have a different timbre, as though muffled and lost) and especially the smell of manure, of ploughed earth, of cowsheds, which reveal the proximity of large hidden vegetable gardens, all contribute to the impression of being outside the circle of the city walls, on the edge of the open countryside.

The restful voices of animals, of chickens, dogs, even oxen, distant bells, agricultural effluvia: sounds and smells even drifted down to the depths of the carpenter's storehouse where Lida and Maria Mantovani worked in men's tailoring. Seated just beside the window, almost as motionless and silent as the grey pieces of furniture behind them—as the table, that is, and the raffia armchairs, and the long narrow beds, the cradle, the wardrobe, the bedside table and three-legged washbowl with the ewer of water beside it, and further back, barely visible, the little door under the stairs which hid the small kitchen and toilet—when they raised their heads from the fabric, it was only to address the odd word to each other, to check that the baby didn't need anything, to look up outside at the rare passers-by, or, at the sudden shriek of the doorbell hung above the drab rectangle of the street entrance, to decide by a rapid exchange of glances which of the two would have to go upstairs to open it . . .

They passed three years like this.

And it might be supposed that many more would have passed in just the same manner, without any disruption or significant change, when life, which seemed to have forgotten them, suddenly recalled their existence through the person of a neighbor: a certain Benetti, Oreste Benetti, the owner of a bookbinding workshop in Via Salinguerra. The peculiar insistence with which he began to pay them visits in the evening after supper almost immediately assumed, at least for Maria, an unequivocal meaning. Yes—she thought, getting flustered—that Benetti's coming round expressly to see Lida . . . After all Lida was still young, very young indeed. At once she became lively, bustling, even happy. Without ever interrupting the talks between her daughter and the guest, she confined herself to walking about the room, glad to be there, it was clear, content to be present but self-contained, and to await and observe the emergence of a rare and delightful event.

In the meantime the one who spoke was nearly always the bookbinder. About the years gone by: it seemed that he had no interest in any other topic.

"When Lida was a little girl"—he said—"just this high," she often came to his workshop. She would enter, come forward, raise herself up on tiptoes so her eyes could be at the level of the workbench.

"Signor Benetti," she would ask him in her little voice, "would you give me a small piece of wax paper?"

"Gladly," he'd reply. "But may I know what you want it for?"

"Nothing. Just to cover my exercise book."

He would tell the story and laugh. Although he didn't speak to either of the women in particular, his looks were directed exclusively toward Lida. It was her attention and agreement that he sought. And while she observed the man in front of her (he had a very big head, which fitted his stout torso, but was out of proportion with the rest of his body), and in particular his large bony hands, forcibly clasped together on the tablecloth, she felt that at least in this respect she could hardly do other than try to please him. Facing him with a reserved courtesy, she spoke calmly, composedly and—deriving from this a strange, unaccustomed pleasure—in a somehow submissive manner.

Of nothing was the bookbinder more acutely aware than of his own importance. Nevertheless he was always in search of further kudos.

Once, on one of the few occasions when he addressed the old woman, even calling her by her Christian name, it was to remind her of the year she'd come to settle in Ferrara. Do you remember—he said—the cold we had that year? He did, very clearly. The abundant heaps of dirty snow that remained along both sides of the city streets until mid-April. And how the temperature had dropped so low the river Po itself had frozen.

"The Po itself!" he repeated with emphasis, widening his eyes.

It was as though he could still see it, he continued, the extraordinary sight of the river gripped in the sub-zero winds. Between the snow-heaped banks the river had ceased to flow, had totally seized up. So much so that, toward evening, instead of making use of the iron bridge at Pontelago-scuro to cross the river, some laborers—they must have been transporting firewood to a sawmill in Santa Maria Maddalena and were returning to Ferrara—preferred to risk their then-empty carts across the huge sheet of ice. What madmen! They advanced slowly, a few meters in front of their horses, holding the reins gathered in one fist behind their backs, as with their free hands they scattered sawdust, and meanwhile they whistled and yelled like the damned. Why were they whistling and yelling? Who knows? Perhaps to embolden the beasts, perhaps themselves. Or else simply to keep warm.

"I remember that famous winter," he began one evening, with the respectful tone he always assumed when he spoke of people and things with any religious connection (orphaned as a child and brought up in a seminary, he had retained for the priests there, for priests as a whole, a filial reverence), "I remember that famous winter, poor Don Castelli led us out every Saturday afternoon to Pontelagoscuro to look at the Po. As soon as we'd passed Porta San Benedetto the children broke out of their lines. Five kilometers there and five back—it wasn't just a stroll round the garden! And yet even to mention the tram to Don Castelli was big trouble. Although, given his age, he was gasping for air, he was always in front, always at the head of the whole troop with his fine soutane flowing and with yours truly at his side . . . A veritable saint, sure enough, and a real father to my humble self!"

"I had just given birth to the baby," Maria Mantovani put in, softly, in dialect, making the most of the silence that followed the bookbinder's speech. "In town I felt lost," she continued in Italian, "I didn't really know anyone. But on the other hand how could I go back home? You know how it was, Oreste: in the country, it's mainly the mentality that's different."

It seemed as though Oreste hadn't heard her.

"Apart from in 1917, there's never again been cold like that," he reckoned, deep in thought. "But what am I saying!" he added, raising his voice and shaking his head. "It's not even comparable. In the winter of 1917 it was warm—on the Carso!* You'd have to ask those on sick leave how it was

---

* The Carso was part of the Italian Front in the First World War, on mountainous terrain in what is now Slovenia; the terrible conditions were equivalent to the hardships of the trenches on the Western Front.

here, those shirkers—whom we all know—" these final words he stressed with a sarcastic tone—"never saw the Front, not even on a postcard."

Taking in the unusually brutal dig directed at Andrea Tardozzi, the blacksmith at Massa Fiscaglia who had been let off service because of pleurisy and for that reason hadn't been sent to war (in 1910 he had moved to Feltre, the Feltre up near the Alps, where he had settled with his family), Maria Mantovani stiffened, offended. And for the rest of that evening, cast out to brood alone in her corner over the innumerable events in her life that might have happened and that didn't, she spoke not another word.

As far as the bookbinder was concerned, having established, as he felt impelled to, the proper distance between them, he briskly resumed all the courtesy and gallantry that was his by nature. It was usually on himself and his own past that he dwelled. Till he was twenty, twenty-five, all had gone badly—he sighed—from every point of view. But afterward, work had changed that, his work, his craft, and from then on things turned around completely. "We craftsmen," he used to say, with no lack of pride, looking Lida straight in the eyes. Never distracted, Lida quietly received his gaze. And he was grateful, one could see it, that she always sat there, on the other side of the table, so silently, so serenely, so attentively, thereby corresponding in her whole aspect to his secret ideal of womanhood.

The bookbinder often talked on till midnight. Having exhausted his store of personal anecdotes, he began to talk of religion, of history, of the economy and so on, lapsing into frequent, bitter observations—expressed of course in a low tone—about the anti-Catholic politics of the Fascists. During the first period of his visits, without ceasing to listen to him, Lida would use the tip of her toe to rock the cradle in which Ireneo slept until he was four years old. Later, when he had grown a bit and had a little bed of his own (he grew up slight and frail, having contracted a long infectious illness when he was five that, apart from permanently weakening his health, undoubtedly influenced the frailty and lack of conviction of his character), Lida would get up from her chair every now and then and, approaching the child who was asleep, would lean over and place a hand on his forehead.

4.

IN THE summer of 1928, Lida had her twenty-fifth birthday.

One evening, while she and Oreste Benetti sat in their usual places, divided as ever by the table and the lamp, suddenly, very simply, the bookbinder asked her if she would marry him.

Soberly, without showing the least surprise, Lida stared at him.

It was as if she were seeing him for the first time. She considered with extraordinary care every detail of his face, his very black, watery eyes, his tall, white forehead topped by an arch of iron-grey hair cut short, like a toothbrush, in the style of certain priests and soldiers, and she was astounded to find herself there, to be taking note of all this only now, so late. He must have been about fifty. At least.

She was suddenly stricken by a wave of anxiety. Not able to say anything, she turned in search of help toward her mother, who, having risen to her feet, had come to the table and was leaning on it with both her hands. The grimace of impending tears that was already pulling down the corners of her mouth only added to her confusion.

"What's wrong with you?" she shouted angrily at her daughter in dialect. "Would you say what's wrong?"

Lida rose abruptly to her feet, rushed toward, then up the stairs—she left, slamming the door, and went down the other staircase to the entrance.

Having finally reached the street, she immediately leaned her back against the wall beside the dark gaping cavity of the wide-open doorway, and looked at the sky.

It was a magnificent starscape. In the distance a band could be heard. Where were they playing? she asked herself, with a sudden, spasmodic desire to mingle with the crowd, happy, dressed in a pinafore and holding an ice cream in her hand like a young girl without a care in the world. Was the sound coming from San Giorgio, in the clearing beside the church? Or else from Porta Reno, perhaps the Piazza Travaglio itself?

But by then her breathing was no longer so labored. And there it was, coming through the walls of old brick against which she rested the whole of her spine, there it was, reaching her, the whispering voice of Oreste Benetti. He was speaking to her mother, now, quietly as though nothing had happened. What was he saying? Who could tell? Whatever the words, his voice, the placid, subdued hum of his voice was enough to persuade her to calm down, to encourage her to go back inside. When she reappeared at the stair landing she was once again mistress of herself, of her thoughts and her gestures.

Having shut the door, gone down the stairs neither too hurriedly nor too deliberately, taking care not to catch the eyes of either the bookbinder or her mother—during her absence the two of them had remained in their places, he seated at the table, she standing: and there they still were, silent, examining her face with inquisitive gazes. She passed close by the table, sat down again in her place, and almost imperceptibly narrowed her shoulders. And the topic of marriage—for the nearly two hours that their guest still remained—was not broached again, nor was it in the course of the innumerable other evenings that were to follow.

This doesn't mean to suggest that Oreste Benetti nurtured any doubt whatsoever about what Lida's response would sooner or later be. Quite the contrary. For him, from that moment on, it was as though Lida had already consented, as though they were already fiancés.

This was evident from the different way he treated her: always solicitous and kind, yes, but within, deep down, there was an air of authority which had been lacking before. At this juncture, he alone—it seemed as though he wanted to declare—was in a position to guide her through life.

In his view, Lida's character had a serious defect—he was willing to say it openly, in such cases, not hesitating to call on Maria Mantovani as a witness with a sideways glance—which was always to be looking backward, always to be chewing over the past. Why not, for a change, force herself to look a little the other way, toward the future? Pride was a great ugly beast. Like a snake, it slithered in where you least expected it.

"You need to be reasonable," he sighed by way of conclusion. "You need to stay calm and keep going forward."

Other times, however, in apparent self-contradiction, even if by nods, by hints and carefully veiled insinuations—Lida following the skilful, tireless workings of his mind without ever reacting, as though hypnotized—it was actually he who showed her the picture of her youth: unregulated,

anarchic, unaware of the urgent need to achieve a higher maturity, a dignified and tranquil way of life.

And on this topic, yes, certainly—he also let it be understood—since
he loved her, he naturally understood, made excuses for her, forgave everything. His feelings, however, were not so blinded, she should realize, as
to stop him remembering (and making her remember) that she had committed a gross error, a mortal sin from which she would only be absolved
the day she was married. What on earth had she imagined? Had she perhaps dreamed that a man of her own breed—who, besides, as she was well
aware, was almost thirty years older—could think of love outside of marriage, of a Catholic marriage? Marriage was a duty, a mission. The true
believer was incapable of conceiving of life, and consequently of the relationship between man and woman, in any other way . . .

All three of them, however, were in such a state of nervous tension,
were so continually on the alert, that it would have needed little indeed
to throw the fragile balance of their relations into crisis. After every clash,
they remained uneasy, sulky, holding on to their grudges.

On one occasion, for example, referring to Ireneo, the bookbinder said
that truly he wished the baby well: just as if he were his father. Betrayed by
the heat of the moment, he had let himself go a shade too far.

"But just a second, aren't you Uncle Oreste?" exclaimed Ireneo, who
was already seven years old, and had acquired the habit of showing him his
homework before he was put to bed.

"Of course . . . you understand . . . It was only a manner of speaking.
What strange things go through your mind!"

The bookbinder's confusion suddenly gave Lida a clear sense of her
own importance. While, a bit breathlessly, the good man kept on talking
to the child, she and her mother exchanged glances and smiled.

But the moments of silent tension and malice were, all considered,
quite rare. To avert them, or leave them behind, presents always played
a useful role. Right from the start, Oreste Benetti had always been lav-
ish with those. Although he had made it clear that after the wedding they
would all move together to a little villa beyond Porta San Benedetto (for
which he was negotiating terms of sale with a building firm, but, despite
that, he had promptly had the electric lights installed and the walls white-

washed and had bought various bits of furniture, a cheap cast-iron stove, a picture, some kitchen utensils, a couple of flower vases and so on), it was as if the marriage, about which, it was evident, he never for a moment stopped thinking, were something he hadn't the slightest intention of rushing. He was in love—he said so with his presents—which were often useless, it was true, and sometimes a bit absurd. If he married her, it was because he loved her. He had never in his life been engaged before, not even once. Neither as a youth nor later as a man had he ever tasted the inebriating pleasure of giving presents to a fiancée. Now that this pleasure was allowed him, he had every right to see that things proceeded slowly, gradually, with a rigorous respect for all the rules.

He came round every evening at the same time: at nine-thirty on the dot.

Lida would hear him coming from afar, from as far as the street. And there it was, the vigorous ringing of the bell that announced him, and there were his steady footsteps on the staircase, on the entrance side, and up there, at the level of the landing, his cheerful greeting.

"Good evening, ladies!"

He would begin to descend, still humming that air from *The Barber of Seville* between his teeth, then interrupt himself halfway down the stairs with a polite cough. And suddenly the room would be full of him, of the little man who wore his hair a bit like a soldier, a bit like a priest, and of his heated, brisk and imperious presence.

His arrival scene was always the same—for years it never changed. Although she could predict it in every particular, each time Lida was overcome by a kind of lulled stupefaction.

She would let him come forward, without even giving him a nod or getting to her feet.

But before, how had it been then in those cherished days?

Oh, at that time, when an equally vigorous ringing signaled that David, wrapped in his hefty blue coat with the fur collar, stamping his feet on the cobblestones out of impatience and the cold, was waiting for her, as agreed, outside the front entrance on the street—he had never wanted to come in, never felt the need to be introduced!—then, on the contrary, she'd had very little time to grab her overcoat from the wardrobe, put it on, shut the wardrobe and bring her face up to the mirror on the wall, furiously dab some powder on and adjust her hair. She was only conceded those few, precious seconds. And yet they were more than enough, as in the large mirror, looking small and shiny, with her hair drawn back behind her head (the light behind her made her seem almost bald), she saw the grey head of her mother appear and disappear, rapid and darting behind her back.

"What are you gawping at?" she turned to shout at her. "You know what? I've had enough—enough of you and this whole life."

She went out, slamming the door. David didn't like to be kept waiting.

5.

STILL TREMBLING, grasping his arm, she would let herself be led away.

Rather than turning right and heading toward the city center, they usually went down Via Salinguerra until they reached the city walls, and then from there, walking at a good pace along the path that topped the walls, they would arrive at Porta Reno in about twenty minutes. It was David's preference. Since he had made peace with his family—so as to free himself later, he said, when he was in a better position to do so, but in the meantime he would graduate, he really needed to graduate!—it was worth their being careful for now, at least to avoid being seen around together. At this point, it was indispensable, he kept on repeating. Given the situation, she herself ought to be convinced that certain "ostentatious displays" ought to be well and truly done with. By "ostentatious displays" he was referring to the earliest period of their relationship, when, throwing down a gauntlet, he was even willing to take her to the Salvini cinema in the evenings, when they would go to sit in the main cafes, including the Borsa, in daylight, and he'd proclaim that he'd already had more than enough of the boring and hypocritical life he'd been leading up till now—university, friends, family and so on. Anyway, wasn't it much better this way? he would hurriedly add, with a grin. Aren't hindrances, subterfuges, the best spur and incentive for love? In any case, one fact was for sure: along that path on top of the walls, or, soon after, at the little cinema in

Piazza Travaglio where they were heading, no one from his family or "circle" would ever encounter them.

Regardless of all that, she kept up alongside him in silence, frozen in body and soul.

And yet, after a little while, almost as soon as she found herself in the crowded, smoky stalls of the Diana, seated next to David with her eyes fixed on the screen, her frayed nerves quickly relaxed. Not seldom the films narrated love stories in which, despite everything, she kept dreaming of herself as the heroine: something that in the final moments induced her not only to look round at David (in the penumbra cut in mid-air by the elongated, blue cone of light which sprang from the projector behind, she could discern his long, thin neck, with his large, protruding Adam's apple just above the tie-knot, his unhappy profile, always seeming to be drowsy, his brown, brilliantined hair slightly curly at the temples), but also to seek out his hand and grasp it anxiously. And David? Ready as he was to return her look and give an answering squeeze to her hand, he seemed relaxed, even to be in a good mood. But she could never rely on that. After having let her hold his hand for a while, he would sometimes withdraw it brusquely. He would move his whole body away, or else, if he hadn't already taken off his coat, he would stand up and do so. "It's so hot in here," he'd sigh heavily, "you can hardly breathe."

Intimidated, she would make no further attempt at closeness. She would quickly return her gaze to the screen, and from then on David would be down there, in the middle of the large grey luminescent rectangle that filled the end of the auditorium, intent on lighting a cigarette with his gloved hands, dancing in his dinner jacket, or staring into the eyes of stunningly beautiful women, pressing himself against their breasts, kissing them lingeringly on the mouth . . . The film so entranced her that later, when it was over, and she was outside again, if David slipped an arm under hers and speaking in caressing tones, offered to accompany her home the same way they'd come, she would violently start awake, as from a kind of sleep.

"It's only a little longer, that way," David would urge her.

"But it's late, my mother was expecting me back at midnight," she tried to reply. "And then the cold, it'll be all wet . . ."

How much better it would be, she thought in the meantime, to return home by cutting back through the center of town! With the mist that had descended—in those two hours it had become so dense that the yellow lights of the streetlamps could barely be seen—no one, they could be sure, would have noticed them, not even if they'd passed by the Listone cafe, or if they'd taken the Corso Giovecca. They could have slowly walked along the sidewalks slippery with the damp, their lips and eyelashes laden with the tepid droplets, holding each other tightly like two real, proper fiancés, and talking, God—or rather David—willing. What would he have talked about? Perhaps the film (what a ham the main actor was!—he would have said—and also the star, what a silly thing she was!), or perhaps about himself, his studies, his plans for the future . . . Finally, before parting, they might even have been able to slip into some small cafe, one of those in the Saraceno district or in Via Borgo di Sotto. Seating them both in a corner, David would then have ordered two small drinks. After which, in the warmth, sipping the anisette and thinking of soon going to bed and to sleep, she could have felt, have been infused with, if not happiness, at least a sense of being in tune with herself and with life.

But instead she would give in.

And they would quickly make their way toward the city walls, away from the bicycle bells of the local lads who would hang around the cinema's still wide-open glass doors, talking in loud voices about sports or who knows what, or else eating roast chestnuts bought for a few *centesimi* from the old woman with the black shawl, the woolen half-gloves, the grey overcoat, forever stooped there over her little cast-iron griddle, they would be catcalling to her with whistles, shouts, disrespectful hisses and swear words. It was no use hurrying past. The ever-growing distance seemed to render the cries even more acute and penetrating. They followed her closely. Like cold, clammy hands which tried to grasp her, to touch her under her clothes.

With the first darkness, in the first field they came to, she was pushed down on to the grass. With her chin on his shoulder, without closing her eyes, she let him do what he wanted.

Later, she would be the first to get up. And if, at a certain point, she felt the desire to struggle beneath him, to bite him, do him harm (David never resisted this: instead, relaxing his long back, he would lean on her with his whole weight), that was when her rage, the sort of anger which lately had induced her to push him off her, would suddenly give way to a tremendous feeling of anxiety, of fear. How far away he already was! she thought, while she strained to get up, to smooth down her dress. Nothing at all mattered to him, now! And yet, why consider him the guilty party? Hadn't she herself been perfectly able to imagine how the evening would end? From when they met, in front of the street entrance, hardly exchanging a greeting, from when they had hurriedly walked toward the city walls, everything had been utterly predictable.

They went on their way.

She was fully aware of all this. He was cold and distracted. Nothing he could say now would do anything but wound her. And yet she would provoke him.

For example, she would ask him: "What's your mother's name again?"

As David kept silent, she would reply on his behalf, with slow emphasis: "Teresa."

Wasn't it funny that she'd ask such pointless questions, and then that it should be her replying, stressing each syllable like a schoolgirl being tested?

"And Marina," she continued, "what is your sister Marina called?"

She burst out laughing, then repeated: "Ma-ri-na."

Hastening his steps over the frost-hardened ground, David yawned. But he finally decided to speak.

What he uttered was strange and muffled. There was without doubt some truth in it, but also—and it sufficed to listen carefully to his tone, to realize this—a great deal of fiction. He spoke in general about himself, and especially about his "romantic involvement" with a young lady of the highest society, about whom, without disclosing her name, he kept on boasting, not just about her beauty, but also her urbane manners, her aristocratic and refined tastes. Their meetings, their tiffs (since, it seemed, they often quarrelled) always occurred in the midst of glittering occasions: a charity ball at the Unione Club, that would have been attended by the nobility, a gala showing at the City Theater, a gallop in the country which ended in a spectacular gathering at some beautiful villa encircled by a vast park.

All things considered, it was "a far from smooth relationship," hindered by both families, certainly, but "solely" due to their different religions: a relationship in whose context the "thing" that they had just done, in the field, would never, even by mistake, be mentioned . . . In the meantime, they had come down from the city walls, and entered Via Salinguerra. And if, till that moment she had been listening in silence, almost holding her breath, as soon as she gathered, from the shapes of the houses and the streetlamps, that in a few moments they would have to part, this caused her to suffer a nervous agitation of such intensity as to make her fear she might lose all control. Oh, how she hated, at that moment, her miserable, worn-out coat, her ruffled hair, flattened at the temples by the damp, her common-looking hands, deformed by work and frost! But what could she do then but try to keep calm? Small of stature, without the least attraction, of physique or personality (if only she'd played the tart a bit more!), she might as well accept her fate now, since it had already been sealed. Who knows? If at that point she'd been able to keep her composure, perhaps David would have been grateful to her. Perhaps in the future he'd have been able to treat her like an old friend to whom every request is conceded, who'd be able to give him any advice, even the most unwelcome. Not much to ask? Little enough. Still, better than nothing.

By then they'd have gone through the gate and reached the entrance.

Though his voice was reduced to a whisper, David kept on talking. What was he saying?

Soon after he graduated—he might, for example, be saying—he would get the hell out, not only of Ferrara, but of Italy. He was fed up with the tedious life of the provinces, of rotting in this hole of a city. Almost certainly he would be off to America, to stay there and settle, definitively.

With whom would he go to America? she had risked asking him on one occasion. Alone, or with that young lady he liked so much?

"Alone," he'd replied, annoyed.

He wasn't the type to marry, he'd added. Anyone. As things were now, all he wanted was a change of air, he'd already told her. Nothing more than that.

She had said nothing in reply. She'd merely nodded in the dark.

Another time though—and she would regret it later, in bed, when the ticking of the alarm clock on the bedside table and the wheezing noise her mother made while sleeping had kept her awake—she had burst out laughing.

She had asked him: "And if I got pregnant?"

She was well aware that a question of this kind would succeed in detaining David for another five minutes. What he would say in those five minutes didn't matter to her. What mattered was that before going he would feel obliged to kiss her.

6.

THE WINTER of 1929 was unusually hard. To find another to compare to it, Oreste Benetti declared, you'd have to go back as far as the famous winter of 1903, when even the river Po was frozen over, or perhaps to the winter of 1917.

It began to snow before Christmas, and it kept snowing until the eve of Epiphany. Yet the cold was still a long way from the extraordinary levels it would reach in the following months. There was even, just after Epiphany, a brief interlude of sun, almost spring-like in its warmth, and the snow had already begun to melt.

"Can it be trusted?" Maria Mantovani wondered.

From the bed, where since around the start of December she had been confined because of a feverish flu, which had left her face lined and her chest racked by an ugly cough, the old woman listened to the splashing and squelching from the occasional vehicle that passed along Via Salinguerra. No, it couldn't be trusted, she ended by replying to herself, the corners of her mouth turned down in a bitter expression. That spell of warmth, but rather than warmth all that mist which from the early afternoon onward swept in from the surrounding countryside and seemed to drench everything just as if it were rain, didn't help at all in fostering any illusions.

Then, as soon as he came in (he now came in without ringing the bell, as Lida had given him a key some time ago), Oreste Benetti divested himself of his sodden greatcoat, hung it on a nail sticking out of the entrance door. He came down the stairs, happy as can be. At length, after seating himself, as ever, at the head of the table, he began to talk.

For a couple of months, that is, since Ireneo had started going to the seminary, the main topic of his speeches had been the boy himself. Naturally, he was saying, there was no point in rushing to decide. All the same, in his modest opinion, from now on it was worth considering what job Ireneo would do when he was grown-up. The first three years at junior high school—those in any case he ought to do. But afterward? Take him out of school and put him immediately to work somewhere? No—they agreed that wasn't an option. And yet once he'd got his certificate from middle school, a choice regarding the various schools (at Ferrara it wasn't as if there was only the high school, no, there were the Training Colleges, the Technical Institute from which one graduated as an accountant or surveyor, not to mention the Industrial Institute in the Vicolo Mozzo Roversella!), a choice of one kind or another couldn't be avoided.

One evening, on his arrival, not without solemnity, he announced that that very afternoon he had dropped in at the seminary. He was invited in by Don Bonora, the director, who had taken over some twenty years ago from poor Don Castelli, and he had asked him about Ireneo.

"What can I say?" Don Bonora had at first somewhat guardedly replied. "We are just starting out on logical analysis and grammar. We have yet to begin a real study of Latin . . ."

He had then tried to sound out the director on what he thought of Ireneo's character. To which, the priest, although continuing to express himself with great prudence and tact, had replied that yes, effectively, the boy's character gave him some cause for concern. It was too early, you understand, he had added, to formulate any definitive judgement of him . . . but that we were dealing with a slightly weak, distracted character, of this, unfortunately, there seemed to him little doubt.

The bookbinder compressed his lips. Then, all of a sudden, he began to talk of the weather.

"In my opinion, we're not clear of it," he declared, raising his eyes to the ceiling and sniffing the air cautiously, "the worst is yet to come."

And Maria Mantovani, stretched out on her bed at the end of the room (from the table where the bookbinder and Lida usually sat facing each other, one could see nothing but her pallid prominent nose, with the two black vertical holes of her nostrils), immediately nodded in agreement, smiling in silence at some private thought.

Oreste Benetti was right. The worst of the winter was yet to come. At the start of the last third of January, as it happened, the sky once again became overcast, the temperature dropped, and as vicious gusts disturbed the air, it began to snow again with a furious intensity. It was like being high up in the mountains. Reduced to mere pathways, or narrow tracks arduously kept clear by the teams of shovellers the town council had hurriedly employed, the streets, especially the smaller ones, provided thoroughfare only for pedestrians. Since the snow had fallen, and the city walls had become the destination for enthusiastic crowds of impromptu skiers, mainly students, at a certain point it was decided by the Fascist Federation, to promote competitions up there, and especially along that stretch of the walls that runs between Porta San Giorgio and Porta Reno. This meant that Via Salinguerra, usually so deserted and silent, became transformed from one day to the next into a gathering place of much noise and bustle.

Quite suddenly Maria Mantovani's health worsened. Her fever began to run high; she became breathless. A doctor was called, and after a rapid examination, he announced that she was suffering from pneumonia. Was she in danger? Without doubt she was! the doctor confirmed, in reply to the direct question addressed to him by the little man of advanced years, perhaps a relative, who had called him out. The general condition of the patient which, even at a cursory glance, looked precarious, hardly promised a happy outcome.

Predicted and feared, the crisis came on the fifth day following.

Maria Mantovani didn't take her eyes off the window. Beyond the glass, which the daylight struggled to filter through, she could make out the snow falling thickly, in scurries. She seemed to be struggling to hear. Via Salinguerra resounded feebly with happy cries and hurrying footsteps. What was going on out there? she wondered. It was as if the city were having a celebration. But how come every voice, every sound, seemed to reach her from so far away?

"I can't hear clearly," she complained. "I can't hear anymore. It's as if my ears have been stuffed with cotton wool."

"It's snowing," Lida replied softly, sitting at the bedside. "That's why it all sounds so muffled to you."

The old woman gave a knowing little laugh.

"It's not as though it's *because of that*," she murmured, shaking her head and lowering her eyelids.

After a couple of hours her wheezing became a death rattle. A priest ought to be called. And the bookbinder, who had suddenly vanished, in fact quickly returned with the parish priest of Santa Maria in Vado.

In the meantime the room had filled with people.

They were mainly the women of the neighborhood who, although no one had alerted them, spontaneously appeared. How had they got in? Lida found herself wondering. Was it possible that Oreste (Oreste, heavens— she noticed herself calling him simply by his first name, which she had never done before . . .), was it possible that Oreste had forgotten to shut the front door behind him? However it had happened, a half-hour later, when the priest had gone away, the neighbors didn't leave the room. They all stayed: huddled underneath the window with their shawls over their heads and fervently whispering.

Rigid in the center of the room, Oreste Benetti held his hands together.

As soon as the death rattle ceased he came forward and leaned over the sickbed. Lightly and precisely, his hands moved to close the half-open eyes of Maria Mantovani, to cross her skeletal arms over her chest, and then, with a final, dextrous touch, to smooth the rumpled sheet and reposition the coverlet which had slipped almost entirely on to the floor.

All this time, until the bookbinder, having finished his work, was on the point of leaving soundlessly, Lida hadn't made a single movement. But even after those big busy hands had withdrawn, hands that belonged to the man who, soon enough, she knew it as a certainty by now, would become her husband, even afterward, she stayed there seated beside the bed, to stare at the waxen profile of her mother. Her almost closed eyelids, her nose that suddenly appeared too big, too prominent, her lips hinting at a vague, absurdly happy smile: the whole, all-too-familiar physiognomy revealed itself as different at a stroke, so much so that it was as if only then was she able to perceive it in all its particularity. As if she could keep on and on staring at her mother's face. While she did so, she felt something old, something bitter, something hard slowly dissolving within her.

She covered her face with her hands and began to weep silently.

Finally she raised her head, turning her eyes full of tears toward the bookbinder.

"Leave me be," she said in a low voice. "You too, Oreste," she added, nodding, "go away as well."

"Quite, quite, my dear . . ." he stammered, intimidated.

The neighborhood women were already leaving. After he'd tagged along behind their group halfway up the stairs, Oreste was the last to reach the landing and, closing the door, the last to disappear.

With her elbow resting on the sickbed and her cheek on her palm, Lida, left alone, thought about her mother, about herself, about their two lives. But she was mainly thinking of David, and the room in the big apartment block on Via Mortara where, at the beginning of that distant spring, she had gone to live with him.

It had happened like this.

One evening, at the end of winter—that same winter during which, because of the boredom and irritability which showed in David's every word and gesture, she was expecting any moment for him to say to her, "That's enough, Lida, from now on it would be better if we stopped seeing each other," and she was eaten away by this waiting—an evening just like many others, David had suggested to her out of the blue that they "set up house together like any normal working-class couple" in the big apartment block on Via Mortara. He had decided to make a clean break with his family, he had added, in order to "forge a new life for himself." He was prepared to live in a "garret," a "fine, poetic garret under the eaves," with a view not only of the whole city, but also "of the countryside as far as the hills of Bologna." In order "to support his family" he'd be willing "to work in the sugar factory" . . . And she? What else could she do apart from immediately assenting, as she had on that other occasion, the first, when, meeting him by chance in the open-air locale of Borgo San Giorgio (she being at that time little more than sixteen, in every way a mere girl) they had remained together as a couple for the whole evening, and then, toward midnight, ended up in a field close by the city walls? Yet again, she hadn't asked herself a thing, hadn't hesitated for a single moment. A few evenings later, she had left the house with a bundle under her arms which her mother, as usual, hadn't dared to comment on, though had surely noticed. Just like that: Goodbye! What madness! And yet, only later, much later, after having given birth, when she had returned to stay alone in the room at the big apartment block, and the child wouldn't stop crying, and she sensed her breasts every day were producing less and less milk, and she had hardly any lire left, only then did she begin to rouse herself from the long waking dream that her life had been until then.

But David, who was he? she now asked herself after many years. What was he looking for, what did he really want?

In the big apartment block, in a room on the floor below, lived the family of a nurse at the Sant'Anna Hospital. They were called Mastellari, and there were six of them: the nurse, his wife and four children.

Mornings when she went down with the pitcher to bring water from the courtyard, it wasn't unusual for her to bump into Signora Mastellari.

"What does your husband do?" the woman had once asked her. "Does he work in a factory?"

"Yes—but at the moment he's unemployed. Soon he'll be working in the sugar factory," she had replied calmly, utterly sure that David, a student, the son of well-to-do parents, and quite regardless of whether he was late with his graduation and had broken with his family, would never in a million years end up working in that factory.

A factory worker—just imagine it! And yet what was it that David most aspired to be if not a "typical worker." Wasn't that what he kept on repeating?

It was enough that he talked, and then everything became simple, easy, attainable. To get married? He had always considered marriage a joke— he would declare once again—one of the most typical and nauseating "bourgeois idiocies." But seeing that she was at heart drawn to "nuptials," he would quickly add, smiling, that she shouldn't fret, at the most within a year, when he'd found work—"a position at the town hall"—he would undoubtedly be able to make a respectable woman of her. It was certain. He would marry her; he had no hesitation in promising her that. Confronted with her "more than legitimate and comprehensible aspiration" to become his wife, his "wife also as regards the law," not only did he not draw back, but rather he would have done his utmost so that "the time all this would take" should be speeded up . . .

The afternoons, those sweltering summer afternoons, he generally passed stretched out, nearly always asleep. His breathing was so slow, his cheeks so pallid under a few days' growth of beard, that at times she— seated beside his bed exactly as she now was beside her mother's bed— couldn't resist the temptation to take him by the arm and give him a shake. "What is it?" he'd grumble, seemingly unable to lift his eyelids. Then, turning toward the wall—his pyjama top from behind was soaked with sweat—he would fall back into a deep sleep.

Usually, as soon as they'd had their supper, they went out. In search of coolness, they'd adopted the habit of staying out late at Porta Mare. That rather crowded kilometer which separated the big apartment block from Porta Mare was worth putting up with. A little farther on from the Customs barrier, there was an ice-cream kiosk with ten or so small tables in front, and ice cream, as David knew, she'd always loved since she was a baby.

Taking Via Fossato di Mortara, you came to the city walls in a few moments. And it had been up there, on one of those evenings, that she had suddenly stopped walking.

"Listen. I think I'm going to have a child," she said very calmly, putting her hand on David's arm.

At that moment, he didn't seem surprised. Not a gesture from him, not a word.

A little later, though, after they'd reached the usual kiosk, and she stood there with her chest leaning on the edge of the zinc counter and her eyes dazzled by the light of the acetylene lamp, he gently asked her:

"And what would you like? Lemon or chocolate?"

Without showing any desire to sit down, he had already begun to lick his ice cream (as ever a custard-and-vanilla combination). But he seemed sad, disappointed. While he licked his ice cream, he looked at her; he examined her from head to toe.

"The heat's unbearable this evening," he'd exclaimed at a certain point, with a bitter sigh. "To think that, up in the mountains as soon as it gets dark, you have to put on a pullover."

He was evidently referring to his family, who from the first of June had been holidaying up in Cortina d'Ampezzo.

"Where have they gone to stay, your family?" she'd found the strength to ask (as she too began licking her ice cream, having once again chosen a chocolate one). "Have they rented a house?"

"No. They've gone to the Miramonti. Imagine a kind of castle—" he seemed eager to explain—"with a wood all round it, six or seven times the size of the Finzi-Contini garden, that one down there at Piopponi, you know, by the Mura degli Angeli, and at least a dozen times bigger than Montagnone[*] . . ."

Who was David? What was he looking for? What did he want? And why?

To these questions there was no reply, and there never would be. Besides, it was late. Someone, most likely Oreste, was knocking on the window. She needed to get up, force herself up to the street door and tell him he could come back inside.

7.

IT WAS indeed Oreste.

After having caught up with the neighbors down at the entrance, for a good half-hour Oreste had stayed to talk to the women of what had happened and chiefly to listen to them. But then the cluster had moved on into the street and dispersed, and he, left alone, had begun to walk up and down in front of the doorway.

He felt two opposite emotions colliding within him, two conflicting necessities.

On the one hand, he felt the pressing need to rush off and lock up his workshop, so as to be able to confront with the required diligence all that

---

[*] A hill in southeast Ferrara made from the rubble left over from the construction of the city walls that became a public garden.

the death of Maria Mantovani saddled him with. And yet the thought of Lida held him back. Several times, bending down and bringing his face close to the steamed-up windowpane, he had tried to peer into the room. Down there, next to the bed, on the right-hand side, he made out a small, curved, motionless, grey figure.

"What's she up to?" he grumbled after a while, with the affectionate impatience of someone who already considered himself a husband.

The first shadows of evening were falling. It had stopped snowing, but it was still bitterly cold. Through the windows of houses round about could be glimpsed the insides of kitchens, cramped, illuminated dining rooms. He should get a move on and bring things to a head. At last, having yet again bent down to peer into the window (too dark—he concluded: by now he could make out nothing at all), he decided to tap on the window. He stood there, listening, his heart beating dully in his chest, until he seemed to hear Lida's footsteps ascending the staircase inside. In response he was quick to slip through the entrance. A second before she lowered the handle and opened the door, he was already on the landing.

Straight away, at first glance, he was aware that he once again had the upper hand. Her back leaning against the doorframe, and her eyes seeming to surrender themselves to his own, Lida stared at him in silence. That he should protect her: in her whole demeanor there was no other request.

"Good Lord, you really oughtn't to spend the night like this!" he said with lowered voice, in dialect, almost roughly.

Then, still whispering, without crossing the threshold, he began to explain to her what he meant to do.

He had to rush off and close the workshop, and since after that he also had to sort out another small matter, he wouldn't be able to get back for at least a couple of hours. Before going to the workshop, though, he would stop for a minute at the house of one of the neighbors, Signora Bedini. As she had offered to give a hand, he'd ask her to come round.

"Why?" he exclaimed, forestalling a possible objection on Lida's part. "Goodness me, to keep you company . . . to make you a bit of supper . . . Or even just to pray with you!"

At the word "supper" Lida had shaken her head as a sign of refusal.

But the argument that had followed was stronger than her resistance. She lowered her eyes, and he looked at her with a smile.

"So that's agreed then," he warned, "don't put the door chain on. Better still, leave the door ajar. You understand?"

And squeezing her hand, he disappeared up the stairs.

The temperature fell sharply during the night. The thin pinkish light which the following morning tried to pierce through the ice-encrusted windows—Lida was stretched out on her bed, Signora Bedini was curled in an armchair while Oreste, who had spent long stretches of the night in prayer, was on his feet at the window scrutinizing the weather—the light seemed to have arrived from a far-away sun, lost in the vague and misty blue of the sky, a sun that gave no warmth.

Just at that moment—Oreste calculated, with his coat collar raised over the stubbly thick silver hairs on the back of his neck while he blew on his frozen fingers—just at that moment the thermometer must be showing way below zero: ten, fifteen, twenty, who could say? That, however, should have made the weather more stable. During January, and perhaps up till mid February, the cold might drop to an even lower level: so that when the canals in the countryside, the river Reno and even the Po, had frozen over, the pipes of drinking water burst, and so on, in the end the winter would be comparable only with that of 1903. Would the farm produce suffer? Perhaps not. He at any rate felt rather sanguine (and felt not the least bit of embarrassment in admitting it), glad to have figured everything out exactly.

Maria Mantovani's funeral took place late afternoon that same day.

The third-class carriage advanced, unhindered, over the flattened snow, and behind, apart from the priest and a small cleric, Oreste walked alone. Submitting to his advice, Lida had remained at home. As for him, the old schoolboy of the seminary, the favorite of Don Castelli, the veteran of the Carso front, all the extremes of the weather imbued him with energy, restored to him as if by magic the missed hours of sleep from the night before. He walked with lowered gaze. With a pace that he instinctively accorded with that of the priest, he unceasingly studied the grooves cut into the snow by the carriage's tall thin wheels, the little slippages of snow that, detaching themselves from the wheel rims, barely powdered the shiny black varnish of the spokes and the leaf springs.

When he got back it was already night. And from the street, rather than knocking on the windowpanes as he had in the past few days, he wanted to announce himself with the emphatic ring of the bell that was his trademark.

Lida was awaiting him at the bottom of the stairs. She must have been asleep. And yet her face, before marked with the signs of weariness, now seemed refreshed and rested. She was completely transformed.

He sat down in his accustomed seat, leaning his folded arms on the table, and looking over at Lida, who was keeping herself busy about the cheap stove. He didn't miss a single gesture. He observed her with a most particular expression, a mixture of joy and gratitude, which surfaced in his eyes every time he thought he could discern in any phrase or gesture or even in a simple look of hers the attempt or desire to please him.

"Tonight it would best to call on Signora Bedini again," he said after a while. "I'll stop by at hers later. Tomorrow I'm thinking of paying a visit to Don Bonora. I think that for the next couple of weeks the boy should sleep round at his house. And then we shall see."

Already it was he who decided, who chose what would happen in the future.

After supper, they remained seated at a remove from the table that still had to be cleared, to discuss things. Limiting himself to Maria Mantovani and her life, Oreste spoke at length and with much tenderness. He remarked that she had suffered a great deal in her lifetime, poor thing, because she had loved very much, because she had had too much heart. He then described the plot in the Municipal Cemetery where tomorrow morning she would be laid to rest.

It was a really lovely place, he assured her, very respectable. Had she not seen it yet, the recently constructed arcade added to the right side of the San Cristoforo Church, making a great symmetrical curve identical to the arcade next to Via Borso, which had been built also to complete the colonnade in front of Certosa, on the Mura degli Angeli side? Well, her mother would be buried there, under those new arches. No, no—he confirmed—at midday, with the sun that would shine there from dawn to dusk, as in a greenhouse, the spot was really splendid.

"It's true that those places there, on that side," he added after a pause, and tightening his lips, "will cost a tidy packet."

But immediately, fearing that he might have been misunderstood, he explained that God forbid, she, Lida, shouldn't worry in any way about the expense.

"After working for so many years," he exclaimed, "thank heavens I've been able to save up a little something!"

And since she, he continued, without quite being able to suppress a slight trembling of his lips, had let him hope, had made him believe . . . and considering besides that this would without doubt have pleased her poor mother . . .

"In short, what is mine from now on will count as yours," he concluded, lowering his voice.

He leaned a little forward, staring her in the eyes—and it was the first time that he had addressed her with the informal "*tu*"! At last, he stood up, and hurriedly excusing himself, promised to be back in the morning.

They had such a lot to talk about!

8.

"WE HAVE such a lot to talk about"—Oreste would declare at every leave-taking, or at least his serious tender expression would affirm it.

But the one talking, if the truth be told, was always him.

When he didn't let himself be carried away on the wave of his habitual memories regarding both the years he spent as a boy in the seminary and the war he had later fought in the trenches of the Carso, he embarked on long monologues centered on his religious preferences, and most of all on the recent, decisive political developments, which had such a close bearing on religion.

After the signing of the Lateran Pact, in the February of that year, his patriotism had begun to overflow, liberally, enthusiastically. Good for the Church!—he said—which for the sake of Italy and the world had been able to set aside every trivial doctrinal matter and any sense of rivalry. But good for the Italian State as well, which deserved the highest praise for being the first to set out on the path of reconciliation. And it was clear, while he expressed himself in this manner, that the Church and the State stood before him in the form of a man and a woman, who, leaving behind a prolonged and difficult relationship, often perturbed by violent crises, had finally decided to get married.

And from that point on, how many splendid things would come to pass!—he would pursue the topic with an exultant expression. The spring that was already coming would see the onset of an era of peace and perpetual joy, a return of the legendary golden age. According to the Bible and the evangelist, according to the dream and prophesy of Dante, Church and State would acknowledge each other in perfect accord. The priest would no longer be persecuted nor held in suspicion. Civil society would no longer rebuff him, but welcome him like a father who should be heeded and revered. And if, today, as things stood, the rebirth of an actual and proper Catholic party, one such as the Partito Popolare, would be a perilous thing to hope for, it didn't matter: for now the results already achieved were more than enough. It was no little thing, if the truth be told, that the Catholic Action Party and those young fellows of the Federazione Università Cattolica Italiana were to be left in peace! It wasn't a small thing at all, but rather a momentous one, to find oneself able serenely to bless the Fatherland's flag displaying so much of the Savoyan coat-of-arms!

Carried along by the intense emotion these speeches awoke in him, but changing the tone, he would at last begin to talk of the two of them, of him and Lida, and in particular of the small villa outside Porta San Benedetto where in May, the day after their wedding, they would take up residence.

He would complain. He would take issue with the plasterer because a wall freshly skimmed, and seeping moisture, was showing stains in various places; with the carpenter because a shutter didn't close properly; with the surveyor because of his brusqueness and bad manners. But then, as soon as he began to describe the place where the villa was being constructed, how his face would relax and become clear again! The little dwelling was situated at the end of Corso San Benedetto—he repeated for the umpteenth time, and it seemed as though he was girding himself to describe certain very special details, almost arcane ones, of a far-away city, a city infinitely more lovely, agreeable and hospitable than Ferrara. He was referring to that district beyond the walls, situated between the Customs barrier and the railway bridge, where a series of houses large and small had been built in the preceding years. Whether larger or smaller, each had at its disposal its own land, to cultivate as a garden or kitchen garden. The two of them, installed there, would be able to breathe clean air—ah! country air. And here, as though overcome, he would then fall quiet—now that the happiness which they had long been awaiting was already in sight, within his grasp, he evidently preferred not to describe it.

May arrived.

In the last few days Oreste had lost his calm. He seemed suddenly riddled with fear, anxiety. He had always referred indirectly to their marriage: by sign, by indirect allusion, nothing more. Now, however, after having been contented for years by a promise that had not even been made in so many words, after having consented to any prevarication, he wanted to expedite everything, not to lose a single day. The date of the ceremony had been decided some time back: they were to be married the third week of the month. And yet, why not get married earlier?—he found himself suggesting. What else did they have to do in preparation?

Lida stared at him, astonished. She didn't understand.

"Why all this fret just now?" she asked him. "Why had he changed so much?"

He paused a little before replying. He stared at her with desperation in his eyes, then said slowly: "I'm like one of those horses that collapse at the finish line."

He then spoke of marriage, of what marriage meant to him. He said that he considered it the supreme aim of his life, so that only after they were married—not before!—he might perhaps have the courage to ask for Divine Providence to protect them. It was true, he admitted, nodding gravely. Up till now, he had had no rush. But, on the other hand, how could he have pushed things forward, feeling as he did that he couldn't count on his own strength?

Lida heard him out. She still didn't understand. Yet it was enough for her to raise her eyes once more, and she suddenly realized: Oreste was still afraid of losing her! Stretching across the table, she placed her hand on his hands, more tightly clenched than ever in their characteristic convulsion. And a moment later, for the first time, she found herself in his arms.

The years that followed, arduous, calm, largely happy, were marked by no momentous events. Even the winters, Oreste would say—though he was to die quite soon, in the spring of 1938—even the winters seemed to have finally become more settled.

It's true that every year, toward the end of autumn, he still loved to stand before the window, with the air of a meteorologist. But, of this one could be sure, he did this not because of any doubts about the truth of his predictions, of the now stable, or almost stable good weather, but rather the better to savor the intimate pleasure procured for him by the ownership of a new, modern house equipped with everything necessary for a comfortable life of modest luxury, including an excellent central heating boiler.

It was evident that the future no longer worried him in any way. After the marriage, Lida had immediately adapted herself to his devout habits, and began regularly to frequent the not-far-off church of San Benedetto, just within the city walls. The thin girl eaten away by anxiety, of those years when he had begun to visit a certain room in Via Salinguerra, had now become a beautiful wife, calm, serene, more than a bit chubby. What else could he desire from then on? What could be better?

Sometimes they joked together about this topic of Lida's beauty.

More inclined to believe it than she tried to appear, she would pull a face.

"Me, beautiful?"

"To say the least!" he would reply, smiling, while, with an expression of pride, he gazed into her eyes.

And yet—he would continue, serious once more—there was absolutely no reason to be surprised by that. This new beauty of hers, so right and timely, so much that of a wife, for which in the end it didn't seem presumptuous on his part to assign himself some portion of the credit, arrived on cue to demonstrate, had there been any such need, that the Good Lord had not only approved their union, but had taken pleasure in it.

9.

"He was happy," Lida sometimes told herself.

And yet, as soon as she happened to frame these words in her mind, an echo would break in on her to deform and distort them. Flecked with doubt, with painful rancor, the words would change into a question to which no one, herself least of all, would be able to reply other than in the negative.

Poor Oreste. He, too, had not been happy. No. In truth something had always been missing for him as well. Sufficient proof was the tender, more than paternal care that for years, for all the years of their marriage, he had lavished upon Ireneo.

When Ireneo had left the seminary with the intermediate diploma in his pocket, Oreste had immediately taken him on, in the workshop, and had installed him at his own little bench between the trimming machines and the glass door. He had wanted to teach him the trade. And some late afternoons, at dusk, when Lida would cross half of the city to reach the binding shop in Via Salinguerra—later, all three of them would return up the Corso Giovecca or Via Mazzini, but each time passing by in front of the Caffè della Borsa, right in the center—it seemed to her as though she could still see him as he brooded behind the big bench with his eyes shining with affectionate zeal over that apprentice, who was so sad, so mute, and yet so ready to be distracted by the least thing happening in the square outside. It seemed to her that she could still see him, still hear him: with that vigorous torso of his, out of keeping with his short legs, that loomed up from the stool on the other side of the bench, with his big, hard hands, oddly become more delicate since his marriage vows (he could never be parted from his wedding ring—not even in 1935 at the time of the sanctions!*), with his strong, chirpy, piercing voice . . . Oh, how hard he must have struggled so that she, Lida, remained unaware of his desire for a son! How he must have secretly tormented himself, almost as though to punish

---

* In October 1935, in response to Italy's invasion of Ethiopia, the League of Nations began to impose limited sanctions on Italy.

the desire itself, to smother it within him: at a certain point he had even pressed for Ireneo to assume his surname!

And yet, despite everything, Lida thought, Oreste never gave up hope. For her to be sure of this she only needed to remember the look he gave her every time she entered the workshop: a questioning but calm look, full of unbending faith.

If not now, his look said, then soon, very soon, she would come to him with the great news. She would give him a son, without doubt, a son that was really his, of his blood, and thus different physically and in character from the son she had before marrying him, who, although he had given him his own surname, although he was instructing him in his own trade with all the enthusiasm he was capable of, had nevertheless never wanted to call him anything but uncle: "Uncle Oreste."

A son that was really his—Lida pursued the thought—that was what was missing for him, that was the only shadow that had disturbed the serenity of their married life.

Regarding that golden age of which, in February 1929, he had predicted the return, he evidently awaited nothing so eagerly as to hear her declare: "I'm pregnant."

It was equally evident, though, that death, taking him by surprise, had prevented the possibility of this hope turning into despair.

The Stroll before Dinner

1.

EVEN today, rummaging through some small second-hand stores in Ferrara, it's not unlikely that you could turn up postcards almost a hundred years old. They show views that are yellowed, stained, sometimes, to tell the truth, barely decipherable . . . One of the many shows Corso Giovecca, the main city thoroughfare, as it was then, in the second half of the nineteenth century. To the right and in shadow, in the wings, looms the buttress of the City Theater, while the light, typical of a golden spring-time dusk of the Emilia Romagna, congregates entirely on the left-hand side of the image. There the houses are low, having for the most part only a single floor, with their roofs covered with thick russet tiles, and below them some little shops, a grocer's store, the entrance to a coal merchant's, a horsemeat butcher and so on: all of which were razed to the ground when, in 1930, the eighth year of the Fascist Era, almost opposite the City Theater, the decision was made to build the enormous structure of the General Insurance in white Roman travertine.

The postcard has been adapted from a photograph. As such it reveals, and not inaccurately, the look of the Corso Giovecca around the turn of the twentieth century—a kind of wide carriageway amid the rather shapeless surroundings, with its rough cobbles, more fitting for a large village of Lower Romagna than of a provincial capital, divided in the middle by the fine parallel lines of the tram rails—but it also reveals just as clearly how life was going on along the entire street in that moment when the photographer pressed the button. The street thus captured extends from the corner of the City Theater and the Gran Cafe Zampori beneath it, to the right, a few yards away from where the tripod had been set up, as far down there as the distant, pink sunlit facade of the Prospettiva Arch at the very end.

In the foreground the image seems crammed with detail. One can see the boy from the barber shop peeping from the threshold and picking his teeth; a dog sniffing the sidewalk in front of the entrance to the horsemeat butcher's; a schoolboy running across the street from left to right, just managing to avoid ending up under the wheels of a calèche; a middle-aged gentleman, in frockcoat and bowler hat, who, with lifted arm, pulls back the curtain which shields the interior of the Cafe Zampori from any excessive intrusion of light; a splendid coach and four which is moving forward at a fast trot to attack the so-called Castle ascent. Except that as soon as one begins to search, perhaps half-closing one's eyes, the slender central space of the postcard which corresponds to the furthest part of the Corso Giovecca, everything then becomes confused, things and people merge together in a kind of luminous dusty haze, all of which would help explain why a girl of around twenty years of age, at that very moment walking quickly along the left-hand sidewalk, having arrived at not more than a hundred meters from the Prospettiva Arch, would have been unable to transmit as far as to us contemporary spectators the least visible sign of her existence.

We should declare right away that the girl was no beauty. Her face was more or less that of many others, neither beautiful nor ugly: rendered, if that's possible, even more average and insignificant by the fact that in those days the use of lipstick, rouge and powder was not generally acceptable among the working classes. Dark-brown eyes in which the beams of youth only rarely shone, and then almost stealthily, with a frightened, melancholic expression, not that different from the sweet, patient look in the gaze of some domestic animals; chestnut-brown hair that, drawn back at the nape, laid bare rather too much of the bulging, bulky, peasant forehead; a squat, busty torso, belted by a black velvet ribbon, that ended in a slender, not to say graceful neck . . . in a fashionable street such as Corso

Giovecca, and during, moreover, that especially animated and bustling hour which, in Ferrara, no less today than at that time, has always preceded the intimate evening ritual of supper, it's fair to suppose that even to a less indifferent eye than the photographic lens, the passing by of a girl like this might easily be overlooked.

It now remains to establish what thoughts, on a May evening some seventy years ago, might have been entertained by a girl like this, a trainee nurse of less than three months standing at the City Hospital of Ferrara.

Yet turning back to examine in that same postcard, this time with a slightly warmer sense of real involvement, the general look of Corso Giovecca at that moment of the day and of its history, paying attention to the combined effect of joy, of hopefulness, produced in the very foreground by that blackish spur of the City Theater, so like a dauntless prow that advances toward freedom and the future, it's hard to dispose of the impression that some tinge of the naive fantasy of a girl—of that and no other girl—heading home after many hours of no doubt uncongenial work, will somehow be ingrained within the image we have before us.

At the end of a whole day spent in the sad wards of the former convent, where, soon after 1860, the Sant'Anna Hospital had found temporary and inadequate lodging, it was, one could deduce, with real eagerness that Gemma Brondi abandoned herself to her adolescent dreams and imaginings. She would be walking, one might say, without seeing. So much so that, approaching the Prospettiva, when, as was her habit each evening, she mechanically raised her eyes to the three arches of the architectural obstruction, a phrase that was whispered in her ear at that exact moment ("Good evening, Signorina" or something of the kind) found her unready and defenceless, only able to blush and then go pale, and to look around timidly in search of escape.

"Good evening, Signorina," the voice had whispered. "Allow me to accompany you."

The phrase had been this or, as already said, something very similar. Speaking thus, and engaging Gemma Brondi in a conversation that forced her to avoid the black and penetrating eyes of her interlocutor, was a sturdy young man of around thirty years of age, dressed in dark clothes, gripping the handlebars of a heavy Triumph bicycle: a young man with a thin face on which gleamed silver-rimmed spectacles, and a moustache, no less black than his eyes, that drooped around his mouth.

But at this point, traveling at speed along the track which these two young people are about to walk, let us betake ourselves a little way from the Prospettiva on Corso Giovecca, and more particularly inside the big, rustic dwelling where the Brondis, a country family, have lived within the city since time immemorial. The house rises in the shelter of the city walls, separated from them only by virtue of the little dusty street that runs along that stretch of the walls. It is already almost night. In the ground-floor rooms, whose windows look back toward the open space of the vegetable gardens, they have just now turned on the lights.

2.

THE ONLY person in the house who had taken any notice right from the start of Dr. Corcos, Dr. Elia Corcos, was Ausilia, the elder sister.

Every evening, there she was again.

After having laid the little dining room's round table, and then, after going into the kitchen and lighting the stove under the pot and the frying pan, as soon as the voices of her father and brothers, who were still working in the vegetable garden in the dark and were now about to come in, began to be more distinctly audible, just at that moment Ausilia vanished, only to reappear later, when the others were about to finish their meal.

Where exactly Ausilia had gone to hide, her mother had almost immediately figured out. But why should she feel any need to speak of it? Seated, in the manner of an *arzdóra*,* with the kitchen door at her back, she only allowed herself an inner smile at the image of her eldest daughter leaning on her elbows at the window of the room she shared with her sister, with Gemma, and perhaps unburdening herself of a loud sigh. As regards old Brondi and his three sons, they, bent over their plates, kept on eating with their customary appetite. The novelty of these regular, recurrent disappear-

---

* Ferrarese dialect word for the formidable peasant housewives of the neighboring countryside. Plural form: *arzdóre*.

ances of Ausilia at suppertime seemed not to hold any interest for them. Why should we bother about that?—their aspect seemed to be saying. After a short while, Ausilia, like the capricious spinster she was well on her way to becoming, would reappear of her own accord, whenever it suited her.

Having come down the internal stairs without making the least sound, Ausilia at last presented herself at the doorway of the dining room, light-footed as a ghost. Her mother was the only one to raise her head. Was this whole affair dragging on? she was silently asking, with the rapid look she threw toward the shadows, where, waiting to approach and be seated, Ausilia usually hovered for a moment. Nor was Ausilia's response ever slow in coming. In acute expectation of the subsequent entry of Gemma, always a bit ruffled and out of breath, Dolores Brondi would receive the information that she sought and that had been weighing on her. No doubt about that, Ausilia would assure her, by her imperceptible shrug of assent. The affair was certainly dragging on, and was showing no signs at all of ending.

Some words passed between mother and daughter about a month later while, as the sun had nearly set, they went to Vespers as usual at the nearby church of Sant'Andrea.

To reach Via Campo Sabbionario where the church was more quickly, they tended to take the path behind the house that led straight across the garden till it reached a small green gate down at the end, situated exactly halfway along the surrounding wall. Who knows? Perhaps it was the narrowness of the path that encouraged them to share these initial confidences, the first exchange of observations and opinions . . . The fact is that, only after the broken, almost fearful sorties of an opening dialogue between the two women, conducted almost at a running pace, without the confidence even to look each other in the face, concerning the looks of Gemma's "crush"— who, judging by the very pale face and the black moustache that drooped around a carefully shaven chin, could only be a gentleman—only after that was Ausilia allowed to go home, a good twenty minutes before the service's concluding "Amen." Her eyes fixed on the altar, Dolores Brondi sensed her getting up, barely displacing the straw seat at her side. True enough—she reckoned, when left alone and gnawed at by a secret envy—it was unlikely the two of them would be able to discuss their new discoveries with the required leisure before the following evening. Soon, anyway, when the thought of Ausilia stationed at her window-observatory had induced her to prolong her conversation with some women of the neighborhood at the small gate to the vegetable garden a moment or two longer than necessary, if a male voice behind her had shouted from afar, "And so, are we going to eat?" (till then that had never happened, but it might!), she would have turned back to the house without any hurry, displaying the cold, hostile expression of someone prepared to assert their rights whatever it cost. Make no mistake about that. She and Ausilia never went out. Never went out, except at the end of the day, and only so as to finish it in a sanctified manner. Who could complain about that? They'd better come armed! If that had happened, supper would have been eaten accompanied by the silence of the tomb. And then, once Gemma had also come back in and she too had finished eating, everyone to bed.

Summer was approaching. Around the brown, back-lit mass of the apse of Sant'Andrea the bats wheeled, with ever more piercing squeaks. And gradually, as time passed, the image of Gemma's suitor was embellished with fresh details: a splendid, swallowtail blue jacket, gleaming silver spectacles, a fat gold watch which he once, at the point of leaving, drew from his waistcoat pocket, and then, as later additions, a white silk cravat, an ivory-handled cane and a manner, what a manner . . . One evening, and this caused Ausilia to draw back in surprise, the couple, rather than appearing down in the street, had appeared above, among the trees on the city walls almost at the height of the window: it might prompt the suspicion that Gemma and the man had been stretched out till then in the thick grass of a meadow to hold and kiss each other—or even worse! Another evening, again on the verge of saying goodbye and leaving, he, besides lifting his cap, had bowed down ceremoniously, perhaps he'd even kissed her hand. His intentions were only too clear! Ausilia, at once awestruck and scandalized, concluded her account of these recent events. Was it possible, though, that Gemma was unaware of the risk she was running? Was it possible she didn't understand that a gentleman like that . . .? But then who was this gentleman, what was he called?

Of the thirty-year-old Dr. Elia Corcos there is no extant portrait. The only one, conserved by Signora Gemma Corcos, during her lifetime, in a small chest of drawers which many years after her death was sold along with other of her belongings to an antiques dealer in Via Mazzini, would be traceable by cutting out a small head from a group photograph, which she, still a girl, a tiny out-of-focus oval among the many, had taken home from the hospital and then hidden in her lingerie drawer. So, just supposing for the sake of pure conjecture that while exploring the insides of a dusty, worm-eaten piece of furniture extracted from the depths of some storeroom it were possible to recover this photograph (a typical keepsake: with ten or so doctors in white coats seated in a semicircle at the front, and behind, standing, to make a background and as it were a crown, some thirty nurses in grey uniforms), it wouldn't be at all unlikely that, carefully observing the gaunt, hungry and very pale face of Elia Corcos at thirty, one might manage to figure out precisely enough the amazement of Ausilia Brondi to begin with, and very soon after of her mother, when their wide-eyed gaze finally fell on the reality so very different from the one which, little by little, they had built up in their fertile imaginings. "Huh, just one of those little half-starved doctors from the hospital!" they exclaimed together, galled and disappointed. A nothing, a nobody. Seeing as Gemma hadn't done so, it should be their job to inform the family. Would her father and brothers any longer, from then on, allow Gemma to leave the house? Never mind! So that an affair of this kind be brought to a stop, all of them would gladly have renounced the few coppers she brought home from the Sant'Anna.

Between saying and doing, between the intention and the action, however, there remained the usual shortfall. The truth was that as soon as she returned home (each time, walking along the vegetable garden's narrow path, between the small green gate and the flower bed, had a calming effect on her), Ausilia hurried as usual up to her bedroom and, having replaced the photograph in Gemma's drawer, took up her customary stance at the window.

The thrill of spying and reporting, of conjectures and deductions, the secret delights of fantasy, undermining the severe, intransigent resolution just now formulated, had always deferred it to an undefined future, but as it happened just at the end of that same day all these intentions and prevarications were brought to a sudden halt before the weight of facts.

The enamoured couple were proceeding along the little road without showing any awareness of having arrived at the place where, after glancing up at the blinds from behind which Ausilia was observing them, they would promptly go their separate ways. Gemma was at a slight remove from the doctor, who, though walking at the same pace as her, was separated from her by the bicycle. They were not speaking. But there was something in the stiffness of their carriage, the stubborn way they both kept their gaze fixed on the ground, which conferred a weight and a particular solemnity on their silence. In addition, now they had advanced a bit farther, it seemed to Ausilia that her sister's cheeks were streaked with tears.

By this stage they were beneath the window, in front of the doorway. Ausilia suddenly felt herself short of breath. "What now?" she whispered, pressing a hand to her breast. What did their sudden gaze into each other's eyes mean? And why did they remain separated by the bicycle without saying a word?

Then, as if in response, the doctor picked up the Triumph by the saddle and handlebars, turned it round and quickly leaned it against the grassy slope of the city wall on the other side of the road. He stood for a moment there before it, with his back turned and bent over, giving the impression that he was in rapt examination of its chain, or perhaps a pedal. At last, straightening up, he slowly retraced his steps.

Gemma had not moved. With her back to the doorframe, she waited.

The other made a strange gesture: just as though—Ausilia thought— he was combing his moustache.

They kissed for a long time. Again and again.

After which, the doctor once more crossed the road and, having collected the bicycle, wheeled it behind him—time had passed: even in the darkness at the start of the scene it was hard to discern his movements— then he followed Gemma, who had already entered, inside the house.

3.

BROUGHT INTO the small dining room and given a seat just in front of the head of the family, who, at his entrance, had raised his eyes from a game of patience and had kept gazing at him with half-open mouth, the doctor began by introducing himself. His name, surname, his parents, his profession, even his address . . . it was a catalogue of personal data of the most official kind: a long stream which, perhaps, had it not been accompanied by the extraordinary, somehow paralyzing courtesy of his manner, or even without the tension which had suddenly gripped the room, might have appeared irksome, pedantic and in its specificity at the very least gratuitous and extravagant.

Elia Corcos—the four males of the house, who until that moment had no clue even about his existence, were in the meantime thinking—what the hell kind of a name is that? His doctor's frockcoat; the white silk tie; the black cap with large raised rim which, placed on his tightly pressed knees, stood just proud of the table edge (and everything a bit worn, a touch faded, as though it had been bought secondhand); his eloquence peppered every now and then with brief phrases or single words in dialect, which he pronounced almost shyly, as though he were picking them up with tweezers; his face itself, which seemed fashioned out of a special substance, finer and more fragile than the usual material: however modest his family origins may have been, even if now he was living alone as a bachelor, or whatever his present financial circumstances, everything about him, they were only too aware, spoke of his belonging to a different class, the class of gentlemen, and therefore different, fundamentally alien.

Compared to this fact, every other consideration, including that he wasn't a Catholic but Jewish, or rather an "Israelite" as he himself termed it, occupied for the moment a very subsidiary position. Apart from the usual, everlasting sense of inferiority, of respect above all created by a timidity as regards speech which always afflicted the country folk, irrespective of whether or not they lived within the city walls, in whatever relations they had with the middle classes, his presence to begin with provoked no special response at all. But what response could it have been expected to provoke at that particular time? The sun of renown, or rather that of an unwearying, affectionate admiration, quite close to fetishistic idolization, which for three entire generations of Ferraresi from all social classes would accompany Elia Corcos throughout his long life—so much so as to make of him a kind of institution, a municipal symbol—the dawning of that sun, which coincided with the dawn of a new century, was still too distant to be observed in the vast sky above the city.

And likewise:

"A great doctor!" would be another accolade, but only to be heard some ten years later, and not before.

Or even some decades later, from witnesses to the flourishing old age of Elia Corcos:

"A genius, gentlemen! A man who if Ferrara had not at that time been Ferrara, but Bologna . . ."

According to the latter, those forever unsatisfied characters, lamenting among other things, the modern decline of Ferrara, always praising and bewailing the distant Renaissance splendors of the house of d'Este, the determining cause of the inadequate (because merely provincial) fortune of Corcos' medical career was a specific historical event that occurred toward the end of the last century.

Around 1890, an obscure Bologna deputy, a Socialist, by "nefariously" blackmailing Crispi, the great Francesco Crispi, had contrived that the most important northern railway terminus was sited not at Ferrara, but at Bologna. All Bologna's prosperity, all its successive and persisting wealth hinged on that fatal decision, yet the more odious because it had been achieved by the swindle of a Socialist, but for that no whit less advantageous and effective for Bologna, which, thanks to this, became in a trice the major city of Emilia Romagna. So then, like so many of his fellow citizens, like so many equally distinguished gentlemen, guilty of nothing but having been born and brought up in Ferrara, Elia Corcos had only been an innocent victim of political shenanigans. He, too, along with innumerable of his fellow citizens worthy of a better fate, just when he was ready to take flight—Power, Glory, Happiness, and so on: oh, the great eternal words, held back in the throat by fierce pride, but still valid in the imagination, to light up prodigious skies behind the four towers of the Castle that rise in the city center and give the city's first greeting to whoever enters from the countryside, gloriously bright . . . he too, just when everything was at its most promising, had had to renounce, withdraw, surrender. Around the same time he had taken a wife. And his marriage, at the age of thirty, to a working-class girl, undoubtedly gifted with many excellent qualities, though who knows if she even completed the fourth form at middle school, had sealed his defeat and self-sacrifice.

This, then, many decades later, would have been the train of thought of many Ferraresi whose temples had begun to grey between the two wars of this century regarding Elia Corcos and the strange, not to say baffling, marriage of his youth. Having ranged so widely, even evoking the name of Francesco Crispi, these thoughts always led to the same conclusion: that Signora Gemma, the deceased wife of Elia Corcos, had not understood, that Gemma Corcos, née Brondi, had not, poor thing, really been the right choice. But was it fair, or useful, to hold her to account in such an unfeeling manner? For a good while she lived alone at the end of Via Borso, at the Charterhouse. And yet had she not been the only person in Ferrara who had ever penetrated the barrier of the solemn, ironical hat raisings which Elia Corcos, especially in the spring, before dinner, strolling along the Corso Giovecca, would habitually dispense to right and left: a barrier of courtesy which had quickly and inevitably blocked any reflex of curiosity, any tentative investigation. And leaving aside once and for all Ferrara and its progressive decline after the Unification, that very evening of 1888—that far-off summer evening—in the course of which Elia Corcos had asked for her hand and been accepted as her fiancé, who, if not her, was seated in that small, dark, rustic dining room of the Brondi house between him, Corcos, and her father, at an equal distance from both of them? That place which she occupied was the perfect one to catch the very instant in which, leaning suddenly out of the shadow, the face of the guest had entered, drained, into the circle of light.

Everywhere around was shadow. In the center the tablecloth shone immaculately.

No, no one was better placed than Gemma Corcos, née Brondi, to appreciate the time required for that sacrifice to be made. The time required by Elia to state the actual reason for his presence—Gemma would recall this to the end of her days—was no more than would be needed to accomplish a brief series of movements: to bend his back, lean his head forward, offer to the light his pale face, a lot paler even than it usually was, as though all the blood in his veins and arteries had suddenly been sucked back into his heart.

What that face declared—the words that tumbled from his mouth didn't count, didn't have the least importance—was: "Why am I here to ask, as just a moment ago I did ask, that old drunkard for the hand of his daughter the nurse? For what possible motive, in God's name, am I ruining my life by my own hand? Just to make up for a pregnancy? And, to boot, not even one that's 'confirmed?'"

And then: "I still have a choice, should I want it. Changing my mind, I could still leave this place, defy the whole lot of them—father, mother, brother—and never be seen again. As I could, also, should I choose to, play along, from henceforth accept the modest life of a provincial general practitioner, and yet, with the advantage in this case, that when the girl soon accompanies me to the door on to the street, I could start insinuating that she was responsible for everything, that it was they who in a certain sense forced me into this marriage."

And then again: "At this crossroads, the one road rough, hard and uncertain, the other smooth, easy, nice and comfortable, one can't, in all justice, really waver about which to take!"

And finally, while beneath his moustache his lips made a series of lateral tics, clearly sardonic: "Would you really call it smooth, that road I'm heading down? Nice and comfortable, seriously? Just try it yourself!"

4.

THEY WERE married. At first they lodged with his father, Salomone Corcos, the old grain merchant, and there, in Via Vittoria, in the heart of what until not that long before had been the Ghetto, Jacopo was very soon to be born, and then Ruben. Half a dozen years or so would have to pass before the home in Via della Ghiara would be acquired: *"magna, sed apta mihi, sed nulli obnoxia, sed parta meo"** as Elia, whose temples had in the meantime become slightly flecked with white, was wont to say, half seriously, half facetiously.

---

* "*parva, sed apta mihi, sed nulli obnoxia, sed non sordida, parta meo, sed tamen aere domus*": "Small, but adapted to my needs, subject to none, by no means miserable and bought with my own money" is the motto above the door of the house of the poet Ludovico Ariosto in Ferrara. Corcos has curtailed the quotation and has ironically substituted "magna" (large) for "parva" (small).

To arrive there from the Brondi house, after you had got beyond the little alley on top of the city walls and hadn't taken any shortcuts, would require a brisk walk of at least a half hour. You'd begin by leaving behind the Borgo San Giorgio, huddled around the big eponymous church with its brown bell tower. You'd continue by hugging the long, blind and monotonous wall of the mental asylum. At length, on the left, at the farthest extreme of the boundless plain, after the blue, wavy line of the Bologna hills begins to become visible, if you turn your head toward the city, your gaze will immediately be drawn to a grey facade, down there, laced about with Virginia creeper, the green blinds closed to protect the occupants from any intrusion of noise: a facade turned toward the south and so exposed to even the most minimal variation of light, with its blanchings and darkenings, its sudden reddenings and alterations, which very much suggested something living, something human.

If one looked at it, the house, from high up there on the city walls, one would have thought it a kind of farmhouse, with its fine flowerbed separated from the adjacent vegetable garden by a hedge, and with the vegetable garden that, full of fruit trees and divided by a thin central path, descended way down there to the sturdy surrounding wall. And there was certainly no danger of being intimidated while approaching from this side! thought Gemma's father and brothers, who, on those afternoons when they came to chop wood, never failed to take the path along the wall. While, from up there, communicating by shouts and crude, brazen whistles, they never failed to feel, however confusedly, and without having ever said as much, as though between the look which the building itself from the second-floor windows and the dormer windows above gently levelled at the fields, and that look which a still youthful woman with her bust framed in the first floor's wide-open window directed at them in the distance, through the already darkening air, a relationship of some kind existed, a secret similarity and affinity. She lifted an arm to greet them, and waved with festive insistence. They were welcome! she seemed to be saying. They should come in! Good Lord, didn't they realize that the little gate at the foot of the wall, which allowed entry to the house also from the back, had been left ajar till darkness fell, just so that they could, if they wanted to, pass freely through?

From the opposite side of the house, the front, one would have no idea of all this.

It seemed like a dignified little construction of bare redbrick. And each time it seemed incredible to Elia's relatives, when they came to visit, that the countryside whose existence Via della Ghiara, with its reserved and tranquil but still markedly urban aspect, almost made one forget, actually began no more than some fifty or so meters away, only just beyond the final veil of those mainly middle-class, though in some cases even aristocratic, facades, among which, without being harmed by the comparison, was to be found also that of Dr. Corcos.

Corcos, Josz, Cohen, Lattes or Tabet, whichever family it was, none of them, kith or kin, seemed at all intimidated by the brass rectangular plaque on which was inscribed: DR. ELIA CORCOS DOCTOR & SURGEON. When properly polished, it stood out on the street door with its fine, black, capital letters. And even if in their time they had severely criticized Elia for having taken a goy as a wife, and following that had also disapproved of his leaving the Ghetto quarter where he was born to establish himself in such a remote area of the city, this nevertheless, it should be added, was always with a secret sense of satisfaction that the main entrance should be so consecrated to him, Elia, and by extension to themselves. The look of the house, the quiet secluded nature of the district, likewise, even in its contrast to the medieval alleyways from which they'd come, was enough to reassure them. It showed that Elia, after all, had not changed, had remained one of their blood and upbringing: finally, unquestionably a Corcos.

This last fact having been firmly established, and since at this point it was clear that when he'd converted he'd hardly even considered it—what's more, with his growing success as a doctor in both the city and the province, he conferred distinction on his shared origins, and his kin sooner or later would enjoy the benefits—at little more than forty years old, apart from being head of the Sant'Anna Hospital, he had become personal physician to the Duchess Costabili, by far the most chic and influential woman of Ferrara, leaving aside that after the premature death of her consort he was perhaps something more than just a personal physician to the duchess . . . So for everything else he could be excused, justified and, in certain particular cases, even applauded.

What the devil did it matter, for example, they would reason, that personally he issued from a less-than-mediocre family, son as he was of that inept fellow Salomone Corcos, that forgettable and undistinguished little merchant who had never done a thing in his life apart from begetting children into the world (he had a good dozen of them!) and ending up as a useless weight on the shoulders of Elia, the last of the series? And the wife he had chosen as well, a goy and, to make it worse, of low extraction (devoted, though, a capable housekeeper, a harder worker you couldn't easily find, or even ever find, and also an incomparable cook), why should she be considered, as many continued to consider her, a kind of lead weight around his feet? No, no. If he, prudent and circumspect as he'd always been, had decided at a certain point to indulge himself in the luxury of a *mésalliance*, rather than having been merely constrained to make amends for a mistake made during one solitary night shift spent in the company of an exuberant girl (to end up in front of the magistrate on this account had never been considered absolutely remiss in Ferrara!), mightn't it be that he had known exactly what he was doing? However it had actually come about, what was important was that he, despite all his eccentricities and oddities—including that of refusing after a certain date to make any contributions toward a bank established by the Italian School Synagogue, affirming that his conscience did not permit him to pretend to a faith in which he didn't believe (except that, regarding circumcision, he was prepared to lend his full support to that small operation and even once to declare openly in the Temple that he wasn't against the "custom," corresponding evidently to hygienic norms also known in ancient times, and therefore, not unwisely, included within the religion)—what was important in the end was that he, to all intents and purposes, when it came down to brass tacks, continued to conform to the general rules.

And in this respect, in 1902, when little Ruben, only eight years old, died of meningitis, had it not perhaps been for everyone a delightful and consoling confirmation that on that occasion it was actually he, Elia, in contrast to his usual indifference to all things religious, who insisted that his second-born should be interred beside his grandfather Salomone with the most orthodox rites? The goyish wife, no: every now and then she had tried to rebel. Not only had she followed step by step the funeral from Via della Ghiara to the cemetery, but afterward, when the gravediggers had finished filling in the grave, she had thrown herself with open arms on the mound of fresh earth, to the dismay especially of Dr. Carpi, interrupted in the midst of his prayers, and had started crying that she didn't want to leave her baby, her *pòvar putin,*[*] there. Well, of course a mother's always a mother. But what was she, Gemma, thinking? That a Corcos, rather than in the Jewish cemetery at the end of Via Montebello, so intimate, tidy, green and well-tended as it was, should be buried outside the walls, in the endless graveyard of the Charterhouse, where you could spend a whole day just trying to find a gravestone again? And, going back to that fit of weeping, Gemma was surely entitled to that. But her relatives, who arrived in large numbers for the occasion, they and the great horde of friends and acquaintances they dragged along with them, all unaware of the requirement to cover their heads—what made them display such desperation? And that other woman? Who on earth was that odd little woman with a black shawl around her head and that spinsterish air who, helped by Elia and by Jacopo (already so like his father, the boy: dark-haired, pale-faced, refined . . .), was trying in every way possible to lift Gemma up, but she, Gemma, shook her head and refused to get to her feet?

"Ausilia Brondi? Ah yes, her sister."

Bumping into Ausilia by chance arriving at the door of Via della Ghiara, there was always one of Elia's relatives ready to repeat this phrase. Cowed, Ausilia gathered her shawl around her throat. And at the click which the lock made, opened from the upper floors by a hand-pulled lever, she would hurriedly give way.

She stepped aside, the aged girl, lowering her eyes. How she would have preferred at that moment to return to her own house, her own family! But no: she too ended up going in, gently closing the big door, queuing up on the staircase in a huddled group with the others, who were busy chatting away to each other: she moved according to an instinct that, for at least forty years, had always been stronger than any will she had to resist it, to fight against it.

---

[*] Ferrarese dialect: "Poor little boy."

5.

THEY WOULD all find themselves together again on the first-floor landing, in front of another closed door. Even here, before someone came to open it, there was always something of a wait.

Finally, they would all be inside. And yet, remaining again behind—the visiting Jewish relatives had immediately gone directly ahead toward the kitchen—it often happened that Ausilia lingered on her own to roam round the rooms of the whole house, including at times those of the second and top floor, avoiding in her wanderings, apart from the storeroom for wood and the pantry on the ground floor, only the grey, half-empty and slightly scary granary under the roof. She would go through room after room, surveying one by one, with a strange kind of envious love, the innumerable familiar objects which cluttered them, the shelves overflowing with books and the notepads scattered everywhere, even in the passageways and in cabinets and cupboards, the ill-assorted furniture, the tables large and small, with the odd, complicated study lamps, the old canvases, nearly all in a parlous state, hung on the walls beside framed and glazed family and hospital photographs, and so on. In the meantime she kept repeating to herself, not without bitterness, that between them, the Brondis, and that tribe, so proud and reserved, who usually treated her as they did, it wasn't possible to reach a real agreement or understanding of any kind that wasn't merely superficial.

Even before seeing him again, she imagined the face of her brother-in-law.

In the big kitchen, where the copper pots and pans reflected back flames from the walls, and where, from his annual summer trips to Baden-Baden or to Vichy in the retinue of the Duchess Costabili, Elia would return every autumn with such an intense and imperious desire for peace and reflection—there, in a few minutes, he would appear to her again, seated as always at the desk placed under the window farthest from the entrance, perhaps just as he lifted his gaze from his books to look out beyond the vegetable garden, beyond the garden wall, which divided it from the city walls, beyond the walls themselves and to focus finally, smiling vaguely beneath his moustache, on the great golden clouds which filled the skies toward Bologna. Even just to imagine him, Elia, was enough for her to know once and for all that in the big kitchen filled with maids, with nurses from the Sant'Anna Hospital or from his clinic, with various Jewish relatives, with babies and children always shouting, often playing wildly and unrestrainedly, when not even Gemma, although his wife and the woman of the house, had ever managed to penetrate the invisible wall behind which Elia withdrew from everything that surrounded him, she the unmarried sister-in-law would never be able to occupy anything but a place apart, a little, very subsidiary and subordinate space. Her mother had been right to have always refused to enter that house! And her father and brothers, who, when they came there to chop wood, never wanted to go upstairs, so much so that at a certain point food and drink had to be taken down to them in the wood store—weren't they, too, right to avoid any intimacy and confidence?

And yet there had been one who was utterly different from the rest of Elia's relatives—a conviction that the years only strengthened in Ausilia's mind.

The person in question was Elia's father, poor Signor Salomone.

Having been married three times, he had twelve children, and though already very old indeed, and a widower for the third time when Elia got married, and very attached to the rented apartment in Via Vittoria where he had lived for more than half a century, regardless of all this, he had finally agreed to follow his beloved son, the doctor, to the house in Via della Ghiara, just in time, as it happened, to die at almost a hundred years of age.

To give an idea of this personage, let's suppose him out walking. Should he perchance meet a woman whom he knew, it made no difference whether she was wearing the hat of a lady or a proletarian shawl, he would immediately, in a sign of respect, salted with a refined admiration if it was worth the effort, draw back completely against the wall or step down from the sidewalk. However religious and devoutly practicing he was (oh yes, marrying as he did, Elia must have dealt him, at least at first, a heavy blow), he would never speak of religion at home, neither in his own nor in other people's homes. He would speak only in his own particular dialect, similar to Ferrarese, but full of the Hebrew words which were common in the vicinity of Via Mazzini, but that was all. And the fact was that in his mouth even those Hebrew words had nothing strange or mysterious about them. Who knows how, but even they took on the coloration of his continual optimism, his bountiful character.

When asked the time, he would draw from his waistcoat pocket a little silver wind-up watch, which at his death would be passed on to Jacopo, his first-born grandson, and, before checking the hour, raise it to his ear with a beatific expression. And often, even if no one had asked him (he was undoubtedly the meekest man, though at the same time a great patriot) he would tell of the distant time when Ferrara was still part of Austria and, in the main square, the white-uniformed soldiers were guarding the Archbishop's Palace with fixed bayonets at the ready. People looked at these soldiers with scorn, with hatred. He too—he admitted—being at that time, before 1860, still quite young, did the same. And yet, thinking back—he would add—they were hardly to blame, those poor lads, mainly Czechs and Croats put there like stakes to prop up the vineyard of the cardinal-legate. Soldiers must do as they're told, after all. Orders are orders.

Even more frequently, however, he would recall Giuseppe Garibaldi, who, he had no difficulty in admitting, had been the sun, the idol of his youth: he dwelt most of all on the general's voice, strong and melodious like the finest of tenors, and such as to rouse the blood, which, one starry night in June of 1863, he, Salomone Corcos, lost in a crowd of enthusiasts, had heard, lift from the balcony of the Palazzo Costabili, where the hero of two worlds had been a guest for the whole week.

He had gone there with Elia when he was a small child, he used to recount, holding him in his arms for the entire duration of his speech, so that the youngest of his children—too young to remember another miraculous night only a few years earlier, when the gates of the Ghetto had been beaten down by the fury of the people—should from that time on preserve indelibly in his memory the image of the red-shirted, blond-haired Man who had created Italy. Garibaldi! He, Salomone, was carrying a not inconsiderable weight of family responsibilities, something like twelve children. And yet he felt that one word from the general—he always spoke haltingly in saying such things but reaching this point in the story he was almost short of breath—would have been enough, had it been necessary, for him to have followed him to the ends of the earth. The ends of the earth, and that's for sure!—he would repeat with shining eyes. Whoever had heard Giuseppe Garibaldi speaking to the people would have done the same.

With Gemma he had always been gentle, kind and most attentive. And likewise in his relations with her, Ausilia, how affable he had been on every occasion, how courteous! For example: it often happened that, meeting her about the house, he would ask her about the price of vegetables, how much were the peas and the lettuce selling for, how much the potatoes, the beans and so on. But he did this, it was clear, above all to indicate to her that he had the greatest respect and consideration for her family, her family of vegetable farmers. "You are Ausilia, Gemma's sister," he might well have begun by saying. And he seemed quite pleased enough to have been able to figure it out on his own—since for some while his head, he explained, tapping his forehead with a finger and smiling, had been a bit faulty now and then.

But there was something of him, apart from his white curls shiny as silk, and his characteristically big nose, which she recalled in a special way. And that was the smell that wafted from his clothes.

A vague mixture of citrus fruits, of old grain and hay, it had the same smell which she had always noticed when she flicked through the ancient, indecipherable pages of some little books of Jewish rites that he brought with him to the house in Via della Ghiara, for their "eventual" distribution among the guests for the two suppers that followed Passover. They were illustrated by blueish, slightly faded engravings which showed, according to what one could read in the Italian printed beneath each of them, the Ten Plagues of Egypt, Moses before Pharaoh, the Passage through the Red Sea, the Rain of Manna, Moses on the Peak of Sinai speaking with the Eternal, the Adoration of the Golden Calf: and so on up until the Revelation to Joshua of the Promised Land. Elia's frockcoat never smelled of anything but ether and carbolic acid. The clothes and the entire person of Salomone Corcos, by contrast, exhaled a perfume that, for all its different accents, reminded her of incense.

Placed in a chest of drawers in the so-called "good" room, a big shad-

owy place overlooking Via della Ghiara where no one ever set foot, the ritual Passover books had impregnated not just the furniture but the whole
atmosphere with this perfume. Whenever she, Ausilia, went to shut herself
up in there, remaining, seated in the darkness, to think over her own concerns for hours on end sometimes (she had continued to use this room
as a kind of hiding place even after the death of Gemma when, in 1926,
she had come to live with Elia and Jacopo as housekeeper, and even after
both of them were deported to Germany in the autumn of 1943 . . .), she
would always have the feeling that poor Signor Salomone was there too,
within the four walls, present in flesh and blood. Just exactly as if, still in
this world and silently breathing, he was seated beside her.

6.

LOVE WAS something different, Ausilia reflected—no one knew that better than her.

It was something cruel, atrocious, to be spied on from a distance, or to
be dreamed of beneath lowered eyelids.

In fact, the secret feeling that from the very start had kept her bound
to Elia, strong enough to force her for her whole life to be continuously,
fatally, indispensably present, had certainly never given rise to the least
joy. No, truly it hadn't, if every time she entered the big kitchen of the
house in Via della Ghiara where, near the window in the corner, he would
linger over his studies until suppertime (he would study and seemed to
notice nothing, and yet nothing really worth the trouble of being noticed
would ever escape his intensely black, piercing, investigating eyes . . .), she
felt a need to avoid that calm gaze which for a moment, at her entrance,
had detached itself from a book, and the need quickly to summon, as if to
defend her, the good and kind image of Salomone Corcos.

The gaze of Elia! Nothing could really escape it. And yet at the same
time he seemed hardly to see anything . . .

That famous night on which he became engaged to Gemma (it happened in 1888, in August), and having returned very late, he passed his
father's bedroom on tiptoe, he stopped there for a moment, wondering

whether to go in. Extract the tooth and be rid of the pain, he thought to himself. Perhaps it was best to tell his father everything straight away.

He was about to lower the door handle when from the other side he was taken aback by his father's voice.

"Good Lord, where on earth have you been?" he cried out. "You know I haven't been able to get a wink of sleep?"

These words of his father, and especially the keening tone of his voice, made him change his mind. Having climbed up to his own room, a little room which looked out over the roofs, the first thing he did was to open the window and lean out. Realizing it was already dawn (not a murmur from within the house, the city asleep at his feet, and down there one of the four towers of the Castle touched at its very tip by a fleck of pink light), he suddenly decided not only to forgo any sleep but without further delay to start studying.

Science—he then said to himself. Wasn't Science his real calling?

It would be he, several decades later as Ausilia recalled, who told her all this, unprompted, at the end of one of the usual suppers that the two of them would take in the kitchen.

He was in front of her, the other side of the table, his face fully lit by the lamp above. While he spoke, grinning slightly beneath his big, brilliantly white moustache, he seemed to be watching her.

But did he actually see her? Truly see her?

It was—poor Gemma—certainly a very odd expression that he had in his eyes at that moment! It was as if, from the morning following the evening on which he'd promised her sister to marry her, as if from then on he had looked at things and at people in just that way: from above and, in some way, from beyond time.

A Memorial Tablet
in Via Mazzini

1.

WHEN, in August 1945, Geo Josz reappeared in Ferrara, the only survivor of the 183 members of the Jewish community whom the Germans had deported to Germany in the autumn of 1943, and all of whom were generally believed to have ended up in the gas chambers, no one in the city at first recognized him.

Josz. The surname certainly sounded familiar, having belonged to that Angelo Josz, the renowned salesman of wholesale fabrics, who, although a Fascist at the time of the March on Rome, and even remaining in the Ferrarese circle of friends around Italo Balbo at least until 1939, hadn't, for all of that, managed to protect himself and his family from the great raid and roundup that occurred four years later.* Yet how could one believe— many immediately objected—that this man of uncertain age, enormously, absurdly fat, who'd appeared a few days earlier in Via Mazzini right in front of the Jewish Temple had turned up alive from no less a place than the Germany of Buchenwald, Auschwitz, Mauthausen, Dachau, and so on, and above all that he, he of all people, was seriously one of the sons of poor Signor Angelo? And then, even conceding that it wasn't all a sham, a fab-

---

* A mass demonstration in October 1922 that brought Mussolini to power. Italo Balbo was an Italian Blackshirt leader in Ferrara and one of the main organizers of the march.

rication, that among that group of Jewish townsfolk sent off to the Nazi death camps there might indeed have been a Geo Josz, after so much time, so much suffering dealt out more or less to everyone, without distinction of political affiliation, wealth, religion or race, what did this character want just then, at that particular time? What was he after?

But better to proceed in an ordered manner, and, tracking a little way back into the past, to begin with the first moment of Geo Josz's reappearance in our city: the moment where the story of his return should properly begin.

In writing an account of it, there's the risk that the scene might look rather implausible, a piece of fiction. Even I have doubts about its veracity every time I consider it within the frame of what for us is that familiar, usual street: Via Mazzini, the street, that is, which leaving the Piazza delle Erbe, and flanking the quarter of the erstwhile Ghetto—with the San Crispino Oratory at the foot, the narrow cracks of Via Vignatagliata and of Via Vittoria halfway down, the baked-red facade of the Jewish Temple a little farther on, as well as, along its entire length, the crowded rows of stores, shops and little outlets facing each other—still serves today as the main route between the historic center and the Renaissance and modern parts of the city.

Immersed in the brilliance and silence of the early afternoon, a silence which at wide intervals was interrupted by gunshots, Via Mazzini seemed empty, abandoned, preserved intact. And so too it appeared to the young worker who, from one-thirty on, mounted on some scaffolding with a newspaper hat covering his head, had been busy about the marble slab which he'd been employed to affix at two meters height on to the dusty brickwork of the synagogue's facade. His appearance was that of a peasant forced by the war to seek work in the city and stand in as a plasterer, but whatever the telltale signs of this were, they would be obliterated in the blazing light, as he himself was well aware. Nor was this annihilating effect of the big August sun at all counteracted by the small group of passers-by, various in color and behavior, which had gathered on the cobblestones behind his back.

The first to stop were two young men, two partisans with beards and spectacles, in short trousers, red scarves round their necks, submachine guns on gun-belts: students, city gents—the young peasant plasterer had thought, hearing them talk and turning for a moment to peek at them. Soon afterward they were joined by a priest in his black vestments, undaunted by the outrageous heat, and then a sixty-year-old from the middle classes with a pepper-and-salt beard, a jovial air, his shirt open to reveal the skinniest chest and a restless Adam's apple. The latter, after having begun to read in a low tone what was presumably written on the tablet, name after name, had interrupted himself at a certain point by exclaiming with emphasis: "A hundred and eighty-three out of four hundred!" as if those names and those numbers might have a direct bearing also on him, Podetti Aristide from Bosco Mésola, who found himself working in Ferrara by chance, and had no intention of staying a day longer than was necessary, and meanwhile was minding his own business and nothing else. Jews, he now heard it said by a growing number of people. A hundred and eighty-three Jews deported to Germany, who died there, in the usual way, out of the four hundred who lived in Ferrara before the war. So that was cleared up. But just a second. Since those hundred and eighty-three must have been sent to Germany by the Fascists of the Republic of Salò,[*] what if one day or another they, the *tupín*,[†] should return to take control, and were biding their time in the hope of a rematch? It was a fair bet that they'd been walking around the streets for some time and in all likelihood they'd have one of those red handkerchiefs round their neck! Taking that into account, wasn't it better that the Jews, too, pretended not to know anything about it? Ah the *tupín*! You can imagine that at the right moment they could suddenly resurface, clad once more in their mud-camouflage uniforms, with those death's heads on their fezzes and pennants! No, no. Given the state of things, the less one knew about who was a Jew and who wasn't, the better, for all concerned.

---

[*] The Germans restored Mussolini to power in northern and central Italy in September 1943, and set up a puppet state, the Social Republic, in Salò on Lake Garda that lasted until May 1945.
[†] Ferrarese dialect for "mice," but here referring to the Fascist-appointed squads of armed teenagers who patrolled the streets of Ferrara in the latter stages of the war.

And it was that unfortunate boy, so determined to know nothing, as he was happy enough to be working and wasn't interested in anything else, and so diffident about whatever else was going on, imprisoned in his rough Po Delta dialect as he turned his back to the sun, who, at a certain point, feeling his calf touched—"Geo Josz?" asked a mocking voice—twisted round, suddenly, annoyed.

Before him stood a short, thickset man, his head covered up to his ears by an odd fur beret. How fat he was! He seemed swollen with water, a kind of drowned man. Still, there was no reason to be scared since, in an apparent effort to win his sympathy, the man was laughing.

His look turned serious and he pointed at the tablet.

"Geo Josz?" he repeated.

He began to laugh again. But quickly, as if contrite, and seeding his speech with frequent "Pardon me's" in the German fashion—he expressed himself with the elegance of a drawing room orator of another age, and Podetti Aristide stood listening to him with his mouth agape—he confessed himself unhappy, "Believe me," to have disrupted everything with an intervention which had, he was more than ready to recognize, all the qualities of a gaffe. Ah well—he sighed—the tablet would need to be remade, given that the Geo Josz, up there, to which in part the tablet was dedicated, was no other than himself, in flesh and blood. Unless that is—he immediately added while surveying them all with his blue eyes—unless the civic committee, accepting the fact as a hint from destiny, didn't immediately give up the whole idea of a commemorative tablet, which—he grinned—though, affixed in that busy place, it would offer the indubitable advantage of almost forcing passers-by to read it, would also have the adverse effect of clumsily altering the plain, honest facade of "our dear old Temple," one of the few things remaining the same as "before" in Ferrara, thanks be to God, one of the few things that one could still rely on.

"It's a bit like you," he concluded, "with that face, with those hands, being forced to wear a dinner jacket."

And so saying he showed his own hands, calloused beyond imagining, but with their backs so white that an identification number tattooed on to the skin, soft, as if boiled, a little above the right wrist, could be distinctly read: with its five numbers preceded by the letter "J."

2.

IT WAS thus that, pallid and swollen, as if he had emerged from the depths of the sea—his eyes a watery cerulean coldly looked up from the foot of the low scaffolding: not at all threatening, but rather ironic, even amused—Geo Josz reappeared in Ferrara, among us.

He came from far away, from much further away than he had actually come. Returned when no one expected him; what was it he wanted now?

To face a question of this kind with the requisite calm would have needed a different time, a different city.

It would have needed people a little less scared than those from whom the city's middle class devolved their opinions (among them were the usual lawyers, doctors, engineers and so on, the usual merchants, the usual landowners; not more than thirty, to count them one by one . . .): all good folk who, although they had been convinced Fascists until July 1943, and then from December of that same year, had in some fashion said yes to the Social Republic of Salò, for more than three months had seen nothing but traps and pitfalls all around them.

It's true, they would admit, they had taken the membership card for the Republic of Salò. Out of a civic sense they'd taken it, out of patriotic sentiments, and in each and every case not before the fatal 15 December,[*] in Ferrara, and the following outbreak across all of Italy of the fratricidal struggle.

But to get quickly to the point about that young fellow Josz, they would continue, raising their heads and swelling their chests under jackets in the buttonholes of which some of them had attached whatever decoration happened to be at hand—what was the sense in his going on covering his head, regardless of the stifling August heat, with a big fur cap? And his endless grinning? Instead of behaving in that manner, he would have done far better to explain how on earth he'd become so fat. As till then no one had

---

[*] Eleven Ferraresi citizens were shot at dawn by Blackshirts near the Estense Castle on November 15, 1943. Bassani here, and in "A Night in '43," mistakenly but consistently places the massacre a month later, on December 15.

heard of an oedema brought on by hunger—this must have been a joke put about in all likelihood by himself, the one most concerned—his fatness could only mean one of two things: either that in German concentration camps one didn't suffer from the terrible hunger that was claimed in the propaganda, or that he had managed, who knows at what price, to enjoy a very special and respectful treatment. So surely he should behave himself, and stop going around annoying people? Those who go seeking the mote in other people's eyes should look to the proverbial beam in their own.

And what could be said of the others—a minority, to tell the truth— who barricaded themselves in their houses with their ears peeled to catch the least sound from outside?

Among them, there was one with the tricolor scarf around his neck who had offered to preside at the public auctions for the goods seques- trated from the Jewish community, including the furnishings, the silver candelabras and everything from the two synagogues, one above the other, in the Temple of Via Mazzini; and there were those who, covering their white hairs with Black Brigade caps, had undertaken the role of judges in a special court responsible for various executions by firing squad, who had shown, it seemed, no prior sign at all of being in any particular way inter- ested in politics, but rather, in the majority of cases, had led a largely retired life, dedicated to their families, their professions, their studies . . . And yet they were so frightened for themselves at this point, so fearful they might unexpectedly be called to account for their actions, that when Geo Josz, too, asked no more than to live, to start living again, even in such a simple, such a basic request, they found something personally threatening. The thought that one of them on a dark night might be secretly taken out by the "Reds," led to the slaughter in some godforsaken place in the country, this terrible thought returned persistently to unsettle and torment them. To stay alive, to keep going in any way possible. They needed to survive. At any cost.

If only that wreck, they would jeer, would take himself away, would get the hell out of Ferrara!

The partisans, having appropriated what had been the HQ of the Black Brigade, were using the house in Via Campofranco still owned by his father, and therefore now his, his alone, as their barracks and prison. So he made do with carting around his ominous face everywhere it wasn't wanted, with the quite evident aim of continually goading those who, sooner or later, would have to settle all of his accounts. It was scandalous, at any rate, that the new authorities should put up with this state of affairs without so much as batting an eyelid. It would be useless appealing to the prefect, Dr. Herzen, who the day after the so-called Liberation had been made president by that same Comitato di Liberazione Nazionale* over which, after the events of December 15, 1943, he had secretly presided—useless because, if it was true, which it certainly was, that every night behind closed doors they updated lists of proscribed persons in his office in the castle . . . Oh yes, how well they knew that kind of person who, in 1939, had let himself be evicted without a word of protest, as though it were nothing, from the shoe factory a couple of kilometers along the road to Bologna, near Chiesuol del Fosso, which at that point he owned, and which later, during the war, had ended up as a pile of rubble! With his half-bald head, his feeble pretence of being a good paterfamilias, with his eternal smile full of gold teeth, with his fat lenses for myopia encircled by tortoiseshell rims, he presented that meek aspect (apart from the rigid straight spine which seemed screwed to the bicycle saddle he was inseparable from: a spine that was so in keeping with his Jewish surname, with its not-so-distant German origin . . .) characteristic of all who should be seriously feared. And what about the archbishopric? And the English governership? Wasn't it precisely an unfortunate sign of the times that even from such quarters there was never any response, apart from a sigh of desolate solidarity or, worse, a smile poised between mockery and embarrassment?

You can't reason with fear and with hatred. Though had they wanted to understand with the minimum of effort what was turning over in the soul of Geo Josz, it would have been enough for them to return to the moment of his first reappearance in front of the Jewish Temple in Via Mazzini.

That moment will perhaps be best recalled by the middle-class man of about sixty years of age, the one with the sparse little greying beard and the dry-skinned throat, who was among the first to stop under the com-

---

* The Committee for National Liberation was formed in September 1943 in opposition to Italian Fascism and the German occupation.

memorative tablet for the Ferrarese Jews deported to Germany, raising his shrill voice ("A hundred and eighty-three out of four hundred!" he had proudly cried out) to call the attention of all present to the importance of its inscription.

Having been present in silence when the sixteen-year-old survivor made a display of his hands, he immediately made his way through the small crowd to kiss him noisily on the cheeks, the latter, however, with his hands and forearms still nakedly extended before him, merely exclaimed in a noticeably cold tone, "With that ridiculous little beard, my dear Uncle Daniele, I didn't recognize you." A phrase which should have at once been considered very telling indeed. And not only about his identity.

And so he continued: "Why the beard? Have you decided, perhaps, that a beard suits you?"

Tightening his lips, he surveyed with a critical eye all the beards of various thickness and measure which the war, rather like the profusion of fake identity cards, had made such a common feature, even in Ferrara—it really seemed as if he were only concerned with that. But rather than the beards it was clear that there was something else, everything else that was troubling him.

In the immediate vicinity of that which, before the war, had been the Josz house, at whose door uncle and nephew presented themselves that same afternoon, there were to be seen, naturally, a good number of beards. And this contributed not a little in giving to the low building of exposed red brickwork, topped by a slender Ghibelline tower and extensive enough to cover almost the entire length of the secluded Via Campofranco, a grim, military air, fitting perhaps to recall the old owners of the establishment, the marqueses Del Sale, but it didn't in the slightest remind one of Angelo Josz, the Jewish wholesale-cloth dealer who had bought it in 1910 for a few thousand lire, and who ended up in Germany with his wife and children.

The big street entrance door was wide open. In front of it, seated on the steps, with machine guns between their bare legs or lounging on the seats of a jeep parked by the high wall opposite which encircled a huge, burgeoning garden, a dozen partisans were lazing about. But there were others, in greater numbers, some with voluminous files under their arms and all with energetic, determined faces, who kept coming and going. Between the street, half in shadow, half in sunlight, and the wide-open entrance of the old baronial house, in short, there was an intense, vivid, even joyful bustle, fully in keeping with the shrieks of the swallows that swooped down, almost grazing the cobblestones, and with the clacking of typewriters that issued ceaselessly from the barred ground-floor windows.

When this odd couple, one tall, thin and wild-looking, the other, fat, sluggish and sweaty, finally decided to step inside the entrance, they immediately attracted the attention of that company—nearly all of them boys, mostly bearded and long-haired, and armed. They gathered round, some rising from the rough benches placed along the walls. And Daniele Josz, who clearly wanted to show off to his nephew his familiarity with the place and its new occupants, was already briskly replying to every question.

By contrast Geo Josz kept silent. He stared one by one at those suntanned, rosy faces which pressed up close to them, as if beneath the beards he hoped to discover some hidden secret, to investigate some taint.

"And they haven't even offered me a drink," his smile seemed to be saying.

Having become aware, at a particular moment, with a sidelong glance whose meaning was clear, that beyond the vestibule, right at the center of the adjacent, rather dark and narrow garden in disarray, there still shone a big, full magnolia, he seemed to grow more contented and calm. But that only lasted a moment. Since very soon after, upstairs in the office of the young Associazione Nazionale Partigiani d'Italia* Secretary for the region (who in a couple of years would become the most brilliant Communist deputy in all of Italy, so very kind, courteous and reassuring as to provoke wistful sighs from not a few young women of the city's best families), Geo repeated with a slight sneer: "You know that beard of yours doesn't suit you at all."

It was at this moment, however, in the embarrassed chill that suddenly fell upon what, until then, mainly to the credit of Uncle Daniele, had been quite a cordial conversation, in the course of which the future honorable gentleman had brushed aside the polite "*lei*" form used by the

---

* ANPI (the National Association of Italian anti-Fascists) was a partisan organization formed in 1944.

survivor, insisting on the "*tu*" of contemporaries and party comrades, that the motive for which the other was there suddenly became clear. If only all those who in the following days built up so many futile suspicions about him had been present at this point.

That house, his look seemed to say as it shifted away from the typist on whom it had alighted and became suddenly menacing (so much so that the girl at once stopped tapping on the keys), that house where they, the Reds, had settled themselves in for more or less three months, replacing those others who had occupied it before—that is, the Blacks, the Fascists—actually belonged to him, had they forgotten? By what right had they taken possession of it? Both she, the graceful secretary, and he, the likeable and hearty partisan chief, so determined to their credit to make a new world, of a sudden became very careful about how they spoke. What were they thinking? That he would be happy to be lodged in a single room in the house? And would that be the very room in which they were speaking? Was that the one they had in mind to keep him quiet and on his best behavior? If so, they were seriously mistaken.

There was a big sing-song going on down in the street:

> *The wind blows and the storm howls,*
> *Our shoes have holes, but we must march on . . .*

Not a chance. The house was his, make no mistake. They would have to give it back, lock, stock and barrel. And as soon as possible.

3.

DURING THE wait for the Via Campofranco establishment to return effectively and entirely into his possession, Geo Josz seemed happy to occupy a single room. To be a guest.

More than a room, in effect it was a kind of granary built at the top of the crenellated tower that overshadowed the house: a big, bare room into which, after having climbed no fewer than a hundred steps that culminated in a rickety, little wooden staircase, one entered directly into a space once used as a lumber-room. It had been Geo Josz himself, with the disgusted tone of someone resigned to the worst, who had been the first to speak of that "makeshift" solution. All right then, he would adapt himself for the moment, he had said with a sigh. But on the understanding, it should be made very clear, that he could also make use of the lumber-room which was beneath the actual granary, where . . . At this point, without finishing the sentence, he lapsed into a brief, mysterious grin.

From that height, however, through a wide window, it was soon apparent that Geo Josz could follow everything that happened not only in the garden, but also in Via Campofranco. And since he hardly ever left the house, presumably spending hour after hour looking at the vast panorama of russet tiles, vegetable gardens and the distant countryside which extended beneath his feet, his continual presence became for the occupants of the floors beneath, to put it mildly, annoying and irksome. The cellars of the Josz house, all of which opened on to the garden, had been made over into secret prison cells in the era of the Black Brigade. About these, even after the Liberation, many sinister stories continued to circulate in the city. But now, under the probably treacherous surveillance of the guest in the tower, evidently they could no longer serve the purposes of secret and summary justice for which they had once been destined. With Geo Josz installed in that sort of observatory, and perhaps, as was attested by the light of the oil lamp which he kept lit from the first signs of dusk until dawn, vigilant at night also, now there was no chance of relaxing, not even for a moment. It must have been two or three o'clock in the morning after the evening when Geo Josz had appeared for the first time in Via Campofranco, when Nino Bottecchiari, who had stayed up working in his office until that time, had, as soon as he'd reached the street, raised his eyes to the tower. "Beware, all of you!" warned the light of the survivor suspended in mid-air against the starry sky. Bitterly reproaching himself for his culpable frivolity and acquiescence, but at the same time, like a good politician, preparing himself to confront a new reality, the young, future honorable gentleman, with a sigh, climbed on board the jeep.

But it also happened that, at the most unsuspected times of day, Geo soon began to appear on the stairs or down at the entrance, walking past the partisans permanently assembled there and wearing the usual minimal uniforms, clad in impeccable olive-colored gabardines which almost immediately had replaced the bearskin, leather jackets and tight, calf-hugging trousers they had when they arrived in Ferrara. He would slope off without greeting anyone, elegant, scrupulously shaved, with the rim of his brown felt hat on one side tilted down over his ice-cold eye. By the silence and unease provoked each time he appeared, from the outset he displayed his authority as the house-owner, too well brought up to argue but assured of his rights which his mere presence sufficed to assert and to remind the inconsiderate and defaulting tenant that enough was enough, he should clear out. The tenant shilly-shallies, pretends not to notice the steady protest of the proprietor, who for the moment is saying nothing, but the time is sure to arrive when he calls him to account for the ruined floors, the scratched walls and so on, so that month by month his position worsens, becomes ever more uncomfortable and precarious. It was late, the day after the 1948 elections, when much in Ferrara had already changed, or rather changed back to how it was before the war (the deputyship of the young Bottecchiari had by then triumphantly come about), when the ANPI decided to transfer its premises to the three rooms of the former Fascist headquarters on Viale Cavour, where since 1945 the local employment federation had established itself. Given the silent and implacable behavior of Geo Josz, this transfer already seemed more than a little unresponsive and tardy.

He hardly ever went out, as if to make sure that no one in the house should forget him even for a moment. Yet this didn't stop him every now and then from being seen in Via Vignatagliata, where since September he had been granted permission that his father's warehouse, in which the Jewish community had been piling the goods that had been stolen from Jewish houses during the Salò period and had remained for the most part ownerless, should be cleared "due to absolutely indispensable and urgent restoration work," as he wrote in a letter, "and for the reopening of the business." Or more rarely he might be seen along the Corso Giovecca—with the uncertain step of someone advancing into forbidden territory and whose mind is divided between the fear of unpleasant encounters and the bitter desire, perfectly contrary, to have them—taking the evening *passeggiata* which had been resumed in the city center, as lively and vibrant as ever; or else at the hour of the aperitif, at a table at the Caffè della Borsa in Corso Roma, sitting down abruptly, as he would always arrive out of breath and drenched with sweat. His attitude of ironical scorn—which soon enough had even prompted Uncle Daniele, so expansive and elec-trified by the atmosphere of those early post-war days, to give up on any conversation through the trapdoor to the granary above his head—hardly seemed to have discouraged the show of cordial salutations, the affection-ate greetings of "Welcome back!" which now, after the initial uncertainty, began to rain in on him from all sides.

They stepped out from the entrances of the shops next to the ware-house, hands outstretched with the air of people ready for any moral or material sacrifice, or crossed the Corso Giovecca, despite its breadth, and with excessive, histrionic gestures threw their arms round his neck; or they leaped out from the Caffè della Borsa, still immersed in that same subver-sive half-darkness of the depths in which once, every day at one o'clock, had issued the radio announcements of military defeats (announcements that had barely reached the bike of the boy Geo in the days when he would speed past . . .), to sit by his side under the yellow awning, which was inad-equate protection not only against the blinding glare but also against the dust which the wind swept up in broad whirls from the ruins of the nearby quarter of San Romano. He had been at Buchenwald and—the only one—had returned, after having suffered who knows what torments of body and soul, after having witnessed who knows what horrors. So they were there, at his service, all ears to hear him. He recounted; and they—also to show their contrition at having been so slow to recognize him—would never tire of hearing him, willing even to renounce the lunch to which, tolling twice, the Castle clock above was calling them. While they displayed, almost in testimony of their good faith and in support of the evolution that their ideas had undergone in those terrible, formative years, the rough canvas trousers, the partisan desert jackets with rolled-up sleeves, open collars without a trace of tie, feet slipped without socks into shoes and sandals res-olutely unpolished, and, of course, beards—there wasn't one of them with-out a beard—it was as if they were all saying in unison: "You've changed, don't you see? You've become a man, by God, and fat as well! But see—we too have changed, time has passed for us too . . ." And they were undoubtedly sincere in exhibiting themselves for the examination and judgement of Geo, and sincere in being pained by his inflexible rejection of their overtures. Just as sincere, in its way, was the conviction held, at least in part, by everyone in the city, even those who had most to fear from the present and most to doubt from the future, the conviction that, for good or bad, from now on there was going to begin a new era, incomparably better than that other one which, like a long sleep filled with atrocious nightmares, was ebbing away in their blood.

As regards Uncle Daniele, who for three months had been living on his wits without knowing each morning where he would be sleeping that night, the suffocating cubbyhole in the tower had at once seemed, to his incurable optimism, a marvellous acquisition. No one was more convinced than he that with the end of the war had begun the glad era of democracy and of universal brotherhood.

"Now at last one can breathe freely!" he had ventured the first night that he'd come into possession of his little cell. He spoke these words, supine on a horsehair mattress, with his hands gripped behind his neck.

"Now at last one can breathe freely, aah!" he had repeated more loudly.

And then: "Doesn't it seem to you, Geo," he had continued, "that the atmosphere in the city is different, really different than before? It can't be denied. Only freedom can produce such miracles! As for me, I'm really convinced . . ."

What Daniele Josz was really convinced about, however, must have seemed of quite dubious interest, as the only reply Geo vouchsafed to the impassioned apostrophes of his uncle from the opening of the little staircase was either a "Hmm!" or a "Really?", which hardly inspired further utterance. "What on earth will he do?" the old man asked himself, growing silent, while his eyes turned toward the ceiling to follow the slapping back and forth of a pair of indefatigable slippers. And for a short while at least he abstained from further comment.

It seemed inconceivable to him that Geo did not share his enthusiasms.

Having fled from Ferrara during the days of the armistice, he had spent more than a year hidden in an obscure village in the Tuscan-Emilian Apennines, looked after by peasants. Up there, after the death of his wife, who, poor thing, had had to be buried under a false name in the little graveyard, he had joined up with a small band of partisans, assuming the role of political commissar—a circumstance which would soon allow him to be among those suntanned and bearded men who, perched on top of a truck, would be the first to enter liberated Ferrara. What unforgettable days those were! What joy it had been for him once again to be in the city, half in ruins it's true, almost unrecognizable, but utterly cleared of all the Fascists of every kind, the early enrolled as well as the late! What a pleasure to once again be able to sit at a table in the Caffè della Borsa (a place where no sooner had he arrived than he had chosen it as the premises for resuming his old, modest insurance business) without any threatening look to chase him away, but rather finding himself the center of a general sympathy! But Geo?—he wondered. Was it possible that Geo felt nothing of what he himself had felt some months before? Was it possible that having descended into hell and by some miracle returned, he should feel no impulse beyond that of motionlessly reliving the past, as witnessed by the frightening series of photographs of his dead—Angelo and Luce, his parents, and Pietruccio, his little brother who was just ten years old—which one day when he had stealthily slunk up to the big room he had found decorating all four of its walls? And finally, was it possible that the only beard in the whole city that Geo found bearable was that of the old Fascist Geremia Tabet, his father's brother-in-law, so esteemed by the regime that he managed to keep on frequenting even the Merchants' Club, at least every now and then, for at least two years after 1938? The night after the day of Geo's reappearance, he, Daniele Josz, with profound unease, had had to follow him to the Tabet house, in Vicolo Mozzo Roversella, where before then he had never dreamed of setting foot. And then, wasn't it shocking that Geo, when the old Fascist stuck his nose out of a first-floor window, had let forth a shrill cry, ridiculously, hysterically, almost wildly impassioned? And what was that cry for? What did it mean? Did it mean perhaps that Geo, despite Buchenwald and the extermination of all his closest family, had become what his father, poor Angelo, had continued being in all ingenuousness till the very end, even perhaps up till the threshold of the gas chamber: a "patriot," as he frequently loved to declare himself with such stalwart pride?

"Who's there?" had asked the hesitant, worried voice above.

"It's me, Uncle Geremia, it's Geo!"

They were standing below in front of the big closed door of the Tabet house. It was ten o'clock at night and one could hardly see a thing down in the alley. Geo's strangled cry, Daniele Josz recalled, had taken him by surprise, pushing him into a state of extreme confusion. What should he do? What could he say? But there was no time to consider. The big door had opened and Geo, having rapidly entered, was already striding up the dark stairs. He needed to run after him, at least try to reach him.

He managed to do so only at the second staircase, where, to make things worse, before the opened doorway to the apartment, Geremia Tabet himself stood waiting. With the light from inside at his back, the old Fascist, in slippers and pyjamas, was staring at the two of them, perplexed but not dumbfounded, having resumed his habitual calm.

He had stopped at the edge of the landing, half-hidden in the shadow. When he had seen Geo, who, by contrast, had kept advancing and abruptly clasped his uncle in a frenetic embrace, the latter suddenly felt himself again to be the poor relative whom all of them (his brother-in-law Angelo perfectly in agreement about this along with his wife's family) had always kept at a distance mainly because of his political convictions. No, no, Daniele said to himself at this point—not even on this occasion was he going to enter that home. Turning his back, he would have walked away. But, instead, what did he do? Instead, like the idiot he was, he had done the opposite. At his final reckoning, he had thought, poor Luce, Geo's mother, was a Tabet. Who can tell—perhaps it was the memory of his mother, Geremia's sister, that kept Geo from treating the nasty Fascist of the family with the coldness that type of character deserved? Natural enough in the circumstances, after the first affectionate greetings had been exhausted, it wouldn't be surprising that the boy should collect himself and reestablish the right distance . . .

But in this he was to be sadly disappointed. For the rest of the visit, which lasted late into the night (as it seemed that Geo couldn't bring himself to leave), he had had to witness, seated in a corner of the small dining room, shows of affection and intimacy that were little short of disgusting.

It was as if by instinct that between the two of them a binding agreement had been established, to which, before they went to bed, the others in the house also quickly conformed (Tani, the wife, so aged and wasted away! and the three children, Alda, Gilberta and Romano, all of them, as usual, hanging on the lips of their respective consort or parent . . .). The pact proposed by Geremia was the following: that Geo should not even hint indirectly at the political past of his uncle, and he, on his side, should abstain from asking his nephew to recount what he had seen and suffered in that Germany where even he, Geremia Tabet, unless there were proof to the contrary—this too should be remembered by all those who now thought they might confront him with minor errors in his youth, some merely-human mistake of political choice made in times so distant as to now seem almost mythical—had himself lost a sister, a brother-in-law and a much-loved nephew. And that was indisputable: the last three years had been terrible. For everyone. Still, things being as they were, a sense of balance and discretion should prevail over every other impulse—the past is past, and it's futile to dig it all up again! Better look to the future. And as to the future, what did it have in store? Geremia had asked at a certain point—assuming the grave but benevolent tone of a paterfamilias who can look into the distance and make out many things there—what kind of plans did Geo himself have? If he was considering, just to suppose, reopening his father's business—a most noble aspiration that he personally could only approve of, and it was worth remembering the Via Vignatagliata warehouse, that at least, was still there—then all to the good. Of course he wouldn't fail to help secure the indispensable support of some bank or other. But apart from this, if in the meantime, since the Via Campofranco house was still occupied by the "Reds," Geo wanted to stay for a while there with them, they could always no trouble at all, find a place to set up a camp bed, no trouble at all.

It was right then, at the words "camp bed," Daniele Josz recalled, that he had raised his head, focusing all the attention of which he was capable. What was happening? he asked himself. He wanted to understand. He needed to understand.

Streaming with sweat, despite being in pyjamas, Geremia Tabet sat on one side of the big, black dining table, and once more doubtful, perplexed, with the end of his finger worrying at his little pointed grey beard (cut in the classic style of the Fascist squads, which he alone among the old Fascists of Ferrara had had the temerity, the untimeliness or perhaps, who knows, even the shrewdness, to conserve in its proper dimensions). It was on that grey pointed beard and that fat hand which prodded it, that Geo, while he smilingly declined the offer with a shake of his head, fixed his blue eyes with a fanatical stubbornness.

4.

AUTUMN CAME to an end. Winter arrived, the long, cold winter that we're used to in these parts. Then spring returned. And slowly, along with the turning of the seasons, the past also returned.

I don't know how believable what I am about to relate will be. It's true that, not so long after, things occurred that would have induced one to imagine that a secret, dynamic relation existed between Geo Josz and Ferrara. Let me explain. Very gradually he grew thin, dried out, by slow steps resuming, apart from the sparse white hair of an absolute silvery whiteness, a face which his hairless cheeks rendered still more youthful, truly like a boy's. But after the removal of the highest piles of rubble and an initial mania of superficial change had exhausted itself, little by little the city, too, began to reassume its old form of sleepy decrepitude which centuries of clerical decadence succeeding the distant, fierce and glorious times of Ghibelline rule had turned into an immutable mask. In short, everything rolled on and kept going. Geo, on one side, Ferrara and its society (not excluding those Jews who had escaped the massacre) on the other: each of them was suddenly involved in a vast, ineluctable, fatal flurry of activity. In concordance like two spheres attached by gears and spinning in a single, invisible orbit, which nothing could resist, or halt.

Then came May.

So was it just for this? someone smilingly asked. Was it just so that Geo's blind regret for his lost adolescence should not seem quite so blind, that from the first days of the month rows of beautiful girls began once again slowly and gracefully to pedal back from their trips to the surrounding countryside, arriving by various routes at the center of town with their handlebars overflowing with wild flowers? And besides, wasn't it for the same reason that the famous Count Scocca, disgorged from who knows what hiding place to lean his back like a little stone idol against the marble half-column which, for centuries, had kept upright one of the three gates to the Ghetto, had returned to his spot right at the corner of Via Vignata-gliata and Via Mazzini?

And since, one late afternoon around the 15th of the month, a stream of young cyclists had almost finished their slow and graceful ascent of Via Mazzini itself, and were about to flow into the Piazza delle Erbe and beyond, laughing—before such a spectacle, always new and always the same, no one could surely begrudge the fact that at this point the count should be unwilling to abandon his station. The little stage of Via Mazzini presented on one side, against the sunlight, the serried and luminous ranks of cycling girls, and on the opposite side, grey as the ancient stonework against which he was leaning, Count Lionello Scocca. Well, everyone thought, why should one not be moved by the concrete manifestation of such an allegory, sagely and suddenly harmonizing everything: an anguished, atrocious yesterday, with a today so serene and full of promise? Certainly, it would never have crossed the mind of anyone who suddenly noticed the penniless old patrician resume, as though nothing had happened, one of his once customary vantage points—one from which someone with good eyesight and subtle hearing could scan the whole of Via Mazzini from top to bottom—to reproach him for having been a paid informer of the Organizzazione per la Vigilanza e la Repressione dell'Antifascismo[*] for years, or having been from 1939 to 1943 the director of the civilian section of the Italo-German Institute of Culture. That black, visibly re-tinted Hitler moustache—not to mention the unmistakable steeply tilted, dull-yellow straw hat, the toothpick gripped between thin lips, the big, sensual nose raised to sniff the reek of rubble that the evening breeze brought with it—might now inspire only sympathetic, even grateful reflections.

So it seemed scandalous that with regard to Count Scocca, all told

---

[*] OVRA (the Organization for Vigilance and Repression of Anti-Fascism) was a Fascist organization involved in surveillance.

just a harmless old relic, Geo Josz should behave in a manner that one had to consider alien to any basic sense of decency or discretion. The shock and embarrassment it caused were all the more difficult to swallow precisely because for a good while people had gotten used to smiling with benevolence and understanding at Geo and all his eccentricities, including his aversion to the so-called "wartime beards." By the same standard, one could recognize a certain appropriateness that the faces of many gentlemen should now finally dare once more to show themselves in the light of day. And on this topic it was true, true as can be (reasoned one of the better informed) that the lawyer Geremia Tabet, Geo's maternal uncle, had not cut off his beard and perhaps never would. But Good Lord, a poor creature like him! He also deserved a bit of understanding! It wouldn't be that hard. Enough to make the connection between that pathetic, grey, pointed beard and the black Fascist jacket, the shiny high, black boots, the black felt fez which for years and years that fine professional had always displayed when he would turn up between midday and one o'clock every Sunday at the Caffè della Borsa, and whoever there was that might want to make a fuss about that would soon lose the courage to say a word.

From the beginning, what happened seemed impossible. No one could believe it. They just couldn't imagine a scene in which Geo, who entered with his usual padded steps into Count Scocca's field of vision as he stood at the corner of Via Vignatagliata, then, with a sudden bestial fury, delivered to the parchmenty cheeks of that old, resuscitated carrion two dry, really hard slaps, more worthy of a Fascist trooper of Balbo and his companions' times, as someone actually remarked, rather than of a survivor of the German gas chambers. In any case, it really happened—dozens of people saw it. But on the other hand, wasn't it odd that, straight away, different and contrasting accounts as to exactly what had happened should have circulated? It made one almost doubt, not only the basis of each of these accounts but even the real, objective event itself, that same double slap, so full and resounding, according to general opinion, as to be heard for almost the entire length of Via Mazzini, from the corner of Piazza delle Erbe, down there at the end, as far at least as the Jewish Temple.

For many, Geo's gesture remained unprovoked and inexplicable.

A little before, he had been seen walking in the same direction as the girls on bicycles, letting himself be slowly overtaken by this procession and never once looking away from the street, his gaze full of stupefaction and joy. Having thus arrived in front of Count Scocca, and abruptly detaching his gaze from a trio of cyclists who had then come parallel with the Oratory of San Crispino, Geo stood stock still, as if the presence of the count, in that place and at that moment, seemed inconceivable to him. His halt, in any case, lasted no more than a second or two, the time required to knit his eyebrows, clench his lips and teeth, convulsively ball up his hands and mutter some words without sense. After which, as though released by a spring, Geo literally leaped on the poor count, who, until that moment, had showed no sign at all of having noticed him.

Is that the whole story? And yet there had been a motive, others objected, and a good one at that! Agreed, Count Scocca might not have been aware of Geo's arrival. Even if rather strange, that couldn't at all be discounted. But as for Geo, however, how was it possible to believe that just at the moment in which the three girls he was gazing fixedly at were about to disappear into the golden haze of Piazza delle Erbe, he had had the time or even the desire to notice the count?

According to these last, instead of merely observing the already almost vesperal scene, with no other concern than to immerse himself in the vague sense of how much the city and he were in perfect harmony, the count had actually done something provocative. And this something, which no one who was passing at a distance of more than a couple of yards could have possibly observed—for the good reason, among other things, that despite everything, the eternal toothpick continued to shift from one to the other corner of his mouth—this something consisted in a subtle sibilance, so weak as to seem shyly casual, an idle little fortuitous whistle, in short, which would surely have remained unnoticed if the tune it hinted at had been anything other than that of "Lili Marlene":

Underneath the lantern by the barrack-gate . . .

the count whistled softly but clearly, his own gaze also, despite his seventy or more years, fixed rapturously on the cycling girls. Who can say?

Perhaps having stopped his whistling for a moment, he had joined his own voice to the unanimous chorus that rippled along the sidewalk of Via Mazzini, murmuring in dialect, "Praised be the Lord for these beauties!" or even, "Bless you all and the busty saint who protects you!" But what good did it do him? Fortune decreed that that lazy, innocent whistling—innocent, you understand, to anyone else except Geo—rose to his lips just a fraction too soon. And the outcome for him was those two slaps.

There existed a third version, however, and the third, like the first, didn't mention either "Lili Marlene" or any other whistling, whether more or less innocent or provocative.

According to this last interpretation, it had been the count who stopped Geo. "Ah ha!" he had said, under his breath, when he saw him so close. Geo had immediately halted. Then the count had engaged him in conversation, hitting the bull's-eye the first time by announcing his full name: "Look who it isn't!" he had said. "Could it really be Ruggero Josz, the eldest son of poor Angiolino?" For Lionello Scocca knew everything about Ferrara, and the nearly two years he had had to spend in hiding around Piacenza, just the other side of the river Po, under a false name, had not in the least clouded his memory or weakened his famous ability to recognize at a single glance one face in a thousand. And so, well before Geo had leaped on him and given him those violent slaps, for some minutes they had kept on talking calmly, the count interrogating Geo about his father, for whom, he had said, he always had the greatest affection, gathering the most detailed information about the fate of the rest of his family, including Pietruccio, and congratulating Geo on having survived it all; with Geo, on his side, replying sometimes a little awkwardly or reluctantly, it's true, but nevertheless replying. In conclusion, they seemed no different at all from a couple of townsfolk lingering on the sidewalk to talk of this and that, waiting for darkness to fall. And yet the slaps still needed to be explained. How the devil had they come about? In the opinion of those who gave this account, and who never tired of returning to the theme with the most various of analyses and surmises, it was this that revealed quite what a bizarre character Geo was; it was this that showed just what an "enigma" he was.

5.

HOWEVER IT actually happened, what's certain is that after that evening in May everything changed. Whoever wished to understand, understood. The others, the majority, at least realized that something serious and irreparable had occurred, the consequences of which could not now be avoided. They would have to put up with them.

It was the day after, for example, that people truly saw just how thin Geo had become during this period.

An absurd scarecrow—to the general wonder, unease and alarm, he reappeared dressed in the same clothes he had worn when he'd returned from Germany the preceding August, including the fur cap and the leather jacket. Now they fitted him so loosely—it was clear he hadn't made the least effort to take them in—that they seemed to be draped on a clothes hanger. People saw him coming up the Corso Giovecca in the morning sun which gaily and peacefully shone down upon his rags, and couldn't believe their eyes. So that was how he really was! they thought. In the last months he'd done nothing but grow thinner and thinner, bit by bit, till he was nothing but skin and bones! But no one could raise a laugh. To see him crossing the Corso Giovecca at the City Theater, then taking the Corso Roma (he had crossed the road as fearful of the cars and bicycles as an old man . . .), there were very few of them who didn't feel themselves inwardly shudder.

And so, from that morning on, without changing his style of dress again, Geo installed himself, one might say, as a fixture at the Caffè della Borsa in Corso Roma, where even if the general, already fading condemnation of the Black Brigade's recent torturers and assassins still held them at bay, still kept them in hiding, the old club-wielding dispensers of castor-oil purges from 1922 and '24, which the war had somewhat cast into oblivion, began to show themselves again one by one. Clad in rags, Geo stared from his table at the little group of these latter figures with an air between challenge and imploration, and his behavior contrasted, to his disadvantage as you can guess, with the timidity, the evident desire not to draw too much attention to themselves which these ex-despots expressed with every gesture. By now old, innocuous, with the signs of wreckage that the years of misfortune had stamped mainly on their faces, and yet still reserved, well mannered, properly dressed, these latter persons displayed a demeanor that was a great deal more human, more decent, and more deserving of sympathy, even. So what after all did Geo Josz really want? a great many people once again began to ask, all of them in agreement that the period immediately after the war, which was so propitious for an examination of both the private and collective conscience, was now over, and this was a luxury that could no longer be afforded. It was the same old question, but framed with the brutal impatience that life, imperious in its demands, at this point unambiguously reasserted.

For these reasons, with the exception of Uncle Daniele, who was always brimming with indignation and a polemical impulse at the "conspicuous" presence at those same tables of some of the most renowned members of Ferrara's earliest Fascist squads, it became increasingly rare that any of the habitués of Caffè della Borsa would be prepared to lift themselves off their seats, cross the few intervening yards and then sit down beside Geo.

And that's not to take into account the unease which rewarded those few for their willing efforts of sociability—each time they felt an anxiety flecked with annoyance which they were unable to shrug off for at least two or three days. Frankly, it wasn't possible, they would exclaim, to keep a conversation going with someone dressed so ludicrously! And besides, letting him speak, they would continue, meant that, sure enough, he'd again start telling about Fossoli, Germany, Buchenwald, the fate of his whole family and so on, so that it was impossible to know how to extract themselves. At the cafe, under the awning pummelled by the sirocco blowing across, and as ill-protected as the tables, chairs and the figures reckless enough to sit at them were from the full violence of the afternoon sun, while Geo chattered away unstoppably, there was nothing else to do but follow, from the corner of their eyes, the movements of the builder opposite busy plastering over the holes in the Castle moat's parapet from the bullets left by the execution by firing squad on December 15, 1943. And he, Geo, what was he recounting in the meantime? Without assuming that this was already understood, perhaps he was repeating once again, word for word, the phrases that his father murmured to him before fainting on the path back to the Lager from the salt-mine where both of them were working. Or else, raising his hand in exactly the same way as he had done a hundred times before, he demonstrated the little wave goodbye his mother had given him some twenty minutes after the train had stopped in arrival at the deserted ghostly station in the middle of a forest of fir-trees, as she was pushed away bewildered among a group of women. Or else, with the look of someone about to impart some important news, he again began to tell of Pietruccio, his younger brother, seated next to him in the complete darkness of the truck that was conveying them from the station to the barracks, and who suddenly disappeared without a complaint or a cry, for ever . . . Horrible, of course, devastating. Still, there was no need to be hoodwinked, those who'd survived such protracted and depressing encounters would declare—you could tell how forced and exaggerated, in short, how false, these stories of Geo's were. And then what a bore! they would add, puffing. Such things had been heard so many times that to have them administered once again (and by the same person as well!) when the Castle clock up there was ringing out hour after hour, one was frankly inclined to give up the ghost and make a run for it. No, let's be clear, you'd need more than a leather jacket and a fur cap to help you swallow this kind of stale swill.

During the remaining months of 1946, the whole of '47 and a good part of '48, this ever more ragged and desolate figure was unceasingly before the eyes of the whole of Ferrara. In the streets, the squares, the cinemas, the theaters, around the sports fields, at public ceremonies: people would turn their heads and there he would be, indefatigable, always with that shadow of saddened bafflement in his eyes. To start holding forth—that was evidently his purpose. By now there was hardly anyone who didn't keep him at bay, who didn't flee him like the plague.

They continued to speak about him, that much, yes.

After Buchenwald, as could be heard in the nastier kind of gossip, it would make sense if he chose to stay at home or, if he went out, that he'd prefer to plod down the shadowy sidestreets like Via Mazzini, Via Vittoria, Via Vignatagliata and Via delle Volte, instead of the thoroughfares of the Corso Giovecca and Corso Roma. When he brought out his lugubrious deportee's uniform again, never more wearing the fine olive-colored gabardine which Squarcia, undoubtedly the best tailor in the city, had cut to his exact measure, and then contrived to turn up wherever people were gathered to enjoy themselves or simply with the healthy desire to be together, what possible excuse could one find for such eccentric and offensive behavior?

From this perspective, they would continue, the scandal which happened at Club Doro in August 1946 (more than a year, it should be noted, after the end of the war), where, at its opening night Geo had the bright idea of turning up dressed in the same fashion, could stand as an apt example.

Nothing could be said against the place in itself. There was no other way to describe it than with a single word: magnificent. Conceived according to the most modern criteria, it was impossible to criticize, except for the fact that it had been constructed at about a hundred meters from the place where in 1944 the five members of the underground Comitato di Liberazione Nazionale had been executed by firing squad—this last detail without doubt rather unpleasant, as the young Bottecchiari, if one looked at the thing from his personal point of view, was perhaps not wrong to underline in the short, satirical article published by him in the Gazzetta del Po a couple of days after the opening. At any rate, only the mind of a madman like Geo could have conceived of an idea to sabotage a place which was so happy and convivial in that manner. What harm was there in it? If people now, as it would soon enough be clear, felt the need for a locale outside the walls, and somewhere no one would stop them enjoying themselves, somewhere that, immediately after leaving the cinema, it would be possible to go, not only to have a snack, but also to dance to the sound of the radio-gramophone among groups of friends and truck drivers in transit, to stay out even sometimes till dawn—well, didn't people have the right to that? Deranged by the war, and anxious to help on its way the much predicted and wished-for reconstruction, society needed to let its hair down occasionally. Thanks be to God, life had begun again. And when it begins, as one knows, it doesn't look back.

Suddenly faces that had, until then, expressed doubt and uncertainty, became bitterly questioning, lit up with malice. And what if the camouflage and self-exhibition of Geo, so insistent, and so irritating, had had a precise political intention? What if—and here they winked—with the passing of time he'd become a Commie?

That evening at the dance club, as soon as he came in, he began to show photographs of the members of his family who had died in Germany to left and right, reaching such a stage of petulance that he was trying to stop the boys and girls from moving off by grabbing hold of their clothes, and they, in that moment, as the radio had suddenly started madly up again, had to brush him off so as to get back onto the dance floor. These were not inventions at all, a great many of the most reliable people had been witnesses to the fact. So what else had Geo been referring to with those gestures of his, with those demented antics, with that bizarre and maca- bre pantomime, seasoned with his saccharine grins and half-imploring, half-menacing looks, unless it was that he and Nino Bottecchiari, having finally reached an agreement about the house in Via Campofranco, were now in alliance and total agreement about everything else, which is to say politics, which is to say Communism? But then, if he had accepted the role of useful idiot, wasn't it more than justified that the Friends of America Club, which in all the chaos and enthusiasm of the immediate post-war period had thought it opportune to enroll Geo as one of their board mem- bers, had later, with due care, decided to cross him off the list? Let's be clear: it's likely that no one would have dreamed of chucking him out, if he hadn't first of all wanted the scandal, and the moderate sanctions against him that followed. No, this was far from being nonsense! The proof could be seen that other famous night in February 1947—when he showed up at the door of the club dressed as a beggar and with his head shaved like a convict: truly reduced to a human wreck—that's the word—the spitting image of the famous tramp, Tugnìn da la Ca' di Dio—there, in the ves- tibule full of coats and furs, he had started to bawl that they should let him through, since whoever was enrolled and had paid their fees had the right to frequent the club how and when they wanted. Expelling someone is always unpleasant. Of course it is. Besides, wasn't it true quite a while before that—to be exact, from the previous autumn—the board of direc- tors of the Friends of America Club had voted unanimously to return as soon as possible to their old title of the Unione Club, once again reducing the enrolled membership to the aristocratic families of the Costabilis, the Del Sales, the Maffeis, the Scroffas, the Scoccas, etc., as well as the more select members of the bourgeoisie—Catholic, but in certain exceptional cases, also Jewish, drawn from the liberal professions and landowners? Like a swollen river that had broken its banks and hugely flooded the surrounding countryside, the world now needed to return to its original margins: that was the point. This explained, among other things, why even old Maria, Maria Ludargnani, who during the same winter had reopened her house of assignation in Via Arianuova—in just a few weeks, it became clear that this was the only, in some way public, place where it was still possible to gather and meet together without political or even apolitical opinion continually leaping out to poison all relations, and the evenings spent there, mainly chatting or playing gin rummy with the girls, were a reminder of the blessed times before the great upheaval—why even she had thought it necessary, that other time Geo had come to knock on her door, to tell him roundly and clearly, Nix, to go away, and in the end declaring in dialect, after making very sure with her eye to the spyhole that he'd been swallowed up again by the mist: "*Agh mancava sol ach gnéss déntar anch clucalà!*"* In conclusion: if no one had dreamed that Maria Ludargnani, prohibiting Geo's entry to her "house," had defrauded him of some right, then one had to admit that the Unione Club had acted toward him in a manner that was most proper, astute and responsible. And then just think about it! If you can't exclude whomever you want from your own house, where is freedom, what sense is there in talking about democracy?

Only in 1948, after the April 18 elections, after the local ANPI section was forced to transfer to the three rooms in the ex-Fascist HQ in Viale Cavour—and with this the belated proof was given that the rumor of "adhesion" to the Communist Party of the Via Campofranco house's owner was pure fantasy—only in the summer of that year did Geo Josz finally decide to abandon the game. Exactly like a character in a novel, he disappeared without warning, without leaving the slightest trace behind. At once some said he had emigrated to Palestine in the wake of Dr. Herzen, others claimed he'd gone to South America, yet others to some undefined "country beyond the Iron Curtain," and others still that he had drowned himself in the Po, throwing himself at night from the height of the iron bridge of Pontelagoscuro which had been recently reconstructed.

---

* In Ferrarese dialect: "Just what we need—for that one there to be in here!"

This topic continued to crop up for the next few months: at the Caffè della Borsa, at the Doro, in Maria Ludargnani's house of assignation, everywhere, to some extent. Daniele Josz was offered on more than one occasion the opportunity to hold a public enquiry. The lawyer Geremia Tabet also intervened to represent questions concerning the inheritance of his nephew. In the meantime: "What a madman!" was heard again and again.

They would shake their heads benignly, tighten their lips in silence, raise their eyes to the heavens.

"If he'd only had a bit of patience!" they'd add, sighing, and they were now, once again, sincere, once again sincerely regretful on his behalf.

Then they would say that as time heals everything in this world, thanks to which Ferrara itself was rising from the ruins the same as it had once been, so time would in the end have brought some peace even to him, would have helped him return to a normal life, in short, to reestablish him within the city. And yet instead the opposite had happened. He had preferred to go away. Disappear. Even to kill himself. To play the tragic hero. Exactly at this point when, renting out the big house on Via Campofranco and giving the right boost to his father's firm, he would have been able to live very comfortably, like a gentleman, and to consider among other things making a new family for himself. But no, let's be honest: they really had treated him with more than enough patience. The episode with Count Scocca, without even cataloguing the rest, should in the end be enough to reveal that, to demonstrate what kind of an eccentric he was, what sort of living enigma had landed among them . . .

6.

An enigma, that's what it was.

And yet, in the absence of any more certain clues, if we consider that sense of the absurd, and simultaneously that feeling of revelatory truth, which any encounter can have just as dusk is falling, the episode with Count Scocca shouldn't have seemed so enigmatic, shouldn't have been anything that could not have been understood by a heart that felt a little solidarity.

It's true that daylight is boredom, a hard sleep for the spirit, "tedious mirth," as the Poet says. But in the end let the hour of dusk arrive, the hour equally woven of shadow and light of a peaceful dusk in May, and then note how the things and people that before had appeared utterly normal and indifferent can suddenly show themselves as they truly are: it can happen all at once—and then it is as though you've been struck by lightning—that they speak for the first time of themselves and of you.

"What am I doing here with this person? Who is this person?" And I, replying to his questions, playing along with him, who on earth am I?

Two slaps, after some moments of mute bewilderment, had been the thunderous reply to the insistent, albeit polite questions of Lionello Scocca. But to those questions there might well have been the alternate reply of a furious, inhuman cry—so loud that the whole city, as much of it as still remained standing beyond the deceptively intact scene of Via Mazzini, and as far off as the distant, breached walls, would have heard it with horror.

The Final Years
of Clelia Trotti

1.

To call the vast, architectonic complex of Ferrara's Municipal Cemetery beautiful, so beautiful as even to be consolatory, there'd be the risk, even among us, of provoking the usual sniggers, the superstitious gestures to fend off the evil eye always at the ready in Italy to greet any speech that refers to death without deploring it. All the same, once you arrive at the end of Via Borso d'Este, a perfectly straight little road, with the marble-cutting workshops huddled at the start and the florists at the end, and entirely overwhelmed by the thick foliage of the two big private parks on either side, the unexpected vista of Piazza della Certosa and of the adjacent cemetery, gives an undeniably joyful, almost festive impression.

To have an idea of what Piazza della Certosa is like, one should think of an open, nearly empty meadow, scattered as it is in the distance with some occasional funerary monuments for illustrious nineteenth-century lay-persons: a kind of parade ground. To the right, the rugged, unfinished facade of the church of San Cristoforo, and, curving in a wide semicircle until it reaches the city walls, a red, early-sixteenth-century portico on which, some afternoons, the sun beats down to magnificent effect; to the left, small, semi-rustic houses, the low boundary walls of the big vegetable gardens, and orchards of which even now, in this most northerly zone of the city, there is an abundance—only houses and low walls which, in contrast to those on the opposite side, do not offer the least obstacle to the long rays of afternoon or evening sunlight. In the space between these boundaries, there's very little that speaks of death. Even the two pairs of terracotta angels right at the top of the portico, awaiting the signal from heaven to blow into the elongated bronze trumpets they've already put to their lips, have nothing about them that could really be considered threatening. They swell their red cheeks, impatient to blow, eager to play: the baroque artist must surely have found the likeness for the faces of these four robust-looking lads in the surrounding Ferrarese countryside.

It may be because of the dreamy sweetness of the place, and also, it should be said, its almost perfect and perpetual solitude, but the fact is that Piazza della Certosa has always been the favorite site for lovers' trysts. Where would you go in Ferrara, even today, when you want to talk to someone a little away from the world? The first choice is Piazza della Certosa. There, should things proceed as might be hoped, it would be only too easy to move on later to the nearby city walls, where you can find as many places as you like away from the prying eyes of nursemaids that are so vigilant in the piazza around the hour of dusk. And if, on the contrary, the idyll doesn't proceed, it would be just as easy and, at the same time, without any risk of being compromised, to return from there together toward the city center. This is a custom that has been established of old, a kind of ritual, probably as ancient as Ferrara itself. It was in force before the war, as it is today and will be tomorrow. True, the bell tower of San Cristoforo, docked halfway up by an English grenade in April 1945 and remaining thus, a sort of bloody stump, is there to declare that any guarantee of permanence is illusory, and therefore that the message of hope that the sunlit porticoes with their reddened heat seem to express is only a lie, a trick, a beautiful deception. Just as the bell tower of San Cristoforo has ceased to exist, without doubt, sooner or later, even the agile procession of arches that stretch like two arms up toward the light will cease to exist, to lull and delude the souls of those who contemplate it. Even this will come to an end sooner or later. As will everything. But in the meanwhile, only a few steps from the thousands and thousands of citizens who lie in row after row of the cemetery sited behind, on the vast grassy expanse scattered here and there with funerary steles and memorial stones, life's peaceful, indifferent bustle goes on unperturbed, refusing to throw in the towel, to give up the ghost; what prophesy would seem more destined to be erased, to remain unheard in the excited atmosphere of the nearing dusk, than one which promises an inevitable, final nothingness?

The atmosphere of general, almost sporting excitement immediately provoked in Piazza della Certosa by a funeral cortège too different from the usual to pass unobserved, a cortège that one autumn afternoon in 1946 emerged from Via Borso with a big band at its head, couldn't but immediately attract the attention of the habitués of the place—mainly nursemaids, children and enamoured couples, inducing the first, seated on the grass beside prams, to raise bewildered eyes from the newspaper or their sewing, the second to stop running after or playing with balls and the last to release their clasped hands and quickly draw back from each other.

The autumn of 1946. The war now over. And yet the first impression, observing the funeral which in that moment was making its entry into Piazza della Certosa, was to have been transported back to May or June of the previous year, to the fiery period of the Liberation. With a sudden leap of the heart and the blood, it was like once again being called on to witness one of those then typical and frequent examinations of the collective conscience by which an old, guilty society desperately tries to renew itself. No sooner had one noticed the thicket of red flags which followed the coffin, and the scores of placards inscribed with an assortment of slogans: ETERNAL GLORY TO CLELIA TROTTI or ALL HONOR TO CLELIA TROTTI, SOCIALIST MARTYR or VIVA CLELIA TROTTI HEROIC EXAMPLE TO THE WORKING CLASS etc., and the bearded partisans who carried them aloft, and above all the absence in front of the carriage of priests and clergymen, than one's gaze hurried ahead to where the procession was making its way: a grave, that is, dug in the portion of the cemetery exactly in front of the main entrance to the church of San Cristoforo where, apart from an English protestant who had died from malaria in 1917, no one had been buried for more than fifty years.

And yet, returning to the funeral cortège, the head of which was by now only tens of meters from the humble, secular grave which was waiting open—another crowd in the meantime was unceasingly pouring out from Via Borso—even a slightly trained eye would quickly be aware, from innumerable details, how deceptive was that initial impression of a magical return to the atmosphere of 1945.

Let's take, for example, the band. It's worth specifying that it proceeded in front of, but was detached from, the carriage, and played Chopin's funeral march in slow time. The brand-new uniforms worn by the band members, one of the boasts of the Communist administration only recently installed in the municipality, would undoubtedly have enchanted a foreigner, an uninformed newcomer, but not someone who, underneath the large caps with shiny visors in the style of the American police, was able to trace one by one the good-natured and dejected features of the Orfeonica's* old zealots, dispersed who knows where, poor devils, at the time of the shootings and ambushes that followed the break-up of the Front and the popular uprising. But the punctilious staging, so alien to the genial chaos typical of revolutions, was if possible even more evident in the compact formation of some fifteen *arzdóre*†
from the Po delta who, carrying in pairs great wreaths of carnations and roses, surrounded the funeral carriage on all sides like a guard of honor.

To see the earthy faces, deeply marked with fatigue, of these mature female heads of the family, all roughly the same age as Clelia Trotti, would be enough to be able to guess where they had come from and how they had arrived. Gathered together at Ferrara from the furthest villages of the Adriatic coast, at midday in the city they will certainly have found someone to offer them the refreshment of *pastasciutta*, a slice of roast beef and a quart of wine, but not the chance of a much-needed rest. The same bureaucratic mind that had provided a table adorned with red paper flags had then inflexibly decided that after the meal these ancient female farm laborers should clean themselves as best they could from their dusty journey and then put on, over their everyday clothes, a strange kind of tunic: red, naturally, and peppered with lots of tiny black hammers and sickles. Thus clad, they now appeared as it had been decreed that they should—almost

---

* A local orchestra.
† See footnote on p. 41.

like priestesses of socialism. But their heavy, bewildered steps, the wild stares which they cast about, gave them away only too clearly. It made one think that the laborious odyssey which, from the start of the day, they had already undertaken was sadly very far from being over. Shedding those tunics some hours later, then getting back into the same three or four cars that had transported them into the city, they would finally be restored to their impoverished dwellings only late at night. And who knows if before letting them depart anyone might remember to sit them down for a second around the table adorned with flags?

Immediately behind the funeral carriage, the authorities followed in several lines that filled the small space between the carriage itself and the undifferentiated crowd carrying flags and placards.

These were Socialists, Communists, Catholics, Liberals, activists, Repubblicani-storici:[*] in short, the complete ex-directory of the last secret Comitato di Liberazione Nazionale, reconstructed with all its members for the occasion. Added to and mixed in with this group, one noticed some other figures who were not, strictly speaking, political, such as the engineer Cohen, president of the Jewish community, and the newly nominated mayoress, Dr. Bettitoni.

So, even if the honorable Mauro Bottecchiari, usually known in Ferrara as "the prince of our forum," couldn't call himself the city's most representative political figure after the recent administrative elections had seen the crushing victory of the Communists, it was to him, to his uncombed, silver head of hair, to his high-colored, loyal, convivial face that everyone's gaze first turned. It's true that on the actual political plane, at this point, the honorable Bottecchiari signified pretty well nothing ("A reformist à la Turati!" people on the Communist side had begun to call him). But compared to the old lion, what an insipid figure the other members of the ex-directory of the final underground Comitato di Liberazione Nazionale cut! Apart from Dr. Herzen, the so-called prefect of the Liberation, recently emigrated to Palestine, no one else was missing. There was the lawyer Galassi-Tarabini of the Democratic Christian Party, who, worried

---

[*] A political party of the center, but anti-Fascist. For information about the *Comitato*, see footnote on p. 66.

to find himself there at a purely secular, civic funeral—and for this reason he swivelled every which way his washed-out blue eyes that seemed always about to fill with tears—walked beside Don Bedogni, of the Catholic Action Party, who, on the contrary, in a French beret and baggy trousers, even in these circumstances made an effort to display the consummate ease, the unprejudiced, modern suavity which, in the post-war period, made him one of the most renowned public figures of the entire Emilia Romagna. There was the engineer Sears, of the Partito d'Azione,[*] who, as usual, walked a little apart from the others with his small hands clasped behind his back, and was smiling slightly to himself. There was the little group of Repubblicani-storici—the chemist Riccoboni, the tailor Squarcia, the dentist Canella—rather embarrassed, you could clearly see, but still willing to keep up with the times. And finally there was Alfio Mori, the federal Communist of Ferrara: small, dark, bespectacled, with the hint of a smile that revealed his big white upper canines, he advanced in quiet conversation with Nino Bottecchiari, the young, promising provincial secretary of the Associazione Nazionale Partigiani d'Italia.[†] And yet, walking stooped and meek, reduced in appearance to a little band of nobodies, over all of them the honorable Bottecchiari enjoyed the easiest of victories. Seeing him looming over them by a head and continuously turning about that same red, ireful face—before which even Sciagura, the notorious Sciagura,[‡] sent to attack him on the crowded Corso Giovecca in the remote year of 1922, had been forced to beat an ignominious retreat—there was no doubt that he, the lawyer, the honorable Mauro Bottecchiari, was back again, if only for a day, the indisputable, acknowledged leader of Ferrara's anti-Fascists. So nothing could be more natural, after the carriage had stopped beside the grave, and the *arzdóre* of the Po delta had slid out from it the zinc coffin of Clelia Trotti, than that it should be he, the honorable Bottecchiari, who should be the first to move toward the catafalque.

---

[*] The Action Party was a radical Socialist party formed in 1942 and dissolved in 1947. It adopted the name of Guiseppe Mazzini's democratic party from nearly a century before.
[†] See footnote on p. 68.
[‡] Sciagura—meaning "calamity" in Italian—is the nickname of Carlo Aretusi, a prominent member of Ferrara's Fascist squad who reappears throughout *The Novel of Ferrara* and takes center stage in "A Night in '43."

The solemn transferral of the remains of Clelia Trotti, who had died three years before in the prison of Codigoro, during the German occupation, from the Codigoro graveyard to the Communal Cemetery of Ferrara, could not possibly have exempted him from the role of absolute eminence that was his due. It was his responsibility as Clelia Trotti's oldest comrade in the Socialist struggle to open the series of commemorative speeches.

"Comrades!" shouted the honorable Bottecchiari—a raucous, imperious cry which echoed far along under the cemetery's porticoes.

"Comrades," he added in a lower tone, after a pause, as if he were preparing to go full tilt.

He then began to speak, gesticulating. And his words would most certainly have reached the furthest corners of Piazza della Certosa—the face of the honorable gentleman had at once become purple with the effort—if at that very moment a motor scooter in Via Borso hadn't revved up explosively: a Vespa, one of the first to be seen coursing about the city just after the end of the war. The silencer on the Vespa's exhaust pipe was missing. Missing? More than that, the showy chrome metal contraption which stuck out below, on the left-hand side of the scooter, served the opposite purpose: not to suppress the motor's chugging revs but to make them drier and more obstreperous, better suited to the restless adolescent hand that twitched continuously to unleash them.

Interrupted in his oratorical flourish, the honorable Bottecchiari became silent. Contracting his white, bushy eyebrows, he directed his gaze toward the end of the square. He was short-sighted and, not seeing clearly, with a nervous gesture of his big hand that always trembled, took out a tiny pince-nez. The distant image of a young girl on a Vespa—who, having left Via Borsa but now slowing down, was riding along the portico arches of the cemetery behind the mass of persons in a semicircle—soon came into focus. Oh, it must be a very young girl, from a good family, the honorable Bottecchiari said, twisting his lips in a grimace of sadness. Who could she be, whose child? he added, with a reticent but irritated expression, as if he were going over in his mind all the names of the most well-off families of the city's bourgeoisie, among whom the Bottecchiaris were also numbered, as if surveying one by one all those sturdy, tanned, teenage legs which at least two months of swimming at Rimini, Ricci-

one and so on, had pared down—oh yes, the bourgeoisie, after the storm
of the war has passed, quickly resume all their old habits! "What a lack
of decency!" he preached at them, loudly: with the bitterness of one who
feels wounded, misunderstood. "I wonder," he added, pointing with outstretched hand at the very young scooterist, upright in her saddle down
there, the slight, almost masculine torso clad in a black silk shirt and with
a red ribbon in her hair, "I wonder if one can be much more disrespectful than that!" And the crowd, hundreds of scandalized faces, turned all
together to make a hushing hiss.

"Ssh!"

The girl didn't understand, or else didn't care to. Although she had
by now reached that part of the square she was heading for—the honorable Bottecchiari, who had seen her disappear behind a high barrier of
people hoisted up on to the curb-posts around the churchyard the better
to witness the ceremony, had waited in vain for her to reappear into the
open further on—she not only didn't feel inclined to turn off the engine,
but instead, unabashed, every now and then kept up her game of sudden,
clamorous revvings.

"For God's sake, get her to stop!" cried the honorable Bottecchiari in
exasperation.

"Ssh!" repeated an energetic chorus of the men who had climbed on to
the curb-posts: necks that turned, eyes that from above could admonish-
ingly survey a scene that he, Bottecchiari, even on tiptoe, was completely
unable to observe. And yet, in the meantime, no one who wanted to put
an end to that scandal was prepared to get down, and thereby risk losing
their place!

Seated on the stone border of the churchyard, in a good spot to see
everything—the honorable Bottecchiari over there, waiting to be able to
resume his eulogy, and here, two or three meters away from him, the girl
on the Vespa whose blue eyes just in that moment caught his own—Bruno
Lattes gave a start.

He felt uneasy (what follows in this story will explain why) and lowered
his head. When, after a few seconds he raised it again, the girl was already
looking elsewhere. She was now staring, in a clearly ironic way, at a boy
more or less her own age, as ashen-blond as herself and with the same hard,

indifferent look in his bright blue irises. A tennis racket between his legs, and a white pullover tied by its sleeves around his neck, the boy was just in front of her, likewise seated on the churchyard border. The two, it was clear to Bruno Lattes, were going out together—and for that reason had arranged to meet here—in Piazza della Certosa, of course! But who was she, who were her parents? Bruno kept thinking, suddenly, spasmodically attracted to her, to the red ribbon that tied up the girl's hair. Was it possible that the war, the years in which he had been a boy and she a child, had left not the tiniest trace on her? Was it possible that everywhere in Italy the adolescents were like this, as if, unaware of anything, they had been born teenagers from out of the pages of an illustrated American magazine?

"I've been waiting for you for half an hour," said the young tennis player, without giving any sign of meaning to get up.

"And you're complaining!" replied the girl.

She nodded, with a little sneer at the square teeming with people.

"Looks to me like you've found something to keep you happy."

"Ssh! Be quiet!" repeated for the third time the men perched on the posts.

The boy assumed the hard look of a gangster from the movies. With a grin he pointed at the scooter.

"Why not give that little twitchy hand of yours a rest?"

"I'd prefer to go somewhere else," the girl grumbled, though, in the meantime having got down from the saddle and switched off the motor, she had sat down beside her friend. "So what do you want to do? Stick around here?"

"Before this coffin that carries the mortal remains of Clelia Trotti, of our unforgettable Clelia," the honorable Bottecchiari had resumed in a tone of voice which foreshadowed the big tears which would soon begin to roll down his apoplectic cheeks, "comrades, friends, fellow citizens all, I cannot but immediately recall the past we have lived through together. If I'm not mistaken, we came to know each other, Clelia Trotti, and I who address you, in the April of 1904 . . ."

Bruno Lattes slowly turned to look in the direction of the speaker. But once again he gave a start. The little man, dressed all in black, straight as a ramrod, who stood down there at the side of the honorable Bottecchiari—

didn't he know him? Could he be Cesare Rovigatti, the shoemaker of Piazza Santa Maria in Vado?

How little time has passed, he thought to himself with regret, since he, after July 25, 1943, had left Ferrara in August for Rome, and then no more than a year after, for the United States of America! And yet how much had happened in such a short time!

At the start of those last, atrocious three years, his parents, who never believed they would have to flee, never saw the need to provide themselves with false papers, were taken away by the Germans, and both their names now figured among the nearly two hundred others on the memorial tablet which the Jewish community had had fixed on the facade of the Temple in Via Mazzini. And he? He, on the contrary, had escaped from Ferrara. He got away at the right moment not to suffer the same fate as his mother and father, or alternatively not to have been shot by firing squad in the following December at the time of the Salò Republic, with the reward, apart from having saved his skin, of being by now on his way toward a tranquil, dignified university career: he was so far only a lecturer in Italian, rather than having tenure, but soon he'd be given a permanent post, which would result (after some months of waiting) in his acquiring the longed-for American citizenship . . .

In short, the last three years seemed like a lifetime. And yet Rovigatti, thank God—Bruno Lattes continued thinking and, without being aware, nodded his head in the affirmative—didn't seem to have aged at all; even his grizzled black hair had remained more or less the same. Likewise the honorable Bottecchiari and all the other Ferrarese anti-Fascists, today assembled in an official plenary for the funeral of Clelia Trotti, whom he had known personally and spent time with from 1939 on. None of them seemed to have aged, nor had Ferrara itself, which, apart from the wreckage caused by the war, which was being speedily repaired, had seemed to him from the first identical to the city of his childhood and adolescence. Although stripped of all its furnishings, even the house he had been born and brought up in had been restored to him intact, intact like an empty shell . . . Likewise for Rovigatti—perhaps especially for him!—it seemed as though time had passed in vain, or even come to a halt.

There it all was, preserved in Piazza della Certosa, he concluded—the little, old provincial world he'd left behind. Almost like a wax replica: there it all was, exactly the same as itself. But Clelia Trotti?

The last time he'd met her had coincidentally been here, in Piazza della Certosa, nearly in the same spot where her coffin now rested, the day before his departure. In his memory, during the following interminable forty months, Clelia had never changed.

How he would have liked, now, to have found her, too, fixed in wax, motionless like a grotesque statuette that, torn between scorn and compassion, he could position as he pleased! With a smile, he would have told her: "See, wasn't I telling the truth when I promised I'd return? And you were wrong not to believe me."

If only she hadn't changed, had remained forever the same as he had seen her that last afternoon before he went away, before he cut the cord and saved himself. He would have asked this of her, if, in the meantime, she hadn't died.

2.

IN THE late autumn of 1939, almost a year after the proclamation of the Racial Laws, when he decided to go in search of Clelia Trotti, Bruno Lattes still knew almost nothing about her. From what he had heard, she was a small, withered woman, nearly sixty, who didn't take care of herself, with the look of a nun, who, if you passed her on the street, you wouldn't even notice. On the other hand, who in Ferrara at that time could claim to know her personally, or even remember that she existed? Even the honorable Bottecchiari, despite having acted a bit in his youth, and at the beginning of his political career having directed with her the legendary *Torch of the People*—they'd even been lovers, according to the whispered gossip, at least until the First World War broke out—even he, at the outset, gave the impression of having completely lost touch with her.

"Here he is, our young Lattes!" the honorable Bottecchiari had cried out from behind the imposing, Renaissance-style table that served him as a desk on the occasion that Bruno had gone to his office hoping to glean some information about the old school mistress. "Do come in!

Come in!" he had added heartily, seeing him hesitating at the doorway. "How's your father?"

While saying so, he extended his powerful right hand by way of greeting and encouragement, half-rising from his comfy lawyer's seat upholstered in red satin while looking him up and down with a satisfied expression. And yet, as soon as he heard the name of Trotti, he was ready to withdraw into a state of cautious reticence.

"But yes ... just a moment ..." he replied, with obvious embarrassment, "someone, I can't remember who, must have told me that she's living ... that's she's gone to stay in the Saraceno district ... in Via Belfiore ..."

He then changed the subject to speak of other things: about the war, the Phoney War, the likelihood of Italy's entering the war, or rather "of Mussolini" doing so, and about Hitler's next possible "strikes." "Oh yes," could be read in his blue eyes, full of little red veins and lit with triumphant irony, "oh yes! For twenty years you've looked at me with suspicion, even you people have avoided and despised me as an anti-Fascist, as a subversive, an enemy to the regime, and now that your lovely regime is chucking you out, here you are, all penitent, with your ears flat and your tail between your legs!"

He spoke of all kinds of other things, while never straying far from matters of international politics and that kind of commentary about things military which, by this stage, when the radio transmitted the daily news of the war halted at the Maginot Line, overflowed even at the Caffè della Borsa. At least on that occasion, Bruno thought, it was clear he didn't want the conversation to stray from such territory. His tone of bland complicity shouldn't mislead anyone who listened to think otherwise. As justification for this, the friendship that he, Bottecchiari, had always had with Bruno's father, also a lawyer, since their long-ago schooldays—rather than friendship it might be better to call it professional consideration between middle-class and well-off colleagues—this tacit understanding had been maintained between the two of them, even after the March on Rome, even after the assassination of Matteotti, by the solemn and confidential greetings they would smilingly exchange in the Corso Giovecca from the distance of one sidewalk to the other ... So much so that, later, at the end of their "pleasant pow-wow," as the honorable gentleman had put it, it was a big surprise for Bruno that it was he, Bottecchiari, who, unprompted, just as they were saying their goodbyes, should have returned to the topic of Clelia Trotti.

"If you manage to track her down, do send her my greetings," he said with a cordial grin, patting Bruno on the back just as he was halfway to the door.

And then, in a lower tone:

"You don't know Rovigatti, do you—Cesare Rovigatti, the shoemaker who has his workshop in Piazza Santa Maria in Vado, beside the church?"

"We always go to him to get our shoes resoled!" The words escaped Bruno and he felt himself blushing. "Why do you ask?"

"He's someone who'll be able to tell you where Signora Trotti is," explained the honorable gentleman. "Go and find him. Ask him. But be careful—" he added (the crack of the frosted-glass door had closed so it was now merely a spyhole)—"be very careful as she's under surveillance!"

When he was downstairs, hovering at the main entrance, the first thing Bruno did was look up at the faintly lit square face of the clock in the square. It was seven o'clock. Why not go at once to see Rovigatti? If he hurried, he could easily find him still there in his dark little den. He was the kind of person who never closed before eight, eight-thirty.

He waited for the most opportune moment to slip away without drawing any attention to himself. He finally stepped out, and having hurried across the open space in front, as always teeming with people at that hour, he took cover under the Duomo's arches.

He began to walk more slowly now, his hands deep in his raincoat pockets, and at the same time he pondered the ambiguous welcome he'd received from Bottecchiari.

Once again he saw his face as it had last appeared through the half-closed door. He had said "Rovigatti" and given a wink as he spoke. So, what had he meant, the honorable Bottecchiari, with that meaningful wink? Had he wanted, with that rather vulgar sign and the whispered name, to excuse himself indirectly for having kept their whole conversation a bit on the general side? Or alternatively, had he wanted to hint at the bond that had tied him, and perhaps, who knows, still secretly did, to his old Party comrade, a hint which, it's clear, would take away, even from the little that had been said, any political import? In fact this was consistent with the way he usually behaved in Ferrara, when half boastfully, half ashamed of himself, he would confide man to man (but above all to other middle-class persons!) of a relationship he was having with a working-class girl. Exactly in that manner, and from time immemorial. And yet, on the other hand, wasn't it quite odd that the honorable Bottecchiari, an ex-deputy of the Socialist Party, a veteran anti-Fascist, one who gave the impression of never having kowtowed to anyone, should be prepared to adopt—it didn't matter whether for a joke or flirtatiously—the same stupid and cruel sulkiness of the conformist herd which arrogantly occupied the streets, the cafes, the cinemas, the dance halls, the sports grounds, the barbers' shops, even the brothels, excluding from the Imperium whoever was or seemed different? The truth was that not even the honorable Bottecchiari had escaped without being harmed, without his character, the fierce integrity of his youth, being tainted by the pressure of those decades, from 1915 to '39, which had seen in Ferrara, as everywhere else in Italy, the progressive degeneration of every human value. It's true, his fellow lawyers, all of them Fascist in the extreme, literally foamed with anger every time, holding forth in the courthouse, he made it clear what he thought—more than one, without doubt, would have liked to hurl him to the ground, grab him by the folds of his toga, and yell in his face, "You're trying to insinuate such and such, eh? Admit it!" But in reality they'd always let him hold forth, content in the end to have given the old battler free rein once more to indulge his eternal saying-without-saying, his never-ending, tireless hinting, which over the years had become a kind of tic, an addiction, almost the expression of a second nature. If the honorable Bottecchiari, regardless of his past, was always prepared, when leaving his office or the court on his way home every day, to walk down Corso Giovecca defiantly flaunting his mane of almost luminously white hair in the face of his few friends and many enemies, none of this had happened without him too, at some level, having at least partly forgiven us.

Rapt in these thoughts that held his heart in the grip of anxiety, jostling and being jostled by passers-by, Bruno slowly ascended Via Mazzini and Via Saraceno. "How disgusting!" he hissed every now and then between his teeth. He looked with hatred at the sparkling shop windows, the peo-

ple stopped in front of them to look at the goods on display, the shopkeepers that showed themselves in their doorways, more or less the same
in their behavior, he thought to himself, as the shrews who kept watch,
always half in, half out of their huddled little houses in Via Colomba, Via
Sacca and thereabouts. Still ensnared and enslaved by the passion which,
since the August of that year, had tied him to one of the most brilliant
and sought-after girls in Ferrara, Adriana Trentini, the women that passed
him going the other way and brushed against him without noticing him
(the beautiful, the blonde and the elegant especially) seemed to him in
their whole way of being at once adorable and detestable, to carry the
ill-disguised mark of depravity. "What trash! What shameful scum!" he
kept repeating, not even under his breath.

And yet, gradually as he proceeded, and the streets became narrower
and less well-lit, his fury and disgust began to abate. Taking a left turn into
Via Borgo di Sotto, he came out almost level with Via Belfiore and was
about to cross. But from the closed blinds of the houses in Via Belfiore, at
least as far as where the little street made a sharp bend, only a sparse, yellowish light filtered out. Who could he ask, whose doorbell could he ring?
By now everyone would be eating supper—at his own home as well, they'd
be expecting him. Remembering Rovigatti, he ended up going on.

Obscured by fog, the Piazza Santa Maria in Vado suddenly cleared
before him, revealing the sombre facade of the church on one side, the dark
opening of Via Scandiana in front, in the center the little fountain where a
group of women were seated chattering, shabby little workshops and hov-
els all around, from which emanated, together with a faint light and smells
of roast beef and chestnut cake, vague and various sounds: an anvil beaten
weakly, a child's muffled sobbing, a "goodnight" and a "goodbye" exchanged
by two elderly men from deep under an invisible portico, a clinking of
glasses ... His gaze was quickly drawn to the left by a small, slightly better-lit
window. Rovigatti was there, seated at his cobbler's workbench. Beyond the
steamed-up windowpane his familiar outline could be discerned. And as he
made his way toward him, it was as though he stood still and the unchanged
image of the shoemaker was coming toward him through the fog.

He went in, took off his hat, offered his hand to Rovigatti above the
workbench, sat down in front of him and at once and without any diffi-

culty obtained the full and exact address of the schoolmistress: 36, Via Fondo Banchetto, at the house of Codecà. Then they began to talk. So that evening, as well, when he returned home the supper had long been finished.

The very next day, he timidly rang the doorbell of 36, Via Fondo Banchetto. And certainly, if he had been invited in at once, if a fat woman with salt-and-pepper hair and a shy manner—"her sister" as Rovigatti had drily explained—hadn't come to the door to tell him that the schoolmistress was not at home, if she, the same she, in a black satin smock and with the Fascist badge pinned to her breast, hadn't reappeared the next day to tell him that the schoolmistress was giving lessons and therefore couldn't receive any visitors, and the next day again, that she wasn't well, and, yet another day, that she'd gone to Bologna and wouldn't be back before next week, and so on week after week, he wouldn't have had the opportunity to become, as he did in fact become, friends with Rovigatti. He had understood from the first moment that he would be kept waiting at Santa Maria in Vado. But for how long? he had wondered. Had Clelia Trotti come to know him through his attempts to contact her? Had her married sister Codecà told her that he came to the house almost every day?

Each time he pressed the bell his heart would be beating fast, and each time he felt the disappointment anew. Rejected, he would withdraw to Piazza Santa Maria in Vado, not three hundred meters away. He would never find Rovigatti's glass door shut, on that he could rely. He only needed to push it open with two fingers, and there would always be the shoemaker in person, with his tuft of raven hair which still youthfully flopped over to one side of his pale forehead, stippled with blackheads around the temples, with his smile, with his dark, almost feverish eyes which gazed up at him. "Good evening, Signorino Bruno, how are you?" Rovigatti would say. "Do come in please and make yourself at home." And did he not truly do so?

They would sometimes talk till after nine o'clock. In the meantime, seated on the bench facing him, Bruno would watch the shoemaker at work.

Rolling the pack thread in palms as tough as the leather he had cut out in the shape of a sole, Rovigatti drew the needle back and forth with a measured energy. He perennially kept a handful of tacks in his mouth, and his lips and tongue were wonders of precision and promptness in disgorging them one by one into the light as the occasion required. Gripping a shoe tightly between his knees, he hammered the tacks in tirelessly and automatically . . . How skilled and assured he was! Bruno thought. What strength and self-awareness he seems able to derive from manual labor! Making busy with his big, blackened, incredibly calloused hands didn't seem in the least to impede his conversation. Rather the opposite. A tack hammered home through the thickness of leather with a single stroke seemed sometimes to serve his purposes better than any argument.

And yet what was it that still kept them apart? he often asked himself. What stopped him from winning the shoemaker's full and absolute confidence? Class difference, perhaps? Could it really be that?

Speaking ill of Fascism to him—in the end really an expedient to win him over, but mainly to get him to intervene on his behalf so that Clelia Trotti's realm might open up to him a bit earlier than had been decreed— it sometimes happened that the shoemaker only listened, or replied coldly, in an exaggeratedly objective tone.

"No, I wouldn't say that," he went as far as replying one evening, having given a peep outside to check. "No, I wouldn't say that. Even the Fascists have done some good."

He was clearly relishing a victory. Not only because Signorino Bruno, the son of those well-off folk in Via Madama whose shoes he'd resoled for almost twenty years, had come to pay him visits, but also because a moment ago he had enjoyed the luxury of conceding some small merit to a common enemy. He wasn't an upper-class gentleman, no, he seemed to be saying. He, Cesare Rovigatti, had been born and brought up among the poor, the persecuted, the oppressed. And so? Just because Cesare Rovigatti was only a shoemaker, did that now mean you could only expect from him obtuse rancor and blind, indiscriminate hatred? Ah no, that's too easy! Those times were over when the rich and powerful could make use of the working classes as cannon fodder, reserving a monopoly on fine sentiments for themselves! Enough of these misunderstandings! If someone had fooled themselves into thinking they could start these old tricks again now, entrusting the working classes with the noble task of doing their dangerous work for them, well then so much the worse for that someone.

He seemed to much prefer other topics to politics. Literature, for example.

Did Bruno like Victor Hugo? he asked. What an unbeatable book, *Ninety-Three*! And *Les Misérables*? And *The Man Who Laughs*? And *Toilers of the Sea*? Although on a much lower level, only Francesco Domenico Guerrazzi in nineteenth-century Italy had managed to write a novel somewhat similar. And yet, all considered, what a disaster Italian literature was from the proletariat's point of view, taking into account the level of education available to him in our country! Among the poets, who was there to look to except Dante, "the greatest poet in the world"? Those who came after had always written for the upper classes and not for the people. Petrarch, Ariosto, Tasso, Alfieri—oh yes, even Alfieri!—Foscolo: all of them fashioning stuff for the élite. As for *The Betrothed*—too much odor of incense, of the reactionary! No, if you wanted to read something worthy—modest, perhaps, but worthy—you had to leap forward to the Carducci of "The Love Song" or some of the social satires of Stecchetti. But on this subject, now, in the twentieth century, apart from "that degenerate D'Annunzio," apart from Pascoli, how were things faring in the world of literature? He, unfortunately, hadn't the time to keep up. Closing at seven, the city library didn't allow any worker in the evening to profit from that public service. But Signorino Bruno didn't have the same constraints. Although, as a Jew, neither could he any longer frequent the city library, nevertheless he taught in the Jewish middle school in Via Vignatagliata and could consider himself a teacher. And so, educated as he was, and surely informed of all that's new, did he, Signorino Bruno, believe that in Italy, today, there were still any good writers?

Suddenly gripped by a deep sense of futility, almost of impotence, Bruno kept silent.

"In that area, I'd be willing to bet," Rovigatti concluded, shaking his head, "no one today's doing anything good or useful!"

But what Rovigatti was most at ease talking about was his own craft.

His was a humble craft, he said, one of the humblest, even: about this no one could be more convinced than he was. But thanks to it, not only had he been able to make ends meet since he was a boy, but also it meant he'd never had to bow down to anyone through all the years of the dictatorship. And then did Signorino Bruno think that being a shoemaker didn't provide him with interesting challenges? Any activity could provide those. You just need to exercise it with passion, succeed in winkling out its secrets.

He was speaking without the least bitterness at this point. And Bruno, listening to him, and bit by bit forgetting his own sadness, ended up feeling almost cheerful.

In his hands any misshapen and scuffed shoe always came alive. With infallible intuition, Rovigatti was able to reconstruct a character from the way a client had scuffed a toe, twisted an upper or worn down a heel.

"It'll be hard getting this person to pay up," he would say, for example, handling some shoes of the tightest patent leather, which seemed new and yet hid considerable signs of wear under their pointed toes. The caution with which he proffered them for Bruno's inspection over the little workbench, for him to examine them with the interest they deserved, perfectly characterized their owner, who was Edelweiss Fegnagnani, no less, one of the most renowned "decadents" of the city.

"And you, blonde beauty, be careful where you run off to!" he murmured with a sympathetic grin, passing his calloused thumb around the extraordinarily high heel, sharp as a dagger, of a little crocodile-skin shoe which a brisk, exuberant, triumphant style of walking had thoroughly consumed at the edges.

One evening he even showed Bruno, among others, the shoes of the honorable Bottecchiari, "the prince of our forum," as he put it, not without sarcasm.

"He has some flaws, you can see," he added a moment later, his eyes burning with combative enthusiasm, with tenacious loyalty, "but he's someone in whom, thank God, one can still have some faith. What does it matter if he's become a bit bourgeois? He earns money, a great deal of it. He has a lovely house, a lovely wife . . . at least, lovely once, though fifty years will have taken a toll even on her . . . With his intelligence, his gifts as a speaker, even the Fascists respect him and court him. Last year they even wanted to give him a Party card. But you know what he said to them? He gave them a slap!"

Meanwhile his hands kept on turning over the honorable Bottecchiari's footwear, a pair of brown leather shoes with square toes—the shoes of a hearty optimist, weighing more than a hundred kilos, at whose side he had marched in the ranks of the Italian Socialist Party of Giacomo Matteotti, of Filippo Turati and Anna Kuliscioff, and together with him, in 1924, had been attacked in the downstairs salon of the Railworkers Food Co-operative, both of them escaping by sheer miracle through a back door.

He gestured with his chin in the direction of Via Fondo Banchetto.

Neither he nor the other friends from the old days, he continued, still met up with the honorable Bottecchiari, hadn't done so for almost twenty years, that was true. And yet, less than a week ago, seeing him passing the other way along the opposite sidewalk of the Corso Giovecca (the other side of the barricade! Bruno thought, suddenly swept up in a fellow feeling that bound him to Rovigatti, to Clelia Trotti, and to all the betrayed and forgotten poor of the city and of the country he imagined behind them, happy and grateful to be with them, now and forever . . .), less than a week ago, Rovigatti was saying, the honorable Bottecchiari, jovial and easy-going as ever, had shouted out, waving an arm above his head: "Ciao, Rovigatti!"

3.

ONE FINE day the door of the house in Via Fondo Banchetto opened without the usual stout figure of Signora Codecà appearing at the threshold. It had to happen. In any decent fairy tale (it could have been three-thirty in the afternoon: there was indeed something unreal about the silence of that utterly deserted district), it's rare that things don't come to an end with the disappearance or transformation of the Monster. At a stroke the spell was broken: Signora Codecà had vanished into thin air. And, well, who but Clelia Trotti could that person be who had opened the door in her stead? It must surely be her, Bruno told himself. It could only be her, the withered, neglected little woman, a kind of nun, as people had described her! To convince himself, all he needed to do was look her in the eyes. They were still the striking eyes of the free, passionate girl who had modelled herself on Anna Kuliscioff, of the impetuous working-class heroine that the honorable Bottecchiari had loved in his youth . . .

Having shed her dragon skin, and resumed her true features, Clelia

Trotti, now, like the princess in a fairy tale, smiled sweetly at the young man who stood on the cobblestones outside her door, at his air of surprise and perplexity. At this point a "Come in—I know why you're here," would have been enough, and, as the little door closed behind them, shutting out the cottonwool-like hush of Via Fondo Banchetto, the fairy tale would have achieved its perfectly correct ending. But no, that welcome was not forthcoming. That sweet smile, somewhat disavowed by the clear expression in her sky-blue eyes, was merely questioning. It seemed to say "Who are you? And what do you want?" So much so that, at least this time, Bruno had little difficulty in understanding. It was clear, he thought. His name up till now had never been mentioned to Clelia Trotti, neither by Signora Codecà nor even by Rovigatti. It was necessary, then, across the threshold still denied to him, to declare his name and surname: "Bruno" and "Lattes," syllable by syllable. This, in any case, was enough for the puzzlement that covered Trotti's face—sincere puzzlement and a trusting abandon, while her pale eyes seemed washed in a wave of generous compassion—to give way to a clearer, more realistic perspective on the situation.

"Take care as she is under surveillance!" the honorable Bottecchiari had said, lowering his voice to a whisper. He was referring to the police, the Organizzazione per la Vigilanza e la Repressione dell'Antifascismo.[*] But yet again, when considered more closely, things turned out to be different from what they seemed.

"Let's go and talk in the dining room," murmured the old school-teacher once she had ushered Bruno into the hallway and shut the door.

She preceded him on tiptoe down a dark, narrow, damp corridor. Following her in the same manner, trying not to make any noise and at the same time watching her move with all the stealth she could muster, he found it easy to guess why. Clelia Trotti was under surveillance mainly at home. Signora Codecà and her husband (the former a full-time elementary-school teacher, the latter cashier for the Agricola Bank, the stronghold of the city's landowning middle class) were Clelia Trotti's true jailors. And OVRA? OVRA knew perfectly well what it was doing. Assigning the "cautioned" sixty-year-old to the domestic control of this worthy

---

[*] See the footnote about this organization on p. 78.

couple, persons clearly possessing too much good sense to put up with their unwelcome guest of a relative receiving suspect visitors, the organization merely needed to appear every now and then. In the meantime, it could, very tranquilly, doze off.

They entered the small, ground-floor dining room. Bruno looked around. So it was here, he said to himself, that Clelia Trotti spent most of her days, talking herself hoarse giving lessons to the infants and children of the neighborhood! So this was her prison!

The furniture in pale wood was cheap, but not without ridiculous pretensions. The faded green woolen cloth, stained with ink, which covered the table in the center, the Murano-style glass chandelier suspended from the ceiling, the accountant's diploma inscribed to the head of the house, Evaristo Codecà, in ruled lines and in florid gothic script, that hung in its glory among wretched pictures of seascapes and mountain landscapes, the huge dark shape of a grandfather clock in the corner, with a dry, resonant, menacing tick-tock, even the ray of sunlight which—from the solitary window, the custodian of a little huddle of potted plants—penetrated the room, revealing on the opposite side in the center of a small, bare wickerwork sofa, a horse's head painted in oils on the hempen cover of a fat cushion; and there, at last, on the other side of the table, smiling, it was true, but with an apologetic look, as if asking for a bit of indulgence, sat the old revolutionary who had seen Anna Kuliscioff and Andrea Costa with her own eyes, who had argued about Socialism with Filippo Turati, who played a by-no-means-secondary part in the famous Red Week of the Romagna in 1914, now reduced to speaking in muffled tones, raising her eyes now and then to the ceiling to signal that her sister or brother-in-law might at any moment come down from upstairs to surprise and interrupt them. Or else she remained silent, with her open hand half-raised and the forefinger of her other hand at her lips (the pendulum clock chimed hoarsely during one of these silences, and at the same time a low clucking of hens could be heard from the garden), like a schoolgirl scared of being caught out . . . In that place like the depths of a well, in that sort of vulnerable den, everything spoke to Bruno of boredom, of apathy, of long years of stingy, inglorious segregation and oblivion. He couldn't, at a certain point, avoid asking himself,

Was it then really worth the trouble to struggle through life in a way so different from how, for example, the honorable Bottecchiari had behaved, if time, which weakens and overturns everything, had extended its fell, corrupting hand on all alike? Clelia Trotti had never bowed her neck, had always preserved her soul in all its purity. On the contrary, the honorable Bottecchiari, although he never accepted the Fascist Party card, had fully involved himself in society in his maturer years. Without anyone complaining about or being scandalized by it, he had blithely become part of the administrative council of the Agricola Bank. So, considering the outcome, which of the two had made the right choices in life? And what had he come for, involving himself so late in the day, if not precisely for that: to realize that the better world, the just and decent society of which Clelia Trotti represented the living proof and the relic, would never return? He watched her, the pathetic, persecuted anti-Fascist, the pitiful prisoner, and was unable to detach his eyes from the dark furrow, clearly visible, which, just under her white hair gathered in a bun at her nape, ran all around her thin wrinkled neck.

What kind of help, he thought, continuing to stare at that poor, ill-washed neck, could he expect from Clelia Trotti, from Rovigatti, and from that humble circle of their friends of whose existence no one could even be sure? For goodness' sake! To extract himself from that grotesque conversation he would have to get up and go from there as soon as possible, and perhaps from that point on to listen a bit more attentively to what his father never tired of advising him. That might be a good idea. Why not just for once pay attention to what his father said? Since last September, his father had lost no opportunity to tell him to take himself off to Eretz, as he was in the habit of saying, or to the United States, or South America. He was still young, his father would insistently say, his whole life was before him. He should emigrate, put down roots abroad. There was still a chance. Italy would certainly not enter the war before the following summer. And no one would refuse him entry, carrying the passport of a persecuted Jew....

"Be patient, I beg you," Clelia Trotti whispered in the meantime, "but in this house I'm merely a guest. My sister and brother-in-law—" she added, her blue eyes staring into Bruno's, showing once more the joy of confiding, the certainty of not being mistaken in having trusted him—"my sister and brother-in-law, since I returned from internal exile, and so for quite a few years, have taken me in, and have no other thought—" here she shook her head and laughed—"but to stop me committing any further folly."

She twisted her lips.

"They keep me under surveillance—" her gaze suddenly serious, almost severe—"and poke their noses into everything I do, believe me it's worse than being a baby. I understand. For people who don't think as we do . . . who have a political viewpoint utterly different from ours . . . good people, you know, two hearts of gold . . . I understand that behaving the way they unfortunately do toward me might seem the right thing to do. They claim they do it for my own good. Perhaps so. But how annoying it is!"

"Is your sister the one who always comes to open the door?"

"Yes, it's my sister, but why?" replied the schoolmistress in alarm. "Does that mean . . . ? Oh, you poor thing!" she exclaimed, joining her small bony hands together, her right hand's index and middle fingers stained with nicotine. "Who knows how many times Giovanna has forced you to make the trip to no avail!"

"One day she'd say one thing, the next another. They were excuses, I could easily see. But I could only suppose you were aware of that. And now . . ."

"Oh, you poor thing!" repeated Clelia Trotti. "And there I was talking about what was right! No. Within certain limits I can understand it, but this is going much too far. They will hear from me."

She remained silent for some seconds, as though meditating on the seriousness of the judgement that had been imposed on her and the measures she would have to take to assert her rights. And yet, at the same time, you could see she was thinking of something else. Something that, despite herself, gave her some pleasure.

"Listen. How did you come by my address? It can't have been that easy for you to procure it, I imagine."

"A couple of months ago, I had the idea of going to ask for it from the lawyer Bottecchiari," Bruno replied, looking elsewhere.

And since Signora Trotti didn't inquire any further, he added: "Bottecchiari is an old friend of the family. I was counting on him knowing where to direct me. But he didn't know, or didn't want to tell me, anything very clear. He advised me to call in on Cesare Rovigatti, you know, the shoemaker who has his workshop near here in Piazza Santa Maria in Vado. Luckily I knew him very well, and..."

"Our little Cesare, yes, indeed. Very dear to us. But I don't understand how... He himself could easily have spoken to me about you! Don't you see? For one reason or another there's no one who doesn't feel compelled to act in the oddest way toward me. And they don't understand that, with this system, gradually making everything a desert around me, it's as if they're taking away the air I breathe. Better to be in prison, then!"

There was fatigue, disgust and deep bitterness in the tone with which she pronounced these words. Bruno looked her in the face. But her intensely blue eyes, steady and dry under her grey, knitted eyebrows, were full of hope, as though she doubted everything and everybody except him.

Suddenly the door opened. Someone looked in. It was Signora Codecà.

"Who's there?" had asked the familiar, hateful voice before the salt-and-pepper head-of-hair poked in to investigate.

The diffident gaze of Signora Codecà fell on Bruno.

"Ah," she said coldly, "I didn't know you had a visitor."

"But it's a friend! It's Signor Lattes..." Clelia Trotti hurried to explain, agitated. "Bruno Lattes!"

"Pleasure to meet you!" said Signora Codecà, without taking a step forward. "At last you've found her, eh?" she added in a sour tone in Bruno's direction without actually looking at him.

She drew back a little.

From the dark of the corridor a little eight- or nine-year-old child came forward with a frightened look. Three white horizontal lines were drawn across the front of his black smock.

"Go on in," Signora Codecà encouraged him.

And then, turning to her sister: "Don't worry, I'll accompany Signor Lattes out."

When they had once again assumed their familiar positions, with her massive person blocking the door and Bruno looking up at her from the cobbled street, Signora Codecà spoke again.

"I'm not sure if my sister remembered to tell you, but after tomorrow at the latest, Clelia will really have to go away. On a trip, a rather long one. How long? I don't know for sure, perhaps several weeks . . . perhaps several months . . . so for the moment it's useless for you to pay any more visits. Try to understand. You'd be doing us a favor, Signor Lattes, if you'd be considerate about this. I'm saying this also for your own sake . . ."

She stressed these last words with a plaintive, pleading look. Then, as she drew back and slowly shut the door in Bruno's face, she added in a whisper: "We're under surveillance, you understand?"

That very night, returning home as usual, very late, and without even having phoned around eight o'clock to tell them not to expect him for supper—he'd spent the evening first at the cinema and then seated by the billiards table in a bar outside Porta Reno—Bruno was taken by surprise in the street by the snow.

To start with it was a sifting of tiny flakes milling lightly around the streetlamps. But shortly after, in Via Madama, as he tried to fit his key into the front door, the flakes had already become so thick and heavy that in no time his face was drenched.

He kept on fumbling with the key, and in doing so, as the castle clock had begun to toll the hours, he tried to count them. One, two, three, four. Four o'clock: very late indeed, but for all that he had little hope his father would have given up waiting and switched off the light—he would only turn it off after he heard him groping past his bedroom door on tiptoe, and his father would let him understand, by coughing and grumbling, that he had stayed awake and worried till that late hour. On the other hand, all the better. Perhaps this night he could be exempted from the tired, stupid saga of tiptoeing along the dark corridor. If his father was still not asleep, fine. He would turn the main light on and resolutely enter his bedroom. He already knew what his father would speak to him about.

And yet, when he found himself in the large entrance hall, at the end of which, across the dividing wall, he could see the dark garden plants, he became aware of a faint light filtering round the door of the ground-floor room that served him as a study. He drew close. Slowly, he opened the door. His father was there, seated in the armchair next to the table. Wrapped in a woolen blanket, he slept with his head inclined against his shoulder.

He stepped noiselessly into the room, and leaned against the wall beside the door.

He'd never come home, he reflected, as late as this. That was perhaps why at a certain point his father had decided to get up from bed and go downstairs, like this, in his nightshirt and slippers. Who could say? It might have been that he'd thought to take the opportunity of a thorough discussion with him about emigrating to Palestine or America, a topic which every time his father had broached it, he'd responded to coldly or even rudely. If he waited for him down in the study, his father had perhaps told himself, the two of them would be able to talk, or even quarrel, for as long as they wanted. Their voices wouldn't have woken anyone.

He moved on tiptoe, grimacing. And he was about to touch the sleeper's left hand, resting as though dead over the *Il Resto di Carlino,*[*] the newspaper open and unfolded over his knees—his right hand, on which his forehead was resting, was instinctively placed to shield his half-closed eyelids from the light of the table lamp—when a sudden pang of sorrow interrupted his gesture midway.

He retracted his arm and took a step backward.

But instead of turning and leaving, he halted to look at his father's scrawny, frail temples, more cartilage than bone, and his white, feathery, weightless hair, in its lightness and whiteness so similar to Clelia Trotti's. How many more years would his father live? And Clelia Trotti? Would the two of them live long enough to witness the conclusion of the tragedy that was convulsing the world?

Although finished and near to death, both of them in the end were still dreaming their dreams. From her prison in Via Fondo Banchetto, Clelia Trotti was dreaming that the rebirth of Italian socialism would occur thanks to the infusion of youthful blood into the Party's old, decrepit veins. From the Ghetto of Via Madama, where with morose delectation he had holed up—the beloved, irreplaceable Merchants' Club had naturally expelled him, so now he stayed at home reading the newspapers and

---

[*] A Bologna newspaper that was founded in 1885, and was under Fascist control from 1923 to 1943.

listening to Radio London—the lawyer Lattes dreamed of the "brilliant career" which was bound to await his little son in America or in Eretz. But he, Bruno, the little son, what would he do? Stay or go? His Papa was mistaken about the power of discrimination: the police headquarters would never issue him with a passport. And since the war, now only just begun, would last who knows how long, since the trap now sprung had rendered any escape impossible, since the only road now was obviously the one that would lead everyone, without exclusion, toward a future without hope, it was better to join in voluntarily, if only for compassion and humility, in the desperate hobbies, the wretched, miserable delusions of onanistic prisoners that were shared by his fellow travelers.

Still on tiptoe, he went toward the window.

After having half-closed one of the two shutters, he looked out through the steamed-up panes between the slats. The snow continued to fall. After some hours it would be piled high, would have extended its oppressive hush over the whole city, a prison and a ghetto for everyone.

4.

IN THE end, Signora Codecà had her way. She asked that her house should not become a den of conspirators. And, finally, she had revealed herself, had thrown her hand down on the table, all the cards of an undoubtedly zealous jailor, and yet not treacherous, only fearful.

Whatever she said or thought, in all probability OVRA had completely forgotten about 36, Via Fondo Banchetto. For a long time, no policeman had shown up at dusk to check whether the "cautioned" Trotti, Clelia, was to be found at her prescribed and proper domicile. Yet it was better not to contradict Signora Codecà. Better to let her play the role of a strict and incorruptible spy which she herself had assumed. Never to lose sight of her subversive sister, who, after her spell of internal exile, had been sentenced to ten supplementary years of enforced residence with a daily obligation to be indoors by dusk and to report every week at the police station to sign in the special register of the "cautioned"; to rush to the door at every loud ring, without ever forgetting to wear the Fascist badge in full view on top of the black smock of a teacher in regular employment—even Signora Codecà had the right to a small raft of illusions, an element of play, necessary to anyone who wants to survive! And Clelia Trotti? Did she truly want to be visited? To leave the house with a furtive air, peep out through the upstairs shutters, to rapidly turn the corner into Via Coperta—if there was something that gave her pleasure, surely it must be this? Sooner or later it would be she herself who would make an appearance.

One morning, about two months later, while he was teaching in a classroom of the Jewish School in Via Vignatagliata, Bruno saw the janitoress' head peeping gingerly round the door.

"May I?"

"What is it?"

"There's a lady outside who wants to see you."

Scuffing her slippers on the brickwork floor and prompting the usual hum of mirth, the janitoress came toward the teacher's desk.

"What should I tell her?" she asked worriedly.

Of an indeterminable age, short, round, with two oily, shining strips of raven hair which descended from the top of her head to frame a sleepy-looking, sheepish face, she was one of the least ancient of those recruited from the hospice for the old in Via Vittoria by the engineer Cohen when, in October 1938, it was necessary to find space on the second floor of the kindergarten for the older children expelled from the state middle schools.

"Tell her to wait for the bell to go off," Bruno replied, so irritably that the pupils suddenly went quiet. "How many times must I tell you not to disturb me during lessons?"

It was Clelia Trotti, it had to be her.

Continuing to explain things to the pupils and to ask them questions, in his mind's eye he saw her waiting in the adjoining vestibule. She was reading the big tablets full of the names of benefactors affixed to the walls between the washed-out doors of the classrooms; she was contemplating, one by one, the varnished clay busts of Victor Emmanuel II, of Umberto I and of Victor Emmanuel III, placed in the niches of the wall around the

Victory Dispatch.* Every now and then she went to look out of the two big windows opposite, both of them thrown open wide . . .

At last, the bell rang. Pouring out of the classrooms into the hallway, the children rushed headlong down the big central staircase. When Bruno, too, had gone out into the now deserted hallway, spotting the little woman in hat and grey suit down there, standing still, with her back to him looking at Diaz's proclamation, for some moments he was disconcerted. He was hoping that, hearing his steps, she would turn round with a start, and smile at him with that kind smile of hers, as though close to tears, to look him in the face with her blue eyes flashing the same ironic, sad and generous expression they had when he had first told her his name. Only then would he truly recognize her.

"It's been many years since I read the Dispatch of the 4th of November 1918!" said Clelia Trotti, even before she shook his hand, signaling with her chin toward the tablet. "I needed to come all the way here to do that!"

They faced each other by the big window that overlooked the inner courtyard garden, with its stricken little trees in the spring sunlight crowded with chirping sparrows, and they rested their elbows on the iron rail.

"What a lovely time of the year, isn't it?" the schoolmistress said, looking out toward the red vista of roofs that opened before them, beyond the garden walls.

"It is indeed."

He observed her from the corner of his eye. She had taken care to spruce herself up, and applied powder as far down as her neck.

"You feel yourself coming alive again," she continued, half-closing her eyes against the glare.

And then, after a pause, but still with a sense of inner joy: "How right we were though, we Socialists—to tell the truth, it wasn't just a few of us, at that stage, who thought otherwise—to hear our death knell in the bells rung for the Italian victory of 1918! 'The valleys, they had invaded, with

---

* The *Bollettino della Vittoria* was the final address to the army and the nation issued by the chief of staff, General Armando Diaz, at the conclusion of the Battle of Vittorio Veneto, which ended the First World War in Italy.

confidence and pride . . .' Already concealed within those words is the Fascist movement, the arrogant rhetoric of these last twenty years."

Suddenly, emerging out of the stagnant depths of his own bitterness, Bruno felt a violent impulse to hurt her, to do harm to her.

"Why fool yourself?" he interrupted. "Why maintain the deception? As you know, in Ferrara all of us Jews, or nearly all of us, were nothing other than bourgeoisie—I say were, since now, perhaps all for the better, we no longer belong to any class, we make up a social group apart, as in medieval times. We were nearly all of us retail traders or wholesale merchants, professionals of various stripes, landowners, and therefore, as you have taught me, nearly all Fascists. Of necessity. You have no idea how many of us even today have remained fervent patriots!"

"You mean nationalists?" Clelia Trotti gently corrected him.

"Call them what you like. My father, for example, went to fight on the Carso as a volunteer. In 1919, returning from the front, he chanced on a march of workers, who, seeing him in officer's uniform, literally covered him with spit. Today, obviously, he isn't a Fascist any longer, despite the fact that it was actually his Fascist Party card of 1922 that earned us some exemptions. Now he only thinks about the Palestinian fatherland. And yet, I wouldn't swear that General Diaz's sentences, which continue to make such an impression on the imaginations of most of my—what should I call them?—my co-religionists, have entirely stopped having an impact on the imagination of those who share your political faith!"

"What you say seems to me very understandable," Clelia Trotti calmly replied. "You explain it very well."

She didn't seem in the least disappointed, but perhaps, once again, somewhat saddened.

She sighed.

"The First World War has been a great disaster," she said. "How many mistakes even we made! Nonetheless, you seem to me too pessimistic. Fair enough: in general terms, you're right. Why not take yourself into account, though? You're different, you're not like the others, and your example is more than enough to show that every rule has its exception. And you're young, you have your whole life before you. For the young like you who have grown up under Fascism, there is a great deal for you to do!"

Hearing Clelia Trotti using the very same phrases as his father, Bruno raised his head. He had again turned to look out of the window. The future she saw was down there, where the last houses in Ferrara, their roofs a dark rusty color, gave way in the direction of the sea to the blue-green of the endless countryside.

A few months later Fascist Italy also decided to enter the war.

"At last!" Clelia Trotti exclaimed, joyful and breathless, that very evening of June 10, as she entered the study in Via Madama.

"At last!" she repeated, as she dropped into the armchair.

She leaned her neck back on the green velvet headrest and closed her eyes. It wasn't the first time that, making the most of the darkness and defying all prohibitions, she had come to visit Bruno. And yet the intensity of excitement which these clandestine visits gave her from the first showed no signs of diminishing.

When her breathing had returned to normal, she immediately said that Fascism, with that mad gesture of declaring war, had signed its own death warrant. She was sure of it, she affirmed, and began to explain with extraordinary heat and passion why she was so sure of her prediction.

Bruno stared at her in silence.

Her good faith was unquestionable, he thought, no one had the right to doubt it. And yet why not admit it? Wasn't the look that shone in her eyes, above all, the certainty—now that leaving Italy had become truly impossible—that he would no longer be able to dodge the task that she had assigned him in her heart of hearts, nor slip out of her hands, as up until yesterday she had feared he might? Undoubtedly there was something of that. Even though, from the expression her mouth had already taken on, tender but at the same time skeptical, it was more than evident that she first of all—she who might be his mother!—would forbid any comparison to be made between the boy before her and Mauro Bottecchiari, the companion of her youth, whom Italy's entry into the war in long-ago 1915 had offered the political pretext of his being rid of her.

In the early stages, their meetings in his downstairs study were on a fairly frequent basis. Everything was done lightly, of course, as a game, the kind of game prisoners might play, steeped in bitterness and in the absence of everyday consolations, and Bruno took some pleasure from it, even from that air of erotic subterfuge which inevitably hovered over their meetings—always occurring after supper; every now and then she would be late, and he would be reading a book or preparing a lesson while he waited—and especially from her light, complicit knock on the blinds outside, which would startle him.

As soon as she came in, Clelia Trotti would sit herself down in the armchair. But sometimes, without even taking off her grey cotton gloves—despite the heat that soaked her forehead with sweat, she would never take off her hat—she would at once get up again and go toward one of the four glass-fronted bookcases symmetrically disposed along the lower part of the study's walls, and remain there with her nose against the glass. Her unwillingness to open the bookcase doors showed a kind of tact. She confined herself to peering through the glass and reading the titles of the books with the help of an eyeglass she would draw from her big black leather bag.

"Why not take some away with you?" Bruno, from behind a table heaped with papers, would encourage her. "I'd gladly loan you any of them."

She shook her head. With all the lessons she had to give, she wouldn't have time to read them.

"Besides, I'm so behind the times in all cultural matters," she confided to him one evening, "that to get up to date would require an effort beyond me. For example, I've always wanted to read a book by Benedetto Croce;[*] I'm not sure, maybe one of his less abstruse works, one of his historical studies. Year after year, I've put off doing so, a little because I imagine the fear it would cause my sister Giovanna, poor thing, should she find that sort of stuff in the house, and also a little because of reservations . . . to do with socialism. Decades have passed, and here we are, and it no longer seems worth the trouble. When I was a girl, I had a passion for philosophy. In those days it was all Comte, Spencer, Ardigò and Haeckel with his Monism."

---

[*] Benedetto Croce (1866–1952) was an Italian thinker whose ideas had great importance for Bassani and whose voluminous work spanned politics, history, philosophy, aesthetics, and poetry. He was also an active politician, critical of the Fascist regime and the only non-Jewish figure to refuse to answer a Fascist questionnaire enquiring about the racial background of Italian intellectuals.

She smiled.

Then, with a tinge of shyness in her eyes: "You, though, are bound to know the works of Croce well, isn't that so?"

It was a reference to what Bruno himself, though he immediately regretted it, had once been unable to stop himself from saying: that he wasn't a Socialist and in all probability never would be.

Yet stronger than any grief, any regret that she was not at a level to be able to teach him anything, she was undoubtedly consoled by the belief that this itself was as it should be: that he wasn't a Socialist, yes, but something other, something new. Socialists of the old school would not know how to confront the future, the years that were awaiting Italy and the world beyond the war that had just begun, years which would only be reached after having paid who knows what reckoning of blood and tears. "We lot are over the hill, a bunch of dinosaurs," she used to say. It was as though she were attesting that tomorrow, in their stead, there would be a need for the young like him, Bruno, who would be Socialists without being such. Only thus would it be possible, when the moment arrived, for the Communists to be given a hard time, even though they were "giants," for they too, especially in their "methods," now belonged in the past.

Toward the end of September, OVRA unexpectedly reappeared on the scene.

One day, toward dusk, an agent of the political wing in plain clothes came to ask if Signora Trotti was "at her domicile." Winded, Signora Codecà replied that she was at home. But the woman's agitated state must have made the official suspicious, and he wouldn't go away without having assured himself with his own eyes, albeit with a profusion of apologies, that everything was in order. One could no longer be sure. Fearing that this sudden awakening of the police signaled a harsher policy of control toward the "cautioned," Clelia Trotti decided to renounce her nocturnal escapades for some time after. Bruno and she had to see each other in the daytime, as it were by chance, avoiding, naturally, any further visits to the study in Via Madama.

So every now and then, even if not with the same frequency as before, and arranging their appointments by way of Rovigatti—who, being jealously possessive of Trotti, was ill-disposed to help—they began to meet in Piazza della Certosa. From his perspective, Rovigatti wasn't mistaken, Bruno could see that. What had they to say to each other or to do together, he and Clelia Trotti, that was worth the risk? It wasn't as though the two of them saw each other, as Rovigatti insinuated, just to talk about Radio London or Colonel Stevens.[*] Certainly not for that. But in the present, tense situation, was it really worth provoking the police?

He tried to pass on the shoemaker's comments to the schoolmistress, attempting also to offer bland justifications for them. In vain. Every time he returned to the topic, she shrugged her shoulders with annoyance.

"What a bore he is!" she sighed.

"Poor little Cesare!" she laughed one evening, and never before had she seemed so youthful. "He acts like that because he's very fond of me. You know when it was we first got to know each other?"

"Before the First World War, I imagine."

"Oh, much earlier than that! From back in elementary school. We both lived in Vicolo del Gregorio."

"So you came to know Bottecchiari much later."

"Much later," she replied drily.

And she gave him a look with a hint of irony, and seemed more youthful than ever.

In the bright late afternoons of September the huge field in front of the church of San Cristoforo was crowded, as it always was when the weather was fine, with children, nursemaids and young couples. Bruno Lattes and Clelia Trotti would speak, sitting close to each other at the edge of the churchyard for the most part, but sometimes on the grass, in the margin of shadow that grew slowly at the southern limit of the portico with the descent of the sun, on the side of Via Borso.

"It's lovely here, don't you think?" said Trotti, her eyes turned toward the square. "It doesn't at all seem as if we're in a graveyard."

"I've never understood," she said on one occasion, "why the dead are kept segregated from us, as is our custom, so that if you want to visit them

---

[*] An exceptional linguist, abducted to Germany in the Venlo Incident in 1939; actually a major but promoted during his long captivity to lieutenant colonel—thought to have disclosed secrets to the Nazis under interrogation.

you have to get permission, as you would for a prison visit. Napoleon was undoubtedly a great man as he imposed on Europe, as well as on Italy, via our Cisalpine Republic, the democratic and social triumphs of the Revolution. But as far as his famous edict on cemeteries goes, I remain of the same opinion as the poet of *Of Sepulchres.** You believe me? I'd like them to bury me right here outside, in this lovely field, with all this noise of life going on around, even if that would cost me eternal excommunication."

She started laughing.

"It's only a dream, I know," she quickly added, "a pious desire that won't ever come true. Apart from some years in prison, some others in internal exile and now this invigilated freedom, what have I done in my life that's so important to deserve a tomb among the illustrious figures of our city, even the heretical ones? To be sure, I haven't even been beaten up. The Fascists were more refined with me. When I was leaving the Umberto I elementary school in Via Bersaglieri del Po in 1922, they confined themselves to making me drink a half ounce of cod-liver oil and covering my face with soot. And so what! If it hadn't been for the children who were standing there watching, and many of them crying from fear, it wouldn't have upset me that much, I can assure you. There was hardly call to come in a group of twenty or thirty, with cudgels, daggers, skulls on their berets, to subdue a woman on her own. A nice show of force! While I was swallowing my portion of cod-liver oil, I knew that the Blackshirts would have achieved nothing by it except to heap general disapproval on themselves."

But what she always preferred to talk about was her past as a prisoner and internal exile.

"Prison gives you a real schooling," she said on another evening, lighting a Macedonia cigarette with the lit stub of the last (a vice, she explained, that—to illustrate the point—she'd picked up in prison), "at least that's so if it doesn't go on too long and that it doesn't break the will or weaken the moral fiber. As regards my own experience, I'm grateful to fate that I wasn't spared the test. Solitude, concentration, having no company but

---

* Ugo Foscolo (1778–1827), an important Italian poet whose most famous work is *D* sepolcri.

our own . . . these are worth learning. And to know oneself, to struggle with one's own tendencies and to emerge from that sometimes victorious, can only happen within the four walls of a cell. When I got out of prison in 1930, I left my number 36 (you see the coincidence?—the same number as my sister's house) with real sadness, as if I were leaving behind a part of myself. Each wall, each corner, every tiny thing carried a trace of suffering. The truth is that the places where you have wept, where you've suffered, where you've had to find the many inner resources to keep hoping and resisting, are the ones you grow fondest of. Take yourself, for example. You could have left, like so many of your co-religionists, and after what you've had to put up with, you'd have had every right. But you made a different choice. You preferred to stay here, to struggle and suffer. And now this country, this city where you were born, where you grew up and became a man, has become doubly yours. You will never, ever abandon it."

She would always end like this. Having started, as usual, by telling a story about herself and her own life, she would soon steer the talk toward Bruno and what she thought he should be doing in the immediate future.

On his behalf for quite some time she had been preparing useful contacts with the city's principal anti-Fascists, she would say, and so, for this very reason, she'd already entrusted Rovigatti with the task of preparing the ground for his imminent visits.

The first people he should approach were undoubtedly the Socialists. But he should take care. Not the notary Licci, a distinctly sour and cantankerous "maximalist"—better leave him to stew in his own juices until he himself decided to shake off his grumpiness and seek out his old friends. Bruno needed to see first of all the lawyers, Baruffaldi, Polenghi and Tamagnini, all three of them Reformists eager to act, and after, returning to the topic of Bottecchiari, to try to link up with his nephew Nino, who for some six or seven months had been taken on as an assistant in his uncle's office. He was without doubt a very bright and able young man, considering that he'd been able to make an impression even on the Gruppi Universitari Fascisti, where he'd been assigned very important roles in the last two years. She urged Bruno to get in contact with him soon, to avert the possibility that one day or another he'd be lured by some new "totalitarian siren."

But then, after the Socialists, he needed to get to know the Repubblicani-storici, such as the dentist Canella, the tailor Squarcia, the chemist Riccoboni. These, too, had of late shown unambiguous signs of wanting to shift, of being ready, because of the shared aims of the struggle, to forget their everlasting rancor and anti-Socialist prejudices.

As for the Catholics, their circle, in this respect similar to the Communist one, remained something of a self-contained world which would be hard to enter. All the same, the lawyer Galassi-Tarabini, he at least, was a remarkably open-minded type. Already in close contact with both Count Gròsoli and Don Sturzo, opposed by the Fascist clerics since Pius XI exalted Mussolini to the point of calling him the Man of Providence— yes, he was a person of real integrity, not to be overlooked in any way. And the same could be said of the engineer Sears, a liberal, leaning to the right, but still good-hearted, and of Dr. Herzen, a committed Zionist, agreed, but perhaps recruitable to the cause of Italian anti-Fascism, especially if he were to be approached by a fellow Jew.

And finally he ought to meet up with Alfio Mori, the friend and in some ways the disciple of Antonio Gramsci—they'd got to know each other in prison—the person from whom it's said that his comrade Ercoli, every time he secretly reenters the country from the Soviet Union, most willingly accepts advice. Mori was the most important of them all, and, as such, was most keenly under surveillance. He would always need to move with extreme prudence. For example, he might arrange a meeting, and Mori wouldn't turn up. A second one, and Mori would be absent once again. Only on the fifth or the sixth appointment might he finally decide to appear. So it was indispensable to be armed with patience. And if he, Bruno, was prepared to be patient, he might indeed manage also to have a talk with Mori . . .

She talked on and on. The shadows of the steles and gravestones slowly lengthened on the grass, the field little by little shed its crowd of visitors, and some enamored couples moved off in the direction of the city walls.

That evening Bruno was stretched out, as was his habit, at the feet of Clelia Trotti. As he listened without much attention to what the teacher was saying, he noticed a tall, slim, blond boy leaning on the handlebars of his bicycle some twenty meters away.

His head immersed in the pink sheets of the sports pages, he looked as though he were waiting for someone. And there on cue, at the far end of the square, almost running to reach him, was a girl, she, too, blonde and very beautiful, who, while continuing to cross the open field, turned every three or four steps to look back toward Via Borso as if she feared she were being pursued.

But of course it wasn't true. She was merely playacting.

Once she had reached her friend, she was the first, like a good actress, to slip down on to the grass, with the rapid, graceful movements of one hand arranging her pleated, white woolen dress around her legs. With the other hand she tugged affectionately at the boy, who had remained standing, to sit down beside her.

Soon the two of them were sitting close to each other, beside the bicycle with their backs turned. Their young heads were so close as to be touching. Suffused with the mild air, delighted by the light touching of their bodies, it seemed as though they had no need to speak. "Who are they? What are their names?" Bruno was wondering while the voice of Clelia Trotti sounded distantly in his ear, an incomprehensible hum. He couldn't remember their names. He was quite sure, though, that they were both still at school, perhaps at the *liceo classico*, and that they both belonged to one of the city's upper-middle-class families.

Ten or so minutes passed.

Suddenly Bruno saw the boy move. He got back to his feet, calmly picked up the bicycle and then grasped his friend by her wrist. Letting herself go heavy, she now laughed with a lazy flirtatiousness, leaning her whole neck back.

They began to move off in the direction of the walls, crossing the field on a diagonal.

"Why don't we go down there too?" Bruno asked.

Stretching out his left arm, he pointed at the Mura degli Angeli still in full sunlight.

"But it's late. I'm afraid we won't have time," Clelia Trotti, interrupted mid-sentence, replied. "You know I have to turn in along with the hens!"

"What will it matter just this once? We'll be able to see a magnificent sunset."

He had already stood up. He stretched out a hand to help her get up, and then they walked on.

The young couple were about fifty meters ahead of them. The boy was sitting on his bike, and every now and then, to keep his balance, he encircled his companion's shoulders with his right arm. Bruno watched them with an insatiable interest. "Who are they? What are their names?" he kept muttering under his breath. They seemed to him more than beautiful—marvellous, incomparable. There they were: the champions, the prototypes of their race! he said to himself with hatred and a desperate love, half-closing his eyes. Their blood was better than his, their souls were finer than his. If he wasn't mistaken, the girl's hair was tied at the back with a red ribbon. The little light that remained seemed to concentrate itself on that ribbon.

Oh, to be them, to be one of them, despite everything!

"I did well to let you persuade me. From the top of the wall we'll be able to enjoy a truly extraordinary sunset," Clelia Trotti calmly observed.

Bruno turned round. So she had seen nothing. Yet again she'd noticed nothing at all. And now once more she'd continued with what she'd been saying. Talking as if to herself. As if pursuing her dream. Lost, as ever, in the unending, lonely ravings of a convict.

He shivered.

Perhaps one day she would understand who Bruno Lattes was, he thought, turning back to look before him. But that day, if it should ever arrive, was still surely a long way off.

A Night in '43

A T first you might not be aware of it. But once you've been seated for a few minutes at one of the small outside tables of the Caffè della Borsa, with the sheer crag of the clocktower before you and, a bit to the right, the crenellated terrace of the Orangery, the whole thing dawns on you. This is what happens. In summer as in winter, in rain or shine, it's very unusual for whoever crosses that stretch of Corso Roma to prefer keeping to the opposite sidewalk that runs along the dark-brown back of the Castle moat. If anyone does so, then it's sure to be a tourist, finger wedged between the pages of the *Touring Guide* and gaze tilted upward, or a traveling salesman who, with leather bag under his arm, is hurrying toward the station, or a farm worker from the Po delta come to the city for the market who, waiting to take the local afternoon bus back to Comacchio or Codigoro, with evident embarrassment lugs his body weighed down with the food and wine he consumed a little after midday in a dive in San Romano. In short, it could be anyone, except someone from Ferrara.

The visitor goes past, and the cafe regulars stare and grin. Yet, at certain hours of the day, those eyes stare in a strange way, even the breath is shorter. The boredom and laziness of the provinces might germinate all kinds of imaginary massacres. It's as though the sidewalk stones opposite were about to be blown to bits by the explosion of a mine detonated by the unwary visitor's foot. Or else as though a rapid burst of bullets from the Fascist machine gunner who, as it happened, fired precisely from here, from under the portico of the Caffè della Borsa one night in December 1943,[*] murdering eleven citizens on that stretch of sidewalk, should make the incautious passer-by perform the same brief, ghastly jig, all startled twists and jumps, that in the moment of death the victims undoubtedly performed before falling lifeless one on top of the other—those whom History has for years consecrated as the very first victims of the Italian civil war.

Of course, none of this happens. No mine explodes, no machine gun returns to pepper the low wall opposite with bullet holes. And so this visitor who, let's suppose, has come to Ferrara to admire its fine artistic heritage, can pass by in front of the little marble plaques bearing the engraved names of the executed persons without his thoughts being assailed by the least disturbance.

And yet, sometimes, something does happen.

One suddenly hears a voice. It isn't a powerful voice, but rather a raw, cracked voice as boys have at the onset of puberty. And since it emerges from the puny chest of Pino Barilari, the owner of the adjoining pharmacy, who, at one of the windows of the apartment above, remains invisible to whomever is seated below, it really sounds as though it has descended from the heavens. The voice says "Beware, young man!" or "Careful!" or "Whoa there!" It's not, I repeat, as though these words were yelled out. Rather, it sounds like a friendly warning, like advice given in the tone of someone who doesn't expect to be listened to, nor, in the end, who has that much desire to be heard. So the tourist, or whoever else happens at that moment to be treading the sidewalk that every true Ferrarese avoids, usually continues on his way without giving any sign of having understood the warning.

But the customers of the Caffè della Borsa, as I've already said, understand it only too well.

As soon as the absent-minded outsider hoves into view, the hubbub of conversation is quelled. Eyes stare, the breath is held. Will that per-

---

[*] See footnote on p. 64.

son, who has nearly arrived at the paving-stones where the shooting took place, realize that he's about to do something he'd be much better leaving undone? Will he or will he not finally lift his head out of the *Touring Guide*? But above all, at a given moment, will the aerial and absurd, sad and ironic voice of the invisible Pino Barilari descend from above, or will it not? Maybe yes. Maybe no. Awaiting the outcome often has a quality of muscular contraction, no more or less than that which attends a sporting event whose result is especially uncertain.

"Whoa there!"

Suddenly, in everyone's mind's eye the image of the chemist at the upstairs apartment window materializes. So, this time, he's there, seated at the windowsill, on the lookout, with his thin, hairy, very white arms raised to point at the passer-by who hasn't noticed the glint of the field glasses above. Many of those hidden in the protective shadow of the portico experience vivid relief to be where they are, rather than out in the open, utterly exposed.

2.

In 1939, a year that was so decisive for the fate of Italy and the rest of the world, there weren't many people in Ferrara who could recount anything that wasn't merely general about him or his life: about, that is, the man seated in pyjamas on an armchair with his back resting on two big white cushions, whose insistent presence at the window overlooking Corso Roma began to be noticed in the summer of that year.

That he was the only son of Dr. Francesco Barilari, who died in 1936 and bequeathed him one of the best pharmacies in the city, that, yes, was a fact known even to the children of the most recent generation. Many a time, as if weighing the future potential of each of them (for this they'd nicknamed him "Scales"), would the ironic, penetrating gaze of the meditative and bony chemist fall on these boys in the mornings as, running to school, they passed by the outdoor tables of the Caffè della Borsa while taking the last puffs on the most vestigial stubs of their cigarettes. There was little else to add about him other than that he had been a respected

Mason of the 33rd degree who, in the early days, had had some sympathy for Fascism, and that from time immemorial he had been a widower.

The information about the young Barilari, if someone thirty-one years old can be called young, didn't go much further than what has already been said. When, for example, in 1936, at the death of the old Mason, he was promptly seen to take up his post behind the counter of the pharmacy, the surprise had been general. Encased in his white coat, he served the customers with confidence, and let them call him "Doctor." So he'd been to university and actually completed the course! they murmured, amazed. "But where? And when? Who had studied with him?"

There was new surprise and wonderment in the autumn of 1937, on the occasion of his sudden marriage to Anna Repetto, the blonde, seventeen-year-old daughter of a marshal in the Carabinieri, originally from Chiavari, but for some years stationed with his family in Ferrara.

She was quite a wild type, forever going on bike rides or to dances in the local clubs, and always followed, not only by long trains of her contemporaries, but also by the gaze of many older men who were admiring her development from afar. In short, she was a young woman who was very eye-catching and very much in the public eye, so that to have her whisked away from under their very noses by someone like Pino Barilari, all of them felt somewhat swindled, betrayed even.

And then, soon after the wedding, more heated gossip about Pino circulated, but much more, to tell the truth, about his very young bride.

Many had made the most feverish predictions about her. She would be noticed on a beach at the nearby Adriatic Riviera by some bigshot from somewhere exotic, who would fall in love at first sight, then marry her; a film director, also bewitched by her graces, would take her back to Rome to be a star . . . So how could they possibly forgive her for having given in to the temptation to settle down, and in that way? They accused her of pettiness, of petit-bourgeois greed, of innate whorishness. They even taxed her with ingratitude to her family. Oh yes. Ligurians, such moneygrubbers—who knows what disappointment they too had had to face, those poor souls! And then when on earth had those two seen each other before they were married? Where had they met up? If theirs hadn't been one of those worthless affairs, common enough, conducted by telephone, they would surely have been caught every now and then in the vicinity of Piazza della Certosa, or along the city walls, or in Piazza d'Armi, and so on. So once again that sly operator Pino Barilari had acted with incredible flair. Hidden away in his pharmacy, he'd let the others, out there, wear themselves out in contemplation of Anna, who, with her blonde hair thrown back over her shoulders, with her generous lips all bright with lipstick, and, displaying her long, suntanned legs up to her thighs and even further, would parade back and forth in front of the little tables of the Caffè della Borsa. Then just at the right moment, snap, he'd pulled in his net, and tough luck to the rest of them. Besides, was there really any need for him to be seen about with a free and unconstrained girl like Anna Repetto—a girl the city never lost sight of for a moment—if above the pharmacy, after the death of his father, he had an entire apartment at his disposal? Who would ever have noticed if, say, she had discreetly entered the pharmacy at two in the afternoon, when no one would still be sitting under the awning of the Caffè della Borsa? A distasteful story, they concluded with a grimace, and decidedly vulgar. Since things ended as they did, better not to speak any more about it, better to just forget it.

Only the sudden paralysis that no more than two years later deprived Pino Barilari of the use of his legs had had the power once more to concentrate public attention on him. The result was to suspend him high up there, as in a royal box, a half-bust in pyjamas above the animated theater of Corso Roma. From then on, his young wife, though of course for a while commiserated with, was barely considered. The conversations turned back to Pino, and to him alone. But wasn't it exactly this that he had sought, exhibiting himself as he did to the eyes of the world? And in fact he was always there now, seated from morning to evening at the window of the apartment above the pharmacy, and ready to glare at anyone who risked passing by within range along the sidewalk by the Castle moat, in a manner, as those same passers-by claimed, that was both insolent and unabashed. And happy as well!—they would add—as though it were the syphilis itself, which for so many years had lain meekly slumbering in his blood, and had at last broken out to deprive him of his legs, that had transformed his colorless life into something clear, comprehensible to him, in short existent. Now he felt strong, one could see it, even reborn; however, now he was utterly different from that kind of shipwrecked figure grabbing on to a lifebelt who, soon after the marriage, had on two or three occasions toward evening been seen arm in arm with his wife along the Corso Giovecca. "You see, my dear fellows, what a small youthful indiscretion can lead to?" he'd had the air of saying. "This is what, can't you see?" In his now shining eyes there was no shadow to be seen. Of any kind.

But fully to understand the embarrassment, the instinctive suspicion, that this sort of behavior induced in the townsfolk, it's worth at this point dwelling on the sense of stupefaction, uncertainty and general diffidence which had begun to diffuse itself throughout Italy, but especially in Ferrara, from the start of the summer of 1939.

In the eyes of many good people the city had at a stroke transformed itself into a kind of hell.

To begin with, there was what happened with those upper-school pupils, which kept cropping up in conversation—that group of boys, none of them older than eighteen, who, prompted by their philosophy teacher, a certain Roccella (who fled to Switzerland) had arrived at the sterling plan of smashing the windows, one each night, of the most important shops in the city center, with the clear intent to foment panic and disorder among the population. This had meant that for the police to be able to lie in wait and catch the villains red-handed, their numbers had to be swollen by a score of old squad members, personally arranged into voluntary patrols by Carlo Aretusi, the renowned Fascist veteran who had joined up even before the March on Rome. Youthful high jinks they might have been, but regardless of the arrested boys' spirited professions of communism, the Organizzazione per la Vigilanza e la Repressione dell'Antifascismo[*] itself was involved in trying to downplay their political significance. Yet an element of that undoubtedly lingered. Things got worse, and that's for sure. Defeatists, saboteurs and spies were lurking everywhere. That things were not going in the right direction could be read in the faces of certain Jews, for instance, who even then might be encountered in plain sight along Corso Roma, under the portico of the Caffè della Borsa—the whole lot of them ought to be shut up again in the ghettoes, and be done with the

---

[*] See the footnote about this organization on p. 78.

usual inappropriate pieties!—or it could be read in the faces of some of the city's more fanatical anti-Fascists who would stop by the Caffè della Borsa only on occasions of public calamities, and these befell us almost every day: there they were, always there, just like other birds of ill-omen of a similar feather. Only the blind would be unaware of the malicious pleasure that, from under the habitual mask of indifference, issued from their every pore! Only the deaf would not have heard in the voice with which the honorable Bottecchiari, seated some way off, hailed the waiter Giovanni to order his usual aperitif—a strong, calm, crisply articulate voice, which made the customers on the other side of the place jump—the derision of someone already looking forward to and savoring their revenge! And what could it mean, that absurd mania to display himself that had seized hold of Pino Barilari, if not that, as an anti-Fascist, a subversive, he too wanted to expedite the defeat of the nation? In his open display of an unseemly disease, wasn't it possible to descry a subtly offensive and provocative intent, beside which, even the fourteen shop windows left shattered from the stones thrown by the so-called "gang of pupils," was footling child's play?

These worries spread abroad and reached the upper echelons.

Yet despite these things, when asked his opinion by the select court of his most faithful followers that encircled him, Carlo Aretusi, nicknamed Sciagura, drew down his mouth in an expression of doubt.

"Don't let's exaggerate," he replied with a smile.

In the inseparable company of Vezio Sturla and Osvaldo Bellistracci he had maintained his—you could call it permanent—station for, by now, twenty years, at the very same table of the Caffè della Borsa. And so it was to him, as the most authoritative member of what at the time of the "action squads" had been Ferrara's famous Fascist triumvirate, that the most delicate questions were addressed without delay.

Sceptical, nostalgic, Sciagura kept on smiling. Despite the insistence of the others, he couldn't be induced to see that in Pino Barilari's behavior there was anything at all threatening.

"That draft dodger a subversive?" he finally blurted out, laughing. "If only you'd been with us in Rome in 1922!"

Thus it was—it's worth recording because this had never happened before—that the little group of his confidants were able to hear from

Sciagura's lips, twisted into an emotional expression for the occasion, a remarkable abundance of detail about the March on Rome.

Ah yes, Sciagura sighed. He, unlike certain others, was always reluctant to speak at all about the March on Rome!

Why—he continued at once, with emphasis—why ever would he waste his time blathering about an event like that, which if it had meant a seizure of power for many, who consequently accrued personal advantages, for him, as for others like him—and here Sturla and Bellistracci nodded in silent confirmation—it represented one thing only: the end of the revolution, the definitive eclipse of the glorious era of the squads?

And then, when you considered the matter closely, what was it if not a kind of military convoy making for the capital, with stops at all the stations, to gather the platoons of comrades-in-arms (in those days, the tunnels made for the fast trains between Bologna and Florence weren't yet even dreamed of), a proper troop of armed Carabinieri and Royal Guards placed as protection along the whole line? Fat chance that they'd be there to guard the four Fiat 18 BLs which, in 1919, had pushed as far forward as Molinella, deep into the Red zone, to set fire to the HQ of the Workers' Organization. That was some feat—which, for the first time, had drawn all of Italy's attention to the Fascist Federation of Ferrara, and which, to be precise, led to the very first friction between the Ferrara and the Bologna federations, as the latter had considered (and explicitly called) the Molinella expedition a "provocative interference." Fascism was at that time anarchic, Garibaldi-like. Then, as opposed to later, bureaucrats were not preferred to revolutionaries. But in 1919 or '20 the young Sciagura, the young Bellistracci, the young Sturla, armed only with clubs, with knuckledusters or, at the most, with some old SIPE-manufactured hand-grenades left over from the war, would leave by night from Porta Reno looking for a fight with the Communist dockers who crowded the drinking dens of Borgo San Luca—it had actually been them, the Bolshevik workers from beyond Porta Reno, who had nicknamed him Sciagura, Calamity: and he had always boasted of the name, and had always worn it like a medal for bravery. No way were they counting on any assistance, even of an indirect kind, from the police! It wasn't until 1922, or rather '23, that the police began to give a hand to the Fascists. In that later period, before setting out on any punitive raid, they used to assemble with all the trucks and cars in the Castle's central courtyard. After 1923, the farm owners from out of town might also have been seen, rushing to offer their cars, declaring themselves highly honored to put them at the service of the Cause!

But getting back to the March on Rome and the son of Dr. Barilari—in the end it was him, the boy, who provided the only real entertainment for the whole trip. Thinking back, it was actually he who salvaged the March on Rome.

He had joined them at the last moment, when the train was already leaving, so a hand had to be stretched from the window to haul him up like a dead weight. The way he was dressed! He was wearing a grey-green cloak which must have been his father's and reached down to his hocks, military puttees which slipped down his legs every five minutes, big, low-cut, yellow shoes, and in addition a great fez, which, crushed down on his head, made his ears stick out like a bat's. What could you do, seeing yourselves gawped at by his idiot eyes on stalks, but split your sides with laughter? It seemed like the boy thought that he, Sciagura, was a kind of Tom Mix and that the others in the "hand-grenade" squad had been the sheriff's posse. "Who are you? Not by chance Dr. Barilari's son?" someone had soon asked. Too out of breath to reply, he'd nodded in the affirmative. "But does your daddy know you've sneaked away with us?" He shook his head for No, all the while staring at them with his baby eyes as if he'd been dropped into a cowboy film.

At eighteen years old, he was far from being a kid. But he was worse than a kid.

At that age he was still a virgin. Since the train, on the way there as on the way back, stopped at more or less every station, and they made the most of nearly every stop by going in search of brothels, and he, Pino, always stubborn as a mule, refused to set foot inside any of them, it ended up with them hauling him in by force. He resisted, dragged his feet, pleaded with his hands together and wept. "What're you so scared of—you think they're going to eat you?" the others said. "At least come in and have a look. Word of honor we won't make you go upstairs into any of the bedrooms!"

He didn't believe us. At a certain moment he, Sciagura, smiling and winking, intervened and took him aside, and whispered something in his ear. "You really don't want to come in?" he said. "Go on, stop pretending!"

Only then did he decide to go in, even if then, as soon as he'd entered the salon with all the others, he huddled down in a corner all on his own. The girls, egged on and touched by him being so scared—it should be said they always had a weakness for Fascists!—were all in competition to pet him; you can't imagine what lengths they went to. Listening to him, you'd think those girls had turned the brothel into a home for abandoned children. And sure enough the madam came in to sort things out. "Now what's going on here, girls?" she yelled at them. "Are we running a wet-flannel factory?" Every time they stopped off, it was a comedy, a farce of this kind.

The mother of all scenes happened at Specchi, a brothel in Bologna, on the return journey.

The Porrettana line* was never-ending—they'd been bored to death on the way there—so at Pistoia, before they had to cope with the Apennines, they'd got out in twos and threes to buy up all the flasks of Chianti they could get their hands on. Up in the mountains it gets cold, and so misty you can't see ten meters ahead. To pass the time, there was nothing to do but drink and sing songs, the result being that when they arrived at Bologna toward midnight, all of them, Pino included, were completely drunk.

At the end of Via dell'Oca, pressing his back against the knocker made of nail-heads on the small entrance door, Pino once again started going through his usual theatrics of resistance. It was then, that he, Sciagura, perhaps because of the alcohol, or the boredom of the journey, or the anger at having taken part in that great travesty that was the March on Rome—at Rome, they'd stayed barely a couple of days, for most of that time stuck in the barracks and never getting even a glimpse of Il Duce, because, they said, he was haggling with the king about forming a government—anyway, suddenly, without knowing quite how, he found himself with the Mauser in his fist pointed at the boy's throat, saying that if Pino didn't stop whining and go in right away, or even, when they'd gone in to the little salon upstairs, if he refused to go up to a room with a prostitute, he'd have to face a lot worse than syphilis. As things turned out, it was probably then that he actually did catch it!

It had been he who accompanied the boy upstairs, to make sure that

---

* The Porrettana railway line runs from Pistoia to Rome, over 300 kilometers.

the two of them did their business and that properly. Lucky Pino had done as he was told! If he hadn't, then he, Sciaguro, drunk as he was and levelling that revolver at him, well, anything might have happened.

3.

WHO IN Ferrara does not remember the night of December 15, 1943?[*] Who could forget the slow creep of the hours that night? For everyone it was an anxious, interminable vigil, with burning eyes peering through the slats of blinds at streets cloaked in the darkness of a blackout, and the heart leaping every minute at the crackle of machine-gun fire or the sudden passing, even noisier, of the trucks packed with armed men.

> *Death holds for us no fear,*
> *Long live death and the cemetery . . .*

sang the unseen men in the trucks. It was a cadenced, rather than warlike song, but that lilt, too, was full of desperation.

News of the assassination of Consul Bolognesi, the ex-Federal Secretary (who, since September, after the interval of the Badoglio period,[†] had been called upon to reorganize the Fascist Federation and assume its governership), had spread around the city in the early afternoon of the 15th. A little later, the radio supplied the details: the Topolino car found on a country road near Copparo, the left-side window wide open; the victim with his head slumped on the steering wheel "as though sleeping"; the "classic" shot to the back of the neck, "more telling than a signature"; and the contempt, "the unstoppable tide of contempt," which the news, as soon as it was received, had provoked in Verona, in the heart of the Constituent Assembly of the New Social Republic assembled in Castelvecchio. Toward

---

[*] See footnote on p. 64.

[†] Pietro Badoglio, who led the Italian military campaign in Abyssinia and defeated the Ethiopian troops with mustard gas, was proclaimed prime minister of Italy in September 1943 and signed an armistice with the Allies. After the German invasion restored Mussolini, he was dismissed in early June 1944.

evening, it was possible to hear a live recording from the session in Verona. A thin, high voice had suddenly taken over from the deep, sorrowful voice of the speaker, who, having informed the listeners of the death of Consul Bolognesi, had begun to fashion his eulogy, shouting angrily and sorrowfully like a child throwing a tantrum: "We shall avenge our comrade, Bolognesi!" The radios were switched off, people stared at each other with frightened expressions, and already the dull rumbling of distant tanks approaching and the lacerating rat-a-tat of the first bursts of machine-gun fire could be heard outside.

No one went to bed, no one even thought of sleeping. There wasn't, in short, a single person in Ferrara who didn't fear that their house would be raided. But it was above all in the city's middle-class apartments that feverish discussions and arguments raged.

What was happening? What would happen now?

It's true, they reasoned, seated torpidly around those same tables, the tablecloths still covered with crumbs and only half-cleared of the lunch's dirty dishes, on which, at a given time as on every other evening, they were vainly attempting to eat supper—it's true that the city was resounding with the noise of gunfire, with lugubrious songs that spoke of death and cemeteries. But this shouldn't make them think that the Fascists—who had, even in Ferrara, shown remarkable moderation, confining themselves since the previous September to rounding up the hundred or so Jews they'd managed to get their hands on and a mere ten anti-Fascists, locking them up in Piangipane Prison—had now suddenly switched tactics and wanted to bring about a general and radical turn of the screw, beginning in the city itself. Good Lord, they might be Fascists, but they were also Italians! And, to tell the truth, a lot more Italian than many others who liked to expatiate on Freedom while polishing the shoes of the foreign invader. No, surely there was nothing to fear. If the Fascists were kicking up a bit of a fuss, swaggering about looking fierce, with skulls on their berets, they were doing it mainly to keep the Germans at bay, who, left to themselves, wouldn't have hesitated to treat Italy like some kind of Poland or Ukraine. What poor devils the Fascists were! You had to understand the predicament they were in, and the personal tragedy of Mussolini, also a poor fellow, who hadn't yet retired from public life to his summer residence, the

Rocca delle Caminate, as he perhaps hoped to, due to Italy's dire plight. But the king, the king! On September 8, all the king could do, along with Badoglio, was cut the cord. By contrast, in the hour of crisis, Mussolini, as a good Romagnolo (the Savoy royal family and Badoglio were Piedmontese, and the Piedmontese had always been a stingy, untrustworthy lot!), hadn't hesitated for an instant to wade into the waves, rush up the gangplank and grab the tiller . . . And frankly, how should the assassination of the Consul Bolognesi be judged—a paterfamilias, besides, and a man who'd never harmed a hair on anyone's head? No true Italian could approve of a crime like that, which was, it was obvious, a servile imitation of Yugoslavia or France, intended to spread the flames and all the horrors of a partisan war into Italy too. The destruction of all the finest Western and Mediterranean values: in short, Communism—that's the real aim of a partisan war! If the Yugoslavs and the French, despite the recent experience of Spain, wanted Communism, well, they had their Tito and their De Gaulle. For Italians today, as things were, there was a single obligation: to stay united and save what could be saved.

Finally, and mercifully, daylight returned. And with the light, the songs and shooting ceased.

And at the same time, at a stroke, the nervous chattering behind doors and windows ceased. But the anxiety did not abate. Daylight, restoring even to the blindest a clear sense of reality, made it even more acute. What did that sudden silence portend? What was it hiding or preparing? It could easily be a trap fashioned to trick people into coming out so that they could then be rounded up. They stayed cooped up inside their houses for at least two hours, before vague news of the massacre had gradually spread, as if by its own momentum. The victims of the reprisal were said to be fifty, a hundred, two hundred. If the most desperate predictions were to be given any credit, not just Corso Roma, but the whole city center would be strewn with corpses.

And yet there were only eleven, laid in three separate heaps along the wall of the Castle moat, on that stretch of sidewalk exactly opposite the Caffè della Borsa. To count and identify them, which was done by the first who dared approach—from a way off they didn't even look like human bodies: rags, poor rags at that, or bundles thrown there in the sun and the dirty melting snow—it was necessary to turn those that lay face down over on to their backs and separate, one from the other, those who fell embracing each other and had become a tight tangle of rigid limbs. There was only just time to count and recognize them. Because soon after, emerging from the corner of the Corso Giovecca, a small military van came to a halt with a theatrical screech of brakes in front of the group who had gathered around the bodies. "Away! Move away!" the Blackshirts militia who were riding in the van yelled out. Still pursued by their shouts, nothing remained for those who were present but slowly to retreat toward the two ends of Corso Roma, and from there, under the sun now already high, their eyes still on the four militia men down there who kept guard over the dead with machine guns in their hands, to let the whole city know by telephone what they'd risked and what they'd seen.

Horror, pity, crazed fear: all of these were mingled in the impression which the announcement of the names of the dead awoke in every household. There were only eleven of them, agreed. But they were persons only too well known in Ferrara, persons about whom, beyond their names, a surfeit of details both physical and moral were too familiar for their end not to appear from the first a terrifying event, of an almost incredible brutality. It will seem strange that the nearly unanimous abhorrence of the murder could at once be accompanied by an equally widespread intention to treat the murderers respectfully, to make a public show of supporting and submitting to their violence. Yet this is what happened, and it would be futile to try to conceal the fact, if it's true, as it was, that in no other city of northern Italy could the Fascism that was reborn in Verona have been able to count such a large number of enrolled Party members as might be seen on the morning of the 17th in long, silent lines in the courtyard of Ferrara's Fascist headquarters in Viale Cavour, waiting for the Federation offices to open. Bent, submissive, disheartened under the worn-out greatcoats made of autarchic fabrics, they were the same silent tide of people who, the afternoon of the day before, had step by step followed the coffin of Consul Bolognesi along Corso Giovecca, Via Palestro, Via Borso, up to Piazza della Certosa, and in whose leaden features the few who had remained inside their houses to watch the cortège from behind their blinds had, with a shudder, been able to recognize their own faces. What else was there to do but give in? The Germans and Japanese, even if for the moment they seemed in retreat, would reverse the situation, uncovering an arsenal of secret weapons of unheard-of power, and win the war with a lightning strike. No, there was only one road left to take.

But those who committed the massacre, who were they? The whole city had started to wonder the following day. There was no doubt: the first perpetrators, those materially responsible for the massacre, could be none other than the men from the military cars, four of them with licence plates "VR," from Verona, and two "PD," from Padua—the same ones that throughout the night had filled Ferrara with their songs and firing, and then, toward dawn, had disappeared. The avengers predicted by the radio had certainly been they. And in fact it was they, the squad members from the Veneto, who presented themselves at the entrance of the prison in Via Piangipane, and it was they, and they alone, who, with guns in their hands, had forced that poor chap, the director, to hand over the lawyers Polenghi and Tamagnini, both of them Socialists and veteran trade union organizers, and also the lawyers Galimberti, Fano and Forlivesi of the Partito d'Azione,[*] all of them detained since September, all awaiting investigation.

And yet, to belie the rumor which was already circulating, according to which no Ferrarese had participated in the atrocity, no Ferrarese was stained with that blood, it was quite enough to ponder the other six dead, National Councillor Abbove, Dr. Malacarne, the accountant Zoli, the two Cases, father and son, and the worker Felloni, at least five of whom were taken from their own houses. Apart from Felloni (a little-known employee of the Electric Company, who had been rounded up with the group of victims only because a little before dawn, the hour at which he usually went to work, he'd happened to run into one of the patrols which were blocking the way to the city center), no one who wasn't from Ferrara—a point argued by many—could possibly have been able to track down National Councillor Abbove, who was not then in his home in Corso Giovecca, but in the office-*garçonnière*, which he had recently had built, having very cheaply bought the site within a narrow medieval cloister in the quiet and secluded Via Brasàvola, and in whose discreet shade, filled with the

---

[*] For information about this political party, see the footnote on p. 95.

most various of art objects, the old epicure was wont to repair, on certain afternoons, to enjoy his declining years. No one who wasn't from the city (very well informed indeed about what had been going on there over the previous years) could possibly have known of the secret meetings which, during the forty-five days of the Badoglio period, had been held in that big trap belonging to the National Councillor Abbove. Dr. Malacarne and the accountant Zoli had always attended, but old Sciagura, no—he had declined each and every invitation. These meetings were thought to be intended to work out a strategy for all those Fascists who, with the fall of the regime, only wanted to send word to the king, attesting to their "unconditional loyalty"—in short, to change their views as swiftly as a weathervane. And the two Cases, father and son, especially, two of the few Jews to have escaped from the big roundup in September, leather merchants who had never had a political thought in their lives and had lived, since September, hidden away in the barn of their old house in Vicolo Mozzo Torcicoda, provided with food through a hole in the floor by their wife and mother, respectively, who was as Aryan and Catholic as could be . . . who else but someone who had the most intimate knowledge of their place of refuge could have been able to point the four cut-throats sent to capture them just there, atop that dusty labyrinth of half-crumbled little staircases? Who else but . . . ?

Carlo Aretusi, yes, him, Sciagura. As to why suspicion should immediately have alighted on him (since the morning of the 16th he had resumed command of the Federation, and his name was spoken henceforth as it had been before 1922, in an instinctively hushed tone), it's enough to recall how he had appeared at the funeral of Consul Bolognesi on the afternoon of that day.

He had never participated in the many clandestine meetings which in August had been held at the house of National Councillor Abbove, even sending word to his ex-comrades that he, not wanting to renege at fifty on what he had done at twenty years of age, had no wish to attend. And so, while he walked at the head of the interminable cortège just in front of the gun carriage which bore the coffin of Consul Bolognesi and kept casting glances of scorn and hatred in the direction of the houses in Corso Giovecca and in Via Palestro—how free and easy he seemed, wearing, despite the cold, only his black shirt with his beret of the Tenth Assault Flotilla, disbanded in 1923, his temples only just beginning to turn grey— he seemed to be exactly as he'd been as a young man at twenty. "Damned vermin, cowardly, boot-licking bourgeoisie! I'll show you! I'll flush you all out!" his furious eyes and curled lips seemed to be threatening. In Piazza della Certosa, before the coffin was borne into the church, he had harangued the crowd in this very tone. Grey and inert, the crowd listened. He seemed to become more and more infuriated, perhaps most of all infuriated because of that inertia.

"The bodies of the eleven traitors shot in Corso Roma at dawn this morning," he had yelled in conclusion, "won't be removed until I give the order. We want to be sure that their example will have the desired effect!"

In that paroxysm of rage could he have boasted anymore explicitly of having administered justice himself, with his own hands?

A little after, in Corso Roma, when he had unexpectedly arrived to call to attention the Black Brigade militia, who were guarding the bodies of the slain, how should one interpret his behavior, which seemed so at odds with that of a half-hour earlier in Piazza della Certosa, except that, reconsidering, it added up to more than a hundred confessions?

Sullenly he got out of the car, barely sparing a glance at the corpses stretched out on the pavement, and at once one of the soldiers took a step forward to inform him, with the air of congratulating him for having arrived at the right moment, of all that had been happening.

The whole day, the militia man explained, speaking on behalf of himself and his companions, the three of them had managed to keep at bay anyone who had tried to approach. More than once, with the aim of dispersing them—they were most likely the traitors' relatives, women weeping and crying out, men who were swearing; it wasn't in the least bit easy to make them obey!—they'd been forced to fire a few bursts of bullets into the air to drive them off down there to the far corners of Piazza Cattedrale and Corso Giovecca, where even now, as Comrade Aretusi could see, a few of them still seemed determined to stay. But what else could they have done—the soldier went on and, raising his arm, pointed to the window, behind which one could make out the motionless shape of Pino Barilari— about that gentleman up there, a really weird guy, I can tell you, when no hint or threat, no burst of machine-gun fire has made him budge an inch? Who knows, perhaps he was deaf? Still, if they'd known how to reach him, even if it meant breaking through the shutters down there in the pharmacy, one of them would surely have gone up to tell him from close up, politely or otherwise, to move the hell away . . .

As soon as the soldier had said "that gentleman up there," Sciagura, with a start as though he'd been bitten by an adder, had raised his eyes to the window the young man was pointing at. It was dark by then. Seeping up over the rim of the Castle moat, minute by minute, the fog was thickening. Along the whole length of Corso Roma that window up there was the only one lit.

Still looking up at it, Sciagura let out a stifled curse and made a scornful gesture. He then turned round, and in a muffled voice, a kind of timorous murmur, ordered the three soldiers, in some twenty minutes' time, when the men he had sent to remove the bodies arrived, to let them do it, and not to get in their way.

4.

PEOPLE IMAGINED things.

They imagined entering the apartment above the pharmacy, where no one from Ferrara, not even the Freemason brothers of the deceased Francesco, had ever even once set foot. A little spiral staircase linked the back workroom to the upstairs floor, which consisted of only four rooms: a dining room, a drawing room, a double bedroom and finally the little room which Pino had had as a boy, and to which, since being struck down by paralysis, he'd once again returned . . . By the sheer effort of imagining it, it was as though they had come to know the apartment intimately—to the extent of being able to point to the very wall on which hung the portrait photograph of Scales in a heavy, gilded, nineteenth-century frame, and to describe the shape of the central chandelier which every evening cast its strong, white light over the table's green cover and on the cards of the game of patience, or to tell of the effect of the modern furniture and objects, scattered here and there, but mostly in the double bedroom, which had been introduced by the young Signora Barilari, or to expound on the little room adjoining the bedroom where, soon after supper, Pino retired to sleep, with a child's iron bed in one corner, a small desk against one wall, a wardrobe against the opposite wall, and at the foot of the bed, covered with a blanket of Scottish wool in red-and-blue tartan, the big armchair with adjustable back which every morning his wife replaced beside the light-filled dining room window, and on which Pino sat from morning to evening. If they'd wanted to they could even have listed one by one the authors shelved in the glass-fronted bookcase next to the radiator beside the door—Salgari, Verne, Ponson du Terrail, Dumas, Mayne Reid, Fenimore Cooper, and so on. Among the other books there was also *The Narrative of Arthur Gordon Pym* by E. A. Poe, in an edition whose cover depicted a tall white ghost armed with a sickle looming over a little whaling sloop. Yet this latter volume was not behind the glass of the bookcase alongside the other books, but, rather, face down on the bedside table's shelf beside a fat stamp album, a bundle of crayons upright in a glass, a cheap penknife, a half-consumed eraser; the volume placed, then, so that the spectre on the cover, while still being present, being there, was invisible, and did not arouse any fear.

But this wasn't enough.

"Where are you going?" Pino had asked on the evening of December 15, raising his head from a game of patience.

Having got up from the table, his wife Anna was already moving toward the door. And it was from the shadowy corridor, at the end of which the trapdoor opened on to the spiral staircase, that her calm voice reached him in reply.

"Where do you think I'm going? I'm going down to close the shop."

Who knows? Perhaps he hadn't heard on the radio, early that afternoon, the report from Verona. What is certain is that at nine o'clock, when the chimes of the Castle clock had faded over the whole city with the slow sweetness of a benediction, one would have expected Pino to be huddled up in his child's bed, the covers drawn up to his ears. Closing his eyes, going to sleep. Hearing his wife get up from the table to go down to the pharmacy—at that hour there was always something to do down there: tot up the day's earnings and, finally, having drawn down the shutters, to lock up from inside—and seeing her about to leave through the drawing room door, so tall and beautiful and indifferent, what would Pino be thinking about except that? To fall into a deep sleep. And that evening, perhaps, even earlier than usual.

They also imagined everything else, naturally, everything else that happened.

They saw the eleven men lined up in three distinct groups against the little wall of the Castle moat, the coming and going of the blue-shirted legionnaires in that space between the portico of the Caffè della Borsa and the opposite sidewalk, the desperate sneer of the lawyer Fano, when, an instant before the firing began, he had shouted "Murderer!" at Sciagura, who was standing a little apart lighting a cigarette, that clear light, that incredibly clear moonlight which, since midnight, with the wind's sudden change, had made every stone of the city a piece of glass or coal, and Pino, finally, whom only the cry of the lawyer Fano had managed to drag at the last moment from his child-like deep sleep, hidden up there, shaking on his crutches, behind the windowpanes which overlooked the scene . . . And it was thus, for months and months, the whole time it took from December 1943 to May '44 for the war to slowly advance up the Italian peninsula, as if the collective imagination needed to return to that spot, to that fearful night, and to have before its eyes the faces of the eleven men who were shot just as Pino had seen them from his lofty vantage-point.

The Liberation came, and finally Peace, and for many Ferrarese, for almost all of them, came the anxious need to forget.

But can one forget? Is it enough to want to?

In the summer of 1946, when in the conference room of the ex-Fascist HQ in Viale Cavour the trial began of the twenty or so presumed perpetrators of the massacre of three years earlier (most of them from the Veneto, collared in the Coltano concentration camp and the prisons), and when, hiding under a false name in the refuge in Colle Val d'Elsa where he had been tracked down by the young and very active provincial secretary of the Associazione Nazionale Partigiani d'Italia,[*] Nino Bottecchiari, Sciagura too made his entry into the big cage, the dock of the accused, this seemed

---

[*] See footnote on p. 68.

the most auspicious occasion finally to place a covering stone over the past. It was, however, true, they sighed, that no other city in northern Italy had supplied as many adherents to the Republic of Salò as Ferrara had, no other middle class had been so ready to kowtow to the dismal banners of its various militia and special corps. And yet it would have needed very little indeed for that error of calculation which many had made under the pressure of such exceptional circumstances, and which the Communists of the region, taking control of the town hall in 1945, had tended to turn into a stain of eternal infamy, for that simple, only human error to become along with everything else just a bad dream, a terrible nightmare from which to awake full of hope, faith in themselves and in the future! Sufficient to this end would have been the condemnation of the assassins, and then every memory of that night of December 15, 1943, that fatal, decisive night, could be rapidly and finally erased.

The trial inched forward in the heat and boredom, provoking in the jostling crowd which gathered for every sitting a growing sense of futility and impotence.

Made restless and uneasy by the loudspeakers placed in the avenue outside which broadcast the proceedings as far away as the city center, as the middle of Corso Roma, the court interrogated the accused one by one. From behind the bars of the big cage placed along one side of the courtroom, between two windows, the accused kept responding in the same way: none of them had been involved in the punitive expedition of December 1943; none of them had even been to Ferrara. They all seemed so sure they had nothing to fear that some of them even risked the odd joke. There was one from Treviso, for example, with long curly dark hair and a jutting, unshaven jaw, who admitted that, yes, he had in fact once been to Ferrara, but twenty years earlier, on a bike to meet his girlfriend—a joke which didn't fail to elicit a sly and good-natured, typically Neapolitan grin from the presiding judge, who always seemed inclined to distance himself from that aura of populist, revolutionary justice the trial had begun to assume. If he had allowed the sittings to take place in the ex-Fascist HQ—so he had said on the first day—it was only because the courthouse, half-destroyed by a bombardment in 1944 and in the process of reconstruction, was still unfit for use.

As for Sciagura, not only did he too deny any direct or indirect involvement in the "event" of December 15, 1943, but from the first moment that the Carabinieri put him in the cage, he never lost an opportunity to display, along with the most punctilious respect for the court called to judge his "actions," his deep disdain for the crowd down in the public space, whose behavior, he said at a certain point, revealed only too clearly the baleful effect "of the present state of affairs." So was it, he added, with factional hatred, with the thirst for revenge that could be seen on all those faces that the much hoped-for national pacification was to be achieved? Was this the climate of freedom to enable the court to pass a cool and unprejudiced judgement on a man like him, only guilty of having been "a soldier in the service of an Idea"?

All this was merely blowing smoke in the eyes of the court, evasive tactics meant to delay and to stop the proceedings from becoming too legalistic, which would be to his disadvantage, whereas a political trial could only work in his favor.

"I was the foot soldier of an Idea," he kept repeating in a self-pleased way, "not the system's hired assassin nor the servant of foreign powers!"

Or in a maudlin tone: "Everyone now speaks ill of me!"

He didn't need to add anything more. But each time it was as though he hinted that his persecutors of today shouldn't fool themselves that condemning him would draw a veil over what they themselves had been yesterday. Every one of them had been just as much a Fascist as him, and no court verdict was going to wipe away that fact.

"And in the end what was it he was being accused of?" he said, going on the offensive one day. If he'd not misunderstood, he was accused of having supplied the list of eleven persons who were shot on the night of December 15, 1943, and of having personally directed the execution of those "unfortunates." But to convince a "proper," a "responsible" court that he, Carlo Aretusi, had really done those two things, proffered the list and directed the execution, proof was required—not mere suppositions! "There's no point in chattering about the slaughter, since I myself am ready to assume full and complete responsibility for it!" It seemed he'd declared as much some days after the "famous night," and it may indeed be that, on that or on another occasion, those had been his words. And so? Once again, proof is required, proof! As for the sentences he may have spoken then, "in the heat of the moment," they were "in all probability" intended to assure "our German allies" of the commitment and unconditional loyalty of Italy. After September 8 the Germans had become the real rulers of Italy, and, as we know, they wouldn't have had any hesitation in reducing every town in the land to a pile of rubble. So what counted wasn't words, and words, remember, spoken in public so that others might hear and heed them. What counted were facts and deeds, not to mention the medals for valour that he, during the First World War, had won fighting against those very Germans to whom he was now accused of being a lackey—he, a lackey?—a stormtrooper on the Piave! And since the stockholders of the Agricola Bank had been referred to, why not also remember that the honorable Bottecchiari, the Socialist lawyer Mauro Bottecchiari, who until the fall of the "Badoglio government" had served on the board of directors of that bank, had been released at Christmas from the Via Piangipane prison due to his, Carlo Aretusi's, direct intervention? Also the schoolmistress Trotti, another Socialist, had been set free on the same occasion, and it's a shame that now she's no longer with us to testify on his behalf. But the honorable Bottecchiari is still enjoying the best of health. So why not call on him at once and ask him to relate all that he knows of the matter? The honorable Bottecchiari is a good man, utterly trustworthy and above any pettiness, and for this reason he, Sciagura, had always had the utmost respect for him since the remote times of 1920, and '22. The truth is that compared to how things were once, nowadays everywhere in Italy political conduct has massively deteriorated! Another truth ought to be told: that today they wanted to condemn Carlo Aretusi mainly because he had been "promoted" to lead the federal Fascist secretariat of Ferrara on the day after Consul Bolognesi's assassination. For a reason of this kind, of "scheming politics" today, they wanted to make a scapegoat of Carlo Aretusi. A "proper" court, a "responsible" court, a court that wouldn't let itself be "swayed by factional prejudices" would at once have understood that he had accepted the directorship with the exclusive aim of hindering certain "lawless desperadoes" from instigating a reign of terror. And, in fact, what had been the first step he had taken as soon as he was appointed but to restore without delay the bodies of the victims to their respective families?

Every now and then, to be fair, the presiding judge would remember to interrupt him, mildly calling him to order, and he, for his part, always showed himself ready to let go of the bars of the cage, which he kept gripping hold of while he spoke, to desist from giving fiery looks toward the public space at the end of the court, and to sit back down on the bench alongside the other accused. But these concessions of his lasted a very short time. At the first phrase from the public prosecutor that displeased him, or at any witness's testimony that he considered "erroneous" or at the slightest murmur from the public, or, most of all, at the tiniest hint made about his active participation in the shooting on the night of December 15, 1943, he would once more spring to his feet, wildly grab hold of the bars of the cage, and again raise his heavy, grating voice, the voice of an old commander, which the loudspeakers outside broadcast in a wide arc across the city.

"Let's see the witnesses!" he yelled like a madman. "Let's see who has the guts to say such a thing to my face!"

Yet he suddenly fell silent when he saw Pino Barilari in person, making his way through the crowd, holding with one hand the arm of his wife, with the other a big, knotty, rubber-tipped walking stick; his legs in baggy, seroual breeches were thin as twigs and moved in a strange lateral sweep with the effort of walking.

From that moment on, as though hypnotized, he neither moved nor took his eyes off the chemist, for whom, as well as for his wife, Nino Bottec-chiari, never absent from the courtroom, hurriedly found a space in the section reserved for the witnesses—it had been him, besides, who had suggested in a letter to the court that the paralysed man be called as a witness. Sciagura actually did move, but only very slowly, to keep smoothing down his iron-grey hair with his right hand. At the same time, he was thinking—you could see it in his face—he didn't stop thinking for a moment.

At last it was Pino Barilari's turn to take the stand.

Still supported by his wife, he came forward and was duly sworn in, though he was barely audible.

But in the second before he answered the presiding judge's question and pronounced with almost pedantic clarity the brief phrase "I was sleeping," which like a pin bursting a balloon filled with air had shrivelled to nothing the huge tension that held the entire court—the silence was absolute, no one breathed and even his wife leaned anxiously forward to

scrutinize his face—in that second, quite a few observers distinctly saw
Sciagura give Pino Barilari a rapid, propitiating look. And a wink of shared
understanding, an almost imperceptible wink.

5.

FOR THE last word to be said on this question, some further years had
to pass. In the meantime everyone found a way of resuming their life.
Pino Barilari began to pass the most part of his days sitting in front of his
usual window once more, but he'd become embittered and ironic, with
field glasses always within reach, and implacable in fulfilling the role he
seemed to have assigned himself: of forever surveying the passers-by on
that stretch of sidewalk below. And all the other, old habitués together
with the next generation of youths (Sciagura, of course, included, since
his trial had resulted in a full acquittal) had returned to share out between
them the tables and chairs of the cafe beneath him.

In 1948, just after the elections of April 18, Anna Barilari left her hus-
band's house and at once began proceedings to obtain a legal separation.
People assumed that she would return to live with her family in Marshal
Repetto's house. But they were mistaken.

Instead she went to live alone in a little apartment at the end of the
Corso Giovecca, near the Prospettiva Arch: two windows, encased in
bulging ironwork that directly overlooked the sidewalk. And although she
was now almost thirty years old, and, shapely though she still was, seemed
even older, she once again began going for bike rides as she had as a girl,
when she had attracted droves of school companions, and there were many
in Ferrara who still remembered such things well.

Enrolled in the Drawing Academy in Via Romei, she wore low-necked
pullovers which displayed her imposing bust, her long, mustard-blonde
hair thrown back behind her, and used more make-up than ever. She probably aspired to the look of the Existentialist young women of Paris and
Rome. In reality, she was on the game, and no joke!—as those who should
know attested, if their account was true—that she frequented the restau-

rants and cheap eating places of San Romano on Mondays with the evident aim of picking up a client among those who came to Ferrara for market day.

She would sometimes disappear, though, for periods that varied from one to as much as three weeks. When she popped up again it wasn't rare that she'd be accompanied by a woman, befriended who knows where, with whom, sometimes for a whole month, she'd be seen walking arm in arm up and down the streets, awakening ever-replenished ripples of interest round about. Who on earth was that brunette with the malicious eyes who was now with Anna? was asked everywhere. Was she by chance from Bologna? Or from Rome? And that other one there with the blue eyes, and the pale, refined features, the heelless and almost, it seemed, soleless shoes, was she from Florence or, if not, from abroad?

On the same evening there was no shortage of men willing to trek to the end of the Corso Giovecca to check up on these facts. Having reached the apartment occupied by Signora Barilari, they would discreetly tap on the windowpanes in winter so they could be let in, in summer simply to have a chat through the window from the sidewalk. So, in that vicinity, at some midnights in July or August it wasn't unusual to come across three or four men standing in a group, flirting with Anna or whatever friend she might have with her.

These were usually men between thirty and forty, not a few of whom had a wife and children. They had known Anna since she was a girl, and some of them had even been at school with her. As a result, later, around one or two in the morning, when they reappeared at the Caffè della Borsa and, hot and tired, with the sleeves of their linen jackets rolled up, slumped into the chairs, they would talk and tell stories chiefly about her until it was time to turn in.

She wasn't a straightforward character, Anna! they'd sigh.

It may well have been to do with the fact that until very recently she had been a respectable housewife, or else because they were ill-equipped to fathom certain mysteries of the female mind: the truth was that they never knew what tone to adopt. You could be talking away to her from the sidewalk and she'd suddenly slam the window in your face, and then a minute later open it again if, instead of shrugging and cursing her, you'd stayed and knocked on the window again and whistled. But it was the same old tune if you went inside. Afterward, for example, it was never clear whether or not you ought to insist on her taking the thousand lire. And the long sentimental preludes you had to put up with? And the unease her continuous, endless, tireless chatter induced? While she was still getting dressed again, she'd resume talking about herself, about Pino Barilari, about the years spent with her husband in the apartment above the pharmacy, the reasons why she got married and those which had led to her legal separation. She and her husband, her husband and her: she spoke of nothing else. After he'd been struck down by paralysis, she explained, she'd begun to cheat on him with this or that person, because he was a sort of child, a sick child, or else a kind of old man, while she was a normal woman. The chaos of the war, with the sirens, the bombardments, every kind of fear, had certainly contributed, later, to bringing things to a head. And yet she'd always loved him, as if he were a younger brother. If she'd cheated on him, she'd done so on the quiet, taking every possible precaution. And not even that often.

It was very late when they'd mull over these conversations with Anna. Corso Roma would be so empty and silent that their voices resounded as if in a hall. Nothing else was audible, save the odd train whistle in the distance and, at every quarter hour, the chimes released into the air from the Castle clock in front.

There was a night, however, toward the end of August 1950, when one of these men related something new.

A little earlier, he began to tell in a low tone, he had been at Anna's house with two friends they had in common, so-and-so and such-and-such. That evening she'd been especially irritating. So much so that, bored that she was once again rehearsing the same old stuff, he'd interrupted her.

"A fine way to show you love your husband!" he'd cut in, laughing. "You loved him and then went with anyone you felt like. Give it a rest—you've always been nothing but trouble!"

All hell broke loose.

"Filthy shameless cowards! Pigs!" she began yelling. "Get the hell out of my house!"

She'd turned into a wild beast. Then the other girl, who was from Modena, she too started shouting as if she were having her throat cut.

But soon enough, when apologies had been offered, both of them calmed down. And this, more or less, was what he heard soon after from Anna.

She had always loved Pino, she started saying again in her usual, tearful tone, and, in fact, for quite a few years they had come to a perfect agreement.

From the time that he could no longer walk, he spent his days in front of the dining room window, solving one by one all the games in *Puzzles Weekly* and other magazines of that sort, for which he had a passion. He had nothing else to do—which explains why, with all those hours of practice, he'd achieved an extraordinary skill in that sort of pastime. So, sometimes, to show her how good he was, he would drag himself on his crutches to the little spiral staircase that linked to the back workroom, and from up there, leaning out over the trapdoor, he would start calling her so impatiently and insistently that she had to close the till immediately, rush upstairs and wait for him, eyes shining with pleasure, to explain how he had solved the puzzle. It was she who had to give him the long series of injections which he needed because of his illness, she who put him to bed every night before nine o'clock. What did it matter if they no longer slept together? Even before his illness he hadn't been that keen to sleep together; it made her think, actually, that he was glad to go back to sleeping alone in the little room he'd had as a boy. No, two people could sleep together all the time and not love each other at all.

However, starting from the night of December 15, 1943, everything had suddenly changed between them.

When the shooting was over she had rushed outside. Having run the length of the Corso Giovecca, it was only at the corner of Corso Roma that she stopped for a moment to get her breath back. And while she paused under an arch of the City Theater's portico, just there, piled up along the sidewalk opposite the pharmacy, she had suddenly seen the dead bodies.

She remembered every detail of the scene as if it were still before her eyes. She could see Corso Roma utterly empty under the full moon, the snow, hardened into ice, scattered like a kind of brilliant dust over everything, the air so bright and clear you could read the hour on the Castle clock—exactly twenty-one minutes past four—and finally the corpses, which from where she was looking seemed like so many bundles of rags, and yet they were human bodies, she understood that at once. Without being aware of what she was doing, she moved away from under the theater portico, stepping out into the open toward the bodies.

It was when she was halfway there, by now in full light, and five or six meters away from the nearest heap of the dead, that the thought of Pino had crossed her mind. So she turned. And Pino was up there, motionless behind the panes of the dining room window, a barely visible shadow that was watching her.

They remained like that, staring, for some moments, he from the dark of the room, she from the street; and her not knowing what she should do.

Finally she decided, and entered the house.

While she climbed up the spiral staircase, she tried to think what would be the best thing to tell him. It wouldn't have been too hard for her to invent some nonsense, to act in such a way that Pino believed it. He was a child, and she, in the end, was his mother.

And yet on that occasion, Pino didn't let her invent any bullshit excuse. When she came into the dining room, he was no longer there. Instead he was in his little room, in bed, with his face turned to the wall and the covers drawn up to his ears; and to judge from the way he was breathing you would have thought him asleep. Waking him up, it's true, would have been the right thing to do! But what if he really were asleep, and what if all she had seen from the street, just before, had been a hallucination?

Full of doubt she had gently closed the door and had gone back to her own room, where she threw herself on the bed. She thought that in a very few hours, if not from Pino's mouth, at least from her own face, the truth would be known. And yet that wasn't to be. Not a word from him, not a look that would help her understand. Not that morning, nor ever after.

Why all of this, why? If he'd been awake, why had he never admitted it? Was he afraid? But of whom exactly, of what? As far as the appearance of their relationship went, nothing had changed. Except from that time on, obsessed with his field glasses, he would pass the days surveying the sidewalk opposite and without ever again calling her upstairs as he once did, to show her how brilliantly he'd solved his puzzles and crosswords.

He would snigger and mutter to himself. Had he gone mad? That was a possibility, considering the disease he had. But on the other hand, how could she keep living with him without, little by little, going mad herself?

: || :

The Gold-Rimmed
Spectacles

1.

TIME has begun to thin them out, and yet it would be wrong to claim that only a few people in Ferrara still remember Dr. Fadigati. Oh yes, Athos Fadigati—they would recall—the ENT specialist who had a clinic and his own house in Via Gorgadello, a short walk from Piazza delle Erbe, and who ended up so badly, poor man, so tragically. It was he who, when he left his native Venice as a young man, and came to settle in our city, had seemed destined to follow the most regular, the most uneventful, and for that reason, the most enviable of careers . . .

It was in 1919, just after the other war. Because of my age, I who write this can only offer a rather vague and confused picture of that period. The town-center cafes spilled over with officers in uniform; lorries bedecked with flags continually passed by along Corso Giovecca and Corso Roma (today rechristened Martiri della Libertà); on the scaffolding covering the facade of the Palazzo delle Assicurazioni Generali, then undergoing reconstruction, in front of the north face of the Castle, a huge, scarlet advertising banner had been unfurled, inviting the friends and enemies of Socialism to come together to drink aperitif lenin; scuffles broke out almost every day between farm workers and extremist laborers on the one side and ex-combatants on the other . . . This climate of fever, of political agitation, of general distraction, which colored the early infancy of all those who would become adults some twenty years later, somehow worked in favor of the Venetian Fadigati. In a city such as ours, where after the war the youth from good families were more reluctant than anywhere else to enter the liberal professions, it's easy to understand how he could have put down roots almost unnoticed. The fact is that in 1925, when the fever began to abate even among ourselves, and Fascism, organizing itself into a large national party, was able to offer advantageous positions to all late-comers, Athos Fadigati was already solidly grounded in Ferrara, the owner of a magnificent private clinic, and moreover director of the ENT department of the big, new Sant'Anna Hospital.

He'd made it, as they say. No longer young, and with the air, even then, of never having been so, he was glad to have left Venice (he once confessed this himself) not so much to seek his fortune in a city other than his own, as to have escaped the stricken atmosphere of a vast house on the Grand Canal in which he had witnessed within the space of a few years the deaths of both his parents and of a much-loved sister. His courteous, discreet manners were much appreciated, as were his evident disinterestedness and the fair-minded spirit of charity toward his poorer patients. But even more than for these reasons, he was appreciated for what he was: for those gold-rimmed spectacles that gleamed agreeably upon the dark earthen color of his smooth, hairless cheeks, for the not at all off-putting chubbiness of that corpulent frame which belonged to someone with a congenital heart condition, who had miraculously outlived the crisis of puberty and was always, even in summer, wrapped up in thick English wool. (During the war, owing to his poor health, he had not been able to serve in anything other than the Office of Postal Censorship.) In short there was something in him that immediately attracted and reassured people.

The clinic in Via Gorgadello, where he saw patients from four until seven o'clock every day, would later crown his successes.

It was a very modern clinic, the like of which until then no doctor at Ferrara had ever had. Furnished with an impeccable surgery which, as far as cleanliness, efficiency and even size go, could only be compared with those of the Sant'Anna, it also prided itself on a good eight rooms in the adjoining private apartment in addition to as many small waiting rooms for the public. Our townsfolk, especially the more socially respected, were dazzled by all this.

Having suddenly become intolerant of what could be described as the picturesque, but overfamiliar and finally questionable clutter in which the other three or four aged local specialists continued to see their respective patients, it induced in them a particular respect. At Fadigati's, they never tired of repeating, there was none of the interminable waiting, heaped on top of each other like animals, hearing through the flimsy dividing walls the nearer or further voices of large and almost always happy families, while in the feeble light of a twenty-watt bulb, the eye coursing over the sad walls had nothing to rest on but some majolica tile announcing "Don't Spit," some cartoon of a university professor or fellow doctor, or even more inauspicious and doleful images of patients being subjected to horrendous enemas in front of an entire medical school, or of laparotomies at which, grinning, Death himself officiated dressed as a surgeon. How on earth had they—until then—put up with such medieval treatment?

Soon enough, going to Fadigati's became more than a fashion, became a distinct pleasure. Especially on winter evenings, when the icy wind, whistling, threaded its way from Piazza Cattedrale down Via Gorgadello, it was with frank satisfaction that the rich bourgeois, wrapped up in his fur coat, using the pretext of the faintest of sore throats to slip inside the half-closed little door, would climb up the two staircases and ring the bell at the glass door. Up there, beyond that magical luminous hatch, at which presided a nurse in a white apron, who was always young and smiling, he would find radiators going at full steam, warmer than at his own house, or even, perhaps, than at the Merchants' Club or the Unione Club. He would find armchairs and sofas aplenty, occasional tables always furnished with the most up-to-date papers and journals, shutters that diffused a strong, white, generous light. He would find carpets that, when one grew tired of being there, snoozing in the warmth or leafing through the illustrated reviews, beckoned him to pass from one waiting room to the next to look at the multitude of paintings and prints, both ancient and modern, hung on the walls. He would find a good-natured and sociable doctor who while personally ushering him "in there" to examine the sore throat, seemed above all anxious to know, like the truly refined gentleman he was, whether his patient had had the opportunity to hear, some evenings before, at Bologna's Teatro Communale, Aureliano Pertile in Lohengrin; or else, who knows?—if he had looked closely at the De Chirico or that little Casorati hung on such-and-such a wall in whichever waiting room, and if the painting by De Pisis had appealed to him; and then he would express profound surprise if his patient, in response, confessed to not knowing who Filippo de Pisis was, let alone that he was a young and very promising artist from Ferrara. A comfortable, pleasing and refined setting, and mentally stimulating to boot. A place where time, accursed time, which is always an insuperable problem in the provinces, passed in a delightful way.

2.

NOTHING SO excites an indiscreet interest among the small circle of respectable society as that rightful impulse to keep the private and the public separate in one's life. So what on earth did Athos Fadigati get up to after the nurse had shut the glass door behind the last patient? The far from evident or at least hardly normal use that the doctor made of his evenings added to the curiosity that surrounded his person. Oh yes, in Fadigati there was a hint of something hard to fathom. But even this, in him, had an appeal, was an attraction.

Everyone knew how he spent his mornings, so no one had anything to say about them.

By nine he was already at the hospital, and with visits and operations (because he also did operations: there was not a day in which he didn't have to take out a pair of tonsils or take a scalpel to a mastoid) he kept at it until one o'clock. After which, between one and two, it was not unusual to meet him once again walking up Corso Giovecca with a bag of tuna in oil or a packet of sliced ham hanging from his little finger, and with the Corriera della Sera jutting out of his coat pocket. So he ate lunch at home. And since he didn't have a cook, and the part-time maid who kept his house and study clean only showed up around three, an hour before the nurse arrived, it must have been he—in itself a bizarre phenomenon—who prepared the indispensable plate of pasta.

Even for supper his presence would have been vainly awaited in the few town-center restaurants which were judged to be of certain decorousness: Vincenzo's, Sandrino's, at the Tre Galletti—or even at Roveraro's, in the Vicolo del Granchio, whose authentic home-cooking appealed to so many other middle-aged bachelors. This did not at all mean, though, that he ate at home as he did at lunchtime. He never seemed to stay at home in the evening. Around eight o'clock, or a quarter past, on Via Gorgadello, it was easy to catch sight of him just as he was leaving. He would linger a moment on the threshold, looking up, looking right, then left, as if unsure of the time or of which direction to take. At last he would set off, merging into the stream of people who at that hour, in summer just as in winter, unhurriedly passed by the lit-up windows of Via Bersaglieri del Po, much as they would along the Mercerie in Venice.

Where was he off to? He was taking a turn, strolling about, here and there, apparently without any particular end in view.

After an intense day's work he certainly liked to be among the crowd: the noisy, happy, undifferentiated crowd. Tall, fat, with his homburg hat, his yellow gloves, or even, if it was winter, with his overcoat lined with opossum fur and with his stick slipped into the right side pocket near the sleeve, between eight and nine o'clock at night he might be seen at any place in the city. Every now and then, one was surprised to find him standing still before some shop window in Via Mazzini or Via Saraceno, looking intently over the shoulders of whoever had stopped in front of him. Often he paused beside the stalls selling trinkets or confectionery, arranged in rows of ten along the southern flank of the Duomo, or in Piazza Travaglio, or in Via Garibaldi, staring fixedly and without a word at the homely goods on display. However, it was Via San Romano's crammed and impoverished sidewalks that he preferred to frequent. It was strange to bump into him there, under those low arches, with their acrid reek of fried fish, salt pork, wine and cheap yarn, and above all crowded with lower-class women, soldiers, boys, cloaked peasants, and so on; to see his eyes so vivid, joyful, satisfied, a vague smile spread across his face.

"Good evening, Doctor!" someone might shout from behind him.

And it was a miracle if he heard; if, already carried away by the current, he should turn to reply to the greeting.

Only later, after ten o'clock, would he reappear, in one of the town's four cinemas: the Excelsior, the Salvini, the Rex or the Diana. But even there, he preferred the back rows of the stalls to the seats in the circle, where those of some social distinction gathered together as though in a drawing room. And how embarrassing for those respectable gentlefolk to see him down there, so well dressed, lost among the worst of "the seething mob"! Was it really in good taste—they sighed, turning their saddened gaze elsewhere—to take the spirit of bohemianism that far?

So it is quite understandable that around 1930, when Fadigati was already going on forty, not a few began to think it was high time he found himself a wife. This view was whispered between patients on adjacent armchairs in those same waiting rooms in the Via Gorgadello clinic, as they waited for the unsuspecting doctor to show his face in the little doorway reserved for his periodic appearances, and to invite one of them to "come on through." It was referred to later at supper by husbands and wives, taking care that their children, with their noses in the soup and their ears pricked up, should be unable to guess what they were speaking of. And later on too, in bed—but here speaking quite openly—the topic had often already engrossed five or ten minutes of those precious half-hours sacred to confidences and ever-more lengthy yawns, which normally precede the exchange of kisses and conjugal "goodnights."

To the husbands as to the wives it seemed absurd that a man of such quality should not have thought once and for all of establishing a family.

Apart from his temperament perhaps being a bit "artistic," but overall so serious and staid, which other resident in Ferrara with a degree, under fifty years of age, could boast of a better position than his? Good-natured toward everyone, rich (oh yes, as far as money was concerned, he could earn what he wanted!), an active member of two of the more important Ferrara clubs, and so equally welcome to the middle and the lower-middle classes of the professions and the shopkeepers as to the aristocracy, with or without coats of arms, with inherited wealth or estates. He had even been provided with a Fascist Party card which, despite his mild declaration that he was "apolitical by nature," the Federal Secretary in person had at all costs wanted to give him. What was he lacking, now, but a beautiful woman to take to the church of San Carlo or the Duomo every Sunday morning, and to the cinema in the evening, wrapped in furs and bedecked with jewels as is right and proper? And why did he not bother to look around and find himself one? Perhaps, that would be it, perhaps he was embroiled in relations with some working-class woman he couldn't confess to seeing, like a seamstress, a governess, a servant or some such. As happens to many doctors, perhaps he was attracted only to nurses: and precisely for this reason, who knows?—those who passed through his clinic were always so good-looking, so provocative! But even admitting that something like this was indeed the truth (and, on the other hand, it was curious that nothing more specific on this matter had ever come to light!), what motive could have prevented him from marrying? Did he want the same fate that, in his time, had befallen Dr. Corcos, the eighty-year-old director of the hospital, the most illustrious of the Ferraresi doctors, who, according to what was recounted of him, after having had an affair for years with a young nurse, at a certain point was forced by her family to keep her for life?

And in the city intense speculations abounded as to which girl might truly be worthy of becoming Signora Fadigati—but this one was unconvincing for one reason, that one for another: none of them ever seemed quite right enough for the solitary home-bound figure, who on certain nights could be glimpsed among the crowd leaving the Excelsior or the Salvini in Piazza delle Erbe, or down there, in the depths of the Listone, a moment before he disappeared into the dark lateral crack of Via Bersaglieri del Po . . . Then all of a sudden—no one knew who started them—strange, no, quite extraordinary rumors began to circulate.

"Didn't you know? It seems that Dr. Fadigati is . . ."

"Wait till you hear the news. You know that Dr. Fadigati who lives in Via Gorgadello, almost at the corner of Bersaglieri del Po? Well, I've heard it said that he's . . ."

3.

A GESTURE, a look was enough.

It was enough even to say that Fadigati was "like that," was "one of them."

But sometimes, as happens in speaking of unseemly questions, and particularly of sexual abnormalities, there would be someone who, grinning, would have recourse to a dialect word, which even in our region carries a more malicious edge than the language of the upper classes. And then to add, not without a touch of melancholy:

"Oh, it all makes sense."

"What a weird type, that's for sure."

"How come we never thought of that before?"

Overall, though, it wasn't as if they were too unhappy to have figured out Fadigati's secret vice so late (it had taken them more than ten years to get there, imagine that!), but rather as if they were at some level reassured and, for the most part, amused by it.

In the end—they exclaimed, shrugging—why should they not be able to acknowledge the sheer style of the man even in the most shameful of irregularities?

What above all disposed them to indulgence toward Fadigati and, after the first recoil of alarmed dismay, almost to admiration, was precisely that, his style, and by style first and foremost they meant one thing: his discretion, the evident care he had taken and continued to take in concealing his tastes, so as not to cause scandal. Yes—they said—now that his secret was no longer a secret, now that everything was clear as could be, at last one could be sure how to behave toward him. By day, in the light of the sun, to show him every respect; in the evening, even if pressed chest to chest against him in the throng of Via San Romano, to show no sign of recognizing him. Like Fredric March in *Dr. Jekyll and Mr. Hyde*, Dr. Fadigati had two lives. But who doesn't?

Knowing amounted to understanding, to no longer being curious, to "letting things be."

Earlier on, entering a cinema, what used to worry them most—they recalled—was making sure whether he was right at the back as was his custom. They knew his habits, and had noticed that he was never seated. Fixing their gaze on the shadows, beyond the circle's balustrade, they sought him out down there, along the sordid sidewalls, near the security doors of the exit or of the toilets, without finding any peace until they had glimpsed the fitful, characteristic glint of his gold-rimmed spectacles in the smoke and darkness: a tiny intermittent flash emitted from an astounding, really an infinite, distance . . . But now! What was the point now, having just come in, of checking to confirm his presence? And why had they ever waited uneasily each time the lights came on? If at Ferrara there was a middle-class man to whom was conceded the right to frequent the lower-class stalls, to immerse himself as he wished and in full view of everyone in the unappealing underworld of the one-lire-and-twenty-*centesimo* "seats," it could only have been Fadigati.

Their behavior was exactly the same in the Merchants' Club or in the Unione Club on the two or three evenings each year when Fadigati would appear (as I have already mentioned, he had been a member of both social organizations since 1927).

While, in the past, to see him crossing the billiards room, and moving on without stopping at the poker and écarté tables, every face was ready to assume an expression somewhere between astonishment and consternation, now it was otherwise: it was rare for any gaze to detach itself from the green baize to follow his steps toward the library door. He was quite entitled to shut himself in the library, where there was never a living soul, where the leather of the Frau armchairs was lit by the tremulous gleams of the fireplace; he was welcome to immerse himself until midnight or beyond in reading the scientific book he had brought with him from home: who would dream, at that point, of having anything to say against this kind of oddness?

There was more. Every now and then he would travel, or, to use his own words, he would permit himself "a truancy": to Venice for the Biennale, to the Maggio concert hall in Florence. Well then, now that people knew, it might fall out that one met him on a train late at night, as happened in the winter of 1934 to a small gathering of townsfolk who had gone to the Berta Stadium for a soccer match, without anyone maliciously exclaiming "Look who it isn't!" as was the fashion among Ferraresi as soon as they found themselves outside the territories hemmed in by the parallel banks of the Reno and the Po. After they had invited him, with great solicitude, to have a seat in their compartment, our good sporty types, who were far from being music lovers (the very name of Wagner made them plunge into an ocean of sadness!), sat there good as gold listening to Fadigati's impassioned account of Tristan which Bruno Walter had directed that very afternoon in Florence's Teatro Communale. Fadigati spoke of the music of Tristan, of the admirable interpretation that the "Teutonic maestro" had given it, and in particular of the opera's second Act, which—he declared—"was nothing but a long lament for love." Holding forth about the little bench completely encircled by a rose bush's flowering boughs, and thus clearly symbolic of the bridal chamber, on which Tristan and Isolde sing for three quarters of an hour running before plunging themselves, enthralled, into a night of voluptuousness eternal as Death itself, Fadigati half closed his eyes behind his glasses, and smiled ecstatically. And the others let him talk without breathing a word. They limited themselves to exchanging the occasional secret look of dismay.

Yet it was Fadigati himself, with his unimpeachable behavior, who fostered around himself such a general spirit of tolerance.

After all, what could be said about him of any weight or concreteness? In contrast to what one might rightly expect to hear on such topics as that of Maria Grillanzoni, to pick a name out of the hat, a lady in her seventies from our finest aristocracy, whose impetuous acts of seduction, perpetrated among the boys from the chemists' or butchers' who came round to her house in the morning, were tales frequently on the lips of everyone (and now and then the city would learn something new about her, to laugh about and, of course, to deplore)—in contrast to this, Fadigati's erotic life gave every guarantee that it would always remain within the precise demarcations of the seemly.

Of this his many friends and admirers declared themselves more than sure. In the cinemas, it's true—they were forced to concede—he would position himself not too far away from the groups of soldiers, which was the apparent basis for an insinuation regarding his presumed "weakness" for the military. All the same it was equally true that never—they would energetically resume—had the poor man been seen to approach them beyond a given limit, never had he been seen to accompany one of them into the street, nor, even less, had a young lancer from the Pinerola Cavalry, with the high busby fallen over his eyes, and the heavy, noisy sabre under his arm, ever been noticed at a suspicious hour slipping over the threshold of the doctor's house. His face was still there, for sure: pudgy, but grey, and its features drawn by a secret and continuous anxiety. It was uniquely his face that reminded one that he was searching. As for finding (how and where), who was in a position to speak with any certain knowledge of the case?

From time to time, though, even of this one would hear rumors. As the years passed, with the very same almost reluctant slowness with which, rising from the muddy depths of certain stagnant pools, the odd bubble of air comes to the surface and silently bursts on reaching it, in just such a way, every now and then, names would be named, particular persons and circumstances indicated.

In 1935, or thereabouts, I can clearly recall that Fadigati's name was often linked to a certain Manservigi, a traffic policeman with blue unwavering eyes, who, when he was not solemnly directing the bicycles and cars at the crossroads of Corso Roma and Corso Giovecca, we boys sometimes were surprised to come across at Montagnone, where, rendered almost unrecognizable by his plain, civilian clothes, with a toothpick in his mouth, he would join our interminable soccer games, often extended beyond dusk. Later, around 1936, one heard stories about another: a doorkeeper at the Town Hall, a certain Trapolini, a sweet and mellifluous character, married and weighed down with children, whose Catholic zeal and passion for the opera were renowned in the city. Still later, during the first months of the Spanish Civil War, to this frugal list of Fadigati's "friends" was also added the name of an ex-soccer player who had played for SPAL.[*] Dark-skinned, now overweight, short of breath, with greyed temples, it was indeed Baùsi himself, Olao Baùsi, who in the decade between 1920 and 1930 had been—who could fail to remember?—an idol of Ferrara's sporting youth, and who in the space of only a few years had been reduced to living by any desperate means at his disposal.

So, no soldiers. Nothing enacted in public, even as regards the maneuvers of an initial approach; never anything scandalous. Some relationships of a carefully clandestine kind with middle-aged men who were not that well off, who were socially subordinate. In short, his associations were with discreet individuals, or at least with those somehow persuaded to be so.

Around three, four o'clock in the morning, filtering through the shutters of Dr. Fadigati's flat, there was always a small glow of light. In the

---

[*] SPAL (Società Polisportiva Ars et Labor): the principal Ferrara soccer club.

silence of the alley, interrupted only by the raucous wheeze of the owls that nested far up there along the Duomo's dizzying, barely visible entablature, there would fly faint tatters of celestial music, Bach, Mozart, Beethoven, Wagner: Wagner most of all, perhaps because Wagnerian music was the most apt to evoke a certain atmosphere. The idea that the traffic policeman Manservigi, or the doorkeeper Trapolini, or the ex-soccer player Baùsi should at that very moment be guests of the doctor was unlikely, except as a passing joke, to cross the mind of the last night-walker, on his way at that hour down Via Gorgadello.

4.

IN 1936, some twenty-two years ago, the local Ferrara–Bologna train, which left every morning from Ferrara a few minutes before seven, covered the line's forty-five kilometers in no less than an hour and twenty minutes.

When things ran smoothly, the train reached its destination around eight fifteen. But more often than not, even if it sped along the straight line after Corticella, the train entered the broad curve of the approach to Bologna Station some ten or fifteen minutes late (and if it had to stop for the entry lights there, the delay could easily extend to thirty minutes). These were no longer the times of old Ciano, that's for sure, when, on arriving, certain trains could expect to find the Minister of Transport in person, entirely absorbed in the quaint and solemn activity of measuring out the station with impatient strides and of grumblingly checking the hour on the face of the stationmaster's big fob watch which he was forever fishing out of his waistcoat pocket. It was true, however, that the six-fifty Ferrara–Bologna express train always, in actual fact, took its own sweet time. It seemed to ignore the Government, to be utterly unconcerned about its boast of having forced even the State railways to observe a rigid respect for the timetable. And, on the other hand, who paid any attention to this or was in the least concerned about it? Half carpeted with grass and roofless, Platform 16, reserved for the train, was the furthermost in the station and bordered the countryside beyond Porta Galliera. It had the air of being completely forgotten.

Usually the train comprised only six carriages: five third class and one second.

Not without a shiver, I remember the December mornings of the Padano, the dark mornings of the years in which, as students at Bologna University, we had to wake up with alarm clocks. From the tram, which rattled along at a breakneck speed in the direction of the Customs barrier of Viale Cavour, we would hear the repeated whistle of the train, far off and out of sight. It seemed as though it was warning us "Hurry up! I'm leaving!" Or even "There's no point rushing, boys and girls, I'm as good as gone!" It was generally only the first-year students, male and female, who urged the conductor to speed things up. All the rest of us, including Eraldo Deliliers, who had enrolled that very year for Political Sciences but who already behaved with the lordly nonchalance of a veteran, well knew that the six-fifty express train would never have left without us. The tram would finally stop in front of the station; we'd leap out and in a few moments board the train, which would be puffing white jets of steam from every pore, or else be standing calmly at the platform as expected. As for Deliliers, he always arrived last, dawdling along and yawning. And, in the event that he had dozed off, as often happened, we would have to drag him off the tram.

One could say that the third-class wagons were dedicated entirely to us. Apart from the odd commercial traveler, the occasional, down-at-heel variety-show company who had spent the night in the station, and whose dancers, during the journey, we would sometimes try to befriend, no one else ever left from Ferrara at that hour.

Yet it would be wrong to assume from this that the six-fifty train would always reach Bologna with only half of its seats filled!

In the course of its lazy progress from the thick darkness of Ferrara to the light of Bologna mornings—often intense and dazzling, on the hill of San Luca white with snow, and with the churches' verdigris cupolas standing out almost in relief against the red sea of roofs and towers—the train gradually gathered more and more passengers from the small and the even smaller stations scattered along the line.

They were girls and boys from middle school; elementary school-teachers of both sexes; smallholders, sharecroppers, various cattle- and sheep-sellers, distinguishable by their ample cloaks, their felt caps drawn down over their noses, with toothpicks or Tuscan cigars fixed between their lips: country folk, from regions closer to the city, who spoke a coarse version of the Bolognese dialect. To fend off any contact with them we would barricade ourselves into two or three connecting carriages. The onslaught of "peasants" began at Poggio Renatico, a kilometer before the left bank of the Reno; was renewed at Galliera, a little beyond the iron bridge, and again at San Giorgio di Piano, San Pietro in Casale, Castelmaggiore and at Corticella. When the train arrived in Bologna, from the doors that opened with an almost explosive violence, a small tumultuous crowd of some hundreds would flow out on to Platform 16.

That left the one and only second-class carriage: which, at least until a certain time, until, to be specific, the winter of 1936/7, never disgorged a single soul.

The train guards, a fixed quartet who would travel on the express trains between Ferrara and Bologna five or six times a day, had established in that carriage a card school every morning to play *scopa* and *tresette*. For our part, we were so accustomed to the fact that this second-class carriage was reserved for the train master, the ticket controller, the brakesman and the non-commissioned officer of the railway militia—however winking and friendly all four of them were, they could be very inflexible in preventing any illegal traveling in the wrong class, especially if they sniffed out GUF students*—that it seemed natural to us to see it function as a kind of after-hours railwayman's leisure club. So at first, when Dr. Fadigati started to travel to Bologna twice a week, and always bought a second-class ticket, we took no notice nor were even aware of him.

This state of affairs, however, lasted only a short while.

I close my eyes. I see once more the wide, asphalted avenue of Viale Cavour completely deserted from the Castle to the Customs barrier, with its street lamps arranged in a long vista some fifty meters from each other, all still lit. The conductor, Aldrovandi, of whom inside the tram one can discern nothing but his bristling hunchback, pushes the decrepit vehicle

---

* GUF (Gruppi Universitari Fascisti): an organization that enrolled Fascists among university students as a kind of ideological elite.

to its limits. But a little before the tram arrives at the barrier, swooping down from behind us, with the characteristic stifled rustling that the engine of the Lancia makes, once again the car, the taxi, overtakes us. It is a green Astura, always the same one. Every Tuesday and Friday it overtakes us more or less at the same point on the Viale Cavour. It's so fast that when, with our tram scarily pitching from side to side in the final sprint, we break into the station square, not only has it already set down its passenger—a chubby gentleman with a white-bordered homburg hat, gold-rimmed spectacles and a fur-collared overcoat—but it has turned round and is heading off in the opposite direction to ours, toward the city center.

Which of us, I wonder, was the first to direct our general curiosity toward the gentleman in the taxi: the gentleman rather than the taxi itself? It's true that in the tram, with his curly blond hair flowing over the wooden back of the seat, Deliliers was usually asleep. And yet I'm inclined to think it was actually him, one morning about halfway through February 1937, while various hands, always a few more than were necessary, reached out through the door to pull him into the train, I'd swear it was actually Deliliers who announced that the second-class carriage had found in the guy in the Astura a permanent and paid-up passenger, and that he was no other than Dr. Fadigati.

"Fadigati? Who's that?" asked one of the girls with a bewildered air. Bianca Sgarbi, to be precise, the older of the two Sgarbi sisters. (The other, Attilia, three years younger and still at the *liceo*, at this point, the beginning of 1937, I had yet to meet.)

Her question was received with peals of laughter. Deliliers had sat down and was lighting a Nazionale cigarette. He had the habit of lighting them where the brand mark was, as careful as could be never to miss.

At that time Bianca Sgarbi, who with the utmost reluctance was doing her third year in the Literature Department, was almost engaged to Nino Bottecchiari, the nephew of the Socialist ex-deputy. Although they went out together, they didn't get on that well. By nature exuberant, and yet at the same time with an almost premonitory sense of the far from bright future awaiting the young of our generation—the poor girl would become the widow of an Air Force officer shot down over Malta in 1942, with two sons to bring up, and would end up in Rome, a part-time employee of the Ministry of Aeronautics—Bianca bridled at anything that tied her down, and kept herself amused by making eyes at anyone she felt at ease with, more or less drifting from one flirtation to another.

"May one ask who that is?" she softly insisted, leaning toward Deliliers, who was seated in front of her.

Huddled up beside the latter in the corner seat next to the door, the unfortunate Nino suffered in silence.

"Oh, just an old queer," Dililiers calmly declared after a pause, lifting his head and staring straight into the eyes of our companion Bianca.

5.

FOR QUITE some time, during the whole journey, he kept apart in his second-class carriage.

Taking it in turns, profiting from stops the train made at San Giorgio di Piano or San Pietro in Casale, one of our group would leap out with the task of buying something to eat from the bar of the small station: wrapped rolls filled with freshly sliced salami, almond-studded chocolate that tasted of soap, half-moldy Osvego biscuits. Turning to look at the stationary train, and then walking past carriage after carriage, at a certain point we could distinguish Dr. Fadigati, who, from behind the thick glass of his compartment, would be watching people crossing the tracks and hurrying back toward the third-class carriages. Judging by his expression of heartfelt envy, the looks of regret with which he followed the small rustic crowd, so unappealing to us, he seemed nothing less than a recluse: a political prisoner under guard, being transferred to Ponza and the Tremiti to stay there for who knows how long. Two or three carriages farther on, behind equally thick glass, one could make out the guard and his three friends. Unperturbed, they continued with their card game—thick as thieves, they kept on arguing, laughing and gesticulating.

However, soon enough, as we might have predicted, we would begin to see the doctor stroll about in the third-class carriages.

The communicating door was locked. The first few times, to have it opened (he himself would later explain) he always had to seek out the guard.

He would put his head into the gambling-den compartment.

"Do excuse me," he asked, "but might I please move into the third-class section?"

It annoyed them, he could see. Proceeding along the corridor with the key in his hand and with the gait of a jailer, the guard made a show of muttering and sighing. At a certain point Fadigati decided to arrange things on his own. He waited for the first stop, the one at Poggio Renatico. The express train remained there for three to five minutes. There was easily time to get off and enter the next carriage.

All the same, I'm absolutely sure it was not on the train that the first contacts between us were established. My impression remains that it happened at Bologna, on the street, even if, as will be seen before long, I could not be sure on exactly which street. (Perhaps at that time I was away from my studies, and was informed about the occasion later by others? Or else, so many years afterward, it's my own failure to distinguish, to remember with any exactitude?)

It could well be that it happened as we were leaving the station, or waiting for the Mascarella tram. Ten or so of us altogether, taking up most of the tram platform one came to just before the rank for taxis and coaches. The sun was shining on the heaps of dirty snow that at regular intervals punctuated the huge square. The sky above was of an intense blue, vibrant with light.

And suddenly Fadigati, who had arrived last of all, just a moment before, and was also waiting for the tram on the same platform, to start up a conversation, found nothing more inspired than some observation upon the "splendid day, almost springlike," not to mention a remark on the Mascarella tram being "so comfortable that it would probably be easier going by foot." Generic phrases, said in a low voice not to any one of us, but to all of us en masse and to no one in particular: as if he did not know us, or rather did not wish to risk admitting that he knew us, even by sight. But in the end, it was enough that one of us, embarrassed by the hesitancy and the nervous smile with which he had accompanied his vague remarks about the season and the tram, should have replied with a minimum of civility, calling him "Doctor." Then the truth was out: that he knew all of us well, by Christian name and surname, regardless of the fact that in such a short time we had become teenagers. He knew exactly whose sons and daughters we were. And how could he not, how could he have forgotten, to be sure, since from infancy "to the age when all children of good families have to struggle with sore throats and earache"—he laughed—he had seen all of us, some more often, some less, pass through his clinic?

Frequently, however, instead of taking the tram and speeding off straight to the university in Via Zamboni, we preferred to go by foot under the arches of Via Independenza until we reached the center. Only rarely would Deliliers be among us. As soon as we were outside the station, he would cut loose on his own, and generally until the morning of the day after no one would see him again: not in the university, nor in the little restaurants, nor anywhere at all. Scattered in twos and threes along the sidewalk, the rest of us could always be found together. There was Nino Bottecchiari, who was studying law, but who, often enough, because of Bianca Sgarbi, could be found hanging about in the corridors and lecture rooms of the Literature Faculty, sitting through the most indigestible classes: from Latin grammar to librarianship. There was Bianca herself, in a blue beret and short rabbit-fur coat, now arm in arm with one or another boy: almost never with Nino, and then only to argue. There were Sergio Pavani, Otello Forti, Giovannino Piazza, Enrico Sangiuliano, Vittorio Molon: students either of Agriculture or of Medicine, of Economics or Commerce. And finally there was me, apart from Bianca the only other student of Literature.

It is not inconceivable that one of these mornings, while we were walking under the endless arches of Via Independenza, lofty and dark as the nave of a church, stopping every now and then in front of a sports shop window, or at a newspaper kiosk, or perhaps mixed up within a group of people who, drawn hypnotically to the oxyhydrogen flame, crowded together in silence around a crew of workers intent on adjusting a tram rail—it's not at all inconceivable that on one of those late-winter mornings, when any pretext could serve to postpone the moment of being shut inside a lecture hall, Dr. Fadigati, who for some time had been behind us, suddenly came up alongside us: perhaps alongside Nino Bottechiari and

Bianca Sgarbi who, a little apart but as usual heedless of being noticed, kept up their ceaseless wrangling and bickering.

Constantly hovering around us, Fadigati had been following us step by step. We were well aware of it. Grinning, nudging each other, we had even pointed it out.

All of a sudden, there he was alongside Nino and Bianca, clearing his throat.

He could be heard speaking with that neutral, impersonal tone of voice which he always adopted when approaching people from whom he was unsure what reception to expect.

"Be good now!" he had cautioned them: and even in this case it was more as if he were talking mainly to the air, rather than to anyone in particular.

But then, directing a shy, hesitant glance, and yet at the same time complicit, peevishly complicit and supportive, toward Bianca:

"And, young woman, you should try to behave yourself too," he added, "be a bit more compliant. It's something expected of women, don't you know?"

He was joking, it was only meant as a joke. Bianca burst out laughing. Even Nino laughed. Chatting away about this and that, we had thus arrived all together at Piazza del Nettuno. But that wasn't all. Before going our separate ways we necessarily had to accept his offer of a coffee.

In short we became friends: however it happened, from that time on, that is, from the end of April 1937, in the two or three carriages in which we used to barricade ourselves—framed by the window the countryside rushed past, already green, cool and luminous—on Tuesday and Friday mornings there was always a place also for Dr. Fadigati.

6.

HE HAD decided to take the university teaching degree—he said—for this reason, "and no other": that he could then travel to Bologna twice a week. But now that he had discovered some traveling companions, those twice-weekly journeys no longer seemed to weigh on him.

He sat quietly in his place, and would take only a minor part in our daily discussions, which ranged from sports to politics, from literature and art to philosophy, and sometimes touched on affairs of the heart, or even on relationships that were "exclusively sexual." He would let fall a remark every now and then, looking at us from his seat with a paternal and indulgent eye. To many of us he was, in a certain way, a friend of the family: our parents had been visiting his clinic in Via Gorgadello for near-on twenty years. It was also of them that he would be thinking, watching us.

Did he know that we *knew*? Perhaps not. Perhaps on this question he still deceived himself. In the poised manner, however, in the polite and troubled reserve that he arduously maintained, it was only too easy to read the steady resolve to behave as if nothing about himself had ever been discovered in the city. For us, above all for us, he had to remain the Dr. Fadigati of old, when as children we saw, half hidden behind the circular head mirror, his large face lean over our own. If anyone in the world existed before whom he had to maintain a proper front, it was us.

Besides, seen from close up, his face did not appear greatly altered. Those ten or twelve years that now distanced us from the age of tonsillitis, of middle-ear infections, of adenoidal growths, had not left on him any more than the slightest traces. His temples had turned grey—that was the difference. But that was all. Perhaps a little fatter, a little more baggy, his cheeks were suffused with the same earthen color as before. The skin, with pronounced pores, had the same thick, shiny quality, and always gave the same impression of leather, of well-cured leather. No, in this respect, we were the ones who, by comparison, were much more markedly altered: we who slyly, absurdly (while he, perhaps, took out of his overcoat pocket a copy of the Corriere della Sera and quietly and sweetly began to read it in his corner), went in search across that familiar face for the proof, the signs—I was about to say the visible stains—of his vice, of his sin.

With time, however, he gained confidence with us, and began to speak a little more. After a brief spring, the summer arrived almost precipitantly. Even early in the morning it was hot. Outside, the green of the Bologna countryside had become darker, richer. In the fields bordered by rows of mulberry trees, the hemp was already high, the wheat growing golden.

"I feel like I'm a student again," Fadigati often repeated, gazing out through the train window. "I feel like I've gone back in time to when I too used to travel each day between Venice and Padua . . ."

That was all before the war—he told us—between 1910 and 1915.

He studied Medicine at Padua, and for two years had made the daily shuttle between the two cities: just as we were doing between Ferrara and Bologna. Though from the third year on, his parents, unceasingly anxious about his heart, had insisted that he set himself up in Padua, in a rented room. And so: in the three years that followed (having graduated with the "great" Michele Arslan and got a First) he pursued a far more sedentary life than before. He spent only two days a week with his family: Saturday and Sunday. At that time Venice was certainly not a lively city on Sundays, above all during the winter. But Padua, with its lugubrious black arches, forever redolent of a peculiar odor of boiled beef! . . . Returning to Padua by train, every Sunday evening, cost him a huge effort—he had to steel himself in preparation.

"We can only imagine, Doctor, what a nerd you must have been!" Bianca once exclaimed. So ingrained was her habit, she even tried flirting with Fadigati.

He did not reply, only smiled graciously at her.

"These days you have soccer games, the movies, all kinds of healthy activities," he said. "You know what the mainstay of Sundays was for the youth of my generation? The dance hall!"

He twisted his mouth, as though he had conjured up an abomination. He added that in his case, at least in Venice, he had a home, his father and mother, above all his mother: in short, the "heart's sacred affections."

How he had adored her—he sighed—his poor mother!

Intelligent, cultured, beautiful, pious: she was the sum of all virtues. One morning, even, and his eyes grew watery with the emotion, he brought out from his wallet a photograph which he passed around the circle of hands. It was a small faded oval, portraying a middle-aged woman in nineteenth-century dress: of a gentle expression, certainly, but generally rather undistinguished.

Vittorio Molon was the only one of us whose family was not from Ferrara. Landowners in Fratti Polesine, the Molons had moved from the far side of the River Po only five or six years ago. And one could hear it: Vittorio, especially when speaking in Italian, retained a strong Veneto cadence.

One day Fadigati asked him if his family (using the polite plural "you" form) were by chance from Padua.

"I'm asking," he explained, "because when I was living in Padua, I was lodging with a widow who was called Molon, Elsa Molon. This lady's small house was in Via Francesco, close by the university, and gave on to a big vegetable garden behind. What a life I had there! In Padua I had no relatives, no friends, not even school friends."

After which, apparently wandering from the subject (but it was the only time he allowed us a glimpse of his ample literary culture: as though, also in this respect, he had imposed a strict rule of discretion), he began to speak of a short story—by he couldn't remember which English or American nineteenth-century writer—set, this was the point, in Padua toward the end of the seventeenth century.

"The main character of the short story," he said, "was a student, a student as lonely as I was thirty years ago. Like me, he lived in a rented room which looked out on an enormous vegetable garden, full of poisonous trees—"

"Poisonous?!" Bianca interrupted him, widening her bright blue eyes.

"Yes, poisonous," he nodded. "But the garden on which my window opened," he went on, "wasn't at all poisonous: don't worry, Signorina. It was a very standard vegetable garden, tended to perfection by a family of farmers, the Scagnellatos, who lived in a decrepit little house leaning against the apse of the church of San Francesco. Many a time, with a book in my hand, I'd go down there for a stroll; especially during the afternoons in late July, with exams looming. The Scagnellatos, who often invited me for supper, were the only Paduan family with whom I became friends. They had two sons: two good-looking boys, so lively and open, so . . . They worked among the plants and sown grain until they were lost to sight. At that hour they generally watered the plants. Ah, the good smell of manure!"

The air of the carriage was grey with the smoke from our Nazionali. But he breathed it deep into his lungs, half closing his eyes behind the lenses of his spectacles and widening the nostrils of his plump nose.

There followed a somewhat prolonged and oppressive silence. Deliliers opened his eyes and yawned loudly.

"Good—the smell of manure?" Bianca said in the meantime with a small nervous laugh. "What an idea!"

Leaning forward, Deliliers let fall on Fadigati a sidelong glance full of disdain.

"Give the manure a rest, Doctor," he sneered, "and instead tell us about those two boys in the vegetable garden who you liked so much—what you all got up to together."

Fadigati winced. As if he'd been suddenly given a mighty slap, his large brown face twisted itself beneath our eyes into a look of pain.

"Eh . . .? What's that . . .?" he stammered.

Disgusted, Deliliers stood up. Opening up a route past our legs, he reached the corridor.

"Playing the peasant as ever!" Bianca huffed, touching one of her knees.

She threw a look of disapproval at Deliliers, standing in exile in the corridor, beyond the glass door. And then, turning again to Fadigati:

"Why not finish telling us about that short story?" she proposed in a kindly manner.

He didn't want to, however much Bianca insisted. He claimed that he couldn't properly remember the plot. And besides—he concluded, with a hint of afflicted gallantry, which sounded especially forced—why would she want to hear a story which ended, he could assure her, so badly?

A tiny unguarded moment had cost him very dear. From then on, you can imagine, he feared ridicule more than ever.

7.

HE WAS happy, in the end, with the least thing, or so it seemed. He wanted no more than to stay there, in our third-class compartment, with the air of an old man silently warming his hands in front of a big fire.

At Bologna, for example, no sooner had we made our way out on to the big square in front of the station than he would get into a taxi and be away. After the first couple of times when he accompanied us to the university, there was never an occasion when we found it tricky to lose him. He was well aware, because we had told him, of the small, cheap restaurants where around one o'clock he could have found us again: the Stella del Nord, in Strada Maggiore, or Gigino's, at the foot of the two towers, or the Gallina Faraona, in San Vitale. This, however, never happened. One afternoon, entering an establishment to play boccette,* we noticed him seated alone, with a coffee and a glass of water in front of him, immersed in a newspaper. He was undoubtedly aware of us. Yet he pretended not to be, and even, after a minute or so, called over the waiter with a sign, paid, and discreetly slipped out.

In short, he was never intrusive or burdensome.

And yet, little by little, despite the fact that big as he was he would huddle up so much on the carriage's wooden bench that he occupied less than an eighth part of it, little by little, without meaning to, almost all of us began to show him scant respect.

To be honest, it was he who once again made a mistake: when one morning, while the train waited at San Pietro in Casale, he suddenly wanted to get off to buy us the usual sandwiches and biscuits at the station bar. "It's my turn," he'd declared, and there had been no way to stop him.

So from the train we watched him clumsily crossing the rails. We were willing to bet that he would forget how many sandwiches to buy, and how many packets of biscuits. And yet he had most carefully verified this point: with the outcome that we leaned out of the window shouting and grinning without restraint, like drunken conscripts, to give him the most contradictory orders, and that he, more and more confused and out of breath as the minutes passed, barely managed to bundle himself back on to the train before it departed.

I'll have more to say later about Deliliers, who never addressed a word to Fadigati, but tormented him whenever the occasion was offered with transparent hints and brutal innuendos. And even Nino Bottecchiari, whose tonsils he had taken out when Nino was a child, and the only one of us he addressed with the "*tu*" form, even he began to treat him coldly. And

---

* An Italian game played on a pocketless billiards table with nine balls, using hands instead of cues.

Fadigati? It was odd to observe him, and even painful: the more Nino and Deliliers heaped on their incivilities, the more he exerted himself in the vain attempt to be likeable. To win one kind word, a nod of agreement, an amused smile from those two, he would have done practically anything.

With Nino, who was by unanimous agreement considered the intellectual of the group, and had taken part the year before in the Venice Culture and Arts Littoriali*—he came fifth in Fascist Doctrine, and second overall in Cinema Studies—Fadigati tried to broach topics of discussion which would give our companion a chance to shine: on cinema, as you would expect, and even on politics, although on this subject, as he often told us, he himself was far from being an expert.

But he was defeated in this—his aim always went astray.

He would begin talking about the cinema (about which he was very knowledgeable: besides, for years he'd been spending his evenings in cinemas!), and Nino would set about him with hysterical cries, as though not even conceding him the right to speak about it, as though to hear him declare, for example, that the old farces of Ridolini were "wonderful"—even if Nino himself had more than once judged them "fundamental"—was provocation enough to make him radically change his "position" on this question.

Put to flight on this matter, Fadigati would then try his luck with politics. The Spanish Civil War was by now about to end with victory for Franco and Fascism. One morning, having scanned the first page of the Corriere della Sera, evidently confident he would not be saying anything that might give offence to Nino or to any of us, absolutely sure, on the contrary, to find us all in agreement, Fadigati expressed what was then not in the least an outlandish view, that the triumph of "our legionaries" should be considered a great cause of celebration. And instead, all of a sudden, the most unexpected scene erupted. As though galvanized by an electric current, and raising his voice so much that Bianca, at a certain point, thought it best to put her hand over his mouth, Nino began to bawl that "perhaps" it was a disaster, the opposite of a triumph, that "perhaps it was the begin-

---

* Italian cultural, artistic and sporting events organized by the National Fascist Party and the GUF between 1932 and 1940.

ning of the end" and that he, the doctor, should be ashamed at his age to be so "irresponsible."

"I'm sorry, my dear boy . . . you see . . . if I may say . . ." Fadigati kept repeating, white as a sheet. Utterly lost beneath the raging of this storm, he just could not understand. His eyes skittered round as if in search of an explanation. But even we were too disconcerted to pay attention to him—especially me, who, the year before, in the course of our usual arguments had been accused by Nino himself—a follower of Gentile, and a passionate advocate for the ethical State—of being infected by "Crocean skepticism"[*] . . . And, by the end of it all, the doctor's round eyes were directed at the floor, shining damply beneath the lenses of his spectacles—or were they filled with a bitter satisfaction, with a childish, inexplicable, blind joy?

On another occasion we were all talking about sports.

If on questions of culture, Nino Bottecchiari was considered our resident expert, Deliliers indisputably held sway on all questions about sports. Ferrarese only on his mother's side—born in Imperia, I believe, or Ventimiglia, his father had been killed in 1918 on the Grappa, at the head of an Arditi company—like Vittorio Molon, he too had only studied at Ferrara for the upper-middle school, that is, for the four years at the *liceo scientifico*. Whatever other purpose they had served, those four years had been enough to elevate Eraldo into a princely local hero. In 1935 he had won the regional schoolboys' boxing championships, middle weight, and apart from that he was an extraordinarily handsome boy, six foot tall, and with a face and body like a Greek statue. Already, at not yet twenty years of age, he had won three or four famous victories. A girl, who was a friend of his at school, had killed herself for love of him the same year he had won the title in the Emilian Championships. All of a sudden he had stopped even looking at her, and then she, the poor girl, ran and threw herself into the river Po. It was clear that, in university circles as well, Eraldo Deliliers was more than loved—he was idolized. When we dressed we imitated his clothes, which his mother brushed, took the stains out of, and tirelessly ironed. To

---

[*] Giovanni Gentile (1875–1944) was also a philosopher, who had an early association with Croce. He became the Minister for Public Education under Mussolini and ghost-wrote the latter's essay "The Doctrine of Fascism" (1932).

stand next to him on Sunday mornings, at the Caffè della Borsa, leaning against a column at the entrance and looking at the legs of passing women, was considered a special privilege.

So, on one of those train journeys, toward the end of March, we were discussing sports with Deliliers. After athletics we ended up talking about boxing. He always kept his distance from everyone, Deliliers. But that day he was unusually open. He said that studying didn't suit him, that he needed too much money "to live," and so, if he succeeded in a certain little coup that he was planning, he hoped to devote himself entirely to the "noble art."

"What, as a professional?" Fadigati had dared to ask.

Deliliers looked at him as if he were a cockroach.

"Naturally," he replied. "Are you worried I'll ruin my face, Doctor?"

"Your face doesn't concern me, although I can see it's already quite marked with scars around the eyebrows. I feel duty-bound to warn you, though, that boxing, especially in the professional realm, in the long term ends up being deleterious to the organism. If I were in the Government, I'd have pugilism banned: even amateur fighting. Rather than a sport, I consider it a species of legal assassination. Pure organized brutality—"

"Oh, do me a favor!" Deliliers interrupted him. "Have you ever watched a fight?"

Fadigati was forced to confess he hadn't. He said that, as a doctor, violence and blood horrified him.

"Well then, if you've never seen a fight," Deliliers cut him short, "why are you talking about it? Who asked for your opinion?"

And once again, while Deliliers, almost shouting, hurled these words at the doctor, and then, turning his back on him, explained to us in a much calmer voice, that boxing, "the opposite of what certain idiots may think," in essence is a sport of the legs, of timing and fencing, above all of fencing, once again I saw shining in Fadigati's eyes the absurd but unmistakeable light of an interior joy.

Nino Bottecchiari was the only one among us who did not revere Deliliers. They weren't friends, but they respected each other. In front of Nino, Deliliers considerably diluted his usual wise-guy antics, just as Nino, on his side, acted far less the professor.

One morning Nino and Bianca weren't there—it was in June, if I remember right, during the exams. There were only six of us in the compartment, all men.

I had a bit of a sore throat, and was complaining of it. Recollecting that as a boy, while I was growing fast, he had had to treat me on various occasions for inflamed tonsils, Fadigati immediately offered to give me a "look-over."

"Let's see."

He raised his glasses on to his forehead, took my head in his hands and began to examine my throat.

"Say aah!" he ordered, in his professional tone.

I complied. And he was still there examining my throat, and at the same time recommending in a friendly, paternal manner that I should take care not to get overheated and sweat, since my tonsils "although by now quite reduced in size" clearly remained my . . . "Achilles heel," when Deliliers suddenly came out with:

"Excuse me, Doctor. When you've finished, I wonder if you'd give a little look at mine?"

Fadigati turned round: evidently much surprised by the request, and the gentle tone with which Deliliers had phrased it.

"What do you feel?" he asked. "Does it hurt to swallow?"

Dililiers stared at him with his blue eyes. He smiled, showing a glint of his incisors.

"It's not my throat that's bothering me at all," he said.

"Well, what is it then?"

"Here," said Deliliers, pointing at his own trousers at groin level.

He explained in a calm, indifferent manner, but not without a trace of pride, that he'd been suffering for about a month from the effects of a "gift from the little virgins of Via Bomporto—it's no joke, I can tell you"— because of which he had had to give up work in the gym "as well." Dr. Manfredini, he added, was treating it with blue meths and daily poultices of permanganate. But the treatment was taking too long, and he had to get fit as quickly as possible.

"My womenfolk are beginning to complain, as you can imagine . . . And so, would you mind taking a look at it as well?"

Fadigati had gone back to his seat.

"My dear fellow," he stammered, "you know very well that with this kind of illness I have absolutely no expertise. And besides, Dr. Manfredini—"

"Don't tell me that—you understand such things only too well!" grinned Deliliers.

"Not to mention that here on a train . . ." continued Fadigati, giving a frightened glance toward the corridor, "here on the train . . . how could it be done . . . ?"

"Oh, as for that," replied Deliliers, ready for him, curling his lip in disdain, "there's always the toilet, if you'd prefer."

There was a moment of silence.

It was Fadigati who first broke into a loud laugh.

"You're joking!" he cried out. "Do you never stop joking? You must take me for an idiot."

This, leaning forward and slapping his knee.

"You ought to take care," he said. "If not, one day or another you'll come to a bad end!"

And Deliliers, in return, but with a serious tone:

"It's you who should be worried about that."

Some days afterward, at around six in the evening, we were all at Majano's in Via Independenza. It was very hot. Nino was the one who first suggested going for an ice cream. If we didn't buy them—he said—we'd soon, no, "immediately" have reason enough to regret it.

Even then, before the modernization of 1940, the Pasticceria Majano was one of the biggest pastry shops in Bologna. It consisted of an enormous, dimly lit hall, from whose high and shadowy ceiling hung a solitary, gigantic chandelier of Murano glass. It was rose-shaped, two or three meters in diameter. It was crowded with a vast quantity of little dusty light bulbs from which an extraordinarily dingy light filtered down.

No sooner had we entered than our eyes sought out at the end of the hall the source of the loud laughter we heard.

There must have been twenty or so boys there, most of them in navy-blue tracksuits: some sprawled in seats, some standing around, and each of them gripping an ice cream either in a cup or a cone. Meanwhile they were talking loudly, in the widest variety of accents: Bolognese,

Romagnolo, Veneto, Marchigiano, Tuscan. At a glance, you could tell they belonged to that particular category of university students far more enamoured of sports stadia and swimming pools than of lecture halls and libraries.

Except for Deliliers, who immediately greeted us from the distance by raising his right arm in a friendly wave. To begin with we couldn't make out among the company anyone else that we recognized, but after a few moments, when we'd grown used to the dim light, we discerned, half hidden within the group, an older gentleman sitting next to Deliliers with his back turned to the entrance. He was there, wearing his hat, his hands linked over the handle of his cane, without eating anything. He was just waiting. Like a tender-hearted father who had agreed to pay for ice creams for a noisy herd of sons and nephews, and who waits in silence, a little ashamed of himself, until the darling kids have finished licking and sucking to their hearts' content, to ferry them all home . . .

That gentleman was obviously Fadigati.

8.

THAT SUMMER too, we went on our holidays to Riccione on the nearby Adriatic coast. Every year the same thing happened. My father, having vainly tried to entice us up into the mountains, the Dolomites, to see the places where he had fought in the war, in the end resigned himself to another trip to Riccione, renting the same little villa next to the Grand Hôtel. I remember it all perfectly. My mother, Fanny, our younger sister and I left Ferrara on the 10th of August, accompanied by our maid—Ernesto, my brother, had been in England since mid-July staying with a family in Bath to improve his English. As for my father, who had stayed in town, he was going to join us later: as soon as his duties administering the land at Masi Torello allowed him to leave.

The same day we arrived we immediately heard about Fadigati and Deliliers. On the beach, even then crowded with Ferraresi on their family holidays, they spoke of nothing else but them and their "scandalous friendship."

Starting from the first days of August, in fact, the two had been seen moving from one hotel to another in the various seaside towns between Porto Corsini and the Punta di Pesaro. They had appeared first of all in the Milano Marittima, beyond the dockland canal of Cervia, having rented a lovely room in the Hôtel Mare e Pineta. After a week, they had moved to Cesenatico, to the Hôtel Britannia. And then, inspiring fierce indignation and endless rumors everywhere, they gradually progressed to Viserba, Rimini, Riccione itself and Cattolica. They travelled by car: a red two-seater Alfa Romeo 1750 of the Mille Miglia type.

Around the 20th of August, apparently without a care in the world, there they were once more in Riccione, set up in the Grand Hôtel as they had been some ten days earlier.

The Alfa Romeo was brand new. Its engine gave a kind of growl. As well as for traveling, the two friends also employed it for the *passeggiata* every evening, when, at sunset, the crowd of bathers returned from the strip of sand to saunter along the promenade. Deliliers always drove. Blond, tanned, beautiful in his tight-fitting T-shirts and cream-colored woolen trousers (his hands, negligently draped over the steering wheel, were adorned with fretted, shammy-leather gloves about whose cost no one could harbor any doubts)—clearly it was only to him, to his exclusive whims, that the car responded. The other did nothing.

Wearing passenger goggles (he was never separated from them, not even when the automobile, cutting through the crowd with some difficulty, had to idle along a stretch of the avenue outside Cafe Zanarini at a walking pace), he would let himself be chauffeured up and down, seated complacently next to his companion.

They continued to sleep in the same room, to eat at the same table.

And they sat at the same little table even in the evenings, when the Grand Hôtel's orchestra, having had their instruments transported from the ground-floor dining hall to the terrace exposed to the sea breeze, moved on from strains of light music to modern and jazz numbers. Soon the terrace would fill up—often enough I even went there myself with friends I had met on the beach—and Deliliers would never miss a single tango, waltz, two-step, nor a "slow" dance. Of course, Fadigati never danced. Every now and then taking to his lips the straw tilted above the rim of the glass, with his round eyes he never stopped following the suave moves that his distant friend accomplished, his arms always embracing the most elegant, the most conspicuous girls and women. Returning from their drives, both of them would immediately go up to their room to don their smoking jackets. Sober, heavy black material, Fadigati's; Deliliers's a white jacket, close fitting and cut short at the sides.

Life at the beach they also shared together: except that in the morning it was usually Fadigati who left the hotel first.

He would arrive when there was almost nobody else around, between eight thirty and nine o'clock, respectfully greeted by the bathing attendants, to whom, by their own account, he was always very generous with tips. Dressed from head to toe in normal city clothes (only later, when the heat increased, would he decide to shed his tie and shoes, but never his white panama hat, with its brim lowered over his eyes—that he kept on), he would go to sit under the solitary beach umbrella which he had asked to be planted farther forward than all the rest, just a few yards from the shore. Stretched out on a reclining deckchair, his hands linked behind his neck and a detective story open on his knee, he would remain like that for a good two hours, staring at the sea.

Deliliers never joined him before eleven o'clock. With his svelte stride of a lazy animal, made still more elegant by the slight impediment of clogs, there he would be, crossing without hurry the clearing of burning sand between the beach huts and the bathing tents. He, by contrast, would be almost naked. The white bathing trunks which he was just at that moment finishing lacing up on his left hip and the same gold chain which he always wore round his neck, and from which dangled a pendant of the Madonna at the top of his chest, somehow only served to accentuate his nakedness. And though, especially the first few days, it seemed to cost him some effort to greet even me when he saw me there in the shade of our tent; and though passing through the narrow passage between the tents and the umbrellas he never failed to furrow his brow in a show of annoyance, there was no real reason to take this performance seriously. It was clear he felt himself admired by most of those present, by the men as well as the women, and this was a source of considerable pleasure to him.

Without doubt everyone admired him, men and women alike. But it fell to Fadigati to pay for the indulgence that the Ferrarese sector of the beach at Riccione reserved for Deliliers.

Our beach-tent neighbor that year was Signora Lavezzoli, the wife of the lawyer. Having lost her former status, she is now just an old woman. But then, in the ripe splendor of her forty years, surrounded by the unstinting deference of her three adolescent children, two boys and a girl, and that, equally unstinting, of her worthy consort, the illustrious civil lawyer, university professor and ex-deputy in the Salandra camp,* she was considered one of the principal and most authoritative fonts of the city's public opinion.

Pointing her lorgnette toward the beach umbrella under which Deliliers had come to rest, Signora Lavezzoli, who had been born and raised in Pisa, "on the banks of the Arno," and made use of the exceptional skill of her quick Tuscan tongue, kept us continually abreast of everything that was happening "over there."

With the technique, almost, of a radio sports commentator, she would note for example that "the newly-weds," having just got up from their deck-chairs, were wending their way toward the nearest pleasure boat: clearly the young man had expressed the desire to dive into the open sea, and "Signor Dottore," so as not to remain on his own, "in the throes of anxious passion," awaiting his return, had received permission to accompany him. Or else she described and commented on the freestyle gymnastic exercises that Deliliers, after his swim, would execute on his own, to dry himself, while "the beloved," immobile there beside him with a towel in hand, would only too willingly have offered to do the drying himself, the rubbing down, the touching . . .

Oh, that Deliliers—she would then add, always speaking from tent to tent, but directing her speech to my mother in particular—perhaps believing that she was lowering her voice in such a way that the "children" would not be able to hear her, though actually speaking louder than ever—that Deliliers was just a spoiled boy, a "young good-for-nothing" for whom mil-

---

* Antonio Salandra (1853–1931) was an Italian politician who as prime minister took Italy into the First World War, despite a parliamentary majority in favor of neutrality, and who later supported Mussolini.

itary service might prove more than useful. But not Dr. Fadigati. For a gentleman of his standing, of his age, there was really no excuse. He was "that
way"? So what—live with it! Who'd been that bothered about it anyway,
until now? But to put on such an exhibition, especially here at Riccione,
where he could not pretend he wasn't known, to make such a spectacle
of himself; especially here when, had it been his desire, Italy could have
furnished him with thousands of beaches where there'd be no danger of
bumping into someone from Ferrara. Not a bit of it. Only from "a dirty old
man" (and so saying, Signora Lavezzoli shot forth flames of real indignation from her queenly blue eyes), only from an "old degenerate" like him
could one expect behavior of this sort.

Signora Lavezzoli talked on, and I would have given much if just once
she could have kept quiet. I felt she was being unfair. Fadigati, it's true,
annoyed me, but it was not by him that I found myself offended. I knew
Deliliers's character perfectly. In that choice of the Romagnolo beaches, so
close to Ferrara, all his malice and arrogance could be seen. Fadigati was
irrelevant, I was quite certain. He was ashamed before me. If he failed to
greet me, or even pretended not to see me, it was for that reason.

In contrast to the lawyer Lavezzoli, who came to the seaside the first
days of August, and so along with the others was au courant regarding
the scandal (inside the tent, however, while his wife held forth, he never
stopped reading *Antonio Adverse,*[*] nor was ever heard to intervene), my
father arrived in Riccione only on the morning of the 25th, a Saturday, even
later than expected, and was obviously in the dark about the whole affair.

He almost immediately went up to greet Fadigati. Before my mother or
the Lavezzoli family could hold him back, he was happily making his way
toward him.

Fadigati winced, and turned away. My father had already stretched out
his hand as the doctor was still trying to raise himself up from the reclining deckchair.

At last he managed to. After which, for at least five minutes, we

---

[*] *Anthony Adverse* is a very long American novel by Hervey Allen published in 1933,
which the lawyer is reading in translation. It was made into a film in 1936.

watched them talk, standing up under the beach umbrella with their backs turned to us.

They were both watching the motionless strip of sea, smooth, palely luminous, without the crimp of a wave. And my father, in whose whole person could be seen the joy of having "closed up shop"—the expression he would use at Riccione to refer to all the unpleasant things left behind in town: business, empty house, summer heat, melancholy lunches at the Roveraro, mosquitoes, and so on—with raised arm was pointing out to Fadigati the hundreds of pleasure boats scattered at various distances from the shore, and then very far away, barely visible on the horizon, almost suspended in mid-air, the rust-colored sails of the fishing-trawlers and the smaller fishing-boats.*

Finally they came toward our tent. Fadigati was letting my father lead the way by about a yard, and his face contorted into an odd expression, somewhere between beseeching, distaste and guilt. It must have been eleven o'clock, and Deliliers had not yet made his appearance. While I got up to go toward them, I noticed the doctor threw a rapid glance full of disquiet toward the line of beach huts, from which at any moment he expected, or feared, to see his companion emerge.

9.

HE KISSED my mother's hand.

"You know the lawyer Signor Lavezzoli, don't you?" my father immediately said, in a loud voice.

Fadigati hesitated for a moment. He looked at my father, nodding his head affirmatively; then, in intense discomfort, he turned toward the Lavezzoli tent.

The lawyer appeared more than ever absorbed in his reading of Antonio Adverse. The three "children" were stretched out face down on the sand a couple of steps away, in a circle around a blue bathing towel, taking

---

* Bassani refers to "paranze" and "bragozzi": the first, one-mast trawlers with sails, the second, smaller two-mast vessels restricted to the Adriatic.

the sun on their backs, motionless as lizards. The signora was embroidering a tablecloth, which draped itself in long folds down from her knees. She looked like a Renaissance Madonna on a throne of clouds.

Well known for his naive spontaneity, my father was utterly unaware of the so-called "situation" until he found himself waist-deep in it.

"*Avvocato*," he called out, "look who's here!"

Forestalling her husband's response, Signora Lavezzoli was ready to step in. She raised her eyes at once from her tablecloth and hurriedly stretched out the back of her hand to Fadigati.

"Of course . . . of course . . ." she trilled.

Fadigati stepped forward dejectedly into the sunlight, and as usual staggered a little because of his shoes and the sand. Still, having reached the Lavezzoli's tent, he kissed the signora's hand, shook hands with the lawyer who in the meantime had stood up, then one by one shook the hands of the three children. Finally he returned to our tent, where my father had already prepared a reclining deckchair for him alongside our mother's. He seemed much more serene than he had a moment before: relieved as a student after a particularly taxing exam.

As soon as he had sat down, he breathed out a sigh of satisfaction.

"But how glorious it is here," he said, "what a wonderful draft of cool air!"

He turned three quarters round to speak to me.

"Do you remember that scorching weather we had last month in Bologna?"

He then explained to my mother and father, whom I had never told of our regular meetings on the six-fifty express train, or of how in the last three months we had become "such good friends." He spoke with worldly negligence. It hardly seemed possible to him, one could see why, to find himself here with us, next to the feared Lavezzolis even, suddenly restored to his set, brought back into the polite and cultured fold to which he had always belonged. "Ah" he kept sighing, broadening his chest to gather in the morning breeze. It was evident he felt happy, free, and brimming with gratitude toward all of us for allowing him to feel this way.

Soon my father had steered the conversation back to the incredible heat of August in Ferrara.

"At night you couldn't sleep," he said, twisting his face into a grimace of suffering: as though even the memory of that urban heat were enough for him to feel once more its sheer oppressiveness. "Believe me, Doctor, you just couldn't sleep. There are those who consider the modern period to have begun with the invention of bug spray. I won't argue with them. But bug spray means having the windows closed. And closed windows means the sheets stick to you with sweat. I'm not joking. Until yesterday I was waiting in a state of terror as night drew near. Damned mosquitoes!"

"It's different here," said Fadigati in a fit of enthusiasm. "Even on the hottest nights you can always breathe."

And he began to hold forth on the "advantages" of the Adriatic coast compared to the other coasts of Italy. He was a Venetian—he admitted as much—and had spent his childhood and adolescence at the Lido, and so perhaps his judgement could be accused of bias. But the Adriatic still seemed to him a great deal more restful than the west, the Tyrrhenian coast.

Signora Lavezzoli had pricked up her ears. Concealing her malicious intent behind a bogus municipal pride, she vehemently took up the defence of the Tyrrhenian. She declared that if she were offered the choice between a holiday stay at Riccione and one at Viarreggio, she wouldn't hesitate for a second.

"Mark my words," she added, "some evenings passing the Cafe Zanarini one feels one's never moved a mile from Ferrara. At least in the summer, let's be honest, one has the desire, just for a change, to see different faces than those on offer the rest of the year. Here it's like walking down the Corso Giovecca, or the Corso Roma, beneath the arches of the Caffè della Borsa. Don't you think?"

Uneasy, Fadigati shifted on his deckchair. Once again his eyes took flight toward the beach huts. But still no sign of Deliliers.

"You may be right. You may be right," he replied with a nervous smile, turning to gaze at the sea.

As it did every morning between eleven and noon, the water had changed color. It was no longer the pallid, oily mass of a half-hour earlier. The brisk wind that came from the open sea, the sun almost at its height, had transformed it into a blue expanse, scattered with innumerable glints of gold. The rush of the first bathers had begun to cross the beach. And even the three Lavezzoli children, after having asked permission of their mother, made their way toward their beach hut to change into their swimming costumes.

"You may be right," Fadigati repeated. "But where can one find, my dear Signora, afternoons of the kind that the sun allows us here, when it starts to drop behind 'the deep blue vision of San Marino'?"*

He had declaimed the line by Pascoli in a lightly nasal, singsong voice, detaching every syllable and making sure not to elide the diaresis of "visïon." An embarrassed silence followed; but the doctor had already embarked on a further discourse.

"I'm well aware," he went on, "that the sunsets of the west coast are magnificent. But still, one has to pay a high price to see them: the price, I mean, of scorching afternoons, with the sea transformed into a kind of burning glass, and with everyone forced to be corked up inside their houses, or else having to take refuge in the pinewoods. By contrast, you must have noticed the Adriatic's color after two or three o'clock. More than blue, it becomes black: in short, it stops one being dazzled. The water's surface absorbs the sun's rays rather than reflecting them. Or rather, it does reflect them, yes, but in the direction of . . . Yugoslavia! As far as I'm concerned," he concluded, absent-mindedly, "I can't wait to finish eating so as to get straight back to the beach. Two o'clock in the afternoon. There's no more beautiful time to enjoy in holy peace our divine, beloved Adriatic!"

"I suppose you'll be enjoying it with that . . . with that inseparable companion of yours," Signora Lavezzoli said in an acid tone.

Brought rudely down to earth, confused, Fadigati kept silent.

Just then, a sudden gathering of people a hundred meters or so away toward the town drew my father's attention.

"What on earth's going on?" he asked, raising a hand above his eyes to see better.

Over the gusts of wind arrived the mixed sounds of congratulatory cries and clapping.

---

* "l'azzurra visïon di San Marino": a line from "Romagna," a poem by Giovanni Pascoli (1855–1912).

"It's Il Duce taking a dip," Signora Lavezzoli explained demurely.

My father twisted his mouth.

"It would seem not even the sea can save us," he complained between his teeth.

Romantic, patriotic, politically naive and inexperienced like so many Jews of his generation, my father, returning from the Front in 1919, had also enrolled in the Fascist Party. He had thus been a Fascist from the "very beginning," and at heart had remained one despite his gentleness and his honesty. But since Mussolini, after the early scuffles, had begun to reach an agreement with Hitler, my father had started to feel uneasy. He never stopped thinking about the possibility of an outbreak of anti-Semitism in Italy as well, and suffering from it, he would allow the odd bitter word against the Regime to escape him.

"He's so straightforward, so very human," Signora Lavezzoli went on without paying any attention to my father. "Like a good husband, every Saturday morning he starts out in his car and off he goes—able to drive from Rome to Riccione in one go."

"Truly a good husband," my father sneered. "Who knows how happy 'the lady' Rachele is!"*

He was looking meaningly at the lawyer Lavezzoli, seeking his support. Wasn't the lawyer Lavezzoli one who had refused to carry the Party card? Hadn't he signed the famous Benedetto Croce manifesto in 1924, and at least for some years, at least until 1930, hadn't he been dubbed a "liberal democrat" and a defeatist? But it was all in vain. Although the lawyer's eyes finally unglued themselves from the thick pages of Antonio Adverse, they remained insensible to the mute appeal in my father's. Stretching his neck, lowering his eyelids, the illustrious lawyer and professor stubbornly gazed seaward. The "children" had hired a pleasure boat, and were driving it too far from the shore.

"Last Saturday," Signora Lavezzoli meanwhile recalled, "Filippo and I were returning home arm in arm along the Viale dei Mille. It was half past seven, or a little earlier, when suddenly, from the gate of a villa, who

---

* Rachele Guidi ("la donna Rachele") married Mussolini in 1915, and remained with him despite his various mistresses.

should I see emerging? Il Duce in person, dressed in white from top to toe. I said: 'Good evening, Your Excellency.' And he replied, polite as can be, raising his hat: 'Good evening, Signora.' Isn't it true, Pippo," she added, turning toward her husband, "isn't it true he was so wonderfully polite?"

The lawyer nodded.

"Perhaps we should have the grace to recognize our errors," he said gravely, turning back toward my father. "The Man, let's not forget it, has given us the Empire."

As though they had been etched on a magnetic tape, I find in my memory, one after the other, every word that was said on that distant afternoon.

Having pronounced his judgement—on hearing it my father's eyes widened—the lawyer Lavezzoli turned back to his reading. But the signora by now could not contain herself. Spurred on by her spouse's remark, and in particular by that word, "Empire," which she had perhaps never before then heard on his austere lips, she plunged into an endless panegyric on Il Duce's "great heart," his generous Romagnolo blood.

"Speaking of which," she said, "I'd like to tell you about an event which I myself witnessed three years ago, right here in Riccione. One morning Il Duce was taking a swim with his two elder boys Vittorio and Bruno. About one o'clock, he came back out of the water, and what did he find waiting for him? A telegraphic dispatch had arrived a moment before, apprising him of the assassination of the Austrian Chancellor Dollfuss. That year our tent was just a few steps away from Mussolini's: so what I'm telling you is the gospel truth. No sooner had he read the telegram than Il Duce let out a loud swear word in dialect—there's no getting away from it, temperament will out! But then he began to weep. I saw with my own eyes the tears that scored his cheeks. They were great friends, the Mussolinis and the Dollfusses. More than that: Signora Dollfuss, a tiny woman, slim, shy, very pretty, was a guest in their villa that very summer, along with her very young children. And he wept, Il Duce, undoubtedly thinking of what, a few minutes later, when he returned home for lunch, he would have to say to that poor, wretched mother . . ."

Fadigati suddenly stood up. Humiliated by Signora Lavezzoli's poisonous remark, from that moment on he had not opened his mouth. He had kept on anxiously biting his lip. How come Deliliers was so delayed? What could have happened to him?

"If I may . . ." he stammered in an embarrassed manner.

"But it's early yet!" Signora Lavezzoli protested. "Aren't you going to wait for your friend? There are still twenty minutes to go before the church bell sounds!"

Fadigati murmured something incomprehensible. Going in a circle, he shook hands with everyone, then trudged off toward his beach umbrella.

Having reached it, he leaned down and gathered up the detective novel and the bathing towel. After which, we saw him once again cross the beach under the one o'clock sun, but this time going back toward the hotel.

He walked uneasily, holding the book under his arm and the towel on his shoulders, his face discomposed by sweat and anxiety. So much so that my father, who had been quickly brought up to date with everything, and who was watching him with a compassionate eye, murmured beneath his breath:

"Puvràz."*

10.

SOON AFTER lunch I returned alone to the beach.

I sat down under the tent. The sea had turned a dark blue. That day, though, starting a few yards from the shore and as far away as the eye could see, the tip of every wave hoisted a plume whiter than snow. The wind still blew from the sea, but now slightly across. If I lifted my father's military binoculars so as to frame the spur at the Punta di Pesaro which ended the arc of the bay to my right, I could see the pine trunks up there swaying, their tops being wildly ruffled. Driven by the so-called Greek wind of the afternoon, the long breakers advanced in closed and successive ranks. Before they began to lower their high crests of foam, which all but vanished in the last few yards, it seemed as though they were rushing in to

---

* Ferrara dialect: "Poor thing."

attack the land. Stretched out on the reclining deckchair, I listened to their muffled crash against the shore.

The desert of the sea, from which even the sails of the little fishing-boats had disappeared—most of them could be seen, the next morning, a Sunday, in rows on the wharves of the canal docks in Rimini and Cesentico—was mirrored by the almost equally deserted beach. Under a tent not far from our own someone was playing a gramophone. I couldn't tell what music it was: perhaps jazz. For more than three hours I remained like that, with my eyes fixed on an old clam fisher who was raking the seabed there in front of me, very close to dry land, and no less dejected and tireless with that music in his ears. When I got up, a little after five o'clock, the old man was still searching for clams, and the gramophone still playing its music. The sun had greatly lengthened the shadows of the tents and the beach umbrellas. That of Fadigati's umbrella had now almost reached the sea.

On the seafront, the rotunda of the Grand Hôtel bordered directly on the dunes. As soon as I set foot on them I saw Fadigati seated on one of the concrete benches in front of the hotel's outside stairway.

He spotted me at the same time.

"Good afternoon," I said, walking toward him.

He gestured at the bench.

"Why not sit down? Sit down for a moment."

I obeyed.

He moved his hand to the inside pocket of his jacket, drew out a packet of Nazionali, and held it out to me.

In the packet there were only two cigarettes left. He realized that I was reluctant to accept.

"They're only Nazionali!" he exclaimed, with a strange gleam of enthusiasm in his eyes.

He had also understood the reason for my hesitation, and smiled.

"Oh, go on, take one! As good friends do—one for you and one for me."

Whistling on the curve's asphalt, a car burst on to the big square. Fadigati turned to look at it, but without hope. It was not, as it happened, the Alfa, but a Fiat 1500, a grey saloon.

"I think I ought to go," I said.

However, I took one of the two cigarettes.

I examined my clogs.

"I see that you've come from the beach. How wonderful the sea is today!"

"Yes, but not for swimming in."

"Don't dream of diving in until an hour after eating—take my advice!" he exclaimed. "You're a boy, without doubt you'll have the strongest of hearts, lucky chap, but coronary disease can strike you down like that, can cut down even the most robust."

He proffered the lighted match.

"You have something planned for now?"

I told him that I was expected at six o'clock by the young Lavezzolis. We had arranged to play then at the tennis court behind the Cafe Zanarini. Although it was still some twenty minutes before six, I had to go by my house, change and pick up the racket and tennis balls. I was worried that I wouldn't arrive on time.

"Let's hope that Fanny doesn't decide to come along too!" I added. "My mother won't let her go without redoing her braids, which means I'll be a good ten minutes late."

As I spoke, I saw him involved in a curious maneuver. He took the Nazionale from his lips, turned it round and lit it at the other end, where the trademark was. Then he threw away the empty packet.

Only at this point did I realize the ground in front of us was scattered with butts, more than a dozen of them.

"Have you seen how much I'm smoking?" he said.

"Indeed."

I was longing to ask him a question. "And Deliliers?" But I wasn't up to it.

I got to my feet and made to shake hands.

"If I'm not wrong, you didn't use to smoke at all."

"I'm trying to make my own modest contribution to the spread of . . . maladies of the throat," he laughed miserably. "I thought it might help me."

I walked a few paces away.

"You said the tennis court near the Zanarini, didn't you?" he called out from behind. "I might just come along later to watch you all."

As became clear shortly after, nothing serious had happened to Deliliers. Instead of going for a swim at Riccione, he had suddenly felt the desire to do so at Rimini, where he knew some sisters from Parma who were staying in the sumptuous Hôtel Vittoria. He had taken the car and disappeared without even bothering to leave a couple of lines to inform his roommate. Then he had come back at around eight o'clock—recounted Signora Lavezzoli who, together with her husband, found herself by chance in the lobby of the Grand Hôtel drinking an aperitif. Unexpectedly they had seen "that Deliliers" crossing the hall with long strides, looking furious, and with Fadigati almost in tears at his heels.

It was Deliliers who approached me that very evening on the terrace of the Grand Hôtel.

I had gone there with my parents and with the ubiquitous Lavezzolis, lawyer and wife. Still tired after tennis, I did not feel like dancing. I listened in silence to Signora Lavezzoli who, although she was certainly not unaware of how much it could offend us, had begun to hold forth, proclaiming her "objectivity" on the subject of Hitler's Germany, arguing that one finally had to accept and recognize its "undeniable greatness."

"But, Signora, you should take note that your Dollfuss, it seems, was disposed of by Hitler himself," I said with a sneer.

"That's of no importance!" she snorted.

She took on the complacent and long-suffering expression of a schoolmistress inclined to overlook any foible committed by her favorite in the class.

"Such things unfortunately are political necessities," she proceeded. "Let's leave aside any personal prejudices for or against. The fact is that in certain circumstances a Head of State, a true Statesman worthy of the name, must also be capable of moving beyond the delicate feelings of the common people, of the small people like ourselves."

She broke into a smile full of pride, in stark contrast with these last words.

Astonished, my father opened his mouth to say something. But as usual Signora Lavezzoli brooked no interruption from him. With the air of changing the topic, and addressing herself directly to him, she had already begun to expound on the contents of an "interesting" article which had appeared in the last issue of *Civiltà Cattolica*, signed by the celebrated Padre Gemelli.

The theme of the article was the "ancient and vexed question *juive*." According to Padre Gemelli—the Signora continued—the recurrent persecutions to which the "Israelites" had been subjected everywhere in the world for almost two thousand years could not be explained other than as a sign of celestial ire. And the article concluded with the following question: is it permitted for a Christian, even if his heart recoils, as one can understand, from every idea of violence, to venture a judgement on historic events through which the will of God is so clearly manifest?

At this point I got up from the wicker sofa and without too many courtesies made myself scarce.

I was then standing with my back leaning against the frame of the big glass screen that separated the dining room from the terrace, and the orchestra had just struck up, if I'm not mistaken, the opening chords of "Blue Moon."

> *Ma tuu ... pallida luna, perchèe ...*
> *sei tanto triste, cosèe ...*

sang the habitually saccharine voice. Suddenly I felt the hard touch of two fingers on my shoulder.

"Hello," Deliliers said.

It was the first time that he had bestowed a word on me in Riccione.

"Hello," I replied. "How are things?"

"Today a bit better," he said, winking. "And you, what are you up to?"

"I've been reading ... studying ..." I lied. "I have to take two exams in October."

"Ah, so you do!" sighed Deliliers, his little finger scratching pensively among his locks shining with brilliantine.

But this was of no interest to him. At a stroke his face changed expression. In a low voice, with the air of sharing an important secret with me, and looking behind him every now and then as if he were afraid of being taken unawares, he gave me a brief, jocular account of the swim he had had at Rimini and of the two girls from Parma.

"Why not come along too, tomorrow morning in the car? I'm going back for more. Go on, be a sport and help me! I can't be expected to take on two girls at once. And give the studying a rest!"

Fadigati appeared at the end of the hall, in his smoking jacket. Narrowing his short-sighted eyes behind the lenses of his spectacles, he was looking round. Where was the white jacket of Deliliers? Well-suited for "Blue Moon," the almost lunar half-dark prevented him from seeing clearly.

"I don't know if I can," I said.

"I'll be waiting for you in the hotel."

"I'll try to make it. What time should we leave?"

"Nine thirty. Agreed?"

"OK, but I can't promise."

I nodded with my chin toward Fadigati.

"So that's settled then?" Deliliers said, turning on his heels and making his way toward his friend, who was intently and feverishly polishing his glasses with a handkerchief.

And only a few moments later, the unmistakeable throaty hum of the Alfa Romeo rose from the big square beneath to inform the whole hotel that the two "lovebirds," perhaps to celebrate their apparent reconciliation in proper style, had decided to reward themselves with a special night out.

11.

THE NEXT morning, I have to admit, I was tempted for a moment or two to go with Deliliers to Rimini.

What most drew me was the prospect of the drive along the coast road. But then what?—I almost immediately began to ask myself. Those sisters from Parma, what kind of girls would they really be? The usual sort to take secretly into the pinewoods (without any let or hindrance), or else two well-brought-up young ladies from a good family to entertain on the beach under the vigilant eyes of another Signora Lavezzoli? In either case (although some eventuality between the two couldn't entirely be discounted . . .) I didn't consider myself a good enough friend of Deliliers to accept his invitation light-heartedly. Strange. Deliliers had never shown me much friendliness or real consideration, and now he was asking, almost begging, me to go out with him on an amorous excursion. Strange indeed. Wasn't he, primarily, using me to broadcast that he was with Fadigati not because of any vice but only to have him pay for the holiday, and that anyway he always preferred girls?

"*Và la, patàca!*"* I grumbled in Romagnolo dialect, having already decided not to go.

And a little later, on the beach, making out the doctor under his umbrella in the distance, abandoned to a solitude that suddenly struck me as unbounded, irremediable, I felt a great inner relief at having renounced the trip. At least I hadn't treated him as a dupe. Rather than assisting someone keen to betray and exploit him, I had had the strength to resist, and had showed him at least a minimum of respect.

A moment before I reached the umbrella, Fadigati turned round.

"Ah, it's you," he said, without surprise. "It's kind of you to pay me a visit."

Everything about him expressed the weariness and pain of a recent quarrel. Regardless of the promises he had most likely made the evening before, Deliliers had still gone off to Rimini.

He closed the book he had been reading and put it down on a stool next to him, half in the shade, half in sunlight. It was not the usual detective novel, but a slim volume in an antique cover adorned with flowers.

"What were you reading?" I asked, nodding at the volume. "Poetry?"

"Take a look, do."

It was a scholastic edition of the first book of *The Iliad*, supplied with an interlinear translation.

"*Mènin aèide, theà, peleiàdeo Achillèos,*"† he slowly recited, with a bitter smile. "I found it in the suitcase."

My father and mother were arriving exactly at this moment, my mother holding Fanny by the hand. I raised an arm to let them know I was there, and gave a version of our family whistle: the first bars of a Schubert *lied*.

Fadigati turned, half raised himself from the reclining deckchair and

---

* Ferrarese dialect: "Get lost, you idiot!
† The first line of *The Iliad*: "Sing, Goddess, of rage, of Achilles' rage."

lifted his panama hat deferentially. My parents replied in harmony: my mother by drily nodding her head and my father by touching the visor of his shining, brand-new, white canvas cap. I immediately understood that they were unhappy to find me in Fadigati's company. As soon as she saw me, Fanny turned to ask my mother something: I was sure it was whether she could come over to me. My mother visibly held her back.

"She's such a delight, your little sister," said Fadigati. "How old is she?"

"Twelve. Exactly eight years younger than me," I replied in embarrassment.

"But there are three of you, aren't there?"

"That's right. Two boys and a girl: four years between each of us. Ernesto, the second, is in England . . ."

"What an intelligent little face!" Fadigati sighed, continuing to look in Fanny's direction. "And how well that tiny pink costume suits her. It's such good luck for a girl to have grown-up brothers."

"She's still very much a little girl," I added.

"I see what you mean. I would have thought her only ten at the most. Still, that doesn't mean much. Little girls mature all at once . . . You will be taken by surprise . . . Is she at junior school?"

"Yes, in the third form."

He shook his head in melancholic disapproval as though he was weighing up within himself all the trouble and pain it cost every human being to grow and become an adult.

But his thoughts were already elsewhere.

"And the Lavezzolis?"

"Hmm. I don't think we'll be seeing them this morning until noon. Because of the Mass."

"Ah, it's true, today is Sunday," he said, startled.

"Well, given this chance," he went on after another pause, while standing up, "let's go and say hello to your parents."

We walked side by side on the sand that was already unbearably hot.

"I have the impression," he said en route, "I have the impression that Signora Lavezzoli hasn't the most friendly feelings toward me."

"Oh no, I don't believe that."

"Still, it's better, I think, to make the most of her absence."

In the Lavezzolis' absence, my mother and father were incapable of sustaining their firm resolve to keep their distance. Especially my father, who in no time started up a conversation of the most cordial kind.

A light wind was blowing from landward, the *Garbino*.* Although the sun had not yet reached its zenith, the sea, without a sail in sight, was already dark: a compact mantle, the color of lead. Perhaps because he was fresh from a reading of the first book of *The Iliad,* Fadigati spoke of the Greeks' feeling for nature and the meaning he thought should be given to epithets such as "purple" and "violet," which Homer bestowed on the waters of the ocean. My father, in his turn, spoke about Horace, and then about the *Odi barbare,*† which represented, as he would repeat in his almost daily arguments with me, the highest ideal in the field of modern poetry. In short, their conversation showed how much in sympathy they were with one another—the fact that Deliliers was not about to emerge from the beach huts from one moment to the next seemed to have a calming effect on the doctor's nervous system—so that by the time the Lavezzolis, fresh from Mass, joined our gathering, just before midday, Fadigati was strong enough to withstand the inevitable barbed remarks of the signora, and even to respond, not ineffectively, to some of them.

We would not see Deliliers again on the beach: not that day or any of the following. He never returned from his drives before two o'clock in the morning, and Fadigati, left on his own, came to seek out our company more and more often.

It was thus, then, that as well as frequenting our tent in the hours before noon—all things considered, to my father it seemed an unimaginable boon to be able to discuss music, literature and art with him, rather than politics with Signora Lavezzoli—in the afternoon Fadigati adopted

---

* Warm southwest wind, whose regional name "garbino," or "garbin," is elsewhere called the "libeccio."
† A three-volume work, published between 1878 and 1889, by the Italian poet and Nobel Prize–winner Giosuè Carducci (1835–1907).

the habit, at least when he knew that I and the Lavezzoli children had gone there, of visiting the tennis court behind the Cafe Zanarini.

Our feeble contests, the four of us—a men's pair against a mixed pair—were certainly nothing to get excited about. If I managed to play rather indifferently, Franco and Gilberto Lavezzoli hardly even knew how to hold the racket. Then, as far as Cristina, their blonde, rosy, delicate, fifteen-year-old sister, was concerned—she had just left a college run by Florentine nuns, and the whole family kept her under constant scrutiny— as a player she was even worse than her brothers. Her face was wreathed with a little crown of tresses which Fadigati himself, once, in paternal admiration had described as "in the style of Melozzo's musician angel." Rather than dishevel a single curl, she would have renounced even the act of walking. So she was hardly going to care about the style of her forehand drive or dedicate herself to an effective backhand!

And yet, even though our play was so lethargic and dull, Fadigati seemed to greatly appreciate it. "Good shot!" "Out by a whisker!" "Oh, hard luck!"—he was overflowing with praises for us all, with some comment, albeit often irrelevant, forever ready for each and every shot.

Sometimes, however, the warm-up became a bit too unbearably languid even for him.

"Why not play a game?" he would propose.

"Oh, please!" Cristina would immediately complain, blushing. "When I can't even hit one ball back . . . !"

He wouldn't hear of it.

"Put your backs into it!" he would exclaim spiritedly. "Dr. Fadigati will reward the winning couple with two delicious bottles of San Pellegrino Orangina!"

He would then rush off to the groundsman's hut, bring out a decrepit, wobbly umpire's chair, at least two meters high, carry it in his arms with difficulty to one side of the court, and finally clamber up on top. The air little by little grew dark; his hat, against the light, appeared encircled by an aureole of midges. But he, perched like a big bird on a high branch, stayed up there, to announce point after point in his metallic voice, determined to play out to the end his self-assigned role of impartial umpire. It was clear: he didn't know what else to do, in what way to fill the vast emptiness of his days.

12.

AS OFTEN happens on the Adriatic coast, in the first days of September the season suddenly changed. It rained only one day, the 31st of August. But the beautiful weather of the following day fooled no one. The sea was restless and green, the green of vegetation; the sky had the exaggerated translucency of a precious stone. Even the lukewarm air bore within itself a small persistent hint of cold.

The number of holidaymakers began to dwindle. On the beach the three or four rows of tents and umbrellas quickly reduced to two, and then, after another day of rain, to only one. From there to the cabins, a good proportion of which by this stage had been taken down, on the dunes, covered until only a few days before by a parched and stunted growth of brush, an incredible multitude of marvelous, budding yellow flowers appeared, long-stalked as lilies. To understand the full significance of that sudden flowering one needed to have a passing knowledge of the Romagnolo coast. The summer was over: from that moment on it would be nothing but a memory.

I made the most of it by settling down to my studies. I was hoping to take my Ancient History exam the following October, at least that one. So I remained shut in my room until almost midday, reading the prescribed textbooks.

I did the same in the afternoon, awaiting the time of the tennis match.

One day, after lunch, when I was thus studying—that morning I had not even gone to the beach: as soon as I was up, the distant crash of the waves had immediately discouraged any idea of swimming—I heard rising from the garden the sharp voice of Signora Lavezzoli. I couldn't make out her words. I understood, though, from the tone, that she was indignant about something.

"But really . . . the scandal of yesterday evening . . ." I managed to catch.

Who had made her so cross? Why had she come to visit us?—I asked myself with irritation. And immediately, instinctively, I thought of Fadigati.

I resisted the temptation to go down to the breakfast room and eavesdrop behind the door that gave on to the garden, and when I emerged an hour later Signora Lavezzoli was no longer there. My father was sitting in the shade as usual under the pine tree. As soon as he heard the noise of my footsteps on the gravel, he put down the newspaper that was unfolded on his knees.

I was kitted out for tennis. With one hand I held the handlebars of my bike, with the other the racket. And yet still he asked me:

"Where are you off to?"

Two summers before, as always at Riccione, a fortnight after having acquitted myself splendidly in the exams for high school graduation, I ended up in bed (and it was the first time ever!) with a thirty-year-old married woman from Milan who was an occasional acquaintance of my mother. Uncertain whether to be proud or worried by my adventure, for two whole months my father had ceaselessly watched my every movement. I only had to be leaving the house, or even to move away from the beach tent, to feel his eyes glued to me.

Now once again that same expression was in his eyes. I could feel my blood rising.

"Can't you see?" I asked.

For some moments he remained silent. Rather than troubled, he seemed exhausted. Signora Lavezzoli's visit, evidently unexpected, had stopped him taking his usual afternoon nap.

"I don't think you'll find anyone there," he said. "Signora Lavezzoli was just here. She came to tell us that her children wouldn't be playing. Her two sons have to study, and she wouldn't let Cristina go on her own."

He turned his head toward Fanny, curled up at the bottom of the garden, playing with her doll. From the back, with her little shoulder blades protruding from under a T-shirt, her braids made blonde by the sun, she seemed even more frail and immature than usual. He pointed at last at the wicker armchair opposite his.

"Sit down for a moment," he said, and smiled anxiously.

He wanted to talk to me, it was clear, but it made him uneasy. I pretended not to have heard.

"It was kind of her to take the trouble, but I'll go anyway," I said.

I turned my back on him, and made off toward the gate.

"Ernesto's written," my father added, in a louder, complaining tone. "Don't you even want to read your brother's letter?"

At the gate I turned round, and at that moment Fanny raised her head. Although so far away, I clearly discerned in her look an expression of reproach.

"Later, when I get back," I replied, and pedaled off.

I arrived at the tennis court. Fadigati was there. Standing by the umpire's chair left there from the afternoon before, he was staring straight ahead, smoking.

He turned.

"Ah, you're on your own!" he said. "And the others?"

Having leaned my bicycle on the metal fence-surround, I went toward him.

"They aren't coming today," I replied.

He gave a feeble smile, his mouth twisted. His upper lip was rather swollen. A double crack crossed the left-side lens of his fine, gold-rimmed spectacles.

"I'm not sure why," I added. "It seems that Franco and Gilbert have to study. But it sounds like an excuse to me. I hope, though, that –"

"I can tell you why," Fadigati interrupted me bitterly. "It will be because of the scene that happened yesterday evening."

"What scene?"

"Don't take me for a fool, I beg you!" he grinned, desperately. "Well, who knows? I didn't see you at the seaside this morning. But is it possible that your parents didn't say anything about it later, at lunch for example?"

It was necessary for me to try to convince him to the contrary. I had, certainly—I told him—heard Signora Lavezzoli enunciate the word "scandal," and I explained when and how, but I knew nothing more than that.

Then, after a strange, rapid, sideways glance, and a subsequent narrowing of the eyes as though he had suddenly been struck by something vague in the distance behind my shoulder, he began to relate how, in the drawing room of the Grand Hôtel, "in front of everyone," he had had an "argument" with Deliliers.

"I reproached him, but under my breath, as you can imagine, for the life he'd been leading these last few days . . . always gadding about here and there . . . forever driving off . . . so much so, one could say, that I almost never had a chance to see him. And he—do you know what he did at a certain point? He stood up, and bang, he loosed a peach of a punch right in my face!"

He touched his swollen lip.

"Here, see?"

"Does it hurt?"

"Oh, no," he replied, shrugging a shoulder. "It's true I ended up flat on my back, and for a while I couldn't understand a thing. But in the end, a punch, what does it matter? And the scandal itself, what does even that matter compared to . . . to the rest of it?"

He went silent. And I likewise, out of sheer embarrassment. I was thinking about his words "compared to the rest of it." I was left to construe the image of his pain as a scorned lover, an image which at that moment, I have to confess, repelled me rather than awakened my pity.

But I had understood only the half of it.

"Today at one o'clock when I went back to the hotel," he was saying, "an even more bitter surprise awaited me. Look at what I found up there in the room."

He dug out of his jacket pocket a small folded sheet of paper and held it out to me.

"Read it, go on, read it."

There was little to read, but it was enough. At the center of the sheet, written in capitals with a pencil, only the two lines.

These:

THANKS AND BEST WISHES
FROM ERALDO

I refolded the note in four and gave it him back.

"He's left, yes, he's gone away," he sighed. "But the worst," he added with a tremor of his swollen lip and of his voice, "the worst is that he's taken all my things with him."

"All of your things?" I exclaimed.

"Yes. As well as the car, which was his anyway—I bought it for him as a gift—he's taken all my stuff, clothes, underwear, ties, two suitcases, a gold watch, a chequebook, the thousand lire I kept in the bedside cupboard. He hasn't overlooked a thing. Not even the headed paper, not even the comb and toothbrush!"

He ended with a strange cry, almost of exultation. As though, finally, listing the objects stolen by Deliliers had had the effect of transforming his torment into a still more powerful sense of pride and pleasure.

People were arriving. Two boys and two girls, all four on bicycles.

"It's five forty-five!" one of the girls shouted brightly, consulting her wristwatch.

"We booked the court for six o'clock, but seeing as no one's playing can we start anyway?"

After having left the court, Fadigati and I silently took the little lane of locust trees that reached the dead-end of Zanarini's red wall. Down in the courtyard you could see waiters coming and going across the concrete dance floor.

"So now what do you intend to do?" I asked.

"I'll go this evening. There's a fast train that leaves Rimini at nine and gets into Ferrara at around half past twelve. I hope there's enough left to pay the hotel bill."

I stopped in my tracks and stood, eyeing him up and down. He was dressed in his city clothes, with his felt hat and everything. I stared at the felt hat. So it wasn't exactly true that Deliliers had taken all his things—I reflected—there was an element of exaggeration.

"Why not report him to the police?" I suggested, coldly.

He stared back at me.

"Report him!" he stammered in surprise.

In his eyes there suddenly gleamed a flash of scorn.

"Report him?" he repeated, and looked at me as one looks at a clueless, slightly ridiculous stranger. "Do you even think that's a possibility?"

13.

WE LEFT Riccione on the 10th of October, a Saturday afternoon.

Around halfway through the month before, the barometer had stuck at Fair/Settled. From then on day after splendid day had followed, with cloudless skies and the sea calm as can be. But who paid any attention to such things? What my father had so long feared had, unfortunately, proved exactly true. No more than a week after Fadigati's departure, in all the Italian newspapers, including the local *Corriere padano*, the crude campaign of vilification, which within the space of a year would bring in its wake the announcement of the Racial Laws, had suddenly begun in earnest.

I remember those first days as a nightmare. My father, distraught, leaving the house early in search of printed matter; the eyes of my mother, always swollen with crying; Fanny still unenlightened, poor little thing, and yet at some level aware; for my part, the painful habit of boxing myself up into a stubborn silence. Always on my own, seething with anger, even with hatred, at the very idea of finding myself in the presence of Signora Lavezzoli enthroned on her reclining deckchair, of having to hear her lecturing us that it was nothing to do with Christianity or Judaism, and still less to do with the guilt that should be laid at the door of the "Israelites" for the crucifixion of Jesus Christ (in principle the signora had quickly declared herself against the Government's new policies in relation to us, but nevertheless even the Pope—it was as if I could hear her saying it—in a certain speech he gave in 1929 . . .). By this point, I was not even prepared to show my face on the beach. It was enough, more than enough, to be forced during mealtimes to listen to my father, who, in futile polemic with the venomous articles that he ceaselessly read in the newspapers, compiled a list of the "patriotic merits" of Italian Jews, all, or nearly all of them—he would keep repeating, with his blue eyes opened wide—having always been the "most distinguished Fascists." In short, I too was desperate. I forced myself to persevere with the revision for my exam. But above all I went on interminable bike rides on the hills of the hinterland. Once, without warning anyone, I had gone as far as San Leo and the Carpegna, staying away in all for almost three days: with the result, on returning, that I found both my father and mother in tears. I gave myself no respite in brooding over our fast-approaching return to Ferrara. I thought of it with a kind of terror, with an ever-increasing sense of intimate laceration.

In the end it started to rain again, and we had to leave.

As always happened with me every time I came back from holidays, immediately after arriving home I couldn't resist the desire to go on a tour round the city. I borrowed a bicycle from the house porter, old Tubi, and even before setting foot in my room, or telephoning Vittorio Molon and Nino Bottecchiari, I went for a leisurely ride, without any particular destination.

I ended up toward evening on the city walls, the Mura degli Angeli, where I had spent so many afternoons of my childhood and adolescence; and, in short, pedaling along the path on top of the walls, I drew level with the Jewish cemetery.

I got off the bike, and leaned against a tree trunk.

I looked at the cemetery below, in which our dead were buried. Among the occasional gravestones, made small by the distance, I saw a man and a woman, both middle-aged, walking about: most likely two visitors delayed between one train and the next—I told myself—who had managed to obtain from Dr. Levi the permit required to visit the cemetery. They were passing between the tombs with the care and detachment of guests, of foreigners. Then suddenly, watching them and the vast urban landscape which displayed itself to me at that height in all its breadth, I was struck by a great sweetness, by a feeling of peace and the tenderest gratitude. The setting sun, cleaving through a dark cope of cloud that lay low on the horizon, vividly lit up everything: the Jewish cemetery at my feet, the apse and bell tower of the church of San Cristoforo only a little farther on, and in the background, high above the vista of brown roofs, the distant bulk of the Estense Castle and the Duomo. It was enough for me to recover the ancient, maternal visage of my hometown, to reclaim it once again all for myself, for that atrocious feeling of exclusion that had tormented me in recent days to fall away instantly. The future of persecution and massacres that perhaps awaited us—since childhood I had heard them spoken of as an always possible eventuality for us Jews—no longer made me afraid.

And then, who knows?—I repeated to myself, turning toward home—Who can tell what the future holds?

But all those hopes and illusions I had would not last long.

The next morning, when I was passing beneath the arches of the Caffè della Borsa, in Corso Roma, someone shouted out my name.

It was Nino Bottecchiari. He was seated alone at a little table outside, and, rising, he almost overturned his cup of espresso.

"Welcome back!" he exclaimed, coming toward me with his arms wide. "Since when have we had the honor and pleasure of your presence among us?"

Hearing I'd been back in Ferrara since five o'clock in the afternoon the day before, he complained that I hadn't telephoned.

"Of course you'll say that you were about to call me at lunchtime today," he smiled. "Deny it if you can."

I would have phoned him, I was actually thinking of that when he called me over. For this very reason I grew silent, embarrassed.

"Come on, forget it, I'll buy you a coffee!" Nino cleared the air, taking me by the arm.

"Come back home with me," I proposed.

"So soon? It's not even midday!" he replied. "*Ach bazòrla:** surely you wouldn't want to miss them coming out of Mass!"

He went in front of me, opening the way for me through the seats and little tables. All the same, after a few steps I stopped dead. Everything disturbed and bruised me.

"What's up?" asked Nino, who had already sat down again.

"I have to go, I'm sorry," I stammered, lifting a hand to say goodbye.

"Wait!"

His shout of greeting, and the long procedure he had to go through to pay (the waiter Giovanni did not have the change for the fifty-lira note: the old man, shuffling along and muttering to himself, had to go and change it at the nearby chemist's, Barilari) distinctly drew the attention of the other customers to Nino and myself. I felt myself being observed by a host of eyes. Even around the two small contiguous tables permanently reserved for the members of the Fascist action squad, who had enrolled in the Party at the earliest date—occupied as well, that day, by the usual triumvirate Aretusi–Sturla–Bellistracci, by the Federal Secretary Bolognesi and by Gino Cariani, Secretary of the GUF—the conversation came to an unexpected halt. Having turned right round to steal a glance at me, Cariani, servile as ever, leaned forward to whisper something in Aretusi's ear. I saw Sciagura give a faint grimace and nod gravely.

---

* Ferrarese dialect: "What a fool."

While waiting for Nino finally to receive his change I moved a few paces away. It was a beautiful day, Corso Roma looked gay and vivid as never before. From under the colonnade I was idly gazing toward the center of the street, where dozens of bicycles, mainly ridden by pupils from the upper school, paint and chrome-work glinting in the sun, glided through the Sunday crowd. A blond boy of twelve or thirteen, still in short trousers, passed by at full tilt on a grey Maine racing bike. He lifted up his arm in greeting and shouted, "Hi there!" I started, and turned to see who it was, but he had already disappeared round the corner of Corso Giovecca.

At last Nino came over.

"Sorry to keep you," he said, out of breath, "but that sluggard Giovanni would test the patience of a saint."

We moved off in the direction of the Duomo, walking side by side on the sidewalk.

As ever, they had been on holiday at Moena, in the Val di Fassa—Nino was saying, meanwhile, of himself and his family. Meadows, fir trees, cows and cow bells: so much the same as it always was, he'd considered it superfluous to send me the ritual postcard, though now he regretted it. Basically, from the very start, a complete bore. But good fortune had willed it that in August they'd had as a guest for a fortnight his uncle Mauro, the Socialist ex-Member of Parliament who, from the first moment after his arrival, had created havoc within the family circle with his wildly exuberant character. He was never still for a second, his eagle eyes forever fixed on the highest peaks. If he, Nino, had not been there to keep him company, who could have held him back? He would have been more than capable of hiking off on his own into the Dolomites.

"Eh! The old fellow is still in great form, I can tell you," he continued, and winked knowingly. "What a character! It was a pleasure to watch him clambering up the mountain, singing "Bandiera Rossa" at the top of his voice. We promised each other to stay friends. He assured me that immediately after I graduate he'll take me into his office as an internee . . ."

We had come up before the main entrance of the Archbishop's Palace.

"Let's go this way," Nino suggested.

He went first into the cool, dark entrance hall. In the background, in full sunshine, the courtyard garden shone motionlessly. The noise from

Corso Roma was by now distant: a weak, confused hum in which the bells of passing bicycles could barely be distinguished.

Nino stopped in his tracks.

"On the subject of holidays," he asked, "have you heard about Deliliers?"

I felt a strange sensation of guilt.

"Well, yes . . ." I stammered ridiculously. "I saw him at Riccione last month . . . Since at the beach we weren't in the same group of people, I must have spoken with him only a couple of times—"

"I'm not talking about that, for God's sake!" Nino interrupted me. "News that he was in Riccione on his honeymoon with that graceless old pederast Dr. Fadigati travelled fast even as far as Moena, as you can guess. No, no, of course it wasn't that I wanted to make sure you knew about."

He began then to tell me how a week before he had received a letter from Deliliers in Paris, no less. It's a pity he didn't have it with him. He meant to show it to me, though: it was truly worth my while. He'd never before held in his hands a document of such arrogant *sfattísia*,[*] and he couldn't decide whether the most fitting response was revulsion or laughter.

"How disgusting!" he exclaimed.

He began to discourse in detail on the letter: on its tone, and of the heavy insults directed at all of us former traveling companions in those journeys back and forth between Ferrara and Bologna, myself included. To tell the truth, he specified, laughing, rather than insult us, the big jerk was trying to make fun of us. We were all good little mummy's boys, provincials, pampered bourgeoisie . . .

"Do you remember what he was planning?" he went on. "Sooner or later he was going to pull off a real coup, after which he'd dedicate himself exclusively to boxing. Just imagine it. Instead he must have found himself some new, well-heeled pansy, perhaps this time of the international variety. But this time he'll play it out as long as possible, I'm sure of that, or at least until he too has been squeezed completely dry. So much for boxing!"

He then went on to speak about France. If it hadn't been the complete disaster it was—Fascism pronounced a thoroughly unfavorable judge-

---

[*] Ferrarese dialect for scorn or dismissiveness that echoes the Fascist political term for "defeatism."

ment on France that he fully shared—it would have put in place an absolute ban on adventurers of his type.

"As for us, in Italy," he concluded, suddenly becoming almost serious,
"you know what we ought to do with people like that? Avail ourselves of
the full powers permitted by the law and put them up against a wall, and
there's an end to it. But Italy, could you call it a society . . . ?"

He had finished.

"Wonderful," I commented, calmly. "I suppose he refers to me as a
nasty Jew."

He was hesitant about answering. In the half-light of the entrance hall
I saw him blush.

"Let's go," he said, turning to take me by the arm. "The Mass will be
over by now."

And he dragged me, using some force, toward the smaller exit of the
Archbishop's Palace: the one that, exactly at the corner of Via Gorgadello,
opens on to Piazza Cattedrale.

14.

THE MIDDAY Mass was about to finish. A small crowd of boys, of young
men, of layabouts, idled as always in front of the Duomo's entrance.

I watched them. Until a few months before, I would never have missed
the Sunday congregation leaving San Carlo and the Duomo at half past
twelve, and even today—I reflected—it wasn't as if I'd missed it.[*] But
would this suffice for me? Today was different. I wasn't down there, in
among the others, in the usual part-mocking, part-anxious wait for the
Mass exodus. Leaning against the doorway of the Archbishop's Palace,
stuck in a corner of the piazza—the presence of Nino Bottecchiari, if
anything, only increased my bitterness—I felt set apart, irremediably an
intruder.

---

[*] The exit from Sunday Mass was, at least until recently, a social event in Italian towns
not unlike the evening *"passeggiata,"* though usually, as here, a chance more specifically
for men and boys to eye the women leaving church.

In that moment the raucous cry of a newsvendor resounded.

It was Cenzo, near enough a halfwit, of an indefinable age, cross-eyed, slightly lame, always on the go walking the sidewalks with a fat bundle of dailies under his arm, and treated by the entire city, and sometimes even by me, to hearty thumps on the back, affectionate insults and sardonic requests to forecast the imminent destiny of SPAL, and so on.

Scuffing his big, nailed soles on the paving stones, Cenzo steered himself toward the center of the piazza with his right hand holding aloft an unfolded newspaper.

"Latest measures of the Great Council taken against the *Jews!*" his cavernous voice hurled out with indifference.

And while Nino remained in a most uneasy silence, I felt in me, with inexpressible repugnance, the first inklings of the Jew's ancient, atavistic hatred for everything that was Christian, Catholic, in a word *goyische*. *Goy, goyim*: what a sense of shame, what a humiliation, what a loathsome falling-off: to think in these terms. And yet I had already managed this— I told myself—becoming exactly like any Jew whatsoever from Eastern Europe who had never lived outside his own ghetto. I thought of our own ghetto, of Via Mazzini, of Via Vignatagliata, of the blind alley Torcicoda. In a near enough future, they, the *goyim*, would once more have forced us to swarm there, in the narrow, twisting lanes of that wretched medieval quarter from which, when all was reckoned up, we had emerged only some seventy or eighty years ago. Piled one on top of the other behind the gates like so many frightened beasts, we would never again manage to escape.

"It annoys me to speak of it," began Nino without looking at me, "but you have no idea how much what's happening distresses me. My uncle Mauro is pessimistic, there's no point in concealing it from you: on the other hand that's to be expected—he has always hoped things would go from bad to the worst possible. Myself, I don't believe it. Despite appearances, I don't believe that Italy will go down the same road as Germany with these policies against your people. You'll see that it will all burst like a soap bubble in the end."

I should have been grateful that he brought up the subject. In the end, what else could he have said? And yet I wasn't. While he was speaking, I barely managed to mask the annoyance his words provoked in me, and the tone especially, the disappointed tone of his voice. "It will all burst like a soap bubble in the end." Could you be any clumsier, more insensitive, more obtusely *goyische* than that? I asked him why, in contrast to his uncle, he was optimistic.

"Oh, we Italians are too buffoonish for that," he replied, without showing he was aware of my irony. "We may imitate the Germans in some things, even the goose-step, but not the tragic sense they have of life. We're just too old, too skeptical and worn out."

Only at this point must he have figured out, from my silence, how inopportune what he had just said was, how inevitably ambiguous. Immediately the expression on his face changed.

"And just as well, don't you think?" he exclaimed with forced joviality. "For all its faults, long live our millennia of Latin wisdom!"

He was sure—he went on—that among us Italians anti-Semitism would never be able to take on a serious, political form, and so take root. The conviction that there was some neat separation between the Jewish "element" and that of the "so-called Aryan" could not be practically feasible in our country—you had only to think of Ferrara, a city that, "as regards its social profile," one could consider more or less typical. The "Israelites" in Ferrara, all or nearly all, belonged to the city's bourgeoisie, of which they even constituted in a certain sense the center, the backbone. The very fact that the majority of them had been Fascists, and not a few of them, as I well knew, among its first adherents, showed their unquestionable solidarity and identity with the whole society. Could one imagine anyone more Jewish and at the same time more Ferrarese than the lawyer Geremia Tabet, just to name one figure that sprang to mind among the small circle of people (with Carlo Aretusi, Vezio Sturla, Osvaldo Bellistracci, the Councillor Bolognesi and two or three others) who in 1919 had founded the first local section of the Veterans' Fascist Movement? And who could be more "one of us" than old Dr. Corcos, Elia Corcos, the famous clinician—so much so that, strictly speaking, his personage could have been perfectly included in the municipal coat of arms? And my father? And the lawyer Lattes, Bruno's father? No, no: just going through the telephone directory, where the Jewish names inevitably appeared accompanied by their professional and academic titles, doctors, lawyers, engineers, owners of big and small commercial companies, and so on, you'd immediately see the impossibility of putting into effect here in Ferrara a racial policy with any chance of success. That kind of policy could "operate" only if there were more cases like that of the Finzi-Contini family, with their most atypical impulse to segregate themselves and live in a grand, aristocratic house. (Although he himself knew Alberto Finzi-Contini very well, he had never succeeded in getting himself invited to play tennis at their house, on their magnificent private court!) But in Ferrara the Finzi-Continis were exactly that: an exception. And then, weren't even they following a resurgent "historical imperative," in acquiring the big house in Corso Ercole I, and all their lands, as well as in their way of living apart, just like certain ancient Ferrarese aristocratic families now extinct?

He said all this, and more that I can't recall. While he was speaking, I did not even look at him. The sky above the piazza was full of light. I had to squint to follow the flight of the doves that crossed it from time to time.

Suddenly he touched my hand.

"I need some advice," he said. "The advice of a friend."

"Willingly."

"Will you be absolutely straight with me?"

"Of course."

Then I had to know—he began, lowering his voice—that a couple of days ago he had been approached by "that snake" Gino Cariani, who, without much preamble, had proposed to him that he take on the role of "Cultural Attaché." So far he had neither accepted nor refused the post. He had asked only for a little time to reflect on it. Now, however, he had to make a decision. That very morning, at the cafe, just before I had arrived, Cariani had brought up the topic again.

"What should I do?" he asked after a pause.

I pursed my lips, perplexed. But he had already begun another speech.

"I belong to a 'clan' with traditions of which you're well aware," he said. "And yet you can be sure that when my father comes to hear that I've declined Cariani's proposal, he'll put his head in his hands, that's what he'll do. And do you think my uncle Mauro will behave any differently? All that's needed is for my father to ask him to send for me, and he'd be only too happy to oblige, if with no other intention than to free himself from any charge of bias. I can already see his face at the moment he blithely asks me to revoke the decision. I can just hear what he'll say. Pressing me not to behave like a baby, to think again about it, because in life . . ."

He laughed, with distaste.

"Look," he added: "I have so little faith in human nature, and in the character of us Italians in particular, that I don't even feel sure about myself. We live in a country, my dear fellow, where the culture of Rome, in its old proper sense, has only remained with us in the form of a raised-arm salute. Which makes even me ask: *à quoi bon*? At the end of the day, if I were to refuse—"

"You'd be making a big mistake," I interrupted calmly.

He stared at me with a flicker of diffidence in his eyes.

"You mean that?"

"Of course I do. I don't see why you shouldn't aspire to have a career in the Party, or through the Party. If I were in your shoes . . . I mean, if I were studying Law like you . . . I wouldn't hesitate for a moment."

I had taken care not to let anything of what I felt show through. The expression on Nino's face cleared. He lit a cigarette. My objectivity, my disinterestedness, had evidently impressed him.

He thanked me for the advice, releasing into the air a first, dense mouthful of smoke. He'd allow, he said, a few more days to pass before he followed it. He wanted to have a clear view both of himself and how things were. Fascism was without doubt in a state of crisis. But was this a question of something wrong *in* the system, or *with* the system? It's good to get on in life. But how? Was it possible to change things from within, or else . . . ?

He finished with a vague wave of his hand.

In the next few days—he began again—he would come round to my house to see me. I was a literary figure . . . a poet . . . he smiled, trying once more to assume the half-protective, half-affectionate tone, the tone of the politician, that he often used with me. At any rate he would greatly appreciate the chance to go over the whole question with me. We must make an effort to phone, see each other, keep in contact with one another . . . above all to react!

I sighed audibly.

"By the way," he asked out of the blue, furrowing his brow, "when is it you have to do your first exam in Bologna? Oh, no! We'll have to renew our railway-travel cards . . ."

15.

I saw Fadigati again.

It was on the streets and at night: a humid, misty night about halfway through the following November. Coming out of the brothel on Via Bomporto with my clothes impregnated with the usual scent, I lingered there, in front of the doorway, undecided as to whether I should go home or follow the impulse to take to the city walls in search of some clean air.

The surrounding silence was perfect. From inside the brothel at my back filtered the weary conversation of three voices, two of them male and one female. They were talking about soccer. The two men were complaining that SPAL, which in the years after the First World War had been a great team, one of the best in northern Italy—in 1923 it had failed by a hair's breadth to win the First Division Championship: they had just needed to draw their last away match at Pro Vercelli—had now ended up in *Serie C*, and each year was struggling even to stay there. Ah, the years of the centerfield player Condrelli, of the two Banfi brothers, Beppe and Ilario, of the great Baùsi, that, yes, that was the great era! The woman only occasionally interrupted. For instance, she said, "That's rubbish, you Ferraresi like sex too much." Or "The trouble with you Ferraresi is not so much ball control, as talking and watching rather than playing!" The other two let her speak, but just went on unfazed with the same argument. They must have been old customers, of about forty-five, fifty: veteran smokers. The prostitute was obviously not from Ferrara, but from the Veneto, probably in the vicinity of Friuli.

Lurching over the sharp cobbles of the alleyway, slow, heavy footsteps could be heard approaching.

"What on earth do you want? Are you hungry, is that it?"

It was Fadigati. A while before he finally made me out in the thick fog I had recognized him by his voice.

"You're just a stupid thing, and filthy too! I've nothing to give you, and you know it!"

Who was he speaking to? And why that tone of complaint, drenched in mannered tenderness?

At last he appeared. Haloed by the yellow light of the single street lamp, his plump form loomed out of the vapors. He advanced slowly, inclined slightly to one side and still declaiming. I saw he was leaning on a cane.

He stopped about a yard away.

"So, then, are you going to leave me in peace, or aren't you?"

He stared the creature in the eyes, raising his finger in a threatening gesture. And the creature, a medium-sized mongrel bitch, white with brown spots, made her reply from below, desperately wagging her tail, eyeing him with a watery, fearful gaze, while dragging herself over the cobbles toward the doctor's shoes. In a moment she would have rolled on her back with her belly and legs in the air, completely at his mercy.

"Good evening."

He detached his eyes from the dog's and looked at me.

"How are things?" he said, placing me. "Are you well?"

We shook hands. We were standing facing each other in front of the nail-studded exit of the brothel. Good Lord, how he had aged! His sagging cheeks, obscured by a shaggy, grey beard, made him seem in his sixties. From his reddened, rheumy eyelids, you could tell that he was tired, that he had not been sleeping. And yet the gaze from behind his glasses was still lively and brisk . . .

"Did you know you've grown thinner?" he said. "But it suits you, it makes you look more of a man. You know, sometimes in life just a few months make all the difference. A few months count for more, at times, than entire years."

The nail-studded door opened, and four or five young men came out: types that might have been from the suburbs, if not from the country. They remained there in a circle to light their cigarettes. One approached the wall beside the entrance to urinate. All of them, including him, kept insistently peering at us.

Passing between the open legs of the young man standing at the wall, a small snaking rivulet flowed rapidly in descent toward the center of the alley. The dog was attracted by it. Cautiously she approached it to sniff.

"It would be better if we went," Fadigati whispered with a light tremor in his voice.

We moved away in silence, while at our backs the alley echoed with laughter and obscene taunts. For a moment I was afraid that the little gang would come up behind us. But luckily there was Via Ripagrande, where the fog seemed even thicker. We just needed to cross the street, step up onto the opposite sidewalk, and I was sure that we would have disappeared from sight, covering our tracks behind us.

We walked on at a slow pace side by side toward Montagnone. Midnight had sounded a good while before, and there was no one to be seen on the streets. Row after row of blind, closed shutters, bolted doors and, at intervals, the almost underwater light of the street lamps.

It had got so late that perhaps we two, Fadigati and I, were the only people left wandering around the city at that hour. He spoke to me with a sad, subdued air. He narrated all his misfortunes. They had dismissed him from the hospital with some perfunctory excuse. Even at the clinic in Via Gorgadello, entire afternoons could pass without the visit of a single patient. For him, it was true, there was no one in the world he had to look after . . . provide for; he had no immediate hardships as far as his finances were concerned . . . but was it possible to keep on living like this, in the most utter solitude, surrounded by general hostility? The time wasn't far off, at all events, when he would have to sack the nurse, make do with a smaller surgery, begin to sell off his pictures. Then perhaps it was best that he should leave at once, try to find work elsewhere.

"Why don't you do that?"

"Of course, you're right," he sighed. "But at my age . . . And then, even if I had the strength and courage to take such a step, do you think it would really make any difference?"

Having arrived close to Montagnone, we heard from behind us the sound of a light trotting. We turned round. It was the same mongrel as before, who had caught up with us, panting.

She stopped, happy to have tracked us down by scent in that sea of fog. And laying back her long, tender ears, whimpering and festively wagging her tail, she was already once more performing, mainly in honor of Fadigati, her pathetic little displays of devotion.

"Is it yours?" I asked.

"Not likely. I found her this evening near the aqueduct. I stroked her and, Lord knows why, she took it to heart! From then on I haven't been able to shake her off."

I noticed her udders were fat and pendulous, swollen with milk.

"She has some little ones, see?"

"It's true!" exclaimed Fadigati. "You're absolutely right!"

And then, turning to the dog:

"You wretch! Where have you left your babies? Aren't you ashamed to go out on the town at this hour? Unnatural mother!"

Once more, the dog flattened herself with her belly on the ground a few inches from Fadigati's feet. "Beat me, kill me if you want!" she seemed to be saying. "It's only right, and besides I like it!"

The doctor knelt to stroke her head. In a fit of genuine passion, the creature kept on licking his hands. She tried to reach his face with the sudden upward ambush of a kiss.

"Calm down, will you? Calm down . . ." Fadigati kept repeating.

Still followed or led by the mongrel, we resumed our stroll. By this stage we had drawn near to my house. When she was in front, the dog stopped at every crossing as though fearful of losing us again.

"Will you look at her!" said Fadigati, pointing. "Perhaps one ought to be like that, able to accept one's own nature. But on the other hand how does one accomplish that? Isn't the price too high? There's a great deal of the animal in all men, and yet can we give in to it? Admit to being an animal, and only an animal?"

I broke into loud laughter.

"Oh, no," I said. "It would be like asking: can an Italian, an Italian citizen, admit to being a Jew, and only a Jew?"

He gave me a humiliated look.

"I understand what you're saying," he replied after a while. "In these times, believe me, I've many times thought about you, and your family. But, allow me to tell you that if I were in your—"

"What should I do?" I interrupted him heatedly. "Accept that I am what I am? Or would it be better to mold myself into what others want me to be?"

"I don't see why you shouldn't," he replied quietly. "My dear friend, if being what you are is what makes you so much more human—you wouldn't be here keeping me company otherwise!—why reject it, why rebel against it? My situation is different, the exact opposite of yours. After all that happened last summer I can't bear myself any longer. I can't, I shouldn't go on. Would you believe that I can't even bear to shave in front of the mirror. I could at least dress in a different fashion! All the same, could you imagine me without this hat . . . this overcoat . . . these glasses, this uniform of respectability? And yet, dressed up like this, I feel so ridiculous, grotesque, absurd! Eh, no, 'inde redire negant'* couldn't be more apt. There's nothing to be done for me, don't you see?"

I kept silent. I thought of Deliliers and Fadigati, one the executioner, the other the victim. The victim as usual forgave and gave his consent to the executioner. But not me: Fadigati was wrong about me. To hatred I could never respond in any other way than with hatred.

As soon as we had reached the entrance to my house, I took the keys from my pocket and opened the door. The mongrel stuck her head in through the crack as if she wanted to enter.

"Out!" I shouted. "Away with you!"

The creature whined with fear, quickly taking refuge between the legs of her protector.

"Goodnight," I said. "It's late, and I really must go."

He returned my handshake with great effusiveness.

"Goodnight . . . Keep well . . . And all best wishes to your family," he repeated several times.

I crossed the threshold. And since, smiling and holding up his arm in salutation, he still had not made his mind up to go away—and seated on the sidewalk even the dog was looking up at me with an interrogative air—I began to shut the double-door.

"Will you phone me?" I asked lightly, before completely closing it.

---

* A quote from Catullus (Carmina 3): "illud, unde negant redire quemquam" ("to the place from whence they say no one returns").

"Who knows?" he said, smiling somewhat mysteriously through the last gap. "Time will tell."*

16.

HE CALLED me up two days later, at lunchtime. We were just sitting down at the table. Since she was the only one not yet seated, it was my mother who answered. She leaned her head out from the little telephone cupboard, searching me with her eyes. "It's for you," she said.

"Who is it?"

She came toward me, shrugging her shoulders.

"A gentleman . . . I didn't catch his name."

Distracted, impractical, forever in a dream, she was never very good at managing this kind of thing, and since we had returned from the seaside, she was worse than ever.

"All you need do is ask," I replied irritably. "It's not that difficult."

I got up with a sigh of annoyance. But a secret quickening of the pulse had already warned me who it might be.

"Yes, who is it?"

"Hello, it's me, Fadigati," he said. "I'm sorry to disturb you. Were you already having your lunch?"

I was surprised by his voice. In the receiver it sounded sharper. Even his Venetian accent was more marked.

"No, no . . . sorry, could you hold on a moment?"

I opened the door again, thrust my head out as my mother had, and without saying who was on the line, nodded to my mother, with an attempt at a smile, to cover my soup bowl with a plate. Fanny was quick to forestall her. Astonished, immediately jealous, my father stared at me, lifting his chin as if to ask "what's going on?" But I had already shut myself up again in the dark little room.

"Please continue."

---

* In the context, the Italian proverb that Fadigati uses—"Chi vivrà vedrà" ("Who lives will see")—is slightly more ominous.

"Oh, it's nothing," the doctor said with a faint laugh from the other end of the line. "You asked me to call you, and so . . . but I've called at a bad time, tell the truth!"

"Not at all," I protested. "Quite the opposite—it's a pleasure to hear from you. Would you like to meet?"

I hesitated briefly, which he was sure to have noticed, and then added: "Listen, why not come round to visit us. I know my father would be really happy to see you. Do you think you might?"

"No, but thank you . . . you're very kind . . . it's so kind of you! No . . . perhaps later on, it would be a real pleasure . . . provided that . . . it would be wonderful!"

I did not know what to say. After a rather long pause, during which nothing reached me through the receiver except a heavy, heartfelt sigh, it was he who began to speak.

"Speaking of meeting, that dog followed me home, do you remember?"

For a moment I could not understand him.

"What dog?"

"You know, the dog the other night . . . the unnatural mother!" he laughed.

"Oh, that one . . . the mongrel."

"Not only did she accompany me all the way home," he continued, "but when we got to the door there, in Via Gorgadello, there was no refusing her, she absolutely had to come in. She was hungry, poor thing! From the cupboard I scraped together a scrag-end of salami, some old bread crusts, a rind of cheese . . . You should have seen the appetite with which she bolted it all down! But that's not all. After that, just imagine it, I had to take her with me into the bedroom."

"What, to bed as well?"

"Well, almost . . . we arranged ourselves with me on the bed, and her on the floor in a corner. Every now and then she woke, started whining with a tiny voice, and went to scratch at the door. "Lie down!" I shouted at her in the dark. For a while she'd be good and keep quiet, for a quarter of an hour, half an hour. But then she'd start again. A hellish night, I can tell you!"

"If she wanted to go, why didn't you let her?"

"What can I say? Laziness. It annoyed me to have to get up, take her all the way down . . . you know how it is. But as soon as it was obvious what she was after, I quickly did what she wanted. I got dressed and accompanied her outside. That's it, it was me accompanying her this time. It struck me that she might not know the way home."

"You came across her near the aqueduct, isn't that right?"

"Exactly. But listen to this. Right at the end of Via Garibaldi, at the corner of the Spianata, at a certain point I heard someone crying "Vampa!" It was a baker's-boy, a dark-haired lad on a bicycle. The dog immediately threw herself into his arms, and I'll spare you the details of all the hugs and kisses. In short, great reciprocal celebrations. Then off they went, he on his bicycle, she trotting behind."

"You see what women are like?" I joked.

"There's some truth in that!" he sighed. "She had already gone some distance, they were about to enter Via Piangipane, when she turned to look at me—can you believe it?—as if to say: 'Sorry to dump you, old man, don't be upset, but I really have to go off with this young fellow here.'"

He laughed on his own, not in the least embittered.

"You'll never guess though," he added, "why all through the night she'd wanted to go."

"Don't tell me the thought of her little ones had kept her awake."

"You've guessed right. Exactly that—the thought of her little ones! Do you want the proof? In my room, in the corner I wanted her to stay in, I later found a large puddle of milk. During the night she'd been suffering from the so-called surfeit of milk: that was why she was so restless and kept whining. The spasms she must have been suffering only she could tell, the poor thing!"

He kept on talking: of the dog, of animals in general and their feelings, which are so like those of people—he said—even if "perhaps" they're more straightforward, more directly subject to the laws of nature. As for me, by then I was feeling an intense discomfort. Worried that my father and mother, undoubtedly all ears, would have worked out whom I was talking to, I confined myself to monosyllabic replies. I was hoping, in this way, to encourage him to cut it short. But no luck. It seemed as though he was unable to detach himself from the receiver.

It was Thursday. We arranged to see each other the following Saturday.

He would phone me just after lunch. If the weather was fine, we would take the tram, go to Pontelagoscuro and see the Po. After the last rains the river must have reached close to the flood-warning level. Just imagine what it looks like!

But finally he wound up:

"Goodbye, my dear friend . . . keep well," he repeated several times, emotionally. "Good luck to you, and to your family . . ."

17.

IT RAINED all Saturday and Sunday. Perhaps also for that reason I forgot Fadigati's promise. He did not phone me, nor did I call him: but only out of forgetfulness, I would like to stress, not from any deliberate decision. It rained without a moment of truce. From my room I watched the trees in the garden through the window. The torrential rain seemed to mount a particular assault on the poplar, the two elms and the chestnut tree, from which it gradually tore the last leaves. Only the black magnolia, at the center, intact and dripping in the most exuberant manner, seemed to visibly enjoy the downpour that was battering it.

On Sunday morning I helped Fanny go over her Latin homework. She had already started again at school, but was having difficulties with the grammar. She showed me a translation from Italian that was chock-full of mistakes. She just did not understand, and it infuriated me.

"You're an idiot!"

She burst into tears. The suntan from the seaside had already vanished; the skin of her face had returned to its pallid, almost diaphanous state, so much so that the blue veins in her temples showed. Her straight hair fell gracelessly over her sobbing shoulders.

Then I hugged and kissed her.

"Won't you tell me why you're crying?"

I promised her that after lunch I would take her to the cinema.

But I left alone. I entered the foyer of the Excelsior.

"Circle?" asked the ticket-seller, who recognized me, from the height of her pulpit.

She was a shapely woman of uncertain age, with dark curly hair, and wearing a thick layer of powder and make-up. How long had she been there, lazily surveying us from under her heavy lids, a grotesque urban idol? I had always seen her there: from when my mother had sent us, as children, to the cinema with the maid. We usually went on Wednesday afternoons, as there was no school on Thursday; and every time we would go up to the circle.

The plump white hand, with its lacquered nails, proffered me the ticket. There was something very assured, almost imperious, in the gesture.

"No, could you give me a ticket for the stalls?" I replied coldly, not without having to overcome an unexpected feeling of shame. And at that very moment I had an image of Fadigati.

I showed the ticket to the usher, slipped into the stalls, and despite the crowd quickly found a seat.

A strange feeling of unease kept drawing my eyes away from the screen. Every now and then I thought I had spotted his homburg hat, his overcoat and his shining lenses in the smoke and darkness, and I waited for the intermission with increasing anxiety. Finally the lights came on. And then, in the light—having looked round everywhere, in the rows of seats where green-grey uniforms stood out most numerously, or in the side aisles, by the heavy curtains draped at the doorway, or even up there in the circle, filled to the rafters with young men returned from the match, with women of all ages in hats and furs, with army or Militia officers, with old or middle-aged men all more or less dozing off—then, in the light, I came to realize at each suspected sighting that it was not him, that he was not there. No, he was not there, I told myself, trying to feel reassured. But why on earth should he have been? In Ferrara, after all, there were three other cinemas. And had he not always preferred to watch films after dinner?

When I left, toward seven thirty, it was no longer raining. Torn into strips, the mantle of clouds allowed zones of the starry sky to be seen. A cold, tense wind had rapidly dried the pavements.

I crossed the Listone and took the Via Bersaglieri del Po. From the corner of Via Gorgadello I looked round toward the five windows of his apartment. All shut, all dark. I then tried to phone him from the public telephone booth in Via Cairoli. But nothing, silence, no reply.

I tried again a little later from home, and again from the public phone booth the next morning, Monday: always with the same result.

"He must have gone away," I told myself on this last occasion, stepping out of the booth. "When he gets back, he's bound to let me know."

I descended Via Savonarola in the sunny quietness of one o'clock in the afternoon. A few people were scattered along the sidewalks; from open windows came snatches of radio music and cooking smells. Walking, I raised my eyes every so often to the perfect blue sky against which were sharply etched the profiles of cornices and guttering. Still wet with the rain, the roofs around the small square of the church of San Girolamo seemed more brown than red, almost black.

Exactly in front of the entrance to the Maternity Hospital I bumped into Cenzo, the newsvendor.

"How is SPAL doing this year?" I asked him, stopping to buy the local Padano. "Is there a chance of making it into Serie B?"

Perhaps suspicious I was making fun of him, he gave me a sidelong glance. He folded the paper, handed it to me along with the change, and went off, shouting the headlines at the top of his voice.

"Bologna's resounding defeat at Turiiiin! SPAL ends up beaten in Carpiii!"

I inserted the key into the lock of the door to our house, and could still hear his distant voice echoing through the deserted streets.

Upstairs, I found my mother happy and excited. My brother, Ernesto, had sent a telegram from Paris, telling them that he was returning to Italy that very evening. He would be staying in Milan for half a day, but was meaning to be in Ferrara by supper time.

"And has Papa heard?" I asked, slightly vexed by her tears of joy as she kept examining the yellow sheet of the telegram.

"No. He went out at ten o'clock. He had to go to the Town Hall first, then to the bank, and the telegram arrived at about eleven thirty. How happy he'll be! Last night he could hardly sleep. He kept saying, "If only Ernesto were home as well!""

"Has anyone phoned for me?"

"No ... or, wait a moment, yes they did ..."

She screwed up her face in the effort to remember, while looking to the left and the right: as though the name of the person who had called might be written on the walls or the floor.

"Oh, yes . . . it was Nino Bottecchiari," she finally recalled.

"And no one else?"

"I don't think so. Nino made a point of asking you to phone him back . . . Why not go to see him sometime? He seems such a good friend."

We sat down at the table, just the two of us—as Fanny was out with a school friend of hers who had invited her to lunch. My mother spoke of Ernesto. She had already started worrying. Should he enroll for a course in Law or rather Medicine? In any case English, which by now he knew to perfection, would without doubt be of great use to him, in his studies, his life . . .

That day my father was later than usual. When he arrived, we had already started on the fruit.

"Great news!" he exclaimed, throwing wide the breakfast-room door.

He let his full weight fall into the chair with a satisfied "Aah!" He was tired, pale, but radiant.

He looked toward the kitchen doorway to assure himself that Elisa, the cook, was not about to enter. Then, opening his blue eyes wide in excitement, he leaned forward over the table with the evident intention of spilling the beans.

He had no success. My mother was at the ready and put the unfolded telegram beneath his nose.

"We too have some important news," she said, and smiled proudly. "What do you think of that?"

"Ah . . . it's from Ernesto," my father replied, distractedly. "When does he arrive? So he's finally made up his mind!"

"What do you mean—when does he arrive!" my mother shouted, offended. "Haven't you read it? It's tomorrow evening, isn't it?"

She grabbed the telegram from his hand. Sulking, she began to fold it up again carefully.

"It's as if it wasn't to do with your own son!" she grumbled with lowered eyes, while she replaced the telegram in her apron pocket.

My father turned to look at me. Enraged, he was calling me to his aid as a witness. But I kept silent. There was something that stopped me intervening, stopped me trying to reconcile this petty, childish quarrel.

"Come on then, let's hear," my mother finally yielded, although with the air of doing so mainly for my benefit.

18.

THE NEWS my father wanted to give us was the following.

A half-hour earlier, at the Credito Italiano bank, he had happened to meet the lawyer Geremia Tabet who, as we well knew, had not only always been "privy to the secrets" of Ferrara's Fascist Party, but also notoriously enjoyed the "friendship" and the good opinion of His Excellency Bocchini, the Chief of Police.

While they were leaving the Credito together, Tabet had taken my father by the arm. Recently he had been in Rome on business—he confided to him—which gave him the opportunity to "peep for a moment over the threshold of the Viminale."* Given the times and the circumstances, he feared that His Excellency's private secretary would not have announced him. On the contrary. The Prefect Dr. Corazza had immediately introduced him in the great hall where the "boss" was working.

"My dear fellow!" Bocchini had exclaimed, seeing him enter.

He had stood up, walked halfway across the big room to meet him, had warmly shaken his hand and made him sit down in an armchair. After which, without too much preamble, he had confronted the much-publicized question of the Racial Laws.

"Don't let this disrupt your own peace of mind, Tabet," he had said in those words, "and instil, I beg you, calmness and confidence in as many of your co-religionists as is possible. In Italy, I'm authorized to guarantee to you, legislation on racial matters will never be passed."

The newspapers, it's true, were still speaking ill of the "Israelites"— Bocchini had continued—but only for ulterior motives, only for reasons of foreign policy. That had to be understood. In these last months, Il Duce had found himself faced with the "un-a-void-ab-le" necessity of making

* The Palazzo del Viminale in Rome has housed the Italian Ministry of Home Affairs since 1925.

the Western democracies believe that Italy was now joined in two-step with Germany. What topic then would be more persuasive to this effect than a bit of anti-Semitism? We should keep calm. It would be enough for a countermand from Il Duce himself for all the useless watchdogs like Interlandi and Preziosi*—the Chief of Police held them in the most extreme contempt—to stop barking from one day to the next.

"Let's hope!" sighed my mother, her big brown eyes turned to the ceiling. "Let's hope Mussolini decides to give it soon, his countermand!"

Elisa entered with the oval plate of pastasciutta, and my father fell silent. At this moment, I slid my chair back from the table, and, standing up, moved toward the little radiogram. I switched it on. Then off. At last I went to sit in the wicker armchair near by.

Why did I not share the hopes of my parents? What was it about their enthusiasm that rubbed me the wrong way? "Good God . . ." I said to myself, clenching my teeth. "As soon as Elisa leaves the room, my father will start one of his usual speeches."

I was desperate, absolutely desperate. And certainly it was not because I thought the Chief of Police had been lying, but because my father was suddenly so happy, or rather because he seemed so anxious to be happy again. So was it this, then, that I couldn't bear?—I asked myself. I couldn't bear him being happy? That the future should smile upon him as it had once, as it had before?

I took the newspaper out of my pocket and, having given a glance at the front page, I moved directly on to the sports coverage. Despite trying with all my might to concentrate my attention on the report of the Juventus–Bologna match that had been played in Turin and ended with Bologna's "resounding defeat," just as I had heard Cenzo crying out, I kept finding my thoughts drawn elsewhere.

My father's joy—I was thinking—was that of a little schoolboy unjustly thrown out of class, who, at his master's call, returns from the empty corridor where he had had to remain a short stretch in exile, and finds himself suddenly, beyond all his hopes, permitted back into the classroom: not

---

* Telesio Interlandi and Giovanni Preziosi were two of the foremost racist and anti-Semitic ideologues of the Fascist regime.

only absolved, but declared innocent and fully rehabilitated. And yet, in the end, was it not right for my father to rejoice just like that child? As for myself, I felt no such joy. The sense of solitude that during the last two months had never left me, at that very moment became, if that were possible, even more acute: absolute and definitive. From my exile, I would never return. Never.

I lifted my head. Elisa had left, the kitchen door was again properly closed. But still my father remained silent, or almost so. Bent over his plate, he confined himself every now and then to exchanging some pointless remarks with my mother, who smiled at him with gratification. Long shafts of early-afternoon sunshine transfixed the gloom of the breakfast room. They shone through from the adjoining drawing room, which was overflowing with light. When he had finished eating, my father would retire there to sleep, stretched out on the leather sofa. I could just see him there—set apart, enclosed, protected. As though in a luminous pink cocoon. With his ingenuous face offered up to the light, as he slept wrapped in his cape . . .

I went back to my newspaper.

And there, at the bottom of the left-hand page, opposite the sports reports, my eyes fell on a middling-sized headline.

It read:

WELL-KNOWN FERRARESE PROFESSIONAL
DROWNED IN THE WATERS OF THE PO
NEAR PONTELAGOSCURO

I believe that for a moment or two my heart stopped. And yet I had not understood; it still hadn't got through to me.

I took a deep breath. And then I understood, yes, I had already understood before I began to read the little half-column beneath the headline, which did not at all speak of suicide, it should be understood, but, according to the style of the times, only of misfortune (it was not acceptable for anyone, in those days, to kill themselves: not even for the long dishonored, who had no reason whatsoever to remain on the earth . . .).

I did not finish reading it, however. I lowered my eyelids. My heart had begun again to beat regularly. I waited for Elisa, who had reappeared for a moment, to leave us alone once more, and then said in a lowered but abrupt tone:

"Dr. Fadigati is dead."

: III :

The Garden of the Finzi-Continis

Prologue

FOR many years I have wanted to write about the Finzi-Continis—about Micòl and Alberto, Professor Ermanno and Signora Olga—and about the many others who lived at, or like me frequented, the house in Corso Ercole I d'Este, Ferrara, just before the last war broke out. But the impulse, the prompt, really to do so only occurred for me a year ago, one April Sunday in 1957.

It was during one of our usual weekend outings. Ten or so friends piled into a couple of cars, and we set out along the Aurelia soon after lunch without any clear destination. A few kilometers from Santa Marinella, intrigued by the towers of a medieval castle which suddenly appeared on our left, we had turned into a narrow unpaved track, and ended up walking in single file, stretched out along the desolate sandy plain at the foot of the fortress—this last, when considered close up, was far less medieval than it had promised to be from the distance, when from the motorway we had made out its profile against the light and against the blue, blazing desert of the Tyrrhenian sea. Battered by the head-on wind, and deafened by the noise of the withdrawing tide, and without even being able to visit the castle's interior, as we had come without the written permit granted by some Roman bank or other, we felt deeply discontented and annoyed with ourselves for having wanted to leave Rome on such a day, which now on the seashore proved little less than wintry in its inclemency.

We walked up and down for some twenty minutes, following the curve of the bay. The only person of the group who seemed at all joyful was a little nine-year-old girl, daughter of the young couple in whose car I'd been driven. Electrified by the wind, the sea, the crazy swirls of sand, Giannina was giving vent to her happy expansive nature. Although her mother had tried to forbid it, she had rid herself of shoes and socks. She rushed into the waves that beat on the shore, and let them splash her legs above the knee. In short, she seemed to be having a great time—so much so that, a bit later, back in the car, I saw a shadow of pure regret pass over her vivid black eyes that shone above her tender, heated little cheeks.

Having reached the Aurelia again, after a short while we caught sight of the fork in the road that led to Cerveteri. Since it had been decided we should return immediately to Rome, I had no doubt that we would keep straight on. But instead of doing so, our car slowed down more than was required, and Giannina's father stuck his hand out of the window, signaling to the second car, about twenty-five meters behind, that he intended to turn left. He had changed his mind.

So we found ourselves taking the smooth narrow asphalted street which in no time leads to a small huddle of mainly recent houses, and from there winds on farther toward the hills of the hinterland up to the famous Etruscan necropolis. No one asked for any explanations, and I too remained silent.

Beyond the village the street, in gentle ascent, forced the car to slow down. We then passed close by the burial mounds which have been scattered across that whole stretch of Lazian territory north of Rome, but more in those parts toward the hills than toward the sea, a stretch which is, therefore, nothing but an immense, almost uninterrupted cemetery. Here the grass is greener, thicker and darker colored than that of the plain below, between the Aurelia and the Tyrrhenian sea—as proof that the eternal sirocco, which blows from across the sea, arrives up here having shed en route a great part of its salty freight, and that the damp air of the not too far-off mountains begins to exercise its beneficent influence on the vegetation.

"Where are we going?" asked Giannina.

Husband and wife were sitting in the front seat with the child in between them. Her father took his hand off the wheel and let it rest on his daughter's dark-brown curls.

"We're going to have a look at some tombs which are more than four or five thousand years old," he replied, with the tone of someone who is about to tell a fairy tale, and so doesn't mind exaggerating as far as numbers go. "The Etruscan tombs."

"How sad," Giannina sighed, leaning her neck on the back of the seat.

"Why sad? Haven't they taught you who the Etruscans were at school?"

"In the history book, the Etruscans are at the beginning, next to the Egyptians and the Jews. But, Papa, who d'you think were the oldest, the Etruscans or the Jews?"

Her father burst out laughing.

"Try asking that gentleman," he said, signaling toward me with his thumb.

Giannina turned round. With her mouth hidden behind the back of the seat, severe and full of diffidence, she cast a quick glance at me. I waited for her to repeat the question. But no word escaped her. She quickly turned round again and stared in front of her.

Descending the street, always at a slight gradient and flanked by a double row of cypresses, we came upon a group of country folk, lads and lasses. It was the Sunday *passeggiata*. With linked arms, some of the girls at times made exclusively female chains of five or six. How strange they look, I said to myself. At the moment we passed them, they peered through the windows with their laughing eyes, in which curiosity was mingled with a bizarre pride, a barely concealed disdain. How strange they looked, how beautiful and free.

"Papa," Giannina asked once again, "why are old tombs less sad than new ones?"

A yet more numerous brigade than those that had passed us earlier, which took up almost the whole thoroughfare, and sang in chorus without thinking of giving way, had almost brought the car to a halt. Her father put the car into second gear as he thought about this.

"Well," he replied, "the recent dead are closer to us, and so it makes sense that we care more about them. The Etruscans, they've been dead such a long time"—once again he lapsed into the fairy-tale voice—"it's as though they'd never lived, as though they were always dead."

Another pause, this time a longer one. At the end of which—we were already very close to the widened space in front of the necropolis's entrance packed with cars and mopeds—it was Giannina's turn to become the teacher.

"But now that you say that," she gently put it, "it makes me think the opposite, that the Etruscans really did live, and that I care about them just as much as about the others."

The whole visit to the necropolis that followed was infused by the extraordinary tenderness of this remark. It had been Giannina who had helped us understand. It was she, the youngest, who in some way led us all by the hand.

We went down into the most important tomb, the one reserved for the noble Matuta family: a low underground living room which accommodated a score of funeral beds disposed within the same number of niches carved in the tufa walls, and densely adorned with painted murals that portrayed the dear departed, everyday objects from their lives, hoes, rakes, axes, scissors, spades, knives, bows, arrows, even hunting dogs and marsh birds. And in the meantime, having willingly discarded any vestige of historical scruple, I was trying to figure out exactly what the assiduous visits to their suburban cemetery might have meant to the late Etruscans of Cerveteri, the Etruscans of the era after the Roman conquest.

Just as, still today, in small Italian provincial towns, the cemetery gate is the obligatory terminus of every evening *passeggiata*, they came from the inhabited vicinity almost always on foot—I imagined—gathered in groups of relatives and blood kindred, or just of friends, perhaps in brigades of youths similar to those we had met head-on in the street before, or else in pairs, lovers, or even alone, to wander among the conical tombs, hulking and solid as the bunkers German soldiers vainly scattered about Europe during the last war, tombs which certainly resembled, from outside as much as from within, the fortress dwellings of the living. Yes, everything was changing—they must have told themselves that as they walked along the paved way which crossed the cemetery from one end to the other, the center of which, over centuries of wear, had been gradually incised by the iron wheel-rims of their vehicles, leaving two deep parallel grooves. The world was not as it once was, when Etruria, with its confederation of free, aristocratic city-states, dominated almost the entire Italic peninsula. New civilizations, cruder and less aristocratic, but also stronger and more war-like, by this stage held the field. But in the end, what did it matter?

Once across the cemetery's threshold, where each of them owned a second home, and inside it the already prepared bed-like structure on which, soon enough, they would be laid alongside their forefathers, eternity did not perhaps appear to be such an illusion, a fable, a hieratic promise. The future could overturn the world as it pleased. There, all the same, in the narrow haven devoted to the family dead, in the heart of those tombs where, alongside the bodies, great care had also been taken to furnish many of the things that made life beautiful and desirable; in that corner of the world, so well defended, adorned, privileged, at least there (and one could still sense their idea, their madness, after twenty-five centuries, among the conical tombs covered with wild grass), there at least nothing could ever change.

When we left it was dark.

From Cerveteri to Rome is not that far; normally an hour by car would be enough. That evening, however, the journey was not so short. Halfway, the Aurelia began to be jammed with cars coming from Ladispoli and from Fregene. We had to proceed almost at a walking pace.

But once again, in the quiet and torpor (even Giannina had fallen asleep), I went over in my memory the years of my early youth, both in Ferrara and in the Jewish cemetery at the end of Via Montebello. I saw once more the large fields scattered with trees, the gravestones and trunks of columns bunched up more densely along the surrounding and dividing walls, and as if again before my eyes, the monumental tomb of the Finzi-Continis. True, it was an ugly tomb—as I'd always heard it described from my earliest childhood—but never less than imposing, and full of significance if for no other reason than the prestige of the family itself.

And my heartstrings tightened as never before at the thought that in that tomb, established, it seemed, to guarantee the perpetual repose of its first occupant—of him, and his descendants—only one, of all the Finzi-Continis I had known and loved, had actually achieved this repose.

Only Alberto had been buried there, the oldest, who died in 1942 of a lymphogranuloma, while Micòl, the daughter, born second, and their father Ermanno, and their mother Signora Olga, and Signora Regina, her ancient paralytic mother, were all deported to Germany in the autumn of 1943, and no one knows whether they have any grave at all.

I

· 1 ·

THE tomb was huge, solid and truly imposing, a kind of temple, something of a cross between the antique and the oriental, such as might be encountered in those stage-sets of Aida or Nabucco very much in vogue at our theaters only a few years back. In any other cemetery, including the neighboring municipal cemetery, a grave of such pretensions would not have provoked the slightest wonder, might even, mixed in among the rest, have gone unheeded. But in ours it stood out alone. And so, although it loomed some way from the entrance gate, at the end of an abandoned field where for more than half a century no one had been buried, it made an eye-catching show of itself.

It seems that a distinguished professor of architecture—responsible for many other eyesores in the city—had been commissioned to construct it by Moisè Finzi-Contini, Alberto and Micòl's paternal great-grandfather, who died in 1863, shortly after the annexation of the Papal States' territories to the Kingdom of Italy, and the resulting abolition of the Jewish ghettos, in Ferrara as well. A big landowner, "Reformer of Ferrarese Agriculture"—as could be read on the plaque, eternalizing his merits as "an Italian and a Jew," that the Community had had set above the third landing on the staircase of the Temple in Via Mazzini—

but clearly a man of dubious artistic taste: once he'd decided to establish a tomb *sibi et suis* he'd have let the architect do as he liked. Those were fine and flourishing years—everything seemed to favor hope, liberality and daring. Overwhelmed by the euphoria of civic equality that had been granted, the same that in his youth, at the time of the Cisalpine Republic, had made it possible for him to acquire his first thousand hectares of reclaimed land, it was easy to understand how this rigid patriarch had been induced, in such solemn circumstances, to spare no expense. It is likely that the distinguished professor of architecture was given a completely free hand. And with all that marble at his disposal—white Carrara, flesh-pink marble from Verona, black-speckled grey marble, yellow marble, blue marble, pale green marble—the man had, in his turn, obviously lost his head.

What resulted was an extraordinary mishmash into which flowed the architectonic echoes of Theodoric's mausoleum at Ravenna, of the Egyptian temples at Luxor, of Roman baroque, and even, as the thickset columns of the peristyle proclaimed, of the ancient Greek constructions of Cnossos. But there it stood. Little by little, year after year, time, which in its way always adjusts everything, had managed to make even that unlikely hotchpotch of clashing styles somehow in keeping. Moisè Finzi-Contini, here declared "the very model of the austere and tireless worker," passed away in 1863. His wife, Allegrina Camaioli, "angel of the hearth," in 1875. Then in 1877, still youthful, their only son, Menotti, Doctor of Engineering, followed more than twenty years later in 1898 by his consort Josette, from the Treviso branch of the baronial family of the Artoms. Thereafter the upkeep of the chapel, which gathered to itself in 1914 only one other family member, Guido, a six-year-old boy, had clearly fallen to those less and less inclined to tidy, maintain and repair any damage whenever that was required, and above all to fight off the persistent inroads made by the surrounding weeds that were besieging it. Tufts of swarthy, almost black grass of a near-metallic consistency, and ferns, nettles, thistles, poppies were allowed to advance and invade with ever greater licence. So much so that in 1924, in 1925, some sixty years from its founding, when as a baby I happened to see the Finzi-Continis' tomb for the first time—"a total monstrosity," as my mother, holding my hand, never failed to call it—it already looked more or less as it does today, when for many years there has been no one left directly responsible for its upkeep. Half drowned in wild green, with its many-hued marble surfaces, originally polished and shining, dulled with drifts of grey dust, the roof and outer steps cracked by baking sunlight and frosts, even then it seemed changed, as every long-submerged object is, into something rich and strange.

Who knows from what, and why, a vocation for solitude is born. The fact remains that the same isolation, the very separateness with which the Finzi-Continis surrounded their deceased, also surrounded the other house they owned, the one at the end of Corso Ercole I d'Este. Immortalized by Giosuè Carducci and Gabriele D'Annunzio, this Ferrara street is so well known to lovers of art and poetry the world over that any description of it would only be superfluous. As is well known, it is in the very heart of that northern zone of the city which the Renaissance added to the cramped medieval quarters, and which for that reason is called the *Addizione Erculea*. Broad, straight as a sword from the Castle to the Mura degli Angeli, flanked its whole length by the sepia bulk of upper-class residences, with its distant, sublime backdrop of red bricks, green vegetation and sky, which really seems to lead you on toward the infinite: Corso Ercole I d'Este is so handsome, such is its touristic renown, that the joint Socialist–Communist administration, responsible to the Ferrara Council for more than fifteen years, has recognized the obligation to leave it be, to defend it against any and every possible disruption by speculative building or commercial interests, in short to conserve the whole original aristocratic character of the place.

It is a famous street: and what is more, it remains effectively undisturbed.

All the same, with regard to the Finzi-Contini house itself, even today it has to be approached from Corso Ercole I—only, to reach it, one must go more than an extra half kilometer through a vast space which is barely cultivated or not at all—and though the house still incorporates the historic ruins of a sixteenth-century building, once a residence or pleasure palace for the Este family, acquired by that same Moisè in 1850, and later transformed, adapted and restored by his heirs into an English-style, neo-Gothic manor: despite so many interesting features that still survive, who knows anything about it, I wonder, and who even remembers it anymore? The Touring Club Guide does not mention it, and this lets any passing tourists off the hook. But even in Ferrara itself, the few Jews left that make up the dwindling Jewish community seem to have forgotten it.

Although the early twentieth-century Touring Club Guides never failed to recognize it, in a curious tone poised between the lyrical and the worldly, the current edition does not mention it, and this is certainly unfortunate. Still, to be fair: the garden or, to be more precise, the vast parkland, which before the war encircled the Finzi-Contini house and stretched for almost ten hectares up to the Mura degli Angeli on one side and the Barriera di Porta San Benedetto on the other, and representing in itself something rare and exceptional, no longer exists, literally speaking. All the broad-canopied trees, limes, elms, beeches, poplars, plane trees, horse chestnuts, pines, firs, larches, cedars of Lebanon, cypresses, oaks, holm oaks, and even the palm trees and eucalyptuses, planted in their hundreds by Josette Artom during the last two years of the First World War, were cut down for firewood, and for some time the land had returned to the state it was in when Moisè Finzi-Contini acquired it from the Marquis of Avogli: one of the many great gardens ringed within the city walls.

Which leaves the house itself. Except that the huge, singular edifice, badly damaged by a bombardment in 1944, is still today occupied by fifty or so families of evacuees, belonging to the city's wretched sub-proletariat, not unlike the plebs of the Roman slums, who continue to cluster especially in the entrance of the Palazzone of Via Mortara: an embittered, wild, aggrieved tribe (some months back, I heard, they greeted the Council's Inspector of Hygiene with a hail of stones, when he came on his bicycle to survey the place). And so as to discourage any future eviction on the part of the Overseers of the Local Monuments of Emilia and Romagna, it seems they had the bright idea of scraping the last remnants of antique murals from the walls.

So why, now, send unsuspecting tourists into such a trap?—I figure the compilers of the last Touring Club Guide must have asked themselves. And in the end what exactly would there be left to see?

· 2 ·

IF THE tomb of the Finzi-Contini family could be mocked as "a monstrosity," then their house, islanded down there among the mosquitoes and frogs of the Panfilio canal and the drainage ditches, and enviously nicknamed the *magna domus*, no—not even after fifty years was that really a fit subject for mockery. Oh, little enough was required to get all het up about it. All you needed to do, I suppose, was to find yourself walking along the interminable outer wall which separated the garden from Corso Ercole I d'Este, a wall interrupted, almost halfway, by a solemn, darkened oak gate, lacking, as it happens, any door handles; or else, from the other side, from atop the Mura degli Angeli girding the park, to gaze deep into the wild intricacy of trunks, branches and foliage, as far as a glimpse of the strange sharpened profile of the manor house, with, far behind it, the edge of a clearing, the grey stain of the tennis court—and then the ancient injury of their aloofness and seclusion would once again return to torment, to burn inside almost exactly as it had before.

What a typically nouveau-riche notion, what presumptuousness!—my father liked to repeat, with a kind of impassioned rancor, every time he felt called on to confront this question.

Yes, yes, I know—he'd admit—the former owners of the place, the family of the Marquis of Avogli, had the "bluest" blood running in their veins, the garden and the ruins flaunted *ab antiguo* the highly decorative title of Barchetto del Duca—all very well and good, I wouldn't argue with that, and all the better that Moisè Finzi-Contini, who should take the undeniable credit of having "spotted" the bargain, set himself back no more than the proverbial few coppers in clinching it. But so what?—he added immediately—just for this was it really necessary that Menotti, Moisè's son, aptly named in dialectal *matt mugnaga*, the apricot nutcase, from the color of his eccentric fur-lined overcoat, was it really necessary for him to move himself and his wife Josette to such a far-off inconvenient part of the city, unhealthy even in those days not to mention now, and on top of everything else to such a deserted, melancholy, utterly inappropriate place?

It was no great hardship for them, the parents, who belonged to a different age, and who could, after all, easily bear the luxury of spending all the coppers they cared to on those old stones. Especially not for her, Josette Artom, of the Treviso branch of the Artom barons (in her day a magnificent woman, blonde, big-breasted, blue-eyed, and in fact her mother was from Berlin, an Olschky). Besides being so crazy about the House of Savoy that in May 1898, a little before she died, she took the step of sending a congratulatory telegram to General Bava Beccaris, who fired on those poor devils, the socialists and anarchists in Milan, and besides being a fanatical admirer of Bismarck's Germany, the land of the spiked helmet, from the time her husband Menotti, forever prostrate before her, installed her in his Valhalla she'd never bothered to hide her aversion to Jewish social life in Ferrara (for her it was always too claustrophobic, as she'd say) nor to hide, which is the truth however bizarre it may sound, her fundamental anti-Semitism.

But as for Professor Ermanno and Signora Olga, all the same (he a studious man and she a Herrera of Venice, and thus born into a very good Western Sephardic family, without doubt most respectable but rather fallen in the world, and besides which highly orthodox), what kind of people did they mean to become? Real aristocrats? Certainly, one can understand that the loss of their son Guido, the first-born who died in 1914, only six years old, following a very sudden attack of infantile paralysis, American variety, against which even Corcos could do nothing, must have been a terrible blow for them—most of all for her, Signora Olga, who from then on never stopped wearing mourning. But setting that aside, wasn't it the case that, due to living in such a cut-off way, they too had started acting like grandees and had fallen into the same deluded and inflated notions of Menotti Finzi-Contini and his worthy consort? Aristocracy—tell us another! Instead of giving themselves such airs, they'd have done much better, the both of them, not to forget who they were, and where they came from, if we're to believe that the Jews—Sephardic and Ashkenazi, Western and Levantine, Tunisian, Berber, Yemenite and even Ethiopian—in whatever part of the world, under whatever skies history has scattered them, are and will always be Jews, which is to say close relatives. Old Moisè wasn't one to give himself airs, not him! He didn't have aristocratic mists befuddling his brain! When he was living in the ghetto, at no. 24, Via Vignatagliata, at the house where he'd have been quite content to end his days, withstanding the pressures brought to bear by his snooty Treviso-born mother-in-law, impatient to transfer the family with all haste to the Barchetto del Duca, it was he who went shopping every morning in Piazza delle Erbe with his shopping basket under his arm; he who brought his family up from nothing and for this very reason was nick-named in dialect *al gatt*, the cat. Because yes—if it was true that "Her Lady-ship" Josette had come down to Ferrara accompanied by a considerable dowry, which consisted of a villa in the Treviso province with frescos by Tiepolo, of a huge allowance and jewels, make that a heap of jewels, which on opening nights, against the red velvet backdrop of their private box, drew the gaze of the entire theater to her swelling décolletage, then it was no less certain that it had been *al gatt*, and he alone, who had assembled in the Fer-rara plain, between Codigoro, Massa Fiscaglia and Jolanda di Savoia, the thousands of hectares on which even today the main part of the family patri-mony depends. The monumental tomb at the cemetery—that was the only mistake, the only failing (above all of taste) of which one could accuse Moisè Finzi-Contini. That and nothing else.

This was how my father would go on—particularly at Passover, during the lengthy dinners that continued to be given at our house even after the death of grandpa Raffaello, attended by a score of friends and relatives, but also at Yom Kippur, when those same friends and relatives came back round to our house to end their fast.

But I remember one Passover supper during which my father added something new and surprising to his usual grumblings—bitter, generic, always the same, made above all for the pleasure of recollecting the time-worn tales of the Jewish community.

It was in 1933, the year of the so-called *infornata del Decennale.*[*] Thanks to the "clemency" of Il Duce, who had suddenly had the inspired idea of opening his forgiving arms wide to every "agnostic or enemy of yester-day," even in the circles of our Community the number of those enrolled within the Fascist Party had managed to rise at a stroke to ninety percent. And my father, who sat down there, at his usual place at the head of the

---

[*] Tenth anniversary of the Fascist Party's assumption of power. This 1933 decree opened up the Fascist Party to public membership, and many Ferrarese Jews joined it at this time.

table, the same place from which for long decades grandpa Raffaello had been wont to hold forth with a completely different authority and severity, had not failed to congratulate himself on this turn of events. The rabbi Dr. Levi had done very well to refer to it in the speech he recently gave at the Italian School synagogue when, in the presence of the major civic dignitaries—the Prefect, the Fascist Party's Federal Secretary, the *Podestà** the Brigadier-General of the local garrison—he had commemorated the Albertine Statute!

Yet he wasn't entirely happy, Papa. In his boyish blue eyes, full of patriotic ardor, I could detect a shadow of disappointment. He must have perceived a small hitch, a little unforeseen and displeasing hindrance.

And in fact, having begun at a certain point to count on his fingers how many of us, of us Ferrarese *Judim*, still remained "outside," and having at last arrived at Ermanno Finzi-Contini—who had never taken up Party membership, that's true, but considering the very sizeable agricultural estates he'd inherited it was hard to figure out why he hadn't—all of a sudden, as though fed up with himself and his own discretion, my father decided to disclose two curious bits of news: between them there was perhaps no direct relationship—he began by saying—but they were no less significant for that.

First: that the lawyer Geremia Tabet, when, in his role as Sansepolcrista[†] and intimate friend of the Federal Secretary, he presented himself at the Barchetto del Duca to offer the Professor a membership card with his name already on it, it was not only returned to him, but, shortly after, of course most politely but equally firmly, he was shown the door.

"And with what excuse?" someone asked faintly. "No one ever dreamed that Ermanno Finzi-Contini was such a lion."

"With what excuse did he refuse it?" my father burst out laughing. "Oh, with one of the usual ones: that he was a scholar (I'd love to know of what!), that he was too old, that he'd never in his life been involved with politics, etc., etc. But the good fellow was canny about it. He must have noticed that Tabet had gone black in the face, and so, just like that, he slipped into his pocket five thousand in notes."

---

* Municipal chief of justice and police during the Fascist era.
† One of those who were Fascists before the 1922 March on Rome.

"Five thousand lire?"

"Absolutely. To be spent on the Seaside and Mountain Summer Camps for the Opera Nazionale Ballila.* He'd thought it through perfectly, no? But listen now to the second piece of news."

He then went on to inform the whole table exactly how, a few days earlier, with a letter he'd sent to the Community's Council by way of the lawyer Renzo Galassi-Tarabini (in the whole world could he have found anyone more groveling, ass-licking and bigoted than that?) the Professor had officially asked permission to restore at his own expense, "for the use of his family and anyone else who should be interested," the small, old Spanish synagogue in Via Mazzini, which for at least three centuries had had no religious function and now served as a storeroom.

· 3 ·

IN 1914, when little Guido died, Professor Ermanno was forty-nine years old, and Signora Olga twenty-four. The child felt ill, was put to bed with a very high fever, and quickly fell into a profound torpor.

Dr. Corcos was called out urgently. After a silent, interminable examination conducted with furrowed brow, Corcos brusquely lifted his head and solemnly stared first at the father then at the mother. The looks that he gave them were long, severe, and strangely disdainful. At the same time, beneath his thick, Umberto-style, down-curved mustache, already completely grey, his lips shaped themselves into a bitter, almost vituperative grimace, for use in desperate cases.

"There's nothing to be done," the doctor meant by those looks and that grimace. But also perhaps something else. And this was that he also, ten years earlier (and maybe he spoke of it that same day before taking his leave or only did so five days later, as without doubt happened, turning to grandpa Raffaello, as the two of them slowly walked together at the imposing funeral), he also had lost a young boy, his Reuben.

---

* Fascist youth organization.

"I've been through this torture myself, I too know what it means to watch a five-year-old child die," Elia Corcos suddenly declared.

With lowered head and hands resting on his bicycle handlebars, grandpa Raffaello walked alongside him. He seemed to be counting one by one the cobblestones of Corso Ercole I d'Este. At those truly unexpected words coming from the lips of his skeptical friend, he turned round, astonished, to look at him.

But what did Elia Corcos himself really know? He had given the child's motionless body a lengthy examination, reached his own baleful prognosis, and then, lifting his eyes had fixed them on the petrified ones of the two parents: the father an old man, the mother still just a girl. Down what roads would he have to journey to read those hearts of theirs? And who else would ever do so in the future? The epitaph dedicated to the little dead child in the tomb-monument at the Jewish cemetery (seven lines blandly enough carved and inked in on a humble upright rectangle of white marble) would say nothing but:

HERE LIES

GUIDO FINZI-CONTINI

(1908–1914)

CHOICE SPIRIT AND FORM

YOUR PARENTS WERE READY

TO LOVE YOU EVER MORE

NOT TO GRIEVE FOR YOU SO SOON

Ever more. A suppressed sob, that was all. A weight on the heart to be shared with no other person in the world.

Alberto was born in 1915, Micòl in 1916: more or less my contemporaries. They were neither sent to the Jewish elementary school of Via Vignatagliata, which Guido had attended without completing the first grade, nor later to the *liceo ginnasio** G. B. Guarini, crucible for the city's finest and most precocious, Jewish and not, and therefore a choice that

---

* A type of middle school in Italy that pupils attended from the ages of fourteen to sixteen.

was at least pragmatic. Instead, both Alberto and Micòl were educated privately; Professor Ermanno every now and then breaking off his own solitary studies of agriculture, physics and the history of Italy's Jewish community in order to supervise their progress himself. These were the mad, but in their way generous, early years of Emilian Fascism. Each and every action, everyone's behavior, had to be judged—even by those who, like my father, willingly quoted Horace and his *aurea mediocritas*—by the crude markers of patriotism or defeatism. To send one's children to the state schools was in general considered patriotic, not to send them, defeatist, and therefore to all those who did send their kids there, in some way offensive.

Notwithstanding this, although utterly cut off, Alberto and Micòl Finzi-Contini had always kept up a tenuous rapport with the outside world, with children like us who went to the "public" schools.

There were two teachers from the Guarini who acted as go-betweens.

Professor Meldolesi, for example, who in the fourth year taught us Italian, Latin, Greek, history and geography, on alternate afternoons would take his bicycle and, from the suburb of little villas that had sprung up in those years beyond Porta San Benedetto, about whose views and prospects he would frequently boast to us, and where he lived alone in a furnished room, would ride it as far as the Barchetto del Duca, to remain there sometimes for as long as three hours. And Signora Fabiani, the math teacher, would do likewise.

From Fabiani, to tell the truth, we never got to know anything. Of Bolognese origins, a childless widow in her fifties, with a churchy air, she always seemed rapt to the point of ecstasy whenever she questioned us. She would continuously roll her light-blue, Flemish eyes and whisper to herself. She was praying. Praying, no doubt, for us poor things, almost all of us utterly incompetent at algebra, but also perhaps to expedite the conversion to Catholicism of those genteel Israelites to whose house she repaired twice every week. The conversion of Professor Ermanno and of Signora Olga, but above all of the two children, Alberto, so very clever, and Micòl, so vivacious and pretty, must have seemed to her an event too significant, too urgent, for the probability of its success to be jeopardized by some silly lapse of discretion at school.

Professor Meldolesi, by contrast, was not in the least discreet. He was born at Comacchio of a farming family, and for his whole school career educated in a seminary (he had very much the typical characteristics of a priest, of a small, sharp-eyed, almost feminine country priest). He then went to study Arts at Bologna in time to be present at the final lectures of Giosuè Carducci, of whom he boasted to be the "humble scholar." The afternoons spent at the Barchetto del Duca, in an atmosphere saturated with the Renaissance, with tea served at five among the whole gathered family—and Signora Olga would very often return from the park at that hour, her arms weighed down with flowers—not to mention later, perhaps, upstairs in the library, sometimes after darkness had fallen, enjoying the erudite conversation of Professor Ermanno, those extraordinary afternoons evidently represented for him something too precious to deprive himself of the chance to turn them into a series of little speeches and digressions for our benefit.

From the evening in which Professor Ermanno had revealed to him how Carducci, in 1875, had been the guest of his parents for some ten days, then had shown him the room he had occupied, let him touch the bed he had slept in, and gone as far as to give him, to take home, so that he could scrutinize it at his leisure, a "sheaf" of letters in his own hand sent to the Professor's mother by the poet, his agitation, his enthusiasm knew no limits. He went so far as to convince himself, and to try to convince us, that that famous verse from the *Canzone di Legnano*:

O bionda, o bella imperatrice, o fida[*]

which clearly prefigures the still more famous lines:

Onde venisti? Quali a noi secoli
sì mite e bella ti tramandarono ...[†]

---

[*] O blonde, O beautiful empress, O trusted one.
[†] Where have you come from? Which past centuries / Have bestowed you on us, you so mild and beautiful ...

and at the same time, the great Maremman poet's clamorous conversion to the Savoyard "eternal, regal feminine," were inspired precisely by the paternal grandmother of his two private pupils, Alberto and Micòl Finzi-Contini. Oh, what a magnificent topic this would have been— Professor Meldolesi had once sighed in class—for an article to send to that same *Nuova Antologia* where Alfredo Grilli, his friend and colleague Grilli, had for some time been publishing his subtle glosses on Serra! Sooner or later, employing, it hardly needs to be said, all the tact such a situation demanded, he might even signal this possibility to the owner of the letters. And, heaven permitting, given the years that had passed since, and given the importance and, it goes without saying, the perfect decorousness of a correspondence in which Carducci addressed the lady only as "adorable Baroness," or "most genteel host," and suchlike, one could only hope that this latter gentleman would not withhold his permission. In the happy prospect of a yes, he, Guido Meldolesi, would take care of the whole thing and, should he be given an explicit agreement by the one who had every right to bestow or withhold it, he would copy the letters out, one by one, accompanying those blessed shards, those venerated sparks of the great wordsmith with a minimal commentary. And what did it need, in fact, the text of this correspondence? Little else but a general introduction, glossed if at all with some sober historical and philological footnotes...

Apart from the teachers we had in common, there were also the exams held for private students—exams that took place in June at the same time as the other exams, those of the state schools—which brought us at least once a year into direct contact with Alberto and Micòl.

For us at school, especially if by passing we would be going up a year, these were perhaps the most enjoyable days. As though suddenly regretting the lessons and homework we'd just been rid of, we seemed unable to find a better place to meet up in than the school vestibule. We would hang about this vast entrance hall, cool and twilit as a crypt, crowding around the great white sheets which recorded our final results, fascinated by our own names and those of our companions, and to read them like that, transcribed in lovely calligraphy and exposed behind glass on the other side of a fine metalwork grating, induced in us a state of wonder. It was great to have nothing more to dread from school, great to be able to go out soon after into the bright blue light of ten in the morning that lured us through the entry postern, great to have in front of us long hours of laziness and liberty to spend however we pleased. Everything was utterly delight-ful, those first days of the holidays. And what happiness at the constant thought of our imminent departure for the sea or the mountains, where all notion of study, which still hung over and harassed others, would for us be all but wiped away!

And so it was, among these others (mainly big rough country lads, sons of peasants, prepared for the exams by local village priests, who, before crossing the threshold of the Guarini would look around bewildered like calves being led to the slaughterhouse), there would be Alberto and Micòl Finzi-Contini: not in the least bewildered, accustomed for years, as they were, to presenting themselves and acquitting themselves triumphantly. Perhaps they were a shade ironic, particularly toward me, when, crossing the entrance hall, they discerned me among my school friends and greeted me with a wave and a smile. But always polite, perhaps fractionally too polite, and good-natured. Exactly like guests.

They would never come on foot, much less by bicycle, but in a carriage, a dark-blue brougham that had huge wheels with tyres, red axles, and was all shiny with varnish, glass and nickel-plating.

The carriage would wait in front of the big entrance gate of the Guarini for hours and hours, only moving to seek out shade. Moreover, it should be said that to look closely at all the details of the equipage, from the big pow-erful horse, with its clipped tail and cropped and combed mane, which every now and then gave a majestic back-heel, to the miniature coat of arms that stood out in silver against the blue field of the doors, even at times to be given permission by the indulgent coachman in his informal livery, yet perched on the box seat as on a throne, to climb up onto one of the steps of the footboard, and thus to contemplate at our leisure, our noses pressed against the glass, the entirely grey interior, sumptuously padded and in semi-darkness (it seemed like a drawing room: in one corner there were even some flowers threaded into a thin-necked oblong vase shaped like a calyx . . .), this too could be a real pleasure, and indeed it was: one of the many adventurous pleasures which abounded in those marvelous late spring mornings of our adolescence.

· 4 ·

SO FAR as I was personally concerned, in my relationship with Alberto and Micòl there was always something more intimate. The knowing looks, the confidential nods that brother and sister both directed toward me whenever we met in the grounds of the Guarini, were signs, I fully realized, of just this private understanding between us.

Something more intimate. But what exactly?

Certainly, to start off with, we were Jews, and this on its own would be more than enough. Nothing at all need ever have actually transpired between us, not even what little came from having exchanged the odd word. But because we were who we were, at least twice a year, at Passover and Yom Kippur, we came with our respective parents and close relatives to a particular doorway in Via Mazzini—and it often happened that having crossed its threshold together, the hallway we entered next, severe and dimly lit, would unleash a rite of hat-lifting, hand-shaking, obsequious bowing among grown-ups who, for the rest of the year, had no other occasions to practice such things; to us children this alone would be enough for us, meeting elsewhere, and above all in the presence of the uninitiated, to prompt the shadowy look or the smile of special complicity or connivance.

That we were all Jewish, however, and enrolled in the registers of the same Jewish community, in our case counted for little. What, after all, did that word "Jewish" mean? What sense could expressions such as "The Jewish community" or "The Jewish Faith" possibly have, for us, seeing that they entirely left aside the existence of a far greater intimacy, a secret one, to be valued only by those who shared it, which derived from the fact that our two families, not by choice, but by virtue of a tradition more ancient than any possible memory, belonged to the same religious observance, or more accurately to the same "School"? When we met each other at the Temple's entrance, generally at dusk, after the proper, dutiful exchange of civilities in the dim entrance hall it was almost always as a group that we climbed the steep stairs which led to the second floor. Commodious, crowded with all kinds of people, reverberant as a church with organ notes and singing—and so high, up among the rooftops, that some May evenings, with its great windows flung open west toward the setting sun, we would find ourselves at a certain point basking in a kind of golden mist . . .—that was the Italian synagogue. So Jews certainly, but Jews who had grown up observing the same particular rite, we alone could truly realize what it meant to have your own family bench in the Italian synagogue, up there on the second floor, rather than down on the first floor, in the German one, so severe and contrasting in its almost Lutheran gathering of prosperous, burgherly Homburg hats. Nor was that the whole story: since it might well be understood even outside Jewish society that an Italian synagogue is distinct from a German one, with all the social and psychological details such a distinction implies, who else could begin to precisely delineate—to give just one example—"the Via Vittoria bunch"? This phrase usually referred to the members of four or five families who had the right to attend the small, separate Levantine synagogue, also known as the "Fanese," situated on the third floor of an old Via Vittoria house, and so to the family Da Fano of Via Scienze, to the Cohens of Via Gioco del Pallone, to the Levis of Piazza Ariostea, to the Levi-Minzis of Viale Cavour, and to who knows which other isolated family group: all of them anyway people who were slightly odd, types always a shade ambiguous and evasive, whose religion, which in the Italian School had taken a more working-class and theatrical, almost Catholic turn, that was clearly reflected even in the character of the people themselves, largely extrovert and optimistic, typical of the Po valley, had in their case remained essentially a cult to be practiced by the few, in semi-secret oratories at which it was opportune to arrive by night, in small numbers, slinking down the darkest and least known alleys of the Ghetto. No, no, it was only we, born and brought up *intra muros*, only we who could know and fully understand these things—things that were so elusive and irrelevant, but not for that any less real. As for the others, all the others, and first among them my much-loved daily companions from both school and play, it was futile to think they might be instructed in such an occult zone of knowledge. Poor things! On this subject, they could only be considered crude simpletons, irretrievably condemned to live out their whole lives in the deepest pits of ignorance, or to being, as even my father would say, benignly grinning, *negri goìm.*[*]

So, on these occasions we climbed the stairs together, and together we made our entrance into the synagogue.

And since our benches were close by, down there at the bottom of the semicircular enclosure entirely bounded by a marbled balustrade at the center of which loomed the *tevah*, or lectern, the rabbi would read from, and both of them in plain view of the monumental cupboard of carved black wood which guarded the scrolls of the Law, the so-called *sefarim*, together we would cross the great hall's sonorous floor paved with white-and-pink lozenges. Mothers, wives, grandmothers, aunts, sisters, etc. had separated from us men in the vestibule. They disappeared in single file inside a little opening in the wall that gave onto a small dark room, whence, with the help of a spiral staircase, they climbed even higher into the women's gallery, and in a short while we could see them again peeping down from between the openings of their hen-coop's grille, right up under the ceiling. But even like this, dwindled in our company to only males—which meant myself, my brother Ernesto, my father, Professor Ermanno, Alberto, and occasionally Signora Olga's two bachelor brothers, the engineer and Dr. Herrera, down from Venice for the occasion—even like this we made a large enough group. And an imposing one at that. So much so that whenever we arrived during the ceremony we would awaken the most intense curiosity before we'd got halfway across the floor.

As I said, our benches were neighboring, one behind the other. We had the foremost one, in the first row, and the Finzi-Continis sat immediately behind us. Even if we'd wanted to, it would have been hard to ignore each other.

Attracted by the difference between us, as much as my father was repelled by it, I was always on the alert for the slightest gesture or whisper coming from the bench behind. My vigilance was unfaltering. I picked up the chatty asides of Alberto, who, although he was two years older than me, had still to enter the *Minyan*,[†] and who nevertheless hurried, as soon

---

[*] Ferrarese dialect: literally, "black (or benighted) Gentiles."
[†] Congregation of a minimum of ten adult males.

as he arrived, to wrap himself in the large black-striped and white wool *tallit** which once belonged to "grandpa Moisè"; but I was equally attentive to Professor Ermanno, affectionately smiling at me through his thick lenses, who would beckon to me with a sign of his finger to look at the copper etchings that illustrated an old Bible he had brought out especially for me from the small drawer. Likewise I would listen open-mouthed to Signora Olga's brothers, the railway engineer and the phthisiologist, chirruping away to each other half in Venetian dialect, half in Spanish ("*Cossa xé che stas meldando? Su, Giulio, alevantete, ajde! E procura de far star in píe anca il chico . . .*"†), and then they'd suddenly stop, to intone together in an extraordinarily high-pitched voice the Hebrew replies to the rabbi's litany. My head was nearly always turned to one side or the other. In a line on their bench, the two Finzi-Continis and the two Herreras were there, little more than a meter away, and yet remote, unreachable, as though all round them was a protective wall of glass. There was little resemblance between the two pairs. Tall, thin, bald, their long pale faces shadowed with beards, always dressed in blue or black, and besides habitually imparting to their devotions an intensity, a fanatical ardor of which their brother-in-law and nephew, one could tell at a glance, would never be capable, the Venetian relatives seemed to belong to a world that was utterly removed from Alberto, with his tobacco-colored jersey and long socks, and from Professor Ermanno's English knitwear and ochre linen, his air of a scholar and a country gentleman. All the same, however different they were, I sensed a deep kinship between them. What did they have in common, all four of them seemed to say, with the distracted, whispering, *Italian* congregation, who even in the Temple, before the wide-open doors of the Ark of the Lord, remained trapped in all the pettiness of their daily lives, of business, politics, even sports, but never concerned with the soul and with God. I was a small boy then, between ten and twelve years old. A confused impression, admittedly, but still essentially true, joined in me with a feeling of scorn and humiliation, equally confused but which stung nevertheless, that I

---

* Prayer shawl; plural, tallitot.

† Mixture of Spanish and Venetian dialect: "What are you up to? Come on, Giulio, get up, will you! And make the boy stand up as well . . ."

belonged with the others, the congregation, the rabble to be kept at bay. And my father? Facing the glass wall behind which the Finzi-Continis and the Herreras, always courteous but distant, effectively kept on ignoring him, his behavior was the opposite of mine. Instead of trying to approach them, I saw him (medical graduate and free-thinker, army volunteer, since 1919 card-holder of the Fascist Party, and sports enthusiast, in short the modern Jew) deliberately exaggerate his own healthy intolerance of any fawning or saccharine profession of faith.

When the serene procession of the *sefarim* began to pass along the aisle (wrapped in rich copes of embroidered silk, their silver crown askew and sporting little tinkling bells, the sacred scrolls of the Torah seemed like a display of royal infants exhibited to the people so as to prop up a tottering monarchy) the doctor and the engineer Herrera were ready to duck forward from their bench, kissing whatever corner of the cope came within reach, eagerly, with an almost indecent greed. What did it matter that Professor Ermanno, copied by his son, confined himself to covering his eyes with a border of the *tallit*, and to whispering a prayer, barely moving his lips?

"What a mawkish fuss, what *haltud!*"* my father would comment later, with disgust, at the dinner table, without this in the least impeding him, immediately afterward, from once again returning to the theme of the Finzi-Continis' hereditary pride, the absurd isolation in which they lived, or even to pronounce on their aristocratic, subterranean, persistent anti-Semitism. But at that moment, without having anyone else to hand on whom he could vent his spleen, he took it out on me.

As usual, I had turned round to stare.

"Would you kindly keep still for just one moment?" he hissed between his clenched teeth, exasperated and fixing me with his blue, choleric eyes. "You don't know how to behave properly even in the Temple. Just look at your brother—he's four years younger than you, and could teach you manners!"

But I took no notice. Soon after, I would be doing the same thing again, turning my back on the psalm-chanting Dr. Levi, oblivious of the warning.

---

* Ferrara Jewish dialect: "bigotry."

Now, if he wanted to regain control of me—physically, I mean, only physically—all my father could do was wait for the solemn blessing, when all the sons were gathered under the paternal *tallitot* in a series of tents. And then, finally (the synagogue verger Carpanetti had already begun his rounds with his long taper lighting one by one the thirty silver and gilded bronze candelabras—the whole room ablaze with lights), as we awaited in awe, Dr. Levi's voice, usually so colorless, suddenly assumed the prophetic tone in keeping with the consummate, final moment of the *berachah*.*

"*Jevareheha Adonai veishmereha . . .* "† slowly began the rabbi, bent down almost prostrate over the *tevah*, after having once more covered his towering white biretta with the *tallit*.

"Come on then, boys," my father would say, brisk and joyful, snapping his fingers, "Come on in under here!"

True, even at that moment, escape was still a possibility. Papa had his work cut out, for all his strong grip—his hard sportsman's hands on the scruff of our necks, of mine in particular. Although vast as a tablecloth, grandpa Raffaello's *tallit*, which we used, was altogether too worn smooth and full of holes to guarantee the kind of hermetic seal my father would have liked. And so, through the holes and tears which the years had wreaked on the fabric, frail as could be and pungent with must and antiquity, it was not difficult, at least for me, while there beside him, to observe Professor Ermanno, his hand resting on Alberto's brown hair and the fine light-blond hair of Micòl, who had just rushed down from the women's gallery, as he pronounced, one by one, following behind Dr. Levi, the words of the *berachah*. Above our heads, our father, who knew no more than twenty words in Hebrew, the usual ones of family conversation— and besides he would never have bowed down—kept silent. I could guess the suddenly embarrassed expression on his face, his eyes, half sardonic, half intimidated, raised toward the ceiling's modest stucco work or the women's gallery. But meanwhile, from where I was, I could peer up with ever replenished awe and envy, at the lined and sharp visage of Professor

---

* Hebrew: "blessing."
† Hebrew: "God bless and keep you . . ."

Ermanno, who at that moment seemed transfigured. I watched his eyes, which I could have sworn were full of tears behind his glasses. His voice was thin and sing-song, but utterly tuneless, his Hebrew pronunciation, often doubling up the consonants, and with the "z"s, "s"s and "h"s far more Tuscan than Ferrarese, seemed to have been filtered through the dual distinction of culture and class.

I watched him. For the entire duration of the blessing, Alberto and Micòl—they too—never stopped exploring among the breaches in their tent. And they smiled and winked at me, both of them strangely inviting, especially Micòl.

· 5 ·

ONCE, HOWEVER, in June 1929, the very day on which the marks for the yearly exams were posted up on the Guarini vestibule noticeboards, something special, something far more direct, took place.

In the oral exams I hadn't done that well.

Despite the fact that Professor Meldolesi had bent over backward to help me, going so far as to ensure, against all the rules, that it was he who would examine me, I hardly ever reached the heights of the many sevens and eights which adorned my school report in the literary subjects. Questioned in Latin on the *consecutio temporum*, I made a whole series of gaffes. In Greek, too, I had answered with some difficulty, particularly when a page of the Teubner edition of the *Anabasis* was put under my nose and I was asked to translate a few unprepared lines. Later I redeemed myself a bit. In Italian, for example, besides having been able to give a résumé, with some nonchalance, of the contents of both *I promessi sposi* and *Le ricordanze*, I had recited by heart the first three octaves of *Orlando furioso* without once tripping up. And Meldolesi, at the ready, rewarded me at the end with a "Bravo!" loud enough to cause the whole examining board, even myself, to smile. Overall, though, I repeat, my performance, even in the Arts, fell way short of the reputation I enjoyed.

But the real fiasco was in math. Since the year before, I just couldn't get any grip on algebra. And worse still, having banked on Meldolesi's unfailing support for the final grades, I had always treated Professor Fabiani rather shoddily: I studied the minimum to scrape a six, and often enough not even to that minimum level. Of what earthly use could math be for someone who'd be applying to study literature?—I continually told myself, even on that morning, as I cycled up Corso Giovecca toward the Guarini. Alas, for the orals in algebra, as in geometry, I'd hardly bothered to open my mouth. Which meant . . . ? Poor Signora Fabiani, who during the last two years had never dared give me less than a six, and in the examiners' meeting she surely wouldn't have dared to . . . here I avoided even mentally pronouncing the word "fail," so much did the idea of failing, with all its consequences of crushingly tedious private lessons to which I'd have to subject myself all summer long in Riccione, so much did it seem an alien and absurd concept when referred to myself. To me, of all people, who had never suffered the humiliation of being forced to retake the exams in October, and who had even been awarded in the first, second and third years of middle school the position of "Guard of Honor to the Monument of the Fallen and at the Parks of Remembrance" "for hard work and good conduct"—me, failed, reduced to mediocrity, forcibly demoted to the most anonymous masses! And as for my father? Just supposing Signora Fabiani had forced me to re-sit the exams in October (she taught math at the *liceo* too, for which reason she had examined me herself, it being her right!), where would I muster the courage, going from there in a few hours, to return home, sit down in front of my father and start eating dinner? Perhaps he would smack me. That, all considered, would have been the best solution. Any punishment at all would have been preferable to that look of reproach which would have frozen me to the spot from his mute, terrible, clear blue eyes . . .

I entered the Guarini's main hall. A group of boys, among whom I immediately recognized several friends, were quietly milling round the intermediate years' noticeboard. Having leaned my bike against the main entrance's wall, I approached with trepidation. No one had noticed my arrival.

I looked from behind a fence of shoulders stubbornly turned toward me. My sight misted over. I looked again: and the red five, the only number in red ink in a long row of black numerals, seared itself on my soul with the violence of a branding iron.

"So what's the big deal?" Sergio Pavani asked, giving me a gentle thump on the back. "It's not worth making a tragedy out of a five in math! Have a look at mine"—he laughed—"Latin and Greek."

"Don't take it so badly," Otello Forti added. "I have to resit one as well—English." I stared at him, utterly stunned. We had been classmates and had shared a desk from elementary school, and had been used to studying together from that time on, one day at his house, one day at mine, and both of us were convinced of my superiority. Never would a year pass without my going up a year in June, while he, Otello, always had to redo some subject or other.

And now, suddenly, to find myself compared to an Otello Forti, and to make it worse, compared by him! To find myself cast down to his level!

What I did or thought in the four or five hours that followed, starting, as soon as I left the Guarini, with the effect wrought upon me by meeting Professor Meldolesi (hatless and tieless, with striped shirt collar turned out over his jacket lapels, he smiled, the good fellow, and was quick to confirm for me Fabiani's "unbudgingness" toward me, her categoric refusal to "close her eyes yet one more time")—followed by a description of the long, desperate, aimless wanderings to which I abandoned myself, having received a gentle cuff on the cheek in the name of friendship and encouragement from the same Meldolesi, is not worth recounting. It's enough to say that around two o'clock in the afternoon, I was still cycling around along the Mura degli Angeli, in the vicinity of Corso Ercole I d'Este. I hadn't even telephoned home. With my face streaked with tears, my heart overflowing with enormous self-pity, I pedaled away almost unaware of where I was, and entertained vague thoughts of suicide.

I stopped beneath a tree—one of those old trees, lindens, elms, plane trees, or horse chestnuts, which, a dozen years later, in the frozen winter of Stalingrad, would be sacrificed for firewood, but which in 1929 still raised their great umbrellas of greenery high above the city walls.

All around, a complete desert. The little beaten-earth track that like a sleepwalker I'd taken there from Porta San Giovanni snaked on between the century-old trunks toward Porta San Benedetto and the railway station. I stretched out beside my bicycle, face down in the grass, with my burning face hidden in my arms. The warm air wafted round my extended body: my only desire was to remain like that as long as could be, with my eyes closed. Against the narcotic background choir of the cicadas, the odd isolated sound stood out sharply: a cock crowing, the noise of beaten cloth most likely made by a woman out late washing clothes in the khaki waters of the Panfilio canal, and finally, very close, only inches from my ear, the ever-slowing ticking of the bike's back wheel, still in search of stasis.

I was thinking that, at home, by this time, they would surely have known—thanks perhaps to Otello Forti. Were they sitting around the table? Probably; even if, soon enough, they would have finished eating. Perhaps they were looking for me. Perhaps they had already collared that very Otello, the good, the inseparable friend, and given him the task of scouring the whole city on his bicycle, plus Montagnone and its walls as well, so it was not in the least improbable that, out of the blue, I'd find him in front of me, his face schooled to sadness by the circumstances, but in truth happy as a lark—I'd be able to see at a glance—that he didn't have to re-sit anything but English. No, perhaps, overcome by anxiety, at a certain point, my parents would have had recourse to the police station. My father would have gone in person to speak to the police chief in the Castle. I could almost see him: stammering, having grown suddenly, frighteningly old, a mere shadow of his former self. He was weeping. Ah, but if only, around one o'clock, at Pontelagoscuro, he could have seen me as I stared at the Po's currents from the height of the iron bridge (I stayed there a good while looking down. How long? At the very least twenty minutes!), yes, then he'd definitely have been scared and yes, then at last he'd have understood, yes, then he . . .

"Psst!"

I woke up with a start.

"Psst!"

I slowly raised my head, turning it left toward the sun. I blinked. Who was calling me? It couldn't be Otello. Who was it then?

I was about halfway along that stretch of the city walls, which in its entirety extended for three kilometers, starting from the end of Corso Ercole I d'Este and finishing at Porto San Benedetto in front of the station. It had always been a particularly lonely place. So it was, thirty years ago, and it still is today, despite the fact that to the right especially, facing the industrial zone, from 1945 on, scores of variously colored workers' cottages have sprouted, in comparison with which, and with the factory chimneys and warehouses that compose their background, the brown, scrubby, half-rocky spur of fifteenth-century fortifications looks day by day ever more absurd.

I looked and looked, half closing my eyes against the glare. At my feet—only then did I notice—the crowns of its noble trees swollen with midday light like those of a tropical forest, stretched out the domain of the Barchetto del Duca: immense, truly heart-stopping with the little towers and pinnacles of the *magna domus* at its center, half-hidden in green, and its whole perimeter bounded by a wall which was interrupted a quarter of a kilometer farther on to allow for the flow of the Panfilio canal.

"Hey! But you must be blind as well!" came the happy voice of a girl.

Because of those blonde tresses, the distinctive yellow streaked with Nordic flax in the style of the *fille aux cheveux de lin*, which could only have belonged to her, I instantly recognized Micòl Finzi-Contini. She peered over the wall as if over a window sill, leaning over with her shoulders forward and her crossed arms flat. She could not have been more than twenty-five meters away (near enough then for me to see her eyes, which were large and clear, perhaps too large at that time for the little, thin, child's face) and she was looking at me up from under.

"What are you doing up there? I've been here watching you for ten minutes. I'm sorry if you were sleeping and I woke you. And . . . my condolences!"

"Condolences? Whatever for?" I stammered, feeling my face go red all over. I had got up in the meantime.

"What time is it?" I asked, raising my voice.

"I make it three," she said, with an appealing twist of her mouth. And then: "I suppose you'll be hungry."

I was dumbfounded. So even they knew! For a moment I even believed the news of my disappearance had been broadcast to them on the phone by my father or mother, to them and to an endless host of people. But it was Micòl who promptly put me right.

"This morning I went into the Guarini with Alberto to see the results. So are you very upset?"

"And you? Did you get put up a year?"

"We still don't know. Perhaps they're waiting for all the other private students to finish before posting the marks. But why not come down? At least come a bit closer so I don't have to get hoarse shouting."

It was the first time she had spoken to me, the first time I had ever heard her speak. And I immediately noticed how similar her pronunciation was to Alberto's. They both spoke in the same way: stressing the syllables of certain words of which only they seemed to know the true sense, the real weight, but then sliding bizarrely over other syllables which one might have thought had more importance. They made a point of expressing themselves this way. They even gave it a name: Finzi-Continish.

Letting myself slip down the grassy slope, I drew near to the base of the wall. Although there was shade—a shade that reeked of dung and nettles—down there it was warmer. And now she looked at me from up above, her blonde head in the sun, relaxed as though our meeting had not been in the least a casual, utterly fortuitous one, but as though from early infancy we had met in that exact spot on innumerable occasions.

"But you're making such a big fuss about it all," she said. "Why's it so bad to have to do another subject in October?"

She was making fun of me, it was clear. After all, it was not so unheard of for such a misfortune to befall someone of my type, from such a common background, so "assimilated" as to be almost, in fact, a *goy*. What right did I have to make such a fuss?

"I think your head's full of strange ideas," I replied.

"Oh yes?" she sniggered, "Then be so good as to tell me why you haven't gone home to eat?"

"Who told you that?" The words escaped me.

"We know what we know. Even we have our informers."

It was Meldolesi, I thought; it couldn't have been anyone else (and as it happens I was right). But what did it matter? All of a sudden I was aware that the question of my being failed was secondary, a babyish matter that would sort itself out.

"How," I asked, "do you get up there? You look as though you're standing at a window."

"I'm standing on my trusty ladder," she replied, overstressing the syllables of "trusty" in her usual disdainful way.

From over the wall, just then, came a deep, short, slightly raucous volley of barks. Micòl turned her head and cast over her shoulders a bored look, though tinged with affection. She made a face at the dog, then turned back to where I was.

"Uffa!" she calmly sighed. "It's Jor."

"What kind of dog is it?"

"He's a Great Dane. Only a year old, but he already weighs a ton. He follows me everywhere. I often try to cover over my tracks, but in a little while there he is again—quite sure of finding me. He's a pain."

She smiled.

"You want me to let you in?" she asked, becoming serious again. "If you'd like I'll show you how right now."

· 6 ·

HOW MANY years have passed since that far-off June afternoon? More than thirty. And yet, if I close my eyes, Micòl Finzi-Contini is still there, leaning over her garden wall, looking at me and talking to me. In 1929 Micòl was little more than a child, a thin, blonde thirteen-year-old with large, clear, magnetic eyes. And I was a boy in short trousers, very bourgeois and very vain, whom a small academic setback was sufficient to cast down into the most childish desperation. We both fixed our eyes on each other. Above her head the sky was a compact blue, a warm already-summer sky without the slightest cloud. Nothing, it seemed, would be able to alter it, and nothing indeed has altered it, at least in memory.

"Well, do you want to, or don't you?" Micòl pressed me, becoming angry.

"I don't really know . . . " I began, nodding at the wall. "It looks very high to me."

"That's because you haven't looked properly," she replied impatiently. "See over there . . . and there . . . and there," pointing her finger to make me look. "There's lots of notches, and even a nail, up there on top. I put it in myself."

"I see . . . there must be some footholds," I murmured uncertainly, "but . . ."

"Footholds?" she interrupted, bursting out laughing. "Me, I'd call them 'notches.'"

"That's too bad, because they're called 'footholds,'" I insisted stubbornly and tartly. "You can tell you've never been mountaineering."

Since childhood I have always suffered from vertigo and though it was a modest climb it had me worried. As a child, when my mother with Ernesto in her arms (Fanny had not yet been born) took me out on Montagnone, and sat down on the grass on the vast square in front of Via Scandiana, from the top of which one could just barely make out our house's roof from among the sea of roofs around the big jetty of the church of Santa Maria in Vado, it was with considerable fear, I remember, that I went to lean on the parapet that skirted the square on the side nearest the country, and looked down over a drop of some thirty meters. Someone was always climbing up or down that dizzyingly steep wall: farmers, manual workers, young bricklayers, each of them with a bicycle on his shoulders. Amongst them were old men too, moustachioed frog-catchers and catfish anglers, laden with rods and baskets, all of them inhabitants of Quacchio, of Ponte della Gradella, of Coccomaro, of Coccomarino, of Focomorto, all of them in a hurry, and rather than go the long way by Porta San Giorgio or Porta San Giovanni (because at that time, on that side, the ramparts were still intact, without any penetrable breaches for at least five kilometers) they preferred to take, as they called it, "the wall route." They left the city, in that case, by crossing the great square, passing me by without even noticing me, stepping over the parapet and letting themselves drop until the tips of their toes rested on the first outcrop or crevice in the decrepit wall, and then, in no time at all, they would reach the meadow below. They came from the country; and then they would come up with those narrowed eyes that seemed to me to be boring into my own as I peeped timidly over the parapet—but I was quite wrong about that as they were understandably only focusing on the next handhold. Always, in any case, all the time they were thus occupied, suspended over the abyss—a pair of them, usually, one following the other—I would hear them chattering away in dialect, no more or less perturbed than if they had been trudging along a footpath in the middle of some fields. How calm, strong and brave they were!—I'd tell myself. After they had come up to within a few inches of my face, mirroring it in their own sclerotic ones, more often than not I was enveloped in the wine-reek of their breath, as they grasped with their thick callused fingers the inner edge of the parapet, as their whole bodies emerged out of the void and—lo and behold!—there they were safe and sound. I'd never be able to do such a thing, I told myself every time, watching them move away, full of admiration but also a kind of recoil. Never ever.

It was the same type of feeling I was once more experiencing just then in front of the outer wall on top of which Micòl was inviting me to climb. The wall certainly did not look as high as the ramparts of Montagnone. But all the same it was smoother, a good deal less corroded with the years and the inclement weather. And what if, scrambling up there, I thought to myself, my eyes fixed on those "notches" Micòl had pointed out to me, what if faintness overcame me and I was to fall? I might easily be killed.

However it was not so much for that reason that I still hesitated. Holding me back was a different repugnance than the purely physical one of vertigo, analogous but different, and stronger at that. For a moment I began to repent of my so recent desperation, my stupid puerile laments of a boy who had "failed."

"And besides, I don't see why here of all places I should force myself to become an Alpine mountaineer. If I'm being invited into your house, I'm very grateful but, frankly, it seems to me a whole lot easier to enter over there," and saying this I lifted my arm in the direction of Corso Ercole I d'Este, "through the main entrance. It would hardly take a moment. I'll get the bike and be there in no time."

I immediately understood that this proposal was not to her liking.

"No . . . no . . ." she said, contorting her face in an expression of intense distaste, "if you go that way Perotti's bound to see you, and then that will be it, there'll be no more fun in the whole thing."

"Perotti? Who's he?"

"The doorkeeper . . . you know. Perhaps you've already seen him. He's the one who's also the coachman, and accompanies us as a chauffeur. If he sees you, and there's no way he won't see you, since, apart from the times he goes out with the carriage or the car, he's always there on guard, damn him! And after that, it absolutely means I'll have to take you into the house as well, and you tell me if that's . . . what do you think?"

She was looking straight into my eyes, serious now, even though as calm as could be.

"All right," I replied, turning my head and nodding toward the embankment, "but what should I do with my bike? It's not like I can just leave it there, untended. It's brand new, a Wolsit: with dynamo lights, a saddlebag with a repair kit and a pump—do you think I'd let them steal my bike—on top of everything else . . . "

I didn't finish my sentence, struck down once more with anxiety about my inevitable confrontation with my father. That very evening, as late as possible, I'd have to return home. What other choice did I have?

I'd turned my eyes toward Micòl while I was speaking: she had seated herself on the wall, with her back turned toward me. Now she confidently lifted her leg and sat astride it.

"What are you up to?" I asked, surprised.

"I've just had an idea about your bike, and in the meantime I'll show you the best places to put your feet. Pay attention to where I'm putting mine. Look!"

She vaulted nonchalantly over onto the top of the wall, and thence, grabbing hold of the big rusty nail she had shown me before, began to climb down. She came down slowly but surely, searching out the footholds with the tips of her little tennis shoes, now with one, now with the other, and always finding them without apparent effort. She climbed down gracefully. All the same, before touching the ground, she missed one foothold, and slid the rest of the way. She fell on her feet but had hurt the fingers of one hand, and also, grazing the wall, her little pink dress—for the seaside—had been torn slightly under the arm.

"What a fool I am," she grumbled, bringing her hand to her mouth and blowing on it. "It's the first time that's happened to me."

She had cut her knee as well. She drew up a fold of her dress far enough to uncover her strangely white and strong-looking thigh, already a woman's, and she leaned over to examine the scratch. Two long blonde locks, the fairer ones, escaped from the clip she used to keep them bound together, fell down over her face, hiding her forehead and eyes.

"What a fool," she repeated.

"You'll need some disinfectant," I said mechanically, without approaching her, in that slightly plaintive tone that, in our family, we all used for this kind of thing.

"Disinfectant? You must be joking!"

She quickly licked the wound, a sort of affectionate kiss, and immediately sat up straight.

"Come on then," she said, all red and ruffled.

She turned, and began to climb up sideways along the bank's sunlit edge. She used her right hand to steady herself, grasping tufts of grass; meanwhile, her left hand, raised to her head, was undoing and refitting her circular hairclip. She repeated the maneuver several times as fluently as though she were combing her hair.

"Do you see that hole there?" she asked me, as soon as we'd arrived at the top. "You can hide your bike in there. No problem."

She pointed out to me, about fifty meters away, one of those grassy, cone-shaped hillocks, not more than two meters high, with an opening that is nearly always buried, which you come across quite frequently going round the walls of Ferrara. At first sight, they look a bit like the Etruscan burial mounds of the Roman countryside, though obviously on a much smaller scale. Except that the often huge underground chambers which some of them lead to have never housed any of the dead. The ancient defenders of the walls used them to store their arms: culverins, arquebuses, gunpowder and so on. And perhaps also those odd cannon balls of much-prized marble which in the fifteenth and sixteenth centuries had made the Ferrarese artillery so feared across Europe, and some examples of which you can still see in the castle, lying there like ornaments in the central courtyard and on the terraces.

"Who would dream that there could be a new Wolsit hidden down there? You'd have to have been told. Have you ever been inside?"

I shook my head.

"No? I have. Hundreds of times. It's awesome."

She moved on decisively, and having picked the Wolsit off the ground, I followed her in silence.

I drew level with her at the threshold of the opening. It was a kind of vertical crack, cut directly into the mantle of grass with which the mound was thickly clad, and too narrow to permit the entry of more than one person at a time. Immediately beyond the threshold began the descent, and one could only see down into it eight, maybe ten meters, but no more than that. Beyond there was nothing but darkness. As though the underground passage came up against a black curtain.

She leaned in to look, then suddenly turned round to me.

"You go on down," she whispered, smiling weakly, embarrassed. "I'd prefer to wait up here."

She drew back, linking her hands behind her back, and leaning her back against the grassy wall beside the entry.

"It's not like you're scared?" she asked, still in lowered tones.

"No, no," I lied, and bent down to lift the bike onto my shoulders.

Without saying another word I went past her, heading on into the tunnel.

I had to move carefully, also because the bicycle pedal kept knocking against the wall; and to begin with, for at least two or three meters, it was as though I'd been blinded: I could see absolutely nothing. But ten or so meters from the entrance hole ("Be careful," I heard Micòl's already distant shout behind me, then: "Mind the steps there!") I began to make out something. The tunnel came to an end a short space ahead: it only continued for a few more meters in descent. And it was just there, beyond a kind of landing which I sensed, even before arriving, was surrounded by a completely different kind of space, that the stairs which Micòl had warned me of began.

When I reached the landing, I stopped for a moment.

The infantile fear of the dark and the unknown which I'd felt the moment I'd moved away from Micòl as I ventured slowly farther and farther into the bowels of the earth gradually gave way to a no less infantile sense of relief. As though, having left Micòl's company, I had just in time escaped some great danger, the greatest danger a boy of my age ("a boy of your age" was one of my father's favorite expressions) might ever meet. Oh yes, I thought, this evening when I get home my Papa may well beat me. But at this point I could easily face his blows with equanimity. A subject to retake in October, Micòl was right, was just a joke. What was a subject in October compared to, I trembled, all those things that might have taken place between us, down here, in the dark? Perhaps I would have had the courage to give her, Micòl, a kiss: a kiss on the lips. But then what? What would have happened next? In the films I'd seen, and in novels, kisses had to be long and passionate! Actually, compared to "all those things," kisses were merely a not-too-worrying detail, if after lips met, and the two mouths were joined, each seeming almost to enter the other, mostly the thread of the story would not be picked up again until the next morning, or even not until several days later. If Micòl and I had managed to kiss each other in that way—and the darkness might certainly have helped things along—after that kiss time would have continued to move at its usual stately pace without any strange or providential interruption arriving to transport us safely to the morning after. In that case, what would I have had to do to fill up the minutes and hours that lay between? Oh, but that hadn't happened, luckily. It was just as well I'd been saved.

I began to descend the steps. I now realized that some faint rays of light from behind were filtering down through the tunnel. So a little by sight and a little by hearing (the bike had only to knock against the wall, or my heel to slip on a step, and immediately an echo increased and multiplied the sound, measuring out the spaces and distances), I quite quickly came to sense the sheer vastness of the place. It must have been a chamber some forty meters in diameter, round, with a vaulted dome of at least the same height. Who knows, perhaps it communicated by way of a system of secret corridors with other underground chambers of the same type, dozens of them, nestled under the body of the walls. Nothing could have been easier to imagine.

The chamber floor was of beaten earth, smooth, compact and dank. As I groped along the curve of the walls, I stumbled on a brick, and trod down on some straw. At last I sat down, resting with one hand gripping the wheel of the bike I'd leaned against the wall, and the other arm around my knees. The silence was only broken by the occasional rustle and squeak: rats probably, or bats . . .

And if the other things had happened, if they had, would that really have been so terrible?

It was almost a certainty I wouldn't have gone back home, and my parents, and Otello Forti, and Sergio Pavani, and all the others, the police station included, would have then had a real hunt to find me! For the first few days they'd have worn themselves out looking everywhere. Even the newspapers would have reported it, bringing up the usual hypotheses: kidnap, mishap, suicide, clandestine flight abroad, and so on. Little by little, however, things would have calmed down. My parents would have finally been reconciled to the loss (after all, they still had Ernesto and Fanny), and the search would have been called off. And, in the end, the person who'd be held responsible would have been that stupid sanctimonious Signora Fabiani, who'd have been sent off to "some other placement" as punishment. Where? To Sicily or Sardinia, naturally. It would have served her right, and taught her not to be so sneaky and spiteful.

As for me, seeing everyone else had become so reconciled to my absence, I would get used to it as well. I could rely on Micòl outside: she would have been able to provide me with food and everything else I needed. And she would have come every day, climbing over her garden wall, summer and winter. And every day we would have kissed, in the dark, because I was her man, and she was my woman.

And anyway, who was to say I wouldn't go outside ever again? During the day, obviously, I'd sleep, only interrupting my slumbers when I felt Micòl's lips brushing my own, and later I'd fall asleep again with her in my arms. By night, however, I could easily make prolonged sorties, especially if I chose the hours after one or two o'clock, when everyone else would be asleep, and almost no one left on the city streets. It would be odd and scary, but in the end good fun, to pass by Via Scandiana, see our house again, and the window of my bedroom, by this stage converted into a kind of sitting room, and then to make out in the distance, hidden in shadow, my father just then returning from the Merchants' Club, and it wouldn't even cross his mind I was alive and watching him. In fact, there he was taking the keys out of his pocket—opening the door, entering, and then calmly, just as though I, his eldest child, had never existed, shutting the door with a single hefty push.

And Mamma? Would it not be possible, one day or another, for me to try to let her know, perhaps by way of Micòl, that I wasn't really dead? And even to see her, before, fed up of my life underground, I finally left Ferrara and disappeared for ever? Why not? What was to stop me!

I don't know how long I remained there. Perhaps ten minutes, perhaps less. I remember precisely that as I climbed up the stairs and threaded the tunnel again (without the weight of the bicycle I moved far more nimbly) I kept on embellishing these fantasies. And Mamma?—I asked myself. Would she also have forgotten me, like the rest of them?

Finally I found myself in the open air again, and Micòl was no longer waiting for me where I'd left her a little before, but rather, as I saw almost at once, screening my eyes against the sun with my hand, was once more sitting astride the garden wall of the Barchetto del Duca.

She seemed busy arguing and reasoning with someone on the other side of the wall: probably the coachman Perotti, or even Professor Ermanno in person. It was clear what had happened: seeing the ladder leaning against the wall, they must have immediately been aware of her little escape. Now they were asking her to come down. And she wasn't sure whether she wanted to obey.

At a certain point, she turned round, and spotted me on top of the bank. Then she blew out her cheeks as if to say:

"Phew! About time!"

And the last look she gave before disappearing behind the wall—a look accompanied with a smile and a wink, just as when, at the synagogue, she spied me from under the paternal *tallit*—had been for me.

II

· 1 ·

THE time when I actually managed to pass beyond the wall surrounding the Barchetto del Duca, and make my way between the trees and clearings of the great private wood as far as the *magna domus* itself and the tennis court, was something like ten years later.

It was in 1938, about two months after the Racial Laws had been passed. I remember it well. One afternoon toward the end of October, a few minutes after having left the table, I'd received a telephone call from Alberto Finzi-Contini. Was it or wasn't it true, he immediately wanted to know, dispensing with any preamble (it is worth noting that for more than five years we had had no occasion to exchange a single word)—was it or wasn't it true that I "and all the others," with a letter signed by the vice-president and secretary of the Eleonora d'Este Tennis Club, had all been banned from the club: "thrown out" as it were?

I denied this firmly: it wasn't true. At least, as far as I was concerned; I'd received no such letter.

As though he considered my denial of no consequence, or wasn't even willing to listen to it, he immediately proposed that I should come round to play at their house. If I could put up with a white clay court, he went on, with not much in the way of surrounds; and if, above all, given that I was sure to be a far better player than them, I could "be kind enough" to give him and Micòl a knock-up, both of them would be very glad and "honored." Any afternoon at all would be fine, he added, if the idea appealed to me. Today, tomorrow, the day after—I could come when I wanted, bringing with me whoever I wanted, even on Saturday, if that was better. He had to stay in Ferrara for at least another month, since the Milan Polytechnic courses wouldn't be starting until November 20 (as for Micòl, she was taking things easier and easier—taking an extra year for her History exams, and having no need to go around begging official signatures, who knows if she'd even set foot in the department at Ca' Foscari) and didn't I see what lovely weather we were having? While there was still time, it would be a real waste not to make the most of it.

He sounded these last words with less conviction. It seemed as though he had felt the chill of some less pleasant thought, or a sudden, unmotivated feeling of boredom had descended to make him wish that I wouldn't come round or take any notice of his invitation.

I thanked him, without clearly committing myself to anything. What was the call about?—I asked myself in some consternation, putting down the phone. All considered, since the time he and his sister had been sent to study outside Ferrara (Alberto in 1933, Micòl in 1934, more or less the same years that Professor Ermanno had been given permission by the Community to restore for "the use of the family and others concerned" the former Spanish synagogue which was incorporated in the Via Mazzini Temple, and from then on the bench behind ours in the Italian School synagogue had remained empty) we hadn't seen each other except on rare occasions, and those only briefly and at a distance. During this whole time we had become so remote from each other that one morning in 1935, at Bologna station (I was already in the second year of my Arts course and I went back and forth almost every day by train), having been brusquely shouldered aside on platform one by a dark-haired, pale-faced young man, with a tartan blanket under his arm, and with a porter laden with baggage at his heels, who was propelling himself with big strides toward the fast train to Milan about to leave, for a moment I completely failed to recognize this figure as Alberto Finzi-Contini. And that time—I continued thinking—he had not even felt the least need to greet me. When I had turned round to protest at being knocked over, he merely gave me a distracted glance. And now, by contrast, what was all this effusive and slippery courtesy about?

"Who was it?" my father asked, as soon as I had entered the dining room.

There was no one else in the room. He was sitting in an armchair next to the sideboard with the radio, as usual anxiously awaiting the two o'clock news.

"Alberto Finzi-Contini."

"Who? The boy? Such an honor! And what did he want?"

He scrutinized me with his blue, bewildered eyes, which a long time ago had lost hope of my obedience, trying to guess what was going on in my mind. He well knew—his eyes were telling me—that his questions got on my nerves, that his continual attempts to meddle in my life were without discretion or justification. But good God, wasn't he my father? And hadn't I noticed how he'd grown old this last year? It wasn't possible for him to confide in Mamma and in Fanny: they were women. Nor could he do so in Ernesto—too much of a baby. So who then could he talk to? Was it possible I didn't understand it was me he needed?

Through clenched teeth I told him what the call had been about.

"And will you be going, then?"

He didn't give me a chance to answer him. Regardless, with all the animation I saw in him at the slightest chance offered him to drag me into any kind of conversation, especially of a political nature, he'd already rushed headlong into a résumé of what he called "the real point of the situation."

It was unfortunately true—he had begun to recapitulate in his tireless way—last September, on the 22nd, after the first official announcement on the 9th, all the newspapers had published that additional circular from the Party Secretary which spoke of various "practical measures" of immediate application for which the provincial Federations would be responsible with regard to us. In future, "the prohibition of mixed marriages remaining statutory, the exclusion of all youths, recognized as belonging to the Jewish race, from all state schools of whatever kind and level," as well as the exemption, for the same, from the "highly honorific" duty of military service, we "Israelites" would then not even be able to place our death announcements in the newspapers, let alone be listed in telephone directories, or keep domestic help of the Aryan race, or frequent "recreational clubs" of any kind whatsoever. And yet, despite all this . . .

"I hope you won't want to start on the usual story," I interrupted him, shaking my head.

"What story?"

"That Mussolini is more *good* than Hitler."

"I know, I know," he said. "But you have to admit it's true. Hitler's a bloodthirsty maniac, whereas Mussolini is what he is, as much of a Machiavellian and turncoat as can be, but . . ."

Again I interrupted him. Did he or did he not agree, I asked, looking him straight in the face, with the idea of Leon Trotsky's essay I'd "passed" to him a few days earlier?

I was referring to an article published in an old issue of the *Nouvelle Revue Française*, a magazine several entire years of which I jealously guarded in my bedroom. What had happened was that, I can't remember why, I had treated my father disrespectfully. He was offended, had gone into such a sulk that, at a certain point, hoping to re-establish normal relations, I could think of no other strategy than to make him privy to my most recent reading. Flattered by this sign of respect, my father did not need to be persuaded. He read the article straight away, rather he devoured it, underlining with a pencil a great many lines, and filling the margins with pages of dense notes. Basically, and this he declared openly, the writings of "that reprobate and ancient best mate of Lenin" had been for him, too, a real revelation.

"But of course I agree with it!" he exclaimed, happy, and at the same time disconcerted, to see me inclined to have a discussion. "There's no doubt about it—Trotsky's a magnificent polemicist. What vividness and powers of expression! Quite capable of composing the article straight in French. Sure," here he smiled with pride, "those Russian and Polish Jews may not be very likeable, but they've always had an indisputable genius for languages. They have it in their blood."

"Let's drop the question of language and get down to the arguments." I cut him short with a sour professorial tone which I immediately regretted.

The article spoke clearly—I continued, more placidly. In its phases of imperialist expansion, capitalism is bound to manifest its intolerance regarding all national minorities, and the Jews in particular, who are the minority par excellence. And now, in the light of this general theory (Trotsky's essay was written in 1931, which shouldn't be forgotten: that is, the year in which Hitler's real ascent to power began), what did it matter whether Mussolini was a better person than Hitler? And anyway, was it really true that he was better, even in terms of character?

"I see. I see . . . " my father kept on meekly repeating as I spoke.

His eyelids were lowered, his face screwed up into a grimace of pained forbearance. At last, when he was quite sure I had nothing further to add, he placed his hand on my knee.

He could see—he repeated once again, slowly raising his eyelids. If I'd just let him speak: I took everything too grimly, I was too extreme.

How come I didn't realize that after the communiqué of September 9, and more particularly after the additional circular of the 22nd, things at least in Ferrara had gone ahead almost as before? It was quite true, he admitted, smiling melancholically, that during that month, among the seven hundred and fifty members of the Community there had been no deaths considered worthy of record in the *Corriere padano* (if he wasn't wrong, only two old ladies from the Via Vittoria Hospice had died: a certain Saralvo and a Rietti, and the latter wasn't even from Ferrara but from a Mantuan village—Sabbioneta, Viadana, Pomponesco, or something like that). But we should be fair: the telephone directory had not been withdrawn to be replaced by a newly purged edition. There had not yet been any *havertà*,[*] maid, cook, nanny or old governess, in service to any of our families, who, all of a sudden discovering in themselves "a racial awareness" had felt it imperative to pack her bags. The Merchants' Club, which had had the lawyer Lattes as its vice-president for more than ten years, and which he had frequented constantly on an almost daily basis, had recorded no such walk-outs to date. And Bruno Lattes, son of Leone Lattes, had he by any chance been expelled from the Eleonora d'Este Tennis Club? Without giving the least thought to my brother Ernesto, who, poor thing, had been all this time watching me with his mouth ajar, imitating me as though I was who knows what great

---

[*] Hebrew: "handmaid."

haham,* I had given up playing tennis, and I had done wrong, if I'd let him say so, very wrong to close myself off, to segregate myself, not to go out to see anyone anymore, and then, with the excuse of university and a seasonal rail card, to continually sneak off to Bologna (and I wasn't even willing to spend time with Nino Bottecchiari, Sergio Pavani and Otello Forti, up until last year my inseparable friends, here in Ferrara, yes, they hadn't stopped phoning me, first one and then the other, poor boys!) I should consider, in contrast, young Lattes. If the *Corriere padano* was to be believed, he had not only taken part in the open tournament but also in the mixed doubles, playing with his partner, the lovely Adriana Trentini, daughter of the province's chief engineer. He was doing exceptionally well—they'd already got through the first three rounds and were now getting ready for the semi-finals. No, you can say what you want about good old Barbicinti, such as that he sets too much store by his own petty nobility's coat of arms and too little store by the grammar of the tennis propaganda articles which the Federal Secretary gets him to write every now and then for the Padano. But that he was a gentleman, not at all hostile to Jews, a harmless enough Fascist—and in saying "harmless enough Fascist" my father's voice trembled, a little tremor of timidity—as far as that's concerned there's no doubt or cause for dispute.

As regards Alberto's invitation, and the behavior of the Finzi-Continis in general, what was it for, out of the blue, all their fussing, all their almost frantic neediness to make contact?

What had happened the week before for Rosh Hashanah at the Temple had already been strange enough (as usual, I hadn't wished to go, and once again had put myself in the wrong). Yes, it was already strange enough, at the climax of the service and with the seats almost all taken, to see Ermanno Finzi-Contini, his wife and even his sister-in-law, followed by the two children and the inevitable uncles, the Herreras from Venice—in short, the whole tribe, without distinctions of gender, make their solemn return to the Italian School after a good five years of scornful isolation in the Spanish synagogue. They had a look about them too, benign and satisfied, no more or less than if they had meant, by their presence, to reward

---

* Hebrew: "sage" or "teacher."

and pardon not only the assembled company but the entire Community. And this alone was apparently not sufficient. For now they'd reached the point of inviting people to their home, to the Barchetto del Duca, just imagine, where since the days of Josette Artom, no fellow citizen or outsider had ever set foot, except perhaps in situations of dire emergency. And did I care to know why? Of course, because they were pleased with what was happening! Because to them, *halti** as they'd always been (anti-Fascist, sure, but above all *halti*), deep down the Racial Laws gratified them! Had they been good Zionists one could have understood! Given that here in Italy, and in Ferrara, they always found themselves so ill at ease, so out of place, they could at least have benefited from this situation and taken themselves off, once and for all, to Eretz! But not at all. Apart from fumbling every now and then for a wee bit of cash to send to Eretz (which was nothing to boast of, anyway), the thought of going had never even crossed their minds. They had always reserved their serious bits of spending for aristocratic baubles: as when, in 1933, to find an *hekhal* and a *parokhet*[†] worthy of a place in their private synagogue (authentic Sephardic furnishings, I ask you—not Portuguese, or Catalan, or Provençal, but real Spanish and to the exact measurement!), they rushed off in a motor car, dragging a Carnera truck behind them to no less a place than Cherasco, in the province of Cuneo, a village which up until 1910 or earlier had been the dwelling of a small Jewish community now extinct, and where the cemetery was only still functioning because some Turin families who'd originated there, Debenedetti, Momigliano, Terracini and so on, kept on burying their dead there. Likewise Josette Artom, Alberto and Micòl's grandmother, in her time, unceasingly imported palms and eucalyptuses from the Botanical Gardens of Rome, the one at the foot of the Janiculum—and because of this and needless to say for reasons of prestige, had forced her husband, poor Menotti, to at least double the width of the already exaggerated gateway that gave onto Corso Ercole I d'Este. The truth is that their mania for collections, of things, of plants, of whatever, little by little ends up with them wanting to do the same with people. Huh! And if they, the

---

* Hebrew: *halti*, "bigotry."
† Hebrew: *hekhal*, "Ark"; *parokhet*, "curtain before the Ark."

Finzi-Continis, so missed being stuck in a ghetto (and the Ghetto—that's where they clearly want to have everyone locked away, even if it meant making a sacrifice for this wonderful ideal and parcelling out bits of the Barchetto del Duca to make a kind of *kibbutz* of it, of course under their noble patronage), they should feel perfectly free to go ahead and make one. Speaking for himself, and quite sincerely, he'd much prefer to go to Palestine. Or better still Alaska, Tierra del Fuego or Madagascar . . .

That was a Tuesday. I can't explain how, a few days later, on the Saturday, I decided to do exactly the opposite of what my father wanted. I'd deny that it had to do with the typical filial mechanism of contradiction and disobedience. What suddenly prompted me to drag out my racket and tennis gear from the drawer they had lain in for more than a year had been nothing other than a luminous day, the light and caressing air of an early autumnal afternoon, unusually sunny.

But in the meantime certain things had happened.

First of all, two days after Alberto's call, I think, and so it must have been Thursday, the letter that "welcomed" my resignation as a member of the Eleonora d'Este Tennis Club had actually arrived. Typed, but with the signature, in full spread, of NH* Marchese Barbicinti at the foot of the page, the express delivery did not descend to personal or particular details. In the driest tone, and a mere few lines, clumsily mimicking a bureaucratic style, it went straight to the point, declaring it without doubt "inadmissible" (sic) any further attendance of my "esteemed person" at the Club. (Could the Marchese Barbicinti ever rid himself of the habit of peppering his prose with certain spelling mistakes? It seems not. But taking note of and laughing about them was a bit more difficult this time than it had been in the past.)

And secondly, the next day, there had been another phone call for me from the *magna domus*, and not from Alberto, this time, but from Micòl.

The outcome was a long, no, an extremely long conversation, the tone of which was maintained, thanks mainly to Micòl, along the lines of a normal, ironic, rambling chat between two seasoned university students who, as children, might even have had a bit of a crush on one another, but who

---

* Nobil Huomo, a title of the Italian nobility.

now, after something in the region of ten years, have nothing else in mind than to bring about an innocent get-together.

"How long is it since we've seen each other?"

"At the very least five years."

"And so, what are you like now?"

"Ugly. A spinster with a red nose. And you? On the subject, I read, I read . . ."

"Read what?"

"That's it. Two or so years ago, in the Padano, must have been the culture page, that you'd participated in the Venice Littoriali della Cultura e dell'Arte. . . Making a bit of a splash, eh? My compliments! But then you always did very well in Italian, even at upper middle school. Meldolesi was truly spellbound by some of your class essays. I seem to recall he even brought us one to read."

"No need to make fun of me. And you, what are you up to?"

"Nothing. I should have graduated in English at Ca' Foscari last June. But instead—fat chance. Let's hope I can get through this year, idleness permitting. D'you think they'll let the students who are late for their exams finish anyway?"

"I haven't the least doubt about that, though my saying so won't cheer you up. Have you chosen the subject for your thesis yet?"

"I've chosen, so far no more than chosen, to do it on Emily Dickinson— you know, the nineteenth-century American poet, that archetypally awful woman . . . but what can you do? I'll have to be tied to the Professor's apron strings, waste a whole fortnight in Venice, the Pearl of the Lagoon—but a short while there's enough for me . . . All these years I've stayed there as little as possible. Besides, to be honest, studying's never been my forte."

"Liar. Liar and snob."

"No. I swear it's true. And this autumn, trying hard to be as good as gold, I feel even less cut out for it. D'you know what I'd rather do, dear boy, instead of burying myself in the library?"

"Why not tell me."

"Play tennis, go out dancing and flirting, you can imagine."

"All of them healthy recreations, including tennis and dancing, which if you cared to you could just as easily pursue in Venice."

"Sure I could—with that pair of governesses Uncle Giulio and Uncle Federico always at my heels!"

"Well, you can't claim anyone's going to stop you playing tennis. As for me, whenever I can, I take the train and make off to Bologna . . . "

"Go on, tell the truth, you make off to make out, round at your true love's."

"No. Not at all. I have to graduate myself next year, I'm still not sure whether in Art History or Italian—but now I think it'll be Italian—and whenever I feel like it I permit myself an hour of tennis. I hire an excellent paying court in Via del Castello or at the Littoriale, and no one can stop me. Why don't you do the same at Venice?"

"The question is that to play tennis or go dancing you need a *partner*,* but in Venice I don't have anyone remotely suitable. And I tell you, Venice may well be beautiful, I wouldn't deny it, but I don't feel at ease there. I feel provisional, displaced . . . a bit as though I'm abroad."

"Do you stay at your uncles'?"

"Yeah. Just to sleep and eat there."

"I see. All the same, two years ago, when the Littoriali were held at Ca' Foscari, I'm grateful you didn't come along. I mean it. It was the ghastliest day of my life."

"How come? After all . . . I should tell you that at one moment, finding out you were performing, I did think of rushing off to be a bit of a claque for . . . the local flag. But listen, changing the subject: d'you remember that time on the Mura degli Angeli, out here, the year you were made to retake your math exams in October? You must have sobbed your eyes out, poor little fellow: you had such eyes! I wanted to console you. It even crossed my mind to get you to climb over the wall and come into the garden. And what reason did you have for not coming in? I know you didn't, but I can't remember why."

"Because someone disturbed us at the crucial moment."

"Oh, yes, Perotti, the gardener, that dog of a Perotti."

"Gardener? Coachman, I seem to recall."

"Gardener, coachman, chauffeur, doorman, everything."

---

* In English in the original.

"Is he still alive?"

"Are you kidding?!"

"And the dog, the actual dog, the one that barked?"

"Who? Jor?"

"Yes, the Great Dane."

"Yes, he's also alive and vegetating."

She had repeated her brother's invitation ("I don't know if Alberto has called you, but why not come round for a bit of a knock-up at our house?"), but without insisting, and without the slightest mention, in contrast to him, of the Marchese Barbicinti's letter. She mentioned nothing but the real pleasure of seeing each other again after such a long time, and of enjoying together, in the teeth of so many things that might prevent it, whatever good times were still possible while the season lasted.

· 2 ·

I WASN'T the only one to be invited.

When, that Saturday afternoon, I emerged at the end of Corso Ercole I (I'd avoided the Corso Giovecca and the town center, and come round by way of the near-ish Piazza della Certosa), I immediately noted in the shade in front of the Finzi-Continis' gateway a small group of tennis players. There were five of them, four boys and a girl, who'd also come by bike. My lips drew back in a wince of disappointment. Who were these people? Apart from one whom I didn't even know by sight, older, around twenty-five, with a pipe between his teeth, long white linen trousers and a brown corduroy jacket, the others, all of them in colored pullovers and shorts, had the look of regular players at the Eleonora d'Este. They had just arrived and were waiting to be let in. But since the gate had still not been opened, every now and then they would leave off their loud chatter and laughter and, as a sign of light-hearted protest, rhythmically ring their bicycle bells.

I was tempted to slope off. Too late. They'd already stopped ringing their bells and begun to stare at me with interest. One of them whom, as I approached, I recognized with a glance to be Bruno Lattes, was even greeting me by waving his racket at the end of his long and extremely skinny arm. He wanted to show he'd recognized me, though we had never been great friends—he was two years younger than me, and we hadn't seen much of each other even at Bologna, in the Literature Department—and at the same time to usher me forward.

By this stage I'd come to a halt, face to face with Bruno, my left hand leaning on the smooth oak of the gate.

"Good afternoon," I said and grinned. "What brings this gathering here today? Has the open tournament ended by any chance? Or have you all been knocked out?"

My tone and words had been carefully chosen. In the meantime I was observing them one by one. I looked at Adriana Trentini, her lovely, very blonde hair, her long tapering legs—magnificent legs, admittedly, but their skin was too white and speckled with strange red patches that always surfaced when she was hot. I looked at the taciturn young man in the linen trousers and brown jacket (certainly not from Ferrara, I told myself). I looked at the other two boys, much younger than him and even than Adriana, the two of them still at school perhaps or at the Technical College, and so, having "moved up" during the last year when, bit by bit, I'd removed myself from every circle of the city, they were pretty well unknown to me. And I turned at last at Bruno, there in front of me, ever taller and drier, and because of his ever swarthier skin, looking like a vibrant, nervous, young black man. And that day, too, he was prey to such nervous agitation he was able to transmit the force of it through the light contact of the two front tyres of our bikes.

Between the two of us passed the inevitable quick glance of Jewish complicity which, partly in anxiety and partly in distaste, I had already foreseen. Still looking at him, I then added:

"I trust that before venturing out to play on foreign soil you have asked Signor Barbicinti's permission."

The unknown young man, the one not from Ferrara, astonished at my sarcastic tone or because he felt uneasy, moved a little to the side of me. Instead of holding me back, this only spurred me on.

"Please, put my mind at rest," I insisted, "that this is an absence with proper leave and not a great escape."

"What are you saying!" Adriana interrupted with her usual recklessness—quite innocent, but no less irritating for that. "Don't you know what happened last Wednesday, during the mixed doubles finals? Don't tell me you weren't there, and why not give your eternal Vittorio Alfieri pose a rest. While we were playing, I saw you among the spectators. I saw you clearly."

"I wasn't there at all," I replied drily. "I haven't hung around the place for at least a year."

"And why not?"

"Because I was sure one day or another I'd be chucked out anyway. And in fact I wasn't wrong. Here's the little document of expulsion."

I took the envelope out of my jacket pocket.

"I assume you'll have received one too," I added, turning to Bruno.

It was only then that Adriana seemed to remember. She twisted her lips. But the chance of breaking important news to me, which I was evidently uninformed about, quickly banished any other thought of hers.

"He needs to be told," she said.

She sighed, lifting her eyes toward the sky.

Something very unpleasant had happened—she then began to tell me in a schoolmistressy voice, while one of the younger boys turned to press the gate's sharp little buzzer made of black horn. All right, I didn't know but, in the open tournament which started halfway through last week and was now over, she and Bruno had reached the finals—no less—a thing of which no one had ever dreamed they might be capable. And then? The final was under way when things took the strangest of turns (honestly, it would make your eyes pop out: Désirée Baggioli and Claudio Montemezzo, two great hopes of the game put in difficulty by a non-classified pair, so much so that they'd lost the first set ten–eight, and were finding the going very tough in the second) when suddenly, by an unprecedented decision of the Marchese Barbicinti, acting on his own behalf, as ever the arbitrating judge of the tournament, and once more, in short, the Big Chief, the game was brought to a sudden halt. It was six o'clock, and admittedly the visibility wasn't good. But not so bad that they couldn't have gone on for at least another couple of games. Good Lord, was this the way things should be done? At four games to two in the second set of an important match, he had no right, in the absence of proof to the contrary, to suddenly shout "Stop play!" to rush onto the court with his arms spread wide, proclaiming the match suspended because of "the impending darkness" and postponing the continuance of play and the conclusion of the match to the afternoon of the day after. And besides, the Marchese was hardly acting in good faith. Even if she hadn't already noticed at the end of the first set that he was in cahoots with that "black soul" Gino Cariani, the GUF* secretary—they had drawn slightly apart from the crowd alongside the small pavilion for the changing-rooms—and that same Cariani, perhaps to be less conspicuous, had been standing with his back completely turned to the court—if this wasn't enough to tell you, the expression on the Marchese's face when he bent to open the little entry gate, so pale and shocked she'd never seen anything like it, "he looked a right little wimp," it would have been clear as day to her that the "impending darkness" was nothing but the feeblest excuse, "utter bullshit." Was there really any doubt about it? Nothing further was said of the interrupted match, although Bruno, the morning after, had also received the same registered delivery letter that I'd had; "the one I wanted to show her." And she, Adriana, had been left so disgusted and indignant with the whole thing that she'd sworn never again to set foot in the Eleonora d'Este, at least for a good while. Did they have something against Bruno? If they did, they could easily have stopped him entering the tournament in the first place. They could have been straight with him and said: "Because of the way things are, we're sorry but we can't let you take part." But with the tournament already begun, and nearly finished, and not only that: him a mere hair's breadth away from winning one of the titles, they should never have behaved the way they did. Four–two. What daylight robbery! The kind of filthy trick you'd expect from complete Zulus, not civilized, well-brought-up people.

Adriana Trentini talked on, ever more fervently, and now and then Bruno would put in a word and add some details.

In his view the match was stopped thanks mainly to Cariani, from whom, as anyone who knew him could tell, one could hardly expect anything else. It was only too obvious: a half-pint nobody like him, with his

---

* Gruppo Universitario Fascista: Fascist university students' organization.

bird-boned look and consumptive's chest, whose only thought, from the first moment he'd got into the GUF, had been to carve out a career for himself, and so he'd never missed an opportunity, in public or in private, of licking the Federal Secretary's boots. (Hadn't I seen him at the Caffè della Borsa on the rare occasions he managed to sit at the small table of the "old heavies of the Bombamano"?[*] He'd puff himself up, curse, unleash swear words bigger than himself, but as soon as the Consul Bolognesi, or Sciagura, or some other bigshot of the group contradicted him, you could see him quickly put his tail between his legs and, just to be forgiven and return to favor, he'd be ready to fawn and take on the most servile tasks, like scurrying off to the tobacconist to buy a packet of Giubek for the Federal Secretary, or telephoning the "Sciagura household" to warn his "ex-washerwoman wifey" of the great man's imminent return . . .) A "worm of that ilk" would certainly not pass up a chance, you could bet your life on it, to ingratiate himself with the Party once again! The Marchese Barbicinti was what you'd expect—a venerable sort, agreed, but rather lacking in "grey matter," and anything but a hero. If they kept him on to run the Eleonora d'Este they did so because he looked the part, and above all for his name, which to them must have represented some glorious lure for the unwary. So it must have been a great laugh for Cariani to put the wind up the doddery old gent. Perhaps he'll have said to him, "And tomorrow? Has it crossed your mind, Marchese, what will happen tomorrow evening when the Federal Secretary'll be here for the dance party, and will have to give a . . . Lattes that splendid silver cup and the customary Roman salute? For my part, I can foresee a terrible scandal. And big trouble, endless trouble. If I was in your place, given that it's starting to get dark, I wouldn't hesitate to stop the match." It wouldn't have needed anymore than that, for dead sure, to have prompted him to bring the tournament to that grotesque and abrupt end.

Before Adriana and Bruno had finished bringing me up to date with these events (and while doing so Adriana even managed to introduce me to the burly stranger: Malnate he was called, Giampiero Malnate, a recently qualified chemist working at one of the new synthetic-rubber fac-

---

[*] Hand-grenade. The "old heavies" are a Fascist squad.

tories in the industrial zone), the big gate finally opened. A man of about sixty appeared on the threshold, big, stocky, with grey hair cut short, from which the half-past-two sun, gushing in a bright stream through the vertical gap behind him, extracted luminous metallic reflections. He had a mustache equally short and grey under a fleshy, violet nose—a bit like Hitler's, it struck me, both the nose and the little mustache. It was him in person, old Perotti—gardener, coachman, chauffeur, doorman, the whole lot and more, just as Micòl had described him. He had not changed in the least since my time at the Guarini when, enthroned on the box-seat, he waited impassively till the school's dark and menacing cave mouth, which had swallowed up his little, fearless, smiling "charges," finally decided to restore them, no less serene and self-confident, to the vehicle made of glass, varnish, nickel-plating, padded material, fine pla-nished hardwoods—exactly like a precious casket—whose conservation and conveyance were entirely his responsibility. His little eyes, sharp and grey as his hair, sparkling with a Venetian peasant's canny hardness, still seemed to be laughing good-naturedly beneath his thick, almost black, eyebrows, exactly as they had been. But at what, this time? Because we had been left there waiting for at least ten minutes? Or at himself, kit-ted out in a striped jacket and white gloves—all brand-new and perhaps donned especially for the occasion?

And so we entered, and were welcomed on the other side of the gate, which was shut with a sudden massive bang at the hands of the assiduous Perotti, by the heavy barking of Jor, the black-and-white Great Dane. He came down along the driveway, the huge dog, then trotted alongside us with an air that wasn't in the least intimidating. But nevertheless Bruno and Adriana fell silent.

"He doesn't bite, does he?" asked Adriana fearfully.

"Don't worry yourself, Signorina," Perotti replied. "With the three or four teeth he still has left, it's not like he's fit to bite anything, not even polenta some days . . . "

While the decrepit Jor, halted in the middle of the drive in a sculptural pose, fixed us with his frosty, expressionless eyes, one dark, the other light-blue, Perotti began to offer excuses. He was sorry to have made us wait—he said. It wasn't his fault, but the fault of the electric current, which didn't always work (but luckily Signorina Micòl had suspected as much and had sent him to check whether by chance we'd arrived), apart from the distance, which regrettably was more than half a kilometer. He couldn't ride a bicycle, but once Signorina Micòl got something into her head . . .

He sighed, rolled his eyes, and once more smiled, who knows why, disclosing from between his thin lips a toothscape as compact and strong as the Great Dane's was feeble. Meanwhile, with his raised arm, he pointed out the driveway which, after a hundred meters, advanced into a thicket of rattan palms. Even for those who could use a bicycle, he warned, it would take three or four minutes just to arrive at the "Palazzo."

· 3 ·

WE WERE really very lucky with the season. For ten or twelve days the weather remained perfect, held in that state of magical suspension, of glassy, luminous, soft immobility which is the special gift of some of our autumns. In the garden it was hot, just slightly less than if it was summer. Whoever wanted to could go on playing tennis until half past five or later, without fear that the evening damp, so marked toward November, would damage the gut strings of the racket. At that hour, naturally, you could hardly see a thing. And yet the light that continued to shed a golden hue down at the foot of the grassy inclines of the Mura degli Angeli, which were overrun, especially on Sundays, with a quiet, many-colored crowd (kids chasing a ball, maids knitting away beside prams, soldiers on leave, lovers in search of places where they could kiss), that last light tempted you to keep on playing, regardless of whether you were all but blind. The day was still not over; surely it was worth playing on just a little longer.

We came back every afternoon, announcing our visits by a phone call at first, then not even that; and always the same group, with the occasional exception of Giampiero Malnate, who had known Alberto since 1933, in Milan, and contrary to what I'd thought that first day, meeting him in front of the Finzi-Continis' gate, not only had he never before set eyes on the four youngsters who accompanied him, but neither had he anything at all to do with the Eleonora d'Este, or with its vice-president and secretary, the Marchese Ippolito Barbicinti.

The days seemed excessively beautiful and yet at the same time undermined by the approaching winter. To lose even one of them would be a real crime. Without making an appointment with each other, we always arrived around two, immediately after lunch. Often, in the first days, it so happened that we all once again found each other in a group in front of the gate, waiting for Perotti to come and open it. But the introduction, after something like a week, of an intercom and a remote-controlled unlocking device meant that, the entry into the garden no longer being problematic, we would arrive in ones or twos, as chance would have it. As for me, I didn't miss a single afternoon; not even to follow one of my usual courses in Bologna. As far as I can recall the same was true of the others: Bruno Lattes, Adriana Trentini, Carletto Sani, Tonino Collevatti, whose number was increased by another three or four boys and girls as well as my brother Ernesto. The only one, as I've said, who came less regularly was *the* Giampiero Malnate (as Micòl began to call him, and soon enough the rest of us followed suit). He had to keep to the factory's hours, he explained on one occasion: it wasn't that strict, admittedly, considering that the Montecatini plant where he worked had not, to date, produced a single kilo of synthetic rubber, but all the same it was a schedule. Whatever the cause, his absences never lasted for more than two days in succession. Besides, he was the only one, myself excepted, who did not seem that bothered about playing tennis (and to be honest he was not much of a player), and was often quite content, when he appeared on his bike after work, to umpire a match or to sit apart with Alberto, smoking a pipe and talking.

Our hosts were even more assiduous than we were. We might sometimes arrive before the Piazza's distant clock struck two: however soon we got there, we were sure to find them already on court, not playing each other, as they had been doing that Saturday when we came out into the clearing behind the house where the court was, but busy checking that everything was in order, the net at the right height, the clay well rolled and the lines swept, the balls in goodcondition, or else stretched out on two deckchairs with wide straw hats on their heads, motionlessly sunbathing. They could not have behaved better if they had been the owners of the house, although it was clear that tennis, as physical exercise, as a sport, interested them only up to a certain point. Despite this, they stayed on till the final match (always at least one of them, but sometimes both) without ever taking their leave earlier on the pretext of an engagement, or because of some duty, or feeling unwell. Some evenings it was actually they, in almost total darkness, who would insist on playing "another couple of points, the last ones!" and would shepherd back on court whoever was on the point of deserting it.

As Carletto Sani and Tonino Collevatti had immediately declared, without bothering to lower their voices, it wasn't as if the court itself was anything special.

Being fifteen-year-olds, too young to have had any experience of tennis courts other than those which deservedly filled the Marchese Barbicinti with pride, they immediately began to expatiate on the many shortcomings of this kind of "potato patch" (as one of them had called it, curling his upper lip with distaste). These were: practically no run-back especially behind the far service line; a bumpy surface and, to make things worse, poor drainage, so even a little rain would turn it into a quagmire; no evergreen hedge to reinforce the surrounding wire fence.

No sooner had they finished their "duel to the death" (Micòl hadn't managed to stop her brother reaching five-all, and at this point they stopped play) than they leaped in to denounce these same defects, not just without a shadow of reserve but with a sort of bizarre self-lacerating enthusiasm, as though the two of them were in competition.

Oh yes, Micòl had remarked, while she was still drying her hot face with a thick towel, for people like us, "spoiled" by the red-clay courts of the Eleonora d'Este, it must be very hard to feel at ease on their dusty potato patch! And the backcourt space? How could we play with so little room behind us? What an abyss of decadence we poor folk had fallen into! But she had no reason to reproach herself. She had told her father innumerable times that the wire netting all round needed to be set back at least another three meters. But would he listen? He, her father, had always hedged, falling back each time on a typical farmer's perspective, which thinks that earth not used for planting things in is merely thrown away (also predictably bringing up the fact that she and Alberto had played on this sorry excuse for a court since they were children and so they could perfectly well continue to play on it as grown-ups). All that effort for nothing! But now things had changed. Now they had guests, "illustrious guests." A good reason for her to take up the cause again with renewed vigor, wearing down and tormenting her "grey-haired progenitor" so much that by next spring she felt confident she could guarantee that she and Alberto would be able to offer us "something more worthy."

She spoke more than ever in her characteristic mode, and grinned. We had no other option but to deny it, and reassure her in unison that on the contrary everything, the court included, was absolutely fine, better than fine, also praising to the skies this green corner of the grounds, beside which the remaining private parks, Duke Massari's included (it was Bruno who remarked on it, just at the moment when Micòl and Alberto were leaving the court, holding hands), faded into so many neatly tended, bourgeois gardens.

If the truth must be told, the tennis court was far from "worthy," and besides, being just one, it forced us all to take overlong breaks off-court. Thus, at four o'clock on the dot every afternoon, perhaps above all so that the two fifteen-year-olds of our very mixed company should not pine for the hours of much more intense sporting activity that they might otherwise have passed under the wing of the Marchese Barbicinti, Perotti would invariably appear, his bullish neck tense and flushed from the effort of holding upright in his gloved hands a huge silver tray.

That tray was overflowing: rolls of anchovy spread, smoked salmon, caviare, pâté de foie gras, pork prosciutto; with little vol-au-vents filled with a sauce of chicken and béchamel; with tiny buricchi which must have come from the prestigious little kosher pastry shop which Signora Betsabea, the famous Signora Betsabea (Da Fano), had run for decades in Via Mazzini to the pride and delight of the entire citizenry. And that wasn't the end of it. The good Perotti had still to lay out the contents of the tray on the wickerwork table already prepared for this, in front of the court's side entrance, beneath a broad parasol in red-and-blue segments, which was attended to by one of his daughters, either Dirce or Gina, both about the same age as Micòl, and both in service "at home," Dirce as a maid, Gina as cook. (The two male children, Titta and Bepi, the first about thirty, the second eighteen, took care of the park in the dual role of park and kitchen gardeners, and the most we ever saw of them was their bending figures, working in the distance, when they would turn the beam of their blue ironic eyes in our direction as we passed by on bikes—we never managed any contact beyond that.) She, the daughter, in her turn, had brought along with her, down the path which led from the *magna domus* to the tennis court, a trolley with rubber wheels, also laden with decanters, jugs, beakers and glasses. Within the porcelain and pewter jugs were tea, milk and coffee, and within the Bohemian cut-glass decanters, beaded with pearls of moisture, was lemonade, fruit juice and Skiwasser—this last a thirst-quenching drink made of water and raspberry syrup in equal measures, with the addition of a slice of lemon and a few grapes, which Micòl preferred to all other drinks and on which she particularly prided herself.

Oh, that *Skiwasser*! In the breaks between games, besides guzzling the odd roll which always, and not without a show of religious nonconformism, she chose from among those filled with pork prosciutto, Micòl would often throw back a whole glass of her favorite "drinkette," continually prompting us to do the same, "in homage,"as she would say laughing, "to the deceased Austro-Hungarian Empire." The recipe, she told us, had been given to her in Austria itself, at Offgastein, in the winter of 1934: the only winter that she and Alberto "in coalition" had been allowed to go on their own for a fortnight to ski. And though *Skiwasser*, as the name testified, was a winter drink, for which reason it should have been served boiling hot, still, even in Austria there were some people who in summer, so as not to stop drinking it, drank it this way, in icy "drafts" but without the slice of lemon, and then they called it *Himbeerwasser*.

However that was, we should take note, she added and raised a finger with comic emphasis, it was by her own initiative that the grapes—"indispensable!"—had been added to the classic Tyrolean recipe. It was her idea, and she stood by it—it was no laughing matter. The grapes stood for Italy's special contribution to the holy noble cause of Skiwasser, or rather of this, to put it more precisely, special "Italian variant, not to mention Ferrarese, not to mention . . . etc., etc."

· 4 ·

IT TOOK some time before the other denizens of the house let themselves be seen.

Speaking of which, something strange occurred even that first day, which I only remembered halfway through the week after, when the fact that neither Professor Ermanno nor Signora Olga had turned up made me suspect that all those whom Adriana Trentini called, en masse, "the old guard," had reached a unanimous decision to keep their distance from the tennis playing—perhaps so as not to embarrass us, or, who knows, so as not to disturb by their presence parties which in the end were not really parties but simply gatherings of the youngsters in the garden.

The curious event occurred right at the start, a short while after we had taken our leave of Perotti and Jor, who remained there watching us cycle into the distance along the driveway. Having crossed the Panfilio canal by way of a strange, stocky bridge of black girders, our two-wheeled patrol had then come within two hundred meters of the lonely neo-Gothic hulk of the *magna domus*, or, to be more precise, of the sad, gravel-covered forecourt which, completely in the shade, extended before it, when all our attention was drawn to two motionless figures right in the middle of the forecourt: an old woman seated in an armchair, with a heap of cushions supporting her back and a young woman, blonde and buxom, who looked like a maid, standing behind her. As soon as she saw us advancing, the old woman was shaken by a kind of start. After this, she immediately began a series of sweeping gestures with her arms to signal no, we shouldn't keep going ahead toward the forecourt where she was, given that there, behind her, there was nothing but the house itself, but rather we should take a left turn down the path covered by a trellis of small climbing roses which she pointed out to us, at the end of which (Micòl and Alberto were already playing: couldn't we hear from where we were the regular thunks their rackets made as they knocked the ball back and forth?) we should immediately arrive at the tennis court. She was Signora Regina Herrera, Signora Olga's mother. I had already recognized her from the singularly brilliant whiteness of the thick hair gathered up at the nape of her neck, hair which

I'd admired every time I'd seen it at the Temple since I'd first glimpsed it through the grating of the women's gallery as a young child. She waved her arms and her hands with hectic energy, at the same time signing to the girl, who it turned out was Dirce, to help her up. She was tired of being there: she wanted to go back in. And the maid obeyed her order with unhesitating solicitude.

One evening, however, contrary to all expectations, it was Professor Ermanno and Signora Olga who appeared. They gave the impression of having passed the tennis court by sheer chance, returning after a long stroll in the grounds. They were arm in arm. Smaller than his wife, and much more stooped than he had been ten years earlier, at the time of our whispered conversation from one bench to another in the Italian School synagogue, the Professor was wearing one of his usual light linen suits with a black-banded panama hat tilted down over the thick lenses of his pince-nez, and leaning, as he walked, on a bamboo cane. Dressed in mourning, the Signora was carrying in her arms a thick bunch of chrysanthemums gathered in some remote part of the garden during their walk. She pressed them against and across her breast, wreathing them with her right arm in a tenderly possessive, almost maternal manner. Although still straight, and a whole head taller than her husband, she too had aged considerably. Her hair had grown uniformly grey—an ugly, dismal grey. Beneath her bony projecting brow her coal-black eyes shone as ever with a stricken, fanatical ardor.

Those of us who were sitting around the sunshade rose to our feet, and those who were playing stopped.

"Please don't put yourselves out," the Professor began in his kind and musical tones. "Do please sit down, and don't let us disturb the game."

He was not obeyed. Micòl and Alberto, but especially Micòl, saw to introducing us. Besides announcing our names and surnames, she lingered over whatever details concerning each of us might rouse her father's interest: most of all our occupations and studies. She had begun with me and Bruno Lattes, speaking about both of us in a distant, remarkably objective manner, as though to stop her father, in this particular circumstance, from showing any possible sign of special recognition or favor. We were "the two literary figures of the gang," "salt of the earth." She then moved on to

Malnate. Here before us was a great example of devotion to science!—she exclaimed with ironic emphasis. Only chemistry, for which he nursed an evidently irresistible passion, could have induced him to leave a metropolis as full of opportunities as Milan (*"Milàn l'è on grand Milàn!"**) to bury himself in a "mini-city" like our own.

"He works in the industrial zone," Alberto explained, straightforward and serious. "For a Montecatini plant."

"They're meant to be producing synthetic rubber," Micòl sniggered, "but up till now it seems they haven't managed it."

Professor Ermanno coughed. He pointed his finger at Malnate.

"You were a university friend of Alberto's, isn't that right?" he asked gently.

"Well, in a way," he replied, agreeing with a nod. "We were in different faculties, and I was three years ahead, but all the same we became great friends."

"Of that I'm sure. My son has spoken of you very often. He's also told us of having been at your house many times, and of the great kindness and hospitality of your parents. Would you thank them on our behalf when you see them next? In the meantime we are delighted to have you here at our house. And do please come back . . . come here any time you'd like."

He turned toward Micòl, and asked her, pointing to Adriana:

"And who is this young woman? If I'm not wrong she must be a Zanardi . . . "

The conversation proceeded in this manner until all the introductions had been made, including those of Carletto Sani and Tonino Collevatti, characterized by Micòl as "the two great promises" of Ferrara's tennis circles. Finally Professor Ermanno and Signora Olga, who had stayed at her husband's side the whole time without saying a word, limiting herself to the occasional benevolent smile, made their way, still arm in arm, toward the house.

Although the Professor had taken his leave with a more than cordial "See you soon!" it would not have crossed any of our minds to hold on too literally to that promise.

---

* Milanese dialect: "What a big place Milan is!"

But the following Sunday, while Adriana Trentini and Bruno Lattes on one side of the net and Désirée Baggioli and Claudio Montemezzo on the other were most keenly contesting a match whose outcome, according to the declarations of Adriana, who had promoted and organized it, should "at least morally" recompense her and Bruno for the dirty trick played on them by the Marchese Barbicinti (but the event was not turning out the same as before: Adriana and Bruno were losing, and rather badly): toward the end of the match, the entire "old guard" emerged from out of the path of the climbing roses. They seemed like a small cortège. Leading them were Professor Ermanno and Signora Olga. They were followed, a little after, by the Herrera uncles from Venice: the first, with a cigarette between his thick protruding lips and his hands clasped behind his back, looking around him with the slightly embarrassed air of a town dweller who, against his will, has found himself in the countryside; and the second, a few yards farther back, supporting Signora Regina on his arm and adjusting his stride to the snail-like pace of his mother. If the phthisiologist and the engineer were in Ferrara, I said to myself, it must be to attend some religious ceremony. But what? After Rosh Hashanah, which fell in October, I couldn't remember what rite there was in autumn. Succoth maybe? Probably. Unless the equally probable firing of the engineer Federico from the state railways had prompted the calling of a most unusual family reunion . . .

They sat down in a dignified manner, hardly making any noise, the only exception being Signora Regina. As soon as she had been settled down in a deckchair, she boomed out in a deaf person's voice a few words in their household jargon. She bewailed the mucha humidity of the garden at that time of day. But beside her, her son Federico was in attendance, and in an equally loud voice was ready to hush her up (though his had a neutral timbre: a tone of voice that my father also paraded on occasion when, in "mixed" surroundings, he wanted to communicate exclusively with some member of the family). She should keep callada, that is, quiet. There were the musafir.

I moved close to Micòl's ear.

"I can manage to make out 'callada.' But what on earth does 'musafir' mean?"

"Guests," she whispered in reply. "But *goyische* ones."

Then she smiled, childishly covering her mouth with her hand and winking: style Micòl 1929.

Later, at the end of the match, and after the "new acquisitions" Désirée Baggioli and Claudio Montemezzo had been introduced in their turn, I happened to find myself apart with Professor Ermanno. The day was dying away across the park in its usual milky diffused shadows. I had moved some yards away from the court's little entrance gate. My eyes fixed on the distant Mura degli Angeli, I heard behind my back Micòl's sharp voice prevailing over all the others. Who knows who she was angry with or why.

"*Era già l'ora che volge il disìo . . .*"* an ironic quiet voice recited, very close by.

I turned round astonished. It was Professor Ermanno himself, seemingly happy to have startled me, and smiling good-naturedly. He gently took me by the arm, and thence, very slowly, keeping some way away from the wire-netting surround and every now and then coming to a halt, we began to walk round the tennis court. Having almost effected a complete tour, we retraced our steps. Back and forth, the darkness gradually deepening round us, we went through this same maneuver a number of times. Meanwhile we talked, or rather, for the most part, he, the Professor, talked.

He began by asking my opinion of the tennis court, if I really found it execrable. Micòl had no doubts on this subject: if he were to follow her advice, they'd have to give it a complete overhaul, utterly modernize it. For his part, he remained unsure. Maybe, as usual, his "dear little whirlwind" was making too much of it. Maybe it wasn't absolutely necessary to turn everything upside down, as she seemed to want.

"In any case," he added, "in a few days it'll start to rain, no use pretending otherwise. Don't you think it might be better to put off whatever needs to be done until next year?"

This said, he went on to ask me what I was doing, and what my plans were for the immediate future. And how my parents were.

While he was asking me about my "Papa," I noticed two things. First of all, that he was reluctant to address me with the informal "*tu*"; in fact, after

---

* "It was already the hour when longing returns . . ." (Dante, *Purgatorio*, canto viii).

a little while, coming to an abrupt halt, he explicitly asked me if this was all right, and straight away, with some warmth and sincerity, I begged him not to use the formal *"Lei"* with me, or I'd be upset. Secondly, that the interest and respect which showed in his voice and face while he was asking how my father was (especially in his eyes—the lenses of his glasses, magnifying them, emphasized the gravity and meekness of their expression) didn't seem at all forced, or the least bit hypocritical. He reminded me to pass on his best wishes. And his "congratulations" as well—for the many trees that had been planted in our cemetery since my father had taken over responsibility for it. Regarding this, would some pine trees be of any use? Some cedars of Lebanon? Some fir trees? Or weeping willows? I should put it to my father. If by any chance they would be useful (these days, with the methods of modern agriculture, transplanting broad-trunked trees had become a simple matter), he would be only too pleased to provide whatever number were required. It was a wonderful idea, I had to admit! Thickly planted with lovely tall trees, even our cemetery would be able, in the course of time, to rival that of San Niccolò del Lido in Venice.

"Don't you know it?"

I replied that I didn't.

"Oh, but you must, you really must try to go there as soon as you can!" he insisted with much animation. "It's a national monument! Besides, as a literary man, you'll most certainly remember the start of Giovanni Prati's *Edmenegarda*."

I was forced once again to confess my ignorance.

"Well," the Professor continued, "it's precisely there that Prati begins his *Edmenegarda*, in the Lido's Jewish cemetery, which in the nineteenth century was considered one of the most romantic sites in Italy. But make sure, if and when you do go, that you don't forget to tell the cemetery caretaker straight away (he's the one with the entrance keys) that you want to visit the old one, this is important, the old cemetery, where no one's been buried since the eighteenth century, and not the other, the modern one, next to it but quite separate. I discovered it in 1905, just imagine. Even though I was almost twice your present age, I was still unmarried. I was living in Venice (I'd been living there for two years), and I would go and visit the place, even in winter—whenever I wasn't at the State Archives burrowing through manuscripts concerning the various so-called "Nations" into which the sixteenth- and seventeenth-century Venetian Jewish Community were divided: the Levantine Nation, the Northern, the German and the Italian. It's true I hardly ever went there on my own," here he smiled, "and that, in a certain sense, deciphering the gravestones one by one, many of which date back to the early sixteenth century, and are written in Spanish or Portuguese, I was continuing with my archival researches in the open air. Oh, they were delightful afternoons I spent there . . . what peace and serenity . . . with the small entrance, facing the Laguna, which opened only for us. We became engaged right there within the cemetery, Olga and myself."

He remained silent for a short while. I took the opportunity to ask him what exactly was the subject of his archival research.

"At the outset I began with an idea of writing a history of Venetian Jewry," he replied, "a subject which Olga herself had suggested to me, and which Roth, the English Jew Cecil Roth, had treated so brilliantly some ten years later. But then, as often happens with historians who become too . . . passionately involved, some particular seventeenth-century documents which I came across began to engross all my attention, and ended up taking me off course. I'll tell you, I'll tell you all about it if you come back . . . It has the makings of a real novel, however you look at it . . . but, anyway, instead of the fat historical tome which I aspired to write, at the end of two years' work I hadn't managed to put together (apart from marrying, that is) anything but two pamphlets: one, that I still believe may be of use, in which I've gathered together all the cemetery's inscriptions, and the other in which I've made public the existence of those seventeenth-century papers I was telling you about, but only that, narrating the facts, without venturing on any interpretation with respect to them. Would you be interested in looking at them? Yes? One of these days you must let me present you with copies. But besides all this, please do go, I really recommend it, to the Jewish cemetery at the Lido (the old section, I repeat!). It's worth the trouble, you'll see. You'll find it just as it was thirty-five years ago, exactly the same."

We turned back slowly toward the tennis court. At first sight, it seemed as though no one was left there. And yet, in the almost total darkness, Micòl and Carletto Sani were still playing. Micòl was complaining: apparently "Cochet" was hitting the ball too hard, hardly the behavior of a "gentleman," and in that darkness it was "frankly too much."

"I heard from Micòl that you weren't sure whether to graduate in Art History or in Italian," Professor Ermanno was saying to me in the meantime. "So have you decided yet?"

I told him that I had, that I'd made up my mind to do my thesis in Italian. My uncertainty—I explained—had been due to the fact that up until a few days ago I'd still been hoping to be supervised by Professor Longhi, who had the chair in Art History, but that, at the last moment, he had put in for a two-year study leave away from teaching duties. The thesis I would have wanted to write under his supervision would have looked at a group of Ferrara painters in the second half of the sixteenth and the early seventeenth centuries: Scarsellino, Bastianino, Bastarolo, Bonone, Caletti, Calzolaretto and some others. Only with Longhi's guidance, writing on material like this, would I have had a chance to produce something of quality. And so, since he, Longhi, had obtained two years of leave from the Ministry, it had seemed to me a better idea to fall back on some other thesis, but in the Italian department.

He had stood there listening to me, deep in thought.

"Longhi?" he asked finally, twisting his lips in doubt. "What does this mean? Have they already appointed the new chair in Art History?

I didn't understand.

"But surely', he insisted, "the professor of Art History at Bologna, I've always heard that it was Igino Benvenuto Supino, one of the most illustrious figures of Italian Jewry. So then . . . "

He had been—I interrupted—had been, until 1933. But after 1934, in place of Supino, put out to pasture long after the age of retirement, they had called in Roberto Longhi. Didn't he know, I proceeded—happy this time to find him lacking in information—the crucial essays of Roberto Longhi on Piero della Francesca and on Caravaggio and his school? Didn't he know the Officina ferrarese, a work that had created such an uproar in 1933, at the time of the Ferrara Renaissance Exhibition held the same year in the Palazzo dei Diamanti? My thesis would have been based on the last pages of the Officina, where the theme had been touched upon, albeit magisterially, but without full development.

I talked on, and Professor Ermanno, more hunched than ever, stood and listened to me in silence. What was he thinking about? About the number of "illustrious" university figures which Italian Jewry had supplied from the Unification to the present time? Probably.

Suddenly I saw him grow animated.

Looking around, and lowering his voice to a stifled whisper, as if he were letting me into something no less than a state secret, he divulged the big news: that he possessed a batch of Carducci's unpublished letters, written by the poet to Professor Ermanno's mother in 1875. If I would be interested in seeing them, and if I considered them a fitting subject for a graduation thesis in Italian, he would be only too pleased to let me have them.

Thinking of Meldolesi, I couldn't help smiling. What had become of that essay he'd meant to send to the *Nuova Antologia*? After talking so much about it, had he actually managed to do nothing? Poor Meldolesi. Some years back he'd been transferred to the Minghetti in Bologna—to his great satisfaction, as one can imagine! One day I really would have to track him down . . .

Despite the darkness, Professor Ermanno realized I was smiling.

"Oh, I know, I know," he said "for some time you youngsters have had a low opinion of Giosuè Carducci! I know that you prefer figures such as Pascoli or D'Annunzio."

It was easy for me to convince him that I'd been smiling for quite a different reason, that being disappointment. If I'd only known that some of Carducci's unpublished letters were to be found in Ferrara! Instead of proposing to Professor Calcaterra, as unfortunately I had already done, a thesis on Panzacchi, I could easily have suggested a "Carducci in Ferrara" theme which would undoubtedly have been of more interest. But who knows: perhaps if I was to speak frankly to Professor Calcaterra, who was a very decent person, he might still let me switch from Panzacchi to Carducci without making too much of a fuss about it.

"When are you hoping to graduate?" Professor Ermanno finally asked me.

"I'm not sure. I'd like it to be next year in June. Don't forget that I, too, am studying independently."

He nodded several times in silence.

"Independently?" he then sighed. "Well, that's not so bad."

He made a vague gesture with his hand, as if to say that, with all that was happening, both his children and I would have plenty of time on our hands, if not too much.

My father had been right. He didn't in the end seem all that distressed by this fact. Quite the reverse.

· 5 ·

IT WAS Micòl who wanted to show me the garden. She was very keen on the idea. "I'd say I had a certain right to do so," she'd sniggered, looking at me.

It was not on that first day. I'd played tennis until late, and it was Alberto, when he had finished competing with his sister, who accompanied me as far as a kind of Alpine hut in miniature, half hidden in a thicket of fir trees and about a hundred meters away from the court—the *Hütte* as he and Micòl called it—and in this hut or *Hütte*, used as a changing-room, I'd been able to change, and later, as darkness fell, to take a hot shower and get dressed again.

But the next day, things fell out differently. A doubles match with Adriana Trentini and Bruno Lattes playing against the two fifteen-year-olds (with Malnate perched atop the umpire's chair playing the role of patient scorer) had quickly assumed the guise of one of those games that never end.

"What should we do?" Micòl had asked me at a certain point, rising to her feet. "I've the impression that it'll be a good hour before you, me, Alberto and our friend the Milanese will get a chance to swap places on court. Listen: what if during the wait us two were to slip off for a brief tour of the plants?" As soon as the court's free—she had added—Alberto will be sure to call us. He'd stick three fingers in his mouth, and honor us all with his famous whistle!

Smiling, she had already turned toward Alberto, who was stretched out nearby on a third deckchair with his face hidden beneath a straw hat and dozing off in the sun.

"Isn't that so, Sir Pasha?"

From under his hat Sir Pasha had agreed with a nod of his head, and we went off together. Yes, her brother was remarkable—Micòl meanwhile continued explaining. When circumstances required, the whistles he could come up with were so ear-shattering that beside them those of shepherds were merely laughable. It was odd though, wasn't it, that someone like him could do that? Just looking, you wouldn't think much of him. And yet . . . who knows where he drew all that breath from!

And so it was, nearly always whiling away the wait between one match and the next, that we began our long forays together. The first times we took our bikes with us. The garden being "some" ten hectares in size, and the driveways, large and small, extending over a dozen or so kilometres, a bicycle was, to say the least, indispensable, my fellow had promptly declared. True, today—she admitted—we'll limit ourselves to a "survey" down there, toward the sunset, where she and Alberto, as children, often used to go to watch the trains being shunted in the station. But if we went on foot, how, even today, would we manage to get back? We'd risk being caught out by Alberto's "oliphant" whistle, without the chance of getting ourselves back with the required dispatch.

So that first day we went to watch the trains maneuvering in the station. And then? Then we turned back, round by the tennis court, across the forecourt of the *magna domus* (deserted as always and sadder than ever) and, doubling back, we went beyond the dark wooden bridge over the Panfilio canal, took the entrance driveway back till we reached the tunnel of rattan palms and the gate on Corso Ercole I. Having arrived here, Micòl insisted that we thread our way down the winding path that followed right round the surrounding wall: first to the left, alongside the Mura degli Angeli, so far that in a quarter of an hour we had again reached that zone of the park from which the station was visible, and from there we explored the opposite side, far more wild and rather dark and melancholy, which flanked the deserted Via Arianuova. We were there, making our way with some difficulty through the ferns, nettles and thorny bushes, when suddenly in the distance behind the thick mesh of tree trunks Alberto's sheep-herding whistle was heard, calling us back with all haste to our "hard labors."

With a few variations in the route, we repeated these far-flung expeditions a number of times in the afternoons that followed. When space permitted it, we pedalled alongside each other. And meanwhile we talked—mostly about trees, at least to begin with.

This was a subject I knew nothing, or almost nothing, about—which caused Micòl no end of astonishment. She looked at me as though I was some kind of monster.

"Is it possible you can be so uninformed?" she exclaimed. "Surely you must have studied a little botany at school!"

"Let's see now," she pursued the point, her eyebrows ready to rise at some further, shocking lapse. "May I enquire, please, what kind of tree milord thinks that one down there is?"

She might just as well have been singling out an honest elm or a native lime tree as some exceptionally rare African, Asiatic or American plant which only a specialist would be able to identify, since they had everything there, at the Barchetto del Duca, absolutely everything. As for me, I always replied at random: partly because I seriously couldn't distinguish an elm from a lime tree, and partly because I realized that nothing gave her more pleasure than seeing me make a mistake.

It seemed absurd to her that such a person as myself existed in the world without sharing her own feelings of passionate admiration for trees, "those huge, quiet, strong, profound beings." How could I not understand, good Lord, how come I didn't feel it? At the end of the tennis clearing, for example, to the west of the court, there was a group of seven slender, extremely tall *Washingtoniae graciles*, or desert palms, separated from the rest of the greenery behind (the usual thick-trunked trees of the European forest: oaks, ilexes, plane trees, horse chestnuts, etc.), and surrounded by a good stretch of lawn. Every time we passed nearby, Micòl always had some new words of tenderness for the isolated group of *Washingtoniae*.

"There they are, my seven dear old men," she might say. "Look what venerable beards they have!"

But seriously—she would insist—didn't they seem even to me like the seven hermits of the Thebaïd, dried up by the sun and by fasting? What elegance, what saintliness they had in their brown, dry, curved, scaly trunks! Truly they seemed like so many John the Baptists, dieting on nothing but locusts.

But her sympathies, as I've already said, were not limited to exotic trees.

For one enormous plane tree, with a whitish, warty trunk thicker than any other in the garden, and I believe than any in the entire province, her admiration overflowed into reverence. Naturally it hadn't been her "grandma Josette" who'd planted it, but Ercole I d'Este in person, or maybe even Lucrezia Borgia.

"It's almost five hundred years old, can you imagine that?" she sighed, narrowing her eyes. "Just think for a moment all it must have witnessed since it first saw the light!"

Then it seemed as though the gigantic plane tree also had eyes and ears: eyes to see us with, and ears to hear us.

For the fruit trees, for which a large tract of ground had been reserved, protected from the north winds and exposed to the sun in the immediate shelter of the Mura degli Angeli, Micòl nursed an affection very like—I'd noticed—that which she showed toward Perotti and all the members of his family. She spoke to me of them, of those humble domestic plants, with the same good nature, the same patience, and often in local dialect, which she adopted only in her relations to Perotti, or to Titta and Bepi, whenever we happened to meet them, and stopped to exchange a few words. We ritually stopped every time before a large plum tree with a mighty trunk like an oak's—her favorite. "*Il brogn sèrbi,*" the sour plums, which grew on that plum tree over there, she told me, had always seemed extraordinary to her, since her childhood. She preferred them to any Lindt chocolate. Then, when she was sixteen, she lost all desire for them, they no longer gave her any pleasure, and today she'd rather have Lindt chocolates or for that matter non-Lindt chocolates (but dark ones, only dark ones) to "*brogne.*" In the same fashion, apples were "*i pum,*" figs "*i figh,*" apricot "*il mugnàgh,*" peach "*il pèrsagh.*" Only dialect could do justice to these things. Only the dialect word would allow her, in naming trees and fruits, to bunch up her lips in a heartfelt expression somewhere between tenderness and mockery.

Later, when tree-spotting was exhausted, "the pious pilgrimages" began. And since all pilgrimages, according to Micòl, had to be undertaken on foot (otherwise what kind of pilgrimages would they be, for heaven's sake?), we stopped using our bikes. And so we would walk, nearly always accompanied every step of the way by Jor.

To start with I was taken to see a small, lone landing-stage on the Panfilio canal, hidden amongst a thick growth of willows, white poplars and arum lilies. From that tiny dock, completely encircled by a mossy terracotta bench, it was likely that in the old days they might have set sail for the River Po as well as for the Castle Moat. And she and Alberto themselves had even set sail from there when they were children, Micòl told me, for long excursions in a two-paddle canoe. By boat, they had never got as far as the foot of the Castle towers (I was quite aware that nowadays the Panfilio only reached the Castle Moat by way of underwater channels). But that hadn't stopped them getting as far as the Po, right up to Isola Bianca. Now, *ça va sans dire*, there was no point in thinking of using the canoe anymore: it was partly stove in, covered in dust, reduced to being "the ghost of a canoe." Sometime I'd be able to see it in the coach-house when she remembered to take me there. However, the landing-stage bench she'd always, always, kept going back to. Perhaps because she was still using it to prepare for her exams, utterly undisturbed, when it was hot, or perhaps because . . . The fact was that this spot had always remained in some way hers, and hers only—her own secret refuge.

Another time we ended up at the Perottis, who lived in a real farm-house between the big house and the fruit groves.

We were received by old Perotti's wife, Vittorina, a sad, wan-looking *arzdòra*,[*] thin as a rake and of an indefinable age, and by Italia, the wife of Titta, the elder son. She was a plump, robust thirty-year-old from Codigoro, with light-blue, watery eyes and red hair. Seated on the threshold in a wicker chair, and surrounded by a crowd of chickens, she was breast-feeding, and Micòl leaned down to caress the baby.

As she did so, she asked Vittorina in dialect: "And so, when are you going to ask me back to eat some more of that bean soup?"

---

[*] See footnote on p. 41.

"Whenever you'd like, *Sgnurina*. Long as you're happy with . . ."

"We should really arrange it one of these days," Micòl replied seriously. "You ought to know," she added turning to me, "that Vittorina makes these monster bean soups. With braised pork crackling of course . . ."

She laughed and said:

"D'you want to have a look at the cowshed? We have a good half-dozen cows."

Preceded by Vittorina we made our way toward the cowshed. The *arzdòra* opened the door with a huge key she kept in the pocket of her black apron, then stepped aside to let us pass. As we crossed the threshold I was aware of a furtive look she gave the two of us—a look that seemed troubled but at the same time secretly pleased.

A third pilgrimage was devoted to the sacred places of the "*vert paradis des amours enfantines.*"

In the previous days we had passed by those parts several times, but always on bikes, and never stopping there. There it is—Micòl then told me, pointing with her finger—the very spot on the outer wall where she used to lean the ladder, and there were the "notches" ("Yes sir, the notches") she'd use when, as it fell out, the ladder wasn't available.

"Don't you think we should have a commemorative plaque placed here?" she asked me.

"I suppose you'll have already worked out the wording."

"It's almost there. 'Here in this place, avoiding the vigilance of two enormous hounds . . .'"

"Stop. You were mentioning a plaque, but from the way it's going I reckon you'll need a big inscription stone like the *Bollettino della Vittoria*. The second line's far too long."

A quarrel sprang from this. I took the part of the stubborn interrupter, and she, raising her voice and behaving like a spoiled child, went on to accuse me of the "usual pedantry." It was clear—she cried out—that I'd sniffed out her intention to leave my name off the plaque, and so, out of pure jealousy, I wasn't even willing to hear her out.

Then we calmed down. She began once more to talk of when she and Alberto were children. If I really wanted to know the truth, both she and

Alberto had always felt equally envious of those, like me, who had the good fortune to study in a state school. Didn't I believe her? It had come to such a point with them that every year they anxiously awaited exam time just for the pleasure of being able to go to school like other children.

"Then how come, if you both so wanted to go to school, you went on studying at home?" I asked.

"Papa and Mamma, particularly Mamma, were dead set against it. Mamma has always had an obsession with germs. She claimed that schools were specially made to disseminate the most frightful diseases, and it never helped at all that Uncle Giulio, whenever he came here, tried to persuade her that this wasn't so. Uncle Giulio would tease her, even though he's a doctor, and doesn't have much faith in medicine, but rather believes in the inevitability and usefulness of diseases. There was no way that he could convince Mamma, after the great misfortune of Guido, our little older brother who died before Alberto and I were born, in 1914. After that he didn't dare touch on the subject! Later, as you can guess, we rebelled a bit: we managed to go to university, the two of us, and even to Austria to ski, one winter, as I think I've already told you. But as children, what could we do? I often used to escape (but not Alberto—he's always been a good deal more placid than me, and much more obedient). Besides, one day I stayed out a bit too long, on a trip round the walls, getting a lift from a group of boys on their bicycle crossbars. When I got home, and saw how desperate they were, Mamma and Papa, from that time on (as Micòl was such a good sort, with a heart of gold!) from that time on, I decided to be well behaved and have never slipped off again. The only relapse was that June of 1929 in your honor, my dear sir!"

"And I thought I was the only one," I sighed.

"Well, if not the only one, certainly the last. And besides, as far as entering the garden goes, I've never invited anyone else in."

"Is that the truth?"

"I swear it is. I was always looking in your direction, at the Temple . . . when you turned round to talk to Papa and Alberto you had such blue eyes! In my heart of hearts I'd even given you a nickname."

"A nickname? And what would that be?"

"Celestino."

"*Che fece per viltade il gran rifiuto . . . ,*"* I stammered.

"Exactly!" she exclaimed, laughing. "All the same, I think for some time I had a little crush on you."

"And then what happened?"

"Then life separated us."

"What an idea though—to put up a synagogue just for yourselves. Was that still all because of a fear of germs?"

She signaled agreement with her hand.

"Well . . . more or less . . . " she said.

"D'you mean more?"

Yet there was no way to make her confess the truth. I was well aware that the reason Professor Ermanno, in 1933, had asked to restore the Spanish synagogue for his and his family's use had been the shameful *infornata del Decennale*. It was this that made him do it. She, however, maintained that once more the crucial factor was her mother's will. The Herreras, in Venice, belonged to the Spanish School. And since her mother, grandma Regina and her uncles Giulio and Federico had always been most attached to family traditions, her father, to keep her mother happy . . .

"But now, how come you've returned to the Italian School?" I objected. "I wasn't there at the Temple on the evening of Rosh Hashanah—I haven't set foot in there for at least three years. Though my father, who was there, has described the event to me in the smallest detail."

"Oh, have no fear, your absence has been greatly noticed, Sir Free-Thinker!" she replied. "By me as well."

She became serious again and said:

"What d'you expect? . . . now we're all in the same boat. At this point even I'd find it rather ridiculous to keep on trying to preserve so many distinctions."

On another day, the last, it began to rain, and while the others took refuge in the *Hütte* playing rummy or ping-pong, the two of us, unconcerned about getting soaked, ran halfway across the park to shelter in the coach-house. The coach-house served now only as a storeroom—Micòl

---

* "Who out of cowardice made the great refusal..." (Dante, *Inferno*, canto iii), commonly interpreted as a reference to Pope Celestine V.

had told me. At one time, however, a good half of the inner chamber had been kitted out as a gym, with climbing poles, ropes, symmetrical bars, rings, wall bars and so on—all this with the sole intent that she and Alberto might present themselves well prepared for the annual exam in physical education. They weren't exactly serious lessons, the ones Professor Anacleto Zaccarini, who had been pensioned off years before and was more than eighty (just imagine it!) came to give them every week. But they were certainly amusing, perhaps more so than all the others. She never forgot to bring along to the gym a bottle of Bosco wine. And old Zaccarini, gradually turning from his usual ruddy-nosed and red-cheeked self to a peacock-purple, would slowly drain it to the last drop. Some winter evenings when he left, he looked as though he was actually emitting his own light . . .

It was a long, low construction of brown bricks, with two side windows defended by sturdy grilles, a leaking tile roof and its external walls almost entirely covered by ivy. Not far from Perotti's hayloft and the glassy parallelepiped of a greenhouse, its approach was through a broad, green-painted gate which looked out toward the opposite part of the Mura degli Angeli in the direction of the main house.

We stopped for a while on the threshold with our backs to the big door. The rain was pelting down in long diagonal streaks, on the lawns, on the huge black masses of the trees, on everything. It was cold. Our teeth chattering, we both looked around us. The enchantment which had till then held the season in suspense had been irreparably broken.

"Should we go in?" I finally proposed. "It'll be warmer inside."

Within the vast chamber, at the end of which, in shadow, shone the tops of two polished, blond climbing poles that stretched to the ceiling, a strange smell diffused itself, a mixture of petrol, lubricating oil, old dust and citrus fruits. It's such a good smell, Micòl suddenly said, aware that I was inhaling it deeply. She also liked it very much. And she pointed out to me, leaning against a side wall, a kind of high scaffolding of dark wood, groaning under the weight of big, round, yellow fruit, bigger than oranges and lemons, which I hadn't noticed before. They were grapefruit, hung there to season, she explained, produced in the greenhouse. Had I never tried them?—she then asked, taking one and offering it me to sniff. It was a shame she didn't have a knife with her to cut it into two "hemispheres." The taste of the juice was a hybrid: it was both like orange and lemon, with an additional bitterness all its own.

The center of the coach-house was taken up by two vehicles: one long grey Dilambda and a blue carriage whose uplifted shafts were only just lower than the climbing poles behind.

"Now we don't use the carriage anymore," Micòl remarked. "On the few occasions Papa has to go into the country he goes by car. And the same for me and Alberto when we have to go—he to Milan, me to Venice. It's the unflagging Perotti who takes us to the station. At home the only ones who can drive are him (and he's a terrible driver) and Alberto. I can't—I haven't got my licence yet, and I'll really have to decide next spring . . . because . . . the problem is also this huge beast of an engine drinks like a fish!"

She drew close to the carriage. Its appearance was just as shiny and efficient as the car's.

"D'you recognize it?"

She opened one of the doors, got in and sat down. Then, patting the material of the seat next to her, she invited me to do likewise.

I entered accordingly and sat on her left. No sooner had I made myself comfortable than, slowly turning on its hinges with the sheer force of inertia, the carriage door shut on its own with the dry, precise click of a trap.

Now the beating of the rain on the coach-house roof became inaudible. It truly seemed as though we were in a small drawing room, a cramped and suffocating one.

"How well you've kept it," I said, unable to suppress the sudden emotion which registered in my voice as a slight tremor. "It still seems new. The only thing missing is a vase of flowers."

"Oh, as for flowers, Perotti sees that they're in place when he takes Grandma out."

"So you still use it then!"

"Not more than two or three times a year, and only for a tour of the garden."

"And the horse? Is it still the same one?"

"Still the same old Star. He's twenty-two. Didn't you see him, the other day, at the back of the stall? By now he's half-blind, but harnessed to the carriage, he still cuts a . . . *lamentable figure*."

She burst out laughing, shaking her head.

"Perotti has a real mania about this carriage," she continued bitterly. "And it's mainly to please him (he hates and despises motor cars—you've no idea how much!) that every now and then we let him take Grandma out for a ride up and down the driveways. Every fortnight or so he's in here with buckets of water, sponges, doeskins and rug-beaters—and that explains the miracle, that's why the carriage, especially when seen at dusk, still manages more or less to hoodwink everyone."

"More or less?" I protested. "But it looks brand-new."

She snorted with boredom.

"Do me a favor, and don't talk drivel."

Spurred by some unpredictable impulse, she brusquely moved away, and huddled up in her corner. Her brow furrowed, her features sharpened with the same rancorous look with which, sometimes when playing tennis, and utterly focused on winning, she would stare straight ahead. Suddenly she seemed to have grown ten years older.

We stayed for a few moments like this, in silence. Then, without changing position, her arms hugging her sun-tanned knees as though she was freezing (she was in short stockings, a light cotton T-shirt and a pullover tied by its sleeves round her neck), Micòl started to speak again.

"Perotti would like to waste vast quantities of time and elbow grease on this ghastly old wreck!" she said. "No, listen to what I'm saying—here where the light is so dim you can make a great fuss about the wonder of it, but outside, by natural light, there's nothing to be done about it, thousands of little defects glare at you, the paintwork stripped in many places, the spokes and hubs of the wheels are all eaten away, the material of this seat is worn away practically to a cobweb (now you can't see it but I can assure you it's so). And so I ask myself: what's Perotti bursting his blood vessels for? Is it worth it? The poor creature wants to have Papa's permission to repaint the whole thing, to restore and beaver away at it to his heart's content. But Papa's dithering about it as usual and can't decide."

She fell silent; and moved very slightly.

"Consider, in contrast, that canoe," she went on, at the same time pointing out to me through the carriage-door window, which our breath had begun to mist over, a greyish, oblong, skeletal shape leaning against the wall opposite the grapefruit frame. "Consider the canoe, and admire how honestly, with what dignity and moral courage, it's faced up to the full consequences of its utter uselessness, as it needed to. Even things, even they have to die, my friend. And so, if even they have to die, it's just as well to let them go. Above all, there's far more style in that, wouldn't you say?"

III

· 1 ·

COUNTLESS times during the following winter, spring and summer, I kept thinking back to what had happened (or rather hadn't happened) between Micòl and me, inside that carriage so beloved of old Perotti. If on that rainy afternoon, in which the luminous Indian summer of 1938 had suddenly come to an end, I had at the very least managed to say what I was feeling—I thought with bitterness—perhaps things between us would have gone differently from the way they did. To have spoken to her, to have kissed her: it was then—I couldn't stop telling myself—then, when everything was still possible, that I should have done it! But I was forgetting to ask myself the crucial question: whether in that supreme, unique, irrevocable moment—a moment that, perhaps, had shaped both my life and hers—I was really ready to risk any act or word at all. Did I already know then, for example, that I was truly in love? The truth is: I didn't know it. I didn't know it then, and I wouldn't know it for another two full weeks, when bad weather, having set in, had irremediably dispersed us and the occasions for which we'd gathered.

I remember how the insistent rain, falling uninterruptedly for days and days, as a prelude to winter, the rigid, gloomy winter of the Po valley, had made any further visits to the garden out of the question. And yet, despite the change of season, everything proceeded in such a way as to deceive me that nothing had substantially changed.

At half past two on the day after our last visit to the Finzi-Continis'—more or less the time when, one after the other, we would have emerged from the tunnel of little climbing roses, shouting out "Hi!" or "Hello!" or "Greetings!"—the telephone at my house rang and put me in contact, as though with the real thing, with the voice of Micòl. That same evening it was I who telephoned her, and the next afternoon it was again she who took the initiative. We might have kept our conversations going just as we had on those latter occasions, grateful now as we were before that Bruno Lattes, Adriana Trentini, Giampiero Malnate and all the others had left us alone and shown no sign of remembering us. Besides, when had we, Micòl and I, ever given a thought to them during our long excursions in the park—so long that often when we returned we found no trace of them, either on the court or in the *Hütte*?

Pursued by the worried looks of my parents, I closed myself up in the cupboard that housed the telephone. I dialled the number. It was almost always she who answered—with such alacrity that I suspected she must be forever carrying the phone around with her.

"Where are you speaking from?" I once tried to ask her.

She started to laugh.

"Well . . . from home, I guess."

"Thanks for that information. I just wanted to know how come you always manage to answer in a flash, so quickly, I mean. Do you have the phone on your desk like a businessman? Or from morning till night do you pace around the apparatus like the caged tiger in Machatý's *Nocturne*?"

I seemed to detect a slight hesitation from the other end of the line. If she got to the phone before the others did, she then replied, that was, apart from the famous speed of her reflexes, because of her gift of intuition—an intuition which, every time the thought of phoning her passed through my mind, ensured that she was in the vicinity of the telephone. She then changed the subject. How was my thesis on Panzacchi going? And Bologna—when would I be resuming my usual journeys back and forth, if only for a change of scene?

Sometimes, however, someone else answered—either Alberto, or Professor Ermanno, or one of the two maids and even, on one occasion, Signora Regina, who displayed a surprising acuity of hearing when it came to the telephone. In such cases, of course, I was forced to announce my name and to state that it was "Signorina" Micòl I'd like to speak to. After a few days, though—at first this would embarrass me even more, but I gradually got used to it—it was enough for me to drop my "Hello" into the receiver for the person on the other end hurriedly to pass me on to the one I was seeking. Even Alberto, when it was he who picked up the phone, did not behave any differently. Micòl was always there, ready to snatch the receiver from whoever's hand it was in, as though they were always gathered together in a single room, a "living room," drawing room or library, each of them sunk into a vast leather armchair within a few steps of the telephone. I really began to suspect that. To inform Micòl, who, at the trilling of the phone (I could almost see her) would suddenly look up, they perhaps confined themselves to offering her the receiver from a distance, Alberto, when it was he, no doubt doing so with a wink poised between the affectionate and the sardonic.

One morning I decided to ask her to verify my guesswork, and she heard me out in silence.

"Isn't it true?" I pressed her.

Apparently it wasn't. Since I was so keen to know the truth—she said—here it was, then. Each of them had a telephone line in their own room (after she'd got one for herself, the rest of the family had also ended up having them installed). They were the most useful mechanisms, she wholeheartedly recommended them: they let you phone out at whatever time of the day or night without disturbing anyone or being disturbed, and they were especially convenient at night-time. Saved you even putting a foot out of bed. What a weird idea!—she added, laughing—whatever made me think that they'd all be gathered together as though in a hotel lobby? Why on earth would they be doing that? It was strange though that when it wasn't she who answered directly, I never heard the click of the phone being lifted.

"No," she categorically reiterated. "To safeguard personal liberty, there's nothing like a private phone line. Honestly—you should get one yourself, in your own room. Just think how we'd be able to talk, especially at night!"

"And so you're phoning me now from your bedroom?"

"I certainly am. And from my bed as well."

It was eleven in the morning.

"You're not exactly an early bird."

"Oh, not you as well!" she complained. "It's one thing for my father, who's worn down with worries and seventy years old, to keep getting up at six-thirty to set us a good example, as he puts it, and to stop us loafing around in feather beds, but it's honestly a bit much when our best friends start preaching at us. Do you know what time yours truly got up, my dear boy? At seven. And you dare to wonder that I'm back in bed again at eleven! Besides, it's not as though I was sleeping—I've been reading, scribbling some notes for my thesis, and looking out of the window. I always do a whole lot of things when I'm in bed. The warmth of the blankets undoubt-edly spurs me into activity."

"Describe your room for me."

She clicked her tongue three times as a sign of refusal.

"No way. That's *verboten. Privat.* Though, if you insist, I could tell you what I can see from the window."

She could see through the glass, in the foreground, the bearded tips of her *Washingtoniae graciles* which the wind and the rain were beating at so "vilely." Who knows if the solicitude of Titta and Bepi, who had already begun to wrap the usual straw coats around their trunks as they did every winter, would be enough to protect them in the succeeding months from a frostbitten death which threatened every year, when the grim weather returned, and which till then they'd always luckily avoided. Then, farther off, partly hidden by wisps of wandering mist, she could see the four tow-ers of the Estense Castle which the heavy rainshowers had turned black as clinker. And behind the towers, with a bruised look that would make you shudder, and that too hidden every now and then by the mist, the distant marble stonework of the Duomo's facade and bell-tower . . . Oh, that mist! She couldn't bear it when it was like this—it made her think of dirty rags. But sooner or later the rain would cease, and then the mist, in the morning, pierced by weak rays of sunshine, would be turned into something precious, something delicately opalescent, which in its changing reflections of tone was exactly like those *làttimi* which her room was full of. Winter was a pain, it's true, not least because it put an end to tennis, but it had its compensations. "Since every situation, however sad and annoying it is," she concluded, "in the end offers certain compensations, and often significant ones."

"*Làttimi?*" I asked. "What are they? Something to eat?"

"No. Not at all," she protested petulantly, appalled as usual by my ignorance. "They're things made with milky glass. Normal glasses, champagne glasses, ampoules, dainty vases, little boxes, stuff you might find among the junk in antique dealers' shops. In Venice they call them *làttimi*, and elsewhere *opalines* or even *flûtes*. You've no idea how much I adore these things. There's nothing at all I don't know about the subject. Try testing me and see."

It was in Venice, she went on, perhaps prompted by the local mists, so different from our big gloomy Paduan fogs, mists which are infinitely more lovely and luminous and which only one painter in the world had managed to do justice to—and that wasn't late Monet but "our" De Pisis— it was in Venice that she'd first got so interested in *làttimi*. She had spent hours going round antique shops. There were some, especially in the San Samuele district, around Campo Santo Stefano, or in the Ghetto, at the far end toward the station, that practically sold nothing but. Her uncles Giulio and Federico lived in the Calle del Cristo, near San Moisè. Late afternoons, not knowing what else to do, and naturally with the housekeeper Signorina Blumenfeld glued to her side—a prim *jodé** sixty-year-old from Frankfurt-am-Main, who'd been in Italy for more than thirty years, a real bore!—she would go out into Calle XXII Marzo in search of *làttimi*. From San Moisè, Campo Santo Stefano is a short walk. Unlike San Geremia, which is in the Ghetto—if you go by San Bartolomìo and the Lista di Spagna it takes at least half an hour to get there, and yet it's very close indeed. You just have to take a *traghetto* along the Grand Canal as far as Palazzo Grassi and then leap off at the Frari . . . But returning to the *làttimi*, what a thrill, the thrill of a dowser, she got every time she managed

---

* Ferrara Jewish dialect: "Jewish woman."

to unearth a new and especially rare one! Did I want to know how many pieces she'd collected? Almost two hundred.

I carefully avoided telling her that what she was saying hardly seemed consistent with her declared aversion to any, even the briefest, attempt to keep things, objects, from the inevitable death which—even for them— lay in wait, and to the mania for preserving them that Perotti in particular had. I wanted her to go on describing her room, and to forget her earlier prescriptions of "*verboten*" and "*privat.*"

I succeeded. She kept on talking about her *làttimi* (she had arranged them neatly on three high, dark mahogany shelves which stretched almost the whole length of the wall which faced the one alongside which her bed had been placed) and as she did so, her room, I'm not sure how conscious she was of this, was gradually taking shape, and all its details were being delineated.

Thus: of windows, there were two. Both of them faced south, and were so high off the floor that to look out from them, with the park stretching out beneath and the roofs which beyond the park's edge extended out of sight, it seemed as though one were looking out from the deck of a transatlantic liner. Between the two windows was a fourth shelf—the shelf for English and French books. Against the left-hand window was an office-type desk, flanked by a small table for the portable typewriter on one side, and on the other by a fifth bookshelf, this one for Italian literature, classic and modern, and for translations: mainly from Russian—Pushkin, Gogol, Tolstoy, Dostoevsky, Chekhov. On the floor, a large Persian carpet, and at the center of the room, which was long but rather narrow, three arm-chairs and a chaise longue to stretch out on while reading. Two doors: one for the entrance, at the end, by the left-hand window, which directly com-municated with the staircase and lift, and another a few inches from the opposite corner of the room which led to the bathroom. At night she slept without ever fully closing the shutters, keeping a little lamp at the bedside table always on, and the trolley with a thermos of *Skiwasser* (as well, of course, as the telephone!) so they could be reached merely by stretching out an arm. If she woke up in the night, all she needed to do was take a sip of *Skiwasser* (it was so comfy always having it ready nice and hot—why didn't I too get myself one, a thermos?). After which, she would slump back down, and let her eyes rove over those misty, luminescent, treasured *làt-timi*. That way, sleep would creep up on her as stealthily as a Venetian "high tide," and quickly submerge and "prostrate" her.

But these were not our only topics of conversation.

As though she also wanted to deceive me into thinking that nothing had changed, that everything between us was the same as "before" when, that is, we had been able to see each other every afternoon, Micòl never missed a chance to remind me of that series of "incredible," wonderful days we had spent together.

We'd always spoken of a whole range of things, back then, while walking around in the park: of trees, plants, our childhoods, our relatives. In the meantime, Bruno Lattes, Adriana Trentini, *the* Malnate, Carletto Sani, Tonino Collevatti and, with them, those who visited later, hardly merited more than the odd reference, the whole group of them designated in the cursory and rather disdainful phrase "those others."

Now, however, on the telephone, our talks continually harked back to them, and especially to Bruno Lattes and Adriana Trentini, who, according to Micòl, had a "thing" going on. Was I serious?—she kept saying to me. How could I not have noticed that they were going out together? It was so blatant! His eyes never left her for a moment, and she too, though she treated him like a slave, while she played the flirt a bit with everyone, with me, with that bear of a Malnate, and even with Alberto, she too was obviously smitten. Dear Bruno! With his temperament (let's be honest, a bit impressionable, or how else explain the way he reveres two well-meaning blockheads of the calibre of little Sani and that youth Collevatti!), with his temperament these last months can hardly have been easy on him, given the situation. No question about it, Adriana was up for it (one evening, in the *Hütte*, she had happened to see them half stretched out on the sofa kissing like there was no tomorrow) though whether she was the type of person to be able to keep something so demanding alive, in defiance of the Racial Laws, and of both his and her relatives, that was another question. Bruno truly can't have been having an easy time of it, this winter. And it's not as though Adriana was a bad catch, far from it! Almost as tall as Bruno, blond, with that lovely skin like Carole Lombard's—at another time she might have been exactly what Bruno dreamed of, given how much he clearly went for the "decidedly Aryan" type. That she was also a bit of an empty-headed flirt, and unconsciously cruel, couldn't be denied. Didn't I recall the look she'd given poor Bruno that time when, as a pair, they lost the famous return match against the duo Désirée Baggioli and Claudio Montemezzo? It was mainly her, and not Bruno at all, who lost the match for them, with that endless series of double-faults she contrived—at least three every time she was serving! And yet, completely unaware, for the whole match she did nothing but berate him with foul mutterings as if he, the poor creature, wasn't done in and depressed enough on his own account. Seriously, it would have been a total joke if it wasn't for the fact that, all considered, the whole event had ended up as rather a bitter one! But so it goes. Without doing it deliberately, moralists like Bruno always fall for little Adriana-types, and from this springs a whole flood of jealous scenes, furtive tailings, unpleasant surprises, tearful episodes, sworn denials, even comings-to-blows, and infidelities, I'm telling you, endless infidelities. No, in the end, Bruno ought to have lit a candle in gratitude to the Racial Laws. He would have to face up to a difficult winter, it was true. But the Racial Laws, not always without some consolations then, would have saved him from committing the most blatant stupidity—of getting engaged.

"Don't you agree?" she once added. "And also because he, like yourself, has literary ambitions, he's someone who's drawn to writing. I seem to remember having seen, two or three years ago, some of his verses published in the literary pages of the Padano all under the title "Poems of an Avant-gardist.""

"Alas!" I sighed. "But what are you trying to say? I don't understand."

She silently laughed—I could clearly hear her.

"Yes indeed, at a final reckoning," she went on, "a bit of gall and wormwood won't do him much harm. '*Non mi lasciare ancora, sofferenza*'* as Ungaretti says. He wants to write? Let him take what's coming to him, and then let's see. Besides, you just have to look at him to tell—it's as clear as day that pain is what he fervently desires."

"You're disgustingly cynical. You and Adriana make quite a pair."

---

* "Suffering, don't leave me yet."

"You're wrong about that. And actually you've offended me. Compared to me, Adriana's blameless as an angel. Capricious perhaps, but unconscious, innocent like '*tutte/le femmine di tutti / i sereni animali / che avvicinano a Dio.*'* Whereas Micòl's good, I've told you already and I'll tell you again, and she knows what she does—remember that well."

Although far less often, she did also mention Giampiero Malnate, toward whom she'd always behaved curiously, basically in a critical and sarcastic way, as though she were jealous of the friendship that bound him and Alberto (a bit exclusive, to tell the truth), but at the same time was reluctant to admit it, and for that reason was driven to "smash the idol."

In her view, even physically Malnate wasn't that impressive. Too big, too bulky, too much like a "father" to be taken seriously in this respect. He was one of those excessively hairy men who, however many times a day they shave, still always look dirty, a bit unwashed—and this, let's be honest, wouldn't do. Perhaps, as far as one could see through the thick lenses of his glasses, his camouflage (it seemed that they made him sweat, and that made you want to take them off him), his eyes weren't really that bad: grey, "steely," the eyes of a strong, silent type. But too serious and severe. Too constitutionally marriageable. Belying their effect of scornful misogyny, they were full of the threat of feelings so eternal that they'd scare off any girl, even the quietest and meekest.

He was always so sulky, that's it; and not nearly as original as he seemed to think himself. Did I want to bet that, with the right line of questioning, he'd not come out and claim that he felt ill at ease in city clothes, and much more at home anywhere in the windjammer, plus-fours and ski-boots that he'd be kitted out in for his unmissable weekends on Mottarone or Monte Rosa? His trusty pipe, when seen in this light, was fairly revealing—it stood for a whole system of sub-Alpine, masculine austerity, like a flag.

He was great friends with Alberto, but as for Alberto, with his temperament passive as a punchbag, he always befriends everyone and no one. They'd lived whole years together at Milan, and that certainly had to be given weight. Didn't I also find a bit too much, all the same, their endless confabulations? Pst! Pst! Woof! Woof! No sooner would they meet

---

* "All/the females of all / the serene animals / closest to God" (Umberto Saba).

each other than they were at it again, drawing apart from everyone else and muttering away. And heaven knows what about! Girls? She somehow doubted it. Knowing Alberto, who had always been rather reticent—not to say mysterious—about such matters, honestly, she wouldn't place the smallest bet on it.

"Are you two still seeing him?" I got round to asking one day, throwing off the question in the most unconcerned tone I could muster.

"Oh yes . . . I think he comes round every so often to visit his Alberto . . ." she answered calmly. "They shut themselves up in his room, take tea, smoke their pipes (even Alberto started puffing away at one a short while back), and talk and talk, happy as sandboys, doing nothing but talk."

She was too intelligent, too sensitive not to have guessed what I was hiding under my indifference: and that being, all of a sudden, a sharp, and symptomatic, desire to see her again. Yet she behaved as though she had understood nothing, without signaling even indirectly the chance that, sooner or later, I too might be invited round.

· 2 ·

THAT NIGHT I spent in turmoil. Fitfully, I slept, I woke up, I slept again, and every time I slept I kept on dreaming of Micòl.

I dreamed, for example, of finding myself, just like that very first day I set foot in the garden, watching her play tennis with Alberto. Even in the dream I never took my eyes off her for a second. I kept on telling myself how wonderful she was, flushed and covered with sweat, with that frown of almost fierce concentration that divided her forehead, all tensed up as she was with the effort to beat her smiling, slightly bored and sluggish older brother. Yet then I felt oppressed by an uneasiness, an embittered feeling, an almost unbearable ache. I asked myself in desperation—what was left of that young girl from ten years ago in the twenty-two-year-old Micòl, in her shorts and cotton T-shirt, this Micòl who had such an athletic, modern, free and easy air (above all free!) that she made you think she'd done nothing else for the last few years than swan around in the Meccas of international tennis—London, Paris, the Côte d'Azur, Forest Hills? But yes, I answered myself, the weightless blond hair, with streaks verging on white, the blue, almost Scandinavian irises, the honey-colored skin, and on her breastbone, every now and then leaping out from her T-shirt collar, the little gold disc of the *Shaddai**—they're still there from the child she was. But what else?

Then we were closed inside the carriage, in that stale, grey penumbra: with Perotti sitting in the box-seat up front, looming, motionless, mute. I reasoned with myself that if Perotti was up there, with his back stubbornly turned toward us, he was obviously doing this so as not to have to see what was—or what might be—going on inside the carriage, no doubt out of a servile discretion. Yet he was nevertheless aware of everything, of course he was, the sinister old bumpkin! His wife, the wan Vittorina, prying through the partly ajar double doors of the coach-house—every now and then I could make out the woman's little reptile head, lustrous with plastered-down, crow-black hair, as she peeped round the edge of the door—his wife stood as a sentry there, fixing him with her fretful, discontented eye, and making stealthy gestures and coded expressions at him.

Next we were in her room, Micòl and I, but not even then were we alone, but rather "plagued"—as she herself had whispered to me—by the habitual third party, which this time was Jor, crouched in the center of the room like a gigantic granite idol, who stared at us with his two frosty eyes, one black, the other blue. The room was long and narrow, full like the coach-house of things to eat: grapefruits, oranges, mandarins and above all *làttimi*, ranged in a row like books on the boards of vast black shelves, severe and ecclesiastic, reaching up to the ceiling. Only the *làttimi* were not at all the glass objects that Micòl had told me about, but, just as I'd supposed, cheeses—little round driplets of off-white cheeses shaped like bottles. Laughing, Micòl insisted that I try one of them, one of her cheeses. At this she stood on tiptoe, and was about to touch with the stretched-out index finger of her right hand one of those which had been set on the topmost shelf—those were the best ones, she explained to me, the freshest. But not at all, I wasn't going to have one—I felt anxious not only because of the dog's presence but also because I realized that outside, while we were

---

* One of the names of God, here inscribed on a pendant.

arguing, the lake tide was rapidly rising. If I were to delay any further, the high water would have locked me in, would have stopped me being able to leave her room unnoticed. For it was secretly and by night that I had come into Micòl's bedroom. Secretly hidden from Alberto, Professor Ermanno, Signora Olga, grandma Regina, her uncles Giulio and Federico, and the earnest Signorina Blumenfeld. And Jor, who was the only one to know, the sole witness of the thing that was between us, couldn't tell anyone about it.

I also dreamed that we spoke openly together, at last without any dissimulation, with our cards on the table.

As usual we quarreled a bit, Micòl arguing that the thing between us had begun from the first day, that is, from when she and I, still utterly surprised to meet again and recognize each other, had made off to see the park, and I, for my part, claiming instead that in my opinion, the thing had begun a good while earlier, on the telephone, from the moment she had announced that she'd become "ugly," "a spinster with a red nose." Obviously I hadn't believed her. All the same she couldn't even have a glimmer, I added with a catch in my throat, of how much those words of hers had tormented me. In the days that followed, before I saw her again, I had gone over them again and again, and couldn't rid myself of the unease they caused.

"Well, perhaps it's true," at this point Micòl seemed to agree, placing her hand on mine. "If the idea that I'd become ugly and red-nosed caused you such distress, then I give in—it means that you're right. But now, what's to be done? That excuse of playing tennis isn't going to wash anymore, and here at home, besides, with the risk of being stranded by the high water (d'you see how it's like Venice?)—it's neither right nor proper that I should let you come in."

"Why should you need to?" I parried. "You could go out yourself, after all."

"Me, go out?" she exclaimed, widening her eyes. "Just think for a moment, *dear boy*. Where would I go out to?"

"I . . . I'm not sure," I stuttered in reply. "To Montarone, for example, or Piazza d'Armi near the Aqueduct, or, if you're unhappy to be seen with me, the Via Borso side of Piazza della Certosa. Everyone who's going out together has always gone there—I don't know about your parents, but mine, in their time, did. And to go out a bit together, honestly, what was the harm in that? It's not like we're making love! It's just the first rung, on the brink of the abyss. But from there to the bottom of the abyss, there's still a long way to go!"

I was on the point of suggesting that if, as it seemed, not even Piazza della Certosa suited her, we could always meet up in Bologna, having taken two separate trains. But I kept quiet, drained of courage, even in dreams. And besides, shaking her head and smiling, she immediately declared that it was useless, impossible, "*verboten.*" She would never have gone with me, outside her home and the garden. And what was all this about?—she winked at me, amused. After she'd let herself be dragged around all the usual "open air" resorts beloved of "the Eros of our wild native town," was I perhaps hoping to take her to Bologna now? Perhaps to some "grand hotel" there, one of those favored by her grandma Josette, like the Brun or the Baglioni, where we'd have to show at the reception—had I thought of that?—our fine documents complete with racial provenance.

The next evening, as soon as I'd returned from a quick, unexpected trip to Bologna, to the university, I tried to telephone.

Alberto answered.

"How are things?" he crooned ironically, showing this once that he'd recognized my voice. "It's ages since we saw each other. How are you? What are you up to?"

Disconcerted, with my heart racing, I began to blather away. I bundled up a whole bunch of things: news about my graduation thesis that loomed above me like an unscalable wall, and comments on the weather, which after the last bad fortnight seemed to be offering some hope of improvement—but it wasn't worth trusting: the sharp air made it quite clear we were now in the middle of winter, and we might as well forget those fine days of October. Most of all, I dwelled on my brief trip to Bologna.

In the morning, I told him, I had passed by Via Zamboni, where, after having sorted out various things in the secretary's office, I'd been able to check out in the library a certain number of entries from the Panzacchi bibliography which I was preparing. Later, around one o'clock, I'd gone to eat at the Pappagallo—certainly not the so-called "*pastasciutta*" restaurant at the foot of the Asinelli which, besides being extremely dear, as far as its cooking went seemed distinctly inferior to its reputation, but rather to the other Pappagallo "*in brodo*," in a little side street off Via Galliera, which, as its name suggests, was famous for its vegetable soups and boiled meats, as well as for its very modest prices. Then in the afternoon I'd seen some friends, gone round the bookshops of the city center, drunk tea at Zanarini's, the one in Piazza Galvani, at the end of the Pavaglione. It had been a reasonably good trip—I ended up saying—"almost as good as it was when I used to attend regularly."

"Just imagine," I added at this point, inventing the whole thing—who knows what devil had suddenly prompted me to tell a story of this kind, "before going to the station I even had time to have a quick look around the Via dell'Oca."

"The Via dell'Oca?" Alberto asked, suddenly becoming animated, although at the same time a bit reserved.

That was all I needed to be spurred on by the same sour impulse which sometimes made my father appear, set beside the Finzi-Continis, far more boorish and "assimilated" than he actually was.

"What?" I exclaimed. "You mean to say that you didn't know that in Bologna's Via dell'Oca there's one of the most famous brothels in all Italy!"

He coughed.

"No. I didn't know it," he replied.

He then mentioned, in a different tone of voice, that in a few days' time he too would have to leave for Milan, where he'd be staying for at least a week. June wasn't after all as far away as it seemed, and he still hadn't found nor, to tell the truth, had he even sought out, a professor who would let him cobble together "any old bits for a thesis."

After which, once again changing the subject, he asked if by chance, not long ago, I'd passed by along the Mura degli Angeli on my bicycle. He'd been out in the garden to see what damage the rain had done to the tennis court. But partly because of the distance and partly because of the already fading light, he hadn't been able to determine whether or not it was me, the guy who was up there, stock still, not having got off the saddle, and leaning a hand against a tree trunk to look. Oh, so it was me, then? He went on, after I'd admitted, not without some hesitation, having taken the Mura route back home from the station: that was because, I explained, of the inner disgust I always felt coming across certain "ugly mugs" that would be gathered in front of the Caffè della Borsa, in Corso Roma, or strung out along the Corso Giovecca.—Ah, so it was me, he repeated. He was sure it had been! Anyway, if it was me, why on earth hadn't I answered his shouts and whistles? Hadn't I heard them?

I hadn't, I once again lied. In fact, I said, I hadn't even been aware that he'd been in the garden. At this stage we really had nothing more to say to each other, nothing at all to bridge the sudden gulf of silence that had opened between us.

"But you . . . weren't you wanting to speak to Micòl?" he said at last, as though remembering.

"That's right," I replied. "Would you mind putting her on?"

He would gladly do so, he told me, if it wasn't for the fact that (and it was truly odd "the little angel" hadn't even let me know) Micòl had left early in the afternoon for Venice, she too meaning to break the back of her thesis. She had come down for lunch all dressed up for the journey, with her bags and everything packed, to announce her intention to her "astonished little family." She had said how bored she was of being weighed down with this task hanging over her. Instead of taking her degree in June, she was aiming for February: which at Venice, with the Marciana and the Querini-Stampalia libraries at hand, she could easily manage, whereas at Ferrara, for a host of reasons, her thesis on Dickinson would never press on at anything like the required speed. This is what the girl said. But who knows whether she would be able to hold out against Venice's spirit-dampening atmosphere, and against a house, the uncles' house, which she didn't care for. It would be easy to imagine her back at base in a week or two with nothing to show for it. He'd think he was dreaming if ever Micòl managed to keep herself away from Ferrara uninterruptedly for twenty days . . .

"Oh, well!" he concluded. "But what would you say (only, this week's impossible, and so is next week, but the one after, yes, I really think that would work), what would you say to the idea of us all taking a roadtrip as far as Venice? It would be fun just to land on her unannounced—let's say, you, me and Giampi Malnate!"

"It's an idea," I said. "Why not? We can talk about it later."

"In the meantime," he went on, with an effort in which I sensed a desire to compensate me for what he'd revealed to me, "in the meantime, sorry—that's if you've nothing better on—why not come round here, let's say tomorrow, around five in the afternoon? Malnate should be there too. We'll have some tea ... listen to some records ... have a chat ... I'm not sure how you, as a literary man, will feel about spending time with an engineer (as I'll be) and an industrial chemist. But if you'd do us the honor, compliments aside, do come—it would be a pleasure for us."

We carried on for a while longer, Alberto ever more keen and excited about this idea of his, which he seemed to have thought up on the spot, to have me round to his house, and I drawn but at the same time put off. It was quite true, I remembered, that a little while before, I had spent almost a half-hour staring at the garden from the Mura, and, especially, at the house, which I could see, through the almost bare boughs of the trees, cut out against the evening sky with the fragile, shimmering air of a heraldic emblem. Two windows on the mezzanine floor, at the level of the terrace from which one went down into the park, were already lit up, and electric light also glowed farther up, from the solitary, topmost little window which barely opened beneath the apex of the peaked roof. For a long while, my eyeballs aching in their sockets, I stood there staring at the little light from that high window (a small, tremulous glow, suspended in the ever-darkening air like starlight); and only the distant whistles and Tyrolean yodeling of Alberto, awakening in me, as well as the fear of being recognized, the anxiety once more to hear Micòl's voice on the phone without delay, had, at a certain point, been able to dislodge me from the spot.

But now, on the other hand—I disconsolately asked myself—what did it matter to me to go round to their house, now, when I would no longer find Micòl there?

Yet the news my mother gave me as I left the small telephone cupboard, which was that just before noon Micòl Finzi-Contini had asked for me ("She asked me to tell you that she had to leave for Venice, to say goodbye, and to say that she'll write," my mother added, looking elsewhere), was enough to make me quickly change my mind. From that moment the time that separated me from five o'clock of the next day began to move with extraordinary slowness.

· 3 ·

IT WAS from then that I began, you could say on a daily basis, to visit Alberto's personal flat—he called it a studio—and it was a studio in fact, with the bedroom and bathroom adjoining it. It was from there, behind the door of that famous "chamber," passing in the corridor alongside, that Micòl would hear resound the indistinct voices of her brother and his friend Malnate, and where, during the course of the whole winter, apart from the maids arriving with a tea trolley, I never caught sight of any other family member. Oh, that winter of 1938–9! I remember the long and motionless months which seemed to be suspended above time itself, and my feelings of desperation—in February it snowed, Micòl postponed her return from Venice—and even now, at a distance of more than twenty years, the four walls of Alberto Finzi-Contini's studio still represent for me a kind of vice, a drug as necessary as it was unconscious each day I went there . . .

It wasn't as though I was at all desperate that first December evening in which I once more rode by bike across the Barchetto del Duca. Micòl had left. And yet I pedalled along the entrance drive, in the mist and darkness, as if in a short while I was expecting once more to see her and only her. I was excited, light-hearted, almost happy. I looked ahead, with the front light planing over those sites that belonged to a past which, though it seemed remote, was still recuperable, was not yet lost. There was the grove of rattan palms, there, farther on, on the right the hazy shape of Perotti's farmhouse, from one first-floor window of which leaked a faint yellowish glow, and there still farther in the distance was the ghostly scaffolding of the Panfilio bridge, and there, finally, heralded a fraction before by the screak of tyres on gravel, was the enormous hulk of the *magna domus*, impervious as a solitary rock, utterly dark except for a vivid white light that streamed from a little door on the ground floor, apparently left open to welcome me.

I got off the bike, stopping to examine the deserted threshold. Within, part blacked out by the left-side door which was shut, I could see the steep staircase covered by a red carpet—a fiery, bloody, scarlet red. At every step there was a brass stair rod, glowing and glinting as though it was gold.

Having leaned the bike against the wall, I bent down to secure the padlock. I was still bent there, in the dark, next to the door from which, besides the light, the hearty warmth from a radiator gushed forth—in the darkness I didn't seem able to close the lock, so I'd just thought of lighting a match—when the unmistakable voice of Professor Ermanno sounded from somewhere very near.

"What are you up to? Are you locking it?" asked the Professor as he stood on the threshold. "Not a bad idea, that. One never knows. You can never be too careful."

I immediately straightened up, as usual unsure whether behind his slightly querulous kindness he was making fun of me.

"Good evening," I said, taking off my hat and stretching out my hand.

"Good evening, my dear boy," he replied. "But keep your hat on, please keep it on!"

I felt his small plump hand rest inertly in my own and then as quickly withdraw. He was not wearing a hat but an old sporting beret tilted down over his spectacles, and a woolen scarf wrapped round his neck.

He gave a diffident glance toward the bicycle.

"You have locked it, haven't you?"

I said that I hadn't. Then, upset, he insisted that I went back, and obliged him by locking it properly, since—he repeated—one never knows. A theft would be unlikely—he went on from the threshold as I once again attempted to hook the lock around the spokes of the back wheel. One couldn't entirely trust to the garden wall. Along its outer perimeter, especially on the side of the Mura degli Angeli, there were at least a dozen points where a moderately adept boy would have no difficulty in climbing over. Then making a getaway, even weighed down by the bicycle over his shoulders, would be almost as straightforward an operation for such a boy.

Finally I managed to click the lock shut. I raised my eyes but the threshold was once again deserted.

The Professor was waiting for me inside the little entrance lobby, at the foot of the stairs. I went in, shut the door, and only then realized that he was looking at me with a troubled, regretful air.

"I'm wondering," he said, "if it wouldn't have been better for you to actually bring the bicycle in . . . Yes, take my advice. The next time you come, bring the bicycle in with you. If you put it there beneath the stairs it won't give the slightest trouble to anyone."

He turned round and began to walk up the stairs. More hunched than ever, still with that beret on his head and scarf round his neck, he ascended slowly, holding on to the banister. All the while talking, or rather muttering, as though his words were directed to himself rather than to me.

It was Alberto who had told him I was coming round that day. For this reason, since Perotti was suspected of having a touch of fever (it was only a minor attack of bronchitis, but it needed looking after to avoid the spread of infection) and since Alberto—always so forgetful, distracted, with his head in the clouds—was really not to be relied on, he had had to assume the responsibility himself of "standing at the ready." Doubtless, if it had been Micòl, he would have had no cause for worry, since Micòl, who knows how, always found time to look after everything, taking care not only of her own studies but also of the general running of the whole household, even of the kitchen "stoves." She had a passion for that almost as strong as for novels and poetry—it was she who at the end of the week would do the accounts with Gina or Vittorina, she who would *schecht** the poultry with her bare hands, and this despite the fact that she really loved the creatures, poor thing! But unfortunately Micòl wasn't at home today (had Alberto warned me she wasn't here?), having had to leave for Venice yesterday afternoon. His not being able to rely either on Alberto or on their "angel of the hearth" nor even, as if that wasn't enough, on the indisposed Perotti, explained why this time he'd had to stand in as doorman.

He also spoke of other things I don't remember. I do recall, though, that in the end he came back to Micòl, but this time to complain about her "restlessness of late," due of course to "many factors," though . . . here he broke off suddenly. During all this time in which not only had we reached the top of the stairs, but had gone down two corridors, and crossed various rooms, Professor Ermanno had always preceded me, never letting me overtake except when he was turning off the lights in passing.

Rapt with all I was hearing about Micòl (that detail about her, with her bare hands, being the one who'd cut the throats of the chickens in the

---

* Yiddish: "ritually slaughter."

kitchen strangely intrigued me), I looked around but almost without seeing. Besides, what we were passing through was not so unlike other houses
which belonged to Ferrara's high society, Jewish or not, laden like them with
the usual furnishings, monumental wardrobes, heavy seventeenth-century
chests of drawers with feet carved in the shape of lions' paws, refectory-type
tables, old Tuscan leather chairs with bronze studs, Frau armchairs, intricate glass and ironwork chandeliers hanging from the center of coffered
ceilings, thick carpets the color of tobacco, carrot and ox-blood stretched
out everywhere over darkly lustrous parquet. Here, perhaps, there were a
greater number of nineteenth-century paintings, landscapes and portraits,
and of books, most of them rebound, in rows behind the glass doors of
huge, dark mahogany bookcases. The mammoth radiators released heat on
a scale which at home my father would have declared plain crazy (I could
just hear him saying it!): a heat redolent of a luxury hotel rather than a private home, and of such intensity that, almost immediately breaking out in
a sweat, I'd had to take off my overcoat.

With him in front and me in tow, we crossed at least a dozen rooms of
differing size, some vast as real halls, some small, even tiny, and linked to
each other by corridors which were not always straight nor on the same
level. At last, having reached halfway down one such corridor, Professor
Ermanno came to a halt in front of a door.

"Here we are at last," he said.

He flicked his thumb toward the door and winked.

He apologized for not being able to come in himself, as—he
explained—he had to go over some accounts of their holdings in the country. He promised to have "one of the girls bring up something hot," and
then, having been assured that I'd come again—he had put aside for me
the copies of his little studies on Venetian history, I wasn't to forget!—he
shook me by the hand, and speedily disappeared at the end of the corridor.

I went in.

"Ah! You're here!" Alberto greeted me.

He was slumped in an armchair. He levered himself up with both
hands on the armrests, got to his feet, put down the book he had been
reading, leaving it open with its spine up on a little low table beside him,
and came toward me.

He was wearing a pair of vicuña grey trousers, one of his fine pullovers the color of dry leaves, brown English lace-ups (they were real Dawsons— he would later inform me—which he'd found in a little Milanese shop near San Babila), a flannel shirt, without a tie, open at the collar, and was carrying a pipe between his teeth. He shook my hand without too much warmth, as he stared at a point behind my back. What was attracting his attention? I had no idea.

"Excuse me," he murmured.

He let go of me, bending his long back sideways, and as he brushed past I realized that I'd left the double door half open. Alberto was already there, however, to see to it personally. He grasped the handle of the outer door, but before drawing it toward him he stuck his head out into the corridor to look around.

"And Malnate," I asked. "Isn't he here yet?"

"No, not yet," he replied as he came back.

He took my hat, scarf and coat from me, and disappeared into the small adjoining room. Through the communicating door I was thus able to see something of it: a part of the bed with a woolen coverlet in sporty red and blue squares, a pouffe at the foot of the bed, and, hanging on the wall beside the little doorway to the bathroom, this also half open, there was a small male nude by De Pisis in a simple frame of light-colored wood.

"Do sit down," Alberto said meanwhile. "I'll be back in a moment."

He did indeed return immediately, and now, seated in front of me, in the armchair I'd seen him pull himself out of with the faintest show of fatigue, perhaps of boredom, he considered me with that strange expression of detached, objective sympathy which was a sign in him, I knew, of the liveliest interest in others of which he was capable. He was smiling at me, revealing the large incisors he'd inherited from his mother's family: too large and strong for his pale, long face, and for the gums they were set in, as bloodless as the face.

"Would you like to listen to a bit of music?" he proposed, turning on a radiogram placed in a corner of the studio at the side of the entrance. "It's a Philips, really the best."

He made as though to get up again from the armchair, but then abandoned the attempt.

"No, wait," he said, "perhaps later."

I looked around.

"What records have you got?"

"Oh, a bit of everything: Monteverdi, Scarlatti, Bach, Mozart, Beethoven. I also have at my disposal a good deal of jazz, but don't be put off: Armstrong, Duke Ellington, Fats Waller, Benny Goodman, Charlie Kunz . . . "

He went on listing names and titles, cool and courteous as ever but without much interest, no more or less than if he'd been offering me a selection of dishes which he himself had made sure of tasting beforehand. He only became more animated, fractionally more, in demonstrating to me the virtues of his Philips. It was—he told me—a rather exceptional player, thanks to certain particular "technical improvements" he'd worked out himself and which a skilful Milanese technician had put into effect. These modifications principally concerned the quality of the sound, which now didn't merely come through a single loudspeaker, but from four separate sources of sound. There was, in fact, one speaker which only picked up bass notes, a second for the mid-range sounds, a third for the treble, and a fourth for the very high. So that from the chosen speaker, let's say, the highest notes, even whistles—here he sniggered—would "come through" to perfection. And don't, for heaven's sake, think for a moment that the speakers can be placed close up to one another! In the radiogram unit there are only two of them: the speaker for the medium-range sounds, and the one for the treble notes. The one for the very highest range he'd had the idea of hiding there at the end of the room, near the window, while the fourth one, for the bass, he'd fitted in under the sofa on which I was sitting. All this with the design of producing a certain stereophonic effect.

Dirce entered at that moment, in a blue canvas blouse and white apron, tight at the waist, dragging behind her the tea trolley.

I saw an expression of slight quarrelsomeness cross Alberto's face. The girl must also have noticed it.

"It was the Professor who ordered that I bring it immediately," she said.

"It doesn't matter. We might as well have a cup ourselves."

Blonde and curly-haired, with the flushed cheeks of the Veneto's Alpine foothills, Perotti's daughter, silently and with lowered eyes, prepared the tea cups, placed them on the small table and finally withdrew. A good scent of soap and talcum powder remained in the room. Even the tea, it seemed to me, was flavored with it.

As I drank, I kept looking round me. I admired the room's furnishings, all so rational, functional, modern, in complete contrast with the rest of the house, and yet, all the same, I couldn't quite work out why I was afflicted by an ever-increasing sense of unease, of oppressiveness.

"D'you like the way I've arranged the studio?" asked Alberto.

He seemed suddenly anxious to have my approval: which, naturally, I didn't begrudge, praising the simplicity of the furniture—having got to my feet, I went to examine more closely a large draftsman's table set alongside and near the window, sporting a finely turned and jointed metal lamp—and especially the side-lighting which—I said—I not only found very relaxing but also excellent for working by.

He let me run on and seemed pleased.

"Did you design the furniture yourself?"

"Not exactly. I copied a bit from Domus and Casabella, and a bit from Studio, you know, that English magazine . . . and a carpenter from Via Coperta made them for me."

Hearing me approve of the furniture—he added—couldn't fail to gratify him. For a place to work or just hang out in, what was the point of surrounding oneself with ugly stuff or even antique junk? As for Giampi Malnate (he colored very faintly as he named him), he'd insinuated that, furnished in this manner, it resembled a *garçonnière* more than a studio, besides arguing, like the good Communist he was, that *things* can at the most only provide some palliativeor surrogate, himself being opposed in principle to any kind ofsurrogate or palliative, and even to technical expertise, whenever it assumed that a drawer which closes perfectly, just to give an example, might offer a resolution to all the individual's problems, including those of morality and politics. He, however—touching his chest with a finger—had a different opinion. While respecting Malnate's views (he was a Communist—absolutely, didn't I know that?), he found life already confused and tedious enough without the household goods and furniture, the silent, faithful companions of our domestic life, having to be so as well.

It was the first and last time that I would ever see him become heated, and take sides with one set of ideas rather than another. We drank a second cup of tea, but by then the conversation had languished, to such an extent it was necessary to have recourse to some music.

We listened to a couple of records. Dirce returned, carrying a tray of pastries. At length, toward seven o'clock, a telephone on a desk next to the draftsman's table began to ring.

"D'you want to bet it's Giampi?" Alberto murmured, rushing toward it.

Before lifting the receiver he hesitated for a second: like a gambler who, having been dealt his cards, puts off the moment of discovering his luck.

But it really was Malnate, as I quickly gathered.

"So what are you doing? You're not coming then?" Alberto said with disappointment, with an almost puerile whine in his voice.

The other spoke rather at length (stuck between Alberto's shoulder and neck, the receiver vibrated with the force of his calm Lombard voice). At the end I heard a "Bye" and the conversation was over.

"He's not coming," Alberto commented.

He slowly returned to the armchair. He let himself drop into it, stretched himself, and yawned.

"It seems he's been kept in at the factory," he added, "and will be there for another three or four hours. He says he's sorry. And asked me to send you his regards."

· 4 ·

RATHER THAN the generic "See you soon" I exchanged with Alberto, while taking my leave of him, it was a letter from Micòl, arriving a few days later, which convinced me to return.

This letter was witty, neither too short nor too long, written on the four sides of two sheets of blue paper which her impetuous fluent handwriting had rapidly filled, without hesitations or corrections. Micòl begged me to forgive her: she had left unexpectedly. She hadn't even said goodbye to me, and this had not been very stylish of her, she was only too willing to admit. She had tried to phone me, however—she added—before she'd left, and in the eventuality that I couldn't be contacted, she'd asked Alberto to track me down. Since this had happened, had Alberto kept his promise of finding me, "at the cost of his life"? Famous as he was for his phlegmatism, he always ended up letting all of his contacts drop, and yet he had such a real need of them, poor thing! The letter went on for another two-and-a-half pages, explaining about her thesis which was by then "sailing on toward the finishing-line," referring to Venice—which in winter "simply made one want to weep"—and coming to an unexpected conclusion with a verse translation of an Emily Dickinson poem.

This:

> Morii per la Bellezza; e da poco ero
> discesa nell'avello,
> che, caduto pel Vero, uno fu messo
> nell'attiguo sacello.
>
> « Perché sei morta? », mi chiese sommesso.
> Dissi: « Morii pel Bello. »
> « Io per la Verità: dunque è lo stesso
> – disse –, son tuo fratello. »
>
> Da tomba a tomba, come due congiunti
> incontratisi a notte,
> parlavamo così; finché raggiunti
> l'erba ebbe nomi e bocche.*

It was followed by a postscript which said, word for word: "Alas, poor Emily. Such are the kind of consolations one's forced to find in abject spinsterhood!"

I liked the translation, but was struck most of all by the postscript. Who was it referring to? To "poor Emily" or was it, rather, to a Micòl in self-pitying, depressive mode?

Replying, I took care, once again, to hide behind a thick smokescreen.

---

* "I died for Beauty – but was scarce" by Emily Dickinson.

After having referred to my first visit to her house, and kept silent on how disappointing it had been for me, and after promising that I should very soon be returning there, I prudently confined myself to literature. Dickinson's poem was wonderful—I wrote—but her translation was also excellent, particularly in the way it showed a somewhat dated taste, a bit "Carduccian." Most of all I appreciated her faithfulness. With dictionary in hand, I had compared her version with the original text in English, finding nothing questionable except, perhaps, one detail, which was where she had translated "moss" which actually meant *muschio, muffa, borraccina* with *erba,* "grass." I continued by saying that all the same, even in its present state, her translation worked very well, and in such things a beautiful inaccuracy was always better than a ploddingly correct ugliness. The fact I'd pointed out was, however, easily remedied. All that was needed was a small change in the final stanza, such as:

> *Da tomba a tomba, come due congiunti*
> *incontratisi a notte,*
> *parlavamo; finché il muschio raggiunti*
> *ebbe i nomi, le bocche.*

Micòl replied two days later with a telegram in which she thanked me "truly, with heartfelt gratitude!" for my literary advice, and then, the next day, with a letter containing two new typed versions of the translation. In turn, I sent a letter of some ten pages which quarrelled, word by word, with her postcard. All considered, by letter we were far more clumsy and lifeless than on the telephone, so much so that in a short while we stopped corresponding. In the meantime, however, I had taken up visiting Alberto's studio, regularly, more or less every day.

Assiduous and punctual, Giampiero Malnate would also come with almost the same regularity. Talking, disputing, often arguing (in short, hating and loving each other from the first moment), it was thus that we got to know each other deeply, and we very quickly adopted the "*tu*" form of address.

I remembered how Micòl had expressed herself on the subject of his "physique." I too found Malnate bulky and oppressive. Like her, I too very often felt a kind of acute intolerance for his sincerity, his loyalty, for the eternal plea he made for manly openness, for that calm faith of his in a Lombard and Communist future which shone from his grey, too-human eyes. Despite this, from the first time that I sat in front of him, in Alberto's studio, I was filled with a single desire: that he should respect me, that he should not consider me as an interloper between himself and Alberto, that, finally, he would not deem as utterly mismatched the daily trio of which, certainly not from his own initiative, he found himself a part. I think that my own habit of smoking a pipe goes back precisely to that period.

The two of us spoke of many things (Alberto preferred to listen), but, obviously, most of all about politics.

These were the months that immediately followed the Munich Agreement, and it was this, and its consequences, which was the most recurrent topic of our conversations. What would Hitler do now that the Sudeten lands had been incorporated within the Greater Reich? In what direction would he strike next? For myself, I wasn't a pessimist, and every now and then Malnate would think I was right. In my opinion, the entente which France and England had been forced to subscribe to at the end of the crisis that had occurred last September wouldn't last for long. True. Hitler and Mussolini had induced Chamberlain and Daladier to abandon Beneš's Czechoslovakia to its fate. But then what? With the change of Chamberlain and Daladier for younger, more decisive men (that's the advantage of the parliamentary system!—I exclaimed), within a short while France and England would be in a position to dig in their heels. Time would surely play in their favor.

Yet if the conversation turned to the war in Spain, now on its last legs, or if there was any reference to the Soviet Union, Malnate's behavior toward the Western democracies and toward me, to all intents and purposes ironically considered their representative and paladin, would abruptly become less flexible. I can still see him thrusting his big brown head forward, his forehead shining with sweat, to fix his gaze upon mine with his usual, unbearable attempt at emotional blackmail, caught between moralism and sentimentalism, to which he willingly had recourse, while his voice took on a low, warm, persuasive, patient tone. Who were they, then—he'd ask—who were the people truly responsible for the Francoist rebellion?

Weren't they by any chance the French and English right, who'd not only tolerated it, at the start, but then, later, even supported and applauded it? Just as the Anglo-French response, correct in its form but actually ambiguous, had allowed Mussolini in 1935 to swallow up Ethiopia in a single mouthful, so in Spain it had mostly been the blameworthy dithering of Baldwin, Halifax and Blum that had swung the balance of fortune in Franco's favor. It was pointless to blame the Soviet Union and the International Brigade, he insinuated ever more gently, pointless to make Russia the easy scapegoat for every idiot, responsible if events down there were now at the point of collapse. The truth was quite different: only Russia had understood, from the very beginning, exactly what Il Duce and the Führer were. She alone had clearly foreseen the inevitable alliance between them, and had consequently acted in time. On the contrary, the French and English right wings, subverting the democratic order as did every right wing of every country in every period, had always looked on Fascist Italy and Nazi Germany with ill-concealed sympathy. Sure, to French and English reactionaries, Il Duce and the Führer might seem slightly inconvenient types, a shade crude and exaggerated, but still in every way preferable to Stalin, because Stalin, as we all know, has always been the devil. Having attacked and invaded Austria and Czechoslovakia, Germany was already pressing on the borders of Poland. So, if France and England were reduced to the level of gawping and accepting everything, the blame for their present impotence fell squarely on the shoulders of those fine, worthy, eye-catching gentlemen in top hats and tail-coats (so well suited at least in their manner of dressing to the nineteenth-century nostalgia of so many decadent, literary types ...) who were now in government.

But Malnate's polemics became even more heated every time the topic of Italian history over the last decades cropped up.

It was obvious—he said: for me, and for Alberto too, Fascism in the end represented nothing but the sudden, inexplicable illness which afflicts and betrays the healthy organism, or else, to use a phrase dear to Benedetto Croce, the guru you share (here Alberto never failed to shake his head desolately, as a sign of denial, but Malnate paid no attention to this), "the Invasion of the Hyksos." For us two, in conclusion, the Liberal Italy of Giolitti, Nitti, Orlando and even that of Sonnino, Salandra and Facta, had all been fine and dandy, the miraculous product of a golden age to which, in every respect, if only that were possible, it would be desirable to return. And yet we were wrong, just see how wrong we were! The illness had not arrived in the least bit unannounced. It began a long way back, in fact, in the earliest years of the Risorgimento, which were characterized by—let's admit it— an almost total absence of the people's participation—the real people—in the cause of Liberty and Unity. Giolitti? If Mussolini had been able to get over the crisis caused by the murder of Matteotti, in 1924, when all around him seemed to be losing their heads and even the King started swithering, we had our Giolitti to thank for that, and Benedetto Croce too—both of them quite willing to install in power whatever monstrous toad happened to be around—anything to make sure the progress of the working classes would be impeded and slowed down. It was actually them, the Liberals we worshipped, who gave Mussolini the time to get his second wind. Less than six months later, Il Duce had repaid them for their services by crushing the freedom of the press and dissolving the other parties. Giovanni Giolitti retired from political life, withdrawing to his country estates in Piedmont. Benedetto Croce went back to his precious philosophic and literary studies. But there were others, far less responsible, in fact entirely guiltless, who had had to pay far more painfully for all this. Amendola and Gobetti were bludgeoned to death. Filippo Turati was snuffed out in exile, far from the Milan where but a few years earlier he had buried his poor wife Anna. Antonio Gramsci had been thrown into one of our illustrious jails (didn't we know that he'd died in prison last year?). Italy's urban proletariat and its agricultural laborers, together with their natural leaders, had lost every effective hope of social justice and human dignity, and now for almost twenty years had been vegetating and dying in silence.

It was not easy for me to oppose these ideas, for various reasons. In the first place because Malnate's political knowledge, the Socialism and anti-Fascism which, at home, he'd taken in with his mother's milk, quite overpowered my own. In the second place because the role he'd boxed me into—the role of literary decadent, as he said, whose political formation had been under the guidance of Benedetto Croce's writings—seemed to me inadequate and inaccurate, and therefore had to be refuted before any further disagreement between us could get under way. The truth was that

I preferred to be silent, molding my face into a vaguely ironic smile. I submitted to him, and kept quiet.

As for Alberto, he too said nothing; in part because as usual he had nothing to say, but mainly to facilitate his friend's attacks on me—this was the main advantage, I reckoned. When three people are shut up for days arguing in a room, it is almost always the case that two of them end up in alliance against the third. So as to be in agreement with Giampi, to show his solidarity, Alberto seemed ready to accept anything from him, including the fact that he, Giampi, would often tar us with the same brush. It was true: Mussolini and his ilk were gathering together all kinds of slurs and defamations against the Jews—Malnate would, for example, claim. Last July's infamous Race Manifesto, drawn up by ten so-called "Fascist scholars"—it was hard to know whether it was more shameful or more ridiculous. But having admitted this—he added—could either of us tell him how many anti-Fascist "Israelites" there had been in Italy before 1938? Very few indeed, he feared, a tiny minority, if even at Ferrara, as Alberto had told him many times, the number of those enrolled in the Fascist Party had always been extremely high. I myself had taken part in the *Littoriali della Cultura*. Wasn't I already reading "the great" Croce's *History of Europe* just at that time? Or had I been waiting, before plunging into it, for the following year, the year of the *Anschluss* and the first warnings of Italian racism?

Though occasionally I rebelled, more often than not I yielded, smiling. Despite myself, I was overcome by his candor and sincerity, sure, a bit crude and relentless, a bit too goy-ish—I'd tell myself—but after all compassionate, because, essentially egalitarian and fraternal. However, when Malnate sometimes turned on Alberto, not entirely in jest, and accused him and his family of being "at the end of the day" filthy landowners, evil proprietors of country estates and, on top of that, aristocrats clearly nostalgic for medieval feudalism, one reason why "at the end of the day" it wasn't so unjust that now they should in some way pay the penalty for all the privileges they had hitherto enjoyed; and when Alberto, bent over double to protect himself from these hurricane blasts, would laugh till the tears came to his eyes, meanwhile nodding his head to show that yes, he, personally, was more than willing to pay the price, then I'd experience a surge of secret glee as I listened to him thundering against his friend. The child of the years before 1929, who walking beside his mother along the paths of the cemetery had always heard the Finzi-Continis' solitary monumental tomb defined as "a total monstrosity," would suddenly reemerge from the very depths of my being to applaud maliciously.

There were times when Malnate almost seemed to forget my presence. These generally occurred when he started recalling with Alberto the "times" they had had in Milan, the shared male and female friendships of that era, the restaurants they had been to together, the evenings at La Scala, the soccer matches at the Arena or at San Siro, the weekend trips to the mountains or to the Riviera. They had both belonged to a "group"—one evening he honored me with an explanation—whose demand on its members was a single one: intelligence. A truly wonderful time! He sighed. Characterized by scorn for every kind of provincialism and rhetoric, that time might be best defined, not only as that of their happy youth, but as the time of Gladys, a ballerina at the Lirico who had for some months been a friend of his—seriously, Gladys wasn't at all bad, a great laugh, "good company," at heart utterly without designs on anyone, and blithely promiscuous . . . and then having lucklessly fallen for Alberto, she'd ended up breaking off all contact with both of them.

"Poor Gladys, I've never understood why Alberto always rejected her," he added with a slight wink. Then he turned to Alberto:

"Come on. Spit it out. Three years have passed since then, and the scene of the crime is almost three hundred kilometers from here. Why don't we finally put our cards on the table?"

But in response Alberto only blushed, and warded off the question. And Gladys was never mentioned again.

He enjoyed the work that had brought him to our part of the world—he would often say—even Ferrara he liked, as a city, and it seemed absurd to him, to say the least, that Alberto and I looked on it as a kind of tomb or jail. Obviously our situation could be considered a rather special one. And yet we were wrong to believe ourselves the only minority group in Italy being persecuted. What were we thinking? The workers in the plant where his job was, what did we think they were—beasts without any feelings? He could name many of them who not only had never enrolled themselves in the Fascist Party but who were Socialists or Communists, and for this had often been beaten up or given the castor-oil "treatment," and yet continued, uncowed, to stand by their principles. He had been at one of their meetings, and was delighted to find there not only the workers and farm laborers who'd come specially, on bikes perhaps, from as far away as Mésola and Goro, but also two or three of the most renowned lawyers in the city. Which went to prove that even here, in Ferrara, not all of the bourgeoisie were on the side of the Fascists, that not all of its ranks were filled with traitors. Had we ever heard Clelia Trotti spoken of? No? Well, she was an ex-primary school teacher, an old woman who when she was younger, they'd told him, had been the pillar of Ferrara's Socialist movement, and continued to be so—and what a force she was! Not a single meeting was held without her lively and vivid contributions. That was how he'd met her. Regarding her humanitarian kind of Socialism, the type of Andrea Costa, it might be better left without comment, and little could be expected of it. But what passion there was in her, what faith and hope! She reminded him, even physically, especially those blue eyes of hers, that hinted at the blonde she must once have been, of Signora Anna, Filippo Turati's companion, whom he'd got to know as a boy in Milan around 1922. His father, a lawyer, had served almost a year in prison with the Turati couple in 1898. A close friend of both of them, he was one of the few who, on Sunday afternoons, still dared to call on them in their small flat in the Galleria. And Malnate would often go along with him.

No, let's be honest, Ferrara was not at all the prison that someone overhearing us might think it was. It's true that seeing it from the industrial zone, shut up as it seemed to be within its old walls, especially on days of bad weather, the city might easily give the impression of solitude and isolation. Yet all round Ferrara was the countryside, rich, abundant, fertile, and beyond it, less than forty kilometers away, was the sea, with empty beaches bordered by lovely pine and ilex woods. And the sea is always a great resource. But this apart, the city itself, once you threw yourself into it as he'd decided to, once you considered it without prejudice, was like every other city, hiding treasures of human virtue, intelligence and goodness of heart, and even of courage, which only the deaf and blind, or rather the sterile, could ignore or misconstrue.

· 5 ·

AT FIRST, Alberto kept on announcing his imminent departure for Milan. Then, bit by bit, he stopped mentioning it, and his graduation thesis ended up becoming a thorny question we had to skirt around with some caution. He made no further reference to it, and it was clear he wanted us to follow suit.

As I've already suggested, his interventions in our arguments were rare and almost always irrelevant. He was on Malnate's side, of this there was no doubt, happy if he should triumph, worried if, on the contrary, I seemed to be getting the upper hand. But mainly he kept silent. At the most, he would come out with some exclamation every now and then ("Ah, that's good, though! . . . ," "Yes, but, if looked at another way . . . ," "Hold on a second, let's be calm about this . . . "), following up with a short laugh or a little bit of embarrassed throat-clearing.

Even physically, he had the tendency of cringing back, of cancelling himself out, of disappearing. Malnate and I would generally sit facing each other, in the middle of the room, one on the sofa and the other on one of the two armchairs, with the table in the middle and both of us right under the light. We would only get up to go to the small bathroom next to the bedroom, or else to check what the weather was like through the big broad window which looked out over the park. By contrast, Alberto preferred to stay down there at the end of the room, protected by the double barricade of the desk and the draftsman's table. Those times he bestirred himself, we would see him wander up and down the room on tiptoe, his elbows drawn in to his sides. He would change the records on the radiogram, one after the other, careful that the volume did not drown out our voices, survey the ashtrays, and empty them in the bathroom when they were full, regulate the brightness of the side-lighting, ask in an undertone if we could do with a little more tea, straighten out and reposition certain objects. In short, he adopted the busy, discreet air of the master of the house concerned only about one thing: that the acute minds of his guests should be allowed to function properly within the best possible surroundings and conditions.

I'm convinced, though, that it was he, with his meticulous orderliness, with his stratagems, with his cautious unpredictable maneuvers, who was responsible for diffusing the vague sense of oppression which shadowed the very air we breathed there. It was enough for him, in the pauses of the conversation, for instance, to start expatiating on the qualities of the armchair in which I was sitting, whose back "guaranteed" the most correct and favorable "anatomical" alignment for the spine; or, offering me the small, dark leather pouch for pipe tobacco, to catalogue the various kinds of cut according to him indispensable for our Dunhill or GBD to obtain the optimum flavor (such-and-such a quantity of sweet, of strong, of Maryland); or, for motives never quite made clear and known only to himself, to announce with a vague smile, lifting his chin toward the radiogram, the temporary exclusion of sound from one of the loudspeakers—in every case of such or similar kind, I would experience a bristling of nerves which was forever lying in wait, forever ready to burst forth.

One evening I didn't manage to suppress them. Certainly—I shouted out to Malnate—his dilettante-like behavior, essentially that of a tourist, let him assume toward Ferrara a tone of tolerance and indulgence which I envied. But how would he, he who spoke so much about the treasures of human virtue, goodness, etc., how would he judge something that had happened to me, personally, only a few mornings ago?

I'd had the bright idea—I began to tell them—of taking myself, my papers and books, to the Reading Room of the Public Library in Via Scienze—a place I'd hung around since my school days and where I always felt at home. Everyone always treated me very courteously there, within those ancient walls. After I'd enrolled in the Faculty of Arts, the Director, Dr. Ballola, had begun to consider me a scholar like himself. As soon as he spotted me, he'd sit down beside me to keep me abreast of the progress of some of his by now ten-year-old research material to do with a biography on Ariosto, filed away in his private study, research about which he declared himself confident "of going some way beyond the renowned efforts of Catalano in the field." So also with the various other staff members there, who acted toward me with such confidence and familiarity as not only to let me dispense with the boredom of filling out forms for the books, but even to let me smoke the occasional cigarette there.

Well, as I was saying, that morning I'd had the bright idea of spending some hours in the library. Except that I'd only just had time to sit myself down at a table in the Reading Room and get out all the stuff I needed, when one of the staff, a certain Poledrelli, a man in his sixties, fat, jovial, a famous eater of pasta and incapable of putting two words together which weren't in dialect, came up to me to suggest that I leave, and forthwith. All puffed up, trying to keep his belly in and even managing to speak in proper Italian, the good Poledrelli had explained in a loud official voice how the Director had given him very definite orders on this matter, and therefore—he repeated—would I be so kind as to get up and be gone. That morning the Reading Room was particularly full of boys from the middle school. The scene had been followed, in a sepulchral silence, by no less than fifty pairs of eyes and the same number of ears. As you can imagine, I went on, it was no joy to drag myself up, gather together all my things from the table, replace them in my briefcase and then to reach, one step at a time, the big glass entrance door. It's true—that poor wretch Poledrelli was only following orders. But he, Malnate, should take great care, in case he should get to meet him (who knows if Poledrelli himself didn't also belong to the schoolmistress Trotti's circle!), take great care not to be taken in by the deceptively amiable look of that big plebeian face. Inside that chest as huge as a wardrobe there lived a little heart no bigger than this. It might well pump good working-class blood, but it was no more dependable for that.

And then, and then!—I grew yet more heated—wasn't it at the very least out of place for him to come here preaching at, let's leave aside Alberto, whose family has always kept itself apart from the communal life of the city, but at me who, on the contrary, was born and brought up within a family that might even have been too inclined to be open, and to mix with others of every class? My father, a volunteer in the war, had joined the Fascist Party in 1919, and I myself until yesterday had belonged to the GUF. Then since we ourselves had always been very normal people, even banal in our normality, it would be absurd to expect us now, out of the blue, to start behaving abnormally. Called into the Federation to hear himself expelled from the Party, then chased out of the Merchants' Club as an undesirable person—it would be very odd for my father, poor fellow, to respond to such treatment with an expression any less anguished and bewildered than the one I saw on his face. And if my brother Ernesto wanted to go to university, should he apply to the Polytechnic in Grenoble? And should my sister Fanny, just thirteen, continue with her schooling at the Jewish College in Via Vignatagliata? From them too, abruptly torn away from their school friends, from the friends of their childhood, was it also fair to expect some especially appropriate behavior? What nonsense! One of the most odious forms of anti-Semitism was precisely this: to complain that Jews aren't sufficiently like other people, and then, the opposite, once they've become almost totally assimilated with their surroundings, to complain that they're just like everybody else, not even a fraction distinguished from the average.

I had got carried away by my anger, had moved somewhat outside the topic of our disagreement, and Malnate, who had carefully followed everything I'd been saying, did not fail to make a point of this. He an anti-Semite?—he stammered: it was frankly the first time he'd ever been referred to in that way! By now over-heated, I was about to return to the fray, to redouble my attack. Just at that moment, as he passed behind the back of my opponent with the ruffled speed of a frightened bird, Alberto cast a begging look toward me. "Please stop!" that look was saying. That he, unbeknownst to his bosom buddy, should this once make such an appeal to what was most secretly and exclusively shared between the two of us, struck me as extraordinary. I held back and said nothing more. Just at that moment, the first notes of a Beethoven quartet played by the Busch lifted into the smoky atmosphere of the room to seal my victory.

The evening was not only important because of this. Around eight o'clock it began to rain with such violence that Alberto, after a speedy telephone exchange perhaps with his mother, speaking in their usual jargon, asked us to stay for dinner.

Malnate said he'd be very glad to accept. He'd been dining at Giovanni's nearly all the time, he told us, "lonely as a dog." It seemed almost unbelievable to him to be able to spend an evening "with a family."

I also accepted, but asked if I could phone home first.

"Of course!" Alberto exclaimed.

I sat down where he usually sat, behind the desk, and dialled the number. As I waited, I looked to the side, through the windowpane striped with rain. Against the thick darkness, the dense trees hardly stood out at all. Beyond the black gulf of the park, hard to say where, a small light glimmered.

Finally my father was heard to reply in his usual complaining tones.

"Oh, it's you, is it?" he said. "We were beginning to get worried. Where are you phoning from?"

"I'm staying out for supper," I replied.

"In this rain!"

"Exactly. Because of it."

"You're still at the Finzi-Continis'?"

"Yes."

"Whenever you get back, stop in to see me, will you? Anyway, I can't get to sleep, as you know . . . "

I put down the receiver and lifted my eyes. Alberto was looking at me.

"Done?"

"Done."

All three of us went out into the corridor, crossed through various large and small rooms, descended a big staircase at the foot of which, in a dinner jacket and white gloves, Perotti was waiting, and from there we passed directly into the dining room.

The rest of the family were already there. There was Professor Ermanno, Signora Olga, Signora Regina and one of the Venetian uncles, the phthisiology specialist, who, seeing Alberto come in, got up, went toward him and kissed him on both cheeks. After which, while distractedly tugging at his lower eyelid with a finger, he began to tell him what had brought him there. He'd had to go to Bologna for a consultation—he said—and then, on the way back, between trains, had thought it a good idea to stop for supper. When we came in, Professor Ermanno, his wife and brother-in-law were sitting in front of the lighted fire, with Jor stretched out at their feet in all his considerable length. Signora Regina was, however, seated at the table, exactly under the central light.

Inevitably, the memory of my first meal at the Finzi-Contini house (I think it was still January) tends to get confused with the memories of the many other dinners at the *magna domus* to which I was invited in the course of that winter. I do, however, recollect with unaccustomed clarity what we ate that evening: and that was a chicken liver and rice soup, minced turkey in jelly, corned tongue with black olives and spinach stalks in vinegar as side dishes, a chocolate cake, fresh and dried fruit, nuts, peanuts, grapes and pinenuts. I also remember clearly that almost at once, no sooner had we sat down at the table, Alberto decided to announce the story of my recent expulsion from the Public Library, and that I was once more struck by the lack of surprise with which this news was greeted by the four old people. The comments which followed on the current situation and on the Ballola–Poledrelli duo, brought up again every now and then throughout the meal, were not even, on their part, especially bitter, but, as usual, elegantly sardonic, almost light-hearted. And joyful, decidedly joyful and pleased, was the tone of voice with which, later, putting his arm round me, Professor Ermanno suggested that from that time on I should make the most of the almost twenty thousand books in the house, a large number of which—he told me—concerned mid- and late-nineteenth-century literature.

But what struck me most, from that first evening on, was undoubtedly the dining room itself, with its floral-style furniture of dark red wood, its vast fireplace with a sinuous, arched, almost human mouth, its walls panelled with leather, except for one which was entirely of glass framing the dark, silent storm of the park like the *Nautilus'* porthole—the whole thing so intimate, so sheltering, so—I was about to say—buried, and above all so well suited to who I was then—now I understand!—a shield for that kind of slow-burning ember which the hearts of the young so often are.

Crossing the threshold, both Malnate and I were received with great cordiality, and not only by Professor Ermanno, kind, jovial and lively as ever, but also by Signora Olga. It was she who showed us to our places at the table. Malnate was given the seat to her right, and I, at the other end of the table, to the right of her husband. The place on her left, between her, his sister, and their old mother, was reserved for Giulio. Even Signora Regina in the meantime, looking lovely with her rosy cheeks and her white silky hair thicker and shinier than ever, bestowed a friendly and amused gaze on all around.

The setting which faced me, complete with plates, glasses and cutlery, seemed to be waiting there prepared for a seventh guest. While Perotti was already doing his rounds with the soup tureen with the *riso in brodo*,

I asked Professor Ermanno in a low voice for whom the seat at his left had been prepared. He just as quietly replied that now the seat was "presumably" waiting for no one—he checked the time on his big Omega wristwatch, shook his head and sighed—it being the seat which Micòl, or to be exact "my Micòl," as he said, usually occupied.

· 6 ·

PROFESSOR ERMANNO was not exaggerating. Among the almost twenty thousand books in the house, many of them on scientific, historical or a variety of scholarly topics (the latter mainly in German), there were many hundreds devoted to the literature of the New Italy. As for whatever had been published relating to Carducci's *fin-de-siècle* literary circle, from the decades in which he had taught in Bologna, there was practically nothing missing. There were volumes in verse and in prose not only by the Maestro himself, but also by Panzacchi, Severino Ferrari, Lorenzo Stecchetti, Ugo Brilli, Guido Mazzoni, by the young Pascoli, the young Panzini, the very young Valgimigli—generally first editions, nearly all of them bearing signed dedications to the Baroness Josette Artom di Susegana. Gathered in three separate glass bookcases which occupied a whole wall of a huge first-floor reception room next to Professor Ermanno's personal study, there was no doubt that these books together represented a collection of which any public library, including Bologna's Archiginnasio's, would be glad to boast. The collection even housed the little volumes, rare as hen's teeth, of the prose poems of Francesco Acri, the famous translator of Plato, till then only known to me as a translator: not such "a saint," then, as Professor Meldolesi (who had also been a scholar of Acri's work) had, since the fifth form, insisted to us he was, as his dedications to Alberto and Micòl's grandmother were, out of the whole chorus of them, perhaps the most gallant and showed the most heightened masculine awareness of the proud beauty to which they alluded.

With an entire, specialized library at my disposal, and besides that, being oddly keen to be there every morning, in the great, warm, silent hall which received light from three big, high windows adorned with pel-

mets covered in red-striped white silk, and at the center of which, under a
taupe cover, stretched the billiards table, I managed to complete my thesis
on Panzacchi in the two-and-a-half months which followed. If I'd really
wanted to, who knows, I might have been able to finish it earlier. But was
that really what I wanted? Or rather hadn't I tried to eke out the time for as
long as possible so as to have the right to visit the Finzi-Contini house in
the mornings as well? What is certain is that around the middle of March
(news having in the meantime been received of Micòl's graduation, with
the marks of 110 out of 110), I still remained torpidly attached to the meagre
privilege of these additional morning visits to the house from which she
insisted on keeping such a distance. By this time only a few days separated
us from the Catholic Easter, which fell that year almost at the same time as
Pesach, the Jewish Easter. Although spring was almost at our doors, a week
earlier it had snowed with extraordinary abundance, after which the cold
had returned with a vengeance. It almost seemed as though the winter had
no intention of ever ending. And I myself, my heart haunted by an obscure,
shadowy lake of fear, held tight to the little desk which the previous January Professor Ermanno had had placed for me beneath the central window
in the billiards room, as though, in so doing, I might be able to halt the
inexorable progress of time. I would stand up, walk to the window and look
down over the park. Buried under a mantle of snow half a meter deep, perfectly white, the Barchetto del Duca seemed turned into a landscape from
a Norse saga. At times I surprised myself by hoping that the snow would
never melt, would last for ever.

For two-and-a-half months my days remained virtually unchanging.
Punctual as a government clerk, I would leave home at half past eight in
the cold, nearly always by bike, though occasionally on foot. After at most
twenty minutes, there I would be ringing at the big gate at the end of Corso
Ercole I d'Este, and from there I'd cross the park, which was infused,
around the beginning of February, with the delicate scent of the yellow
flowers of the calycanthus. By nine I was already in the billiards room
where I'd remain until one o'clock, and where I'd return around three in
the afternoon. Later, at about six, I would call in on Alberto, sure of also
finding Malnate there. Finally, as I've already stated, both of us were often
invited to stay for supper. In fact, very soon it had become so customary

for me to stay to eat, that I no longer even phoned home to tell them. I might perhaps have told my mother as I left: "I'll probably be staying out for supper there." "There" required no further clarifications.

I worked for hours and hours without seeing another soul, except Perotti who, around eleven o'clock, would come in bearing a small cup of coffee on a silver tray. This too, the eleven o'clock coffee, had almost immediately become a daily ritual, an acquired habit about which there was no point in either of us wasting any words. What Perotti would talk about, as he waited for me to finish sipping the coffee, was, if anything, the "running" of the house, in his view seriously undermined by the over-extended absence of the "Signorina," who, no doubt about it, had to become a teacher and everything, but . . . (and this "but," accompanied by a look of doubt, might have alluded to a host of things: to the fact that his masters, fortunate creatures that they were, had really no need at all to earn their living, or perhaps to the Racial Laws which in any case would have turned our degree diplomas into mere bits of paper, without the slightest practical use) . . . even if a bit of a leave, seeing as without her the house was quickly going "to the dogs," a bit of a leave, maybe a week away then a week back here, was something she could easily have sorted for herself. With me, Perotti always found some way to complain about his employers. As a sign of mistrust and disapproval, he tightened his lips, winked and shook his head. When he referred to Signora Olga, he even went as far as tapping his temple with his rough forefinger. Naturally I didn't encourage him, and stubbornly blanked his repeated attempts to have me join him in a servile complicity which, besides repelling me, were offensive to me personally. And so, in a short while, in the face of my silences, of my chill smiles, Perotti had no other option but to make off, leaving me once again alone.

One day his younger daughter, Dirce, arrived in his place. She too waited beside the desk for me to finish the coffee. I drank it and looked her up and down.

"What's your name again?" I asked her, giving her back the empty cup, as my heart began to beat rapidly.

"Dirce," she smiled, and her face was suffused with a blush.

She was wearing her usual blue cotton blouse, its thick fabric strangely redolent of the nursery. She scurried off, ducking my gaze which had been seeking hers out. A moment later I'd already begun to feel ashamed of what had happened (but what after all had happened?) as the vilest and most squalid of betrayals.

The only family member who would occasionally appear was Professor Ermanno. With special caution he would open the study door at the far end of the room, and then, on tiptoe, he would make his way across the room, so that more often than not I only became aware of his presence when he was already at my side, leaning respectfully over the papers and books I'd laid out before me.

"How are things going?" he would ask in a contented voice. "It seems like you are going ahead full steam!"

I would make as if to get up.

"No. No. Please keep on working," he'd exclaim. "I'll be leaving you straight away."

Usually he stayed no more than five minutes, during which time he always found some way of showing me all the sympathy and respect he felt for the way I stuck to my work. He looked at me with fiery, shining eyes, as though from me, from my literary future, my future as a scholar, who knows what great things could be expected, as though he was counting on me to fulfil some secret design which transcended not only himself but me as well . . . And, *à propos*, I remember that this behavior of his toward me, although flattering, also upset me a bit. Why did he have no such expectations about Alberto—I'd ask myself—who's actually his son? And why had he accepted without any protests or complaints Alberto having given up his degree? And what about Micòl? In Venice, Micòl was doing exactly the same thing as I was doing here—finishing her thesis. And yet he never had occasion to name her, Micòl, or, if he referred to her it was by way of a sigh. He seemed to be implying: "She's only a girl, and it's better for women to be concerned with the home, rather than literature!" But should I really have believed him?

One morning he stayed to talk longer than usual. In a roundabout manner, he began to speak once again of Carducci's letters and his own "little works" on the Venetian topic: all the stuff—he said, nodding toward his study behind me—which he kept "back there." He smiled mysteriously as he mentioned this, his face assuming a sly, inviting expression. It was obvious he wanted to lead me "back there," and at the same time wanted it to be me who proposed I should be taken there.

I made haste to oblige him.

So we went to the study, which was a room hardly less grand than the billiards room, but reduced, rendered almost shrunken, by an incredible accumulation of disparate things.

To start with, there was an abundance of books. Those on literary subjects mixed up with the scientific (mathematics, physics, economics, agriculture, medicine, astronomy and so on); books on local history, Ferrarese or Venetian, with those on "ancient Jewish history"—the volumes chaotically crowded the usual glass-fronted bookcases, and took up a good part of the big walnut table (behind which, if he were seated, Professor Ermanno would most likely show as little more than the top of his beret); they were heaped up in perilously unsteady piles on the chairs, stacked into towers even on the floor, and scattered around almost everywhere. An enormous map of the world, then a lectern, a microscope, half a dozen barometers, a steel safe painted dark red, a small white bed like you see in doctors' surgeries, several hourglasses of different sizes, a brass kettle-drum, a little German upright piano topped by two metronomes shut in their pyramidical cases, and beyond, many other objects of uncertain use which I don't now recall, lent the surroundings the look of a Faustian laboratory, which Professor Ermanno himself was the first to make fun of and to excuse himself for as if it represented a personal, private weakness of his: almost as if it was all that remained of his childish fads. However, I was forgetting to mention the fact that as far as pictures went, in contrast to all the other rooms of the house, which were generally overladen with them, here there were none to be seen except one: a huge life-size portrait by Lenbach, weighing on the wall behind the table like an altarpiece. The magnificent blonde lady bodied forth in this, standing upright, her shoulders bared, a fan in her gloved hand and with the silken train of her white gown brought to the fore to emphasize her length of leg and fullness of form, was obviously no other than the Baroness Josette Artom di Susegana. What a marmoreal forehead, what eyes, what a scornful lip, what a bust! She truly looked like a queen. Among that host of objects in the study, his mother's portrait was the only thing Professor Ermanno did not joke about—not that morning, not ever.

That very morning, though, I was at last presented with the two Venetian tracts. In one of them—the Professor explained to me—all the inscriptions of the Jewish cemetery at the Lido were assembled and translated. The second, on the other hand, was on a Jewish woman poet who had lived in Venice in the first half of the seventeenth century, and as renowned to her contemporaries as she was now, "sadly," forgotten. She was called Sara Enriquez (or Enriques) Avigdòr. For some decades, at her house in the Old Ghetto, she had held an important literary salon, assiduously frequented not only by the extremely gifted Ferrarese-Venetian rabbi Leone da Modena but also by many first-rate literary figures of the age, foreign as well as Italian. She had composed a considerable number of the "finest" sonnets, which still now awaited a scholar capable of reassessing and reasserting their beauty. She had undertaken a brilliant correspondence with the famous Ansaldo Cebà, a gentleman from Genoa, who had written an epic poem on Queen Esther, and had become fixated on the idea of converting her to Catholicism, but then, in the end, seeing how futile all his insistence had been, had had to renounce this plan. A great woman, all considered: the honor and boast of Italian Jewry at the height of the Counter-Reformation, and in some way a part of the "family"—Professor Ermanno had added as he was writing a couple of lines as a book dedication for me—since it seemed certain that his wife, on her mother's side, was one of her descendants.

He got up, walked around the table, took me by the arm and led me into the window bay.

There was, however, something—he continued, lowering his voice as though he feared someone might overhear us—which he felt obliged to warn me about. If, in the future, I should ever happen to concern myself with this Sara Enriquez, or Enriques, Avigdòr (and the subject was such as to merit a far more deep and detailed study than he in his youth had been able to give to it), at a certain point, I would inevitably have to confront some contrary opinions . . . disagreements . . . in fact some writings by third-rate literary figures, most of them the poetess's contemporaries (libellous things that were glaringly envious and anti-Semitic), which insinuated that not all the sonnets signed by her in circulation, and not even all the letters written by her to Cebà were, let's say, written by her own hand. Well, he, if his memory served him well, had obviously been unable to ignore the existence of such slanders and had, in fact, as I'd see, properly documented them. In any case . . .

He broke off to look me in the eyes, uncertain of my reactions.

In any case—he continued—even if I should think "sometime in the future" . . . umm . . . if I should ever attempt a reevaluation . . . a revision . . . he advised me even then not to give too much credit to these malicious rumors. They might well be intriguing, but in the end they were misplaced. What, finally, was it that made an excellent historian? He must set himself the ideal of arriving at the truth, without in the process losing a sense of what's right and appropriate. Didn't I think so?

I nodded my head to show I agreed, and he, relieved, patted me on the back with the palm of his hand.

This done, he moved away, hunched up, across the study and bent to tinker with the safe, which he opened. He then drew from it a small casket covered in blue velvet.

He turned round, once more all smiles, toward the window, and before opening up the small casket, he said that he could see that I'd already guessed its contents—within, indeed, was kept the famous Carducci correspondence. It amounted to fifteen letters: and not all of them—he added—would I perhaps judge to be of the most pressing interest, as at least five of the fifteen were concerned with a special "blood sausage from hereabouts" of which the poet, having received it as a gift, had been "so greatly" appreciative. All the same, I would without doubt be struck by one of them. It was a letter of autumn 1875, written therefore at the time when the crisis of the Historic Right was looming on the horizon. That autumn Carducci's political stance seemed to be that as a declared democrat, Republican and revolutionary, he was unable to join the ranks of Agostino Depretis's left. On the other hand, *"l'irto vinattier di Stradella"** and the "crowd" of his friends seemed to him common folk, "little men."

---

* "Stradella's bristly wine seller" (Carducci, "Roma").

People who would never be capable of restoring Italy to its calling, of making Italy a Great Nation, worthy of its ancient Forefathers . . .

We stayed there talking until dinnertime. The result, at the end of all this, was that from that morning on the communicating door between the billiards room and the next-door study, till then always shut, now often remained open. Most of the time, the two of us stayed in our respective rooms. Yet we saw each other a lot more than before, Professor Ermanno coming to seek me out, and I making my way to him. Through the door, when it was open, we even exchanged the odd word: "What time is it?" "How's the work going?" and such things. Some years later, during the spring of 1943, in jail, the phrases that I would exchange with an unknown neighboring cellmate, shouting up toward the air-hole of the "wolf's mouth," would be of this kind: spoken in just this way, above all from the need to hear your own voice, to sense that you are alive.

· 7 ·

AT HOME, that year, Passover was celebrated with a single dinner.

It was my father who wanted it this way. Also, given Ernesto's absence—he'd said—we'd best forget having a Passover like those of previous years. And then, apart from this, how could we have done otherwise? They, my Finzi-Continis, had once more managed things perfectly. With the excuse of the garden they had succeeded in keeping all their servants, from the first to the last, letting them pass as farm-workers adept in the cultivation of vegetable-garden produce. And ourselves? From the time we had been forced to give notice to Elisa and Mariuccia, and to assume in their place that dried fish of an old Cohen, in practice we had no one to call on. In such circumstances, even our mother would be unable to work a miracle.

"Isn't it true, my angel?"

My angel didn't nurse any warmer feelings for the sixty-year-old Signorina Ricca Cohen than my father did. Instead of being delighted, as usual, to hear one of us speak ill of the poor old woman, Mamma had consented with heartfelt gratitude to the idea of a low-key Passover. All right then—she had agreed: just one dinner, and that's all, a meal for the first evening. So what do we need to make it? She and Fanny would take care of everything, almost unassisted, without "that one"—here she tilted her chin toward Cohen, shut in the kitchen—getting into one of her usual tempers. Plus, why not, so "that one" wouldn't have to scramble to and fro with so many plates and pans, at the risk, among other things, weak in the legs as she was, of some disaster or other, why not arrange it in another way—rather than eat in the dining room, so far away from the kitchen, and this year, with the snow, chilly as Siberia, rather than the dining room why not lay the table here in the breakfast room . . .

It was not a happy meal. At the table's center, the hamper which apart from the ritual "snacks" contained the tureen of *haroset*, the tufts of bitter herbs, the unleavened bread and the boiled egg reserved for me, the first-born, uselessly enthroned beneath the blue-and-white silk handkerchief which grandma Ester had embroidered with her own hands forty years ago. In spite of all the care taken, or rather because of it, the table had assumed a look closely resembling the one it wore those evenings of Yom Kippur, when it was set out only for Them, the family dead, whose mortal remains lay in the cemetery at the end of Via Montebello, and yet made their presence decidedly felt, here, in spirit or effigy. Here, that evening, in place of them, we, the living, sat to eat. But fewer of us compared to before, and no longer light-hearted, laughing, loud-voiced, but rather sad and wistful like the dead. I looked at my father and my mother, both of them much aged in those last months. I looked at Fanny, who was then already fifteen, but, as though some ancient fear had arrested her development, she seemed no more than twelve. I looked around, one by one, at uncles and aunts and cousins, a great number of whom, within a few years, would be swallowed up by German crematoria ovens, and never would they have dreamed of ending up like that, nor would I myself have dreamed it, but all the same, then, that evening, already, even though I saw them looking so insignificant, their pitiful faces topped with dowdy bourgeois hats or framed by bourgeois perms, even if I was aware how obtuse their minds were, how utterly unable to grasp the realities of that present moment or to read anything of the future, already they seemed to me swathed in the same aura of statue-like, mysterious fate that still, in memory, encircles them today. I looked at old Cohen, the few times she dared to peep out from behind the kitchen door: Ricca Cohen, the distinguished spinster in her sixties who had come from the old people's home at Via Vittoria to serve in the house of well-off co-religionists, but who wanted nothing other than to return there, to the home, and, before the times got any worse, to die. Finally I looked at myself, reflected within the dark waters of the mirror opposite, and even I was already a little grey-haired, even I was caught up in the same cogs, but reluctantly, still unresigned. I wasn't dead yet—I told myself—I was still bursting with life! And yet, if I was still alive, how come I was there with them, for what purpose? Why didn't I immediately leave that grotesque and desperate gathering of ghosts, or at least stop up my ears so as not to hear any more talk of "discrimination," of "patriotic awards of merit," of "certificates of ancestry," of "proportions of Jewish blood," so as not to have to listen to the narrow-minded keening, the grey, monotonous, futile dirge that relatives and kin were meekly intoning all around me? The meal would drag on like that, chewing over the same familiar sayings for who knows how long, with my father frequently bringing forth, in his bitter, relishing style, the various "affronts" he'd had to submit to in the course of these past months, beginning with the time when in the Party Headquarters the Federal Secretary, Consul Bolognesi, with a saddened, shifty look, had announced to him that he had been forced to "cancel" him from the list of Party members, and ending up with the time when the president of the Merchants' Club, with an equally sorrowing look, had called him over to tell him that he should consider himself "struck off." Oh, he could tell us some stories! To keep us up till midnight, till one or two!

And then, what would follow? The final scene, the communal good-byes. I could already see it. We would have gone down the dark stairs all together, like a besieged flock. Having reached the entrance hall, someone—perhaps me—would have gone on ahead to leave the street door ajar, and then, one final time, before separating, on everyone's part, and mine included, there would be a renewal of the goodnights, the best wishes, the hand-shakings, the embraces and the kisses on both cheeks. But then, suddenly, from the street door left half open, there, against the blackness of the night, a gust of wind would sweep through the entrance hall. A hurricane wind that came from the night. It would crash down the hallway, cross, then pass beyond it, whistling through the gates that divided the hall from the garden, and meanwhile disperse with its force any of the guests who might have wanted to delay, with its savage howl would suddenly quell and hush any who might still have wished to linger and talk. Thin voices, faint cries, immediately overwhelmed. All of them blown away—light as leaves, as bits of paper, as hairs from a head of hair turned grey with age and terror . . . Oh, in the end, Ernesto had been lucky not to have gone to university in Italy. He had written from Grenoble to say that he was suffering from hunger, and that, with the little French he knew, he could hardly understand anything of the lessons in the Polytechnic. But lucky him to be suffering from hunger and being scared he wouldn't pass his exams. I had stayed here, and for me who had stayed, and who'd once again chosen out of pride or sterility a solitude nourished by vague, nebulous, impotent hopes, for me there really was no hope at all.

But who can ever foretell the future?

Nearing eleven o'clock, as it happened, while my father, with the evident intent of dispelling the general low spirits, had begun singing the happy nonsense-verses of "Caprét ch'avea comperà il signor Padre"* (his favorite song, his "battle-steed" as he would put it), it happened that at a certain point, by chance, lifting my eyes to the mirror opposite, I caught sight of the telephone cupboard's door very slowly opening a little, behind my back. Through the hatch cautiously jutted the face of old Cohen. She was looking right at me, and it seemed almost as though she was begging for my help.

I got up and went over.

"What's wrong?"

She nodded at the telephone receiver dangling on its wire, and disappeared through the doorway that gave onto the entrance hall.

Left alone, in utter darkness, before even lifting the receiver to my ear, I recognized the voice of Alberto.

"I can hear singing," he was crying out in a strangely festive voice. "At what point in the proceedings are you?"

* "The little goat the father bought."

"At the 'Caprét ch'avea comperà il signor Padre' point."

"That's good. We've already finished. Why don't you drop round?"

"Right now?" I exclaimed astonished.

"Why not? Here the conversation has begun to enter the doldrums and you, with your much acclaimed resources, would doubtless be able to lift it up again."

He sniggered.

"And also . . . " he added, "we've prepared a surprise for you."

"A surprise? And what might that be?"

"Come and see."

"Such mysteriousness."

My heart was beating furiously.

"Put your cards on the table."

"Go on, don't make me have to beg. I repeat: come and see."

I immediately went to the entrance, took my overcoat, scarf and hat, stuck my head around the kitchen door, asking Cohen in a whisper to say, in case they asked where I was, that I'd had to go out for a moment, and two minutes later I was already on the street.

It was a magnificent moonlit night, frozen, clear as could be. There was no one, almost no one on the streets, and Corso Giovecca and Corso Ercole I d'Este, smooth, empty and of an almost salt-like whiteness, opened up in front of me like two huge ski-tracks. In the bright light, I swayed down the middle of the street, my ears numbed by the icy air. At supper I'd drunk a fair few glasses of wine, and not only could I not feel the cold, but I was actually sweating. My bike's front tyre barely rustled over the hardened snow, and the dry snow-dust it raised filled me with a sense of reckless joy, as though I was skiing. I raced on, without fear of skidding. Meanwhile I thought of the surprise, which, according to Alberto, would be awaiting me at the Finzi-Continis'. Had Micòl perhaps returned? Odd if she had. Why wouldn't she have come to the phone herself? And why, before supper, had no one seen her at the Temple? If she had been at the Temple, I would already have known of it. My father at the dinner table, making his usual survey of those present at the service—he'd done this especially for me: as an indirect reproach for my non-attendance—would certainly not have neglected to mention her. He had gone through the whole list, naming them one by one, of the Finzi-Continis and the Herreras, but not her. Was it possible she had come on her own at the last minute, on the direct, quarter-past-nine train?

In an even more intense brightness of moonlight and snow, I went on across the Barchetto del Duca. Halfway, a little before the bridge crosses the Panfilio canal, a gigantic shadow suddenly appeared before me. It was Jor. There was a moment's delay before I recognized him, just as I was about to cry out. But no sooner had I done so than the fear I felt was transformed into an almost equally paralyzing sense of foreboding. So then it was true—I told myself—Micòl was back. Forewarned by the street bell, she must have got up from the table, gone downstairs and now, sending Jor out to meet me, was waiting for me at the threshold of the side door reserved exclusively for family and close friends. A few more pedalings, and there was Micòl herself, a small dark figure etched against an electric-light background of sheerest white, her back encircled by the protective breath of the central heating. Another moment or two and I would hear her voice, her "Hi."

"Hi," Micòl said, motionless on the threshold. "It's good of you to come."

I had foreseen everything most exactly: everything except for the fact that I would kiss her. I had got off my bike, and replied, "Hi. How long have you been here?" and she had just enough time to say, "Since yesterday afternoon—I travelled down with my uncles," and then . . . then I kissed her on the mouth. It happened all of a sudden. But how? I was still there with my face hidden in her warm and scented neck—a strange mixed scent of a child's skin and talcum powder—and already I was asking myself how. How could it have happened? I had embraced her; she had managed a feeble effort to resist, and then let me carry on. Is that how it happened? Perhaps that was it. But what now?

I drew back slowly. Now she was there, her face a few inches from mine. I stared at her without speaking or moving, incredulous, that's it: incredulous. Her back against the door jamb, her shoulders covered with a black woolen shawl, she too stared at me in silence. She looked me in the eyes, and her steady, straight, hard look entered me with the shining ease of a sword.

I was the first to look away.

"I'm sorry," I murmured.

"Why sorry? Perhaps it was my mistake coming down to meet you. It's my fault."

She shook her head. Then tried to give a good-natured, affectionate smile.

"Such a lot of lovely snow!" she said, nodding toward the garden. "Just imagine, in Venice not even a centimeter. If I'd only known so much had fallen here . . . "

She stopped, making a gesture of her hand, her right hand. She had drawn the shawl out from below, and I immediately noticed a ring.

I took her by the wrist.

"What's that?" I asked, touching the ring with my fingertip.

She winced, as though with distaste.

"I'm engaged. Didn't you know?"

She immediately burst out in a loud laugh.

"No, don't take it like that . . . can't you see I'm joking? It's just any old ring. Look."

She took it off with an exaggerated movement of her elbows, handed it over, and it was indeed an insignificant ring: a little circle of gold with a small turquoise stone. Her grandmother Regina had given it to her many years ago—she explained—concealed inside an Easter egg.

Once she had the ring again, she replaced it on her finger, then took me by the hand.

"You'd better come along now," she murmured, "or else, upstairs, they might"—she laughed—"start getting ideas."

As we went, she kept hold of my hand, and never stopped talking for a moment. Only on the stairs she stopped, inspected my lips in the light, and concluded the examination with a detached "Excellent!"

Yes—she was saying—the whole affair of the thesis had gone better than she'd dared hope. In the viva for graduation, she'd "held forth" for a good hour, "orating unstoppably." In the end they'd sent her out, and happily ensconced behind the examination hall's frosted-glass door, she'd been easily able to hear everything the gaggle of professors had said about her work. The majority were opting for a *cum laude*, but there was one, the Professor of German (a dyed-in-the-wool Nazi!) who wouldn't hear of it. He'd made himself very clear, the "worthy gentleman." In his view, the *cum laude* could not be given her without provoking a serious scandal. What were they thinking!—he had shouted. The Signorina was Jewish, and not even excluded as she ought to have been, and now they were talking of awarding her this distinction. What a disgrace! She should be thankful they'd let her graduate at all . . . The chairman, who taught English, also supported by others, had energetically countered by saying the school was a school, intelligence and hard work (so kind of him!) had nothing whatsoever to do with blood relations, etc., etc. However, when the moment came to do their sums, obviously, the Nazi carried the day. And she'd had no other consolation, apart from the apologies which later, running after her down the stairs of Ca' Foscari, the Professor of English had given to her—poor thing, his chin was trembling, he had tears in his eyes . . . —she'd had no other consolation apart from greeting the verdict with the most impeccable Roman salute. In the very act of giving her the title of "Doctor," the president of the Faculty had raised his arm. How was she supposed to have reacted? Limited herself to a charming little nod of the head? Not a chance.

She laughed joyfully, and I laughed too, drawn into her force field. In turn I recounted my eviction from the Public Library, dwelling on all the comic details. Yet when I asked her what had kept her in Venice for another month after her graduation (in Venice—I added—which, to listen to her, not only had she never found agreeable as a city but which was also a place in which she'd never found any real friends, male or female), she turned serious, withdrew her hand from mine, and her only reply was to cast a quick sideways glance.

We had a foretaste of the happy welcome we would receive in the dining room from Perotti, who was waiting in the vestibule. As soon as he saw us coming down the big staircase followed by Jor, he gave us an unusually joyous, almost conspiratorial smile. On a different occasion, his behavior would have annoyed me; I would have been offended by it. But for some minutes I'd found myself in a most peculiar frame of mind. Suppressing within myself every reason for unease, I felt enriched by a strange lightness, as though borne up by invisible wings. At the end of the day Perotti's a good fellow—I thought. He too was happy that the "Signorina" was back home. Why should one blame the poor old man? No doubt from then on he'd stop his grumbling.

Side by side, we made our appearance at the dining room doorway, and our presence was greeted, as I said, with the utmost rejoicing. All the diners' faces were rosy and lit up, expressing warmth and benevolence. And even the room itself, as all of a sudden it seemed to me that evening, was far more welcoming than usual—a rosy glow seemed to have spread over the furniture's polished wood, and the fire's tongue-like flames drew out subtle flesh tones from its grain. I had never seen it so filled with light. Apart from the glow unleashed from the burning logs, the great upturned corolla of the candelabra above the table (from which one could see the plates and cutlery had been cleared away) poured forth a veritable waterfall of light.

"Come on in!"

"Welcome!"

"We were beginning to think you'd decided not to come."

It was Alberto who uttered this last sentence, but I could see that my arrival had filled him with sincere pleasure. Everyone was looking at me. Some, like Professor Ermanno, had turned right round in their seats, others were leaning over the table or pushing away from it with straightened arms, and others still, like Signora Olga, seated alone at the head of the table, with the fireplace behind her, was tilting her face forward and half-closing her eyes. They watched me, they examined me, they looked me up and down, and they all seemed fully satisfied with me, and with the impression I made standing beside Micòl. Only Federico Herrera, the railway engineer, looking surprised, or worried, was slow to school himself to the general delight. But it was only a question of a moment. Having sought some explanation from his brother Giulio—I saw them quickly conferring behind their old mother's back, bringing their two bald heads together— he rapidly beamed his own share of warmth and approval toward me. Besides making a face which showed his outsized upper incisors, he even raised his arm in a gesture which, rather than greeting me, showed his solidarity, an almost sporting encouragement.

Professor Ermanno insisted I sit at his right. It was my usual place— he explained to Micòl who in the meantime had sat down at his left, facing me—where I "normally" sat whenever I stayed for supper. Giampiero Malnate—he went on to say—Alberto's friend, would sit "over there, on the other side," on Mamma's left. Micòl was listening to him with a strangely attentive air, part sardonic, part piqued—as though annoyed to discover how family life had proceeded in her absence, not exactly as she had foreseen, and yet pleased that things had, as it happened, gone in that direction.

I sat down, and only then, shocked to have been mistaken, did I notice that the table had not in fact been cleared. In the middle was a low, round, quite capacious silver tray, at the center of which, surrounded at two hands' breadth away by a circle of small pieces of white card, each inscribed in red crayon with a letter of the alphabet, stood a solitary champagne flute.

"And what's that then?" I asked Alberto.

"That's the big surprise I was telling you about!" he exclaimed. "It's absolutely wonderful. It just needs three or four people in a circle to put their fingers on the rim of the glass, and immediately it gives a reply, moving in every direction, one letter after another."

"Gives a reply?!"

"It certainly does! At a fair pace it writes down all the replies. And it makes sense—you can't imagine how much!"

I hadn't seen Alberto so excited and euphoric for a long time.

"And this new wonder, where has it come from?" I asked.

"It's just a game," Professor Ermanno broke in, placing a hand on my arm and shaking his head. "Something Micòl brought back from Venice."

"Ah, so you're the one responsible!" I said, turning to her. "And can your glass also read the future?"

"You bet!" she exclaimed, laughing. "I'd say that was its real speciality."

Dirce came in at that moment, holding aloft and balancing on one hand a round tray of dark wood, overflowing with Passover sweets—her cheeks also were rosy, shining with health and good will.

As the guest, and the last arrived, I was served first. The sweets, called *zucarìn*, made of shortbread with raisins mixed in, looked almost the same as the ones I had just tasted at home, half an hour before. Nevertheless those *zucarìn* at the Finzi-Contini house immediately seemed far better, much tastier, and I said as much, turning to Signora Olga who, busy as she was choosing from the plate that Dirce was offering her, seemed not to have noticed the compliment.

Next came Perotti, his big farm-laborer's hands clamped round the edge of a second tray (this time, pewter) which bore a flask of white wine and a number of glasses. And then, while we sat around the table, drinking Albana in little sips and nibbling at the *zucarìn*, Alberto went on explaining to me, in particular, the "goblet's divinatory qualities." It was true that for the moment it was keeping its counsel, but just a bit earlier it had been giving them replies of the most wonderful, extraordinary acuteness.

I wondered what they'd been asking it.

"Oh, a bit about everything."

They had asked it, for instance—he went on—if he, sometime or other, would ever get his degree in engineering; and the glass had, straight away, come back with the driest of "No"s. Then Micòl had wanted to know if she would get married, and if so, when; and the glass had become less peremptory—it seemed even a bit confused, giving a classic, oracular response, leaving open the most contradictory interpretations. They'd even interrogated it on the question of the tennis court—"the poor old glass!"—trying to discover whether Papa would finally abandon his rigmarole of perpetually putting off, from year to year, starting the work of refurbishing it. And on this question, displaying considerable patience, the "Delphic one" had reverted again to explicit mode, reassuring them that the longed-for improvements would be effected "immediately," at least within the year.

But it was mainly in the matter of politics that the glass had worked miracles. Very soon, within a few months, it had predicted, war would break out: a long, bloody war, grievous for everyone, such as would turn the whole world upside down, but in the end, after many years of inconclusive battles, it would finish with complete victory for the forces of good. "Of good?" Micòl, who always pounced on any gaffe, had asked at this point. "And what, may I ask, would those forces of good be?" To which the glass, making everyone gawp with surprise, had replied with one word only: "Stalin."

"Can you imagine," Alberto cried out among the general laughter, "can you imagine how that would have pleased Giampi, had he been here? I must write to him about it."

"Isn't he in Ferrara?"

"No. He left the other day. He's gone to spend Easter at home."

Alberto kept on for quite some time about what the glass had said, until the game was begun once more. I too placed my index finger on the "goblet." I too asked questions and waited for the replies. But now, for some reason, nothing comprehensible emerged from the oracle. Alberto became most insistent, tenacious and stubborn as never before. But nothing.

For my part, at least, I wasn't greatly bothered. Rather than attending to him and to the business of the glass, most of the time I was looking at Micòl: Micòl who, every now and then, feeling my gaze on her, would smooth her forehead of the same frown she used to have when playing tennis, to reassure me with a quick, considerate smile.

I was staring at her lips, faintly colored with lipstick. Just before, I had managed to kiss them. But had it happened too late? Why hadn't I done so six months earlier, when everything would still have been possible? Or at least during the previous winter? How much time we'd wasted, me here in Ferrara, and she in Venice! One Sunday I could easily have taken a train and gone to visit her. There was a fast train that left Ferrara at eight in the morning and arrived in Venice at half past ten. As soon as I'd got off the train, I could have phoned her, suggesting she took me to the Lido—so that, among other things, I could tell her, I'd finally get to see the famous Jewish cemetery of San Niccolò. Toward one o'clock, we might have eaten something together somewhere nearby and, after, have made a phone call to her uncles' house to keep the Fräulein sweet (oh, I could just see Micòl's face as she phoned her, the pursed lips, the clownish looks!). After that, we could have gone for a long slow walk along the deserted beach. There would have been time for that too. Then, as far as my return went, I would have had the choice of two trains—one at five, the other at seven, both of them excellent so that not even my parents would have the first idea anything had happened. If only I'd done it then, when I should have, everything would have been easy. What a joke.

What time was it now? Half past one, maybe two. Soon I'd have to go, and most likely Micòl would accompany me down, as far as the garden gate.

Perhaps it was this that she was also thinking of, this that was worrying her. Room after room, corridor after corridor, we would have to walk side by side without having even the courage either to look at each other or to say a word. I could sense we were both fearing the same thing: the leave-taking, the ever nearer and ever less imaginable point of saying goodbye, the goodbye kiss. Otherwise, if Micòl should choose not to accompany me, offloading the job onto Alberto or even Perotti, in what state of mind would I have to bear the rest of the night? And the day after?

But perhaps—I obstinately and desperately went back to dreaming—we wouldn't need to, we'd never have to get up from the table. The night would never have to end.

IV

· 1 ·

SOON enough, the very next day, I began to realize how hard it would be for me to resume the rapport with Micòl that we had had before.

After much hesitation, getting on toward ten, I tried to telephone her. I was told (by Dirce) that both the "Signorini" were still in bed, and would I be so kind as to call again "at noon." To while away the time, I threw myself on my bed. I picked up a book at random, *Le Rouge et le Noir*, but however hard I tried I wasn't able to concentrate. And if I didn't call her at midday? In a short while, though, I changed my mind. All of a sudden it seemed to me that now I only wanted one thing from Micòl: her friendship. Rather than disappearing—I told myself—it would be far better if I behaved as though yesterday evening nothing had happened. She would understand. Impressed by my discretion, utterly reassured, she would quickly reward me with all her full confidence, the delightful confidence she had of old.

At midday on the dot I braced myself and dialled the number of the Finzi-Contini house.

I had to wait a long time, longer than usual.

"Ah, it's you."

It was Micòl herself.

She yawned.

"What is it?"

Disconcerted, my mind a blank, I could think of nothing better to say than that I'd already called up once, two hours ago. Dirce had replied—I continued, stammering—suggesting I call again around midday.

Micòl heard me out. Then she began to complain about the day she had before her, all the many things she'd have to organize after being months and months away, suitcases to unpack, all kinds of papers to put in order, and so on, with the final prospect, not exactly enticing for her, of a second "banquet." That was the trouble with every trip away—that getting back to the usual dull routine cost even more effort than it had in the first place "to take oneself off."

I asked her if she meant to go along to the Temple later on.

She said she wasn't sure. Perhaps she would, but perhaps not . . . The way she felt at the moment she couldn't give me any guarantee it was at all likely.

She hung up without inviting me to come round again in the evening, and without arranging how or when we might see each other again.

That day I avoided ringing her up again. I didn't even go to the Temple. But around seven, passing by Via Mazzini, and noticing the Finzi-Continis' grey Dilambda parked behind the corner of the cobbled stretch of Via Scienze, with Perotti wearing his driver's beret and uniform seated at the wheel waiting, I couldn't resist the temptation of installing myself at the entrance of Via Vittoria to keep watch. I waited a long time, in the biting cold. It was the busiest time of the evening, the pre-prandial *passeggiata*. Along the two sidewalks of Via Mazzini, cluttered with dirty, already partly melted snow, the crowd was rushing in both directions. At last I had my reward. Suddenly, even though at a distance, I saw her emerge from the Temple's entrance and pause there on the threshold. She was wearing a short leopardskin coat, tied at the waist with a leather belt. Her blonde hair shining with the light from the windows, she was looking around her as though searching for someone. Was I the one she was looking for? I was about to emerge from the shadows and come forward, when her relatives, who had evidently followed her down the stairs at a distance, arrived in a group behind her back. They were all there, including grandma Regina. Turning on my heels, I hastily made my way down Via Vittoria.

The next day and the days that followed I kept on with my phone calls, yet only occasionally did I manage to speak to her. Nearly always, someone else came to the phone, either Alberto, Professor Ermanno, or Dirce, or even Perotti, all of whom, with the solitary exception of Dirce who was curt and impassive as a telephone operator, and for that very reason daunting and disquieting, entangled me in long, futile conversations. At a certain point I would cut Perotti short. But with Alberto and the Professor things were harder for me. I let them talk away. I always hoped that it would be they who mentioned Micòl. But in vain. As though they had decided to avoid all reference to her, and had even discussed the matter with each other, both her brother and her father left it up to me to take the initiative. With the result that very often I hung up without having found the courage to ask for what had prompted me to call.

I then resumed my visits, in the morning, with the excuse of the thesis, and in the afternoon, I'd go to see Alberto. I did nothing to make Micòl aware of my presence in the house. I was sure she knew of it, and that one day or another she would appear.

Although my thesis was actually completed, I still had to copy it out. So I would bring my typewriter along with me, and its tap-tapping, as soon as it first broke the silence of the billiards room, immediately called forth Professor Ermanno to the doorway of his study.

"What are you up to? Are you already copying it out?" he called out merrily.

He came over to me, and wanted to have a look at the contraption. It was an Italian portable, a Littoria, which my father had given me a few years earlier when I'd passed my final school exams. Its trade name did not, as I'd feared it might, provoke a smile from him. On the contrary. Claiming that "even" in Italy now they made typewriters, like mine, which seemed to work perfectly, he appeared to be impressed with it. There at home—he told me—they had three of them, one for Alberto's use, one for Micòl and one for him—all three were American Underwoods. Those of his children were undoubtedly hard-wearing portables, but not nearly as light as this one (at this point he weighed it on his hands). His own, on the other hand was the usual kind, an office typewriter. Yet . . .

Here he gave a little start.

Did I know, though, how many copies it let one make, if one wished?—he added, winking. As many as seven.

He led me to his study and showed it to me, lifting, not without some effort, a black, funereal cover, probably made of metal, which till then I hadn't noticed. In front of such a museum item, evidently hardly ever used even when it was new, I shook my head. No thanks—I said. Using my Littoria I'd never be able to make more than three copies, and two of them on the thinnest paper. All the same I preferred to keep on with my own.

I typed out on its keys chapter after chapter, but my mind was elsewhere. And it wandered elsewhere also when, in the afternoons, I went upstairs to Alberto's studio. Malnate had returned from Milan a good week after Easter, full of indignation at what was happening at that time: the fall of Madrid—ah, but it wasn't over yet; the conquest of Albania—what a dreadful disgrace! What a total mess! As for this last event, he told us what certain Milanese friends of his and Alberto's had said to him. Rather than it being a scheme of Il Duce, the Albanian business had been a pet project of "Ciano Galeazzo." Obviously jealous of von Ribbentrop, that disgusting coward had wanted to show the world that he was a match for the German in matters of lightning-diplomacy. Could we believe it? It seems that even Cardinal Schuster had expressed himself on the subject in disparaging, warning terms, and though he had spoken in the utmost secrecy, the whole city soon knew of it. Giampi also told us other things about Milan: about a performance at La Scala of Mozart's *Don Giovanni*, which he had luckily been able to attend, of an exhibition of paintings by a "new group" in Via Bagutti, and of Gladys, herself, whom he'd met by chance in the Galleria all wrapped up in mink and arm in arm with a well-known industrialist who dealt in steel. Gladys, friendly as ever, had while passing him given him a tiny sign with her finger which meant without any doubt "Phone me," or else "I'll phone you." What a shame that immediately after he'd had to return "to the factory!" It would have been a joy to cuckold that famous steel magnate, soon-to-be war profiteer . . . he'd have done it most willingly . . . He talked on and on, as usual addressing me in particular, but, at least in the end, a bit less didactic and peremptory than in the previous months—as though after his trip to

Milan, having enjoyed once more the affection of his family and friends, he had discovered a new temperament, far more indulgent toward others and their opinions.

With Micòl, as I've already noted, I only had the odd brief talk on the telephone, during which both of us avoided reference to anything too intimate. But some days after I had waited for more than an hour in front of the Temple I was unable to resist complaining about her coldness.

"Did you know," I said, "that the second evening of Passover I did see you?"

"Oh, is that right? Were you at the Temple too?"

"No. I was passing by Via Mazzini when I noticed your car, but I preferred to wait outside."

"How odd of you."

"You were most elegant. D'you want me to tell you what you were wearing?"

"No, really, I'll take your word for it. Where were you lurking?"

"On the sidewalk opposite, at the corner of Via Vittoria. At a certain moment you turned to look toward me. Tell me the truth—did you recognize me?"

"Don't be so silly. Why should I wish to deceive you? But as for you, I don't understand what you were thinking of . . . I'm sorry, but couldn't you have managed to *put a foot forward*?"

"I was about to. Then when I realized that you weren't alone, I abandoned the idea."

"What a surprise that I wasn't alone! But you're a strange type. I reckon you could have come over to say hello all the same."

"It's true when you think about it. The trouble is one can't always think clearly. And anyway, would you have been pleased if I had?"

"Good Lord. What a fuss about nothing!" she sighed.

The next time I managed to speak to her, not less than twelve days later, she told me she was ill, suffering from a terrible cold and some signs of fever. What a bore! Why didn't I ever come to visit her? I'd quite forgotten her.

"Are you . . . are you in bed?" I stammered, disconcerted, feeling myself a victim of a huge injustice.

"I certainly am, and between the sheets to boot. Tell the truth—you're refusing to come for fear of catching the flu."

"No, no, Micòl," I replied bitterly. "Don't make me out to be more pampered than I already am. I'm only astonished that you can accuse me of having forgotten you, when the truth is . . . I don't know if you remember," and as I continued my voice came out stifled, "but before you left for Venice phoning you was really easy, while now, I have to admit, it's become a complicated business. Didn't you know that I've come round to your house several times these last few days? Haven't they told you?"

"Yes."

"Well then! If you'd wanted to see me, you knew quite well where to find me—in the billiards room in the mornings, and in the afternoons downstairs with your brother. The truth is you had no desire to see me."

"What nonsense! I never like going to Alberto's studio, especially when he has friends round. And as for looking in on you in the mornings, aren't you hard at work? If there's one thing I hate doing it's disturbing people when they're working. Still, if it's really what you want, tomorrow or the day after I'll call in for a moment to say hello."

The morning of the day after, she didn't come, but in the afternoon, when I was with Alberto—it must have been seven o'clock—Malnate had brusquely taken leave of us a few minutes earlier—Perotti came in carrying a message from her. The "Signorina" would be grateful if I should go upstairs for a moment—he announced, impassively but, it seemed to me, in a bad mood. She had sent her apologies. She was still in bed, otherwise she would have come down herself. Which did I prefer—to go up immediately, or stay for supper, and go up afterward? The Signorina would prefer me to go on up straight away, since she had a bit of a headache and wanted to turn the light off very soon. But if I decided to stay . . .

"Heavens, no," I said, and looked at Alberto. "I'll go right now."

I got up, preparing myself to follow Perotti.

"Please make yourself at home," Alberto said, accompanying me considerately to the door. "I think this evening at dinner Papa and I will be alone. Grandma is also in bed with the flu, and Mamma doesn't leave her room even for a minute. So, if it suits you to have something with us, and go up to see Micòl later . . . it would make Papa happy."

I explained that I couldn't, that I had to meet "someone" "in the Piazza," and rushed out behind Perotti, who had already reached the end of the corridor.

Without exchanging a word we soon arrived at the foot of the long spiral staircase which led up and up to the little tower with the skylight. Micòl's rooms, as I knew, were those situated at the top of the house, only a half-flight below the topmost landing.

Not being aware of the lift, I began climbing the stairs.

"Just as well you're young," Perotti said with a grin, "but a hundred and twenty-three stairs are a fair number. Wouldn't you like us to take the elevator? It does work, you know."

He opened the black external cage, then the sliding door of the cabin, and only then stepped back to let me pass.

Getting into the elevator, which was an antediluvian big tin box all aglow with wine-colored wood and glittering slabs of glass adorned with the letters M, F and C elaborately interwoven; feeling my throat seized by the pungent, slightly suffocating smell, a cross between mold and turpentine, which impregnated the shut-in air of that narrow space, and being suddenly aware of a motiveless sense of calm, of resigned fatalism, even of ironic distance—these all collided and combined into a single sensation. But where had I smelled something like this before?—I asked myself—and when?

The elevator began to ascend quickly up through the stairwell. I sniffed the air, and at the same time looked at Perotti in front of me, at his back clad in pin-striped cotton. The old man had left the plush, velvet-covered seat entirely at my disposal. Standing, at a couple of hand's breadths away, self-absorbed, tense, with one hand grasping the brass handle of the sliding door and the other resting on the button panel—this too of glowing, well-polished brass—Perotti had closed himself once again in a silence open to all kinds of interpretation. But it was then I remembered and understood. Perotti was keeping silent not because he disapproved, as at a certain point I'd conjectured, that Micòl was receiving me in her room, but rather because the opportunity offered him to operate the lift (perhaps rare enough) filled him with a satisfaction as intense as it was private and intimate. The lift was no less dear to him than was the carriage, left down there in the coach-house. On such things, on such venerable witnesses to a past that was by then also his own, he could express his difficult love for the family he had served since he was a boy, the angry loyalty of an old domestic animal.

"It moves very well," I exclaimed. "Who are the makers?"

"It's American," he replied, half-turning his face round, and twisting his mouth in that characteristic grimace of distaste behind which country-men often conceal their admiration. "She's been at it for more than forty years, but she could still haul up a regiment."

"It must be a Westinghouse," I guessed at random.

"*Mah, sogio mi...*"* he stammered. "Some name like that."

After this he started out telling me how and when the contraption had been "put in." But then—to his evident displeasure—the lift shuddered to a sudden halt and forced him to interrupt his story then and there.

· 2 ·

IN MY frame of mind just then—a fragile serenity shorn of illusions—Micòl's welcome surprised me like an unexpected, undeserved gift. I'd been afraid she'd treat me badly, with the same cruel indifference as she had of late. And yet as soon as I entered her room (having introduced me Perotti had discreetly closed the door behind me) I saw she was smiling at me in a kind, friendly, open manner. More even than the explicit invitation to come on in, it was her luminous smile, full of forgiving warmth, which convinced me to move out from the dark end of the room and approach her.

So I came right up to the bed, laying both hands on the bed rail. With two cushions supporting her back, Micòl was sitting with the covers only up to her waist, wearing a long-sleeved, high-necked, dark-green pullover. Above her breasts the little gold medallion of the *shaddai* glinted over the wool . . . When I came in she had been reading—a French novel, as I'd quickly gathered, recognizing from a distance the familiar red-and-white

---

* Ferrarese dialect with Veneto inflection: "Don't ask me!"

covers, and it was probably reading rather than the cold which had made the skin under her eyes look tired. No, she was always beautiful—I told myself then, gazing at her—perhaps she'd never been quite so beautiful, so attractive. Beside the bed, at the height of the bolster, there was a walnut-wood trolley with two shelves, the upper one occupied by a lit articulated lamp, the telephone, a red earthenware teapot, a pair of white porcelain cups with gilded rims and a nickel silver thermos. Micòl stretched to place the book on the lower shelf, then turned in search of the hanging electric-light switch on the opposite side of the headboard. Poor me—she muttered at the same time between her teeth—it's not right I should be kept in a mortuary like this! The increase of light had hardly been effected when she greeted it with a long "Aah!" of satisfaction.

She kept on talking: of the "vicious" cold which had forced her to stay in bed for a good four days; of the aspirins with which, unbeknownst to Papa, and equally to her uncle Giulio, a sworn enemy of all sudorifics—in their opinion, they damaged the heart, but it wasn't true at all!—she'd tried in vain to bring her illness quickly to an end; of the boredom of endless hours being stuck in bed without even the desire to read. Ah, reading! Once, at the time of the famous flu and fever she'd had when she was thirteen, she'd been capable of reading the whole of *War and Peace* in a few days or the complete cycle of Dumas's *Musketeers*, while now, in the course of a miserable cold, though it did affect her head too, she had to be thankful if she managed to put "out of its misery" a little French novel, of the kind printed in big letters. Did I know Cocteau's *Les Enfants terribles*?—she asked, picking up the book again from the trolley and handing it to me. It wasn't bad, quite amusing and chic. But weighed beside *The Three Musketeers*, *Twenty Years After* and *The Viscount of Bragelonne*? Those were real novels! Let's be honest about it—even considered from the point of view of "chic-ness" they worked "much better."

Suddenly she interrupted herself.

"But why are you standing there like a garden pole? Good heavens, you're worse than a baby! Take that little armchair"—as she pointed it out—"and come and sit closer."

I hurried to obey her, but that wasn't good enough. Now I had to drink something.

"Is there nothing I can offer you? Would you like some tea?"

"No thanks," I replied, "it's not good for me before supper—it swills about in my stomach and takes away my appetite."

"Perhaps a little *Skiwasser*?"

"That has the same effect."

"It's boiling hot, you know! If I'm not wrong, you've only tried the summertime version, the one with ice, an essentially heretical version of the *Himbeerwasser*."

"Really, no thanks."

"Good Lord," she whined. "D'you want me to ring the bell and have you brought an aperitif? We never take them, but I believe there's a bottle of Bitter Campari somewhere in the house. Perotti—*honi soit*—will undoubtedly know where to find it . . . "

I shook my head.

"So you really don't want anything!" she complained, disappointed. "What a pain you are!"

"I prefer not to."

I said "I prefer not to" and she burst out laughing loudly.

"Why are you laughing?" I asked, a bit offended.

"You said 'I prefer not to,' just like Bartleby. With the same face."

"Bartleby. And who might that gentleman be?"

"It just goes to show you've never read Melville's short stories."

Of Melville—I said—I only knew *Moby-Dick*, in Cesare Pavese's translation. Then she wanted me to get up, to go and fetch from the bookcase there in front of me, between the two windows, the volume of *Piazza Tales* and bring it to her. While I was searching among the books, she told me the plot of the story. Bartleby was a clerk—she said—a scrivener employed by a New York lawyer (a real professional, busy, capable, "liberal," "one of those nineteenth-century Americans that Spencer Tracy plays to perfection") employed to copy out office work, legal documents and so on. Well, this Bartleby, so long as they got him to copy, would keep scribbling away conscientiously, bent over his desk. But if it crossed Spencer Tracy's mind to entrust him with some other small supplementary task, such as to collate a copy of the original text, or to nip down to the tobacco shop on the corner to buy a stamp, nothing doing—he would confine himself to an evasive smile and reply with stubborn politeness: "*I prefer not to.*"

"And why should he do that?" I asked, returning with the book in my hand.

"Because he wasn't prepared to be anything but a scrivener. A scrivener and nothing else."

"I'm sorry, but," I objected, "surely Spencer Tracy paid him a regular wage."

"Of course," Micòl relied. "But why should that matter? The wage is paid for the work, not for the person who performs it."

"I don't understand," I insisted. "Bartleby had been taken on in the office as a copyist by Spencer Tracy, but also, I suppose, so as to help things along in general. In the end what was he asking of him? A little more that may well have been less. For someone obliged to remain forever seated, nipping out to the tobacconist on the street corner might be seen as a pleasant change, a necessary break in the routine—whichever way you consider it, a perfect chance to stretch his legs a bit. No, I'm sorry. In my view, Spencer Tracy was quite right to protest that your Bartleby shouldn't hang about there playing the victim, and should immediately perform what had been asked of him."

We went on for a long time arguing about poor Bartleby and Spencer Tracy. She reproached me for not understanding the whole point, for being unimaginative, the usual inveterate conformist. Conformist? She must be joking. The fact is that just before, with an air of commiserating, she'd compared me to Bartleby. And now, on the contrary, seeing I was on the side of the "abject bosses" she had begun to laud in Bartleby "the inalienable right of every human being not to collaborate," that is, to liberty. She just kept on criticizing me, but for contradictory reasons.

At a certain point the telephone rang. They were calling from the kitchen to ask if and when they should bring up the supper tray. Micòl declared that for now she wasn't hungry, and that she would ring them back later. Would some minestrone soup be all right?—she replied with a grimace to a detailed question that came to her through the ear-piece. Of course. But, please, they shouldn't start preparing it yet—she never liked food that "had hung around."

Having put down the receiver, she turned to me. She stared at me with eyes that were at once kind and serious, and for some moments said nothing.

"How are you?" she asked at last, in a low voice.

I swallowed.

"Just so-so."

I smiled and looked around the room.

"It's strange," I went on. "Every detail of this room exactly matches how I'd imagined it. For instance, over there's the *chaise longue*. It's as though I'd already seen it. Well, actually I have seen it."

I told her the dream I'd had six months ago, the night before she left for Venice. I pointed to the row of *làttimi*, glowing in the half-dark of their shelves: the only things here, I told her, which in my dream had seemed other than they really were. I explained how they'd appeared to me and she kept listening, serious, attentive, without once interrupting.

When I'd finished, she stroked the sleeve of my jacket with a light caress. I knelt by the side of the bed, embraced her, kissed her neck, her eyes, her lips. She let me do it, but always watching me and, with little maneuvers of her head, always trying to stop me kissing her mouth.

"No . . . no . . . " she kept saying. "Stop it now . . . please . . . Be good . . . No, no . . . someone might come in . . . No."

But all in vain. Gradually, first with one leg and then with the other, I got myself onto the bed. Then I was pressing down on her with my whole weight. I continued blindly kissing her face, but only rarely managing to meet her lips, and never succeeding in getting her to lower her eyelids. At last I buried my head in her neck. And while my body, as though almost independent of me, made convulsive movements over hers, immobile under the covers as a statue, suddenly, in a terrible pang deep within me, I had the precise impression that I was losing her, that I'd already lost her.

She was the first to speak.

"Please get up," I heard her saying, very close to my ear. "I can't breathe like this."

I was literally annihilated. To get off that bed seemed to me an undertaking beyond my powers. Yet there was no other choice.

I dragged myself up. I took some steps around the room, hesitating. At length, I let myself fall once again on the little armchair beside the bed, and hid my face in my hands. My cheeks were burning.

"Why are you doing this?" Micòl said. "Can't you see it's useless?"

"Why is it useless?" I asked, quickly raising my eyes. "May I ask why?"

She looked at me, the shadow of an impish smile playing round her lips.

"Won't you go in there for a moment?" she said, nodding toward the bathroom door. "You're all red, *impizà** red. Go and wash your face."

"Thanks, I will. Perhaps it's a good idea."

I got up in a hurry and made toward the bathroom. Then, just at that moment, the door that gave onto the staircase was shaken by a vigorous blow. It seemed as though someone was trying to shoulder their way in.

"What is it?" I whispered.

"It's Jor," Micòl replied calmly. "Go and let him in."

· 3 ·

IN THE oval mirror above the sink I saw my face reflected.

I examined it carefully as though it wasn't mine, as though it belonged to someone else. Although I'd plunged it several times in cold water, it still looked completely red, *impizàda* red—as Micòl had said—with darker blotches between my nose and upper lip, above and around my cheekbones. I scrutinized with minute attention that large face lit up there in front of me, drawn first by the throbbing of the arteries under the skin of my forehead and temples, then by the dense mesh of tiny scarlet veins which, as I widened my eyes, seemed to lock the irises' blue discs down in a kind of siege, then by the hairs of my beard thickly bristling on my chin and along my jaw, then by a small spot that was barely visible . . . I was thinking of nothing. Through the thin dividing wall I could hear Micòl speaking on the phone. To whom? To the kitchen staff, probably, to stop them bringing up the supper. Good. The impending goodbye would then be less embarrassing. For both of us.

---

* Ferrarese dialect: "flaming."

I came in as she was putting down the receiver, and once again, not without surprise, I realized she had nothing against me.

She leaned from the bed to pour herself a cup of tea.

"Now please sit down," she said "and have something to drink."

I obeyed in silence. I drank with slow deliberate sips, without raising my eyes. Sprawled out on the parquet behind me, Jor was asleep. His thick snoring, like a drunken tramp's, filled the room.

I put down the cup.

It was once again Micòl who started speaking. Without any reference to what had just happened, she began by saying how for a long time, for much longer than I might think, she'd meant to speak frankly about the situation which bit by bit had developed between us. Did I perhaps remember that time—she went on—last October when, so as not to get soaked, we'd ended up in the coach-house, and had gone to sit in the carriage? Well, it was exactly from that time on that she'd become aware of the way our relationship had taken a wrong turn. She'd understood immediately that something wrong, something false and dangerous had started up between us. And it was mainly her fault, she was only too ready to admit, if, since then, the landslide had gathered momentum and kept on rolling downhill. But what could she have done? The simple thing would have been to take me aside and be honest with me, at that point, without delay. But rather than that, like a real coward, she'd chosen the worst course—to escape. Oh yes. It's easy enough to cut the cord. But what comes of it? Especially where it's all become "morbid." Ninety-nine percent of the time, the fire's still glowing under the cinders, with the wonderful result that later, when the two see each other again, for them to speak calmly, like good friends, has become hard as can be, almost impossible.

Even I could understand what she was saying—I put in at this point—and in the end I was very grateful to her for speaking so honestly.

But there was something I wanted her to explain. She'd suddenly rushed off without even saying goodbye to me, and after that, as soon as she'd arrived in Venice, she seemed concerned only with one thing: to be sure that I didn't stop seeing her brother Alberto.

"Why was that?" I asked. "If, as you say, you really wanted me to forget you (forgive the cliché and don't start laughing in my face!), couldn't you have dropped me completely? I know it would have been hard on me. But not impossible that, for lack of fuel, to put it that way, all the cinders might go out, on their own."

She looked at me without hiding a start of surprise, perhaps astonished that I could find in me the strength to move into a counter-attack, even if, all considered, with such small conviction behind it.

I wasn't wrong—she then agreed, with a troubled look, shaking her head—I wasn't wrong at all. But she begged me to believe that, acting as she had, there hadn't been the least intention on her part to stir things up. She valued our friendship, that was all, valued it even in a slightly too possessive way. And then, seriously, she'd been thinking more about Alberto than about me—Alberto who'd been left here with no one, apart from Giampiero Malnate, he could have a chat with. Poor Alberto—she sighed. Hadn't I noticed, spending time with him these last few months, how much he needed company? For someone like him, used to spending the winter in Milan, with theaters, cinemas and everything else on tap, the prospect of being stuck here at Ferrara, shut up at home for months on end, and on top of that having nothing to do, was hardly a happy one, I had to agree. Poor Alberto!—she repeated. Compared to him, she was much stronger, much more independent—able to put up with, if need be, the most awful loneliness. And besides, it seemed to her she'd already told me, Venice was perhaps, as far as squalor goes, even worse in the winter than Ferrara, and her uncles' house no less sad and secluded than this one was.

"But this house isn't in the least bit sad," I said, suddenly moved.

"D'you like it here?" she asked, brightening up. "Then I have to confess something to you (but you mustn't get annoyed with me and accuse me of hypocrisy, or even of being two-faced!)—I very much wanted you to see it."

"And why's that?"

"I don't know why. I can't explain to you why. I suppose it's for the same reason that, even as a child, at the Temple, I would happily have pulled you too under Papa's *tallit* . . . ah! If only I could have done! I can still see you there, under your father's *tallit*, on the bench in front of ours. What a pang I felt seeing you. It's stupid, I know, but I felt the same kind of sorrow as though you'd been an orphan, without a father and mother."

She fell silent for some moments, her eyes fixed on the ceiling. Then, leaning her elbow on the bolster, she began to speak to me again—but this time seriously, almost solemnly.

She said she hated causing me pain, she really hated it. On the other hand she needed me to understand—it was absolutely unnecessary that we spoil, as we were risking doing, the lovely memories of a shared childhood. For us two to make love? Did it really seem feasible to me?

I asked her why she thought that so impossible.

For countless reasons—she replied—but mainly because the thought of making love to me disconcerted, embarrassed her: in the same way as if she were to imagine making love with a brother, with, say, Alberto. It was true that, as a child, she'd had "a crush" on me, and, who knows, it was perhaps precisely this that was now blocking her so utterly with regard to me. I . . . I stood "alongside" of her, didn't I see? rather than "in front" of her, while being in love (at least this was how she imagined it) was something for people who were determined to get the better of each other, a cruel, hard sport—far crueller and harder than tennis!—with no holds barred, with all kinds of low blows, and without any concern, just to palliate things, for the good of the soul or for notions of fairness.

> *Maudit soit à jamais le rêveur inutile*
> *qui voulut le premier, dans sa stupidité,*
> *s'éprenant d'un problème insoluble et stérile,*
> *aux choses de l'amour mêler l'honnêteté!*

—Baudelaire, who well understood, had warned. As for us? We were both stupidly honest, as alike as two drops of water ("and, you ought to believe me, people so alike should never fight each other"), so we'd never be able to try to get the better of each other, us two. Could I really see us wanting to "wound" each other? No way! As the good Lord had made us like this, it meant the whole thing had neither prospects nor possibilities.

But even allowing for the unlikely hypothesis that we were made differently from the way we were, that between us there was in fact even the least possibility of a relationship of the kind that "offered no hostages," how were we then supposed to behave? "To get engaged," for instance, accompanied by an exchange of rings, parental visits, etc.? What an edifying image! If he were still alive, and got to hear of it, Israel Zangwill himself might have had a juicy coda to add to his *Dreamers of the Ghetto.** And what a delight, what a "pious" delight everyone would feel when we appeared together in the Italian synagogue for the next Yom Kippur: a bit wan in the face from fasting, but apart from that so good looking, such a perfect couple! And seeing us, there'd certainly be someone there who'd give thanks to the Racial Laws, proclaiming that, faced with such a lovely union, the only thing to be said was: every cloud has a silver lining. Who knows if even the Secretary of the Fascist Party in Via Cavour might go a bit soft at the prospect! Even if in secret, wasn't that good fellow Consul Bolognesi really a lover of Jews? Pah!

Defeated, I kept silent.

She profited from this pause to lift the receiver and tell them in the kitchen to bring up the supper, but in a half-hour or so, not before, as—she repeated—that evening she wasn't "in the least bit hungry." Only the day after, going over it all, would I remember when, closed in the bathroom, I'd heard her talking on the telephone. So I was wrong—I told myself the next day. She might have been talking with anyone in the house (or even outside) but not with the kitchen.

But then I was immersed in a completely different train of thought. When Micòl put the receiver down I lifted my head.

"You said we were exactly alike," I spoke again. "In what way?"

"But yes, yes we are"—she exclaimed—"in the way, like you, I've no access to that instinctive enjoyment of things that's typical of normal people." She could sense it very clearly: for me, no less than for her, the past counted far more than the present, remembering something far more than possessing it. Compared to memory, every possession can only ever seem disappointing, banal, inadequate . . . She understood me so well! My anxiety that the present "immediately" turned into the past so that I could love it and dream about it at leisure was just like hers, was identical. It was "our" vice, this: to go forward with our heads forever turned back. Wasn't it true?

---

* Israel Zangwill (1864–1926): London-born Jewish writer, pacifist, supporter of women's suffrage, and involved in the Zionist aspiration to found a Jewish homeland.

It was—I had to admit within myself—it was exactly so. When was it that I'd embraced her? At the most an hour before. And already everything had again become as unreal and mythical as ever: an event that was unbelievable, or a source of fear.

"Who knows," I replied. "Perhaps it's all much simpler. Perhaps you don't find me attractive. And that's all it is."

"Don't talk nonsense," she said in protest. "What's that got to do with it?"

"It's got everything to do with it!"

"You are fishing for compliments.* And you know it. But I'm not going to give you the satisfaction, you don't deserve it. And anyway, even if I was now to try telling you once more all the praise I've lavished on your famous blue-green eyes (and not only on your eyes) what would I get from that? You'd be the first to judge me ill, as an utter hypocrite. You'd think, here we go, after the stick comes the carrot, the sweetener . . . "

"Unless . . . "

"Unless what?

I hesitated, and then finally decided.

"Unless," I went on, "there's someone else involved."

She shook her head to say no, looking me in the eyes.

"There's no one else in the least bit involved," she replied. "And who could there be?"

I believed her. But I was desperate and wanted to hurt her.

"You're asking me?" I said, pouting. "It could be anyone. Who can assure me that this winter, in Venice, you haven't met someone else?"

She burst out laughing. Fresh, happy, crystalline laughter.

"What an idea!" she exclaimed. "Given I've done nothing else but huddle over my thesis the whole time!"

"You don't mean to say that in these five years of university you've not been out with anyone. Please! There must have been someone there who was following you around!"

I was convinced she'd deny it. But I was wrong.

"Sure, I've had some admirers," she admitted.

---

* In English in the original.

It was like a hand had grabbed hold of my stomach and twisted it.

"Many?" I managed to bring out.

Stretched out supine as she was, her eyes fixed on the ceiling, she slightly raised one arm.

"I wouldn't really know," she replied. "Let me think."

"So you've had a lot, then?"

She gave me a sidelong look with a sly, decidedly louche expression, which I didn't recognize in her and which completely floored me.

"Well . . . let's say three or four. Five to be precise . . . but all little flirtations, I should make it clear, quite innocuous . . . and also fairly boring as it happens."

"What kind of flirtations?"

"Oh, you know . . . long walks along the Lido . . . two or three routine trips to Torcello . . . every now and then a kiss . . . a great deal of holding hands . . . and going to the flicks. Orgies of cinema."

"All with fellow students?"

"More or less."

"And Catholics, I imagine."

"Of course. Not as a point of principle, though. You understand: you have to make do with what's there."

"But with . . ."

"No. With *Judim*, I have to say, not once. Not that there weren't any in the classes. But they were so serious and ugly."

She turned once more to look at me.

"However, no one at all this winter," she added, smiling. "I could swear an oath on that. I've done nothing else but smoke and work, so much so that Signorina Blumenfeld herself had to prompt me to go out."

She took out from under the pillows a packet of Lucky Strikes, unopened.

"D'you want one? As you can see I've started off on the strong ones."

I silently pointed to the pipe which I kept in my jacket pocket.

"You as well!" she laughed, highly amused. "That Giampi of yours really is growing a crop of disciples!"

"And you, you keep on grumbling about having no friends in Venice!" I complained. "What a lot of lies. It's clear you're just like the other girls."

She shook her head, though I wasn't sure whether in sympathy with me or with herself.

"Flirtations, even insignificant ones, are not to be had with friends," she said with sadness, "and so, when I was speaking to you about friend-ship, you should see I was only being a bit dishonest. But you're right. I am just like other girls—a liar, a deceiver, unfaithful . . . in the end not much different from an Adriana Trentini."

She had said "un-faith-ful" separating each of the syllables in her usual fashion, but with an extra quality of bitter pride. She went on to say that if I had a fault it was that I'd always thought a bit too highly of her. In say-ing this she hadn't the least intention of excusing herself. And yet she'd always seen in my eyes so much "idealism" that it had somehow forced her to appear better than she actually was.

Nothing much else was left to say. A little later, when Gina came in with the supper—it was already past nine o'clock—I stood up.

"I'm sorry, but I have to go now," I said, holding out my hand.

"You know the way, don't you? Or would you like Gina to accompany you?"

"No, there's no need. I can manage it on my own."

"Take the lift, it's a lot easier."

"I shall."

At the door I turned round. She was already bringing the spoon to her lips.

"Bye," I said.

She smiled at me.

"Bye. I'll phone you tomorrow."

· 4 ·

BUT THE worst part only began about three weeks later, when I returned from a trip to France I made in the last fortnight of April.

I'd gone to France, to Grenoble, for a very particular reason. The few hundred lire every month, legally permitted for us to send my brother Ernesto, were only enough, as he kept repeating in his letters, to pay for his rented room, at Place Vaucanson. So it was vital he received more money. For this reason, when I returned home later than usual one night, my father, who had been staying awake especially to speak to me, pressed me to take him the money in person. Why didn't I make the most of the opportunity? A chance to breathe some different air from "what wafts around here," to see a bit of the world, to have a wander: that's what I ought to do! It would be good for my morale, and my body as well.

So I went. I stopped for two hours in Turin, four at Chambéry, and finally reached Grenoble. In the *pensione* where Ernesto went to eat his meals I immediately got to know various Italian students, all in the same situation as my brother and all enrolled at the Polytechnic: a Levi from Turin, a Segre from Saluzzo, a Sorani from Trieste, a Mantuan Cantoni, a Florentine Castelnuovo, a Pincherle girl from Rome. I didn't hitch up with any of them. During the dozen days left to me, most of the time I spent in the Municipal Library, leafing through Stendhal's manuscripts. It was cold in Grenoble, and rainy. The peaks of the mountains at the back of the lodgings, hidden by mists and cloud, were only rarely visible, while in the evenings the blackout trials dampened any desire to go out. Ferrara seemed very far away to me, as though I'd never return. And Micòl? Since I'd left I had ceaselessly heard her voice in my ear, her voice the time she'd said to me: "Why are you doing that? It's no use." One day, however, something happened. As I was reading through one of Stendhal's notebooks and chanced upon these isolated words in English: "All lost, nothing lost," as though by a miracle, I had a sudden feeling of being freed, healed. I got hold of a postcard, and wrote that line from Stendhal on it, just that, and then sent it off to her, Micòl, without adding a single word, not even a signature—she could make of it what she wanted. All lost, nothing lost. How true that was! I told myself. And felt I could breathe again.

I was fooling myself. Returning to Italy in the first days of May, I found the spring in full bloom, the meadows between Alessandria and Piacenza broadly swathed with yellow, the roads of the Emilian countryside thronged with girls on bikes revealing bare arms and legs, the big trees of the Ferrara walls laden with leaves. I'd arrived on a Sunday, toward midday. As soon as I got back home, I had a bath, took lunch with my family and answered a host of questions patiently enough. But the unexpected frenzy that gripped me the very moment when, from the train, I'd seen the turrets and belltowers of Ferrara rise up from the horizon, made any further delays intolerable to me. At half past two I was already on my bike racing along the Mura degli Angeli, my eyes fixed on the motionless green abundance of the Barchetto del Duca, which gradually drew closer on my left. Everything had turned back to how it was before, as though I'd spent the last fortnight asleep.

They were playing, down there on the tennis court—Micòl and a stout young man in long white socks who, it wasn't hard for me to make out, was Malnate. I too was quickly noticed and recognized, for the two of them stopped knocking up and began to wave their rackets in the air with extravagant gestures. They were not alone, however; Alberto was also there. Emerging from the leafy border, I saw him rush to the center of the court, look out toward me and raise his hands to his mouth. He whistled two, three times. Might they be informed what it was I was doing on top of the walls?—each of them, in their own way, seemed to be asking. And why on earth had I not come immediately into the garden, strange creature that I was? So then I steered toward the opening of Corso Ercole I d'Este, pedaling alongside the surrounding wall, and had come in sight of the gate when Alberto unleashed another of his "oliphants." "Make sure you don't slink off!" his ever powerful whistles now seemed to be saying, though they had become in the meantime somehow good-natured, a shade less admonitory.

"Greetings!" I shouted as usual, when I emerged into the open from the gallery of climbing roses.

Micòl and Malnate had gone back to their game, and without stopping, replied together with another "Greetings." Alberto stood up and came to meet me.

"Would you tell us where you've been hiding all these days?" he asked. "I phoned your house a fair few times, but you were never there."

"He's been in France," Micòl replied on my behalf from the court.

"In France!" Alberto exclaimed, his eyes full of an astonishment that seemed to me truly felt. "Doing what?"

"I've been to see my brother Ernesto in Grenoble."

"Oh, of course. It's true. Your brother's studying at Grenoble. And how is he? How is he coping?"

In the meantime we had parked ourselves on two deckchairs, placed one beside the other in front of the side entrance to the court in an excellent position to follow the state of play. As distinct from last autumn, Micòl was not in shorts. She was wearing a pleated, white woolen skirt, very old-fashioned, a shirt that was also white, with its sleeves rolled up, and curious long white cotton socks, almost like those of a Red Cross nurse. Covered in sweat, and red in the face, she was concentrating on striking the balls into the furthest corners of the court, powering her shots. Yet although he'd put on weight and was quite out of breath, Malnate was effortfully holding his own against her.

A tennis ball, rolling along, came to a stop within a short distance of us. Micòl approached to collect it, and for a moment our eyes met.

I saw her pull a face. Evidently annoyed, she brusquely turned back toward Malnate.

"Shall we play a set?" she shouted out.

"We could try," he panted out. "How many games handicap will you give me?"

"Not a single one," Micòl replied, frowning. "All I'll give you is the chance to serve first. Your service, then!"

She threw the ball over the net and got into position to receive her opponent's serve.

For some minutes Alberto and I watched them playing. I felt full of unease and misery. The "*tu*" form with which she addressed Malnate, her show of ignoring me, suddenly and fully revealed to me the length of time I'd been away. And as for Alberto, he as usual had eyes only for Giampi. But every now and then, I noticed, instead of admiring and praising him, he would start running him down.

There you see a type of person—he confided whisperingly, and so surprisingly that, however anguished I felt, I didn't miss a single syllable he said—there you see a type of person who, even if he took tennis lessons every blessed day from a Nüsslein or a Martin Plaa, would still never make a halfway decent player. What was stopping him? His legs? Certainly not that, otherwise he'd never have become the accomplished mountaineer he undoubtedly was. Lungs? Nor them, for the same reason. Muscular power? He had enough of that to spare—you just have to shake his hand to feel it. What was it then? The truth is that tennis—he concluded with extraordinary emphasis—as well as being a sport is also an art, and since every art requires a particular talent, whoever's lacking in that will remain "all elbows" their whole life.

"I ask you!" Malnate shouted out at a certain point. "Will you two keep the noise down a bit?"

"Play on, play on," Alberto retorted, "and try not to let a woman get the better of you!"

I couldn't believe my ears. Was it possible? What had happened to all of Alberto's meekness, all his submissiveness to his friend? I looked at him carefully. His face seemed to me of a sudden wan, emaciated, as though wrinkled with the premature onset of old age. Was he ill?

I was tempted to ask him, but I lacked the courage. Instead, I asked him if this had been the first day they'd started playing tennis again, and why Bruno Lattes, Adriana Trentini and the rest of the *zòzga*[*] weren't there.

"Well, it's clear you know absolutely nothing!" he cried out, revealing his gums in a big laugh.

About a week ago—he immediately launched into the tale—having seen the good weather set in, Micòl and he had made ten or so phone calls, with the worthy intention of restarting last year's memorable tennis meets. They'd called Adriana Trentini, Bruno Lattes, that boy Sani, young Collevatti—and various splendid examples of both sexes selected from among the new generation who, last autumn, they hadn't even thought of. All of them, "young and old" had accepted the invitation with commendable promptness, so that the day of the opening—Saturday, May 1— looked well set to be a triumphal success to say the least. Not only had they played tennis, gossiped, flirted and so on, but they'd even danced, there, in the *Hütte*, to the accompaniment of the "conveniently installed" Philips.

An even greater success—Alberto went on—had attended the second session, Sunday afternoon, May 2. Except that as early as Monday morning things were already coming to a head. Heralded by a sibylline visiting

---

[*] Ferrarese dialect: "gang."

card, toward eleven o'clock the lawyer Tabet arrived on his bicycle—yes, that big Fascist blockhead Geremia Tabet in person, who after being shut away in conference with Papa in his study, had passed on the mandatory order of the Party Secretary to cease forthwith the provocation of those scandalous daily gatherings that for some time had been held at the house, which apart from anything else were entirely lacking in any healthy sporting activity. It was really unacceptable, the Consul Bolognesi let it be known through his "common" friend Tabet, it was really unacceptable, for obvious reasons, that the Finzi-Contini garden was gradually turning itself into a kind of rival tennis club to the Eleonora d'Este—the latter a much-renowned institution of Ferrarese sporting life. So that was that. To avoid official sanctions, "such as a forced stay for an undetermined period of time in Urbisaglia," from this time on no one who was a member of the Eleonora d'Este should be lured away from their natural habitat.

"And what did your father say in reply?" I asked.

"What could he say?" Alberto laughed. "There was nothing left for him but to behave like Don Abbondio.* To bow and murmur 'Your obedient servant.' I think that's more or less how he expressed himself."

"I hold Barbicinti responsible," Micòl shouted out from the court, clearly not far enough away to have stopped her following our conversation closely. "No one will change my mind that it was him who ran off crying to complain at Viale Cavour. I can just see it. But still, you have to sympathize with him, poor thing. When one's jealous, one becomes capable of anything . . . "

Although they were perhaps thrown out without any particular intent, these words of Micòl stung me deeply. I was on the point of getting up and going away.

And who knows, maybe I would have done so, if I hadn't stopped at that very moment, as I turned toward Alberto, almost to invoke his witness and assistance, and again noticed how grey his face was, the afflicted scrawniness of his shoulders lost in a pullover now grown too big for him (he winked, as if telling me not to take it to heart, and began to hold forth on other things—the tennis court, the work to improve it "from the

---

* One of the principal characters in Manzoni's *I promessi sposi*.

foundations up" which, despite everything, would be starting within the week...), and if in that same instant I hadn't seen appearing, down there at the edge of the clearing, the black mournful little figures, close together, of Professor Ermanno and Signora Olga, coming from their afternoon stroll in the park and wending their way slowly toward us.

· 5 ·

THAT WHOLE long period which followed, up until the fateful last days of August 1939, until, that is, the eve of the Nazi invasion of Poland and the phoney war, I remember as a slow progressive descent into the Maelstrom. There were only four of us left in sole possession of the tennis court, which was soon to be covered with a fine coat of red shale from Imola—myself, Micòl, Alberto and Malnate. (Presumably lost in his pursuit of Adriana Trentini, Bruno Lattes was not to be numbered amongst us.) Swapping partners, we spent whole afternoons in long doubles matches, with Alberto, even though he was short of breath and easily tired, oddly driven, unwilling to give either us or himself any quarter.

What was it made me stubbornly return every day to a place where, as I well knew, I'd be rewarded with nothing but humiliation and bitterness? I couldn't say with any clarity. Perhaps I was hoping for a miracle, for a sudden change in the state of affairs, or perhaps I was actually going in search of humiliation and bitterness . . . We played tennis or else, stretched out on four deckchairs in front of the *Hütte*, we argued about the usual topics of art and politics. But when I asked Micòl, who, deep down, remained kindly toward me, sometimes even affectionate, for a turn in the park, it was very rarely that she accepted. If she did, she never followed me willingly, and every time her face would assume an expression poised between distaste and forbearance which made me regret having dragged her away from Alberto and Malnate.

All the same, I wasn't prepared to lay down my arms; I wouldn't give up. Caught between the impulse to break it all off, to disappear forever, and its opposite: not to renounce being there, not to surrender at any cost, in the end I almost always turned up. Sometimes, it's true, a look from Micòl that was colder than usual, an impatient gesture of hers, one of her sarcastic, bored expressions, would be enough for me to feel with utter sincerity that that was it, it was all over. But how long did I succeed in staying away? Three or four days at the most. On the fifth there I was again, parading my face with the good-humored and detached expression of someone just returned from a most rewarding journey—I was always talking of having taken trips, comparing the journeys I'd made to Milan, to Florence, to Rome: it was just as well all three of them gave the impression of believing me!—but all the same I did so with a flayed heart and with eyes that once again began to seek out in those of Micòl some answer which was now impossible. That was the time, as she was to call it, of our "marital rows." During which, if ever the occasion permitted, I would try to kiss her. And she put up with it, never appearing to be uncivil.

One evening in June, however, things were to go differently.

We were seated beside each other on the steps outside the *Hütte*, and though it must have been about half past eight it was still not dark. I was watching Perotti, in the distance, busy taking down and rolling up the net on the tennis court, the surface of which, since the red shale had arrived from the Romagna, never seemed to him sufficiently well looked after. Malnate was taking a shower inside the hut—we could hear him panting noisily under the jet of hot water—and Alberto had taken his leave a little earlier with a melancholy "bye-bye." So the two of us, Micòl and I, had been left alone, and I'd immediately taken advantage of this to resume my eternal, boring, absurd campaign. As ever, I kept on trying to convince her she was wrong to believe a relationship between us would not work. As ever I accused her (in bad faith) of having lied to me when, less than a month before, she had assured me there was no third party involved. I put it to her that there was, or at least there had been, in Venice, during the winter.

"I'm telling you for the thousandth time you're wrong," Micòl said in a low tone, "but I know it's pointless. I know you'll want to return to the fray tomorrow with the same old story. What do you want me to say—that I'm plotting in secret, that I'm living a double life? If you really want that, I could certainly oblige you."

"No, Micòl," I replied in an equally low but far more agitated tone. "I may be all kinds of things, but I'm not a masochist. If only you knew how normal, how terribly banal my hopes are—you'd laugh. If there's one thing I want, it's this—to hear you swear what you've said is true, and to believe you."

"Well, I swear it. Now do you believe me?"

"No."

"So much the worse for you then!"

"True, it's all the worse for me. And yet if I could really believe you . . . "

"Then what would you do? Let's hear."

"Oh, just the most normal, banal stuff—that's the problem. This, for example."

I grasped her hands, and began to cover them with kisses and tears.

For a while she let me. I hid my face in her knees, and the smell of her skin, smooth and soft, slightly salty, numbed me. I kissed her there, on the legs.

"Now, that's enough," she said.

She withdrew her hands from mine, and stood up.

"Goodbye. I'm cold," she went on, "and you should go home. Dinner will be ready by now, and I have to wash and dress first. Get up, come on, and stop acting like a baby."

"Goodbye," she then shouted toward the *Hütte*. "I'm going now."

"Goodbye," Malnate replied from inside, "and thanks."

"See you soon. Are you coming tomorrow?"

"I don't know about tomorrow. We'll see."

Separated by the bicycle whose handlebars I was feverishly grasping, we made our way toward the *magna domus*, standing tall and dark in the summer dusk alive with bats and mosquitoes. We kept silent. A cart brimming with hay, drawn by a pair of yoked oxen, was going in the opposite direction to us. Seated on top of it was one of Perotti's sons who, coming level with us, doffed his beret and wished us good evening. Even though I'd accused Micòl without believing it, I'd still have liked to shout at her—telling her to stop play-acting with me. I wanted to insult her, even to slap her. And if I had? What would I have gained from it?

But I did something just as mistaken.

"It's pointless you denying it," I said, "and anyway I know who the person is."

No sooner had these words escaped me than I regretted them.

Now aggrieved and in earnest, she looked at me.

"I see," she said, "and now, according to your calculations, I'll have to try to get you to spit out the name and surname you've hidden away, if you really have any name in mind at all. But I'm afraid that's it. I don't want to hear anything more. Only that, having arrived at this point, I'd be grateful if from now on you were a little less assiduous in your visits . . . I mean, if you were to come to our house less often. I'm telling you frankly: if I didn't fear being overwhelmed by gossip in the family—how come . . . why ever . . . etc., I'd beg you not to come at all, ever again."

"Forgive me," I murmured.

"No. That I can't do," she replied, shaking her head. "If I did, in a few days you'd only start again."

She added that for a long time up till then my way of behaving had been undignified—both for her and for myself. She had told me and repeated it a thousand times that it was useless, that I shouldn't attempt to shift our relationship onto any other plane than that of friendship and affection. But what good was it? As soon as I could I did the opposite—I'd grab on to her, trying to kiss her and go further, as though I didn't know that in situations like ours there was nothing more disagreeable and ill-advised. Good heavens! Was it really possible I couldn't contain myself? If there'd been a physical relationship of a deeper kind between us than one based on the odd kiss, in that case she might have been able to understand how I . . . how she, so to speak, had got under my skin. But given the relations that had always been between us, my compulsion to embrace her, to rub myself up against her, was the sign of one thing only: my effective heartlessness, my constitutional inability to really care about another person. And what's more, what did my unexpected absences mean, and my sudden returns, the inquisitional or "tragic" looks, the hangdog silences, the rudenesses, the irrational insinuations—the whole repertoire of rash and embarrassing behavior which I tirelessly exhibited, without the least sense of shame? Perhaps she could have put up with it if these "marital rows" had been reserved for her ears alone, apart from the others. But that her brother and Giampi Malnate should have to be witnesses, this no, and again no, she wouldn't put up with.

"Now it seems to me you're exaggerating," I said. "When have I ever made a scene in front of Malnate and Alberto?"

"Always. Continually!"

Every single time I'd come back after a week of being away—she went on—and declare I'd been to Rome or somewhere, and then I'd start laughing, laughing in nervous fits like a nutcase, without the least reason, did I fool myself into thinking Alberto and Malnate would somehow not notice I was talking bullshit, that I'd never been anywhere near Rome, and that my fits of laughter "straight out of *Cena delle beffe*"* weren't all directed toward her? And when in arguing, I'd jump up and start haranguing and screaming like a maniac, frequently taking everything personally—some day or other Giampi would get really annoyed, and he wouldn't be without some justification, poor thing that he was too!—did I think people would somehow not notice that she was the cause, albeit the innocent one, of all my crazy antics?

"I understand," I said, lowering my head. "I really understand that you don't want to see me any more."

"It's not my fault. It's you who, bit by bit, have become unbearable."

"You said, though," I stammered after a pause, "you said that I could come round every so often, rather that I have to. Isn't that right?"

"Yes."

"Well then . . . you must decide. How should I behave so as not to offend you further?"

"I don't know," she replied, shrugging her shoulders. "I'd say that, to start off with, you should leave a space of at least twenty days. Then you can start visiting again, if you want to. But I beg you, even after, don't come round more than twice a week."

"Tuesdays and Wednesdays, would that do? Like for piano lessons."

"You idiot," she muttered, smiling against her will. "You really are an idiot."

---

* *The Feast of the Jesters* (play by Sam Benelli, 1909).

· 6 ·

ALTHOUGH THE effort, especially to begin with, was extremely hard, I made it something of a point of honor to observe Micòl's prohibitions to the letter. Suffice it to say, having graduated on June 29, and having received a warm congratulatory note from Professor Ermanno which contained, among other things, an invitation to dinner, I thought it opportune to refuse, saying I was sorry but I couldn't. I wrote that I'd been suffering from a bout of tonsillitis, and that my father had stopped me going out in the evenings. My refusal, however, was down to the fact that of the twenty days Micòl had imposed on me, only sixteen had passed.

The effort was really hard. Though I was hoping that sooner or later there'd be some recompense, my hopes remained somewhat vague: I felt glad to be obeying Micòl and through this obedience I thought I might once more have access to her and to the paradisal regions I'd been shut out from. If before I'd always had something to reproach her with, now I had nothing. I and I alone was the guilty one. How many mistakes I'd made!—I told myself. I thought back over all the times that, often by force, I'd kissed her on the lips, but always and only to put her in the right, who, even in rejecting me, had put up with me for so long, and to feel ashamed of my satyr-like lustfulness, masked as sentimentality and idealism. The twenty days having passed, I risked showing myself again, and, following that, kept rigorously to the twice-weekly visits prescribed. But even this didn't induce Micòl to descend from the pedestal of purity and moral superiority on which, since being sent into exile, I'd placed her. She continued to stay up there. And I felt myself lucky to keep on being able to admire this distant image of her, no less beautiful inside than she was on the outside. "Like truth itself / like her, sad and beautiful . . . ": these first two verses of a poem I never finished, though they were written much later, in Rome, soon after the war, refer back to that Micòl of August 1939, and the way I saw her then.

Chased out of Paradise, I waited in silence to be let back in. And yet I suffered—some days atrociously. It was with the intention somehow to alleviate the weight of an often intolerable distance and solitude that one week, soon after that final, disastrous conversation with Micòl, I had the notion of going to visit Malnate, to keep in contact at least with him.

I knew where to find him. As Professor Meldolesi once had, he lived in the zone of small villas just outside Porta San Benedetto, between the Canile and the curve of the Doro. At that time, before the building speculation of these last fifteen years wrecked it, this area, even if a bit grey and modest, did not seem at all disagreeable. All on two floors, each one sporting its own little garden, these small villas generally belonged to magistrates, teachers, civil servants, state functionaries, etc., who, should you be passing by in summer after six in the evening, could be spotted beyond the bristling bars of their gates, sometimes in pyjamas, intent on busily watering and pruning their plants or hoeing the soil. Malnate's resident landlord was one of them, a tribunal judge. He was a Sicilian around fifty, thin as a rake, with long, thick grey hair. As soon as he noticed me, still not off my bike and holding on with both hands to the gate's pointed uprights as I peered into the garden, he set down the hose with which he'd been watering the flower beds.

"May I help you?" he asked, approaching.

"Is Dr. Malnate here?"

"He lives here. Why?"

"Is he at home?"

"Who can say. Do you have an appointment?"

"I'm a friend of his. I was passing, and I thought I'd stop by for a moment to say hello to him."

In the meantime, the judge had covered the ten or so meters which had separated us. And now I could only see the upper part of his bony, fanatical face, his black eyes, piercing as needles, looming above the edge of the metal plate linking the gate's uprights at the height of a man. He stared at me with suspicion. All the same, the examination must have ended up in my favor, because almost immediately the lock clicked open and I was let in.

"That way, please," Judge Lalumìa finally said, lifting his skeletal arm. "Just follow the paving that goes round the house. The little ground-floor door is the one to the doctor's apartment. Ring the bell. He may not be in. If he isn't, the door will be opened by my wife, who should be there at the moment, making up his bed."

This said, he turned his back on me, and without taking any further notice of me attended once more to his hose.

Instead of Malnate, a mature, blonde, abundant woman in a dressing gown appeared in the small doorway I'd been directed to.

"Good evening," I said. "I was looking for Dr. Malnate."

"He hasn't come back yet," Signora Lalumìa replied, all kindness, "but he shouldn't be long. Almost every evening, soon as he gets out of the factory, he goes to play tennis round at the Finzi-Continis, you know, the house in Corso Ercole I . . . But he should, as I said, be back here any moment. Before supper," she smiled, lowering her eyes in a rapt expression, "before supper he always drops in at the house to see if there's any mail."

I said that I'd come back later, and began to retrieve the bicycle I'd leaned on the wall beside the door. But the Signora insisted I remain. She wanted me to come in and sit down on an armchair, and in the meantime, standing in front of me, she informed me that she herself was Ferrarese, "a pure-blooded Ferrarese," that she knew my family very well, especially my mother, of whom "something like forty years ago" (so saying she again smiled and bashfully lowered her eyes) she had been a classmate at the Regina Elena elementary school, the one close by the church of San Giuseppe in Carlo Mayr. How was my mother?—she asked. I was, please, not to forget to send her greetings from Edvige, Edvige Santini, and my mother would then certainly know who she was. She made some remarks about the possibly imminent war and, sighing and shaking her head, referred to the Racial Laws, explaining that she had been deprived of "home help" and so had had to organize everything on her own, including the kitchen, and then, having excused herself, she left me alone.

When the Signora had gone out, I looked around. The room was spacious but with a low ceiling and as well as being a place to sleep in served as a study and sitting room. The rays of the sunset, penetrating the big horizontal window, lit up the motes of dust in the air. I looked around at the furnishings: the divan-bed, half divan, half bed, as was confirmed by the wretched cotton coverlet patterned with red flowers which hid the mattress, the fat white pillow, uncovered and set on its own to one side, the small black table, in a vaguely oriental style, placed between the divan-bed and the single armchair, of imitation leather, on which I was sitting, the fake parchment lampshades scattered about the room, the cream-colored telephone that stood out against the funereal black of an unsteady lawyer's desk, full of drawers, the crude oil-paintings hung on the walls. And although I told myself that Giampi had a nerve turning up his nose at Alberto's "twentieth-century" furniture (how could that moral fervor which made him such a stern judge of others let him be so indulgent toward himself and his own things?), suddenly feeling my heart gripped by the thought of Micòl—and it was as though it was she in person gripping my heart, with her own hand—I renewed my solemn resolve to behave well with Malnate, not to quarrel or argue with him anymore. When she found out, Micòl would have to take account of this as well.

Far off, the siren of one of the sugar factories of Pontelagoscuro sounded. Soon after, a heavy tread made the gravel grind on the garden path.

The judge's voice sounded very close by, on the other side of the wall.

"Ah, Doctor!" he was intoning in his distinctly nasal fashion, "you've a friend waiting for you at home."

"A friend?" Malnate said coldly. "And who might that be?"

"Go on, go and see . . . " the other encouraged him. "I said it was a friend."

Tall and fat, taller and fatter than ever, perhaps from the effect of the low ceiling, Malnate appeared at the doorway.

"Who'd have thought it!" he exclaimed, his eyes wide with surprise as he adjusted his glasses on his nose.

He came forward, shook me energetically by the hand, and patted me several times on the back. Having always sensed some hostility in him toward me, since we'd first met, it was very odd to find him now so kind, considerate and communicative. What was happening?—I wondered, perplexed. Had he too come to a decision utterly to change his manner toward me? Perhaps. What was clear was that at this time, in his own house, there was nothing in him of the stubborn gainsayer with whom, under the watchful eyes of Alberto and Micòl, I'd so often done battle. It was enough to see him, and I understood: between us, outside the Finzi-Continis'—and to think that in the last period we had quarrelled to the extent of offending each other, and almost actually came to blows!—every motive for conflict was destined to pass away, to dissolve like mist in the sun.

In the meantime Malnate was talking—in an astonishingly garrulous and cordial way. He asked me if I'd met his landlord while crossing the garden, and if so whether he'd been polite to me. I replied that I'd met him and, laughing, described the whole scene.

"Just as well."

He proceeded to tell me about the judge and his wife, without leaving me time to say I'd already met them both: excellent people—he said— even if, all considered, their common resolve to protect him from the risks and snares of "the big wide world" made them slightly interfering. Though decidedly anti-Fascist—being an ardent monarchist—the judge didn't want any problems, and so was continually on the alert, clearly anxious that Malnate, recognizable at a glance as a likely future client of the Special Tribunal—as he'd said on several occasions—shouldn't secretly bring home any dubious types: for instance any ex-political convict, anyone under surveillance, or some subversive. As regards Signora Edvige, she too was forever on the alert. She spent whole days perched behind the gaps in the blinds at the first-floor window or coming to his door even late at night, when she'd heard him returning. But her fears were of a completely different kind. Like the good Ferrarese she was—for she was Ferrarese, née Santini—she knew only too well, she told him, what the women of the city were like, both married and unmarried. In her view, a young man on his own, a graduate, from elsewhere, furnished with an apartment with its own door, was in great danger. In no time women would have reduced his spine to pulp. And he? He'd always done his very best to reassure her. But it was clear: only when she'd managed to transform him into a sad, beslippered codger in vest and pyjama bottoms, with his nose eternally parked above the kitchen pans, would "Madame" Lalumìa find any peace.

"Well, in the end, what's so wrong with that?" I objected. "I seem to remember you often running down restaurants and trattorias."

"That's true," he admitted with unusual compliance—a compliance that kept astonishing me. "And besides there's no point in it. Freedom's undoubtedly a wonderful thing, but unless there's some limit set to it" (he winked at me as he said this) "who knows where it'll all end?"

It was starting to get dark. Malnate got up from the divan-bed where he'd stretched out his considerable length, went to turn on the light, and then into the bathroom. He needed a shave—I heard from there. Would I give him the time to shave? Afterward we could go out together.

We kept the conversation going in this way—he in the bathroom, I in the sitting room.

He mentioned that also that afternoon he'd been round at the Finzi-Continis', and had in fact just come back from there. They had played for more than two hours—first him and Micòl, then him and Alberto, and finally all three together. Did I like playing American doubles?

"Not much," I replied.

"I can understand that," he agreed. "For someone like you who knows how to play, American doubles doesn't make much sense. But it can be fun."

"So who won?"

"The American doubles?"

"Yes."

"Micòl, naturally!" he said with a snigger. "My respect to anyone who can contain her. Even on the court she's like a whirlwind . . . "

He then asked me why for some days I'd not shown my face. Had I been away somewhere?

Remembering what Micòl had told me, that no one believed me when, after each of my absences, I said that I'd been away on a trip, I replied that I'd got tired of going round and that, often, in the last period, I'd anyway had the impression my presence was irksome, above all to Micòl, and for this reason I'd decided to "keep a bit of a distance."

"What are you saying?" he asked in surprise. "Far as I can see, Micòl has nothing at all against you. Are you sure you're not mistaken?"

"Sure as can be."

He sighed, letting it pass. I too had nothing to add. Soon after, he came out of the bathroom, clean-shaven and smiling. He realized I was looking at the ugly pictures on the walls.

"So then," he asked "how does it strike you, this big mouse-trap of mine? You've yet to bestow your opinion."

He grinned in his old manner, waiting in the doorway for my reply, but at the same time, I could see it in his eyes, determined not to take offence.

"I envy you," I replied. "If only I could have something similar at my disposal. I've always dreamed of something like this."

He threw me a gladdened look. It was true—he consented: even he could clearly see the limits of the Lalumìa couple's sense of furnishings. And yet their taste, typical of the petit bourgeois ("and it's not for nothing"—he added parenthetically—"they represent the very core and backbone of the nation"), always had something lively, vital, healthy about it—and this was probably directly related to its obviousness and vulgarity.

"After all, things are just things," he concluded. "Why become a slave to them?"

Should Alberto be considered in this light—he went on—it would be hard on him! With his determination to surround himself with exquisite, perfect, flawless things, one day or another he too will end up becoming . . .

He made toward the door without finishing his sentence.

"How is he?" I asked.

I too had got up, and had reached him at the doorway.

"Who, Alberto?" he said with a start.

I nodded.

"That's right," I added. "Of late he's seemed to me a bit tired and done in. Don't you think so? I have the feeling he's not well."

He drew in his shoulders, then turned off the light. He went on out into the darkness in front of me and said nothing more till we reached the gate, except halfway there to return a "Good evening" to Signora Lalumìa who had appeared at a window. Then at the gate he suggested I go with him to have supper at Giovanni's.

· 7 ·

I HAD no illusions, however. I realized even then that Malnate was perfectly aware of all the reasons, without exception, which kept me away from the Finzi-Continis. Despite this, in the talks we had the topic never surfaced again. On the theme of the Finzi-Continis we both displayed an exceptional reserve and delicacy, and I was especially grateful that he pretended to believe all I'd said on the subject that first evening—grateful, in short, that he was prepared to play along with me and back me up.

We saw each other almost every evening. From the first days of June the heat had suddenly become stifling and emptied the city. Usually it was I who went round to his house, between seven and eight. When I found nobody there, I waited patiently for his return, sometimes entertained by the chatting of Signora Edvige. But most times, there he was, stretched out on his divan-bed in his vest, his hands joined behind his neck and his eyes fixed on the ceiling, or else sitting writing a letter to his mother, to whom he was attached with a deep, slightly exaggerated affection. As soon as he saw me, he'd rush to the bathroom to shave, and after this, we would go out, it being understood that we would also eat out together.

Usually we'd go to Giovanni's, sitting outside, in front of the Castle's towers which loomed above us like the walls of the Dolomites, and, like them, the tops of its towers were aglow with the last of the daylight. Or else we'd go to the Voltini, a trattoria outside Porta Reno. Sitting at its tables lined up under a graceful colonnade, exposed to the midday sun and, at that time, open to the countryside, it was possible to look out as far as the huge fields of the airport. On hotter evenings, however, instead of heading toward the city, we made our way out along the lovely street of Pontelago-scuro, crossed the iron bridge over the Po, and pedaling side by side to the top of the embankment, with the river on our right and with the Veneto countryside on our left, after another fifteen minutes, halfway between Pontelagoscuro and Polesella, we reached the big, solitary Dogana Vec-chia, famous for its fried eels. We always ate very slowly, and sat on at the table till late, drinking Lambrusco and Vinello di Bosco and smoking our pipes. If we had dined in town, at a certain point we'd put down our napkins, each paying our own bills, and then, wheeling our bikes, we'd begin to stroll along the Corso Giovecca, up and down from the Castle to the Prospettiva Arch, or else along Viale Cavour, from the Castle as far as the station. Then it was he, usually around midnight, who would offer to accompany me back home. He would glance at his watch, announce that it was bedtime (he'd often solemnly remark, that even though the factory sirens only sounded at eight o'clock for them, the technicians, they always needed to be out of bed by quarter to seven "at the latest"), and however much I would sometimes insist I accompany him, there was never an occasion when he let me. The last image I'd have of him was always the same: motionless in the middle of the street, astride his bike, he would be waiting there to check I'd properly closed the door on him.

On two or three evenings, after our meal, we ended up on the city walls near Porta Reno, where, that summer, an amusement park had been put up in the opening which lay between the gasometer on one side and Piazza Travaglio on the other. It was a cut-price affair, half a dozen huts with coconut shies huddled round the grey, patchworked canvas mushroom of a small equestrian circus. The place attracted me. I was drawn to and touched by the sad group of impoverished prostitutes, young thugs, soldiers, and a few wretched pederasts from the outskirts, who customarily frequented it. I quoted Apollinaire in an undertone, and Ungaretti. And though Malnate, somewhat with the air of being dragged along against his will, accused me of "second-hand Crepuscularism,"* deep down it also pleased him, after we had dined at the Voltini, to go up there, into the big dusty square, to hang about eating slices of watermelon near the acetylene lamp of a coconut shy, or to try our luck for some twenty minutes shooting at the bull's-eye. Giampi was an excellent shot. Tall and corpulent, standing out in the well-pressed cream-colored flannel jacket I'd seen him wearing since the beginning of the summer, calm as could be in taking his aim through his thick lenses rimmed with tortoiseshell, he'd obviously taken the fancy of the heavily made-up and foul-mouthed Tuscan girl—a kind of queen there—at whose stall, as soon as we could be seen on the stone staircase which led from Piazza Travaglio to the top of the city wall, we were imperiously invited to stop. While Malnate took his aim, she, the girl, let loose a stream of sarcastic compliments with an undercurrent of obscenity, which he parried with great wit and with that calm detachment typical of someone who has spent many hours of his youth in a brothel.

One particularly airless August evening we happened, instead, to be in an open-air cinema where, I remember, they were showing a German film

---

* A movement in Italian poetry in the early years of the twentieth century, often accused of vagueness and melancholy, whose major figures included Guido Gozzano, Corrado Govoni and Sergio Corazzini.

with Cristina Söderbaum. We had come in when the show had already begun, and without paying any attention to Malnate, who kept telling me to be careful, to stop making a racket, since it just wasn't worth it, I'd already begun whispering ironic comments before we'd even sat down. Malnate was only too right. In fact, suddenly getting to his feet against the milky background of the screen, a man in the row in front of me told me in a threatening manner to shut up. I replied with an insult, and he began to shout in dialect: "Get out, you filthy Jew!" and jumped on me, grabbing me by the neck. Luckily for me, Malnate, without saying a word, was ready to shove my assailant back into his seat and drag me away.

"You're a complete idiot," he shouted at me, after we'd both hurriedly collected the bicycles we'd left in the bike racks. "And now, beat it, and you'd better pray to that God of yours that scumbag in there was only guessing."

In this manner, one after another, we passed our evenings together, with the perpetual air of congratulating ourselves that now, in contrast to when Alberto was present, we managed to converse without coming to blows. It never seemed to cross our minds that with a simple phone call, Alberto might have come out too to stroll around with us.

We set aside all political topics. Both being sure that France and England, whose diplomatic missions had already reached Moscow some time ago, would end up in accord with the USSR—the agreement we believed inevitable would have saved Poland's independence as well as averting a war, provoking as a consequence not just the collapse of the Pact of Steel but also the fall at least of Mussolini—it was now of literature and art that we almost always spoke. While his manner remained calm, without ever becoming polemical (besides—he affirmed—he could only understand art up to a certain point, it wasn't his thing), Malnate upheld a kind of rigid veto against everything I most loved: Eliot and Montale, García Lorca and Yesenin. He'd hear me out as I gave an impassioned recitation of "*Non chiederci la parola che squadri da ogni lato,*"* or passages from the "Lament for Ignazio Sánchez Mejías," and in vain I'd hope to have got through to him, to have converted him to my taste. Shaking his head,

---

* "Don't ask from us the word squared off on every side."

he'd declare that no, Montale's *"ciò che non siamo, ciò che non vogliamo"** left him cold, indifferent; that true poetry shouldn't be founded on negation (don't bring in Leopardi, please! Leopardi's a different matter, and anyway he'd written his *"Ginestra,"* I oughtn't to forget . . .) but rather, on the contrary, it was founded on affirmation, on the Yes that the Poet in the final analysis had no choice but to raise up against the hostility of Nature and against Death. Even Morandi's paintings didn't convince him—he told me: so refined, undoubtedly delicate, but in his view too "subjective" and "unanchored." A fear of reality, a fear of making mistakes: that was what Morandi's still lifes, his famous paintings of bottles and flower bouquets, expressed deep down. And fear, in art as well, had always been the worst adviser . . . Against all this, not without cursing him in secret, I never found any effective counterargument. The thought that the next afternoon, he, the lucky one, would certainly be seeing Alberto and Micòl, perhaps talking to them about me, was enough to make me put aside any empty wish to rebel, and forced me to withdraw into my shell.

Despite this I would sometimes champ at the bit.

"Well, after all, you too," I objected one evening, "you too indulge in the same radical negation toward contemporary literature, the only living one, that you can't abide when it, our literature, shows the same toward life. Does this seem fair to you? Your ideal poets remain Victor Hugo and Carducci. Admit it."

"And why shouldn't they be?" he replied. "In my opinion Carducci's republican poetry, written before his political conversion, or rather, his infantile reversion to classicism and monarchism, still needs to be entirely rediscovered. Have you read those poems recently? Try them, and you'll see."

I answered that I hadn't reread them, and had no desire to do so. For me they too were empty "trumpetings," boringly stuffed full of patriotic rhetoric, and incomprehensible to boot. Though precisely because they were incomprehensible, there was something amusing—and in the end, "surreal"—about them.

---

* "[All that we can tell you today] is what we are not, what we don't want." (Last line of the Montale poem of which the first line was quoted above.)

On another evening, however, not so much because I wanted to cut a good figure, but rather driven by an undefined need to confess, to open myself up, which I'd been feeling the pressure of for some time, I gave in to the temptation to recite a poem of mine to him. I'd written it in the train, returning from Bologna after the graduation thesis viva, and although for some weeks I continued to believe that it faithfully reflected the deep desolation I felt at that time, the disgust I felt for myself, gradually as I recited it to Malnate, I clearly saw, with unease rather than dismay, all the falsity of emotion in it, how "literary" it was. We were walking along the Corso Giovecca, down toward the Prospettiva Arch, beyond which the dark of the countryside was thickening into a kind of black wall. I declaimed the poem slowly, making myself stress the rhythm, overloading my voice with pathos in the attempt to pass off my damaged goods as the real thing, but ever more convinced, as I approached the ending, of the inevitable failure of my performance. And yet I was wrong. As soon as I finished, Malnate looked at me with remarkable seriousness, then, leaving me gaping, assured me that he had liked the poem very much indeed. He asked me to recite it a second time (and I immediately obliged him). After which he affirmed that in his modest opinion my "lyric," on its own, was worth more than all "the feeble efforts of Montale and Ungaretti combined." He could feel real suffering within it, a "moral commitment" absolutely new, and authentic. Was Malnate being sincere? At least on that occasion, I'm convinced he was. And from that evening on he started loudly repeating my verses, and kept on maintaining that in those few lines it was possible to glimpse an escape for contemporary Italian poetry from the sad toils of Calligraphism and Hermeticism. As for me, I'm not ashamed to admit that it wasn't at all unpleasant listening to these views of his. Faced with his hyperbolic praises, I confined myself to launching the occasional feeble protest, my heart overflowing with gratitude and hope. Looking back now, I'm far more inclined to find this moving rather than contemptible.

In any case, on the subject of Malnate's taste in poetry, I feel obliged to add that neither Carducci nor Victor Hugo were really his favorite authors. He respected Carducci and Hugo, as an anti-Fascist, as a Marxist. But as a good citizen of Milan, his great passion was Porta, a poet to whom, before then, I'd always preferred Belli, but I was wrong, Malnate argued; how could I compare the funereal "Counter-Reformation" monotony of Belli with the variety and human warmth of Porta?

He could quote hundreds of his verses from memory.

> Bravo el mè Baldissar! Bravo el mè nan!
> L'eva poeù vora de vegnì a trovamm:
> t'el seet mattascion porch che maneman
> l'è on mes che no te vegnet a ciollamm?
> Ah Cristo! Cristo! Com'hin frecc sti man!*

he liked to declaim in his deep, slightly raucous Milanese accent, every night when, out strolling, we approached Via Sacca or Via Colomba, or dawdlingly made toward Via delle Volte, peeping through the half-closed doors at the lit-up interiors of brothels. He knew the whole of "Ninetta del Verzee" by heart, and it was him who really taught me to appreciate it.

Threatening me with his finger, narrowing his eyes at me with a sly and suggestive expression—suggestive, I supposed, of some remote episode of his Milanese adolescence—he would often murmur:

> Nò Ghittin: no sont capazz
> de traditt: nò, stà pur franca.
> Mettem minga insemma a mazz
> coj gingitt e cont'i s'cianca . . . †

and so on. Or else in a heartfelt, bitter tone he would set about:

---

* *Good on you, Baldissar! Well done at last, you midget!*
  It was about time too you'd come to see me:
  d'you realize, you mad pig, it's nearly
  a month you've not been here to fuck me?
  Ah, Jesus! Jesus! How cold these hands have got!
† All of these poems are in Milanese dialect.
  No, Ghittina: I'm incapable
  of betraying you: no, of that you can be sure.
  You oughtn't to lump me together
  with rascals and disreputables.

> *Paracar, scappee de Lombardia...*[*]

underscoring every verse of the sonnet with winks, directed naturally toward the Fascists rather than Napoleon's Frenchmen.

He quoted from the poetry of Ragazzoni and Delio Tessa with just as much enthusiasm and involvement, especially from Tessa, whose work (as I didn't fail to point out to him) seemed to me not to merit the epithet of "classic" poet, overladen as it was with a "Crepuscular," decadent sensibility. Yet the truth was that anything that had any connection whatsoever with Milan or its dialect always made him uncharacteristically indulgent. Concerning Milan, he was disposed to accept anything: everything to do with it induced in him a tolerant smile. In Milan even literary decadence, even Fascism itself, had some positive attribute.

He would declaim:

> *Pensa ed opra, varde e scolta,*
> *tant se viv e tant se impara;*
> *mi, quand nassi on'altra volta,*
> *nassi on gatt de portinara!*
> *Per esempi, in Rugabella,*
> *nassi el gatt del sur Pinin...*
> *... scartoseij de coradella,*
> *polpa e fidegh, barretin*
> *del patron per dormigh sora...*[†]

and laugh to himself, laugh aloud with tenderness and nostalgia.

---

* *Soldiers, fleeing from Lombardy...*
† *Think and toil, watch and listen,*
  the longer you live the more you learn;
  me, should I be born one more time,
  I'd be born a doorwoman's cat!
  For example, in Rugabella,
  if I were born as Signor Pinin's cat...
  ... [there'd be] bags of heart scraps,
  mince and liver, the master's cap
  to sleep on top of...

Obviously I didn't understand everything in Milanese, and when I didn't I'd question him.

"Sorry, Giampi," I asked him one evening "but what's Rugabella? I've been to Milan though I can't claim to know the place. As you'd understand—of all the cities it's the one I'm most likely to get lost in—it's even worse than Venice."

"How can you say that?" he replied with unexpected passion. "You're referring to a city that's utterly straight and rational. I can't see how you dare compare it with Venice, that oppressive, overflowing shithouse!"

But he rapidly calmed down, explaining to me that Rugabella was a street, an old street near the Duomo, where he'd been born, where his parents still lived and where in a few months, perhaps before the year was out—that's if the Civic Authorities in Milan hadn't binned his request to be transferred!—he was once more hoping to live.

Because, let's be honest—he explained—Ferrara is a delightful, small city, lively, engaging in all sorts of ways, including its politics. He counted the two years' experience he'd gained here as important, not to say essential. But home was always home, there was no one like one's own mother, and as for the Lombard sky, "so adorable when it was fine," there was no other sky in the world with which it could be compared.

· 8 ·

ONCE THE twentieth day of exile had passed, as I've already mentioned, I began once more to visit the Finzi-Contini house, every Tuesday and Friday. But, at a loss as to how I should pass my Sundays—even if I'd wanted to renew my contacts with old school friends such as Nino Bottecchiari or Otello Forti, for example, or with more recent university friends made in the last years at Bologna, there was no possibility since they'd already gone on holiday—after a certain time had lapsed I started going there on Sundays as well. Micòl let this go, and never held me to the letter of our agreement.

We were now most considerate to each other, perhaps over-considerate. Both of us being aware just how precarious the equilibrium we had achieved was, we took pains not to disturb it, to keep ourselves in a safe zone which excluded not only the excessive coldness between us but also any over-familiarity. If Alberto wanted to play—and this happened ever more rarely—I willingly made up the fourth. But most of the time I didn't even bother to get changed. I preferred to umpire the long, hard singles matches fought out between Micòl and Malnate, or else, seated under the big parasol at the side of the court, to keep Alberto company.

Alberto's health was worrying me, deeply. I kept thinking about it. I would stare at his face, which looked longer because of the weight he'd lost. I would find myself checking his breathing as it showed in his neck, which by contrast had become fatter and swollen, and I'd feel my heart contract. I felt oppressed by a hidden sense of remorse. There were moments when I would have given anything to see him return to health.

"Why don't you go away for a while?" I once asked him.

He turned to look at me.

"D'you think I'm low?"

"Well, I wouldn't say low . . . You seem to me a bit thinner—that's all. Is the heat annoying you?"

"Certainly is."

He raised his arms as he breathed in deeply.

"For some time, my dear fellow, breathing has been a real effort. Ah! To go away . . . but where, though?"

"Up in the mountains would do you good. What does your uncle say? Have you been to see him?"

"Of course. Uncle Giulio assures me it's nothing serious, which must be true, don't you think? Otherwise he would have prescribed some remedy or other . . . On the contrary, my uncle thinks I should play as much tennis as I want. What more could I ask? It must be the heat that's bringing me down. Actually I'm hardly eating anything . . . but it's really nothing."

"So, given it's to do with the heat, why not spend a fortnight in the mountains?"

"In the mountains in August? I ask you. And then . . . " (here, he smiled) " . . . and then *Juden sind unerwünscht* everywhere. Had you forgotten?"

"That's nonsense. It's not true, for example, of San Martino di Castrozza. One can still go to San Martino, as you could, if you wanted, go to the Venice Lido or to Alberoni . . . There was something about it in last week's *Corriere della Sera*."

"What a bore. To spend the August bank holiday in a hotel, crammed in with sporty flocks of Levis and Cohens, I'm sorry, I can't say that appeals. I'd prefer to stay where I am until September."

The next evening, making the most of the new atmosphere of intimacy between me and Malnate, after I'd risked his judgement on my verses, I was determined to talk to him about Alberto's health. There was no doubt about it—I said: in my view Alberto had something. Hadn't he noticed the labored way he was breathing? And didn't it seem strange at the very least that no one at his home, neither his uncle nor his father, had made the smallest effort to work out what was wrong? The medical uncle, the one from Venice, had no faith in medicines, so that can be understood. But the rest of them, including his sister? They were all seraphically calm and smiling—not one of them was lifting a finger.

Malnate listened to me in silence.

"You shouldn't be so alarmed," he finally replied, with a slight hint of embarrassment in his voice. "Does he really seem to you so run down?"

"But, good God, can't you see!" I broke out. "In two months he's lost ten kilos!"

"That's going a bit far. Ten kilos are an awful lot!"

"If not ten, it'll be seven or eight. At the least."

He fell silent, lost in thought. He admitted that he too, for some time now, had realized that Alberto wasn't well. On the other hand—he added—were the two of us really sure we weren't getting worked up over nothing? If his own closest family weren't concerned, and if not even Professor Ermanno's face betrayed the least sign of worry, well then . . . That's the point—if Alberto really had been ill, it was fair to assume that Professor Ermanno wouldn't even have considered the possibility of bringing two truckloads of shale from Imola for the tennis court! And talking of the tennis court, did I know that in a few days the work to enlarge its famous surrounds was about to start?

So, taking our cue from Alberto and his presumed illness, we had unwittingly introduced into our night-time conversations the new theme, hitherto taboo, of the Finzi-Continis. Both of us were well aware we were walking over a minefield, and for this reason we always proceeded with great caution, very careful not to put a foot wrong. But it's worth saying that every time we spoke of them as a family, as an "institution"—I'm not sure who first came up with this word but I remember that it gave us some satisfaction and made us laugh—Malnate made free with his criticisms, even the harshest. What impossible people they were!—he'd say. What a strange, absurd tangle of incurable contradictions they represented, "socially"! At times, thinking about the thousands of hectares of land they possessed, and the thousands of laborers who worked it for them, the disciplined, submissive slaves of the Corporative Regime, at times he was tempted to prefer the grim "regular" landlords, those who, in 1920, 1921 and 1922, had hardly paused a moment to fork out for the blackshirt squads with their strong-arm and castor-oil tactics. They "at least" were Fascists. When the occasion presented itself, there wouldn't be any lingering doubts about how to treat them. But the Finzi-Continis?

And he would shake his head, with the expression of someone who, should they wish to, could even understand such subtleties and complications, but who is just not minded to. Such tiny fine discriminations, intriguing and engaging as they might be, at a certain point became irrelevant: they too would be swept away.

After the August bank holiday, late one night, we had stopped for a drink in a small bar in Via Gorgadello, alongside the Duomo, a few steps away from the place that had been the surgery of Dr. Fadigati, the well-known ENT surgeon. Over several glasses of wine I'd told Malnate the story of the doctor, with whom, in the five months preceding his suicide "for love," I had become a close friend, the last and only friend he had left in town—when I said "for love" Malnate couldn't resist a little sarcastic laugh of a typically undergraduate kind. From Fadigati to a more general discussion of homosexuality was just a few steps. On this topic Malnate had very uncomplicated views—like a true *goy*, I thought to myself. For him, pederasts were nothing but "miserable wretches," poor "obsessives," about whom there was no point bothering apart from a medical perspective or with a view to social prevention. By contrast, I maintained that love justified and sanctified everything, even pederasty. I went further, saying that love, when it was pure, by which I meant totally disinterested, is always abnormal, asocial and so on: exactly like art—I added—which when it's pure, and therefore useless, displeases the priests of every religion, including Socialism. Setting aside our good intentions to be moderate, just this once we went back to arguing almost in our ferocious, earlier style, until the moment when, both of us realizing we were slightly drunk, we simultaneously burst out laughing. After that, we had left the bar, crossed the half-deserted Listone, and gone back up San Romano to find ourselves wandering along Via delle Volte with no particular destination in mind.

Without any sidewalk, its cobbled surface full of holes, the street seemed even darker than usual. While we all but groped our way forward, guided only by the light that squeezed through the half-closed doors of the brothels, Malnate had set off again as usual declaiming some stanza of Porta's—this time, I remember, it wasn't from "Ninetta," but from *"Marchionn di gamb avert."*

He recited the lines in a low voice, in the bitter, hurt tone he always assumed for the "Lament":

> *Finalment l'alba tance voeult spionada*
> *l' è comparsa anca lee di filidur . . .* *

but at this point he suddenly stopped.

"What would you say," he asked me, pointing his chin toward a brothel door, "to going in there to look around?"

The proposal was nothing out of the ordinary. And yet, coming from him, with whom I'd only ever had serious discussions, it surprised and embarrassed me.

"It's not one of the better ones," I replied. "I reckon it's one where you pay less than ten lire . . . but why not, if that's what you want."

It was late, almost one o'clock, and the welcome that awaited us was far from warm. An old peasant-like woman, seated on a wickerwork chair behind the door, began to make a fuss about not wanting the bicycles brought in. And then the madam, a dry, raw, little woman with glasses, of

---

* At last the dawn, so long looked out for,
  herself appears between the shutter's slats . . .

an indefinable age, dressed in black like a nun, also started complaining about the bicycles and how late it was. Then a servant girl, who was already cleaning the small reception rooms with a worn-out, dusty brush, the handle of a dustpan under her arm, gave us a look full of scorn as we passed through the entrance hall. And even the girls, all gathered together and quietly talking with a small group of clients in a single room, didn't bother to say hello. None of them came forward to greet us. We waited not less than ten minutes, during which time Malnate and I sat facing each other in the small separate reception room that the madam had taken us away to, not bestowing on us a further word—through the walls the laughter of the girls and the drowsy voices of their client-friends reached us—until a small blonde with a refined air, and hair drawn back above the nape of her neck, soberly dressed like a schoolgirl from a good family, decided to appear in the doorway.

She at least didn't seem too fed up.

"Good evening," she greeted us.

She calmly examined us, her blue eyes full of irony.

"And as for you, Little Blue-Eyes, what can we do for you?"

"What's your name?" I managed to stammer.

"Gisella."

"Where are you from?"

"Bologna!" she boasted, widening her eyes as if vouchsafing who knows what pleasures.

But it wasn't true. Calm and in perfect control of himself, Malnate immediately saw through her claim.

"Bologna like hell!" he interjected. "I'd say you were from Lombardy, but not even from Milan. You must be from somewhere around Como."

"How did you guess that?" the girl asked, astonished.

The madam's ugly mug had meanwhile loomed behind her back.

"Uh-huh," she grumbled. "Here as well I can see all that's happening is a lot of blather."

"Not at all," the girl protested, smiling and pointing at me. "Little Blue-Eyes over there has some serious intentions. So should we go?"

I turned toward Malnate. He too was looking at me in an encouraging, affectionate way.

"And you?" I asked.

He made a vague gesture with his hand, and let out a small laugh.

"Don't think about me. You go on up, and I'll wait for you."

Everything happened very quickly. When we came back down, Malnate was chatting with the madam. He'd brought out his pipe, and was talking and smoking. He was finding out about the "financial status" of the prostitutes, their fortnightly "rota" and their "medical check-ups" etc., and the woman was responding with equal attention and care.

"*Bon,*" Malnate said at last, noticing my presence, and standing up.

We went back into the entrance waiting room, making for the bicycles leaned one on top of the other against the wall beside the street exit, while the madam, now become most considerate, rushed in front to open the door.

"Goodbye, then," Malnate said to her.

He placed a coin in the doorwoman's outstretched palm, and went out first.

Gisella had remained in the background.

"Bye, darling," she said in a sing-song voice. "And come back again!"

She was yawning.

"Bye," I replied as I went through the door.

"Goodnight, then, gentlemen," the madam respectfully murmured behind our backs. As she closed the door I heard the bolt slide home.

Leaning on our bikes, we slowly went back up Via Scienze to the corner of Via Mazzini, and then took a right along the Saraceno. Now it was Malnate who mainly spoke. At Milan, some years back—he was telling me—he'd been a fairly regular visitor to the famous San Pietro all'Orto brothel, but it was only tonight that he'd had the idea of gathering precise information about the laws governing the "system." Christ, what a life whores have to live! And how abject the state was, the so-called "ethical state," to set up such a market for human flesh!

Here he became aware of my silence.

"What's wrong?" he asked. "Aren't you feeling well?"

"No. I'm fine."

I heard him sigh.

"*Omne animal post coitum triste . . .* " he pronounced melancholically.

"Have a good sleep, and you'll see—tomorrow everything'll be as right as rain."

"I know. I know."

We turned left, down Via Borgo di Sotto, and Malnate nodded toward a modest little house on the right, in the direction of Via Fondo Banchetto.

"That's where the schoolmistress Trotti must live," he said.

I didn't reply. He coughed.

"And so . . . " he went on, "how are things going with Micòl?"

I was suddenly overwhelmed by a great need to confide in him, to open my heart to him.

"Badly. I have such a terrible crush on her."

"Well, that we've been able to work out," he said with a friendly laugh. "For some time. But how is it going now? Is she still treating you badly?"

"No. As you'll have seen, of late we've reached a certain *modus vivendi*."

"Sure. I've noticed you don't squabble like you used to. I'm glad you're becoming friends again. It was really absurd."

My mouth twisted into a grimace, while tears misted over my sight.

Malnate immediately realized what was happening.

"Don't take it so badly," he urged me, embarrassed. "You mustn't let yourself go like this."

I made an effort to swallow.

"I don't believe one bit that we'll be friends again," I murmured. "It's utterly futile."

"Nonsense," he replied. "If you only knew how much she cares for you! When you're not there, and are being spoken of, woe betide anyone who dares say anything against you. She's like an adder ready to strike. And Alberto respects and really likes you too. I ought to tell you as well that a few days ago—perhaps it was indiscreet of me, I'm sorry—I even recited one of your poems to them. Good Lord! You've no idea how much he liked it, how much they both, yes, both of them liked it . . . "

"I'm not sure what use either their wishing me well or their high opinion is to me."

We had come out into the little square in front of the church of Santa Maria in Vado. There wasn't a soul to be seen: neither there, nor the whole length of Via Scandiana up to Montagnone. We went along in silence toward the drinking-fountain beside the churchyard. Malnate leaned down to drink, and after him I drank too, and washed my face.

"Listen," Malnate continued as he kept on walking, "in my opinion you're wrong. In times like these, nothing is more important than mutual affection and respect, friendship that is. Besides, it doesn't seem to me ... It's quite possible that in time ... What I mean is—why not come over and play tennis more often, as you did some months back? And anyway, who says absence is the best strategy? I've the feeling, my friend, that you don't know women very well."

"But it was she herself who forced me to make my visits less frequent!" I blurted out. "D'you think I can just take no notice? After all, it is her house!"

He remained silent for a few moments, deep in thought.

"It doesn't seem possible to me," he said at last. "Perhaps I could understand it, if something ... really serious, irreparable, had come between you. But what, in the end, has happened?"

He scrutinized me, unsure.

"Forgive my not too ... diplomatic question," he went on, and smiled, "but have you got so far at least as to kiss her?"

"I have indeed, many times," I sighed desperately. "Unfortunately for me."

I then told him in minute detail the story of our relationship, going right back to the beginning and not concealing that episode of last May, in her room, an episode which I'd come to believe, I said, decisive in its negative impact, and irremediable. Amongst other things I wanted to describe to him how I kissed her, or at least how, time and again, and not only on that occasion in her bedroom, I'd tried to kiss her, as well as her various responses, sometimes more and sometimes less disgusted.

He let me get it all out, and I was so intent on, so lost in these bitter reconstructions that I paid little heed to his silence, which in the meanwhile had become hermetically sealed.

We'd been standing for almost half an hour outside my house.

I saw him give a start.

"Lord," he murmured, checking his watch. "It's a quarter past two. I really have to go. Otherwise how will I get myself up tomorrow?"

He leaped onto his saddle.

"Well, bye . . . " he said, leaving, "and life goes on!"

I noticed his face had a strange grey look. Had my confidences annoyed or angered him?

I remained watching him as he quickly rode away. It was the first time that he'd left me standing like that, without waiting for me to shut the gate.

· 9 ·

ALTHOUGH IT was so late, my father had still not switched off his light.

Ever since the summer of 1937, when the newspapers took up the racial campaign, he had been afflicted by a severe kind of insomnia which reached its most acute phase in summertime, with the heat. He passed whole nights without shutting his eyes, reading for a while, then wandering around the house, listening for a while in the breakfast room to the radio's Italian-language foreign transmissions, chatting for a while with my mother in her room. If I got back after one o'clock, it was rare indeed for me to be able to reach the end of the corridor along which all the bedrooms were disposed (the first was my father's, the second my mother's, then came those of Ernesto and Fanny, and finally, at the very end, my own) without him hearing me. I would get a fair way down on tiptoe, having even taken off my shoes, for my father's very sharp ears would pick up the least creak or rustling.

"That you?"

On that night too, as might be expected, I failed to duck under his radar. Usually, in response to his "That you?" I would immediately quicken my step, going straight on without replying, making as if I hadn't heard. But not that night. Though I could well imagine, and not without irritation, the kind of questions I'd have to answer, always the same for years on end ("How come you're so late?" "D'you know what time it is?" "Where've you been?" etc.), I chose to stop. As the door was shut, I put my head through the hatch.

"What are you doing there?" my father said at once, scanning me above his glasses. "Come on in for a moment."

He was not lying down, but seated in his nightshirt, leaning with his back and his nape against the headboard of blond carved wood, and covered no further than the base of his stomach with a single sheet. It struck me how everything about him and around him was white—his silver hair, his pallid, exhausted face, his white nightshirt, the pillow behind his kidneys, the sheet, the book open on his chest, and how that whiteness (a clinical whiteness, I thought at the time) was in keeping with the surprising and extraordinary serenity, the unexpectedly benign expression, full of wisdom, that lit up his bright eyes.

"How late you are!" he commented with a smile, giving a glance at the Rolex on his wrist, a waterproof affair he would never be parted from, not even in bed. "D'you know what time it is? Two twenty-seven."

For the first time, perhaps, since being given the front-door key at the age of eighteen, this recurrent phrase of his caused me no irritation.

"I've been wandering about," I said quietly.

"With that friend of yours from Milan?"

"Yes."

"What does he do? Is he still a student?"

"You must be joking. He's already twenty-six. He's employed . . . he works as a chemist in the industrial zone, in a Montecatini synthetic-rubber factory."

"Just goes to show. And I thought he was still at university. Why don't you ever ask him round to dinner?"

"I don't know . . . I thought it wasn't right to give Mamma more work than she already has."

"Nonsense! It wouldn't be any trouble. It's just an extra bowl of soup after all. Bring him over, please do. And . . . where did you have dinner then? At Giovanni's?"

I nodded.

"So tell me what dainty dishes you had to eat?"

I complied with good grace, surprised at my own lack of contrariness, listing the various courses—those ordered by myself, and those by Malnate. In the meantime I'd sat down.

"I'm glad," my father concluded, satisfied.

"And after," my father went on after a pause, "*duv'èla mai ch'a si 'ndà a* *far dann, tutt du?** I bet" (here he raised a hand as though to forestall any denial of mine), "I bet you've been running after women."

On this subject, there had never been any exchange of confidences between us. A fierce modesty, a violent irrational need for freedom and independence, had always driven me to stifle at birth any of his timid attempts to broach this subject. But not that night. While I looked at him, so white, so frail, so old, it was if something inside me, a kind of knot, an age-old secret tangle, was rapidly unravelling.

"It's true," I said. "You guessed right."

"You'll have been to a brothel, I suppose."

"Yes."

"Excellent," he gave his approval. "At the age you two are, especially at your age, brothels are the best solution from every point of view, including that of health. But tell me—as regards money, how do you manage it? Does the weekly pocket money Mamma gives you suffice? If it's not enough, you can also ask me for some. Within the limits of possibility, I'd be happy to help."

"Thanks."

"Where have you been? Round at Maria Ludargnani's? In my time she was already holding the fort."

"No. A place in Via delle Volte."

"The only thing I'd advise you," he continued, suddenly switching into the language of the medical profession he had only ever practiced in his youth, having then, after my grandfather's death, devoted his energies exclusively to the administration of the land in Masi Torello and the two houses he owned in Via Vignatagliata, "the only thing I'd advise you is to never neglect the necessary prophylactic measures. I know it's annoying. One would gladly do without. But it takes nothing to catch a nasty blennorrhagia, otherwise known as the clap, or worse. And above all: if you wake up in the morning and find something's not right, come immediately to the bathroom and let me see. In which case, I'll tell you what you should do."

"I understand. Don't worry."

---

* Ferrarese dialect: "Where on earth have the two of you been, out making trouble?"

I could feel he was searching for the right way to ask me more. Now that I'd graduated—I guessed he was about to ask—did I by chance have any ideas for the future, any plans? But instead he took a detour into politics. Before I'd come home—he said—between one o'clock and two, he'd managed to receive several foreign radio stations: Monteceneri, Paris, London, Beromünster. And now, on the basis of the latest news, he was convinced that the international situation was rapidly worsening. Unfortunately, there was no getting away from it—it was a real *"afàr negro."** It seemed as though the Anglo-French diplomatic mission in Moscow was already on the point of breaking up (obviously without having achieved anything). Were they really prepared to leave Moscow just like that? There was reason to fear so. Which left nothing to be done but commend everyone's soul to God's care.

"What did you expect!" he exclaimed. "Stalin's hardly the type to have many scruples. If he found it useful, I'm sure he wouldn't hesitate for a second to reach an agreement with Hitler!"

"An agreement between Germany and Russia?" I smiled weakly. "No, I don't believe it. It doesn't seem feasible to me."

"We'll see," he replied, smiling in his turn. "Let's hope God hears you!"

At this moment a moan was heard from the room next door. My mother had woken up.

"What did you say, Ghigo?" she asked. "Is Hitler dead?!"

"If only!" my father sighed. "Sleep, sleep, my angel, don't worry yourself."

"What time is it?"

"Almost three."

"Send that son of ours to bed!"

Mamma uttered a few more incomprehensible words, and then fell silent.

My father stared me in the eye for a long while. And then in a low voice, almost a whisper:

"Forgive me speaking to you about these things," he said, "but you'll understand . . . both your mother and I have been well aware, since last

---

* Ferrarese dialect: "black business."

year, that you've fallen in love with . . . with Micòl Finzi-Contini. It's true, isn't it?"

"Yes."

"And how is your relationship going? As badly as ever?"

"It couldn't get worse than it is now," I murmured, suddenly realizing with absolute clarity that I was speaking the exact truth, that effectively our relationship really could not have got worse, and that never, despite Malnate's opinion to the contrary, would I be able to clamber back up from the bottom of that slope where I had been vainly groping for months.

My father let out a sigh.

"I know, these things are hard to bear . . . But in the end it's much better this way."

I had lowered my head, and said nothing.

"It's the truth," he continued, raising his voice a little. "What were you really hoping to do? Get engaged?"

Micòl herself, that evening in her room, had also put the same question to me. She'd said: "What was it you were hoping for? Did you really think we should get engaged?" It had taken my breath away. I could think of no reply. Just the same then, I thought, as now with my father.

"And why not?" I managed all the same, and looked at him.

He shook his head.

"D'you think I don't understand you?" he said. "Even I can see how attractive she is. I've always liked her, since she was a baby . . . when she'd come down at the Temple, to receive her father's *berachah*. Attractive, no, beautiful—perhaps even (if that's possible) too beautiful!—intelligent, full of spirit . . . but to get engaged!" here he stressed both syllables, widening his eyes. "To get engaged, my dear boy, means getting married. And in difficult times like these, without above all a reliable profession you can fall back on, tell me if you . . . I imagine you hadn't reckoned on me being able to support your family (and indeed I wouldn't have been able to lend you enough, I mean, to meet the need) nor that you'd planned to depend on her. The girl will certainly come with a magnificent dowry," he added, "there's no doubt about that! But I don't imagine you'd . . . "

"Let's forget the dowry," I said. "If we loved each other, what would that matter?"

"You're right," my father agreed. "You're absolutely right. Me as well, when I got engaged to your mother, in 1911, I took no thought of such things. But the times were different then. We could look ahead, to the future, with a certain amount of tranquility. And even if the future hasn't shown itself as happy and easy as the two of us imagined it would be (we got married in 1915, as you know, with the war having begun, and soon after I had to leave as a volunteer), the society we lived in was different, then, a society that guaranteed . . . Besides, I'd studied to be a doctor, while you . . . "

"While I . . . "

"That's what I mean. Instead of medicine, you chose to study literature, and you know that since the moment came to decide I haven't ever tried to impede you in any way. That was your passion, and you and I, both, have done what we ought to—you choosing the route you felt you had to choose, and I doing nothing to stop you. But now? Even if, as a graduate, you'd aspired to a university career . . . "

I shook my head to say no.

"So much the worse!" he went on. "While it's quite true that nothing, even now, can stop you continuing your studies on your own account . . . to keep on developing so as one day to try, if it's possible, to become a writer, a most risky, difficult career, or a militant critic such as Edoardo Scarfoglio, Vincenzo Morello, Ugo Ojetti . . . or else, why not? A novelist, or . . . "—here he smiled—" . . . or a poet . . . But precisely for these reasons: how could you, at your age, being only twenty-three, with everything before you still to do . . . how could you think of taking a wife, of starting a family?"

He was speaking about my literary future—I told myself—as though it were a lovely seductive dream which could not be translated into something tangible, real. He was speaking as though both he and I were already dead, and now, from a point outside space and time, together we were discussing life, everything which in the course of our respective lives might have happened and yet didn't. Had they reached an agreement, Hitler and Stalin?—I even asked myself. And why not? Most likely they had.

"But apart from this," my father went on, "and apart from a whole pile of other considerations, can I be frank with you, and give you the advice of a friend?"

"Go ahead."

"I know that when someone, especially at your age, loses his head over a girl, he isn't going to enter into a whole set of calculations . . . and I also know that you have a rather special character . . . and don't think that two years ago when that poor wretch Dr. Fadigati . . . "

In our house, since his death, Fadigati's name had never been spoken by any of us. So what had Fadigati to do with all this now?

I looked at his face.

"Please let me go on!" he said. "Your temperament—I reckon you got it from your grandma Fanny—your temperament . . . you're too sensitive, that's what I mean, and so never satisfied . . . you're always in search of . . . "

He didn't finish. A wave of his hand conjured up ideal worlds inhabited purely by chimeras.

"And forgive me," he continued, "but even as a family the Finzi-Continis were not suitable . . . they weren't people cut out for us . . . Marrying a girl of that kind, I'm sure that sooner or later you'd have found yourself in trouble . . . but yes, yes, it's the truth," he insisted, perhaps fearing some word or gesture of mine in protest. "You well know what my opinion has always been on that subject. They're different from us . . . they don't even seem to be *Judim* . . . Eh, I know: she, Micòl, perhaps for this reason was especially attractive to you . . . because she was superior to us . . . socially. But mark my words: it's better it's ended this way. The proverb says: "Choose oxen and women from your own country." And that girl, regardless of appearances, was certainly not from your own country. Not in the least."

I had once again lowered my head, and was staring at my hands poised open on my knees.

"You'll get over it," he continued, "you'll get over it, and much sooner than you think. I am sorry: I can guess what you're feeling at this moment. But, do you know, I envy you a bit. In life, if you want to understand, seriously understand how things are in this world, at least once you must die. And so, given that this is the law, it's better to die when you're young, when you still have so much time before you in which to pick yourself up and recover . . . To come to understand when you're old is unpleasant, much more unpleasant. It's hard to know how. There's no time left to start again from scratch, and our generation has made one blunder after another. In any case, you at least are still young enough to learn, God willing! In a few months, you'll see, all this that you've had to go through will no longer seem real. Perhaps you may even feel happy. You'll feel yourself enriched by this, feel yourself . . . I don't know . . . more mature . . . "

"Let's hope so," I murmured.

"I'm glad to have been able to talk, to have got this lead weight off my chest . . . And now a final bit of advice, if you'll let me?"

I nodded.

"Don't go round to their house anymore. Start studying again, busy yourself with something, maybe set about giving some private lessons— I've been hearing it said there's a great demand for them . . . And don't go round there anymore. Apart from anything else, it's more manly not to."

He was right. It was, apart from anything else, more manly.

"I'll try," I said lifting up my eyes. "I'll do all I can to keep to it."

"That's the way!"

He looked at the time.

"And now go to sleep," he added. "That's what you need. And I myself'll try to shut my eyes for a second or two."

I stood up, and leaned down over him to kiss him, but the kiss we exchanged turned into a long embrace, silent and very tender.

· 10 ·

AND THAT was how I gave up Micòl.

The next evening, keeping faith with the promise I'd made my father, I abstained from going round to Malnate's, and the day after, which was a Friday, I didn't show up at the Finzi-Contini house. A week passed like this, the first, without me seeing anybody: neither Malnate, nor the others. Luckily, in all that time, I wasn't sought out by anyone, and this fact certainly helped me. Otherwise it's very probable I wouldn't have been able to resist. I would have let myself get caught up again.

Ten or so days after our last meeting, around the 25th of the month, Malnate called me. It had never happened before, and as it wasn't me that had answered the phone, I was tempted to have them say I wasn't home.

But I immediately repented. I already felt strong enough: if not to see him again, at least to speak to him.

"Are you all right?" he began. "You've really beached me high and dry."

"I've been away."

"Where to? Florence? Rome?" he asked, not without a flicker of irony.

"This time a bit farther still," I replied, already regretting the pathos of the phrase.

"*Bon.* I don't want to pry. So: are we going to meet?"

I said I couldn't that evening, but that tomorrow I'd almost certainly be passing by his house, at the usual time. But if he saw I was late—I added—he shouldn't wait for me. In that case, we'd meet directly round at Giovanni's. It was at Giovanni's he meant to eat?

"Most likely," he confirmed, curtly. And then:

"Have you heard the news?"

"I've heard it."

"What a mess! Do come, I'm relying on you, and we can talk about everything then."

"Goodbye for now," I replied gently.

"Goodbye."

He hung up.

The next evening, straight after supper, I went out on my bike, and having gone down the whole of the Corso Giovecca, I went and stopped not more than a hundred meters from the restaurant. I wanted to check if Malnate was there, nothing more than that. And, in fact, as soon as I'd ascertained that he was—seated as usual at an open-air table, wearing his eternal flannel jacket—rather than go up to him I doubled back from there to lurk on top of one of the Castle's three drawbridges, the one facing Giovanni's. I worked out that this was the best way to observe him without running the risk that he'd notice me. And so it was. With my chest pressed against the stone edge of the parapet, for a long while I observed him as he ate. I watched him and the other clients down there in a line with the wall at their back, I watched the white-jacketed waiters bustling back and forth between the tables, and it seemed to me, in my suspended state, in the dark above the moat's glassy water, almost as though I was at the theater, a hidden spectator of some pleasant but pointless performance. By now Malnate had started in on the fruit. He was reluctantly nibbling at a big bunch of grapes, one after the other, and every now and then, clearly expecting my arrival, he would turn his head to the left and the right. In doing so, the lenses of his "fat glasses," as Micòl would call them, glinted: nervously, quiveringly . . . Having finished off the grapes, he called the waiter over with a sign, conferring with him for a moment. I thought he had asked for the bill, and I was already getting ready to leave, when I saw that the waiter was returning with an espresso cup. He drank it in a single swig. After this, from one of the two breast pockets of his flannel jacket, he took out something very small: a notebook, in which he immediately began to write with a pencil. What the hell was he writing?—I smiled to myself. Had he too taken to versifying? And there I left him, all bent and intent over that notebook of his from which, at rare intervals, he would lift his head to peer left and right, or else above, to the starry sky, as though searching for ideas or inspiration.

In the evenings that immediately followed, I kept on wandering haphazardly along the city streets, noticing everything, indiscriminately drawn by everything: by the headlines of newspapers that carpeted the newsagents' shops of the center, headlines in big, block capitals, underlined in red ink; by the film photographs and announcement posters stuck up beside the cinema entrances; by the chatting clusters of drunks halted in the middle of the alleyways of the old city; by the number plates of the cars parked in a row in Piazza del Duomo; by the various kinds of people leaving the brothels, or appearing in small groups out of the dark undergrowth of the Montagnone to consume ice creams, beers or fizzy drinks at the zinc counter of the kiosk that had recently been installed on the city walls of San Tomaso, at the end of the Scandiana . . .

One evening, around eleven, I found myself again in the vicinity of Piazza Travaglio, peeping into the half-dark interior of the renowned Cafe Scianghai, almost exclusively frequented by street prostitutes and workers from the nearby Borgo San Luca. From there, soon after, I went up onto the city wall above it to spectate a feeble shooting match between two unprepossessing youths competing under the hard eyes of that Tuscan girl who'd been so taken by Malnate.

I stayed there, at the side, without saying anything, or even dismounting from my bike, so that after a while the Tuscan girl addressed me in person.

"Hey, you there, young man," she said. "Why not step up and shoot a few yourself? Go on, take a risk, don't be scared. Show these two big sissies what you can do."

"No thanks," I replied.

"No thanks," she repeated. "God, what's happening to the young today! Where've you hidden that friend of yours? That one was a real man! Tell me, have you buried him somewhere?"

I kept silent, and she burst out laughing.

"Poor little thing!" she commiserated with me. "Run along home now, or else your daddy'll take his belt to you. Go on, run along to your granny."

The next evening, getting on toward midnight, without even knowing myself why, I was on the opposite side of the city, pedaling along the unpaved track which runs smoothly and sinuously within the circumference of the Mura degli Angeli. There was a magnificent full moon: so clear and bright in the perfectly serene sky as to render the front light unnecessary. I pedaled along briskly. I kept on passing new lovers stretched out on the grass. Some were half-naked, one moving on top of the other. Others, already disentangled, remained close, holding each other by the hand. Others still, embraced but motionless, seemed to be asleep. Along the way I counted more than thirty couples. And though I passed so close to some of them as almost to brush them with my wheels, no one ever gave any sign of noticing my silent presence. I felt like, and was, a kind of strange driven ghost, full both of life and death, of passion and compassion.

Having reached the heights of the Barchetto del Duca, I got off my bike, leaned it against a tree trunk, and for some minutes, turned toward the silver unmoving stretch of the park, I stayed there to watch. I wasn't thinking of anything in particular. I was watching, and, listening to the paltry and immense outpourings of the crickets and frogs, surprised myself by the faint embarrassed smile that stretched my lips. "Here it is," I said slowly. I didn't know what to do, what I'd come there to do. I was suffused by a vague sense of the uselessness of any act of commemoration.

I began to walk along the edge of the grassy slope, my eyes fixed on the *magna domus*. All dark at the Finzi-Contini house. Although I couldn't see the windows of Micòl's room, which were south-facing, I was sure just the same that no light whatsoever would be issuing from them. Having at last come to that point exactly above the garden wall which was "sacred," as Micòl would say, "*au vert paradis des amours enfantines*," I was seized by a sudden notion. What if I climbed over the wall and secretly entered the park? As a boy, in that far-off June afternoon, I hadn't dared do it. I'd been too afraid. But now?

Within a moment I was already down there, at the foot of the wall, encountering once again the same smell of nettles and dung. But the wall itself was different. Perhaps because it had aged ten years (as indeed I too had aged in the meantime, and grown in size and strength) it didn't seem either as unscalable or as high as I remembered it. After a first failed attempt I lit a match. The footholds were still there, perhaps even more of them. There was even that fat rusty nail still sticking out from the stones. I reached it on my second try, and, grabbing it, it was then easy enough for me to get to the top.

When I was seated up there, with my legs dangling on either side, it didn't take me long to notice a ladder leaning against the wall a little beneath my shoe. Rather than surprising me, this fact entertained me. "I'll be damned," I murmured with a smile, "and there's the ladder as well." However, before making use of it, I turned back round toward the Mura degli Angeli. There the tree was, and at its base the bike. It was an old wreck, hardly a tempting prospect for anyone.

I made it down to the ground. After which, leaving the path that ran parallel to the garden wall, I cut down through the meadow scattered with fruit trees, with the intention of reaching the driveway somewhere almost equidistant between Perotti's farmhouse and the wooden bridge over the Panfilio. I trod the grass without making a sound: struck once in a while, it's true, by the glimmer of a misgiving, but every time it surfaced I shrugged my shoulders and shed it before it turned to worry and anxiety. How beautiful the Barchetto del Duca was by night—I thought—and how gently lit by the moon! In those milky shadows, in that silvery sea, what else could I want or look for? Even if I'd been surprised wandering about there, no one could have got that worked up about it. On the contrary. If everything was taken into account, I could even claim a certain right to be there.

I came out onto the drive, crossed the Panfilio bridge, and from there, turning left, reached the clearing of the tennis court. Professor Ermanno had kept his promise: the playing area was already being enlarged. The metal wire surround was pulled down, and lay in a luminous tangled heap beside the court, on the opposite side to where the spectators usually sat. A zone of at least three meters beside the side lines and five behind the backcourt seemed to be all ploughed up ... Alberto was ill. He hadn't long to live. It was necessary to conceal from him in some, even in that way, the seriousness of his illness. "Good idea," I agreed, and went on.

I went on out into the open, meaning to make a big circle round the clearing, nor was I surprised at a certain point to see, advancing toward me at a slow trot from the direction of the *Hütte*, the familiar shape of Jor. I waited stock still for him to arrive, and he too, as soon as he was about ten meters away, came to a halt. "Jor!" I called in a stifled voice. Jor recognized me. After having conveyed to his tail a brief, mildly festive wag, he slowly turned back on his own steps.

Once in a while he would turn round to reassure himself I was following him. I wasn't following him, or rather, although progressively approaching the *Hütte*, I didn't detach myself from the far edge of the clearing. I was walking some twenty meters away from the curving row of huge dark trees that grew in that part of the park, my face continually turned to the left. I now had the moon at my back. The clearing, the tennis court, the big blind spur of the *magna domus*, and then, in the distance, lying above the leafy tops of the apple trees, the fig trees, the plum trees, the pear trees, there was the city wall, the Mura degli Angeli. Everything looked bright and clear-cut, as though in relief, even more so than by day.

Continuing like this, I suddenly found myself just a few steps away from the *Hütte*—not in front of it on the side facing the tennis court but behind among the trunks of the young larches and fir trees it was close up against. Here I stopped. I stared at the black, rugged shape of the *Hütte* against the light. I suddenly felt uncertain, not knowing where to go, what direction to take.

"What should I do?" I was saying in a low voice. "What should I do?"

I kept on staring at the *Hütte*. Then I began to think—without this thought even making my heart beat faster: accepting it with indifference as stilled water lets light pass through it—I began to think that yes, if after all it was here, at Micòl's, that Giampi Malnate would come every night after leaving me at the entrance of my house (why not? Wasn't it perhaps for this that before going out with me to supper he would shave himself with so much care?), well then, in that case the tennis changing-room would have undoubtedly provided them with the best, the most perfect refuge.

But of course—I calmly pursued this line of reasoning in a rapid internal whisper. It has to be. He would go wandering around with me only till it was late enough, and then, having so to speak tucked me up in bed, he would be on his way, pedaling at full speed round to her, already waiting for him in the garden. But of course. Now I understood that gesture of his at the brothel in Via delle Volte! You go ahead. Making love every, or almost every night, it was hardly surprising that there comes a moment when you start missing your Mamma, the Lombard skies and so on. And the ladder against the garden wall? It could only have been Micòl who left it there, in that particular spot.

I was lucid, calm and clear. Everything added up. As in a jigsaw puzzle every piece fitted exactly.

Sure it was Micòl. With Giampi Malnate. The close friend of her sick brother. In secret from her brother and all the others in the house, parents, relatives, servants, and always at night. In the *Hütte* as a rule, but then perhaps even upstairs, in her bedroom, the room of the *làttimi*. Entirely in secret? Or rather had the others as ever pretended not to see, let it go on, even slyly approved of it, considering it only human and right that a twenty-three-year-old girl, if she didn't want to or wasn't able to marry, should all the same have everything that nature required. They, there at the house, even pretended not to notice. Alberto's illness. It was their system.

I listened out. Absolute silence.

And Jor? Where had he got to?

I took several steps on tiptoe toward the *Hütte*.

"Jor!" I called out, loudly.

And then, as if in response, from far away through the night air came a sound—feeble, heartbroken, almost human. I knew it immediately: it was the sound of the dear old voice of the piazza clock, striking the hours and the quarters. What was it telling? It was telling that once again I'd been out very late, that it was stupid and wicked of me to keep on in this way torturing my father, who, that night as well, worried because I hadn't returned home, would probably not have been able to get any sleep, and that now it was time that I gave him some peace. For good. For ever after.

"What a great novel," I grinned, shaking my head as if at an incorrigible child.

And turning my back on the *Hütte*, I made my way off among the plants in the opposite direction.

Epilogue

THE story of my relationship with Micòl Finzi-Contini ends here. And so it is right that this story also has an end, now, since anything I might add to it has nothing to do with her, but only, should it go on, with me.

I've already told at the beginning what was her fate, and her family's fate.

Alberto died before the others of a malign lymphogranuloma, in 1942, after a long agony in which, despite the deep chasm dug between its citizens by the Racial Laws, the whole of Ferrara was concerned at a distance. He suffocated. To help him breathe, oxygen was needed, in ever greater quantities. And since, in the city, because of the war, the canisters for oxygen had grown scarce, in the later stages the family had involved itself in a stockpiling operation across the whole region, sending people out to buy them, at whatever price, in Bologna, Ravenna, Rimini, Parma, Piacenza . . .

The others, in September 1943, were captured by the *repubblichini*.[*] After a brief stay in the jail at Via Piangipane, the following November they were sent to the concentration camp at Fòssoli, near Carpi, and from there, later on, to Germany. With regard to myself, however, I should say that in the four years between the summer of 1939 and the autumn of 1943 I never again saw any of them. Not even Micòl. At Alberto's funeral, from

---

[*] Supporters of the Fascist Italian Social Republic, established under Mussolini in the north of Italy following his rescue by the Germans from captivity.

behind the windows of the old Dilambda, converted to running on methane, which followed the cortège at a walking pace, and which as soon as it crossed the entrance of the cemetery at the end of Via Montebello immediately turned back, it seemed to me, for a moment, that I could make out her ash-blonde hair. Nothing more than that. Even in a city as small as Ferrara it's easy enough, if you should want, to disappear from each other for years and years, to live together as the dead do.

As for Malnate, who had been called back to Milan from November 1939 (he'd tried in vain to phone me in September, and had even gone so far as to write me a letter . . .), I never even saw him again after August of that year. Poor Giampi. He believed in the honest Lombard and Communist future which smiled down on him, then, in the dark days of the impending war: a distant future—he admitted—but one that was sure and infallible. But what does the heart really know? If I think of him, sent off to the Russian Front with the CSIR,[*] in 1941, never to return, I still have a vivid memory of how Micòl would react every time, between one tennis match and the next, he'd start off again "catechizing" us. He would speak in that low, quiet, humming voice of his. But Micòl, in contrast to me, never took much heed of what he said. She'd never stop sniggering, goading, and making fun of him.

"But then, whose side are you on? The Fascists'?" I remember him asking her one day, shaking his big, sweaty head. He didn't understand.

So what had there been between the two of them? Nothing? Who knows.

It was really almost as if, with some presentiment of her own and her family's approaching end, Micòl would continually repeat even to Malnate that she didn't care a fig for his democratic and Socialist future, that for the future, in itself, she only harbored an abhorrence, far preferring to it "*le vierge, le vivace et le bel aujourd'hui*" and preferring the past even more, "the dear, the sweet, the sacred past."[+]

---

[*] Corpo di Spedizione Italiano in Russia: Italian expeditionary force sent to Russia in 1941.

[+] The first quotation is from a poem by Stéphane Mallarmé ("The virginal, evergreen, beautiful today"), and the second ("il caro, il dolce, il *pio* passato") is from Giosuè Carducci.

And since these, I know, were only words, the usual desperate, deceptive words that only a true kiss would have been able to stop her saying, with these words and just these, the little that the heart has been able to recall will here be sealed.

: IV :

Behind the Door

1.

'VE been unhappy many times in my life, as a child, as a boy, as a man; many times, if I think about it, I've touched what are called the depths of despair. And yet I can recall few periods blacker for me than the months from October 1929 to June 1930, when I had just started the *ginnasio* superiore.[*] The years lived since then have not, in the end, been of any use: I haven't managed to remedy the suffering which has remained there like a hidden wound, secretly bleeding. To cure it? To be rid of it? I don't know if that will ever be possible.

From the first days there, I had felt out of place and deeply uneasy. I didn't like the classroom where they had put us, at the end of a dark corridor; such a far cry from the happy and familiar one, on to which opened the thirteen doors of the *ginnasio* inferiore classrooms, which were divided into three lower sections and two higher. I didn't like the new teachers, with their aloof, ironic manner that discouraged any warmth, any friendly relations—they used the formal "*Lei*" with all of us!—even

---

[*] The Italian school system in Bassani's day comprised *elementare* for students aged six to ten years old; *ginnasio inferiore* or lower *ginnasio* (three classes) for students eleven to thirteen years old; *ginassio superiore* or upper *ginnasio* (two classes) for students fourteen to fifteen years old; and *liceo* (three classes) for students sixteen to eighteen years old. The pupils in this novel have just graduated from upper *ginnasio* to the first year of the *liceo* (within the same school) and therefore are around fifteen to sixteen years old (with the exception of two older boys who are resitting the year).

when it didn't actually threaten that in the immediate future we'd be subjected to regimes almost as harsh and severe as a prison, as was the case with Guzzo, the Latin teacher, or Signora Krauss, who taught chemistry and natural sciences. I didn't like my new companions, who had come from 5A and with whom we of 5B had been amalgamated. They seemed so different from us, maybe cleverer than us, better-looking than us and from better families than ours. They were, to sum up, irremediably foreign to us. And so I could neither understand nor condone the behavior of many of our own who, unlike me, had quickly sought to make common cause with them, rewarded, as I noted with consternation, by a reciprocal warmth and an equally easy-going acquiescence. How could that be possible, even conceivable? I wondered with discontent and jealousy. My keeping of the faith, crudely offended even on the first day of school, when I caught sight of Meldolesi, our beloved fifth-form literature teacher, disappearing into the distance at the head of his new fourth form down the school corridor (from now on a forbidden place where we could no longer set foot); my absurd faith would have wanted an invisible line of demarcation to continue, keeping apart the remainder of the two old fifth forms even at upper school, in such a way that we of the B class would be protected and safeguarded from any betrayal, from any contamination.

But the event that undoubtedly embittered me most was that Otello Forti, the old friend I'd shared a desk with from primary school, hadn't managed to pass the fifth-form exam—I myself, the year before, had to retake mathematics in October, but he, although earlier he had only had to retake English, had been failed definitively that October. Not only did I now no longer have him seated as ever on my right, but I couldn't even meet him outside at the school gates, at midday, to walk back along the Corso Giovecca together, each of us going to our respective homes—nor could I meet him at the Montagnone to play soccer in the afternoon, nor at his house, most of all, his lovely, big, happy house, full of brothers and sisters, of boy and girl cousins, where I had passed the greater part of my adolescence—since Otello, poor thing, unable to bear his unfair failure, had got his father's permission to repeat the fifth year at Padua in a boarding school run by the Barnabite Order. Deprived of Otello, no longer able to enjoy his massive, slightly obtuse presence at my side, his body so much bigger and heavier than mine, no longer to be stimulated or even goaded by the gruff, ironic, but still affectionate reserve which he always deployed at my expense, whenever, either at his house or mine, we did our homework together. Right from the start I'd felt that persistent pain, the inconsolable emptiness of the bereaved. What did it matter that he wrote some letters to me from Padua in which, with an eloquence that astonished me—I'd never had him pegged as very intelligent—he poured out all his affection? What did it matter that I replied to him with no lesser effusions? I was now at the *liceo*, he was stuck in the *ginnasio*. I was at Ferrara and he at Padua— this was the insuperable reality which he, with the courage, unexpected clear-sightedness and maturity of all defeated souls, showed himself even more aware of than I was. I wrote to him: "We'll see each other at Christmas." And he replied, that yes, at Christmas, some two and a half months off, perhaps we would meet again (on condition he obtained, as he swore to himself he would, the right grades in all his subjects—something that was by no means certain!), but anyway, ten or so days spent together wouldn't really alter the situation. He seemed to be suggesting: "Go on, forget me! If you haven't made another friend yet, go out and find one!" No, writing to each other achieved very little. So little, in fact, that after the holidays at the beginning of November, after All Saints' Day, All Souls' Day, then Armistice Day, by unspoken agreement, we gave up altogether.

I needed to vent my unhappiness, to show it. So, on the first day of school I made sure that I didn't join the usual stampede to grab the best desks, the ones closest to the teacher's podium, at which, at the beginning of every year, my school companions would launch themselves. Leaving this battle to the others, to ours and theirs, I held back at the doorway of the classroom to observe the scene with distaste, and in the end, went so far as to sit down, down there by the window, at the furthest corner desk reserved for the girls. It was the only seat left unoccupied: a big desk, ill-adapted to my less than average size, but perfectly befitting my intense desire to be in exile. Who knows how many slovenly failures and year-repeaters it had been host to before me! I thought to myself. I read on the tarry surface of the tilted desktop all that had been carved by the penknives of my predecessors (mainly invectives against the whole teaching body, but especially against the head-master, Turolla, nicknamed Halfpint). Looking around, over the thirty-odd heads and necks bent over in an orderly fashion in front of me, I was filled with acrimony. My recent failure in math still riled me. I was in a hurry to reestablish myself, to be considered once again one of the best and bright-est pupils. And yet, for the first time, I understood the perspective of the idlers in the back row. School seen as a prison, the headmaster as its warden, the teachers as its guards and my school companions as fellow jailbirds: a system, in short, in which any eager collaboration should be resisted, while every chance to denigrate and sabotage it should be embraced. Those waves of anarchic scorn that, with a touch of fear, I had felt surging from the back of the class since primary school, how well I now understood them!

I scanned the scene before me and disapproved of all and sundry. The girls, humiliated by having to wear their black smocks, as a group amounted to nothing. Just little girls, the four who occupied the first two double desks, all of whom came from 5A; with their tight pigtails swaying on their slender backs, they seemed like kiddies from the kindergarten. What were they called? Their surnames all ended in ini: Bergamini, Bolognini, Santini, Scanavini, Zaccarini—that sort of thing, which brought to mind, with their diminutives, the most petit-bourgeois of families—milliners, delicatessen shopkeepers, book-binders, council employees and so on. The two girls at the third desk, Cavicchi and Gabrieli, the first very fat, the second bony and skinny with the pallid, spotty face of a thirty-year-old spinster, represented what remained of 5B's "females": hunched and grey-ish, undoubtedly the two ugliest girls, destined to work as pharmacists or schoolmistresses and to be reckoned as mere objects, things. The remain-ing three girls positioned at the fourth and fifth desks—Balboni and Jovine at the fourth and Manoja alone at the fifth—came from outside the city: Balboni from the countryside—you could see that clearly enough from the way she was dressed, poor thing; her mother might well have been the village dressmaker, a position acquired without exacting qualifications, and likely it was she who had constructed those dresses . . . and Jovine came from Potenza, Manoja from Viterbo. These two were probably part of the retinue of low-grade civil servants or railway employees transferred to northern Italy as a reward for special merit. How sad and boring! Was it some kind of rule that girls who continued their studies always had to look like this, dejected, characterless crones (who didn't even wash that often judging by the odor of mold that wafted from them), while beauties such as Legnani and Bertoni, for example, the two vamps of 5B, were promptly failed? But Legnani and Bertoni couldn't have cared less. The former was, it seemed, about to get married; with her wasp waist, her short, shiny black fringe and those wicked eyes like the starlet Elsa Merlini's—fat chance that she'd repeat the fifth form! She was the type to slink off to Rome to become an actress—as we'd often heard her say. She wasn't likely to rot away behind the door of the *liceo*!

But it was the boys who were the main target of my criticism, especially the two pairs who occupied the desks in the center row facing the teacher's podium. Down there, in the first and second desks, 5A had planted all of three interlopers, Boldoni, Grassi and Droghetti, beside whom in the second desk sat Florestano Donaddio from 5B, who seemed an uninvited but tolerated guest, abject as he was in his physique, in his studies, in everything. The son of a cavalry officer, with that irreproachable and stupid look of his that convinced you he was sure to follow exactly in his father's footsteps, Droghetti was certainly a mediocrity. But the two in front, Boldini and Grassi, among the brightest and best of 5A, together represented a real force, and the small-statured, rosy-cheeked and blond Donadio, wee timorous creature that he'd always been, had evidently offered himself as their assistant and vassal. Another baleful combination sat in the third row: Giovannini from B and Camurri from A. For the sake of clarity, it wasn't that Giovannini was any worse than the other—despite coming from the country, the good Walter even managed to speak a reasonably convincing Italian. But Camurri was upper class: ugly, short sighted and sanctimonious, but upper class. His family—who didn't know of the Camurris of Via Carlo Mayr?—was among the richest in the city. They owned hundreds of hectares in the Codigoro area, precisely in that part of the country from which Walter came, so it wasn't at all unlikely that his grandfather and father had once been, or even still were, in service to the Camurri household . . . In the fourth row alone—who knows why, unless it showed that no one had sufficiently aristocratic lineage to be beside him, sat Cattolica, Carlo Cattolica, who from primary school onward had always been the undisputed genius of the A class (regularly receiving top marks in every subject). Although it might seem improbable, it was no sweat for him to communicate, if need be, with the no less trusted Boldini and Grasso in the first row via the dependable backs of Camurri and Droghetti leaning over their desks in front of him. It was a marvel to behold how they managed this in Greek and Latin classes. Messages were passed from the fourth row to the first, and vice versa, with the same ease as if they'd had a field telephone at their disposal.

Behind Cattolica, two of ours: Mazzanti and Malagù, two nonentities, more or less. And, on my right, leaning over their desks with the sole aim of ducking down and escaping the eagle eyes of the teacher as much as possible, sat Veronesi and Danieli, the first at least twenty and the second even older: a pair inured to continually repeating the year, veteran slackers, useless even at sport, and for years regular frequenters of brothels. And even if the places in the row of desks closest to the door, those in front of the blackboard, seemed a slightly better assortment (in the second desk Giorgio Selmi had ended up next to Chieregatti, in the third Ballerini had managed to place himself once again with the inseparable Giovanardi), how could I resign myself to be paired with Lattuga in the fourth desk, the wretched, stinking Lattuga, who throughout his days at school had rarely found anyone willing to sit beside him, and this year too, like Cattolica, though for completely different reasons, had remained all alone. No, no, far better the solitude of the place I had chosen in the row of girls. Bianchi, the Italian teacher, had begun his series of lessons by declaiming one of Dante's "Canzoni," and one verse had especially struck me: "The exile imposed on me I hold as an honor." That could have been my banner and motto.

One day I was distractedly looking out of the big window to my left at the glum courtyard inhabited by starved cats which separated the Guarini School building, a former convent, from the side of the Gesù Church. I was thinking that after all it would have been good if, for example, Giorgio Selmi, who had always seemed at heart a likeable boy, had taken the initiative on the first day of school to ask me to share with him. Selmi was an orphan whose father and mother were both dead. He lived with his brother Luigi at the house of his paternal uncle, the lawyer Armando, a grumpy bachelor of about sixty who couldn't wait to be rid of his nephews,

having found a place for one of them in the military academy at Modena
and the other in the Livorno Naval Academy. And yet, why on earth had
Giorgio preferred to put himself beside that grim hunchback Chieregatti
rather than me? His uncle's apartment in Piazza Sacrati—legal offices
annexed to a few rooms that served as living quarters—certainly wouldn't
have sufficed for the two of us to do our homework in, if it was true that he,
Giorgio, had to study in his bedroom, a broom cupboard of barely three
by four meters. By contrast, at my house, we would have had all the space
we needed at our disposal. My study was big enough for me, him and whoever else might have wanted to join our partnership. Besides, my mother,
delighted that I was now spending my afternoons at home, and not at Forti's house as I had done at the *ginnasio*—would have brought us who knows
what splendid snacks at five o'clock, accompanied by tea, butter and jam!
It really was a shame that Giorgio Selmi hadn't chosen to pair up with me.
No doubt this was a result of envy, of jealousy. My home was too fine and
comfortable compared to his. And then, I had a mother, and he didn't—all
he had was a scurvy old uncle. Every now and then, anti-Semitism proved
to be an irrelevant factor.

"Sss!"

A faint whistle, coming from my right, made me start. I abruptly
turned round. It was Veronesi. Crouched behind Mazzanti's shoulders, he
was signaling to me with his thin, incredibly nicotine-stained forefinger,
to turn round and look in front of me. What was I doing? he seemed to be
asking, half amused, half worried. Did I not know where I happened to be,
mad idiot that I was?

I obeyed. In the absolute silence, barely broken by a ripple of laughter,
the whole class had turned their faces in my direction. Even Guzzo, the
teacher, seated up at the front, was staring at me with a grin.

"At last," he sighed.

I stood up.

"And your name is?"

I stammered out my surname.

Guzzo was famous for his nastiness, a nastiness bordering on sadism.
About fifty years old, tall, Herculean, with big, blazing, greenish reptilian
eyes beneath an enormous Wagnerian forehead, and two long grey side-

burns which grew halfway down his bony cheeks, he was deemed a kind of genius at the Guarini School (it was he who had composed the epigraph for the fallen of the First World War so conspicuously emblazoned on the entrance corridor: *"Mors domuit corpora—Vicit mortem virtus")*.* He wasn't enrolled in the Fascist party and because of this, and only because of this, everybody said, he hadn't been granted the university chair which various of his philological writings, published in Germany, would otherwise surely have warranted.

"What?" he asked, curling a hand behind his ear, leaning forward with his broad chest against the open ledger. "Will you please raise your voice!"

He was enjoying himself, that was clear. He was toying with me.

I repeated my surname.

He brusquely sat up, and carefully checked the ledger.

"Good," he concluded, while he made a mysterious pen stroke in it.

"Now, will you tell me a little about yourself?" he went on, leaning back in his chair again.

"About me?"

"Indeed. About you. To which part of the fifth form did you belong, A or B?

"B."

He made a wry face. "Ah, to B. Good. And how have you got here? With one flying jump or—forgive my poor memory—are you trying a second time?"

"I have to retake math in October."

"And only math?"

I nodded.

"Are you sure you don't have to 'retake'—ugly but serviceable word—any other subjects? Latin or Greek, for example?"

I shook my head.

"Are you quite sure?" he insisted with feline meekness.

I denied it again.

"Well then, my good fellow, pay attention. I wouldn't want for you to

---

* "Death vanquishes the body—Virtue conquers death."

have to retake Latin and Greek as well as math this summer . . . *quod Deus avertat* . . . three subjects . . . you do catch my drift, don't you?"

He asked me how I had done in the *ginnasio*, and if I had ever been held back a year. But he wasn't looking at me. He was looking around as though he thought me untrustworthy and was soliciting testimony from whoever was willing to supply it.

"He always does well. One of the best," someone dared to venture, perhaps Pavani, there, in the first desk in the front row.

"Ah, so one of the best!" Guzzo exclaimed. "But if he belonged to the chosen few in lower school . . . how come this falling off? How did that come to pass?"

I didn't know what to say. I stared at the desk as if the answer Guzzo sought would come to me from that ancient blackened wood.

I lifted up my head.

"How come?" he persisted implacably. "And why have you chosen a desk such as that one? Perhaps to be close to the excellent Veronesi and to the no less excellent Danieli, so as to learn true wisdom from them, rather than from me?"

The class broke out in unanimous laughter. Even Veronesi and Danieli laughed, though less heartily.

"No, no, you should pay heed," continued Guzzo, controlling the turmoil with the broad sweeping gesture of a conductor. "First of all, you must change places."

I looked about, weighed up and narrowed down the options.

"There. In the fourth desk. Next to that gentleman."

He pointed at Cattolica.

"What's your name?"

Cattolica stood up.

"Carlo Cattolica," he replied plainly.

"Ah, good . . . the famous Cattolica, good, good. You come from 5A, don't you?"

"Yes, sir."

"Good, good. A with B. Perfect."

I gathered up my books, stepped into the aisle, reached my new desk, greeted in passing by a cough from Veronesi and welcomed on arrival by a smile from the ace of the A form.

"So be careful, Cattolica," Guzzo said in the meantime. "I'm entrusting him to you. Lead this poor lost sheep back to the straight and narrow."

2.

I HAVE absolutely no idea what became of Carlo Cattolica in these last thirty years.

He's the only one of my school companions about whom I know nothing: what career he took up, if he ever married, where he lives, or if he is still alive. I can only say that in 1933, after he passed the final school exams with the highest marks, he had to leave Ferrara to move to Turin, where his father, an engineer—a little bald chap with blue eyes, maniacally dedicated to opera and stamp-collecting, browbeaten by his math teacher wife who was a whole head taller than him—had unexpectedly been given secure employment in, I believe, a paint factory. Did Cattolica, the son, become an important surgeon, as he had predicted since the beginning of 1930, confident in himself as ever? Did he actually get married to the girl he went on his bicycle to meet every evening in Bondeno, and to whom he was, then, "officially" engaged—Accolti, Graziella Accolti, I think she was called? Our generation has been buffeted about like few others. The war and all the rest of it obliterated a multitude of our intentions and vocations no less resolute than those of Carlo Cattolica. And yet something tells me he is alive, is a surgeon as he dreamed of being and that, even though he left Ferrara when still a boy, all the same he ended up marrying his Graziella. Will we two ever meet again? Who can say? I realize that's a possibility. But I should press on regardless.

I can still see Cattolica's fine-featured, clear-cut profile to my right, precisely modelled as on a medal. He was tall, very thin, with lively black eyes set under arched, rather prominent eyebrows and a forehead that wasn't high but broad, pale, placid, very beautiful. It's odd but the earliest image I have of him is likewise in profile. We both went to the primary school, Alfonso da Varonno in Via Bellaria, even then in different classes, and one morning, in the school courtyard, during recess, I was struck by his way of running. He sped round the perimeter wall, moving his thin legs with the long, regular, scythe-like strides of a middle-distance runner. I asked Otello Forti who he was. "What? Don't you know who that is? It's Cattolica!" Otello had answered, wide-eyed. He ran, I noticed differently from all the others, myself included, as if nothing could distract him or force him to veer off course. He advanced calmly looking ahead, as though he was the only one, he alone among all the others, who was sure of where he was going.

Now we were sitting close together, only a few inches from each other, but a sort of secret border, a demarcation line, stopped us communicating with the relaxed familiarity of friendship. To begin with, to tell the truth, I had made a few tentative attempts. One morning during Latin class work I had asked him, for example, if I might, due to exceptional circumstances, slip the two fat volumes of my dictionary into the space under our desk reserved for him, for his books and exercise books. And yet the chill rotation of a very few degrees which Cattolica, in consenting, performed on the axis of his face, had quickly dissuaded me from any further requests of this kind. What else was I hoping for anyway? I wondered. Wasn't the social significance, the worldly uplift of our union enough for me? Every year of the *ginnasio* from the first to the fifth, he had been the best pupil of the A class, not to speak of elementary school, where the teachers passed around his compositions in the corridors. Yet I too, despite a slip every now and then, had always been a part of the select top group. And so? Being, as we were, the standard-bearers of two historically rival factions, wasn't it better that we behave precisely so, each of us remaining, for all intents and purposes, in our proper places?

As a rule, we displayed ample mutual consideration; the maximum respect and chivalry. Every now and then, after being tested, we'd return to our desk graciously bestowing on each other smiles of approval, congratulatory handshakes; nevertheless, anxious that Mazzanti behind us (who, being aware of the situation and scenting the chance to extract some advantage from it for himself and Malagù, had soon begun his own record-book in which he accurately tallied up the marks each day) hadn't made any errors, and had maintained that unwavering fairness and impartiality in the faithful record-keeping to which he laid claim. But then, during class work, how precipitously those frail castles of opportunistic hypocrisy crumbled away. In such circumstances, no passage of Greek or Latin was hard enough to master that it could ever induce us to join forces. Each of us would work independently, jealously and meanly avid for our own marks, even ready, just so as to owe nothing to the other side, to turn in an unfinished or erroneous version. As I had foreseen, Droghetti and Camurri acted as go betweens for Cattolica and the distant advance posts of Boldini and Grassi. When time was restricted, when our teacher Guzzo, having raised his eyes from the proofs of some essay of his on Suetonius, would announce with a cruel smile that in exactly two minutes, and not a moment more, he would send out the "excellent" Chieregatti to collect the "manuscripts of you gentlemen," you'd have to have seen it to believe with what impudent efficiency the telephone network of the A section was made to work! Goodbye, then, to any exchange of smiles and handshakes; goodbye to any feigned comradely courtesies. The mask fell off. And when it fell, the irreprehensible face of Cattolica, pent up and twisted with factional striving, showed itself to me in all its hostile, hateful reality. Naked, at last.

And yet, even though I loathed him, I admired and envied him at the same time.

Perfect in everything, in Italian as in Latin, in Greek as in history and philosophy, in science as in mathematics and physics, art history and even gymnastics—I was let off religious studies and didn't attend the lessons of Father Fonseca, but I had no doubt that even with "the Priest" Cattolica was impeccable—I hated and at the same time envied his mental clarity, the lucid working of his mind. What an addled klutz I was compared to him! It was true; perhaps in Italian essay-writing I outdid him. But not always, as there was a range of topics, some that suited me, some that didn't, and when an argument didn't appeal to me, there was nothing to be done—then it would be a fluke if I managed to get six out of ten. Perhaps I also outshone him in Latin and Greek orals—after that initial skirmish, Guzzo had begun to warm to me and, reading Homer or Herodotus, especially Herodotus, he almost always turned to me to elicit what he called the "exact translation"—but in the written exercises, especially in translating from Italian into Latin, Cattolica was decidedly better, recalling all the most recondite little rules of morphology and syntax, and practically never making a mistake. His memory was such that when tested in history, he could recite scores of dates without a single error, or in natural sciences, reel off the classifications of invertebrates to the enraptured Signora Krauss with the same sureness and nonchalance as though he were reading them from the textbook. God, how did he do it? I wondered. What was he hiding in his head? A calculator? And Mazzanti didn't hesitate—after such displays of mnemonic bravura he was always prompt to mark down a nine or even a nine-plus in his ledger. And the worst of it was, that it was often me who, turning round, would insist on that "plus" being added.

But my sense of inferiority didn't derive as much from a comparison of our respective scholastic efforts as from everything else.

First, his height. He was tall, slender, already a young man, and dressed in an adult fashion, in long grey vicuña trousers, with non-matching jackets in heavy fabric (in the pocket of which would be a packet of ten Macedonia cigarettes), an organdie cravat around his neck; while I, short and stocky, burdened with the eternal zouave trousers which my mother favored—beside him, how could I seem anything other than an undistinguished little boy? Then sports. Cattolica didn't indulge in any of them, he even looked down on soccer, and not because he couldn't play (once in the churchyard of the Gesù Church we'd improvised a kick around and he'd shown what a stylish player he was), but "just because": because sports didn't interest him he considered it a waste of time. Besides, what course of studies would I pursue at university? I didn't know: one day I inclined toward medicine, the next toward law, the next again toward the arts, while he had not only chosen medicine, but had decided between general medicine and surgery, opting for the latter. And finally, there was the girl he went out with, the young lady from Bondeno. In matters of love, I hadn't had the least, serious, actual experience—would the summertime beach encounters I'd had with those young girls even count as experience? A little holding of hands, staring into one another's eyes, the odd furtive peck on the cheek, and nothing more . . . He, on the other hand, was officially engaged with a conspicuous ring on his finger. Oh, that ring! It was a sapphire mounted on white gold, an important, senatorial ring, especially displeasing. And yet, what would I have given to own one myself! Who knows, I thought to myself, perhaps to become a man, or at least to acquire that basic minimum of self-confidence to pass oneself off as such, a ring of that sort would surely be an accessory, a great help!

Who did he, Cattolica, do his homework with in the afternoons? At first, I couldn't work this out. He seemed so self-sufficient, so aloof, that I was inclined to concede him no real, no close friend. I thought that even his relationship with Boldini and Grassi was based on necessity, and that at his home in Via Cittadella no school friend would ever be invited, not even them.

But I was wrong.

To tell the truth, I'd had an inkling some time before: that morning when, as the last one out, I'd gone down the stairs from the chemistry and biology lab, Krauss's exclusive domain, and then had suddenly seen in front of me that very trio—Cattolica, Boldini and Grassi—halted on a landing in deep conversation. Seeing them there, I immediately guessed that they were arranging to meet up again in one of their houses in the afternoon. In fact, they quickly changed the subject, aware of my approach. They began talking about soccer—just imagine it! As if I didn't know Cattolica had no interest in sports, and would never discuss it.

All the same, I wanted to be sure, I wanted physical evidence. So, that very evening, not having found my father at the Merchants' Club—from the time I'd stopped studying with Otello I'd taken to stopping in at the club almost every evening at about seven—I suddenly made up my mind. Instead of going straight home, I'd rushed off to station myself at the corner of Viale Cavour and Via Cittadella.

It was still some twenty minutes before eight. From the Castle to the Customs Barrier, Viale Cavour sparkled with lights, while Via Cittadella, broad and stony, seemed steeped in a dark mist. I stood at the corner and stared toward the Cattolicas' house, which was a couple of hundred meters away. It was a smallish, red, detached building, recently constructed— undoubtedly graceful, I thought, but with something tasteless about it. Weren't they a bit vulgar, a touch dubious, the pink curtains that adorned the lit-up second floor windows? Some of those little houses in Via Colomba where Danieli and Veronesi spent a good part of their afternoons behind closed shutters gave a hint of something similar.

I waited a quarter of an hour. And I was considering leaving—having begun to suspect that they'd arranged to meet elsewhere, either at Grassi's in Piazza Ariostea or at Boldini's in Via Ripagrande—when the street door opened and, one after the other, the three of them, Cattolica included, trooped out.

All three of them then went back up Viale Cavour on their bikes, slowly enough to allow me to step back from the corner unseen. Once there, however, the trio parted company, Boldini and Grassi turning left, straight toward the city center, and Cattolica to the right, toward the Customs Barrier.

Where was Cattolica off to?

For a good while I tracked him at a distance, my eyes glued to the back light of his shiny, grey Maino bike. It was clear—he was going round to his fiancée's at Bondeno. But the idea that, after a busy day of studying—the morning at school basking in universal approval, then the afternoon at home soothed by the admiration and affection of his closest friends—he could then award himself an evening session smooching with his fiancée was suddenly unbearable to me.

3.

ALTHOUGH OTELLO Forti had received an excellent report at the end of his first term, he wanted to spend no more than three days with his family: Christmas Eve, Christmas Day and Santo Stefano. I hardly saw him—not until a few hours before his return to Padua, and by then he was already utterly taken up with the thought of leaving.

I had gone to see him at his house, number 24, Via Montebello.

He had immediately taken me to admire the big dazzling Nativity scene, arranged as ever in the ground floor drawing room, but as to its construction, that year, for the first time in at least ten years, none of his brothers had thought to invite me round to help. Then we went up to his bedroom. And yet, not even up there, on the top floor, in that little room which I'd always considered somewhat my own, did I manage to make myself useful. As soon as I'd entered, Otello, with unfamiliar courtesy, had made me sit down in the armchair next to the window. Then he busied himself with packing his suitcase. And when I stood up to help him he insisted I sit down again. He preferred to do it himself, he said, he'd get it all done much more quickly on his own.

I did as I was told. In the meantime, I watched him. Without raising his eyes, he kept going back and forth to his suitcase with a slowness that seemed to me studied. I remembered him as blonder, chubbier, with a pinker complexion—and perhaps, aside from the long trousers that made him look slimmer, he had indeed lost some weight and grown an inch or two. But above all in his eyes, behind the glasses he wore for short-sightedness, there had now settled a serious, solemn, bitter expression which pained and wounded me. It's true that he'd never been of an open disposition. It had always been me who took the initiative in everything, in our games, our bike rides into the country, our out-of-school reading (Salgari, Verne, Dumas); he, for his part, letting himself be dragged along, grumbling and resistant, but sometimes even laughing, thank heavens, and secretly admiring me precisely because I managed to make him laugh every now and then. But now? What had changed between us? How was it my fault that he'd been failed? Why didn't he wipe off that resentful scowl?

"What's up with you?" I'd tried to ask him.

"With me? Nothing. Why?"

"I don't know. It really looks as if you've got something against me."

"Lucky you, you're still the same," Otello had replied, with a brief, notional smile that strayed no further than his lips.

He was evidently alluding to my inveterate tendency to worry over trifles, my eternal need to have others like me, as well as to the change brought about in his character by misfortune. If that's what I wanted to do, I could keep on wasting time with my usual childish whims. But not he, he neither had the time nor the inclination. Misfortune had made a man of him, and a man had to deal with serious things.

"I don't know what you mean," I replied. "But, I'm sorry, is this any way to behave? If you'd at least have written . . . "

"It seems to me that I did write. Didn't you receive my letters?"

"I did, yes, but . . . "

"Well, then?"

He raised his eyes and gave me a hard, hostile stare.

"How many times did you write to me? Three letters in the first fortnight. And then nothing after."

"And you?"

He was right, the first who'd failed to reply was me. But how could I explain to him, at this point, the reasons why I hadn't felt like dragging on a correspondence in which our roles had suddenly been reversed? I had thought it was for me to console him for his ill fortune, and yet in some way it had been he, from the start, who'd had to console and chide me.

Later, making the most of the day's mild weather—there was no comparison with the brutal winter of the year before; regardless that the season was well advanced, the cold spell had still not dug in—we had gone down to walk in the garden. In the blue, slightly misty light of dusk we had completed a kind of tour of the treasured sites of our friendship: of the lovely central lawn, now damp and patchy, where he and I, along with his brothers and cousins, had played many a game of croquet; of the rustic shed beyond the lawn, the ground floor of which served for a woodpile and coal cellar, and its first floor for a dovecote; and finally of the wooded rise, down there by the outer wall, on top of which Giuseppe, his older brother, had built a greyish hut, half worm-eaten beams and half wire fencing, once a chicken coop, for his rabbit breeding project. It was mainly Otello who spoke. He gave a sketchy account of his life at school: tough, certainly—he admitted—mainly due to the brutal morning call by the "prefects" (they had to get up at a quarter past five, and then all of them rushed down to the chapel), but "cleverly planned" so they couldn't sit around dawdling, and always had something to do. The curriculum? Much broader than ours of the year before. For Latin, they had to prepare the third book of the *Aeniad*, Cicero's *Letters* and Sallust's *Jugurthine War*. For Greek, Xenophon's *Cyropaedia* and Lucian's *Dialogues* and a selection of Plutarch's *Lives*. For Italian *I promessi sposi* and *Orlando furioso*.

"All of *Orlando furioso*?" I exclaimed.

"The whole lot," he replied drily.

But there was one question I was burning to ask him, and which I only managed to do, in the doorway, just as I was leaving.

"Have you made friends with anyone?"

To which he replied with evident satisfaction that yes, of course—

he had got to know a Venetian boy whom he liked a lot, and they studied together. He was called Alverà, Leonardo Alverà—his father was a count!—a good guy and "also" good at Italian, Latin and Greek, "but" especially good at math and geometry, subjects, that was for sure, in which no one could compete with him. If every now and then I would dash off a poem, a short story, he, with the same ease, just for his own pleasure, solved the most complex equations. What a phenomenon! With a brain like that, who could tell what he'd achieve as an adult—become a scientist, an inventor, in short "a Marconi" . . .

I can't be sure if what I'm about to tell you took place on the eighth of January, as we went back to school after Epiphany. It's likely that it did. In any case, one early morning, a half-hour before the bell rang, I'd gone into the Gesù Church where I'd never before set foot—whenever he was confronted with a tough bit of classwork or an important oral exam Otello went there, as I put it to myself, to "propitiate the gods," but I had only accompanied him as far as the threshold and no farther.

The church seemed empty. I had slowly walked up the right aisle, gazing up and around like a tourist, but the sunlight which shone through the large upper windows stopped me from seeing the large baroque canvases hung above the altar clearly. Having reached the transept, immersed like the rest in semi-darkness, I'd crossed to the left aisle, which was flooded with light. And there my attention was suddenly drawn to a strange gathering of motionless and silent figures, huddled beside the second of the smaller entrances.

Who were they? As I came to realize as soon as I'd come close enough, they were not living people but life sized carved statues of painted wood. They were, as it turned out, the famous Pianzùn d'la Rosa to which as a child I'd been taken many times (though not here at the Gesù, but at the della Rosa Church of Via Armari) by my Aunt Malvina, the only Catholic aunt that I had. Once again, I looked at the ghastly scene: the wretched, bruised body of the dead Christ, stretched out on the bare ground, and around him, petrified in mute attitudes, in soundless grimaces, in endless grief, never to be released in words, were gathered his relatives and friends: the Madonna, Saint John, Joseph of Arimathea, Simon, Mary Magdalene, and two pious women. Looking again at this scene, I remembered Aunt

Malvina, who never managed to restrain her tears at this same spectacle. She would draw her black spinsterish shawl across her eyes, then kneel down, without, of course, daring to make her little unbaptized nephew kneel beside her.

Finally, I roused myself, looking around before leaving.

I spotted Carlo Cattolica down there, kneeling composedly in a pew off the central nave.

My initial impulse was to leave him undisturbed, and make off without being seen. Yet, instead, with my heart beating hard, I went down the left aisle on tiptoe till I came level with him.

He was praying with his satchel of books beside him, his pure, beautiful forehead leaning on his clasped hands, and proffering to my observing gaze the same finely chiselled, indecipherable profile that I would notice every day at school. Why weren't we friends? I wondered, tormented. Why couldn't we become friends? Perhaps he didn't respect me? No, it couldn't be that: even if they were hard-working and bright, Boldini and Grassi certainly weren't better than me. Because of religion, then? No, it wasn't to do with that either. Our different religions had never cropped up between me and Otello. On the contrary, if anything, at the Fortis', even if they were all extremely pious and militantly active in Catholic organizations—the lawyer Forti belonged to the Saint Vincent de Paul Society, and Giuseppe had also joined, two years ago—no one had ever made me feel it mattered that I was Jewish. And Cattolica's parents weren't known to be especially churchy. So why was it? Why?

Cattolica had got to his feet, made the sign of the cross and then seen me.

"Oh! What are you doing here?" he asked in lowered tones as soon as he had come over to me.

I'd signaled with my thumb.

"I was looking at the Pianzùn d'la Rosa."

"Didn't you know it?"

Only too well—I explained—having seen it on many occasions in the della Rosa Church as a child. And as we walked toward the statues I held forth about my Aunt Malvina and her ruling passion—visiting all the churches of Ferrara.

This information seemed to interest him. He wanted to know who this aunt was. Was she by any chance my mother's sister?

"No, my grandmother's," I replied. "My mother's mother. She was called Marchi."

Meanwhile, we'd walked out into the churchyard. It was a few minutes before nine, and both the churchyard and Via Borgoleoni, especially in front of the Guarini School, were already crowded with youngsters. We were leaning against the red facade of the Gesù Church. And as none of our school companions seemed to have noticed us, we'd continued our conversation. For the first time. The event moved me, made me garrulous, and stirred in me a need for friendship.

We began to talk in general about religion, but then he asked me if it was true that we "Israelites" didn't believe in the Madonna, if it was true that, according to us, Jesus Christ was not the son of God, if we were still expecting the Messiah, if in church we wore caps, and so on. And I replied to all of this, point by point, in a more than affable manner, suddenly feeling that his general, somewhat crude, not to say rude curiosity pleased rather than offended me, and was liberating for me.

At the end, it was I who posed him a question.

"Excuse me," I said "but you . . . I mean your family . . . have you always been Catholics?"

His lips briefly stretched in a proud smile.

"I would imagine so. Why?"

"Oh, I don't know. Cattolica is the name of a town, a seaside town near Riccione . . . between Riccione and Pesaro . . . and Jews, as you know, all have the surnames of cities and towns."

He froze.

"You're wrong about that," he had retorted drily, suddenly assuming a knowledgeable air. "It's true that many Israelites bear the names of cities and towns. But not all. Many are called Levi, Cohen, Zamorani, Passigli, Limentani, Finzi, Contini, Finzi-Contini, Vitali, Algranati and so on. What relevance does that have? I could just as easily cite an infinite number of cases of people with surnames that seemed Jewish, but actually weren't at all."

At this point he had begun walking off, still harping on about this topic in an undertone. This let us, for once, slip through the school gates together, and then walk down the long corridor which led to our classroom, and finally to cross the room to reach our desk, each of us keeping pace with the other like the best of friends.

4.

I REMEMBER very well Luciano Pulga's arrival on the first Monday after lessons began.

Everyone had already taken their places. Mondays would invariably begin with two hours of Guzzo, which were dedicated to class assignments, while he, "the boss," often liked to idle by the big window at the end of the corridor till almost a quarter past nine, immersed in apparent contemplation of the field that was growing wild at the foot of the Gesù Church's apse, when, at the doorway, instead of the gigantic form of the teacher, we saw appear the miniscule one of a blond boy, in a green pullover, grey, knee-length short trousers, and long tawny socks. Who was he? Still, as he hovered uncertainly just inside the doorway, casting around his blue eyes, the intense cold blue of mountain ice, in search of a vacant place, I was immediately repelled by his hook nose, and the stick-legged look of someone on stilts, and at the same time moved to pity by his anxiety to find a safe haven. I watched him. Seeing no one next to Giorgio Selmi— Chieregatti was absent that day—he first tried to seat himself in the second desk of the first row. He was blocked. That place was taken—Selmi had quickly warned him—it belonged to someone absent, but who would be back tomorrow or the day after, and would certainly make him move. At which, he instantly stood up again, and moved away. Skinny, with a thin Adam's apple that trembled, half strangled, a little above his white shirt collar, he halted at the end of the girls' row, at the very desk which had remained empty since the start of term, when I'd occupied it in my stab at self-exile, and began once more to look around. Once again he walked down the aisle between the second and third rows with a measured and determined step, with the fixed gaze of someone who sees a sanctuary before him. But he was sweating. Droplets of sweat made pearls along the skin above his slightly retracted upper lip. And this detail, the drops of sweat—which I had noticed in a flash as he passed by almost touching me—once again filled me with a vague sense of repulsion.

I also clearly remember what happened when Guzzo returned to the classroom. He, the teacher, subjected the new arrival to a prolonged inter-rogation. "Good heavens! And who might you be?" he began, "Perhaps a visiting pupil?" The other replied to the despot, "Pulga, Luciano," display-ing an easy, inveigling Italian, that of a traveling salesman, with a markedly Bolognese accent. The class obsequiously rewarded Guzzo's quips with gusts of laughter; and after a while I came to the aid of the poor creature, guilty of having come to school with nothing more than a fountain pen, not only offering him the regulation sheet of school paper so that he could do the class work, but also, swiftly following Guzzo's invitation, I made my way to the back row so that "Signor Pulga, Luciano" might avail himself of my dictionary.

And, finally, I remember the odd feeling I had throughout that hour and a half spent side by side with him, with Pulga, the two of us busy try-ing to solve the puzzle of that Greek translation. Guzzo, while making me change places—"Seeing as you've scored top marks by lending him your foolscap," he'd said, "why not excel yourself by scurrying back to where you came from?"—had given instructions that the dictionary should remain on the desk, visible at all times and placed exactly in the middle to prevent either of us from copying. But Pulga copied away regardless, as and when he wanted. Taking advantage of the teacher's rare moments of distraction, he cast hasty, greedy, sideways glances over the Schenkl, displaying such perfect technique, I thought, that it must have required years and years of practice, an extensive career. And yet, the way he copied my work with such complete confidence, with such a lack of personal judgement, only keen to perform his own work of plagiarism without error, filled me with a complex, trapped sensation, a mixture of gratification and disgust, against which from then on I found myself defenceless, more or less incapable of any proper reaction.

At the midday break I found him close beside me.

Could I come along with him to some bookshop? he asked me. At the Minghetti School in Bologna which he'd attended, they mostly used different textbooks, so now—as though his father hadn't forked out enough in moving here!—he'd have to buy almost a whole new set again. A complete disaster. If only he'd been able to acquire them one at a time, perhaps even on credit . . .

Together we went up Via Borgoleoni in the wan January sunlight, and Pulga, meanwhile, respectfully conceding me a place on his right, kept on talking. Despite the fact that Guzzo, during the lesson, had already elicited almost everything about his family and his scholastic curriculum, he chose to repeat, for my sole benefit, that they came from Lizzano in Belvedere, a small mountain town some eighty kilometers from Bologna, where his father, a doctor, had held a practice for almost ten years; that he had gone to primary school in Lizzano, lower *ginnasio* in Porretta Terme, and started upper *ginnasio* in Bologna, traveling back and forth on the train every damned day, and finally, that his family, the four of them—father, mother and two boys, because of this unforeseen move "into the Ferrara province"—had fallen into serious difficulties. Just imagine—they didn't even have a house to live in!

"How come?" I asked, astonished. "You don't even have a house? So where do you sleep?"

"In the Hotel Tripoli, in that big square behind the castle."

I knew exactly what sort of hotel the Tripoli was. Rather than a hotel, it was a third-rate restaurant, frequented at midday by farm workers and street hustlers, and in the evening by those my mother would call "women of ill repute." The bedrooms were situated above, on the first and second floors. And the owner of the locale—small, fat with a bowler tipped back on his crown and a toothpick between his gold-filled teeth, who, in summer, in his shirt sleeves, almost permanently sat by the entrance astride a kitchen stool—rented them out mainly by the hour, keeping the keys in his own pocket.

"True, it's not one of the finest hotels," Pulga continued, "and by night"—he sniggered—"it seems to be busy enough. And yet, you know, it's far from cheap. D'you want to know how much it costs a day for four people for board and lodging?"

"I wouldn't know."

"Fifty lire."

"Is that a lot?" I asked, uncertain.

"A lot? Do the math: five times four makes twenty. That's two thousand lire total per month. A fair sum, wouldn't you say? If you consider that my father, as a local doctor in Coronello, earned a monthly basic salary of only a thousand lire . . . "

I felt a wave of anxiety.

"And so how do you manage?"

"Well . . . I said a basic salary of a thousand lire. On top of that, though, there are home visits, operations, above all, operations. But even then, in the country, people would prefer to die rather than shell out! Then, take into account competition with the main hospital in Ferrara. Coronella is too close to the city. Ten kilometers is nothing."

He suddenly stared at me with his steady, ice blue eyes.

"But your father, what does he do?"

"He's also a doctor," I said, embarrassed. "But he doesn't practice."

"He doesn't practice?"

"No. Every now and then he pays a home visit, but for free, to friends. A couple of times a year he gets called out farther afield. For circumcisions," I added with an effort.

He didn't understand, and turned round to look at me. But he caught on quickly.

"Oh, I see, that's it . . . So, I guess you live off a private income?

"I think so."

At the Malfatti Bookshop, in Corso Roma, the textbooks he was searching for were all out of stock. They'd have to be ordered, the assistant explained, and given that the term was already far advanced, they wouldn't be likely to arrive for a fortnight.

I was expecting this news to disturb him. But he appeared relieved, or so it seemed to me. He dried the droplets of sweat that the heat of the shop had once again formed above his lip with a small handkerchief, and left the assistant with the list of books. He'd call back in a fortnight, he said, then went ahead of me toward the exit.

He wanted to accompany me back to my house. It was nearly one o'clock. I tried to dissuade him, telling him how far away Via Scandiana was, and that if he went along with me he wouldn't be back at the hotel before two.

"Oh, don't worry about that," he exclaimed, laughing. "The good thing about the restaurant is that you can eat when you want to."

"You and your family don't eat together then?"

"Yes, we do . . . at least in theory. But partly because my father returns from the country only in the evening, when he's finished his clinic, and partly because my mother is always out looking for flats . . . in the end we just eat together at supper and that's all. That must seem strange to you?"

He looked at me and laughed, jutting his protruding jaw sideways (a sure sign, according to my father, of a *"mauvais caractère"*). It was obvious that he envied me, envied me the order, the economic security, the bourgeois stability of my family, but it was clear he felt a slight contempt for me as well.

Perhaps afraid that he might have given himself away, he immediately began to thank me effusively for my help over the class work. If I hadn't been there to give him a hand—he said—who knows how he'd have been able to manage, and with teachers like Guzzo, it's obvious, the first impression you give him has enormous importance. But on that subject, why didn't I ask Guzzo to be transferred, so I could stay in the back row on a permanent basis, or at least until he had got hold of all the textbooks? That Cattolica, whom I shared with, had the look of a very well-behaved, well-brought-up boy. No doubt he's clever as well, exceptionally so. And yet, it has to be said, he's not very likeable. Isn't he perhaps a bit stuck up? His way of behaving, of looking at people, didn't it have a certain . . .

He interrupted himself.

"I don't mean to offend you," he added, scrutinizing me, "perhaps you're good . . . very close friends?" he asked anxiously.

I avoided his gaze.

"No, not especially," I replied.

As far as the books were concerned, I continued, he didn't have to worry, at school I could always lend them to him. But as for moving to sit by him, I wasn't sure I could do that. I didn't get on that well with Cattolica, but we'd sat together now for two months, and just to drop him like that . . . all things considered, we were something of a tried and tested partnership.

"But who do you do your homework with? With him?"

"No. I don't do homework with anyone."

We had almost arrived. We left Via Madama by Piazza Santa Maria in Vado and turned down Via Scandiana. "What was that kind of barrier down there at the end of the street?" Pulga asked me as he kept on walking, and at the same time pointed toward the mist-covered prow of the Montagnone, at which it seemed Via Scandiana came to a halt.

I stopped in front of the entrance to my house, pressed the bell, and turned round to explain to him what the Montagnone was. But he was already distracted by something else.

"Good heavens!" he exclaimed in a serious tone. "It's a mansion!"

He stepped back to the center of the street, keeping his gaze directed upward.

"Is it all yours?"

"Yes."

"It must have heaps of rooms!"

"Quite a few . . . Including the first and second floor, there must be something like fifty."

"And they're all taken just by your family?"

"Oh no. We only live in those on the second floor. There are tenants on the first floor."

"So you and your family live in twenty or so rooms?"

"More or less."

"But how many of you are there?"

"There are five of us. My father, my mother and us three children: that is me, my brother, Ernesto, and my sister, Fanny. Then you'd have to count the maids."

"How many of them do you have?"

"Two . . . and then one more who works part time."

"Twenty rooms! Imagine the cost to heat them. And the tenants?"

At that moment, the latch of the door sprang open. I raised my eyes. My mother was at the window.

"How come you're so late?" she asked, observing Pulga. "Come on in, your father's already sitting at the table."

"Good day, Signora," said Pulga, bowing slightly.

"Good day."

"This is a classmate of mine," I said. "Luciano Pulga."

"Very nice to meet you," my mother said, with a smile. "But come in quickly now if you don't want to make your father angry."

She withdrew from the windowsill and closed the window. And yet Pulga had still not decided to go. He approached the big double door, gently pushed one of its wings and leaned his head into the opening.

"May I come in for a second?" he asked, turning. "I'd like to have a quick look at the garden."

He silently walked ahead of me over the threshold while taking off his sports cap. Then, without taking his eyes off the door at the end, open onto the garden, he took another few steps on tiptoe. I watched him. He walked across the huge floor of waxed green and white tiles, with those cautious steps of his, a little stiff-jointed, like a small, solitary marsh bird.

He stopped. He kept looking around with his back turned to me, and in silence.

My lips moved of their own accord. I said:

"Would you like to come back to do your homework with me today?"

5.

MY MOTHER was delighted that I'd made a new friend.

She very much liked Luciano, from that first afternoon. When she came into the study, not only did he stand up, but he even kissed her hand. The gesture won her over utterly. A short while later, in fact, returning with a pot of tea—exceptionally good tea, accompanied by toast, butter, honey and blackcurrant jam and slices of ginger cake—she sat down to join us with this little feast and her dark eyes caressed Luciano with maternal solicitude while she spoke. She had asked about him, his family, his father's professional duties and, becoming anxious on behalf of his mother—busying herself from morning to night in search of an apartment—she offered any possible assistance to that end. Poor woman! she had sighed. Whatever she needed, she should phone her, please tell her to phone, and she would be more than happy to mobilize not only herself but all her women friends.

"How nice your friend is," she said later at table. "Yes, he really is polite and well brought up."

With that emphatic "he," she was evidently alluding to Otello Forti, whom she, being jealous, had always found too "coarse" and "sulky." Irritated, I didn't reply. It was true—I thought with my eyes fixed on my plate—rather than stay home, I had always preferred to go and study in Via Montebello, at the Fortis' house. But so what? How was it Otello's fault that ever since Roncati, the teacher at primary school in Via Bellaria, had placed us next to each other in the first desk of the central row, right in front of the teacher's podium, I had always preferred studying round at his house? As for hand-kissing and courtly stuff, Otello was an absolute nonstarter. But he was genuine, and sincere, perhaps too sincere . . .

Signora Pulga telephoned, and my mother wasn't slow in relating what she and that lady had talked about.

In a highly refined voice, wearied but very appealing, the lady was profuse in her thanks. She explained she had already found a house—outside Porta Reno was where it was, along the road out to Bologna, Via Coronella, that is—and so, as far as that was concerned there was no need for any kind soul to trouble herself on their behalf. But her Luciano! How could they ever forget, she and her husband, all that we had been doing to help her Luciano?

"Thank you, my deepest thanks, my dear Signora," she concluded. "At the moment, no, as we still have to organize the furnishings, and you know how much it costs to keep things in storage, but in a fortnight my husband and I would like permission to intrude on you with another phone call. My Oswald, as a doctor, would also very much like to make the acquaintance of your husband!"

"As a doctor?" my father grumbled, giving a faint, twisted grin, but happy, you could see, as he was whenever anyone remembered the subject in which he'd qualified. "More likely, they'll be after some money . . ."

Dr. Pulga was not after money at all, at least not from my father. Some days later, having called round (without his wife) at our house, he immediately made his intentions clear: he had come only to get to know a "colleague" and to have a chat. He then began to talk about himself. He had studied medicine in Modena, between 1908 and 1913. In 1914 he had married. From 1915 to 1917 he had fought on the Carso and in 1918 at Montello. In 1920, "due to a shortage of funds," he'd had to take on the practice in

Lizzano in Belvedere, which, after almost ten years in the most difficult conditions, he'd decided to leave, to take up this practice in Coronella. It was obvious—he'd added—that as far as medicine was concerned Ferrara and Bologna couldn't even be compared. But leaving aside Coronella's proximity to Ferrara, the Ferrarese medical establishment didn't at all seem, as it was in Bologna, to be controlled by a tight little mafia and thus hermetically sealed against any "infiltration." He himself knew, it could be said, all of the doctors in Bologna, from old Murri to Schiassi, from Nigrisoli to Putti, from Neri to Gasbarrini. He was even a family friend of the surgeon Bartolo Nigrasoli.

Of short stature, with a red face, "cyanotic" and green rolling eyes with a hyperthyroid aspect that glinted behind small lenses, Dr. Pulga—my father declared—wasn't someone who appealed to him. What a hideous way of talking! To claim to be a friend of this and that person in Bologna, an intimate of half the university and half of Sant'Orsola Hospital, and meanwhile to speak so ill of them, sparing nothing and no one! Bartolo Nigrisoli, for example, perhaps the finest wielder of a scalpel in Italy today, had always been an anti-Fascist. No harm in him remaining faithful to his own views. But to wish, as Dr. Pulga had had the *chutzpah* to wish, that he be thrown out of the Bologna "school," where his teaching risked "corrupting" so many youths—and at the same time proclaiming himself a friend of him and his family—my word, that really was a disgrace! And to cap it all, what kind of behavior was it to pay a visit and remain sunk in an armchair from three-thirty till eight? For heaven's sake, would you get going! If, by chance, Dr. Pulga were to call him on the phone, we had two choices—either tell him he was out or that he was ill in bed and couldn't move.

But Luciano? What was Luciano like?

The first impression of faint, physical repulsion had certainly remained, and daily familiarity had not erased it. Although he was clean, in both his person and his clothes, there was always something in him that perturbed me: it might have been the droplets of sweat that emerged among the blondish hairs above his upper lip at the slightest emotion, or the blackheads, scattered more or less everywhere on the waxy skin of his face, but denser around the temples and just under his nostrils, or the marked sideways movement of his jaw when he pronounced the "z," or else, though I'm not sure, the calloused, yellowy hue that strangely covered the palms of his hands, which were thin and oversized, a bit like a hunchback's. But for all the rest, I have to confess, that, especially in the beginning, his refugee-like humility, his total submissiveness, that of an inferior under protection, gave me an almost inebriated sense of satisfaction. In essence, my relations with Otello had never been so easy. He accepted my superiority, but made me pay for it in countless ways: with his continual muttering, with his mulish stubbornness—if, for instance, he came to my house, and that happened rarely enough, he'd always do so sighing with ill grace. And here we had a fellow of a very different stripe, for whom my house (he even told me so that very first day when I took him on a room-by-room tour of the apartment) was the most beautiful, welcoming and comfortable place he'd ever seen in his life, my mother the nicest and kindest mother of all, and myself a kind of prodigy of cleverness and brilliance, with regards to homework, an oracle before whom he could only listen in silence and awe. Although he was neither stupid nor inept—for in the question-and-answer sessions to which he was subjected for a whole month by all the teachers, from Guzzo to Krauss, from Bianchi to Razzetti, and "that one" who taught history and philosophy, he had always defended himself tooth and nail (and, however reluctantly, even Mazzanti had been unable to award him a lower mark than five)—he left me free to unravel the knotty passages, dictate aloud whatever I decided was right, and when I'd finished, limiting himself—while he was still writing it down in his notebook in his big, neat, slightly angular, feminine hand—to exclamations of applause, such as "Bravo!" "What a knockout!" "I've never seen anyone translate Greek so well!" "Lucky sod!" How relaxing, I would say to myself, what an easy life it is for Luciano Pulga! What a difference between him, who never needed to contribute (in practice, it was I alone who translated, so that if my mother had approached on tiptoe to eavesdrop behind the door—nor was it impossible that she did so, as I had heard the parquet creak in the next room more than once—she would have heard only one voice holding forth, mine), what a difference between him and Otello, who, whenever he opened his mouth, it was to play the contrarian or devil's advocate! But leaving Otello aside, if I'd managed, as at a certain point I was hoping to, to enter and be part of Cattolica's circle, imagine what a struggle I'd have had! The rivalry that divided us at school, sharpened by the irremovable presence of his two cronies, Boldini and Grassi, would certainly have continued round at his place. At Cattolica's house, yes: as for where we'd go to study, there would have been no discussion. Either his place or solitude, take it or leave it...

Luciano would arrive every afternoon around four o'clock, and wouldn't leave before seven-thirty or eight. Yet it's not as if we were always working. Besides the half hour for tea, every now and then we'd stop to chat. This was always up to Luciano to decide, for it was he, suddenly energetic and commanding, who would impose those brief pauses which my poor, tired brain had need of, just as, later, when he considered that I was sufficiently rested and relaxed, he would spur me on to further labors.

During the intervals, he did everything to entertain me, distract me, even amuse me. He was greatly in debt to me—for the protection I'd offered him from the first day, the books that I was still lending him, the hospitality of my home, the homework that, essentially, I did for him. And he therefore—he seemed to be saying—repaid me with the modest, but perhaps not contemptible gift of his presence and with his spectator's role of egging me on. It wasn't much. Little enough, that was true. But of one thing I could be sure—there was nothing more he was able to give.

He was careful not to boast about anything. Very often he would declare that he was without any ambitions, happy to remain confined within the limbo of "those who are suspended between a five and a six,"[*] as, he would add with a smile, standing out in one way or another, for good or for bad, one ended up "paying the price." It was as if he were saying, "I know I don't count for much—no, for even less than that." And yet the way he talked to me about school, for example, putting Mazzanti's fairness in doubt—he was sure that between me and Cattolica, he shamelessly favored Cattolica—or making me aware that down there, from the back row—a lowly position, to be sure, yet not without some advantages—he was afforded a much clearer and more objective vision of the whole class

---

[*] Pulga is quoting Dante's *Inferno*, canto ii, where Virgil in Limbo says he is "*tra color che son sospesi*": among those suspended.

than I could have, involved as I was in the struggle, the competition, in the glorious but also petty daily slog of coming out on top: in every phrase of his I could perceive his determination to be useful to me, even indispensable.

Confident that it would please me, he never missed an opportunity to speak ill of Cattolica.

In his view, Cattolica was nothing but a conceited bighead. Leaving aside the present company, how could I really compare the intelligence of Boldini with Cattolica's, or even that of Giorgio Selmi? The fact was that Boldini didn't want to come out on top—even being an underdog was a vocation!—and even less than that would do for Selmi, who aspired to nothing more than an average of seven. A plodder like Chiereghatti, though better organized and cannier—that was all Cattolica basically was! And, in fact, Guzzo, who was by no means stupid, and didn't let himself be dazzled, like Krauss and Razzetti, by mere feats of memory, when he sought out an answer a little out of the ordinary, usually left Cattolica well alone, and knew who to turn to . . . True, I wasn't especially well disposed to scientific subjects, or to be more precise I only applied myself in subjects I liked—Italian, Latin, Greek etc. But it would just have needed a little effort on my part—only last year in the math retake exam hadn't I passed with a good eight?—and he was willing to bet that even in math, in physics and in natural sciences that "Signor" Cattolica would be made to bite the dust.

"No, really, I don't think so." I weakly warded off the compliment. "I've never been any good at math."

"You've never been any good at it because you've never wanted to be."

"Maybe. But isn't that the same thing in the end?"

"It isn't the same thing. Being able is one thing, wanting to is another."

"In my opinion, it's a question of the grey matter, of the brain's development just not being adapted to it."

When I threw out that phrase with a smile, Luciano jumped up in protest. For me, of all people, to argue such a thing!

The way he looked at me, serious, intense, and at the same time respectful, I understood that he was awaiting my permission to remind me of the mathematical genius of my race—my father too, with an excellent head for figures, was convinced that we Jews were the best mathematicians in the world, attributing my scarce aptitude seriously enough to the peasant blood of my grandmother Maria. I pretended not to understand and let the topic drop.

But he was right, and bit by bit he was becoming indispensable to me. With that in mind, I remember one afternoon toward the end of February when, because of the snow, he was late for our meeting.

Unexpectedly, the snow had begun to fall in the morning, around nine thirty. How beautiful and moving it was to see from inside the classroom, the small silent flakes as they slowly fell against the blackish background of the Church of Gesù, and then, on leaving, to find Via Borgoleoni entirely mantled in white. It caused the usual festivities. At the school gates, a big snowball fight broke out, during which Luciano and I had utterly lost sight of each other, but it didn't matter, as it was understood that at four o'clock we would meet up as usual.

After lunch, rather than abating, the snowfall became heavier. At five, oddly uneasy, I was already wondering if Luciano would have been able to make his way on foot from the remote district of Foro Boario as far as Via Scandiana. Perhaps today he might not manage it—I said to myself, looking out the window. Perhaps it would be better if I started my studies alone.

I sat down at the desk with my notebook and with the textbook open before me, but I couldn't concentrate. The Pulgas still needed to install a telephone at their house. Yet if Luciano had really meant not to come, it was reasonable to suppose he could all the same have found some way of warning me, bothering to walk to the chemist's fifty meters away to phone me. Whenever there was any urgent need, the Pulgas made use of that facility. He had told me so himself.

At a quarter past five, I stood up again, and went to the window once more. Outside it was already dark. And if I were to go to Luciano's house? Besides, that would only be fair.

I opened the window. I leaned out, breathed the air and looked down. The snow continued falling, but more feebly now, reduced to a kind of dust dancing weightlessly around the yellowish streetlamps. Down in the street an immaculate blanket of snow, compact and even, had covered and softened every protuberance. Neither the cobbles nor the curbs could be distinguished anymore.

And then, down there, while my heart was beating madly, beating with a joy mixed as ever with its opposite, I suddenly made out Luciano himself, as he swiftly slipped inside the gate at that very moment.

6.

IN THE early days, to amuse me, Luciano had recourse to two equally inexhaustible repertoires: he told jokes in Bolognese dialect or he dredged up memories from his childhood. These were also comic. They were all centered on Lizzano in Belvedere and the mountain villages thereabout—Poretta, Vidiciatico, Madonna dell'Acero, Corno alle Scale: names which quickly became familiar to me, and invariably figured himself as the main character, including those stories which referred to his father, his mother or his brother Nando. The role he reserved for himself never changed. It was always that of the sly operator, the clever and quick-witted trickster, deft not only with his mind but also his hands and feet. Perhaps they were only pure inventions and fantasies, but I enjoyed them no less for that. I laughed as if I was watching a farce by Ridolini or Charlie Chaplin. Luciano, too, seemed happy enacting them and pleased by their success.

Later there was a change.

It happened by chance, I'd say, one evening in March when a violent storm broke out, and from then on, the nature of his talk completely altered.

At seven o'clock I saw him stand up.

"Are you going?"

"I think I ought to."

"Don't you want to stay for supper? If you'd like I'll go and tell my mother."

He stared at me. He was already tying up his books with his belt, but he paused.

"Thanks, thanks a lot . . . " he stammered, shifting his lower jaw to the side more than ever. "But I don't want to be any bother."

"What d'you mean? I'll go tell her now."

I got up and rushed toward the door.

"Wait a moment!"

I turned. Standing up by the table lamp, he seemed paler than usual, with his blue eyes deeply in shadow in his little bony face, while the base of his aquiline nose and bulbous forehead stood out in the light.

"No, don't bother. They're expecting me at home."

I argued that it wouldn't take much to ring the chemist's near his house.

"Alright, that's fine, but after supper . . . " he said in an unconvinced tone, still staring hard at me, "I won't be able to stay overnight."

I hesitated.

"Why not?" it cost me to ask, turning toward the table. "We could easily put up a camp bed in my room."

He didn't reply. He walked to the window and looked out.

"Is it still raining?" I asked.

"It's eased off a bit."

He moved back to the center of the room and sat down in the armchair.

"All things considered, it was much better when we were staying at the Hotel Tripoli," he said. "Living in the Foro Boario area will be fine in summer, but in winter it's worse than Lizzano. It must be the new built walls, but you've no idea how cold it gets, and how damp."

I asked if they didn't have radiators.

The question was unimportant. And yet when I was asking it, something warned me I was straying into a danger zone. I suddenly felt that we were sliding toward an intimacy which till then we'd kept at a distance, an intimacy which I had to avoid at any price.

But it was too late. Luciano was already explaining how his father, instead of the central heating whose installation remained beyond their financial possibilities for now, had bought two terracotta Becchi stoves. That kind of heater worked perfectly well, on condition, it's clear, that the pipes go directly upward. Instead his father, "stubborn thickhead" that he'd always been, had decided one day that the pipes should be laid crossways from room to room, halfway up the wall. The result: you just had to light a piece of paper and the whole house immediately filled with smoke. So, you die of asphyxiation!

I was shocked by that "stubborn thickhead," by the abandonment of every reserve and caution on his part. What had happened? I wondered, fearfully. What was happening?

Despite recalling the very negative impression Dr. Pulga had made on my father, I tried to take up his defence. Useless. Luciano only redoubled his attacks. Not only was his father a thickhead—he repeated—but a miser and violent to boot. I let him talk on. When he came home in a bad mood, his first instinct was to take it out on his family. He often ended up hitting every one of them.

Were these, too, inventions and fantasies? They might have been. On the other hand, it wasn't the truth that mattered, even here. What mattered was the altered tone in which he spoke to me, the unexpected crudeness, without any tact, the ill mannered bitterness in his voice.

"Really?" I said breathlessly. "He hits your mother as well?"

"Oh, it's mainly her that he hits, the scumbag!" Luciano replied. And yet—he added, grinning—it was obviously her, "wretch" that she was, who wanted to be hit. In essence, his mother liked to be beaten: that was the actual truth. And he, his father, who had understood that perfectly, he kept her happy. As best he could.

He burst out laughing.

"The mysteries of the human heart!" he exclaimed. "What d'you think, that it's only men who are disgusting? Women are too, you can be sure of that, women too!"

Aside from the radiators chugging away at full throttle, the Hotel Tripoli—he went on—was better even in that respect because it offered an accurate picture of things, of life as it really was "without sugaring the pill." Had I ever seen the owner, that pig with a German name, Müller, always sitting there, on the ground floor behind the restaurant till? The couples who came in to "have a little afternoon siesta" didn't even have to stop to eat something. All they had to do was stride past the tables straight up to him, and he, without the slightest pause, would just hand over the key. What a laugh, though, to see some of the couples that turned up! Usually, country folk, with the "cheap whores" who had picked the yokels up in the square. But sometimes, it was a youngster from the city, who'd come in for a quick reconnaissance, take the key and disappear upstairs, to be followed a minute or so later by the girl, the "chick," who would slip in "all guilty looking." Chick? Hardly! Often enough it was more like a "fat old hen," a forty year-old, a mother, perhaps even a grandmother, sweating sin from every pore of her leathery face. These were the "consorts" of engineers, of lawyers, of doctors—recognizable as such at first glance. Women from the best society, in short, who would be quite capable of displaying themselves from the height of their box in the town theater that very evening as if nothing had happened, or boldly prancing about for the crowd and swaying their backsides along Viale Cavour the day after. God's truth, it was a total joke!

The alarm clock on the table showed it was seven thirty. The parquet in the adjoining room creaked. My mother leaned in at the door and observed us with satisfaction.

"Have you finished yet?" she asked.

Lost in reverie, I looked at her. Yes—I confirmed—we've just finished.

With his usual promptitude, Luciano had leaped to his feet.

"Poor thing!" my mother commiserated. "To have to go by foot all the way past the docks in all this rain. Do you have an umbrella? And galoshes? If you'd like to stay for supper, you only have to say."

"Thanks a lot, Signora," Luciano replied, "but as I was just saying to him"—he nodded at me—"I'd prefer not to. If my mother and father don't see me come back . . . well, they'll be annoyed, you know how it is."

My mother insisted. It would be simple to phone to ask their permission. But Luciano wouldn't be persuaded. They spoke, he standing beside the armchair, more suave and saccharine than ever, she in the doorway, enfolding him in the caress of her dark-eyed gaze. Remaining seated, I watched one and then the other. I followed the movements of their lips, but most of their words I couldn't understand or hear.

At last my mother withdrew.

"I tell you it's a total joke," Luciano resumed in a lowered tone, as soon as he'd assured himself with a glance that the door was properly shut, "the way they behave—it's fun to watch, mainly it's a laugh."

It's like the sleaziest port, he continued, the Hotel Tripoli by night! He slept with his brother Nando, who fell so fast asleep, as soon as he was under the covers, not even a bombardment would wake him, because of which he heard nothing—the "poor innocent!"—neither the quarrels that broke out in the adjoining room between their parents every night before they went to bed—quarrels that ended often enough in furious blows— nor the noises of every kind that filtered through the paper-thin wall on the other side. They'd "go to work" flat out, over there. All night there'd be shudders, sighs, creaking springs—a complete disaster if you wanted a wink of sleep. But who even thought of sleeping? Only that meek little mouse of a Nando. As for him, it didn't even cross his mind to go to sleep. He'd be there till the small hours in his nightshirt, his ear glued to the wall, wide awake and alert as could be, checking out when different voices announced "a changing of the guard." Some nights in the next-door room there were as many as five different couples, one after another. Every now and then he'd get up and watch.

"And watch?"

"That's right. Through the keyhole of the communicating door."

"And what could you see?"

"What could I see? Oh . . . sadly, I wasn't always able to because the bed was placed right behind the keyhole and besides, it was really high, you know that type of double bed. But I glimpsed something, you can be sure of that."

For example, once, he continued, he had seen someone's back looming up above the headboard. It was a woman's, moving up and down, "Hup! Hup!" just as if she were riding a trotting horse. Another time he'd seen a couple walking around the room stark naked, so that every so often they'd be in range of the keyhole showing "their fronts and their backsides." On another occasion, a couple, instead of using the bed, had preferred to make love on the floor, very close to the door. And if that time, however desperately he'd strained his eye to look down, he hadn't managed to see a thing, as a recompense he'd been able to hear, which was perhaps even better.

"Better?"

"You bet it was! More than the sighs, the stifled cries, you should have heard the words they said to each other. Juicy stuff! It went on and on."

At that moment, the maid entered. She told us dinner was on the table, so Luciano was forced to interrupt his tale and leave.

But in the following days, taking more and more time off from our homework, it was he who kept returning to this kind of talk. I was weak, passive, unable to react, and he made the most of it.

He told me, among other things, that he was reading an amazing book, *Aphrodite*, by Pierre Louÿs: doubly amazing, he explained, for its literary achievement and its "highly instructive" contents. He recounted how he'd had to read it, just a few pages at a time, mainly at night, with one hand ready to turn the page and the other no less ready to accompany the salient points of the story with "a vigorous royal wave."

"Will you lend it to me?" I asked.

"What?" he replied with a grin. "The book?"

I nodded.

"I don't know . . . if we're talking of the book," he went on, looking hard at me with his enamel-blue eyes, "I'm not sure I can. My father guards his tomes jealously. It's a passion of his!"

To get his "paws on" this or any other book of equal interest which his father kept on a special shelf in his study, under surveillance—he continued—he would generally have to wait until night time, when everyone was asleep, taking great care to put everything back as it was. With this "trick" he had been able to read nearly all of Pigrilli's novels, *The Garden of Punishments* by a French author whose name he'd forgotten, Weininger's *Sex and Character*, and *The Betrothed*, not obviously the one by Manzoni, which in the fourth and fifth year we'd already had up to here, but those other betrotheds written about by my "co-religionist," Da Verona, who were infinitely more worthwhile in his opinion. In any case, he added, raising a hand to forestall any possible protest on my part, in any case *Aphrodite* by the "said" Louÿs beat every one of those other books hands down. Did I want to know what was described in the first part of the novel? It described a garden, the one that surrounded the goddess's temple, where scores of women coupled "in every imaginable way both with men and with each other." And they invented innumerable ways and positions for doing this, so that even he, who, all modesty aside, had a fair knowledge of such things, was left with his mouth agape.

Till then I had never masturbated. When Luciano learned this, he was astonished. How's that possible? At my age! Since he was ten he'd always masturbated at least once a day.

"But doesn't it do any harm?"

"Harm!? On the contrary, it does you nothing but good. It's possible," he said smilingly, "that doing it too much might wear out the memory a bit. But conversely, it broadens the mind incredibly."

In his view, there was nothing better to develop the "intellectual faculties." Of course, one shouldn't go overboard, the same way you shouldn't drink to excess or, say, overindulge in sports. And yet it was good for you. It was a normal and natural "practice," and Nature, if one knew how to interpret "scientifically" the impulses it instilled in us, wouldn't give us such impulses to harm us. But was it possible circumcision had blunted my "sexual proclivities"? Had I ever had any erections? And at night had I ever had any "wet dreams"?

I replied as best I could, admitting everything, even when I hadn't properly understood: which was to say that yes, often in the most unexpected moments, my "thing" got hard, and that one or two mornings I'd woken with my nightshirt covered with wet patches.

One afternoon Luciano unbuttoned his short trousers and showed me his member. He presumed that I would then do the same. I had always been extremely shy and so refused. But he insisted and I ended up doing as he asked.

He inspected it carefully, leaning a little forward, with the dispassionate air of a doctor. "So that's all a circumcision is?"—he burst out laughing. He'd always believed it was a fairly serious operation. It was really nothing, he could now see well enough. In the end, what was the big difference between his and mine?

He unbuttoned himself again to verify.

It went on like this until Easter, with the continual feeling on my part of being impelled step by step toward something unknown and threatening, but without anything in particular ever happening. Luciano talked and talked. His voice held me suspended; shut me up in its low, resonant spirals.

I have few precise memories of that period. I lived as though in an underground tunnel—unable to see the end of it, but fearing that I would suddenly find myself up against it. I recall a sense of abject complicity, which rose in me every time my mother came in. And I also recall one

afternoon during the Easter holidays, perhaps not even an actual afternoon, but only one that I dreamed.

I had gone to play soccer on the Spianata behind the Aquaduct with
half of the class. We began around two o'clock, happy to run on the dry
grass burnt by the winter frosts till we were out of breath, and happy to
have shed our heavy clothes. The lovely sunlight lit up even the dark bell
towers of the military storehouses, gave a shine to the mossy marble of the
statue of Pope Clement, usually so melancholic and lonesome-looking,
and gilded the blue distance of the first houses on Via Ripagrande and Via
Piangipane. Around three, Luciano came along as well, on foot, of course.
Like Cattolica, he wasn't particularly keen to play, and besides he was too
skinny, too puny, and no one wanted him on their team. Stamping his feet
to warm them up, he was left on the sidelines as a spectator. While we were
playing, every now and then we'd hear his commentary—applause, or
hissing and jeering. Every time I looked at him, he seemed to be smiling—
I guessed at, rather than saw, the grin on his pallid little mug. And I knew
why he was staying there. For me. After the match finished he'd want to
perch on the handlebars of my bike and to steer it as far as Via Garibaldi, to
the corner of Via Garibaldi and Via Colomba, where with perfect ease we
could spy on the men who entered and left through the little nailed doors
of the brothels.

It was almost dusk. And then, just as we were about to pack in the
game, I fell and hurt my knee. Nothing serious, I knew that perfectly well,
but still I took some time to get up, in short, making "a bit of a scene," I lay
there with my eyes shut, my aching limbs suffused, little by little, with an
extraordinary sense of wellbeing, glad that the match had ended because
of this accident, and glad that three or four friends gathered round me were
making gentle attempts to set me on my feet. In the pungent evening air,
above my outstretched body, I could hear their lulled voices, and I wanted
never to get up.

"Give over, it's not as if he's dead," someone finally said. "Can't you see
he's just hamming it up? Come on, let's go and get changed." I heard their
steps moving away and half opened my eyes. I peeked through lowered
lashes. Standing in silence beside me—and huge when seen from below,

coldly observing me from head to toe as if I was a mere thing—no one remained but Luciano.

7.

THE DAY before term began I fell ill with tonsillitis.

I had suffered from that from earliest childhood—that was why my Aunt Malvina was so keen to take me on visits to the Church of San Biagio, protector of the weak-throated. But that year the inflammation seemed more acute than usual. It was caused by an abscess, my father declared, and my Uncle Giacomo, immediately called in by my mother, was of the same opinion.

To operate or not to operate?

Often in agreement as far as the diagnosis was concerned, my father and my uncle always quarrelled about the treatment. And so, to resolve the eternal dispute at my bedside between the two doctors of the family (my father favored intervening, my uncle not), my mother thought it best to telephone the throat specialist, Dr. Fadigati. It had been Fadigati who had operated on my tonsils when I was a baby. To placate my uncle, they had only been partly removed. No one, then, was better placed than he to decide on the best treatment . . .

Fadigati arrived, examined my throat, confirmed the diagnosis. As for the treatment, he too, like my uncle, held the view that, for now, with this temperature I had, a "little incision" might be dangerous. We needed to wait. Around the seventh or eighth day, we'd have a better idea whether to make the most of the occasion—here, the doctor, who was already smiling at me, stretched out his hand and stroked my cheek—finally to be rid of "the whole works."

There was no need for that. The fever broke on its own. It was true that the two tonsil stumps might cause trouble if they were left there, but once again the decision was made to take no further action. They might, however, discuss the issue further in June, before we left for the seaside.

I breathed a sigh of relief. And yet I wasn't happy, or, rather, I was made uneasy by the anticipated recovery which would hasten my return to school. I thought nervously about Luciano. He'd only visited me once.

He'd turned up on the second or third day, when I still had a very high fever. Seated composedly by my bedside, even during the brief times when my mother left the room, he spoke of nothing but school matters: which verse they'd got up to in translating *The Iliad*, which of Horace's *Odes* Guzzi had set us, what Krauss was currently teaching, and so on. I kept quiet and listened. At a certain point, speaking with some difficulty, I had asked him if, by chance, given that I was ill, he hadn't thought of doing his homework round at someone else's house? To which he'd replied, smiling affectionately, no, it hadn't crossed his mind "to two time" me. What did I take him for? A Judas? Rather than worry about that, I should make every effort to recover. As soon as I got better—as far as the schedule went I shouldn't worry: clever as I was, I'd catch up in a jiffy—we would resume our "expert tandem team." And it was precisely this last prospect which, in the following days, filled me with an obscure reluctance. School and Luciano. Returning to the first meant continuing with the second also.

Continuing with Luciano. But what would that really mean?

In bed, convalescent, I abandoned myself to strange thoughts without restraint. Again and again, I paced through the dark tunnel of the last months, from that morning on which Luciano had first appeared at the door of the classroom until, conversation by conversation, we had begun to "bite the bullet," as he called it. I knew well enough how it had come about. It had all hung on my question about the central heating. The rest, including the mutual display of our penises, had quickly followed on its own from that. I saw the whole scene again. After he had got me to undress, Luciano had leaned forward to examine me, while adopting an impassive expression, but at the same time seeming a bit disappointed. Was it possible, he seemed to be thinking, that I who was so much more stocky, robust and sporty than him, was so small in that department? And when he in turn had unbuttoned himself—I could never have guessed that a skinny guy like him would be hiding such a disproportionate thing in his trousers—swollen, white, but above all huge—seeing it, I had felt an uncontrollable sense of disgust grip me in the stomach. Disgust, revulsion. If I continued seeing Luciano, every minute spent with him would be steeped in that revulsion. Latin and Greek would be a walk in the park compared to that!

And if I were to ditch him? If, offering some excuse, I were to get him off my back?

At home, that maneuver might perhaps have worked without hindrance. I would only need to tell some fib, letting Luciano be the one who had made the first move that led to the break up, or to invent some quarrel. My mother would almost certainly be consoled by the crucial fact that I kept on doing my homework at home. But at school it wouldn't have been anything like as easy. Even though I had always been a bit ashamed in front of the others of my friendship with Luciano—up there in Krauss's class, unfortunately, we sat next to each other, but when Mazzanti, before giving him a mark, felt obliged to consult me, most often I didn't reply, annoyed and shrugging my shoulders—all the same, everyone knew that he came round to my place to study every afternoon. Then there was Cattolica. There was also Giorgio Selmi. Cattolica had always pretended not to notice my partnering up with that "arse-licker Pulga"—as Luciano was referred to within the exclusive circles of the ex-A section. He had never given me the satisfaction of mentioning it, so that if I were now to break with Luciano his triumph would be too prodigious, too overwhelming, too hard to bear. As for Giorgio Selmi, who recently in gym—Luciano was exempted because of a weakness due to pleurisy in childhood—had had the hypocrisy to come up and complain to me about being on his own and had proposed I share a desk with him next year; he too needed to be kept at a distance. To break with Luciano now, all of a sudden, would be to give him too swift a victory, to drop my trousers in front of him as well.

I went back to school, and immediately after, Luciano began coming round to my house once again.

I had been off school for rather too long and therefore had to make up the lost time, so that it was easy to keep him in line for the first few days: I imposed my authority—"Let's cut the chatter." Yet I knew that soon enough we would once again broach those old topics, oh how well I knew it! There was the vaguely sardonic expression in the depths of Luciano's eyes as confirmation of this; and, even more, there were some imperceptible changes in his behavior—for instance, the way he was much less adulatory toward me, the way he allowed himself periods of distraction which would have been inconceivable earlier on, his humming in a low voice, waiting, while I beavered away at a sentence not perhaps as tricky as I was pretending it was. "Right, go ahead then, if it really means so much to you," he seemed to be saying. "But does it really? Don't think I can't guess what you too would really prefer to concentrate on."

All the same, one afternoon something new happened.

I had gone to a lesson at the gym some way off in Via Praìsolo, after which I'd agreed with Luciano that we would meet up at my house around six. At the end of the lesson, one of our classmates, leaving the gym, had brought out a rubber soccer ball, and then a game immediately kicked off in the huge courtyard in front. Rather than a game, it was a tangled series of scuffles without head or tail, but still. The absolute prohibition—that I should not sweat—the same one that a little earlier, during the gym lesson, had forced me to sit it out on a little bench, returned, to fill me with a searing, aching envy. With my back propped against the surrounding wall which separated the courtyard from Via Praìsolo, I kept watching the others running around, jumping, shouting, sweating, and, more than ever, I felt like a social reject, a weakling, a wretch, in every way deserving to end up with Luciano Pulga as my only companion.

I wasn't alone, though.

Cattolica was there too. Instead of sauntering off home as was his wont, he'd stopped to watch. He too was leaning against the wall, and had lit a cigarette without saying a word. But suddenly he approached me, and most unexpectedly, slipped his arm under mine.

"It annoys you not being able to play, doesn't it?" he said with sympathy.

I replied truthfully that I really wanted to, but that unfortunately I couldn't. For some time, I'd been ill—I added unnecessarily—and my father, who was a doctor, had wanted me not to get hot and sweaty on any account.

Cattolica stood listening to me patiently and attentively. A fair bit taller than me, he listened with his head tilted a little forward—a characteristic posture for him when something or someone interested him.

"Perhaps it's an indiscreet question," he finally said, "but what was the illness you had? I haven't been following the daily bulletins of Pulga," he added ironically. "I thought he mentioned a sore throat."

Daily bulletins? And Luciano hadn't shown his face more than that once, nor, strangely, had he even telephoned to find out how I was!

"I had an abscess," I replied.

He furrowed his brow.

"Is it painful?"

"Fairly." I smiled, staring at him. "I wouldn't wish it on my worst enemies."

He blinked.

"Sorry to hear that," he said. "If I'd known, I too would have come round to see you."

Despite that "too," my heart began beating fast. Cattolica round at my house! The poignant image of him, the repentant and sympathetic rival, beside my sickbed, formed in my mind. But I didn't believe him. I couldn't trust him.

"It hurt like hell," I said, "especially the first few days. It looked as though they'd have to cut it out. Then luckily the abscess burst on its own . . . It's likely they'll have to operate on my tonsils. Not now, but in June, before we go to the seaside."

We kept up the conversation like this, standing next to each other, for a good ten more minutes. Although Cattolica had meanwhile unlinked his arm from mine, all the same I felt his presence, his closeness. What did he want, I asked myself? And it made me doubly uneasy: both on account of what he might want and of the obligation that it put on me, to cut a good figure, to act with dignity.

"You live round here, don't you?" he asked at a certain point.

Yes. In Via Scandiana. Close by the Palazzo Schifanoia. Have you ever seen the Schifanoia frescoes?"

"No. Two or three weeks ago, I went as far as Santa Maria in Vado. We live near the station. In Via Cittadella."

"Oh yes?"

"It's a very nice area," Cattolica went on with the indomitable confidence he usually showed when speaking about anything concerning himself. "Brand-new . . . modern . . . "

He interrupted himself. "Listen—why not come round to my place today to do your homework?"

I turned to look him in the face.

"To your house!"

"Why not?"

He was smiling, chuffed at having made me gawp.

"Call in at your house, collect your books and then come round. 16, Via Cittadella. How long would it take on your bike? Ten minutes, more or less."

"Thanks a lot . . . But, sorry, don't you do your homework with Boldini and Grassi?"

"Of course," he replied with the air of a gambler who, seeing he's been beaten, shows his cards. "But what does that matter?"

"Oh, not at all . . . Only that if there's already three of you, a fourth would be a crowd."

He straightened his back and looked away.

He then replied that, on the contrary, one more wouldn't make any difference; it would be far from crowded. In his room, there was a huge table, so big—he smiled with pride—that if you wanted to, you could seat the whole class around it—"the girls as well." And then—he went on—Boldini and Grassi, he could assure me, would have nothing against me joining them, nothing against me, they three had studied together for years now . . .

He turned to look at me.

"You understand," he said in conclusion.

I had understood only too well. Between Boldini and Grassi on one side and me on the other, he would have to choose them, his old companions, his faithful courtiers and yes-men. Besides, it was similarly obvious and undeniable that between his house and mine, it was his house, his room, his table that I, too, needs must prefer. My house, whatever it might contain, was a place in the city that he, from Via Cittadella, wouldn't dream of considering as something definite, something that actually existed, with a roof, under which I and my family happened to live. And that "ass-licker Pulga" who came round every day to my house? He, too, didn't exist; Luciano too was an abstract being, who could be ignored, a futile, irksome topic on which it wasn't worth squandering a single word.

"Yes, I understand, and thanks," I replied. "But, look, today it's not feasible. Pulga's coming round to my house, and there's no way of rearranging . . . If only I could phone him . . . "

"Doesn't he have a telephone?"

"Not yet. He lives a long way off in the Foro Boario area, beyond the Docks, and to get him on the phone's a nightmare. You have to call a chemist near his house. But better not, there's a good chance the man will get annoyed. And anyway, it's late. As he doesn't have a bike, it's likely he'll be on his way already."

Without saying more, we made our way toward the exit. At the door, we paused, still undecided. I had to go to the left, and he to the right.

"Well, bye, then," he said coldly, extending his hand.

"Aren't you waiting for Boldini and Grassi?"

"No. Those two are on their bikes. I'm taking the tram."

"Unless . . . " I resumed, without letting go of his hand, " . . . unless I could bring him along too. I could go home first, ask him, then we could come together."

That would solve the problem—I thought, looking searchingly into his eyes with ill concealed anxiety. All things considered, that would solve the problem splendidly. For me, anyway.

"Can I bring him along?"

"Him who?" Cattolica said with a scornful grimace, withdrawing his hand. "Pulga?"

"Didn't you just say that your table was so big? So, if there would be four of us, then . . . "

He reacted confusedly.

"No way. Five of us! And Pulga to boot! You must be joking?"

"Joking why?" I replied very coolly. "What's so wrong with Pulga that you people have to treat him like he has the plague?"

I was deeply offended and wanted him to know it.

"He's been coming round to my place every day since January, and I can't see any sign I've caught it from him."

But Cattolica was right—I couldn't help thinking, even while I was still speaking. Luciano really did have the plague, and by having been so close to him, he'd infected me with it too.

Cattolica sighed.

"*De gustibus*. You are free as can be to invite anyone you want to your house. I repeat: if you want to come round to mine, fine, but him, no. Never. Not a chance!"

"Well . . . if that's how it is," I murmured in a trembling voice, near to tears as I was, "I'm sorry, but it's either both of us or neither."

8.

THAT EVENING Cattolica and I parted brusquely, or rather it was him who uttered a terse "goodbye," turned his back, and hurried off toward Corso Giovecca. But, the morning after, he returned determinedly and insistently to the fray. Without once alluding to the strange conversation we'd had, he did his utmost, I couldn't help noticing, to remove the invisible barrier that had separated us till then.

It wasn't as if he ever turned round during lessons. His gaze, as ever, fixed immovably on the teacher seated in front of the class, he continued to show me his finely carved profile, covering his mouth with his hand opened like a fan, whispering under the shadow of his fingers. He was too zealous and disciplined, too attached to his reputation as a model pupil— in regard to behavior as well—to dispense with these basic precautions. And yet I realized that the perfect straightness of his neck and body, which I effortfully tried to imitate, was dedicated not as much to the eyes in front of him as to the more dangerous eyes, because they lay outside his control, of whoever was behind him. If Luciano, back there from his desk by the wall, had realized that there was no longer the former coldness between me and Cattolica, and that we even spoke to each other, continuously, he would perhaps have been able to guess the topic of our whispering. It was absurd from my perspective. I certainly felt guilty enough toward Luciano to sense, almost physically, the icy touch of his blue, interrogating irises on the back of my neck.

Imagine my astonishment the morning that Guzzo himself turned in surprise toward Cattolica.

He was scanning aloud a Catullus poem, the one that begins: "*Multas per gentes et multa per aequora vectus . . .*"*

He stopped suddenly, and in a muted tone gave the order:

---

* "Conveyed through many lands and over many seas," Catullus, 101.

"Cattolica, continue."

"Me?" asked Cattolica, astonished, touching his chest.

"Indeed. None other," confirmed Guzzo, whose anger generally induced him to slip into Tuscan dialect. "Carry on scanning the line, my dear chap. Let's see how you manage."

Cattolica began, breathlessly, to flick through the book, which was open, but not at the right page. Who knows how long his torment would have lasted—motionless at the far side of the desk I didn't dare help him— if, at last, from behind, Malagù's raised hand hadn't come to his aid. "Well done, Malagù," Guzzo remarked. "I'm delighted that you are following, that the good Catullus is of interest even to you . . . But you, Cattolica, tell me: does he not interest you, is he not to your taste, perhaps?"

"No . . . it's not . . . " stammered Cattolica, very pale in the face, slowly getting to his feet.

"No?" Guzzo responded, with a grin.

He arched his thick eyebrows which stood at the base of his vast, Wagnerian forehead like two grey circumflexes—being an atheist, a "pagan," as he had boasted on innumerable occasions, he never lost the chance to make fun of those whom, like Camurri, or indeed Cattolica, he suspected of belonging to clerical families.

"*Passer deliciae meae puellae,*"* he declaimed softly, while winking at the rest of the class. "Is it that little joking gallantry you reproach him for? You won't forgive him for that?"

"I like him a lot," Cattolica heatedly denied the accusation. "It's only that . . . "

"Only that you," Guzzo cut him short, "for a good while, taking advantage, with some hypocrisy, of my good opinion, have taken to paying scant attention. *Scantinamus,* unceasingly. I see you, don't think I don't, you and your good neighbor tirelessly gabbing away *sub tegmine manuum.*† What's wrong with the two of you? Do you think—mistakenly—that you've already well and truly passed? Or is it the spring that's affecting you?"

Cattolica turned, as if to ask me to bear witness. But he said nothing.

---

* "Sparrow, my darling's pet," Catullus, 2.
† *Sub tegmine manuum*: under the cover of (your) hand (Latin).

He turned back toward Guzzo, whose eyes meanwhile were slowly scanning all the desks.

"I wonder," Guzzo said at last, "whether it wouldn't be wise to proceed without further delay to the separation of this pair who by now have grown only too well attuned. In any case, my dear Cattolica, you have been warned. If I catch you chattering once more, I'll send you back there, to the back row, to sit next to that saintly fellow Pulga. Have you understood?"

He unscrewed his pen top, opened his ledger, and immersed himself in writing a long negative report.

Once out on the street, we never tried to stay together, since as soon as we were outside the school the usual configurations reformed, and Luciano was there, ready to glue himself to my side, very often not leaving me until we were at the corner of Via Terranova, halfway up Corso Giovecca. But apart from the afternoons when we saw each other for gym lessons (at least two of them), we began to phone each other in the evening, usually before going to bed.

What did we talk about? I couldn't say; I've forgotten.

I suppose we talked about the teachers, about our schoolmates, about the books we were reading—we had utterly different tastes: I preferred cloak-and-dagger novels of adventure, Dumas, Ponson du Terrail, Verne, and the *Children's Encyclopaedia*; he was more advanced and liked books of popular science and fictionalized biographies. We talked, I suppose, about things without much importance when set beside what was brewing. But how else could we have behaved? The sound of our words was the ink with which the cuttlefish, in order to flee from a threat, darkens the water around it. Under the refuge of that acoustic ink we kept on studying, brushing against each other the cautious tentacles we had extended.

However, what Cattolica told me about Boldini and Grasso, I remember very well indeed.

Against all my expectations, Cattolica displayed an absolute freedom of judgement toward them. In his opinion, Boldini had "an excellent brain." He lacked imagination, though, that flair which always accompanied true intelligence. Very ordered, punctual as a Swiss watch, over-precise, he was too closed up in himself, too egotistical. In the six years he'd known him, he'd never been able to put together a coherent argument, never any proper reasoning. At every attempt of his, Boldini always replied with the usual grunts, the usual whistling through his teeth, the same old pats on the back. He was strong, that was certainly true, more than strong. Last month he had swum across the River Po, up at the Giarina, when the temperature was almost sub-zero. But all considered, he was a mediocrity, and his cultish devotion to building up his muscles was abundant proof of that. As for Grassi, although his mind and character were the opposite of "that other one," he didn't amount to much either. He read a great deal, knew masses of things, but at the end of the day, what did that count for? . . . Boldini never read a single book that wasn't an assigned text, and that, it was clear, was a mistake. But Grassi read too much, at random, with the result that he stuffed his head with junk and made his short-sightedness worse day by day. Was he a good character? He tried hard enough to be considered as such, with that sickly air of a Silvio Pellico!* But at the end of the day he was sincere, a friend you could count on . . . Maturity, balance, a harmony between their various mental and physical qualities, that was what they were both missing, Boldini as much as Grassi.

By such criticism, it became evident that it was his intention to place himself and me on another, higher plane. But I didn't let myself become spellbound. Hearing him hold forth in that way about his best friends made me more distrustful than ever.

I had a burning desire to teach him a lesson. For this reason, too, I often made a point of speaking well of Luciano. He wasn't an idiot at all—I would say—nor was he the hypocrite everyone thought him. I understood that he looked unprepossessing, and from the beginning even I'd had to overcome no small internal resistance. On the other hand, if one were only to choose one's friends on the basis of their physical appearance, what would become of mankind? And goodbye to any Christian charity! When Pulga arrived in Ferrara—I recounted, moved by my own words despite myself—he knew no one and had nothing, not even the school books. His family had yet to find a house—they had to camp out in the Hotel Tripoli: in the condition he found himself in then, how could I refuse the help and

---

* Silvio Pellico (1789–1854): a writer, poet and Italian patriot.

hospitality he was in such urgent need of? True: although he wasn't an idiot at all—he made as if he was, mainly because he was too lazy to make an effort—I didn't get much from studying with him, but not even intellectual capability constitutes the true cement of friendship.

"And what, according to you, does constitute the true cement of friendship?" Cattolica asked me at this point one evening.

We were on the phone. Heralded by a little sarcastic chuckle, the question took me by surprise.

"I don't know," I replied. "It's hard to say. How do two people ever become friends? Because, fundamentally, they like each other, I suppose. But would you tell me why you're asking me a question like that?"

"Just because," he replied mysteriously. "No particular reason. I only wanted to have your learned opinion on the matter. So then the true cement of friendship would consist of"—here he laughed again—"reciprocal feelings. Have I got that right?"

"Absolutely."

For a moment, he added nothing more. But the next evening, again on the phone, it was he who returned to the topic once more. He began by declaring that he'd thought long and hard about what we'd spoken of the day before. It was right that amity and "*amore*" had the same root: "am." And if love is fundamentally a desire to be in accord with, to identify oneself with the other, to feel with the other ("*sun-pathèin*"), it follows that "sympathy" is at the root of friendship as well. But now would I let him put another question to me?

"Of course."

I registered a slight hesitation on the line.

"Let's be frank with each other," he said in a strangely wearied voice. "Do you really like Pulga?"

"I do, yes," I replied with a laugh, relieved. "Why shouldn't I like him? He might not be a high-flyer. Sometimes he can be a bit of a bore, a bit interfering. But at heart he's a good character. You people immediately shut the door in his face, because . . . Poor thing. He really hasn't deserved that kind of treatment."

I was confident he would see I was right, would recognize how wrong he'd been and say sorry.

"Have you ever been to his house?" he asked instead.

"No. Why? He always comes round to mine."

"Well, listen . . . " he went on, once again, hesitantly, " . . . do you think that he likes you?"

I was shaken by the question, but even more by the tone of his voice, at first unsure and subdued, then suddenly resolute: like someone who, after hesitating a long time between two roads, one easy and level, the other steep and perilous, finally decides on the second. I didn't understand. Where was all this going?

I replied that everything made me believe my feelings were reciprocated.

"You're sure of that?"

"I would say so. As I told you, it's always he who seeks me out. If he didn't like me, wouldn't you think that rather than coming round every afternoon to my house, he'd go to someone else's? Even . . . " I added ironically " . . . round to yours."

He sighed.

"How naive you are!"

"Naive?"

But he didn't want to explain it to me. He was so unwilling that, to persuade him, or rather, to use his own phrase—to rid him of the lead weight he was carrying—I was forced to insist a great deal. At last, he burst out by saying that I ought to hear Pulga—my dear Pulga—what delightful things he said about me behind my back!

9.

"Don't take it amiss, but you really are naive," Cattolica had repeated in conclusion. "And that's precisely why I'm so disgusted by his behavior."

I could see he wasn't trying to hoodwink me, that he was telling the truth. And yet although I was hurt (my heart had almost stopped), it was all I could do to stop myself yelling with joy. This was my big chance to get free of Luciano—I suddenly thought—here it was at last!

I managed, somehow, to restrain myself.

"I don't believe it," I said irritably.

"I expected that," he replied. "But I can give you proof if you want."

I didn't reply, and put down the receiver. I was sure he'd ring back. I waited for some minutes, shut in the telephone cupboard. Nothing. Suddenly the door opened and my mother's face appeared.

"What are you doing sitting there in the dark?" she asked, scrutinizing me with worried eyes.

"I was on the phone."

"To whom? Cattolica?"

"Yes."

"Why is it, these last few days, you're always on the phone to him?"

Instead of replying, I gave her a light kiss on the cheek and said goodnight.

It was very hot in my room. As soon as I entered I locked the door and opened the windows wide. It was a lovely, starry night, moonless, but very bright. Down in the garden the shape of the trees stood out sharply: there the magnolia, and farther back the fir-tree, and down at the end where the three arches of the entrance terminated was the lime-tree. Between the flowerbeds was the milky whiteness of the gravel, and in the middle of the even brighter clearing that opened in front of the dark cave of the entrance, a black spot: a stone perhaps, or maybe Filomena, our ancient tortoise, whose awakening from hibernation my mother had joyfully announced at supper.

"Filomena!" I called out in a muffled voice. "Hey!"

I stepped back into the room, slowly undressed, and, without closing the window, stretched out on the bed with my hands linked behind my neck. I was completely naked. From the garden the intense odor of plants and the grass was perceptible. More than ever convinced that Cattolica had not been lying, I thought about Luciano. But of course! I said to myself again and again, gradually taking in the huge injustice Luciano had done me, and yet at the same time feeling glad, lightened, freed of a crushing weight. But of course! How blind I'd been for so long, not to have seen what a traitor Luciano was! I tried to shrug it off, to rise above it. "What a swine!" I muttered between my teeth, "what a bastard!" Tomorrow, at school, I would confront that Judas straightaway. I would ask him point blank: "So it's like that, is it? So it's true you badmouth me behind my back?" and without waiting for him to deny or confirm it, I would give him a slap in front of everyone. I could see the whole scene: me, red in the face with my eyes popping out, fists raised to punch him; he, the little wretch, the despicable little cad, writhing at my feet as he tried to protect his swollen, bruised face, while the others stood around in a circle in silence. I would fly into a fury, rain down blows on him, and Luciano wouldn't defend himself. He would only try to shield his face with those repellent palms of his, without even crying. He would take his punishment, and that would be it.

The next day, as soon as I awoke from a dreamless, leaden sleep, everything took on a different aspect. I was still determined to profit from the opportunity that had been offered me to break with Luciano, to unchain myself once and for all from the enslavement of that hideous nightmare, which had, for some time, secretly and unconfessably, darkened my days. But my role of executioner quickly seemed absurd to me, and, besides, hard to put into practice. And with Luciano standing at the corner of Corso Giovecca and Via Borgoleoni, waiting for me—without doubt, he was waiting for me: and, spotting him, I felt myself seized with an obscure sense of guilt and fear—I tried to behave as if nothing had happened. That cool, sunny morning we walked together to school, speaking of matters both trivial and serious. Every now and then I glanced at him. He seemed smaller than ever, weak and pathetic in his grey vicuña short trousers, with skinny legs like a flamingo. But I could barely bring myself to look at his high, slightly bulging forehead, the seat of so much malice.

Further down the entrance corridor, flanked by his usual cronies, I saw Cattolica. He was walking with Boldini and Grassi, looking tall and slender between them, and he stared at me with a serious, haughty expression. I pretended not to see him. But in class, as we waited for the lesson to begin, it was he who spoke first.

"A fine way to behave," he began, with a look both offended and disgusted. "Might you explain why yesterday evening you slammed the phone down on me?"

"I'm sorry," I murmured. "I'm not sure why myself."

"Do you believe me, or don't you?"

Pale, thin, he scrutinized me with those black eyes of his that burned with fanaticism in the depths of their sockets, like those of a medieval monk. I understood clearly that his motive was only the wish to humiliate me. But I needed him now. No one else besides him could help me.

"I'll believe you when you've given me proof," I replied.

The teacher, I don't remember which, came in, and we had to shut up. But during the morning Cattolica returned to the topic several times. It was hard to talk that way, both of us covering our mouth with our hands, but we did so anyway.

"Fair enough," he began, "it's more than reasonable you should ask for proof. But to have it, you'd have to come round to my house."

"To your house?"

"Definitely. I'll ask Pulga to come as well, and so you'll hear for yourself the kind of stuff he says."

"But what exactly does he say?"

"If you want me to tell you," he replied, with a grimace of distaste, "you'll have to wait till the cows come home. I can't stand gossiping."

The idea of a confrontation now began to frighten me.

"Hear for myself?" I murmured. "But how will I do that?"

"Come to my place, I've told you. I have a very precise plan to make him sing. Don't be scared."

"When should I come?"

"Today, if you'd like."

"At what time?"

"Oh, whenever you please," he said in a considerate tone. "At four, at five, at six, at seven . . . come when you want. All you have to do," and here he smiled, "is tell me exactly when."

I pointed at the backs of Boldini and Grassi.

"Yes," he confirmed. "They'll be there too. For it to work, they need to be."

I still hesitated, but ended up agreeing. I said that I'd get rid of Pulga with some excuse or other and that I'd be at his house at six.

"Be on time," he warned me. "Otherwise there's the risk you'll meet him at the door."

At the exit, there Luciano was, once again at my side. But by then I was calm and determined.

"By the way," I said when we'd come to the top of Via Borgoleoni, "it's better if you don't come round today."

He arched an eyebrow.

"No? Why's that?"

In the school entrance, a little earlier, I had seen Cattolica say something to him, and him replying and then nodding silently. What a hypocrite! I thought. How good he was at faking, the hideous little worm!

"I've an appointment," I replied brusquely, avoiding his bright blue eyes anxiously searching my own, and staring instead at the little droplets of sweat that pearled above his upper lip.

"An appointment?"

I threw out the first thing that came into my head. I had to go to my Uncle Giacomo's to be examined. With my mother.

"Has your sore throat come back?"

"Yes."

I pretended to swallow with difficulty.

"I think my uncle wants to operate."

He stared at me with a strange, dark, saddened expression. As if he had guessed I was lying. As if he had guessed everything.

"I see. And what time do you go to your uncle's? If you were going late, I could come round to yours a bit earlier. Perhaps at three, or three-thirty."

"No, it's better you don't. I'm not sure what time my uncle wants to see me."

We had stopped to talk at the angle of Corso Giovecca, at the same spot where I'd met him that morning, and there we parted.

At six o'clock on the dot I rang the doorbell of Cattolica's house.

It was he who opened the door, and it was he, having come down the three concrete steps in front of the door, who hefted my bike onto his shoulders and went into the small entrance hall before me.

Outside, it was still very light. I had crossed the city with the low sun in my eyes, but in the narrow entrance hall of the Cattolicas' house, without a window and lit only by a solitary low-wattage lamp, it was so dark it was hard to see. I noticed, at a glance, the floor covered with dark, shiny, slippery tiles, an enormous coat rack up against the wall of the entrance door, the bare, ugly, skeletal staircase that, in the same kind of dense concrete as the outer steps, ascended in a spiral to the floor above, and in front of me, beneath the stairs, a half-closed glass door, beyond which I could just make out a small dining room crossed by a melancholy ray of sunlight. Heaped up one on top of the other against the coat-rack, were three bicycles. The first was Cattolica's, a grey Maino. Cattolica added mine to the pile, then, having second thoughts, lifted it back on to his shoulders.

"What are you doing?" I asked in a whisper.

"Wiser to carry it through there into the dining room," he replied, also in a whisper. "Sly as he is, he'd be bound to notice."

He made his way toward the glass door and disappeared into the room.

"The others are here?" I asked, recognizing their bikes.

"What?"

"I wondered if Boldini and Grassi had already arrived."

"Of course," he said, without looking at me, busy cleaning his hands with his handkerchief.

We climbed the stairs without exchanging another word, he in front and I following, until at the top we reached a kind of anteroom, in its unadorned shabbiness similar to the little entrance hall below, and as if hovering above it. From a single window a hesitant light made its way through the pink curtains. Here, too, I made out a black coat-rack leaning against the far wall, hung with dark material. To the left, two doors, both shut. But through the cracks in the wood and through the keyhole of the nearer one filtered a vibrant, vivid, reddish light.

Having opened the door, Cattolica's back was suffused with that light.

"Come on in," I heard him say.

10.

ALTHOUGH DAZZLED—IT wasn't an electric light, as I'd supposed, but the sun, close to setting, which blazed obliquely into the room—I entered, looking about with amazement.

It was big, a kind of reception room, with a large horizontal window which took up most of the wall facing west, and with a second, smaller window looking out toward Via Cavour, the Aqueduct and the Spianata fields. But straightaway, as soon as I'd come in, behind the backlit figures of Boldini and Grassi, I became aware of two pinewood bookcases, one opposite the other, full of beautiful leather-bound volumes; in the center, a dark leather sofa facing a low table; two armchairs upholstered in the same material; the impeccably waxed parquet floor almost entirely hidden by carpets; the bed beside the door which sported a fleecy, carefully folded woolen cover at its foot; and a graceful bedside table level with the top of the headboard. I was struck, in short, by the luxurious appearance of the room, undoubtedly the finest in the house, and beside which, even my study, so admired and praised by Luciano, looked like a cubbyhole. All things considered, he hadn't greatly exaggerated, Cattolica—I thought—when he'd boasted of that table, proclaiming that almost the whole upper school could have sat around it, "girls included!" Yet again, guessing that behind the ease of the spoiled little rich boy, lay the obsession of both his parents determined to make any sacrifice so that he, the adored only son, might scale the highest and brightest reaches of his career and of life—but mainly the obsession of his mother, the mathematics teacher, with whom, some mornings, I'd seen him arm in arm, a tall, pale, thin woman, with glances that darted from cavernous eye sockets, and capable, by all accounts, of giving a dozen or so detentions a day; yet again, I was gripped by that obscure dislike mixed with envy which, from the very start, I'd felt for the classmate with whom I shared a desk.

I exchanged greetings with Boldini and Grassi, and went to sit at the far end of the table. In front of me was Boldini's head, half hidden by a big lamp that wore a green silk shade, Grassi on the left and, to the right, Cattolica, who was also now seated and holding forth. I felt uneasy, full not only of apprehension about Luciano's arrival which I believed to be imminent, but also of suspicion and rancor. Yet Cattolica seemed perfectly calm. He chatted away volubly, entertaining the guest, the outsider. Unfortunately, he couldn't offer me anything to eat or drink—he said, his black eyes shining and excited—as there was no one but us in the house and his mother wouldn't be back before nine . . . Then he came straight to the heart of the matter. Given that he had a distaste—it had never been his habit, his "style" to employ "devious means"—he had to remind me that in the last few days he'd tried his best to open my eyes. And I? How had

I rewarded his efforts? Not only had I listened with obvious reluctance, but I'd behaved toward him as if he, not Pulga, had been the real villain. This had gone on too long. Now I'd finally understood and, thank God, believed in his good faith. But ask either him, pointing to Boldini, or him, pointing at Grassi: Was it or was it not true, that Pulga, the few times he'd come over to study with them—it had happened a month ago during the nearly two weeks that I'd been ill—had badmouthed me continuously and in the most disgusting way? He was seated just there, where I was, copying their texts with impunity and seizing upon any chance he had to attack me. And he went for me, unprompted, it had to be said, without anyone, ever, even dreaming of encouraging him, so much so that on one occasion he couldn't resist asking Pulga if I'd done something to hurt him. To which the bastard had replied, No, not a chance, I'd done nothing to him, but that shouldn't in any way prevent him judging me with objectivity—objectivity, didn't I see?—for what I was and for my true worth.

I listened. When Cattolica, feverishly pointing his bony finger, prompted me to ask Boldini and Grassi, I obeyed. I detached my gaze from him and turned it first on one and then the other. To Cattolica's question—"Was it or wasn't it true?" the former had replied, nodding, with a serious air, while staring at his hands on the table. As for the latter, bent and almost flat against the exercise book in which he was sketching a caricature, he seemed not even to have heard. But his silence meant the same thing: that he agreed, that the facts were just as Cattolica had described them. Both of them were very different—I thought—from how I'd always seen them at school. Boldini's hair wasn't blond, but reddish. And only now that I saw his hands clenched together, almost making a single enormous fist, was the strength that Cattolica had ascribed to him apparent to me. And Grassi? Grassi, too, was different. Cattolica had compared him to Silvio Pellico. He was right. Utterly absorbed in his sketch, every now and then he stuck out the tip of his tongue, leaving it there to linger for a few moments, a grey bud at the corner of his mouth. He was right. The comparison was spot on.

I suddenly got up, walked to the window and pressed my forehead against the glass. Having disappeared briefly behind the sugar refinery opposite the station, the sun was no longer in my eyes and the vista, filled with orchards and gardens which stretched from the Cattolicas' house to the city walls, and then beyond to the endless plain, immediately made me want to be there, with those boys chasing after a ball on the broad walkway on top of the walls, or else there on that fast train which, with its windows lowered, was at that very moment slowly leaving the station, or else there, in the far distance, going along the lovely asphalted street of Pontelagoscuro on that little yellow tram, tiny as a tin can, which was perilously careening toward the black horizontal line made by the banks of the Po. By now it must have begun to cool down outside. If not today, tomorrow, at this very hour, I would take off on my bike and go to see the Po. The Po in full flood. And alone at last. After having exposed Luciano. After having finished with him and with all the others. Alone forever.

"What a total bastard!" Cattolica repeated. "When I think that there are people like Pulga in the world, it makes my blood boil."

I turned round. I couldn't wait to be done with it all.

"But are you sure he's coming?"

"Definitely. Who knows how many miles that creep would be willing to trudge in a day on his little matchstick legs to sneak into other people's houses? You know those mongrels you just have to whistle for and they immediately come running and wagging their tails? Pulga's just like that, a real suck-up. Desperate to sneak about and stick his nose in, you know what I mean? And it's not really as if he does it out of need. It's just a question of character. Maybe because I'm not a bastard or a suck-up, and I can't bear that combination, it makes my skin crawl. I'm only at ease in my own home, while, on the contrary, there are people in the world who can never stay put in their own houses."

"What time did you tell him to come?"

He checked his elegant Eberhard chrome-metal wristwatch and twisted his lips.

"There's time. I told him, and repeated it, not to come before seven o'clock, and since he does as he's told, we still have a good twenty-five minutes to arrange things."

Although he had spoken of his "plan to make him sing," I don't know why, but I was sure he had prepared a kind of trial: with himself playing the role of judge and Boldini and Grassi together as assistant judges, with

Luciano and me battling it out with words under the scrutiny of the court. I had basically imagined a direct confrontation, and in the last hours it had been this prospect that gradually wrung my stomach in an ever more oppressive grip. It was therefore a relief to learn from Cattolica that his famous scheme did not require my presence in the room at all, and so no "scene" was planned. When Luciano arrived, I would simply pass through to the adjacent bedroom—and, so saying, Cattolica pointed to the door I'd noticed behind Boldini's back—and from there with the greatest of ease I could hear everything that creature would undoubtedly, once again, spew forth about me. In short, all I had to do was listen. But in the meantime, why not go through right now for a moment, into the other room—it was his parents' bedroom—taking care to leave the door a fraction ajar? Only in that way could I check beforehand how well I'd be able to hear.

Not to have to see Luciano, to avoid looking at his face, while Cattolica made him talk! Overcome by a sudden sense of euphoria I moved away from the window and, brushing past Boldini's back, entered the adjoining room.

Inside was very dark, or at least so it seemed to me: the thick darkness of a cellar.

I stationed myself at the door, my eyes at the crack, and said blithely:

"Go on, say something!"

"I'm telling you, Gianni," Cattolica began in a relaxed manner, turning to Boldini, "in my opinion it's not true that . . ."

"I can see that," Boldini replied, "yes, I can see that . . ."

"Can you hear us OK?" asked Cattolica, raising his voice.

"Perfectly!" I shouted out. "I can hear every word."

I returned to the study.

I sat down again, but now we didn't seem to know what else to say. Grassi had begun sketching again. Boldini was looking out the window, his attention drawn, it seemed, to the little fluttering black tatters of the bats that flitted so close to the windows they looked as if they'd smash themselves against them.

Dusk was drawing on. Even Cattolica stopped talking. I saw him glance at his watch again.

"What time is it?" I asked.

"Still another ten minutes to go."

He shook his head, as though unhappy about something. I asked if anything was wrong, and he denied it. I pressed him further and he admitted that yes, there was something wrong.

"Perhaps we've been making a mistake all along," he said.

Staring at me, he then added, that should it suit me, having fully heard all of Pulga's spiel, if I was to come out of my hiding place and give him a "flurry of slaps," right where he was sitting, I should feel utterly free to do so. None of them would lift a finger to stop me. Far from it.

"What?" I exclaimed. "D'you mean here?"

"Why not? Postpone the punishment and the guilt is half forgiven. Let's suppose tomorrow morning at school you take him aside and start saying to him, 'D'you know, Luciano . . .'"—and he began speaking, in a nasal, saccharine tone as if that was the way Luciano and I habitually spoke to each other—"'D'you know, Luciano, yesterday evening I was there at Cattolica's too, hidden behind a door?' So, you start telling him like that, that the game's up and he's been caught red handed. Sly little cheat that he is, you can be sure that Pulga will manage to convince you there was nothing amiss, that he didn't mean anything by it, that you hadn't understood at all, and so on. He'd even be capable of losing his temper, arguing that these things shouldn't ever be done, that a friend would never play a dirty trick like that, and that he had been aware of everything immediately anyway, had spoken a little ill of you deliberately, to pay you back . . . I can just see you both," he scoffed. "And everything will vanish like a soap bubble."

He was right. I too could see myself and Luciano playing this out, and a little later, Luciano would be round at my house to do his homework once again. As though nothing had happened. As though nothing at all had changed.

"Alright, then," I said uncertainly, looking around me, "but how could it be done here?"

Cattolica leaped to his feet. "I'll prepare the ring for you."

On his own, in a flash, he dragged the leather sofa and the little table under the window, so they stood against one of the two bookcases, on the other side of the armchairs, then he rolled up the carpet that was in the center of the room and hid it under the bed.

"There we are," he said, turning toward us, all red in the face from his exertions.

From the far side of the table Boldini had raised his blue eyes toward me, of the same icy blue that Luciano's had. He was staring me straight in the face. He tightened his lips, as if fighting against an impulse of shyness, and then said in a serious voice:

"You're not scared, are you?"

I burst out laughing.

But he didn't seem very convinced. He asked me how much I weighed. Then he wanted to know how heavy I thought Luciano was. And without waiting for my reply, he concluded that in his opinion a single "slap," well delivered, would be enough "to knock him down."

He got up, walked behind Grassi, came over to squeeze the muscles of my arms—Cattolica, silent for once, merely nodded—and meanwhile proceeded to reassure me about the outcome of the approaching contest and to advise me how I ought to hit him. I should follow a left to his belly, with the right, a "haymaker," to the jaw.

"Let me show you."

I followed him into the middle of the room, the center of the "ring." And we were still there, facing each other, intent on practicing the "move" before the infantilized gaze of Cattolica and Grassi, when we heard the doorbell ring.

11.

A LITTLE before, for the few moments I'd been there, the bedroom of Cattolica's parents had seemed steeped in total darkness. I was wrong. Once there again, I quickly realized that one could see more than enough.

In the room I'd just left, they had turned on the table lamp. Seeping through the gap of the half-closed door, the light was a white band which extended sharply past my feet, across the floor of dark, hexagonal tiles identical to those on the ground floor, without encountering a single object. The very faint light—that of an underground crypt—which spread uniformly across the room was produced by a tiny low dim lamp beneath a holy image hung in the center of the wall to my right. It was enough to disclose the parallel shapes of two separate beds side by side, and the blackish shadow of a dressing table and a wardrobe beside the image itself—which was of a Jesus with languid blue eyes and a blond helmet of hair perfectly parted in the middle, with vermillion lips barely separated to disclose the tips of two snow-white teeth and with one alabaster, feminine hand raised limply to point at a plump red heart that hung like a monstrous fruit high on his chest.

I was tense, alert, but calm. I focused on the image of Jesus, that extravagant red heart; and also on my own, which from the first had been beating furiously, but now had steadied itself. Besides, I was no longer there in the study, a few yards from Cattolica and Luciano, who, after having slowly climbed the stairs, were still lingering to chat in the anteroom. The bedroom where I had hidden appeared at once infinitely more secret, more remote, even more shadowy than it actually was—a speck lost in the womb of a vast space, wide as the ocean . . .

Once the four of them were seated round the table, Luciano, I guessed, occupying the place where, till just before, I myself had sat, I wondered when and in what way they would get round to talking about me.

They had some two hours at their disposal; and perhaps, for this reason too, apart from enjoying keeping me in suspense, Cattolica seemed unconcerned to hurry things along. Patient and sly as a cat with a mouse, he listened to his prey dispensing his fluent, typically Bolognese chatter. Pulga was speaking about trivial enough things. He too was stalling. And so?—Cattolica had the air of saying, though remaining almost entirely silent—and so? Let the little toad keep croaking, let him do his utmost to appear amusing and intriguing in exchange for the inestimable gift of being invited and accepted there. Sooner or later—from the tone of his sparse replies, of his measured interruptions to the ceaseless hum of Luciano's voice, I understood how sure of himself Cattolica felt—get around to doing exactly what we had all, myself included, agreed to do.

So, for a long time, for a good half-hour, Luciano spoke of things that related to me only indirectly.

He began speaking about their homework. He asked if they'd finished it. And since Cattolica answered in the affirmative, that they had completed it just now, a moment before he'd arrived—Oh well, he sighed, lucky them! He, by contrast, hadn't managed to get through more than a fraction: the Latin and Italian he'd done, but not any Greek yet. No, really, but thanks a lot! he had then exclaimed, allowing me to almost see the rapid lateral shift of his jaw—it wasn't necessary for Cattolica to lend him his exercise book. Apart from the fact that every now and then he liked to try doing it on his own, that is, translating the ninety-eight verses of *The Iliad* assigned us by that "crabby" old Guzzo, he still had the whole evening after supper and tomorrow morning to finish it.

From homework, he changed the subject to philosophy.

Razzetti had yet to quiz him in class—he said—and so tomorrow morning, when he'd finished working on *The Iliad*, he certainly needed to take a look at *Phaedo*, as one could never be sure . . . and speaking of which, Razzetti, sure enough, philosophy wasn't his forte, and he could only teach it by way of the usual smoke and mirrors, relying on those synopses he also resorted to in his history classes. But Plato himself, wasn't he, anyway, every bit as dull as poor old Razzetti? And Socrates! Always pontificating with his smug, know-all teacher's air, and yet as stupid as they come, an utter fool! Just as well that at the end—he'd skipped ahead—they'd given him that famous cup of hemlock to drink. But even leaving aside Plato and Socrates, in his modest opinion, the whole of philosophy was a load of crap.

"What d'you mean?" objected Cattolica. "It's not as though philosophy is religion, there's no need for you to believe in it!"

"Excuse my ignorance, but what is it, then?"

Slowly, good-naturedly, indulgently, Cattolica began to expound his thoughts on philosophy. Grassi, and even Boldini, also chipped in every now and then.

"I daresay all of you are right," Luciano sighed at a certain point.

All the same—he added—with what little grey matter that "after so much cranking the shank" he had left at his disposal, who knows what low marks he'd get tomorrow morning, should it occur to Razzetti to test him. He was no Cattolica, unfortunately, someone who only needed to read something once to understand it! Of little intelligence, as he knew himself to be, with only the faintest glimmer of a memory . . .

But going back to *Phaedo*: it seemed to him, as he'd already said, nothing more than worthless blather. And yet, there was one theory in it that, while probably a load of rubbish, nevertheless had somewhat convinced him.

"I'll bet that was the theory of metempsychosis," Cattolica interposed.

"How did you guess?"

Cattolica replied that if there was one thing in *Phaedo* which he himself could give no credence to, it was precisely the theory of the transmigration of souls from men to animals and vice versa. To believe in that, you'd have to dispose of the whole Catholic religion. And he, as a good Catholic, believed in hell, purgatory and heaven.

"I wouldn't argue with that," Luciano replied contritely, "even though I feel there's an element of truth in metempsychosis."

Listen—he went on—take Guzzo, for example: most likely before being born with two legs and arms, he had been a poisonous snake—an adder or a cobra, take your pick—and would revert to that as soon as, God willing, he breathes his last. And Krauss, who, perched up there in her cupboard among her retorts and alembics, gives herself the grand air of being a wise owl, maybe she used to be a duck instead. You just had to look at her backside. Old Half-pint, who knows, perhaps he used to be an earthworm, the kind you find by the bucket load when you're out in the country and give a clod of mud a kick; tiny, it's true, but lovely and fat and pink.

And moving down the scale to our classmates, it's more than probable that Mazzanti was a rat, only you'd have to decide whether he was a country rat, a cellar rat or a sewer rat; Chieregatti, a pack mule; Lattuga, a pig, obviously, and perhaps a hyena as well, since hyenas feed on corpses, corpses dug up in cemeteries, and they stink even worse than pigs; Donadio, a guinea pig, Camurri, a blind mole; Droghetti, with that nose of his, a camel; Selmi a horse—more of a carthorse, though; Veronesi and Danieli, poor things, two donkeys, with their dicks always dangling, and so on. So, just supposing for the moment that metempsychosis isn't the nonsense it may well be, all of them would in time revert to their original forms, with the exception of Lattuga, who, retaining his identity, would be reborn as a worm, of the sort that squirms about in the intestines; here, he broke into dialect: "*dèinter in la mérda a mèza gamba*"* and also excepting Mazzanti, who instead of being reborn as a rat, even if it was a sewer rat, there's every reason to suppose that he'll find himself turned into a louse trudging his way through someone's pubes.

"You've forgotten the girls," Cattolica observed.

"They don't count. Haven't you seen them? Where d'you think they all come from? Obviously, all of them were geese or hens."

I heard him snigger. He sounded all fired up and very pleased with himself.

"And me?" Cattolica persisted. "What might I have descended from, in your opinion? Go on, don't be shy."

"I dunno, perhaps from a bird: a falcon of the alpine variety, or a sparrowhawk, or even an eagle. That 'over the others'"—he recited Dante through his nose—"'like an eagle, flies ...'"†

"Oh yeah! And Boldini?"

"Give me a moment. He could have been a jaguar, or an elephant seal. While you, Grassi, d'you know what you used to be? You were a beaver, one of those beasts with two big front teeth, always paddling around constructing dams ... "

Anyway—he went on—he was of the same opinion as Plato, that there were very few men and women indeed, whom, when they were reborn, would manage not to regress. He himself had perhaps been a dog. And would always return as a dog, unless, like Mazzanti and Lattuga, he had to descend a great deal lower. For some moments, they remained perfectly silent.

"So, to sum up," Cattolica finally responded. "Lattuga's a tapeworm, Mazzanti's a pubic louse, and you?"

"Hmm. We'll have to wait and see."

He then said if he had to choose what type of parasite he'd be reincarnated as, he'd almost prefer to descend to the very lowest point, and rather than be a flea or a tick, to be reborn as a microbe. That would be a rein-

---

* Ferrarese dialect: "up to his thighs in shit."
† Dante, *Inferno*, canto iv: "che vola sopra gli altri come un'aquila" speaking of Homer's stylistic superiority.

carnation with real privileges! No worries as far as food and drink went, guaranteed invisibility . . . a real godsend, all considered. Responsibilities? Nothing apart from making modest claims, avoiding the behavior of certain microbes, like those of typhoid, rabies, tetanus, pneumonia and so on, those that gloat because in a few days they've ruined everything. Rather than that, it was much more sensible to model one's behavior on those microbes of a better character, who, once they found a quiet little dwelling, stay there happily eating away, for twenty, thirty, forty years, and, at the final reckoning, don't really annoy anyone. The syphilis bacillus or those of certain kinds of tuberculosis: those are the proper gents with brains, able to live and let live! His father always said the same.

He sniggered again. The others didn't breathe a word.

And it was just at this point that Cattolica pronounced my name. It was as if it didn't belong to me, as if it belonged to some unknown person.

"Fair enough," he added. "Let's suppose that you're a dog. How about him?"

"Another dog," he replied without hesitation. "No doubt about it."

With this difference—he went on—that while he himself had once been, he'd bet on it, one of those small worthless mongrels, always trotting about the streets in search of questionable matter to "sniff"—turds, dog piss, etc.,—I, by contrast, must have been one of those "big dogs," far from thoroughbred, but still quite a fine cross breed, one it's always fairly easy to find a good home for. That's it, a big dog, but not one of the very biggest, good looking but not a beauty, strong but not that strong: one of those dogs that when they meet a mongrel of the "Pulga type," weighing a mere couple of kilos and only a palm or so high, often, it falls out that it's the mongrel who drags the other dog along with him wherever he wants to go. And it's not by any means always the case that "the fine big dog" isn't the one sniffing the other's arse. Quite the contrary!

12.

WHEN THEY'D finished laughing—all four of them had burst out laughing, Cattolica included—the conversation continued. Now it was about me that they spoke and, as before, it was the voices of Luciano and Cattolica that were heard above the others.

What were they saying?

Cattolica was asking Luciano how he'd managed to get rid of me. And Luciano replied to him that everything had been as easy as pie, as it was I who had announced that I was busy that afternoon. I had a very sore throat, I'd said—though perhaps that was a fib—and had to go for an appointment with my uncle who was a doctor.

"A fib?" Cattolica asked quietly. "And why would that be?"

"Who can say. He's not that easy to figure out. He seems naive and yet he's so complicated and suspicious! He takes offence over trifles!"

Unfortunately—he continued—between the three of them and me there wasn't the best of relations, and no one knew that better than him, who, caught between enemy lines, had had to work so hard at reconciliation. But on this subject, what had actually happened between us to justify my rancor toward them? What had they actually done to me? He knew, all too well, what weird quirks of character to expect from a Jew. But that much anger!

"That really surprises me," Cattolica replied. "I've never had anything against him. And nor have those two."

"D'you know what I think?"

"Tell us."

"I think," Luciano resumed, lowering his voice, "that he's irked most of all by the fact that he'd like to be your friend, to come round here as well, while instead"—and here he sniggered—"he's been left in the lurch."

"I think you're wrong about that," said Cattolica, with a flicker of impatience. "First of all, we're the best of friends, otherwise I'd like to know why on earth we would have kept on sharing the same desk for so many months. And secondly, if, as you say, he was so keen to come round to study at my house, why has he never asked me? He could very well ask me, don't you think?"

"Of course he could!" Luciano exclaimed. "Only, if you'll let me explain, if it was him that had to ask you, what pleasure would he have got from that? Don't you see?—and I know him well enough to know what I'm saying—he wanted above all for you to invite him. And since you weren't ever inclined to . . . "

From the sound of a chair being shifted I gathered that Cattolica had stood up. Muffled by the carpet, his footsteps suddenly resounded on the bare wood of the "ring," then once more became deadened. Perhaps he'd gone to sit on the bed at the far end of the room, or even stretched out on it.

"But what has he done to you," he said at last from down there, "that you always speak so ill of him?"

Luciano, too, got up from his seat. Most likely he'd felt the need to be nearer Cattolica and, to confirm it, when he spoke, his voice sounded farther off, different.

He said that it was true, that basically he couldn't stand me, but not so much because he found me disagreeable, or because I'd behaved badly toward him. If he criticized me, he did so for much more serious reasons than merely because we were incompatible characters, or out of any trivial, childish, hysterical spite. He was mature enough to suppress any reaction of that kind. But for this very reason, because he was above any such pettiness, not even a sense of gratitude would stop him saying, with objectivity, whatever he thought was right and useful to say about me.

For example, to start off with: my vanity, my incredible, absurd vanity, that of a child in kindergarten.

He'd perceived this straightaway, right from the start.

"Have you ever been to his house?" he asked.

"No," Cattolica replied. "I never go round to other people's houses. It's a principle of mine."

Well—Luciano went on—it's a real palatial spread, as big as four or five normal houses stuck together, and endowed with a magnificent garden besides. My family, on its own, had reserved the whole second floor for itself, an apartment of some twenty or so rooms—who knows the cost of heating it! We were basically made of money, and you could see it. But a gentleman is a gentleman, and a profiteer is something else. Our wealth didn't date back to an earlier era than that of my paternal grandfather, a wholesale textile merchant—that was something I'd confirmed for him on the first day, when, without giving him time to catch his breath, I'd taken him on a room-by room tour of the whole place. I had immediately shown him everything: the salon for parties, the three drawing rooms, the two dining rooms, the seven bedrooms, the four bathrooms, the so-called "office," and even the toilets, one for the owners and one for the servants; and all the time I looked smug and complaisant, disgustingly pleased with myself. On every door frame, my grandfather, who, as I'd told him, was very religious, had had attached certain small rods made of nickel, about the size of a fifty *centesimo* piece, each of which had a little piece of paper with writing in Hebrew rolled up inside it. He'd asked me for some explanation about this, and you should have seen my face as I expounded on the minutiae of the meaning and function of those gadgets. I was blushing with pleasure! What was written inside those rods? Nothing. The name of God the father, and that's it. Such was my vanity that I even transformed our religion into a personal or a family achievement. Our God—I'd used these very words—is the Eternal God, the one and only—in my opinion Christianity should be seen as a more modern version of Judaism. And so it may be. But as I went on about Him, my "Old Man with a Beard," I assumed the same triumphal air with which I might swank about that good old salt, my grandpa, the canny wholesale cloth merchant . . .

We had started studying every day in tandem. But even here, I revealed a conspicuous desire to show off, to be in the lead—everything became a spur to competition for me—at home, as much as at school, I behaved as if I was perpetually in a soccer match, which was enough to induce anyone close to me to let me forge ahead and win, and be done with it. It was quite true that "scholastically speaking" for months he had lived in my shadow, transformed by me into a kind of parasite, a hermit crab. But hold on! The hermit crab is a poor crustacean about whom it's fair to say it "gratefully proffers its backside," but a classmate, even if from a less well-off family, even if less intelligent and knowledgeable, even if in the end not at all unhappy to have found someone prepared to do the work for him, is still always a classmate, which is to say, a human being! I had never considered him either a human being or a friend, and that was the truth. His only purpose had been as a machine for doling out praise, worked with the same detachment as turning on a tap.

He'd barely even seen my brother and sister. The brother was still in the second form of the *ginnasio* and the girl, the youngest, was only in the third form of primary school. But he'd certainly had a chance to see my parents up close. Particularly my mother.

"Have you ever had a look at her?"

"Who?"

"His mother."

"No."

"That's a shame, because as women go she's certainly worth the effort."

She was a lady of around thirty three—he went on—maybe a bit "brassy" as Jewesses always are, but with a stunning mouth, with big, brown eyes, which send out some very particular looks . . .

Although she was dark-eyed and dark-haired, it was mainly her that I looked like. And in the same way that I, vain and in constant need of praise, made use of him as a vaulting horse to measure the strength of my muscles, his mother, too, had made use of him as the best means to ensure that her nice little boy stayed safely home till supper-time. She'd be capable of any sly tricks, that gracious dame, just to achieve this worthy end! She would turn up with huge trays that would have kept hunger at bay for a whole family for two days. Coffee and milk, tea, hot chocolate, whipped cream, pastry, little cakes, petits fours, chocolate sweets: every afternoon a complete panoply. But this was nothing, because apart from that air she always had, "the hussy," while filling your cup or putting cakes under your nose—"Go on, don't be polite," she presses you in her insinuating way, "sweets are nourishing, they build up the muscles and the mind!"—she never failed, afterward, taking her leave, to cast back through the half-closed door a look that was "half maternal and half femme fatale." And the kisses that, so close up, she would often plant on the cheeks of her good little son, all beaming with joy to see he was there, within the warm glow of the radiators, so hard-working, so handsome and clever, what kisses!

One evening last winter, when there was a storm, she went a bit further. To persuade him to stay for supper and perhaps even to sleep there overnight, she suddenly began to stare at him, looking into his eyes so intensely that it would have put the frighteners, not just on him, whom it didn't take much to scare, but the very devil. What was she promising with that look? That's enough, he'd better stop there. One thing for sure was that the summer at the seaside—we'd be going to Cesanatico next summer, take note!—a woman like that, what wouldn't she get up to during the week when her feeble old husband would have to return to the city to sort out his affairs, leaving her in the rented villa with no other company than the servants and the children! With those big fleshy lips, with those languid eyes, half hidden by her hair—her breasts had sagged a bit, true, but the "undercarriage" was perhaps worth a visit all on its own—there was no way that, given the chance, he'd let her escape.

But, going back to me, could they believe that I didn't even know what "jacking off" was?

To tell the truth, he'd always suspected it. And yet, on the occasion when, cornered, I'd had the courage to admit that I'd never done it, he was gobsmacked. At sixteen! And giving himself such airs, as well!

Let's start with having a look at it, he'd said.

After much prevarication, he'd got me to show him my dick—which although a "Roundhead" from circumcision, had seemed to him utterly normal and average. Yet there had been another event which had seemed to him "pretty symptomatic," and that was my reaction when, a bit before, to convince me to unbutton, he'd had the idea of unbuttoning himself.

Well, I went so pale at seeing his, his dick, and then, in the follow-ing days, my manner of behaving was so changed—I became surly and rude all at once, my eyes were shifty, as if he had disgusted me or, I don't know, made me angry—that he couldn't but think the worst. Indeed. I was undoubtedly a "pansy," though perhaps in a latent state: only waiting for the "bell to ring" before "I crossed over," and as yet still ignorant—this being the tragic thing—of the lovely career that would inevitably open before me . . .

13.

ON TIPTOE, slowly leaving the shadow for the light, I moved toward the large glass door that separated the sitting room from the dining room.

My family was having supper. Seated with her back to me, my mother was wearing a light dress of white linen that left her neck, back and arms bare. Around the table were my father, my brother Ernesto, my sis-ter Fanny.

I looked at each of them, one after the other, as if they were strangers—

an odd memory block hindered me from remembering my mother's face, which was hidden from me. Was he my father, I wondered, that poor old man in slippers and pyjama top, who was just finishing up his bowl of soup? Were they my siblings, those two little children with such a grave and solemn air who, within seconds, would burst out laughing? And the lady with her back to me, the beautiful woman with dark hair haloed with light, her left hand glinting with rings when she lifted it to wave it about, was she really my mother? And was it possible that I myself was the son of that mediocrity of a man, both bored and boring, unable to contain himself, especially at home, to act in a dignified fashion, and of that woman who seemed so common, and that, precisely to that union, that physical union, I owed my existence?

The maid arrived carrying the plates of meat and vegetables, and suddenly, from the expression, between surprise and fear, which her face assumed, I realized that my presence had been registered.

"It's the young sir!" she exclaimed.

I had no other option. I pushed down on the door handle, went in and sat at my place beside my mother.

"But, dear, it's nine-thirty!" My mother broke the silence around the table, smiling. "Where have you been?"

She was looking at my face, my hands, checking everything. And through her fearful glances, worried, and at the same time collusive, I understood how far she was an involved participant in the atrocious wound that had been dealt me such a short time ago. Who knows? Perhaps, by mysterious means, she too had suffered at the exact same moment that I had.

I replied that I'd been round at a friend's house.

"At Cattolica's?"

"Yes."

"You two have now become inseparable, eh? I wonder what Pulga has to say about that. Was he there too?"

"What a way to behave!" my father intervened in an indignant tone. "You could have phoned, surely? It would have cost you no effort at all."

"Yes, Pulga was there," I murmured, without lifting my eyes from the empty soup bowl.

My father opened his mouth, but a furtive gesture of her ring-laden hand was at the ready to hush him.

"Would you like some cold soup?" she asked me.

I nodded.

But I wasn't hungry. I ate slowly, with half-spoonfuls, feeling as if my stomach would reject the food. I imagined myself back in the bedroom of Cattolica's parents, my shoulders pressed against the wall and my eyes fixed on the Jesus with that red heart, and could still hear the calm, indefatigable hum of Luciano's voice through the partition. No, I didn't step out, I didn't make an appearance. After I heard Luciano say, with a laugh, "Such prodigious efforts to learn all that Latin and Greek, and what chance does he have of any career but that one?" I finally shook myself, stepped away from the wall, crossed the room, and walked out into the anteroom. In the thick darkness, I went down the stairs, found my bike in the small dining room, and then in the open air began pedaling rapidly with my head down. Via Cittadella, Viale Cavour, Corso Giovecca: onward, without ever stopping, as if down a dark straight endless tunnel . . .

"Aren't you hungry, darling?"

I shook my head.

"He'll have eaten something," my father grumbled.

I got to my feet.

"I feel a bit sick. Best if I don't eat supper."

"What have you been eating"—my father pressed the point—"ice cream?"

"I haven't eaten a thing." I stared at him coldly, with hatred.

"Calm down!" he responded, intimidated. "Did you get out of bed on the wrong side?"

"Goodnight."

Without giving either him or my mother the customary goodnight kiss on the cheek, I quickly left the room.

As soon as I was in my bedroom I stripped, got between the sheets, turned off the light and closed my eyes. I remained like that for some ten minutes. I couldn't sleep. I was about to get up and dressed again when I heard my mother's steps in the corridor.

She stopped before the door. I heard her call me in a low voice, then felt the room fill with her presence. What a bore! I thought to myself in fury, pretending to be asleep. I felt her beside me, tall and silent above my outstretched body, and I wanted to get up, insult her, slap her and chase her away. But then, as cool, as fresh and light as ever, I felt her hand descend through the dark to touch my forehead and rest there. That alone sufficed. Nothing else was needed for me, just a little later, alone again, to fall asleep, to fall once again into the deep curative sleep of a child.

The next morning, entering the classroom, I saw at once that everyone was there, seated at their own desks. Luciano quickly greeted me with a smile and with a festive wave. But from Boldini's and Grassi's behavior, leaning over an exercise book they had between them, and that of Cattolica in particular, whose gaze, as I drew closer to him, didn't leave my face for a second, it was clear to me that even they realized the irreparable gravity of what had happened the evening before. Cattolica waited till I sat down and didn't even greet me: he merely gave a faint grin. I knew him well enough to understand that he felt lost and worried. But why? I wondered. What was making him walk on eggshells? Was it perhaps the hope that I hadn't stayed to the bitter end, and so hadn't heard the worst? It could have been that. In any case, if that had been his hope, I would soon strip away any illusion he was under. Everything was over between us, over forever. And he should understand that as soon as possible.

He covered his mouth with his hand.

"You did the right thing to leave," he said. "It really wasn't worth your trouble staying."

I lowered my head in assent and didn't reply.

He sighed.

"He's crazy. He's a poor fool who can't control himself."

"Leave me alone, and stop bothering me."

Guzzo was at the teacher's desk. I had spoken without troubling to cover my mouth, and was immediately aware the teacher was scrutinizing me.

"Are we at it again?" he said threateningly.

As though inspired, I leaped to my feet and stared him in the face.

"Excuse me," I said, "but could I ask you to let me change places?"

"And why ever should I do that, my dear fellow? Have you perhaps forgotten that there are fewer than ten days before the end of term?"

"I know. But it's precisely because of that I want to change places. Here, with him"—I nodded toward Cattolica—"it always ends up with us continually distracting each other."

My words were received with a prolonged whisper of consternation and disapproval.

"May I ask you all to stay absolutely silent?" Guzzo shouted.

He had the air of not believing what was happening. But there I was, in front of him, standing rigid and straight, determined to get what I was asking for.

He looked around, bewildered.

"And to which desk would you like to be transferred? It doesn't look to me as if any are available."

"I'd like to go again to the back of the class"—pointing at Luciano's desk without turning round—"where Pulga is. But on my own."

"And Signor Pulga?"

"Pulga can easily come and sit here."

"I see. You are proposing a double transfer!" Guzzo exclaimed in amusement. "*Do ut des!*[*] ... Very well, I shall permit it. Have you been following, Luciano Pulga? Up, shift, get a move on. Assemble your splendid chattels and betake yourself up here beside the great Cattolica, who I'm sure will be honored!"

And while Luciano, laden with his books, went past me along the aisle between the second and the third row of desks—brushing against me, he gave me a look full of bafflement and fear—a dry, imperious, sibilant "Ssh!" served to strangle a fresh crop of murmuring at birth.

To return to the complete solitude of the preceding autumn, I had still to manage one further step: to break with Luciano.

Yet at midday, after the end of school bell, when I noticed him walking all alone along the sidewalk of Via Borgoleone in front of me, painfully at a tilt because of the pile of books he carried balanced on his angular

---

[*] Latin for "I give that you may give"—more or less equivalent to English use of the Latin tag *quid pro quo*.

hip, I felt a moment of hesitation. It was true: I had treated him harshly and coldly all that morning in class. And yet, how come, now, I hadn't foreseen this? I even felt I could surmise from the speed of his steps, from the neat precision with which he set down one foot after the other, that he'd guessed everything and wanted to flee. And if he did? All the better.

"Hey!" I cried out. "Wait up!"

He stopped with a jolt and turned his head back. He was very composed, the corners of his thin lips raised in a smile tinged with slightly woeful benevolence.

"Oh! It's you."

We walked on side by side. He said nothing to me, making no reproach, and this began to disconcert me. Where the street met Corso Giovecca, I crossed over determinedly, leaving him some yards behind.

He caught up with me on the opposite sidewalk.

"What's wrong?" he asked in confusion. "Aren't you going home?"

I replied that I was fed up with always taking the same route along the same streets. Today I wanted to walk with him partway to his house.

It was a Friday, market day. Corso Roma and Piazza Cattedrale were thronged with farm workers. We made our way through with difficulty, occasionally losing one another in the bustle, still without speaking a word. He doesn't know—I thought. If I were only to allow him, at four o'clock, there he'd be, sitting beside me at my table.

Before the turning for Porta Reno, right under the clock tower on the square, I stopped.

"Goodbye," I said.

He swallowed, then murmured, "Bye."

Pale as a corpse, he stared at me, the sparse whiskers on his upper lip damp with sweat and his Adam's apple in nervous agitation.

"We'll see each other later today?" he risked.

"I don't think so."

"Are you busy?"

"Just my homework, that's all."

"What . . . what's wrong with you?"

"Nothing. And you?"

He widened his blue eyes.

"Me?"

But I'd already turned my back on him.

14.

THE VERY morning when, in the vestibule of the Guarini School, the marks for the end of year were due to be posted, Otello Forti phoned me.

He had arrived back the evening before—he told me. He had finished his last oral exams at five-thirty in the afternoon, just in time to return to college, pack his suitcase and run to catch the train that left from Padua at seven.

I asked him how he'd done.

"Quite well, I'd say. And you?"

I replied that I didn't know, that I was just then leaving to check the grades.

"Why not stop by at my place?" he suggested. "If you'd like we could go along together."

He was friendly, talkative even, having acquired a light trace of a Veneto accent. But even toward him I now felt only indifference.

"Why don't you stop by at mine and pick me up," I said.

He tried to argue. He said that as his house was halfway between mine and the Guarini it seemed to him more "logical" that I should come round to his. And he was already less friendly, already en route to readopting his ever grumbling, despotic persona, always ready to throw himself into the most stubborn arguments when he got it into his head to get something.

"Fine. Listen," I cut him short, "let's meet in front of the main entrance of the Guarini in half an hour. Would that suit you?"

"Alright, alright . . ."

Naturally I'd passed. With eights in all literary subjects, and with two sixes: in science and in math and physics. But where was I placed? First? Second? Third?

It was eleven-thirty. In the big vestibule, there was no one but ourselves. Otello only needed a glance to work out that battling for first place were me, Cattolica and Grassi. Sure, against my eight in Italian, Cattolica could only boast of a seven, and Grassi a mere six. But Cattolica had an eight in math and physics, and Grassi a nine in science . . .

"You must be second," he concluded, "behind Cattolica by one point. Grassi's third, also just by one point."

Unusually solicitous and helpful, he took a pencil from his pocket and began writing on the wall beside the lists. Luciano had passed, I noted in the meantime. All sixes, but a pass just the same.

"I was right," Otello announced at last with a flourish of triumph in his voice. "Cattolica first, and you second."

We went out into the open air.

"Aren't you going to phone home?"

I said it wasn't worth the trouble. With one hand on the bicycle saddle, the other on the handlebars, I looked him up and down. If, at Christmas, he had seemed so much taller and more grown-up than me, now he appeared small, a kind of child.

"D'you want me to take you on the bike back to your house?" I proposed. "Go on, get on the crossbar."

And in fact, like a child, he obeyed immediately.

Despite the weight, the encumbrance and the cobblestones of Via Mascheraio, I pedalled fast. I looked at the back of Otello's neck. Beneath his blond hair, cut short, I could make out the plump, pink, tender skin. I breathed in the odor of good soap he gave off, and remembered, by contrast, Luciano's scrawny neck, greasy with brilliantine, his big, pale, translucent, wafery ears, a bit like an old man's. I hadn't carried Luciano on the crossbar of my bike more than two or three times in all, Otello hundreds. And yet I understood now that there was no remedy. Even if I had forced myself to re-establish my old relations with Otello, as when we were at primary and then at the *ginnasio*, beneath his good, honest smell I would always sense the other, that revolting, oppressive reek of brilliantine.

As if he too had intuited that in the future we would only see each other rarely, and that from now on the clock of our friendship was ticking away, Otello didn't stop talking for a moment. He pumped me for all kinds of information: who I'd shared a desk with during these months, whose house I'd gone to study at, who I'd become friends with. And I answered him sketchily: referring to Cattolica and to Luciano, but without informing him of anything else. His back was there in front of me, stocky and childlike. To confide in him! I felt as if I was facing a huge, steep, impervious mountain. The very idea of having to scale such a mountain of obtuseness was enough to fill me with nausea and powerlessness.

"Luciano Pulga?" asked Otello. "So who would he be? He's not from around here?"

"No."

"Where?"

I explained.

"And what's he like? How does he do at school?"

"He gets by."

"Did he pass?"

"Yes. All his marks sixes."

On the topic of Cattolica I was less laconic. I told how it came about that we shared a desk. I even said that despite sitting next to each other we'd never really become friends.

"If nothing else he has to be clever," Otello observed at this point. "Did you see how many eights he managed?"

We had arrived. I braked, put one foot on the ground and swiftly, as soon as he'd dismounted, Otello looked me in the eyes.

"Come in for a moment."

I replied that I couldn't, that I had to be going. And saying so, I pressed down on the pedals and left him.

In five minutes, I had reached my house, and having passed through the street entrance I immediately saw my mother seated in the garden under the magnolia. The sudden change from the heat outside to the cool of the entrance made me sneeze. I saw her raise her head. If I'd gone up to my room by crossing the garden—I thought—I would have had to stop to talk. It was just midday. We had plenty of time. And yet what would we have had to talk about?

I sneezed again and blew my nose. From the depths of the entrance, with my bike resting on my hip, I watched my mother half-closing her eyes. Immersed in the sun-speckled shade which gathered around the base of the magnolia, she was nothing but a remote, brightly lit spot.

She raised her arm.

"Oo-hoo!" she cried out, modulating her lovely singer's voice in her preferred call.

I disappeared to the side to put my bike in its usual place under the stairs, turned back and said that I had to rush off to make a phone call.

"Did you pass?"

"Yes."

"What were your marks?"

"I have to make a phone call," I repeated.

Upstairs, I passed through one room after another until I reached my bedroom. I had only just entered when I heard my mother's voice resound once again. She was now talking to the cook who was leaning out of the office window. When I had finished on the phone—she was saying— please ask him to come down here for a moment. And as the cook replied that I wasn't in fact on the phone, but she thought I was in my room, my mother began to call me again. She called out my name two or three times, lingering melodiously on the vowels. Between one call and the next I heard her grumbling.

I lifted the blinds.

"I'm here."

"Will you or won't you, strange fellow that you are, honor us by coming down here for a moment? Go on, hurry up and do as you're told."

She wasn't annoyed, far from it, not even impatient. At the heart of her realm, center-stage, surrounded by her "blessed creatures," the poodle, Lulù, the two smoke-colored Persian cats and the tortoise Filomena, she watched me and smiled. She was sewing the hem of a sheet or a tablecloth. The needle glinted on her lap. The garden, lush as a little jungle, glowed around her.

"I got all eights," I said, "except from Signora Krauss and Signora Fabiana. Six in science and six in physics and math."

"Well done, darling! I can imagine how happy your father will be . . . Come down now and give me a kiss."

She kept staring at me, gracefully tilting her head, her lips shaped in her sweetest and most alluring smile. When I showed no sign of moving from the window, she lamented, "Oh, d'you think it's kind to make your mother beg this much for a little kiss?"

A short while before, as I was walking through one of the drawing rooms, I had stopped to look at an old, silver-framed photograph which was on top of a small table along with many other family photos. It portrayed me and my mother in 1918, during the last summer of the war. Skinny as a girl, dressed in white, my mother was kneeling beside me against the background of the vegetable garden of my grandparent's country house at Masi Torello, where she and I had gone to stay shortly after my father had left for the Front. While she hugged me passionately to her breast, she turned in the direction of the lens an intensely joyous smile, in stark contrast to the severe and scowling expression on my chubby face, framed by long, straight hair cut in a fringe. The photo was taken by my father on one of his brief leaves from the Front—it was his masterpiece, he often said, and my mother would nod in agreement every time. Yet only a minute ago, I had understood the real meaning of that smile of my mother's, a bride of barely three years: what it promised, what it offered, and to whom . . .

I now watched her. My mother was no longer so young, no longer so much a girl, and I felt my heart once again filling with disgust and rancor. With the rapidity of jump-cuts in a film, epic and melancholic visions of storm-beaten, lonely beaches flashed through my mind, of dizzy, unreachable mountain peaks, of virgin forests and deserts . . . Oh, to be gone from here, to flee! Not to see another soul, but most of all not to be seen by anyone else!

"So?" my mother insisted. "Do I have to stay here beneath your balcony, begging, or would His Highness prefer his faithful follower to go all the way upstairs to pay him court?"

No. I'd come down to her. We would talk. I would let her question me, until the moment my father, having returned home and seeing us, would clap his hands to let us know he was there and was in a hurry to have supper. What would it cost me to have lied for half an hour? I would behave perfectly. Every attempt on her part to sound me out would fail.

And if she needed a kiss to deceive herself that I was still a little child, her little child, she would have the kiss she sought.

"No, wait," I replied. "I'll come down straightaway."

Saying this, I withdrew from the window sill.

15.

THE ULCER had begun to fester in secret. Slowly, torpidly, irremediably . . .

I was expecting no epilogue in the near future. I was neither expecting, nor hoping for any explanations whatsoever, not even concerning Luciano. And yet I did see Luciano at Cesenatico, a month and a half later. And with that meeting, I undoubtedly received an explanation of some kind.

One Sunday morning, after a sleepless night spent pacing up and down the few square meters of my little bedroom—I suffered from adolescent acne at that period—I went down to the beach very early and on my own.

It must have been eight o'clock. The vast expanse of sand appeared almost deserted. Stretched out on a deckchair beside a folded beach parasol, I finally dozed off into a fairly light sleep, as I still seemed able to register, one by one, all the small sounds that prefigured the noisy day at the seaside which was just beginning—the coming and going of beach attendants busy setting out tents and parasols, the rhythmic shouts of a group of fishermen drawing their net ashore—but no less restorative for that. And while I was thinking that at around ten I'd rouse myself and go to visit the tent where the children of the Sassòli family from Bologna were camping, and later I would go with them for the usual, very long-drawn-out swim— and then, there he was, before me.

He was standing there studying my awakening, his little skeletal body, utterly hairless, seeming even slenderer beside the abnormal swelling of his sex beneath the grey trunks. He was smiling at me.

"When did you arrive?" I asked, without getting up.

A flash of joy and gratitude lit up his eyes. So I wasn't going to chase him away! So I'd returned to being the nice person I used to be!

"Only about half an hour ago," he replied, with his customary lateral jutting of the jaw.

"Did you come from Ferrara?"

"That's right."

"But when did you leave?"

"When it was still dark!" he laughed. "At quarter to four—just imagine it—there was a local train. Chuff-chuff, chuff-chuff—it took us almost four hours to travel a hundred kilometers."

The train—he went on, all smiles and contentment—didn't miss out on a single station en route. It began its stops after only ten minutes: at Gaibanella. Then Montesanto. And then, one after another: Portomaggiore, Argenta, San Biagio, Lavezzola, Voltana, Alfonsine, Glorie, to "beach itself" at Ravenna, two thirds of the way through the journey, where it decided to have a rest for "a good thirty five minutes." After Ravenna . . .

I lifted my hand.

"How did you manage to find our villa?"

"Every now and then my memory seems to work," he replied with a smile, and winked. "I remembered the address."

That captivating wink, rather than hinting at our intimacy during the last months, meant to reassure me that he hadn't the least intention of reproaching me for anything. Though he did blame me. Affectionately, but still, he blamed me.

"You must be hungry," I said. "Should I fetch you something to eat?"

There was no need. My mother—he said, glad to ramble on once more—had already prepared a snack for him. As soon as she'd seen him, she'd kindly taken the trouble to set before him "an enormous cup" of milky coffee. He'd had the coffee in the dining room, along with my brother and little sister, who had just then got out of bed. But since the two of them wouldn't be coming to the beach before nine, and since he was keen to see me again, he'd hurried along here.

"Where did you change?"

"In your room," he replied, slightly alarmed. "Why? It was your mother who told me I could go in there . . . "

At this point he was sitting beside me on the sand. It was a really beautiful morning. Before us the water and the sky formed a single brightness. The boats in the distance seemed to be suspended in air.

"It's such a great place, this," he murmured after a long silence.

He turned back toward me for a moment, then, in a serious tone, added that he had come to Cesenatico on purpose to see me and have a talk with me. After being so friendly and kind, I had altered of late, and didn't seem the same person. And since his father had finally managed to persuade a friend of his, an old doctor in Bologna, to rent him his medical practice—a circumstance that would force them to leave Ferrara within a month—before moving elsewhere, he'd felt the "pressing need" to come and thank me once again, hoping at the same time to dispel all those misunderstandings that might have got between us. And so, what did I have to reproach him with? He felt his conscience to be "more than clear." In case I had believed some "stupid rumor" about him that had been put about by "malicious persons unknown" I had only to ask him, and he was ready to answer any question whatsoever.

Seated cross-legged like an Indian, he spoke without looking at me. I listened to him. I listened to the hum his words made in that huge expanse of motionless air. He'd said that he and his family were about to leave Ferrara, that we would never see each other again. Good.

"Go on," he persisted. "First question—fire away!"

I replied that there was nothing I had to ask him, not a single thing.

He shook his head.

"Perhaps," he sighed. "And yet I feel that you're hiding something . . . that you're not telling the whole truth."

For a while he stayed silent. At last, after another sidelong glance, he asked me how I spent my days at the seaside and if, during that month or more I'd been here, some seductive married lady hadn't assumed the responsibility of . . . of helping me lose my virginity. How many lovely and well-disposed ladies there must be in Cesanatico! Coming from the station to our house, he'd been able to ogle quite a few "luscious bits" taking a stroll along the avenues. I . . . with my physique . . . all I'd need to do was to take a look around. When on holiday, and especially at the seaside, women only think of enjoying themselves. So whoever . . . wants to enjoy himself with women . . . only has to know how to make the best of the opportunities the time and place have offered him.

I had been expecting him, sooner or later, to return to his favorite topic—I'd had that thought from the first moment I spied him through my half-closed eyelids. But the cautious, oddly anxious tone his voice had assumed was something I hadn't foreseen.

I replied that I hadn't encountered any married women of that kind, and this time the company I'd kept was all male, headed by some brothers called Sassòli from Bologna, and anyway, if I had sighted any such women, the spots erupting on my face would undoubtedly have stopped me from being taken into consideration.

He gave a quick look at my face and once again shook his head.

"What a weird idea!" he exclaimed happily. "You're strikingly handsome, regardless."

In any case—he went on—should I fail . . . ahem . . . to find anything better "out in the streets" I could always, if I wished, have recourse to him. He immediately explained. A few mornings ago, in Ferrara, while he was passing down Via Colomba, "a black-haired beauty" in her dressing-gown leaning out from a first-floor window in the Pensione Mafarka had greeted him with a big smile accompanied by a suggestive gesture. They hadn't actually exchanged any words. But he was sure all he needed to do was to introduce himself one morning wearing long trousers—his mother had resisted buying them for him, but within a week he'd be able to persuade her—better still if he was accompanied by a friend . . . and she, the dark haired doll, would let us "sample the goods" gratis. If the idea appealed— and he stared me in the eyes—I could be that friend.

"Couldn't you invent some excuse to make a trip to Ferrara"—he relentlessly pursued the topic—"that woman, you'll see, would not only let us in, but take us up to her bedroom together."

I looked away and up at the sky. As on every morning at that time, a military aircraft was flying over, some way out from the coast. In the distance, the silver cockpit of the Savoia-Marchetti glinted in the sunlight. How many kilometers out was it from the shore? I reckoned that those four fishing vessels far out at sea, motionless on the horizon, must have had the plane overhead.

I stretched and yawned.

"No," I replied. "First of all, I don't have any long trousers either. And then the idea of a threesome doesn't appeal to me. I would never do it."

"You don't like the idea of a threesome?" he stammered, staring at me, pallid as a drowned man. "But I . . ."

He added nothing more. He started examining the sand in front of his pointed knees.

I too remained silent. Suddenly I stood up.

"Would you like to take out a rowing boat?"

He lifted his face with an enquiring look.

"Gladly," he replied and was already getting to his feet. "But don't forget I can't swim."

"Never fear. Should the need arise, I'll save you."

I rowed. At some hundred meters from the shore, I spotted my mother in a skirt and short sleeved blouse standing in the doorway of the Adele Baths, having just arrived there from our house. With her right hand, she was holding Fanny's hand. With her left hand raised, she was screening her eyes from the sun. Not seeing us under the beach umbrella, she must have quickly surmised that we were in the sea and was trying to work out where.

"Oo-hoo!" I cried, waving an arm above my head.

"Oo-hoo!" she replied. "Oo-hoo!"

"Who is it? Your mother?" Luciano asked.

I didn't reply. I had begun rowing again vigorously, my eyes fixed on my mother, who was already making her way toward our beach cabin. By now she was tiny. In a short while, when she left the cabin wearing her beautiful blue Janzen swimsuit, she would be no more than an indistinguishable speck.

When we had gone about a kilometer from the beach, I stepped up on to the seat and dived in the water. Left alone on the dipping and rolling boat, at first Luciano was overcome by panic. He gripped the seat, looking around bewildered. But he soon seemed to calm down, and I was aware he'd begun to follow my maneuvers in the water attentively and admiringly.

"You looked like a motorboat," he said as soon as I'd climbed back aboard. "What do you call that stroke you were doing?"

"The crawl."

"What is it? Does it come from America?"

"From Hawaii."

"I can believe it!" he exclaimed enthusiastically. "Last week I was at the canal by Via Darsena to watch a swimming race. No one swam like you, making all that foam with your feet. Is it hard to learn, the crawl?"

"Not that hard."

I tried to explain to him how you needed to coordinate your feet with your head and arms.

"And who taught you how to do it?" he asked when I'd finished.

"No one," I replied.

In the meantime I'd started rowing again.

"And what now?" Luciano asked in a melancholic tone, realizing that we were once more heading for the open sea. "Aren't we going to turn back?"

"With the sea this calm it'll be worth the effort to get as far as the nearest fishing boats."

I nodded with my chin toward two of the four fishing vessels that I'd noticed from the shore, and that were now fairly close. If we were alongside when they draw in their nets—I said—perhaps they'd give us some fish to make soup with.

"But apart from the soup," I added, "can't you see how beautiful it is?"

And it was, after all, beautiful. I can hardly remember a sea so calm and so flat—rather than floating on the water it seemed that we were flying, gliding slowly through the air. Was that the shore out there opposite? Hazy, with the blue hills behind, I could barely recognize it.

Luciano too had his head turned toward the distant shore. Silent, shut in his thoughts, he seemed to have forgotten about me.

I watched him. And suddenly, there, in the fiery motionless air, I was shaken by a strange cold shiver. I didn't fully understand. I felt uneasy, suddenly at the edge of things, in some way excluded, and precisely because of that, envious, wretched and petty . . .

And what if, instead, I'd spoken my mind to Luciano? I wondered, staring at his thin, lonely back, a little reddened by the sun above his shoulder blades. If I had been decisive, accepting his recent suggestion, had roughly placed him and myself in front of the truth, the whole truth? Not for an hour yet would the offshore wind begin to make the water choppy. There would be no shortage of time.

And yet in the very moment when, facing his sorry bare back, suddenly distant, unreachable in its solitude, I gave way to these thoughts, already, then, something was telling me that if Luciano Pulga might be able to accept this encounter with the truth, I would not. Slow to understand, nailed by birth to a destiny of exclusion and resentment, it was useless to think I'd ever be able to throw open the door behind which I was yet again hiding. I just couldn't do it—there was no remedy. Not now. Not ever.

: V :

The Heron

I

1.

NOT instantly, but resurfacing with something of a struggle from the bottomless pit of unconsciousness, Edgardo Limentani thrust out his arm in the direction of the bedside table. The small traveling alarm clock which Nives, his wife, had given him three years ago in Basel on the occasion of his forty-second birthday, kept emitting at brief intervals, in the darkness, its sharp, insistent though quite discreet alarm. He needed to silence it. Limentani withdrew his arm, opened his eyes, and turned, leaning on his elbow and stretching out his left arm. And at the very moment that his fingertip reached the Jaeger's delicate, already slightly worn buckskin leather and pressed down the button to stop the alarm, he read the time from the hands on the phosphorescent dial. It was four o'clock: exactly when, the evening before, he had decided to wake up. If he wanted to arrive in Volano in good time he shouldn't waste a single minute. With one thing and another—getting up, going to the lavatory, washing, shaving, dressing, knocking back some coffee and so on it seemed unlikely he'd be in his car before five.

As soon as he had turned on the light and, seated on the bed, had looked slowly around, he became prey to a sudden sense of listlessness and was tempted to give up, to stay at home.

Perhaps it was because of the coldness of the room, or the faintness of the glow diffused from the central light—but what was certain was that the bedroom, where except for a brief stretch just after his marriage and except, of course, for the later year and a half in Switzerland, he'd slept since his boyhood, had never seemed to him so alien and so squalid. The dark wardrobe, tall, wide and bulbous—his mother had always referred to it as "paunchy"—which occupied a good part of the left-side wall; the heavy chest of drawers on the right-side wall, topped by a small oval mirror, so opaque it was good for nothing, not even for knotting a tie; directly in front of him the mahogany glass showcase for rifles, dwarfed by the grey form of the pelmet; the armchairs; the wheeled clotheshorse on which yesterday afternoon, a good half day early, his mother had set out his woolen suit, the proper vest and longjohns—the other articles that comprised the whole hunting outfit including his boots which she had preferred to have ready for him in the bathroom—several mounted pictures (that of his degree certificate and those of his own photographs, chiefly of mountains) here and there randomly hung on the walls: each piece of furniture, each of his household goods, each object which fell beneath his gaze discomfited and vexed him. It was as if he were seeing them all for the first time. Or else, more accurately, as if only now was he able to perceive their petty, irksome and absurd aspect.

He yawned. He passed his hand over his cheek and chin, rough with stubble, pushed back the covers, set his feet down onto the floor, took from a chair his fawn-colored towel dressing-gown, put it on over his pyjamas, shuffled on his slippers; and after a few moments stood before the window and looked out over the courtyard through the glass and the half-closed shutters.

There was hardly anything to be seen. The courtyard was so steeped in darkness that he could barely make out the well at its center. And yet from the kitchen window of the Manzolis, the caretakers, streamed a bar of the whitest light: intense enough to reach the top of the high surrounding wall which faced toward Via Montebello, the upmost branches of the tall climbing rosebush which, in summer, almost completely covered the inner side of the wall. Gusts of the sirocco shook and ruffled it. The gusts were dry and light and sudden as though impelled by an electrical discharge. It wasn't raining. As long as the wind blew it wouldn't rain.

He turned to look toward the entrance. The door of the ground floor apartment the Manzoli family occupied was open. From it another light shone out, though far weaker than that from the kitchen window, and suddenly a bent and burdened figure was seen in profile against it.

"Romeo's already up and about" he muttered to himself.

Attentive and motionless, he followed the caretaker's every move. He saw him go up to the wrought iron gate which divided the entrance from the courtyard, half open one of the wings of the gate, step out into the street, look up at the dark sky, and finally, evidently having become aware of him, the owner, he doffed his beret.

He opened the double casement window, and was caught by a gust of soft, damp, almost warm wind as he swung the blinds wide and leaned out to fix them to the wall.

He straightened up.

"Good morning" he said, addressing the caretaker. "Would you please tell Imelda, if she's already up, to make me a coffee."

"Will you be going anyway, *sgnór avucàt?*"* asked the other in dialect, he too in a soft, lowered tone.

He nodded in the affirmative, and then closed the windows. Moving away from the windowsill, he was in time to notice Romeo once again doffing his beret. How many long years had the Manzolis been in service at their house? he wondered as he entered the bathroom, slightly distracted just as he passed the gun cabinet by the subdued gleam of the rifle barrels behind the glass. They must have been with them, he concluded, for maybe a little more, a little less than forty years.

He took off his dressing gown, hung it on the hook fixed high on the door, let the water in the basin run till it was hot, and took his shaving kit from the leather washbag, all the while observing himself in the mirror.

That face was his own, and yet all the same he stood there observing it as if it belonged to someone else, as if not even his own face belonged to him. He checked every detail meticulously and diffidently: his bald convex forehead; the three horizontal and parallel furrows that were etched almost from one temple to the other; the faded-blue eyes; the sparse, too

---

* *Sgnór avucàt*: Ferrarese dialect for *signor avvocato*, the respectful title given to a lawyer.

emphatically arched eyebrows that gave his whole physiognomy a pereni-
ally uncertain and perplexed expression; the nose rather pronounced, and
yet handsome, well-designed, aristocratic; the lips big and protuberant, a
little like a woman's; the chin disfigured at its tip by a kind of dint in the
form of a comma; the brick-red coloration of his long, lugubrious cheeks,
darkened with stubble that was so black it seemed bluish. How malicious
and unpleasant, how absurd, even his face was! His mother had always
maintained, naturally with gratification, how much it resembled that of
the former King Umberto. That might well be so. One thing for sure was
that, if the current tide of Communism were to keep on swelling—truly
one couldn't see who might be able to halt it . . . De Gasperi?* With a face
like that?—all the proprietors of farms of a certain size, and among these,
as fate would have it, they too, the Limentani, with their La Montina estate
of over four hundred hectares, would very soon be forced to relinquish
their ownership.

He began to lather his face, beginning with the point of his chin. And
as the lines of his face gradually disappeared under the foam, he began to
feel, even more markedly than before, the burden of the day of hunting
that awaited him.

It was he alone who had decided on it. And why had he done so? To
what end? Wouldn't it have been far better once and for all to give up on the
idea of going to the hide to shoot duck. His cousin Ulderico Cavaglieri, for
instance, although he'd settled for good in Codigoro, and therefore within
a stone's throw of the valleys, although, protected as ever by the big patriar-
chal Catholic family he'd assembled over some fifteen years, and although
he could at this stage entirely disregard even the Communists, as earlier
he'd disregarded the Fascists of the Salò Republic and the German SS, all
the same he hadn't considered it wise to hang around waiting all this time.
On the contrary. In 1938, in the autumn of '38, soon after the Racial Laws
had been declared—Ulderico was then forty years old while he himself
was now forty-five—no, he hadn't let that deny him his gun licence. Not
a chance. He hadn't even put in a request as it had simply been renewed.

---

* Alcide De Gasperi (1881–1953) was the founder of the Christian Democracy Party and
prime minister of Italy from 1945 to 1953.

And in '45, just after the Liberation, he had taken care not to make the mistake of reapplying for it.

He shaved with his usual care, after which, waiting for the bath to fill, he slipped out of his pyjama bottoms and sat on the toilet. For some years emptying his bowels in the morning had become a bit troublesome, and when he couldn't go—either because he'd eaten too much the evening before or because he'd got up too early—then for the whole day he'd feel in the worst of moods, and even suffer from palpitations. As he'd expected, today it wasn't going to be easy. But it would hardly be a good idea setting off in this state! There was the risk that he'd have to stop halfway, perhaps without even the possibility of washing.

So he sat there, in the thunderous roar of the water cascading into the bath, and keeping an eye on the level which was rising meanwhile. He thought about the hunt in the valley, about how it had been before the war and how it might be now. Before the war—he remembered—a gentleman from Ferrara could go and fire off a few shots in the region of Codigoro or Comacchio on a Sunday and be quite sure of a good reception and of general respect. More than that, from the practical, the organisational perspective, everything would be precisely prearranged—and one could tell that it had been so for centuries—because the same gentleman would find it straightforward to travel and stay there, and have something to eat, in short to find everything he needed *in situ*. But today? Apart from already being a considerable danger, traveling through the countryside in an automobile—exactly as in 1919 or 1920 there were those who had seen a windscreen smashed by a big millstone thrown by persons unknown from behind a hedge—what else might he expect to find there, with or without a double-barrelled shotgun slung over his shoulder, except dark looks, backs stubbornly turned or even open and challenging sneers? The times of courteous smiles, of the doffing of hats, of respectful bows were over. For everyone—the politically and the racially persecuted alike.

He thought too, as for several months he had been unable not to, of the unpleasant occurrence that befell him, he of all people, last April at La Montina, that day he decided to go and see how the land-levelling works were proceeding.

What a brilliant idea! And, above all, what a glorious scene!

He once again saw himself in the midst of endless fields, seated on the verge of a ditch, with some thirty field hands—familiar faces, for the most part, the majority of whom he'd known for years and years—who, ready to bring their raised hoes down on his skull, demanded the immediate revision of their sharecropping agreements. He'd had no option but to yield, and Galassi-Tarabini, his family solicitor whom he had consulted as soon as he returned to town, had unconditionally approved of his "tactic." And yet this was what had resulted from the advice that his lawyer had then dispensed, not to give the least regard to the promise he had given, but rather to report the threats of violence he'd suffered to the Codigoro *Carabinieri*: from that day on he hadn't dreamed of setting foot in La Montina again, so his manager and accountant Prearo needed to visit the farm on his behalf every now and then to tally his accounts with Benazzi, the farm overseer. And because, since 1939, the entire inheritance of agricultural and real estate of the deceased Leone Limentani was now in the name of his daughter-in-law Nives, Nives Pimpinati, Catholic, Aryan and at that time eight months pregnant, his son Edgardo and his widow Erminia Calabresi, his direct heirs, could now consider, definitively, the over four hundred hectares of the holding, if not also the Ferrara house in Via Mentana where for good or ill they still lived, the property of another person.

Apart from Galassi-Tarabini and his accountant Prearo, he had never spoken to a soul about the incident at La Montina, neither to his mother nor to his wife. His mother for sure—just a glance at her and you could see how unruffled she was—had heard nothing about it up until now. But Signora Nives? Was it possible that she hadn't been informed of everything by Prearo with whom he would so often see her confabulating in the administrative offices? Then with respect to the farming community of Codigoro and its district, as far at least as Pomposa—above all the community of farm laborers—fat chance that they wouldn't have drummed the whole affair into the heads of all and sundry at the local trade union council!

But precisely because of this: if that was how things were, what point would there be in risking worse, what the devil would make him take that chance? Was it worth provoking further trouble, perhaps even of a physical nature, for the simple desire to fire off some shots?

Which was more important, all considered, the hunt or else . . . ?

Abruptly he decided to wait no longer.

"It's all pointless, anyway" he grumbled morosely.

He raised himself, shifted to one side and stretched out over the bath to turn off the taps, and was standing upright once again.

In the meantime the room had filled up with thick tepid steam.

2.

STANDING MOTIONLESS before the closed door, touching the latch without lowering it, he wondered if he might still manage to slope off unnoticed.

His mother and his wife had said goodbye to him the previous evening, when, soon after dinner, he'd left them in the dining room to knit away in silence in front of the smoking coals of the fireplace. It was true: the previous evening he hadn't been able to say goodbye to Rory, his baby girl, since he'd come home from the Unione Club at nine and by nine Rory would already have been asleep for a good hour. Yet now was certainly not the time to hesitate. If giving Rory a kiss meant he'd have to face an additional series of goodbyes from Nives, who occupied the double bedroom next to his own, opposite the baby's room (his mother's bedroom looked out at the front: far enough away and safely isolated, by the grace of God!), then no thanks, he would gladly have done without that kiss.

He opened the door slowly.

As soon as he was outside he switched on the light, turned to shut the door, then made a few tentative steps across the linoleum of the corridor. Although he was wearing short American military boots without nails in their soles, nevertheless he put down his feet with extreme care. His usual weight was about eighty kilograms. But today swathed as he was in his hunting clothes, and laden with the weight of two rifles, the Browning and his old Three Rings Krupp, today without doubt he must have weighed another twenty kilos. The merest creak provoked by his hundred kilos from the parquet beneath the lino, and Nives, who had always been a light sleeper, would in all likelihood awake and call him.

"Dgardo!"

"Ssh!" was his instinctive reply.

Who knows how but Nives had managed to hear him. "What a pain!" he grumbled. If he didn't immediately enter her room, she'd be sure to start yelling for him.

He poked his head into the utterly dark room.

"Ssh! What's wrong? Wait a second."

It irked him to have to enter his wife's bedroom with the rifles, the cartridge belt round his belly, and all his gear: the five-shot rifle in its conspicuous bag of *écru* leather, especially, which despite every announced program of tight economy he had bought the previous September at Gualandi's, the foremost gunsmith in Bologna. Slowly then, taking pains with every movement, he offloaded the Browning, hanging it from its strap on the window handle there at his side. He was about to do the same with the double-barrelled shotgun, but there'd be no harm showing that gun to Nives, he reflected. She had seen it in his hands even as far back as their time in Codigoro, when she was only his mistress, so most likely, she would hardly notice it now. It could also serve to avoid a scene of any kind—an *intention* of that sort wasn't out of the question: she was more than capable of starting a quarrel at just such a moment—by making it clear to her he was just about to leave, and hadn't a minute to spare for a chat or anything else.

He entered the room.

Nives was switching on the bedside table lamp. With his righthand thumb hooked between the gun's leather strap and the bristly tweed of his jacket, he moved toward the center of the room. And so, approaching the double bed of carved pinkish wood where he, the only son, had been conceived, and where from 1939 on he had slept so rarely with his wife, for the second time that morning he felt himself pervaded by a strange sense of absurdity. Once again it was as if between himself and the things he saw around him a thin transparent layer of glass had been interposed. Everything, there, on the other side, and he on this side looking at them one by one in a state of wonder.

Nives yawned. She lazily lifted her naked arm and covered her mouth with the back of her hand. Half buried beneath the waxy fat flesh of her upturned hand, the little gold wedding ring was almost invisible.

"What time is it?"

"Twenty minutes to five" he replied, staring her in the face. "I have to get going."

"Christ almighty—it'll be so cold! Is it really cold?"

"No, not very. I think it'll rain."

"Don't forget to take your raincoat, Dgardo!"

"I've already put it in the car."

"And the wellington boots?"

"Likewise."

While they spoke they were observing each other: he with his hands on the bedstead, she stretched out as always on her side, the righthand side, of the bed. But what they said to each other was of no importance. It served, for her too, only to buy time. In the meantime she too was scrutinizing, studying, weighing things up.

"I really have no idea why anyone would want to go hunting in winter," Nives continued. "Especially between Christmas and New Year! Just see if you don't come home with pneumonia!"

"Why should that be? All I need to do is keep well wrapped up."

"Have you at least put on the woolen suit?"

"Yes. Mamma took care to put it out on the clothes horse."

He hadn't planned to say that, he could swear to it. All the same Nives grimaced.

"Since Mamma Erminia always wants to plan ahead for you," she said, giving a series of curt nods of her head which was full of curlers, "it wouldn't be polite of me to get in her way."

Luckily, she quickly changed her tone.

"How can anyone do that?" she continued, "Staying out soaked through for five or six hours without a break? Good Lord, you could keep in mind that you're no longer a spring chicken! Just thinking about it I get goosebumps. Brrrr."

She laughed, narrowing her eyes. And he, at the end of the bed, while curiously observing their shape and every detail of that face, felt a sense of stupefaction growing within him. He could fully understand how it could have come about that this little countrywoman aged between thirty and forty, with her small grey inexpressive eyes, her short hooked nose like the beak of a raptor, and with that small mouth and its thin almost invisible upper lip and its fat prominent lower lip, had become his wife. Oh how well he understood that! Yet at the same time, watching her play the role of a lady from the most select urban society who had never once set foot in the country, least of all in that of the Bassa region, he couldn't believe it was true. Nives. That Nives. What was she called again, her surname? Ah yes: Pimpinati. Nives Pimpinati.

"What time will you be back this evening?"

"I'm not sure. After five."

"Are you going to visit your cousin as well?"

There was nothing at all strange about her asking a question like that. It was no secret that after almost ten years he had finally decided to reestablish contact with Ulderico—only by telephone, it's true, and with the excuse of asking if he happened to be able to suggest someone to take him by boat through the valley marshes, but the ice had thus been broken. And yet the question must have seemed to her in some way risky and indiscreet. She feigned indifference, but he knew her—though who knows what was going on inside her head now. Poor Ulderico. She was probably still unable to forgive him for doing everything in his power to persuade him not to marry her . . .

"I don't know" he replied. "It's possible."

"And where will you go to eat?"

"I don't know. Perhaps in Caneviè . . . or maybe even in Codigoro, at the Bosco Elìceo restaurant. It's not as if there's a great deal of choice."

Nives wrinkled her nose.

"So you'll go to that nice Fascist Bellagamba?" she exclaimed. "To that thug of a *tupìn*?[*] Sorry but rather than go there you'd do much better eating at our house in the country. You could get Benazzi's wife to make you something, a *pastasciutta*, a cut of meat . . . At the end of the day," she went on, with a harder look in her eyes, and speaking now as if the whole thing concerned her, directly, personally, as though it concerned her more than it did him, "at the end of the day the house at La Montina is still ours if I'm not mistaken!"

---

[*] *Tupìn*: Ferrarese dialect for mouse, but here a reference to violent young Fascists.

What on earth was Nives getting at?

She smiled, tightening her lips.

"Well, it's up to you" she continued. "But you know what I'm thinking? It would be a pleasure to go there, to La Montina, once in a while, perhaps even to be taken there by someone. That's something I might enjoy! You may think everything's fine. But the effort to be polite, not to ruffle anyone's feelings ends up, little by little, with *them* taking possession of it all, of the land. And nothing will stand in their way, just see if I'm wrong."

This meant one of two things: either she didn't know what had happened to him last April at La Montina, and in that case by "*them*"—when she pronounced it, he noticed, her upper lip lifted to form a circumflex—she meant to refer in general to the thousands of Pimpinatis, Benazzis, Callegaris, Callegarinis, Patrignanis, Tagliatis etc. who were in political "agitation" in the whole Bassa region of the Ferrara countryside from the city gates to the sea, always after more and more from the landowners. Or she knew, and so was inviting him to speak about it, to open up, to confide in her.

This latter prospect suddenly filled him with a kind of fear. Confide in Nives! And tell her what exactly?

"Listen to what Prearo told me yesterday evening" Nives continued. "He told me that . . ."

"It's not because of that" he interrupted her. "It's so as not to have to drive another ten kilometers as well. And then, if it rains, there's the risk of getting stuck in the mud."

He moved back brusquely from the bed, and turned his back.

"If you start back later than five o'clock," Nives shouted out behind him, "beware of the fog!"

He turned slightly, lifting a hand to stop her making a fuss.

"Fine, yes, I understand."

Although she was sleeping alone, she was well organized. On the bedside table, apart from an image of the Virgin Mary Help of Christians, to whom the main church in Codigoro, the one in the square, was dedicated, she had also arranged the miniature radio, the basket with her sewing things, the photographs of her parents and a stack of papers. Why did they still live together?—he wondered as he left the room. Why didn't they finally separate?

He paused in the corridor, in front of the Browning, once more unsure what to do. He checked the time on his Vacheron-Constantin wristwatch—another keepsake from Switzerland. It said four fifty-eight. Late, he was late—he said to himself. Still. . . . Suddenly deciding not to shoulder his second rifle, he drew a flashlight from his jacket pocket and walked toward the door of his daughter's bedroom.

He turned off the corridor light, lit the flashlight, lowered the latch, and very slowly entered the room. To separate, yes!—he thought, advancing on tiptoe amid the faint smell of talc, school exercise books, chalk dust and floor wax which always wafted between those walls. To separate—it took nothing to say the words. But in practice how would they manage to accomplish such a thing? How much would it cost in lawyers' fees? Not a little, that was for sure. And in that case, how would it be possible for him, the landowner of nothing, to gather together what was needed? "At the end of the day, La Montina is still ours, if I'm not mistaken," Nives had said just a moment ago, laying the stress on "ours" and "mistaken." Truly she couldn't have found a turn of phrase that was more effective in reminding him how things actually stood.

But aside from that, what about Rory?

Having drawn up to her little bed, he halted. Almost holding his breath as he felt his heart beat throbbing darkly in his throat, he directed the beam of light first at the tiny Christmas tree placed in a pot at the bedside, and then at the small body stretched out under the fluffy pink angora wool blanket—beginning with the slight swelling of her feet and ascending as far as her shoulders and the lower part of her cheek. And while he stood contemplating Rory, astonished as ever at how beautiful, how lively, how strong she was (her face perhaps somewhat resembled his own, especially the eyes, which, however, were bigger than his—they were huge!—and in the shape of the lips) he was suddenly overwhelmed by an inexpressible anxiety, by a sense of inconsolable desolation. He did not know why. It was as though, silently and without warning, it had leaped upon him. As though he had been attacked by a wild beast.

He leaned down to brush his lips against the little girl's forehead, retraced his steps across the room, and went out a third time into the corridor. He turned on the light switch and looked at the time. It was five minutes past five. He went back to pick up the rifle leaning on the window handle, slung it over his left shoulder, and went on his way. And soon after, with the sensation of falling into a well, slowly, and without any sign of haste, he descended the dark spiral staircase which led down to the entrance.

3.

AT THE doorway it was very cold: a damp insidious cold which could really have been that of a well, of an underground cellar. In sudden gusts through the street door, which Romeo for some reason had left wide open, the wind made the little blackened ironwork lamp sway perilously where it hung from the coffers of the dark ceiling.

The caretaker stood still down there at the threshold, intently staring out toward the invisible facade of the house across the way. What was he doing looking out there? With his slightly hunched shoulders, like those of a worker on strike, stubbornly turned, he not only seemed unaware of his presence but also to have forgotten that before leaving he still needed to have his coffee and besides that, always, especially in winter, the motor was meant to be warmed up slowly, without any hurry.

The melancholy, familiar, faithful shape of his dark-blue Lancia Aprilia waited outside the door with its fenders pointed toward the gate that opened onto the courtyard and that had remained half-shut. He went round the car, placed the rifles on the chest which stood up against the wall opposite the staircase, retraced his steps, opened the car's right-hand-side door and sat behind the steering wheel. While he fumbled with the starting key— the motor seemed loath to start up: doubtless due to the cold, but also due to the battery, as ancient as the rest of the vehicle—he didn't detach his gaze from the motionless shape of Romeo reflected in the rearview mirror. For the almost thirty years he'd helped with these early morning departures for the country, never, he said to himself, had he behaved like this. Was he, perhaps, now for the first time, suddenly irritated to have had to get up before dawn and on a Sunday too? Was that what he wanted to convey? Given the times, everything was possible. However it was, here was another novelty, and not in the least a pleasant one.

After a series of coughs, the motor finally came to life. With an effort, thanks to the cartridge belt wound round his waist, he leaned forward to find the choke under the dashboard. When he sat back up again he was surprised to find himself face to face with Romeo. He stood there beside the car door, slightly stooping, looking down at him from under his heavy tortoise-like eyelids.

"Will you be wanting your coffee?" he asked slowly in dialect.

He knew the caretaker's character inside out—brusque, sometimes surly, but still affectionate and unfailingly faithful. And so—he told himself, and his breast expanded with relief—not only did Romeo not harbor the least rancor toward him but, on the contrary, from the vague hint of jokiness hovering around his prominent cheekbones, one could guess that he was content, privately delighted and gratified to see him after so many years once again going off on a duck shoot.

He got out of the car.

"Is it ready?"

Romeo nodded. Then, pointing with his chin toward the two rifles, he asked if he should pack them in the boot.

"If you give us the keys" he said in dialect, "I'll put everything in."

"No, it's not necessary," he replied, trying to maintain the usual tone, between benevolent and self-composed, which typified their relations. "It's better you put them on the back seat. And this as well if you don't mind."

He took off the cartridge belt and laid it on the caretaker's outstretched arm, after which he went with rapid steps toward the lit-up entrance to the Manzolis' apartment.

The apartment where they lived comprised three inter-connecting rooms, railroad-style. On one side the kitchen, which overlooked the courtyard; on the opposite side the bedroom, with its window onto Via Mentana; in between a huge room which, since their daughter Irma had gone to live with her husband, the two old folk had piled up with rows of polished furniture, but which in practice they never occupied. As always happened since that event of last April in La Montina, and now, once again, stepping into the caretaker's flat—and especially into their kitchen which was so pretty and neat, so well-lit and above all so well heated by the glowing plates of the cheap stove—suddenly lifted his morale. That was it—he exclaimed to himself once again—here he felt at ease, truly and completely as if at home! The Manzolis were utterly dependable!

He sat at the table, and began to take slow sips of boiling coffee from the bowl without a handle that was kept for his use—his own *mastèla dal cafe,* his coffee bucket—as Romeo called it in dialect. Meanwhile Imelda, her sharp features hidden behind the black kerchief of a local peasant woman, moved busily about.

He stared at her over the curved rim of the cup, intently following her every move.

Neither she nor Romeo could stand Nives. More or less openly they showed their disapproval of everything to do with her, extending their disapproval to include Prearo, the accountant, as well as the cook Elsa, and even Rory—in short, every new person or thing that had made an appearance at no. 2, Via Mentana since 1938. Whenever they spoke to him about her, they never called her by name. Unfailingly they called her "*your* Signora," the only true ladies of the house being "Signora Erminia," and Lilla, the three-year-old poodle who was his mother's tender companion, and was even allowed in her bed, her only true child to cuddle and spoil in every possible way. They had nothing in the least bit good to say about Nives, ever. He only needed to enter their house for a moment and one or other of them would start up their usual litany of complaints.

Recently, for example, they had begun to refer to Nives's habit, when he was away from home, of not using the entryphone. For their slightest need, both she and Elsa preferred to lean out of the window, and yell so loud that the like of it was never heard even in the big apartments of Via Mortara . . . And now—he wondered, lowering his eyes, as if by doing so it would be easier to draw on the infinite reserves of patience he needed to have at his disposal—what further offence committed by his wife would he have to hear about? Imelda was certainly brooding about something.

He raised his eyelids again.

"What's wrong?"

Once again he was mistaken. Imelda had reddened eyes, continually raising her handkerchief to her nose, but she wasn't thinking about Nives at all. As soon as Romeo had come to the door, she began to inveigh against William "that scrounging Commie William" as she put it in dialect. Although he had all his electrician's diplomas—she was loudly complaining—William refused to work, spent all his money at the brothel, so that they, poor and old as they were, had to carry him and his wife, both, on their shoulders.

He turned toward Romeo.

"Who is this William?" he asked.

"Irma's husband," Romeo replied drily in dialect, bending his silver head under the light.

For a moment he didn't understand—as though, to protect his inner calm, his memory had stopped working.

But then he quickly remembered.

Of course—he reflected—the husband of Irma, their daughter. How had he forgotten about him?

He was a young man of about twenty-five—he recalled—scrawny, straw-blond, with a fluent patter, well-mannered, someone who up until recently he'd often enough seen hanging about the entrance and the courtyard, and who had once not only offered to wash his car but, having done so, had refused any payment. A Communist? He could easily have been: it was enough to look at his thin, pale, avid face eaten up from within by who could guess what secret rage, enough to listen to his Italian that sounded like that of a radio announcer, so smooth and detached, it was true, but also so suspicious and unreliable. It was a source of wonder that Irma, such a meek girl, so refined and well brought-up, raised by the nuns in the sewing school of Via Borgo di Sotto, and ready to blush all over if anyone so much as chanced upon her in the street or greeted her, let alone talked to her, should have let herself fall for a person like that.

Now Irma was six months pregnant—Imelda was explaining to him. And so she, working from morning till night like a "skivvy," then had to fork out for the extravagance of that good-for-nothing husband.

He felt a growing unease, and yet he stayed there. He still couldn't make up his mind to leave. He looked at the time: five thirty-five. On the telephone Ulderico had been very precise about the time. The man he'd hired who was to ferry them from Lungari da Rottagrande to the hunting hide—a man called Gavino if he'd heard correctly—would be waiting for them at Volano, in front of the big Tuffanelli house, from a quarter past six. It was now five thirty-five. He had to be there at a quarter past six. The meeting with Gavino wasn't going to work. He'd be there at the earliest by six thirty, or even a quarter to seven. And that was without taking into account that, to the best of his recollection, from the Tuffanelli house to Lungari di Rottagrande they would have to travel around more than a third of the perimeter of Valle Nuova and so that would mean a good half hour to add on before they arrived. So if everything were to go smoothly, he'd be able to hunker down in the hide no earlier than a quarter past or half past seven when it was already fully light. And that was only if he he didn't hang around another minute and left at once.

He looked at his watch, trying to hurry himself up, to find the necessary energy to get to his feet. Useless. A vast inertia, stronger than any exertion of his will, held him to the woven wicker seat in the Manzoli kitchen, as though he were tied down. Oh, if only, despite everything, he had could just stay there, in the warmth of the caretaker's flat, hidden from his family and from everyone else until the evening! He would have given anything for that.

He raised his eyes to Imelda.

"But why on earth," he asked, "would your son-in-law not want to work?"

Shrugging her thin shoulders, Imelda replied that she didn't know. "Beats me," she said in dialect. She only knew one thing—she went on—that her son-in-law stayed in bed all day and if she, Irma, ever tried to reproach him, "to tell him off," that Communist delinquent was quite prepared to give her a clout.

It was true. That was guaranteed by Romeo's face, suffused with a barely contained rancor and even more so by her face, with its eyes that spoke of fated, perhaps even willing, victimhood.

Bewildered, he made as if to get up.

"If he doesn't work," he tried to object "perhaps it's because he can't find any."

Romeo intervened.

"Not a chance!" he said in dialect, lowering his head. "Doing nothing's the only thing he'd dream of doing."

"But then why"—he persisted, turning to the question of Imelda once again—"don't you get her, your daughter, to come back to live with you?"

The woman sighed. She'd suggested that to her umpteen times—she said. But Irma was stubborn as a mule. She didn't want her mother even to talk of it.

"She's in love," she summed it up, twisting her thin lips into a grimace full of scorn.

Certainly she's in love, as he had anyway already understood. And now even the Manzoli kitchen had become uninhabitable—this too a place one had to vacate. And quickly.

In the silence that followed Imelda's final words—while only the muffled grumbling of the Aprilia's motor idling at the gate reached him through the walls—he looked at his watch once again. Five fifty-two.

"Well, I'd best get moving," he announced.

He grasped the edge of the table with both hands, stood up, and made his way out. And to Imelda who scurried after him begging him to do something for Irma—if he were to speak to the son-in-law, she said, perhaps that "scoundrel" would finally make up his mind to turn over a new leaf—he replied with a "We'll see" which he, more than anyone, knew meant nothing at all.

Go and speak to a fellow like that?—he thought to himself while he went through the door and walked toward the car. Speak to *him*? Imagining the talk he would have with the young electrician with his cadaverous face, he felt invaded by a kind of disgust. A disgust mingled with fear.

He got into his car. He turned on the headlights. Finally, he replied with a wave to Romeo's deferential salute as he slowly negotiated the reverse maneuver which brought him out onto the street, and there, halted at the edge of the pavement, looked back at the caretaker, who was standing in silence with the faint light from the doorway at his back, as he shifted into first and drove away.

4.

ALL HE wanted now was to be there in Codigoro.

For a good part of the journey, from the Prospettiva Arch right up to the outskirts of Codigoro he had driven with his eyes fixed only on the road. The ferryman would be waiting at Volano, so he had to hurry. But besides that, only after Codigoro, after Pomposa, when he saw in the uncertain light of dawn the low deserted landscape broken by stretches of apparently stagnant water—which were actually in flux, joined as they were to the open sea—only then did he begin to relax, to breathe easily.

And yet, just at the outskirts of Codigoro, a hundred meters before turning onto the smoothly asphalted ring road, an acute spasm of pain at the level of his belt, heralded a moment earlier by a faint heart tremor, forced him to bend forward over the steering wheel.

"Just as well that we're here" he grumbled, glancing up through the windscreen at the two looming chimneys, the one of the Eridania sugar factory and the other of the water pump of the Land Reclamation Company.

He was well attuned to his own habits. He could hold off for a maximum of ten minutes. Would that be enough?

He made use of the first, rare municipal street lights, madly swinging above the rough cobbles of the country road, to look at his watch. Six forty. At that time the two cafes on the square would already have drawn up their blinds. Best then to give up his plan to drive on to Volano and stop at Codigoro instead. If he could get as far the square, he'd be safe and sound.

Turning right, he soon reached the town center, and drove into the square. No lights at all he immediately noticed—annoyed and yet, absurdly, with a sense of relief—neither from the two cafes, the one opposite the other, nor from the ten-story building of the I.N.A.* there in front of him, where Ulderico and his family lived, nor from the other houses in the vicinity, large and small. Everything was shut. All dark, with not a soul to be seen.

He parked his car on the left, beside the big, *Novecento* ex-Fascist Head-

---

* Istituto Nazionale delle Assicurazioni: a large Italian insurance company.

quarters, now become a *Carabinieri* barracks. He switched off the head-lights, then the motor, got out and calmly locked the car door. Codigoro. Codigoro's main square. It had been some ten years since he'd been there at such an early hour. And yet he couldn't recall ever seeing it so deserted. What had happened to make it so? Was it because of—he grinned—"the Communist terror." Or simply Christmas time?

It wasn't cold and, here at least, there was hardly any wind. Strange, even his stomach was no longer bothering him. A dog left the shadows of the entrance at the base of the I.N.A. building, a setter to guess from its stride. He saw it move into clear view toward the center of the square—in fact it *was* an old setter—and come to a halt at the statue for the Fallen of the First World War. It sniffed studiously at the figure's boot and urinated on it, then, at the same trot, disappeared down an alley to the left. And if he should try calling round at Bellagamba's?—he wondered, once again alone. True, it might be that not even the Bosco Elìceo would be open. At worst, though, given that it was also a hotel—he had never slept there himself but he'd often heard it said that there were bedrooms upstairs—he could always ring the bell.

He opened the boot and took out a grey Russian-style Astrakhan cap, an old *schmutter* that had served him since he was a youngster both for hunting in the valleys and for skiing in the mountains. He put it on. Then, some twenty meters from his car, he came to the corner of the ex-Fascist Headquarter's facade and the adjoining street. He narrowed his eyes and scanned the street. He wasn't mistaken. Even the Bosco Elìceo was shut. So he really would have to use the bell. As there was no doubt about it, a stop was called for. He had no choice.

Regardless of this, when he came up to the lowered blinds, with the neon sign sizzling above his head, the sudden prospect of finding himself in a face-to-face conversation with Bellagamba, who might very well be the one who opened the door, was enough to hold him back.

He remembered Bellagamba in '38, in '39, in his corporal's militia uniform—he was called Gino, if he wasn't mistaken, Gino Bellagamba—with his fez tilted back on his shaved neck and with the black tassel swinging halfway down his bullish back. He remembered his gritty aspect in those days, his air of a country bully-boy reinstated into active service because of the requirements of the time, his almost perpetual presence in the square in front of the Fascist Headquarters, the threatening and scornful looks that he'd had to put up with as a "Jew," as an "apolitical" and as a landowner, every time that, returning to Codigoro en route to La Montina, he'd had the misfortune to come within range . . . No. To find himself in front of that ugly mug, with whom, apart from all the rest of it, he'd never exchanged a single word in his whole life, to have to ask him for what he would have to, permission to use the toilet, all this would be far from pleasant, that was for sure. If only he had got there a little later, he would almost have preferred to turn on his heels and go and ring the doorbell at the Cavaglieris' house.

But what could he expect to find there? Besides, why go to all that bother? He had always got out of accepting the Fascist membership card, not because he was especially *anti*, if truth be told, but just from that unsociable side of his character, and in this respect his behavior was different from that of Ulderico who, for his part, when they had offered him the card in 1932, had pocketed it straight off. But when all was said and done, were the Fascists before 1943 that much worse than the Communists of today? And the present trade union councils, enforcers of policies to the detriment of those who owned land, were they really any worse than the Fascist Headquarters or the local Fascist groups of those days? As regards Bellagamba, perhaps it was true, as Nives claimed, that after the Badoglio period he had joined up with the forces at Salò. Very likely. In any case, if even the Communists, who were the absolute masters in Codigoro today, left him alone to make a good living, why should he of all people kick up a fuss about him? Besides, it was well known that Nives had it in for her townsfolk. She never missed a chance.

While he stood there, uneasy about the two rifles left in evidence on the backseat of the car—perhaps it would be better to turn back at once and hide them in the boot along with the cartridge belt—he seemed to hear noises filtering out from inside the inn They were murmurs, sighs, tremors, creaks—as though made by someone effortfully shifting furniture about.

He waited a while in silence then knocked with his knuckles on the corrugated iron sheet.

He was assailed by a voice that was violent, irate and at the same time frightened.

"Who is it?"

"A friend," he answered quietly.

"A friend who?"

He hesitated. He heard heavy steps from inside approaching, then coming to a halt.

"Limentani," he said.

"Who?"

"Li-men-ta-ni," he repeated without raising his voice, suddenly marvelling at his own surname, at the way the syllables of his own name resounded in the open air.

With a single tug, the blinds were fully raised.

It was indeed him, Bellagamba—he saw—even bigger, fatter and more bullish than before, with his chest under the leather jacket shaped like a woman's. And seized once more with his old repugnance he was on the point of turning his back and leaving. Perhaps he was still in time.

But he was too late. Bellagamba who was already opening his blue eyes wide, had recognized him.

"What a treat!" he was saying under his breath.

He smiled gleefully, showing the small compact teeth of a boxer.

"You've no idea what a fright you gave me, Signor Avvocato," he went on, still in a whisper, and then as he moved aside he winked at him conspiratorially. "Come in, please. It's cold out there. Do come in!"

He would have expected anything but such a cordial, such a talkative welcome—strange how Bellagamba too, like that William, the husband of Irma Manzoli, spoke an unusually fluent, easy, refined Italian. He would almost have preferred a rougher more hostile reception, so that he could assume the role of the courteous and absent-minded gentleman. What did this conspiratorial behavior of Bellagamba's mean? Once he was taken into the man's den, was he planning to force him, in his presence, to mourn the loss of the golden times of the Fascist era, or even those of the Salò Republic? Bellagamba, like everyone else at Codigoro must have known every detail of what had happened to him last April in La Montina. But if he was now expecting to hear complaints and confidences from him, he was greatly mistaken. He held no grudge against anyone in the world and against Bellagamba least of all. And yet, let's be clear, neither did he have any personal ties to him.

In the meantime he'd entered with the impression, intensified also by the strong stench of fried fish which took him by the throat as soon as he crossed the threshold, of venturing into a cave, into the den of a wild animal. He took off his fur cap and looked around. He found himself in a medium-sized hallway, immersed in an almost complete darkness. On the opposite side from the entrance, on top of a small isolated desk, a table lamp capped with a lampshade of green silk spilled a faint yellowish glow.

He quickly realized that the desk was nothing other than a brand new hotel reception desk. Behind it, on numbered hooks fixed in a double row to a wall of limewashed plaster hung ten or twelve keys. In the semi-dark he could make out nothing else. But that was enough. That desk and those keys were enough to make him aware how little the present inn, transformed by the ex-corporal of the militia into a hotel and restaurant, shared with the unpretentious country eating-house as he remembered it from years ago.

Bellagamba had remained behind him. He heard him muttering, swearing between his teeth at the blinds that refused to shut again. Every now and then he advised him to take care. On the floor there was a half torn open package with something heavy inside—a weighing scale which had arrived the evening before by post from Milan. He might trip up and do himself an injury.

At last Bellagamba drew closer, and as he brushed past, wafting the smell of his armpits, he lightly bumped against his shoulder. He made his way toward the desk and turned a switch mounted beside the keys. Finally in the vague blaze of a fat neon tube that ran crossways along the ceiling they sat facing each other: he occupying a small leather armchair and Bellagamba there behind the desk, his wide jaw divided in two by the yellow light of the table lamp.

With an even stronger sense than before of being outside the world, he didn't know how to begin. It wasn't even thinkable to ask for something to eat. He felt his stomach was clenched like a fist.

Bellagamba came to his aid.

"But what," he enquired in an insinuating tone, suddenly switching to dialect and narrowing his bright watery eyes, "but what, pardon me, brings you here? Have you maybe come to Codigoro to hunt?"

Given the way he was dressed the question was essentially superfluous. But the way it had been posed in that insinuating yet at the same time humble tone—very much that with which a farmworker on his own lands might have addressed him before 1938—was enough to reassure him of his basic safety.

He nodded.

Yes, he then said. He'd come here exactly for that—to fire off a few shots.

He lifted the hem of his sleeve and glanced at his wristwatch.

Though would he be in time to do that?—he wondered and all at once really doubted it. He was too late. He should have reached Volano some time ago—at a quarter past six. While now it was already past seven.

At last he made up his mind.

He got to his feet and looked around.

"Would you mind me using your toilet for a moment?" he asked.

5.

THE STAIRCASE was in front of him, straight and steep.

He went up slowly, step by step, holding on to the smooth wooden banister and staring up at the landing, watching it gradually draw near. Up there, the sky appeared through a kind of open round window in the opposite wall. The sky was dark, crossed by rapid swollen clouds. Dawn was breaking.

Once he had set foot on the landing, he stopped for a moment to get his breath back. To the left and to the right two short, ill-lit corridors led away. All the doors to the rooms were shut. On the floor outside one of them, the last on the right hand corridor, a solitary pair of man's shoes had been set out.

Bellagamba had really gone all out—he thought looking at those shoes. He'd spared no expense. But why be surprised at that? There was a fair amount of cash in circulation, more than a fair amount. For everyone. The only ones to be denied, always excluded from the tide of bank loans, were those few old-style agricultural landowners who still existed, and remained attached tooth and nail, some for one reason, some for another, to the usual corn, the usual hemp, the usual beetroots and therefore, Communism or no Communism, destined soon enough to disappear, to be swept away. Fair enough, it's true—someone else in his place would have paid heed to Nives and Prearo, the accountant, who for quite a while hadn't missed a chance to make him understand that enough was enough, it was time to quit, and once and for all he should decide to be rid of the old traditional crops which had become disastrously unproductive, and turn his estate, as so many others had, into an exclusively fruit-growing enterprise. Someone else in his shoes, not caring a jot for the Communist threats, would have presented himself one fine day at La Montina with a goodly escort of *Carabinieri* and have sacked the lot of them starting with that equivocating overseer Benazzi and ending with the last of the hired hands and cowherds. Someone other than him. Because it wouldn't be him. He agreed with the banks, the Agricultural Bank of Ferrara included, who were ready to give financial support to anyone at all, even to a Bella-gamba, but not to certain "hangovers from the past" a phrase which could be read in even the official newspapers such as the *Giornale dell'Emilia*. It was enough for him to think of himself as a farmer to immediately renounce any such project and see himself as a relic.

In the meantime he had climbed a second staircase. Broken by a small mezzanine landing, this one was less arduous than the one before. He began climbing a third which was once again steep. At last, without once detaching his gaze from another port window identical to the first, he reached the summit of the top floor.

Here, too, were the same empty corridors in semi-darkness, the same closed doors. Slightly to the right of the stairwell he recognized the door he was seeking at once. A little earlier Bellagamba had been explicit. "You'll see it's even written on it," he had specified, with every precaution, as though hoping to cut a good figure, directing him to the only toilet in the hotel he considered befitting such an honorable guest rather than to the "water closet" of the ground floor. It was indeed as he'd said. The straw-colored door sported an enamelled metal plate three-quarter way up on which could be read BATHROOM. It seemed to him like a miniature road sign. The kind that were usual before the First World War, but were now rarer than white flies. The color of the elongated, upright capital letters was the same blackish blue as the thin border.

He went in.

Even before he had turned on the light he noticed that the bathroom did indeed contain a bath. Apart from the lavatory, the room had a rectangular cast-iron tub, a basin with a mirror above it and a bidet with two taps.

The lavatory was on the other side of the bath next to the window. He approached it and examined the seat of blondish wood which had retained some flecks of white paint. He lifted it with his foot. Taking off his jacket and cap which he hung on the window catch, he unbuttoned his trousers and the two pairs of underpants, lowered them and sat down directly onto the freezing porcelain.

But nothing. Once again nothing. His bowels showed no inclination to empty themselves. Regardless of every effort, he felt that not even now would he succeed and if he did any result would be infinitesimal.

On the low window sill, a meter or so from his forearm, there was some newspaper—a small pile of square sheets all cut to the same measure that a dark, porous sea pebble kept orderly and secure. He stretched out his hand and drew out from under the stone the first sheet on the pile. It must have come from a newspaper published some months earlier, he thought, reckoning on the yellow hue of the paper—perhaps an old number of the *Giornale dell'Emilia*. SPERI IN NEW YORK declared a caption in big letters. And so—he tried to remember—when was it that De Gasperi had gone to America to discuss things with Truman and Marshall? In April? May? Or earlier? That visit must have been before then! The Communists had been dismissed from the government *after* the crisis last May. And the crisis, the last of a series, had broken out—this he remembered exactly—when De Gasperi had already been back in Italy for a good while. So was it in January then? Or February?

He picked up at random some other sheets, the provenance of none of which he could establish, but not all of them had been cut from the same newspaper or from the same day. RIGHT TO STRIKE ELEGATION

OF THE COAS declared another headline in even bigger letters than the previous one. And another: ENNI and TOGLIATTI─ATTACK THE GOVERNM And yet another: EDDING OF JEWISH BLOOD─IN TODAY'S POLAND.

He tried to read a passage of the two column article that followed.

It was a report from Cracow. If the reporter was to be believed, in Poland under the Communists in 1949 the persecution of the Jews was proceeding no less bloodily and cruelly than under Gauleiter Frank, Hitler's trusted henchman in Polish affairs. Was that possible? The tone of the article seemed to him excessively strident. The writer was surely exaggerating. And yet there must be some truth in it. Heavens─he grinned─surely it couldn't all be nonsense!

He raised his head and to distract himself looked out of the window. Dark but clear, it was now full daylight. No mist, no fog. Under the window, adjacent to the earthen courtyard where Bellagamba kept his hens, he saw a wretched, overgrown soccer field stretch out in a vertical perspective, with the islanded goal posts at either end. Even from a distance he seemed able to perceive all their grey, frail, woodwormy decrepitude. Beyond the sports field more or less the whole village─its dark roof tiles, so different from the roof tiles of Ferrara (thicker, more irregular as though they had been handmade one by one) and yet seen together so similar, so obviously of the same breed. And out there, the square, the Church of Santa Maria Ausiliatrice on one side, on the other the red facade of the Trade Union Hall between the now lit-up windows of the two cafes and in the middle, as though on the same line of vision, much higher than the roofs of the modest little houses that flanked them, the two massive structures of the ex-Fascist HQ and the I.N.A. building facing each other. And then, farther out, the curve of the river port, hidden by the two banks, but easily surmised from the looming masts of the big cargo ships at the end of the docks. And finally, farther still, much farther away, along the asphalted ribbon of the main road to Ferrara, high against the row of frozen poplars this side of the Volano stretch of the river Po, the northern edge of La Montina, the thin smoke-darkened chimneys of the Eridania sugar refinery and lower down the single chimney of the Land Reclamation Company's water pump . . . Like a land surveyor deprived of his essential equipment he tried to measure the distances and proportions by eye. How far off in a straight line—he wondered, but casually without any real attempt to deduce it— was the square by the river port? And that group of chimneys, down there to the right, how far was it from them to the half-ruined, brown, Gallo watchtower, tiny in the midst of the bare fields of La Montina, just slightly more visible than the farmhands' dwellings scattered at wide intervals around the property?

However hard he tried he couldn't see the little villa—sold at the time of the Racial Laws—where he had installed Nives in 1930 and of which, for years, he had been the owner. No, that he couldn't make out. Isolated at that time on the southern reaches of the village, today it was impossible to distinguish it from the countless other houses put up in that area since, and all of them more or less of the same type. But that didn't matter. How many hundreds of meters separated that quarter, the most modern part of Codigoro, from the central square? And the ash-colored statue of the infantryman which, atop the monument for the Fallen in the main square, was throwing himself into battle waving the torn and bullet-riddled regimental flag, was it bigger or smaller than lifesize?

The direction of his thoughts changed again.

He now thought about Ulderico, his cousin and friend, his great friend, the inseparable companion of the first two thirds of his life at least who, for something like fifteen years, after having rented out the building in Via Montebello, Ferrara, to the Land Reclamation Company, had come to live in Codigoro, within walking distance of his estates, not even in a lovely villa surrounded by a park but in a nondescript apartment, big, comfortable, but nondescript, right in the center of the town. And thinking of Ulderico, and of himself, and of their lives so similar and so different, he decided that sometime late that afternoon, if he didn't feel too tired and had a brace of wild fowl to bring as a gift—with the dark and the mist the chance of being spotted and of having an unpleasant encounter in the street was almost zero—he would certainly go and pay a visit to the Cavaglieris: Ulderico, his wife Cesarina and all their kids. It was true that he hadn't visited them once, neither before the war nor during, nor for that matter in these last three years following his return from Switzerland, and that he hadn't set eyes on even one of their six children—six! But after the two telephone calls he and Ulderico had exchanged last week, after all his cousin's unstinting kindnesses to him, not least of which had been not to appear in the least surprised to hear his voice after so long, what point would there be on either of their parts to persist in not seeing each other? How strange life is! He remembered the huge scandal of 1932, within the family and beyond, when Ulderico had decided point-blank to marry, in church, the seamstress of Codigoro, with whom for ages he had been carrying on a more or less public relationship—what the hell kind of surname did she have?—and on top of that, on the very day of their marriage, to get himself baptised. And he remembered, still thinking about Ulderico, the insistense, the unexpected and unbearable interference, the absurd doggedness with which, ironically, his cousin had tried to make him give up on the idea of marrying, in his turn, his own mistress Nives . . .

No, no—he came to a conclusion. To continue not seeing each other, to persist in maintaining a distance as if they had something to fear from one another, would be utterly meaningless.

6.

LATER, WHEN he had come down again, Bellagamba was not to be found. What a trial it would have been to have to take his leave of the militia's ex-corporal, what a pain. All he wanted to do now was to be off, to distance himself from Codigoro as quickly as possible.

But no sooner had he left and come to the square than he saw Bellagamba himself standing on the edge of the same sidewalk, from which he once used to cast inquisitorial and threatening looks at everyone, townsfolk and outsiders alike. Standing beside the old Aprilia with a foot resting on one of the front tires, he had the air of an expert weighing up the condition of the forecarriage. He realized that it wouldn't be possible to dodge him and that he'd have to put up with wasting even more time.

Approaching, he observed him. There was something almost unrecognizable about him. Over a high-necked, iron-grey sweater like a cyclist's he wore a dark double-breasted coat and, on his head, a soft hat with lowered rim of the same tone. Completely inoffensive, and even as camouflaged and out-of-place as he too felt himself to be, Bellagamba looked quite like Mussolini in his last years, when the Germans took him away in a Storch single-engine aircraft from his Gran Sasso refuge . . .

"Hello" he said.

"This yours?" the other asked in dialect, barely giving him a glance and signaling toward the car.

He nodded. He came up beside him and looked out in front of him. It was eight o'clock. The square was filling up. And while Bellagamba spoke to him about the Aprilia, fulsomely praising the "brand and model" and, it seemed, offering to buy it off him—he'd been looking for a car of this type for some time, he said, robust as well as cheap to run, and preferably one that had had few owners, better still just one, to customize it into a small van, given the growing demands of the restaurant—he couldn't take his eyes off the throng which, gathering in groups, grew ever bigger minute by minute there in front of the low redbrick building of the Trade Union Hall opposite. Others, women, girls, mainly very young girls, were continually being swallowed up by the big dark central entrance to the Church of Santa Maria Ausiliatrice, set alone in a space behind to the left, at the end of the churchyard which was vast as a private square of its own. No one showed any sign of noticing the two of them. Everyone seemed busy with other concerns. With what though? he wondered, feeling reassured, but at the same time strangely unhappy, disappointed. From the top of the belltower which rose slender and pointed at the rear of the church, so tall that on some days of fine weather, coming from Ferrara, one could begin to make it out at least twenty kilometers away, the solemn tones of the great bell were ceaselessly calling the people to Mass.

The bell was tolling. Some moments before, Bellagamba had stopped talking.

Now it was his turn.

"Ok. I'll think about it," he murmured, his gaze still fixed on the belltower. "Perhaps we can discuss it later today."

"You'll be coming for lunch?"

A little earlier, at the entrance of Bosco Elìceo, where he and Bellagamba had parted, there was seated a fellow of about seventy, thin, with a grey mop of hair, the pallid gaunt face of a malaria victim, wearing a filthy, worn-out, striped jacket. Not in the least fazed to see him descending from the upper floors, he had informed him at once that "Signor Gino" had left less than a quarter of an hour before, but without saying where he was going or when he'd return. "Well, would you say goodbye to him for me?" he said to the old man as he made his way out. "Give him my thanks, and tell him I may be coming back for lunch."

For lunch?—he now thought. He had indeed spoken of lunch. But what if instead, abandoning all his plans, he were to return immediately to the city?

In any case he didn't reply. He shifted his gaze from the belfry, immediately below the very tall spire, and looked up at the sky. There were no longer any swollen, swift, low altitude clouds coursing over the village roofs but a uniform, grey, compact mantle. And if he really were to return home?

He turned to Bellagamba.

The latter smiled at him with his usual, ambiguous, sly and vaguely sleepy expression.

"And would you care for a coffee?" he heard him propose in dialect.

He was being treated, he thought, with the same intimate, circumspect patience employed by Romeo. But in neither case was it to make fun of him, or with any obscure intent to provoke him, to test him out. Quite the reverse. If he hadn't misjudged it, he was only trying to reassure him, to make it clear that there was quite simply no need to keep on being disturbed by what were no more than shadows. To suggest to him, as a friend, not to have any unnecessary qualms, worries or fears.

"Where?" he asked.

"Over there. At Fetman's"

With his big chin propped up by the high collar of his sweater he nodded toward the cafe on the left side of the square.

"They serve much better coffee there than at Moccia's" he went on, signaling once again with his chin toward the right, at the square's other cafe. "And also," he added with a wink, "at this time of the day I can assure you that you'll not encounter any unpleasant faces at Fetman's." Then he added in dialect, "On that I give you my word."

As the two locales in the square at Codigoro had been from time immemorial the designated meeting places not only for the various political factions but for all the dealers of the region, he had always avoided frequenting them—both out of instinct and from principle. Fetman's—what a name for a bar! Before the war it had a completely different kind of name . . . He'd not set foot in there even once. And yet why not? Even now, in '47, with the Reds in full spate, to go in at such an early hour, the chance of coming up against some ugly hostile mug would have been roughly the same as before, in other words pretty slim. And then if, having taken his coffee, he really *should* decide to return to Ferrara—in which case he'd have to give up the idea of paying a late afternoon visit to the Cavaglieris'—what more convenient spot could there be than that for him to telephone Ulderico from? If he wanted to simply greet him and nothing more, holding out the possibility of another trip to Codigoro in the near future especially to see him, then he would have to do it soon, before he left.

"Why not?" he replied. "Let's go."

They crossed the square side by side like two old friends—with the constant impression in his mind that everyone was ignoring them and, exactly as happens between friends, without exchanging a single word.

They then stood at the bar waiting to be served. During the wait—at Fetman's there was hardly anyone: a few anonymous, taciturn regulars seated at small tables at the end of the big rectangular room that looked more like a garage than a cafe; a smoky atmosphere impregnated with the smells of expressos, grappa, Tuscan cigars; he could feel his cheeks gradually becoming warm—his attention was once again directed to the I.N.A building. Staring at it through the misted-up window panes, the construction seemed to him like a vague kind of grey-pink outcrop, like something threatening and impervious. It really was an impressive edifice—he thought to himself—as impressive as it was disproportionate. This explained why the street of which it formed the corner and over which it loomed with its ten floors, looked so straitened, wretched and dark. He scanned its ground floor. No visible entrance. In the semi-darkness that still lingered under the arches in front of it were alligned one after the other the three windows of the agricultural machinery salesroom which he had glancingly noticed a moment before while crossing the square. And so, he wondered, how would you enter to reach the floors above? Perhaps at the back? He should remember to ask Ulderico about that when he called him.

In the meantime Bellagamba had resumed his chatter.

He was offering him advice. Confidential but respectful—speaking in rather subdued tones as well, evidently because a bartender was nearby— Bellagamba had begun to find fault with his plan to push on to Volano. What would be the point of that?—he was saying. Apart from the uncertain weather, it didn't seem to him at all likely that he'd arrive and settle himself in the hide before ten o'clock, however fast he went. And there'd be no serious hunters out there that Sunday, as could be seen from the fact that last night only a single person had taken one of his rooms and gone out, and he wasn't even a hunter at all but someone from Reggio, a salesman for barber's razors, and if he, Signor Avvocato, were to go, what would he have to shoot at at ten in the morning? It was pointless. To arrive at the hide so late, you always risk going home empty-handed or worse—out of frustration you'd start taking potshots at a seagull of which unfortunately there were never any shortage.

"Wouldn't you like me to get a nice bed prepared for you instead?" he added, his voice lowered to a whisper. "Just say the word, and I'll go straight to the hotel and get things ready."

Bellagamba had turned to look at him. He had the habit of winking but this time his face was all red as if he were offering him something exotic, if not forbidden. But he was right—he couldn't help acknowledging. There was no denying it. As for the bed, though, not a chance. Far better to get back in his car, and off to Ferrara. In the afternoon, at five-thirty, after a nap, an outing to the Unione Club to while away the time with a game of bridge until supper time, would always be an appealing option.

"No thanks," he replied. "It's kind of you, but it wouldn't be convenient." He took out his handkerchief and dried his mouth.

"Excuse me—I have to make a telephone call," he said, raising his face toward the bartender.

"To Ferrara?"

"No. Here in Codigoro."

The bartender, a forty-year-old with a greasy, sweaty face and sporting a grizzled three-day beard, stared at him coldly.

"Who do you want to speak to?"

"Cavaglieri, the engineer."

"Right away!" the other exclaimed, suddenly obliging, extracting a telephone token from a drawer under the till and proffering him it. "The telephone booth's over there."

He signaled toward a kind of tall narrow wardrobe of dark wood and glass, sited against the farthest wall of the big room, beyond the chairs and small tables. And making his way toward the phone booth, he wondered with envy how the mere name of his cousin could prompt so much deference toward him. But he was wrong to be surprised, he reasoned with himself at once. Good heavens! Fifteen years of fixed residence in a small town of a few thousand inhabitants, with a wife who was local, a gaggle of kids and so on—anyone in like circumstances would end up becoming assimilated, even the least disposed to be so. And then add in Ulderico with his odd but not unpleasant character which made him sure of himself at every turn in his life, and always so calm and cordial! He was probably a regular at the Cafe Fetman, as it was only a few yards from his house.

Having made his way over, he was about to enter the phone booth.

"Do you have his number?" the barman called out.

He turned round. Down there, Bellagamba was intent on lighting a cigarette, his face hidden in his cupped hands; several customers had looked up and were staring at him.

Of course. The number. It doubtless consisted of just two digits. But which?

He shook his head.

"No."

"Dial twelve. One. Two."

He shut himself in and dialled the number. He heard it ringing for a long while at the other end of the line. Only then did he realize it had a different sound to the discreet, muffled tone of the Ferrara telephone network. Insistent, raw, gratingly metallic, and very hard on the ear.

"Who's calling?" a rude voice finally interrupted, a voice that made him even more inclined to put down the receiver.

"Limentani," he replied quite loudly, overcoming with difficulty that sort of surprise mixed with embarrassment he always felt in pronouncing his own surname.

"What was that?"

"Limentani," he repeated.

He was most likely speaking to a housekeeper, an old woman without many teeth in her head, and perhaps a bit hard of hearing. Limentani, Edgardo Limentani. He had to repeat it several times, even breaking it down into syllables. To no avail. The old woman just couldn't understand. Until, finally, she replied that the engineer was still in bed and that Signora Cesarina had just gone into the bathroom.

He hesitated.

"I'm sorry, I don't want to disturb them," he said. "But all the same would you tell the Signora that it's their cousin calling, the one from Ferrara?"

"Wait a moment."

Their cousin from Ferrara—to drag even this out had cost him dearly. And yet he was in no doubt. When she, Ulderico's wife, would come to the telephone, keeping any kind of conversation going would be hard work. What sort of person was this Cesarina? The truth is he could hardly remember her. In all he'd seen her a couple of times when she was a girl, without having any clear impression of her physically and without having exchanged a word. Tall, blonde. Maybe a redhead. After some twenty years—twenty years!—including a marriage of that kind and all the rest of it . . . And how should he address her—with the informal "*tu*" or the polite "*lei*"?

In the meantime no one had picked up the phone, and despite the fact that the apartment—as he could tell from the noise—was in a state of commotion.

The apartment. It must be big, very big, some of the rooms like enormous drawing rooms. In the one with the telephone, for example, some children were playing right at that moment with a rubber ball. There were at least three of them and all were boys. And from the thuds their jumps and sprints and falls made on the parquet it wasn't hard to reach a reasonably exact idea of their surroundings and its dimensions. Far, far away a baby was crying, a baby only a few months old. But then, much closer, he heard the voice of a girl of around fifteen shouting "Clementina!" And as

Clementina, shut away who knows where, perhaps in her room or in the toilet, was slow to reply, the other told her to run to Tonino or Tanino. "Come on out," she said impatiently but with a laugh. "Do come on out, it's not as bad as that . . ."

He was holding his breath, without making the slightest movement. It felt as though he too was in the Cavaglieri house, hidden behind some door to eavesdrop and spy on them.

"Goal!" yelled a boy from very close by.

"It doesn't count!" protested another younger one. "I saw you. Get lost. You sneaked it in with your hand!"

"No—it was a goal!" the first boy insisted.

What a din—he said to himself—what utter chaos. If only they'd just go and play somewhere else . . .

And yet, although of their own accord his lips had twisted into a grimace of disapproval and intolerance—see what happens, he thought, when you load yourself down with kids: however spacious and comfortable it is, no house will be big enough, life will turn into a living hell—he felt compelled to remain there, the receiver glued to his ear, listening to the voices and noises with a tense and defeated sort of hunger.

"Who's there?" suddenly along the wire, a child's slightly hoarse voice asked.

As a general rule, he didn't like small children. Even with Rory herself—it had happened early this morning when he had entered her room for a moment—his throat closed up and he could feel himself choking. On the telephone, though, it seemed to be different. One could always find something to say.

"Edgardo" he replied. "And what's your name?"

"Andrea."

He heard him breathing heavily. It was obvious what had happened: the boy had seen the receiver dangling down the wall. And since his older brothers weren't including him in the argument as to whether it was a goal or not, at a certain point it had occurred to him to make the most of the break in the game and have a go on the telephone. Usually he couldn't reach it by any other means than standing on a chair.

"How old are you?"

"Six."

"And are you already at school?"

"Yes."

"Which class are you in? The first form?"

"No. The preparatory first."

Rory at seven, he recalled, was already in the third form.

"We're a little behind," he attempted to joke. "But you're a good boy at least?"

"So-so."

"What d'you mean so-so? You have to be a good boy. Surely you know that?"

The child did not reply. His silence coincided with the resumption of the soccer game. So more screams, more running, jumping, thudding. And Andrea stayed there, at the other end of the line, with the heavy, determined breathing of a little peasant.

Rain or no rain, whatever it cost, he felt a sudden violent overwhelming desire to be in the midst of the valleys, alone.

He could of course hang up—he thought. Without waiting any longer for the maid who, he could have bet on it, hadn't managed to convey anything at all clear, neither his first name, nor his surname, nor anything else—who knows what she was still saying to the Signora through the shut bathroom door—he could have easily hung up and made himself scarce. Besides, as soon as he woke up, Ulderico would immediately work out who had called . . .

And wasn't this, if anything, the only thing that mattered to him?

He gently put down the receiver.

II

1.

J UST as he was leaving the telephone booth it occurred to him that out
in the valleys he would find everything he needed—serenity, health in
body and mind, the joy of being alive. He should waste no time. He walked
toward Bellagamba who, seeing him approach, cast away his cigarette. He
paid for the telephone token at the till. Then, finally, with the old Fascist
dogging his heels, he strode out.

"Goodbye," he said as soon as they were outside on the sidewalk in
front of the door.

"This morning," the other said in dialect, "they'll be fetching me a fine
turbot from Gorino. Would you like me to keep it for you?"

"Please do," he quickly agreed, only to be free of him.

He stretched out his hand.

"And thanks," he added, "thanks for everything."

He waited for Bellagamba to finish pressing his hand between his two
big hairy paws, then turned his back and began to cross the square.

He walked hurriedly, lifting his face every now and then to sniff the air.
No rain at all, not a drop. As for the air, likewise dry: now he could sense it
was laden with that characteristic lagoon smell, salty and at the same time
sweetish, which stuck so stubbornly and ineradicably to clothes and which
after a short time always made him hungry. Excellent—he said to himself,

in a good mood. During the last quarter of an hour the wind had not only begun to blow but had also changed direction. It came from the opposite direction, from the sea. If it kept blowing from there for a while, the whole sky would become clear.

To take the road for Pomposa he had to drive past the Cafe Fetman once again.

Bellagamba was still there, standing on the sidewalk.

He took the small lateral road, the entry to which was overshadowed by the I.N.A. building. He quickly reached the river port, crowded as it was every Sunday by the brown shapes of the boats one beside another below the dock. Then after a few hundred meters, he took a right turn. Beyond the bend, because of the cobbles, he had to slow down and drive at a walking pace. But down there, just after the intersection with the ring-road, he hoped the surface would again be nice and smooth. As indeed it was. He saw the bluish edge of the asphalt drawing nearer and enjoyed the imminent prospect of being able to put his foot down.

He passed the intersection and, just after, the junction of the short road to the cemetery, crowded, especially toward the far end beside the pinkish surrounding wall, with the usual Sunday visitors. He pretended not to notice the gesture with which a good-looking blonde girl, standing on the corner dressed all in black and with a veil over her face, was asking for a lift. He put the car into third, then into fourth gear. Soon enough, without his going slower than seventy kilometers per hour, the Pomposa abbey came into view.

How long it had been since he last visited this part of town!—he couldn't stop himself sighing as the Aprilia sped along the final straight stretch of road.

He was glad, however. Glad that the abbey, apart from the undergrowth that now clung more thickly to it—this, a sign that the pumps of the Land Reclamation Company had been able to keep on working undisturbed even in the last few years—had survived the war preserving its original aspect intact which was that of a large-scale agricultural enterprise like La Montina. Ah well, he said to himself, staring at the old red stones of the monastery. With that bell tower, from one side spacious as a silo of grain; with that church in the midst of it all which rather than a church made one think of a haybarn; with those other unadorned buildings on the right like big farmhouses disposed around the barnyard: to all intents and purposes, even if on a bigger scale, every element of Pomposa closely resembled La Montina. And meanwhile he was also glad that, remembering La Montina, repeating its name in his mind, his heart wasn't crushed within the usual grip of bitter regret, anxiety and fear.

Having got as far as Pomposa he took a right turn toward Romea then, after a few hundred meters, turned left, all the bends to left and right leading at a slant into the valleys. He breathed deep. Toward the south, as far as the eye could see, he noted the vast, almost marine expanse of the Valle Nuova; toward the north, the stark, reclaimed lands in the distance bordered by the black, uninterrupted line of the Mesola woods. He felt so calm now, so full of energy and faith—it was cold and he'd turned on the heating—and yet it seemed to him all the same that the air of the lagoon had seeped into the closed car to expand his lungs. In short he felt so well that a little later, becoming aware of a sudden acidic taste in his mouth, he considered this detail hardly impinged on his state of well being. He shook his head and smiled. It was only natural. Having taken in nothing but two coffees since he woke up—how stupid of him not to have got Imelda to give him at least a piece of bread before leaving, and then a quarter of an hour ago at Codigoro not to have remembered to buy a packet of Saiwa biscuits or some cake—all things considered it was perfectly normal that he should now be reduced to this condition. It was clear that he'd have to have something to eat before settling into the hide. Were there any eating places at Volano? Good heavens, surely there must be, even nowadays. At the worst, in any case, he'd be able to scrape together half a loaf of homemade bread or a slice of Ciambella cake, the rustic kind with big sugar crystals sprinkled all over it, by knocking at one of the doors in the village. What would it cost him to ask? No one at Volano would ever have recognized him. And of course he could pay . . .

He passed the isolated fish traps at Canaviè, where they used to sell food but which now seemed utterly decrepit and out of commission. He passed Porticino, a place name which as ever corresponded to nothing, nor even showed the slightest sign of human habitation. And finally, after the umpteenth twist and turn, there was Volano, with its little low houses lining both sides of the street that crossed the whole village and far down

there the massive parallelepiped of the big Tuffanelli house against which
the street seemed to come to a halt. There were only some hundreds of
meters to go—he thought accelerating—and then he'd find out if Ulderico's man had indeed waited for him. It was unlikely. But for now he should
take a look. Then, if he was, he could decide what to do.

He passed the semi-deserted village, and slowly, as a sign advised,
crossed the bridge over the Volano stretch of the Po, then stopped beside
the Tuffanelli house, sheltered from the wind, on the side which looked
toward the Valle Nuova, and immediately got out of the car. There wasn't
the faintest sign of Ulderico's man. He looked at his watch: a quarter past
nine. Who knows how long the poor fellow must have had to wait.

He pricked up his ears. Silence. Only the far cries of unseen birds, high
in the sky. Closer, perhaps chained up, a dog howled.

He scanned the huge landscape that surrounded him.

He saw, there, at the edge of the flat terrain of water and small islets
through which he had come and which were brightened by patches of sunlight, the bell towers of Pomposa and Codigoro, the former rough, dark, fat
and heavy, the latter slender, white, and very far off, of an almost metallic
sheen like a needle. To the right, toward the Greater Po and its estuary,
the compact dark mass of the Mesola woods. To the left, the empty stretch
of the Valle Nuova, and the other valleys beyond. Finally Volano, in front
of him, and after the bridge, the two parallel rows of shabby houses, some
still bearing roofs thatched with straw and cane. He looked. And once
again heard the insinuating voice of Bellagamba, the words in dialect with
which an hour before he'd tried to dissuade him from going on. "It's not
worth the bother, mark my word," he'd said. He'd seemed all sympathy,
commiserating with him.

And yet, no. He mustn't give in, resign himself. This time, without any
kind of hesitation, he was ready to ward off the idea of going home immediately, which had once again returned to tempt him. To travel back the
other way along the route full of bends which he had recently taken, to pass
below Pomposa once again, and through Codigoro, or even less appeal-
ingly to take a turn around the town, and finally, toward eleven, to see the
four towers of the Estense Castle loom up before him in the distance: all
of this, he hadn't the least doubt, would effectively plunge him into the

depths of that same dark well of acidic sadness from which at a certain point he thought he'd securely emerged. And what if he went ahead on his own, without the guide? He would be quite able to get as far as Lungari di Rottagrande on his own. As for shooting, well agreed, there'd be nothing to shoot at. But he shouldn't despair.

He could even have stayed at Volano. If not for the whole day, at least for some hours. Who knows, perhaps Ulderico's man, that Gavino, actually lived there. And let's say he did, if for no other reason than to give him the five hundred lire owing to him in person, it would be worth seeking him out. His surname was Menegatti—Menegatti, Felisatti, Borgatti, something of the sort. But apart from that, a private house or an inn, a place to hole up in with a modicum of peace and safety, somewhere far away, it didn't matter for how long, from every perspective equivalent to a hide lost in the middle of the valleys—where on earth better than in Volano could he find something of the kind? Again that acidic taste in his mouth. He had to get some food. And soon.

His attention was suddenly drawn to something. On the far bank of the canal, ten or so meters to the right of the bridge and the road, he'd noticed a long narrow wooden shack, painted green all over and with a metal roof. It had a brand new look to it, witnessed by the almost reflective sheen of the paint and by the roof's corrugated iron sheet that looked fresh from the builder's merchant's. What was it? He tried in vain to read a small sign mounted above the entrance. From a thin tube of *Eternit* cement, held up on top of the roof by four converging steel cables, billowed forth thick curls of black smoke. As soon as it appeared the wind dispersed it. Perhaps that was the very refuge for him—he thought as he observed the smoke closely, studying its composition. It might well be.

He locked the car door, and made his way against the wind toward the shack.

Having got halfway across the bridge, he had only to read above the door SALSAMENTERIA to start salivating profusely. He'd been lucky. He'd be able to find something to eat there, without having to go on any long search. Meanwhile a tall, thin, dark-haired young man appeared at the door, and didn't move off. After he'd closed the door behind him, he simply watched him approach.

2.

FROM HOW the young man was dressed—visored cap, a sheepskin-lined military jacket, rubber waders up to his groin—but most of all from the questioning insistence of his gaze, he worked out at once who it was before him. It was Ulderico's man, Gavino—it couldn't be anyone else.

He raised his arm in a lively wave.

"Good day," he shouted out.

The young man gave a slight bow. A somewhat stiff bow like a soldier's.

"I was beginning to think you weren't coming," he said calmly.

"I'm very late, I know," he replied.

He lowered his head.

"Perhaps it's because I haven't been here in the valleys for at least fifteen years," he added with an attempt at a laugh, "and so, you know how it is, one loses all track of time. My apologies."

"Don't give it a thought."

He'd said "Don't give it a thought." Now he gave the faintest of smiles. Did he think him capable of not paying him for his services?

That would have been absurd: absurd from every point of view. He put his hand on his wallet, determined to fish out the five one-hundred lire notes on the spot which, according to the going rates, he owed him. But the other man was quick to stop him. Certainly not, he said with a slight gesture of annoyance. They had plenty of time to sort out the fee. They could get to that "afterward." Right now it would be much better if they concentrated on getting to the hide. The wind had changed direction, he went on in his calm, precise almost accentless Italian, lifting his blue eyes to scan the sky. And if they hurried there was still the chance they'd shoot something.

He's right, he thought. No doubt about it.

"I forgot to bring along something to eat," he objected nevertheless. "I wouldn't want to get hungry. Would it be alright," he asked, nodding toward the shack, "if I had them make me a sandwich?"

"As you wish," Gavino replied. And he stepped aside to let him pass.

Inside the shack was much bigger than he'd expected.

It consisted of a single room—deep, narrow and in semi-darkness. Along the side walls were widely spaced, cramped windows like embrasures. To the right was a lit fire, and seated motionless in front of it were three old men. Ahead, parallel to the facing wall was a sales counter divided into two parts: one reserved for tobacco, the other for food. And behind this, on the side of the former, her long raven hair haloed by the scarse light from one of the small windows, the gaunt, pallid, bloodless face of a woman. He stopped just over the threshold and, with half-closed eyes, breathed in the odor that pervaded the locale—a mixture of freshly sawn wood and cheap foodstuffs, without Gavino showing the slightest impatience. The half-dark; the dry warmth; those three customers, there, with their glasses in their hands, their decrepit faces on which the flames incised deep wrinkles as though they were sculptures; the head of the woman behind the counter, the smell of the sawmill, of ham and food in oil and so on: it seemed to him exactly as though he'd ended up in a refuge high in the mountains. What bliss if only he could find some way of staying there! he said to himself, now unable to resist that disheartened feeling he'd begun to grapple with from first catching sight of Gavino. How right and quick he'd been to guess the sheer comfort he would feel once he'd got inside the shack!

A little later, reemerging into the air, the light gave him a fortifying, reanimating shock. The baked red of the big Tuffanelli house shone vividly, joyfully: it looked like someone had just finished polishing it. The stretches of water that lay in the Valle Nuova, when he paused for a moment at the peak of the bridge to look at them, astonished him with their extraordinary intensity of blue. They shone blue not only in the distance, where the hard cold wind flecked them here and there with foam, but also near the bank, there, where half-hidden rivulets between foreshore and foreshore twisted their way as near as two or three hundred meters from where some houses stood.

Yet later still, in the car, going along that sandpit of a road, made ever narrower by the water flowing from the Tufanelli house to Lungari di Rottagrande, new motives for unhappiness and regret began to encroach on him.

The dog, first of all; Gavino's bitch. Youthful and exuberant—a cross between an Italian pointer and a setter, medium-sized, brick-red—there was no hope that she'd stay quiet for a single moment. Gavino switched between talking to her soothingly in dialect, while carressing her mud-spattered flanks, or pulling her down beneath his legs, shouting at her, even hitting her. All to no effect. Even when it seemed as though she'd given up making a fuss, only sticking her head up like a seal between her master's boots every now and then, the car was still just as full of her, of her obsessive boisterousness, of her life. Leaving aside the smell she gave off, she kept on whining, trembling and fidgeting. Should he stop the car, let her out on her own, to let off steam and chase behind? Not worth even considering, Gavino said at a certain point. In the state of excitement she was in, it was probable she'd dive into the water—with the likelihood that just when they needed her she'd be nowhere near.

Then there was Gavino—Aleotti Gavino as he himself had found occasion to specify. Or rather there were the thoughts that his presence in such close vicinity prompted.

As they went on their way, he gradually found out more about him: that he was from Codigoro, that he had a wife and a baby boy, that from 1944 until the Liberation he had been a "fighting partisan," and that leaving aside the minor assistance he gave to hunters between November and February under commission to the Land Reclamation Company, for the rest of the year he alternated work as a farm laborer and as a "construction" worker. Not much, in the end, when the main question remained untouched, that being whether or not he was a Communist—courteous, patient, reserved in speech: from his behavior he could well be one. On this topic he was able to determine nothing at all.

All the same this wasn't what most disturbed him—it was his physical presence, even more than the dog's. It was odd. But the calm way in which he felt him occupy the space at his side made him nervous, oppressed him. He observed his right hand, resting a little above his knee on the olive green rubber of his waders. It was a big, dark hand, that of a worker more than a sportsman, with slightly damaged nails and covered in tufts of reddish hair. And every time he looked at that hand, with increasing unease and annoyance, it reminded him of Ulderico. Could he have been his natural son, born before his marriage? he began suddenly wondering, adding to the evidence of the hand his stature, his pale blue eyes, their similarly small heads, and especially the calm and the self-confidence of every gesture that they both displayed. Why not? To wait for some hours practically without moving, and then not say a thing! His adherence to such an undertaking, which was frankly a bit exaggerated, could also be accounted for by this theory.

He glanced at the man's hand, and rapidly scanned his thin, suntanned face with its compact, pointed profile. The wind had changed directions— he noted at the same time. And yet he, like Bellagamba earlier, seemed to find him at the very least an eccentric for presuming that there'd be something to shoot at so late in the day. It was true that, unlike Bellagamba, Aleotti Gavino hardly spoke at all. Yet wasn't that vague air of mockery that hovered round his prominent cheekbones perhaps just as eloquent and depressing as any speech? And while he was thinking about all this, he blamed himself for being the one to insist that he joined him in the car. What a blunder that was! Had he let him drive his motorbike—before deciding to take up the offer, Gavino had entrusted it to the care of the Tuffanelli house with considerable reluctance—later on, he could have dismissed and been rid of him. Now they were bound together. With cords of steel.

For some time the road, narrowed to a path, had been running along a very slender strip of land, straight as far as the eye could see, and flanked on both sides by open stretches of the lagoon. "Here it is, we must have arrived," he said to himself, recognizing the place; and suddenly, to the right, he saw the stern of the punt appear between two stumps of tamarisk bushes.

He slowed down. He steered the car to the right and parked it so that other vehicles, should any appear, could pass. He switched off the motor, applied the handbrake and put the gears into reverse. Finally he opened the door and stepped out into the open air. As Gavino, still wrangling with the dog, gave no sign of moving, he made his way toward the craft alone.

He reached it and touched it with his foot. Painted in dark colors, sloped like a gondola but with a flat bottom, it was exactly like those pre-war boats. Likewise the floating decoys—metal cut-outs, painted wooden waterfowl and so on—piled up there toward the half-submerged prow seemed more or less the usual kind: many-colored, as they used to be, as they always are . . .

He lifted his head.

The wind whistled between the weeping willows and the tamarisks on the shore, bent the thin grey plumed reeds that covered some of the small islets facing him. It was cold, much colder than it was in Volano. But when he'd put on his gumboots and a second pullover under his big Montgomery jacket, which along with the camouflage raincoat he'd had the forethought to pack in the boot of his car the day before, then he'd be fine, and would have nothing to fear from the temperature.

He thought he heard shots from a long way away. He leaned forward. Yes, they were shots. From hunting rifles. They were fired from close by to one another, at regular intervals and continuously.

"Have you heard how they're shooting?" he said, turning toward Gavino who in the meantime had also got out of the car.

The young man merely nodded. He'd already unleashed the dog who, having run off some fifty meters, paused motionless at the edge of the shore, tensely staring at who knows what in the direction of the open water. He had put down the two rifles and the packet with the sandwiches and fizzy drink a few steps farther on.

"We'll need to remove the other stuff from the boot as well," he added. "Take the keys."

And he turned back toward the valley, trying to establish exactly where the noise of the guns was coming from. He strained his hearing to the limit, narrowing his eyes. Was it possible they were shooting in the vicinity of Romea? So far inland?

3.

HE'D ALREADY taken his place in the hide.

He sat crouched up on the small, uncomfortable stool at the back, and was following Gavino's movements some thirty meters in front of him. The Browning and the Krupp were leaning in front just about within reach, and everything immediately outside the hide was occluded by its upper edge—all except the punt which was almost entirely visible—and at the center of the space framed by the two rifles' parallel and upright barrels, down there, with the water reaching his thighs, Gavino could be seen bending over his decoy marsh birds like a puppeteer in his theater. Nothing else was visible.

He lowered his eyes and glanced at the hands of his watch.

It was even later than Bellagamba had predicted—he grimaced to himself—a quarter past ten. But what did it matter to him whether it was early or late? Having slumped back into the exact same state of mind he'd woken up in a few hours before, for now, he restricted himself to looking out and to listening to the muted whines of the dog tied to one of the oarlocks of the boat, the isolated cries of some passing bird, the familiar popping tattoo of shots that started off again in the other part of the valley toward Romea. That was enough for him, and to spare.

He slowly gazed around him.

Considerably reduced in comparison to how it looked when he used to visit with Ulderico—at this rate, in another fifteen years, the Land Reclamation Company's pumps would have drained away all the water that yet remained—the Valle Nuova wore a different complexion. It was far from easy to take one's bearings. Where exactly in the lagoon, for example, was the little islet of a few square meters which housed the hide in which he was hunkering down?

To the right, on the same side as the driveable Pomposa-Volano track, on top of a low embankment, and therefore clearly distinguishable—calculating by sight he'd have reckoned a couple of kilometers away—a long flat foreshore stretched out, covered with a thick, stunted, tobacco-colored vegetation, like the mane of an old workhorse. On the opposite side, against the sun, was a second island, of the same kind and the same size as that of the hide, and the same distance off from the foreshore, about a hundred meters, but no more, and beyond it was the just-emergent line of the Lungari di Rottagrande, about two kilometers away as well, with the little, shining beetle-backed form of the Aprilia right in the middle. Finally, in front of him, at no less distance, lay dry land crowded with poplars. Good. The hide was in the central part of the valley, then, at an equidistant point between the shores . . .

The wait extended. If he had been seated a bit more comfortably—he thought—and not like this as if squatting on the lavatory, perhaps he might have managed to doze off. But, in recompense, he could sort out something to eat. He had arranged it earlier. And all the better, at least for that.

He fumbled below, by the two boxes of cartridges, for the wrapped up sandwiches and the fizzy drink. He put them on his knees and took off his gloves. After which, having opened the wrapping, he fished out a sandwich, but nothing else. Only later would he take out the small bottle.

He sunk his teeth into the sandwich and bit off a piece. But he'd already completely lost his appetite, and besides that he was put off by the fact that the bread—which in the semi-darkness of the shack he hadn't realized was of that French kind, bread that now, it was apparent, had started to make its way into the countryside as well. And then what was that stuff the woman in the hut had filled the bread with? Mortadella? It was greasy, undeniably greasy, yuck. But with a coarse texture. And the taste had something rancid about it that made him recall the years of '42 and '43, and ration books, the time during which he'd tried equally laboriously and willingly to play the role of husband, that of the good husband— effectively the worst years of his life.

Gavino had finished his preparations.

"Just as well," he muttered.

He swallowed with difficulty. And while he continued to eat his lunch off his knees, groping with his fingers in the greaseproof paper, having given up his first idea to throw away the rest of the sandwich, he watched Gavino return to the hide and didn't take his eyes off him.

He strode forward swinging his long legs and raising his eyes toward the sky every now and then. And gradually, as he approached, he seemed to him, when seen from below, taller than he actually was, taller with every step. The dog had suddenly stopped her whining. He couldn't see her, but imagined her still as a statue, waiting for her owner's commands.

Now he was standing over him.

"How many have gone by," he said. "Did you see?"

He was joking—he thought. But no, he was serious, although in a way that looked like it was costing him some effort.

"No, I haven't seen a thing," he replied. "I've been having something to eat."

The other nodded at the Browning.

"There's a fair bit of wind and others will be flying past. But with that gun there you'll be able to bring down as many as you please."

He noticed the pack on his knees.

"How was it?" he asked.

"Not that good."

Perhaps, he added, it was because he wasn't as yet that hungry. But the mortadella wasn't of the best. And he didn't care much for French bread, never had.

He smiled, or thought he smiled, and then offered him the packet.

"Would you like some?" he said. "Do help youself."

He was amazed that he accepted without being pressed any further. He didn't even say thank you. Having slipped the packet into his jacket pocket, Gavino bent over to set down the now empty decoy case and, most likely, to stroke the dog. Had he offended him? He'd offered him some leftovers. And stale ones to boot.

"I'm afraid I've already taken a bite" he said.

"Please! Don't give it a thought."

"Why don't you take one of the rifles?" he proposed.

"A rifle?" Gavino exclaimed.

He had slowly drawn himself up to his full height, and turned to stare at him.

"To do what?"

It was happening again just as it had at Volano, beside the Tuffanelli house when without anticipating he would soon regret it, he had insisted he leave the motorbike there and join him in the car.

Why would he not want to take a rifle? he wondered. From that nearby islet—he pointed to it as he spoke—he could shoot at all the birds that he, on his side, had missed, and for the fifteen years he hadn't been in the valleys, who could guess how many that would amount to!

But Gavino stood firm, and wouldn't be persuaded.

It wasn't as if, let's be clear—he replied smiling and shaking his head— it wasn't as if the idea of shooting didn't appeal to him. Rather the reverse. But each to his own job. His job these days was only to accompany gentlemen to the site—he used the words "these days" and "gentlemen," nodding at the same time in the direction of Romea—and then, when the hunt was over, to go around in his boat to gather the dead and the wounded.

Yet he finally consented.

"Well alright then," he said. "As you please."

4.

HE GRASPED the Browning by its strap, lifted it up and began trying it out for balance.

He treated it with the skill and cool negligence of someone who'd had a great deal of experience with guns, but at the same time with a kind of diffidence, a veiled displeasure. What was he thinking? Perhaps of how much it would have cost. That must be it.

"Fine rifle," he said after a while, making a wry face. "You'll have bought it in Ferrara I guess?"

"No. In Bologna."

"Oh."

For some moments he was rapt in examing the various parts: the barrel, the magazine, the trigger, and mainly the trigger guard below, which was of a special quality of steel—opaque and white, like silver.

"It's new. Have you tried it out yet?"

"I got it last November, and it still hasn't been fired once."

"And what's the other one? A Krupp?"

"Yes," he replied. "It's an old Three Rings rifle from before the war. Made in '28 or '30."

"I could use that if you'd prefer."

"No, no," he quickly replied. "You start with the Browning for now. And we could swap later if you want."

He bent down to rummage on the floor of the hide, and brought forth the leather case containing the choke and a box of cartridges.

"Here they are," he added, holding out both.

He seemed more interested in the cartridges than the choke.

"G.P.," he read from the box in a muffled voice.

But he looked worried, pensive. Having leaned the rifle on his shoulder in his usual phlegmatic manner, he flicked open the lid of the box and drew out a couple of cartridges, then after weighing them distractedly on the palm of his hand, he slipped them into his trouser pocket. Finally, as he leaned down to place the half-opened box in the boat, he frowned slightly.

Why should he do that? Was there something else wrong?

"They're meant to be better than Rottweils and M.B.s. More velocity," he said.

The other didn't reply. He had already turned to stand up. With his body three-quarters twisted round, he was looking up to the right.

He too began to scan the sky in that direction and almost immediately spotted an isolated bird which, about a hundred meters up, was flying toward them.

"What is it?" he asked.

"It must be a heron," Gavino said.

It was quite a sizeable bird—with two large, very large wings, out of proportion with its body which was thin and small. It advanced with some apparent effort, ploddingly. Its long S-shaped neck, drawn in to its shoulders; its huge brown wings, that seemed made of heavy fabric, opened to waft the biggest possible volume of air under its belly—it looked as though it couldn't manage to fly against the wind and appeared at any moment on the verge of being overturned, of being blown away like a rag.

"What a comical creature!" he thought.

He watched it slowly fly over the stretch of the lagoon which separated the sandbank from the hide and then hover perpendicularly above their heads: keeping practically motionless and slowly gaining a little height. It must surely have been the decoys that attracted the bird here. But before that? Just a little while earlier? What a comical creature! It was a fair question as to what had induced it to fly so far and so laboriously against or almost against the wind, what it had come in search of so very far from the shore, in the middle of the valley.

"I don't think it would be very edible," he said

"You're right there," Gavino agreed. "It tastes of fish, or more precisely seagull. But it looks good stuffed."

The heron once again flew lower. Then one could clearly spot its talons thin as sticks and tensely drawn back, its large pointed beak, its little reptilian head. Suddenly, though, as if exhausted by its efforts or as if it sensed some danger, it switched directions and, regaining height, within a few seconds disappeared in the direction of the Pomposa church tower.

"It must be written on high," Gavino said, with a laugh. "Here it's wise to give a wide berth."

It was amusing, he realized, but he didn't have any desire to laugh.

He too gestured toward the opposite shore.

"What's to stop it getting itself shot over that way?" he grumbled.

"No," Gavino replied with one foot already in the boat. "Give it some time, and see if it doesn't fly all the way back here."

He said nothing more, but pushed the boat out into the water and then, sitting in the stern and shoving off with the oar, he began to row away.

He watched him, covering his eyes against the sun with his hand. He saw him arrive at his destination, step onto dry land, let the dog off its leash, bend down to pick up the box of G.P. cartridges from the bottom of the boat and finally, having climbed to the top of the islet, quickly search out cover beneath a thicket of marsh reeds. Before firing at almost everything—he must have found something to sit on as only a bit of his cap appeared out of the mass of reeds—he had raised an arm as if to declare "I'm here." Mechanically, he himself had responded with the same gesture.

5.

FROM THE effort of staring at the long, close row of decoys far out in front of the hide, he became drowsy. He fell asleep, perhaps even dreamed. Then, coming from his left, a brief energetic whistle woke him with a start.

He looked up.

At a height of seventy, eighty meters, a half dozen ducks were crossing the sky above the hide. Ducks—they were ducks, he thought, while he slid out the double-barrelled gun from between his thighs and rested it on the hide's edge. He could tell by the way that they flew, the sudden, urgent, pulsing rhythm of their short, stocky wings. What kind of duck were they?

He'd never been that good at telling right off the various kinds of birds in the valley. And there were dozens of different types of duck.

They were flying in formation—one at the head and the others in a triangle behind like a squadron of small fighter planes. Hurriedly, like someone running a bit late for an important appointment, and they too were headed in the direction of Romea. "Safe journey," he murmured. Unless they were suddenly to change direction they'd be arriving within range of the hunters dug in on the shoreline ahead within a minute or so.

They didn't veer. With the wind blowing behind them it was also unlikely they would turn around. But he had only just formulated this thought and replaced the double-barrelled gun between his legs when he spotted a pair of birds—two almost imperceptible points against the dark wall of cloud growing denser over the dry land—detach themselves from the flock and, after a wide lateral shift, begin their journey back.

He took hold of the Krupp once again. There were indeed just two of them: perhaps a faithful couple, male and female. Passing, they must have spotted the decoys. And now they had returned to take a better look, to make sure of things.

Judging by the slowness with which their forms grew larger, they must have been flying with great difficulty, and you could understand why as this time the wind was against them. But apart from the wind, might they not also have been undecided, wavering about which route to take? Perhaps, who knows, they might give it all up after a while. Another U-turn, and in a few seconds they would have disappeared . . .

For more than an hour he remained like this, with his gun in hand to watch the birds flying past on their way above him. He didn't shoot. He didn't even try a single shot. It was Gavino alone, behind his bush, who would shoot the birds one after the other when they came within range. *Bang-bang. Bang-bang-bang. Bang-bang-bang-bang. Bang-bang-bang-bang-bang.* A series of two, of three, of four, even of five successive shots—it was rare for him ever to miss his target. And for the creatures, killed or wounded, not to fall down into the water with muffled thuds.

The first to fall were those two ducks—two mallards in all probability— which having flown almost as far as the opposite shore had turned back struggling bravely against the wind. Soon after the same fate had befallen a brace of widgeons, these two having arrived from behind them, from the sea, but coming down just a bit beyond the decoys, gliding with their open wings. Next another mallard, this time alone. Then, after various pauses, a long line of coots. The number of birds Gavino had shot had quickly risen to some thirty. In the meantime, crouched within the hide, he had totted up nothing. He was just there to watch, and nothing more.

It was as though, all the while, he'd been dreaming.

The first two ducks, for example—he'd watched them advance until they were almost hanging motionless in front of the hide, at a range of little over a hundred meters. Suddenly, though, they'd plummeted down. Going at full speed, their brown beaks and their little round bloodshot eyes wide open, he had suddenly found them almost on top of him, unexpectedly enormous. He hadn't fired at them. They had passed by almost touching him. But a moment later—*bang-bang*—two shots. His stomach felt the hard recoil.

A little after that, a coot had also whizzed very close by him with the hiss of a bullet—that too had seemed part of a dream. It whistled across and past at who knows how many miles per hour. And yet he had been able to observe its every detail: exactly as though it had been motionless, photographed, stopped in midair forever. The lavender-black feathers, lightly tinted a yellow-olive on its back. Its head, neck and the underside of its tail-feathers black. Its breast very slightly paler. The ends of its wings white. Its flat beak bluish. The feet green, shading into orange nearer the legs. The irises red, barred and glassy. As can happen sometimes in nightmares, in a second—the second before the five shots fired by Gavino took it in mid-flight and made it plump down into the water like a bundle of sticks—he had been able to see and notice everything and to think about every detail except for taking up his Krupp and pulling the trigger.

Nothing else seemed real to him. Gavino, on his little islet, his forehead wrinkled in a frown and his Browning scorching his hands, was busy scanning above and around so as not to be caught unawares. The dog crouched at his feet, but ready after each flurry of shots, to leap into the water to retrieve some fresh birds for his master, holding them tight and high in her dripping mouth, and to add them to the pile of dead birds and those in their death throes. He was sitting in his hide, with his rifle in hand like Gavino, only frozen, unable to make a single move . . . The real and the unreal, the seen and the imagined, the near and the far: everything became blended, tangled up with each other. Even the normal passage of time, measured in minutes and hours, no longer existed, no longer counted.

Suddenly—it must have been one o'clock in the afternoon—he saw the heron.

It was flying there in front of him, about two hundred meters away, and once again coming from the north with its characteristic slow and awkward progress like an old Caproni seaplane. He shook himself. "What an idiot!" he exclaimed. It had very much the air of someone who just out of curiosity, quite needlessly, would end up by and by getting himself into deep trouble.

It began flying lower, much lower than before. How many meters high? Fifty at most. Having swung to the left a short while before, once again lured by the decoys, there was every likelihood it would soon be flying overhead. And with the choke attached to the barrel, his Browning would easily have brought it down.

He looked in Gavino's direction. His whole head was sticking out of the bush. He seemed distracted, his head just moving about. Was it possible he hadn't seen it? That he didn't think it worth a single G.P. cartridge? Could well be.

But he couldn't convince himself of that. He remembered the phrase "It looks good stuffed" and regretted not having clearly and immediately told Gavino that stuffed birds were something he'd never been able to stand.

It flew forward, now, always farther forward, making a display of itself with extraordinary, unbearable clarity. From the back of its perfectly smooth little head sprouted something thin and wire-like, perhaps a kind of aerial. While his heart in the meantime had begun to beat hard against his ribcage, he was wondering about this, about what the devil that strange thing could be, and was screwing up his eyes to see it better when, suddenly, in the vast expanse of sunlit, windy air, he heard the echo of that now familiar double shot.

6.

IT DIDN'T drop immediately. He saw it flutter upward, beat its wide brown wings chaotically, then career toward the islet from which the shots had issued. It struggled to keep itself aloft, to gain height. But then it suddenly gave up, and dropped as though it were breaking into many pieces. It was indeed just like an old-style Caproni seaplane—he had time to say to himself as it plummeted down and into the water—the type used in the First World War, all canvas, wood and wire.

He thought it must be dead and that the dog would rush out to retrieve it. But no. As soon as it had resurfaced, it was ready to rise up on its stilt-like legs and began to turn its tiny head to and fro. "Where have I ended up?" it seemed to be asking itself. "And what's happened to me?"

It still hadn't understood a thing. Or very little, for although one wing, the right one, draped down along its side, soon after it moved its shoulder-blade as though about to take off and fly. Only then must it have realized it was wounded. And in fact from that moment on, it gave up on any further attempt of that kind.

Restless, unceasingly swivelling its smooth, fatuous head, which had the look of a pleasure seeker's—elongated behind the nape by that odd, almost imperceptible spiky antenna—it was clearly trying to orient itself, to recognize at least the objects around it. Only a few yards away, half dry and half in the water, it had noticed the punt. What was it? A boat or the body of a large sleeping creature? One way or the other, better keep clear of it. Better not risk reaching the small beach of fine compact sand which that peculiar and threatening thing lay across. Much better. Besides the stabbing pain at its side wasn't so noticeable anymore. Its wing didn't hurt as long as it wasn't moved. Best keep it still.

He watched it full of anxiety, utterly identifying himself with the creature. He too was in the dark about what had made so many things happen. Why had Gavino fired? And why didn't he stand up now, and fire another shot, the *coup de grâce*? Wasn't that the rule? And the dog? What was Gavino scared of: that the heron, not having yet lost enough blood, might defend itself with its beak? And the heron? What could it do? Waiting there was all well and good, but for how long and to what end? He felt his mind confused, befuddled, crowded with questions to which there were no apparent answers.

Quite a few minutes passed in this state. Until, suddenly, he realized the heron had moved.

It was steering itself in his direction—this he could verify after raising his hand to his eyes to shield them from the water's glare—right toward the hide. This he understood. The heron had spotted the decoys. Brightly colored and catching the oblique sunlight, it was only natural they should have seemed a flock of real birds, busy feeding. It was worth trusting them. There wouldn't be any danger in that neighborhood, that was for sure.

It moved forward dragging its wing in the water, with short rapid successive spurts broken by brief pauses, carefully choosing the shallowest stretches of water. It passed beside the decoys, came on again, ever farther on. And finally it was face to face with him, just a meter away from the hide, about to reach the shore. It stopped once more. All brown, except for the feathers on its neck and breast which were a faint beige and its legs which were the yellowish-brown of bone stripped of flesh, of relics, it dipped its head to one side, looking at him, with curiosity, certainly, but unalarmed. And motionless, hardly breathing—aware that the bird was losing blood from a gash half way along the wing by the joint—he had the chance to stare back for a considerable time.

It was now right up against the hide, just like a frozen old codger hoping to catch some sun, and although he could no longer see the bird he could sense its presence. Every now and then it shifted to find a better place or to clean its feathers with its beak. Big, bony, out of proportion, and impeded to boot, it moved clumsily and kept bumping into the hide.

For minute after minute, though, it did the right thing and kept perfectly still. Tucked well in from the cold whistling gusts of the seawind, and with the warm planks of the hide at its back, what was it up to? Perhaps it had even cheered up a bit. Although even now it hadn't understood very well, it had to keep a sharp eye out for everything. Gather its strength: this for the moment, it was telling itself, must be the main aim. And once it had gathered its strength, *whoosh*, it would suddenly spread its wing and fly away.

More time passed, who knows how much.

All of a sudden, three shots were fired in close succession, followed by thuds which shook him with pain.

He turned his head toward Gavino.

"Isn't that enough now?" he said half-aloud.

He waited for the birds to surface—all three of them coots, lifeless—and looked at his watch.

Unfortunately it was no later than two o'clock, and there would be light good enough to shoot in for at least another hour and a half. But even if, personally, he'd had more than enough at this point, would it be alright to lift his arm and signal to Gavino to call it a day? True, for a while the heron hadn't budged at all. But in case it should still be alive, what could he do with it anyway? Finish it off point-blank—no, that was out of the question. Capture it then? Lean out of the hide, gather it in his arms and then carry it back to town? In the car? And to keep it where? In a cage down in the courtyard? He could foresee Nives's response when she saw him return with a creature like that, and wounded besides, with no end of fees to pay the vet just for starters. He could foresee her shouting, her protests and her whining. . . .

The dog had ended its traipsing back and forth. He'd retrieved the last coot, and carried it to his master. Then, turning by chance to the right, toward the sandbank, as if seeking a prompt of some sort from that direction, she saw the heron once more.

It was now some ten meters away from the hide, and judging by the direction it had taken it looked as if it was heading for the sandbank. The din of the last shots just before had certainly given it a fright. Then it had seen the dog go back and forth three times, each time coming ashore with a coot in its mouth. And although wounded, although weakened with loss of blood, and so, more than ever eager to enjoy the last heat of the sun, shielded from the wind, from one moment to the next the bird had decided it would be sensible to move somewhere safer, and quickly. The broad sandbank there, covered with thick plants more or less the same color as its feathers, and at the same time high enough to allow a way through without being spotted, perhaps represented the best solution to all its problems. To hide in there, for the meantime, awaiting the night which was not far off. And then, after that, to wait and see. Because it wasn't clear that the sandbank was completely surrounded by water. Who could say whether or not it was linked in some way with dry land? And dry land within reach would have meant another possibility of escape, perhaps even of safety, or if perhaps not of absolute safety, the almost certain guarantee of keeping alive at least until tomorrow.

Meanwhile it was moving ever farther away, arduously dragging its broken wing behind it, and he felt able to read this whole series of reasonings from the posture of its stubborn little slender neck. But how wrong it was!—he suddenly exclaimed to himself. It was completely deluding itself—fine as far as reaching the sandbank but the dog, soon to be off the leash and free to follow her nose, with all that blood it kept on losing, wouldn't have the slightest difficulty in flushing it out—it was fooling itself to such an extent, it was obvious, the stupid thing, that if the thought of shooting it hadn't seemed to him the very same in some way as shooting himself, he would have immediately opened fire. So that, if nothing else, it would be all over.

III

1.

H E wanted to return to Codigoro as soon as possible.

"Goodbye," Gavino was saying. "If you need me again, you can always contact me via the engineer."

"Understood."

"And thanks."

"For what? It's me that should be thanking you."

He had already backed the car up. Through the windscreen he could see the humped back of the suspension bridge. In a moment he would be gone.

He wound up the car window, and only at this moment, after a fairly animated disagreement between them about the distribution of the game—he trying to offload the whole lot on to Gavino and the latter obstinately refusing to accept any of it—he began to examine the man's face. Dignified as ever but on the alert—cracked lips, the gaunt face of one who's gone hungry, he was smiling weakly as if asking to be forgiven. Finally he was confident that, even through the dirty window, he could see Gavino for who he really was. Someone paid a wage of five hundred lire a day. In the end an undistinguished peasant, a poor devil.

And yet, a minute or so later on the minor road to Pomposa, going over this again in his mind gave him no comfort. A hired laborer—he kept repeating to himself—a wretch who despite the airs he gave himself of a gentleman and a Communist Party member, despite his pretence of not accepting any gifts, not even a brace of ducks, and especially not the carcass of a heron only fit to hand over to the taxidermist. On his motorbike and with the dog straining to trot along behind him, who knows how long it would take him to reach Codigoro? It was utterly useless; without worrying that the car going at full speed might end up in the valley or else in the wide canal which, after Pomposa, flanked the righthand side of the road, he took the curves so fast that the tyres whistled on the asphalt. It was exactly as if Gavino, the dog, and everything the two of them forced him to remember, were gaining on him or were even now hot on his heels.

He sped along with his hands gripping the steering wheel and his eyes fixed on the road; and kept on thinking.

At Codigoro he would certainly have been able to get rid of the dead birds with which the car boot was crammed: an embarrassing and revolting freight that at every curve he seemed to sense shifting softly from side to side. At Codigoro, in addition, famished as he was—since the moment he'd turned his back on the Tufanelli house and Volano, he had again felt such an appetite that he feared nothing would satisfy it—he could eat a proper meal, and not only the "fine turbot" which Bellagamba had spoken of at eight o'clock that morning, but anything and everything else he cared to order. What's more, the stop at Codigoro, which fitted in perfectly with his plan, would give him an excuse to put off for at least another three hours his return to Ferrara which, with every kilometer, seemed overcast with ever darker and gloomier hues. All considered, between having lunch, offloading the game on to somebody, and relaxing for a while—but Uldrico? Couldn't he also pay a visit to the Cavaglieri household?—he wouldn't have time to hit the road again before six. And if at six, the fog were to come, all well and good. In that case he would arrive when he arrived—with the dinner table already cleared or, maybe, sometime before, all of them would already have gone to bed, the Manzolis downstairs included.

A little before Codigoro, at the level of the cemetery, a compact, black wall of mist suddenly appeared in front of the bonnet obliging him to put his foot down violently on the brake. Fog, no, it didn't seem to him like fog. Perhaps it was only a low cloud which a breath of wind would be strong enough to disperse. In the meanwhile, however, at hardly a quarter past three in the afternoon, it was as if night had already fallen. The clear air that had surrounded him until only a moment ago now seemed in the distant past, so remote as to be unbelievable.

He entered the town at walking pace, headlights ablaze and windscreen wipers on the go. He could hardly see a thing. The smoky dark, his impatience to sit down before a sumptuously laid table and, most of all, the persistent feeling of being pursued, absurd as of course he knew it was but no less real for that, made him unable to turn his gaze away from the unbroken yellowish glare that was revealed before him by the headlights. He progressed laboriously as if through a kind of underground alleyway ever more anxiously impatient to be in the dining room of the Bosco Elìceo. The small lobby of the hotel and the floors above it he more or less knew. But the dining room, doubtless adjoining the lobby on the other side of the wall opposite the staircase, what was that like? He imagined that, by now, at a quarter past three, it was full of loud happy folk, of eaters and drinkers used to eating and drinking for hour after hour, slowly and without pause, in a warm, perhaps overheated atmosphere flooded with electric light and impregnated with the smells of food, damp clothes and greasy leather. And he couldn't but marvel that for such surroundings, which in normal circumstances he would have faced with reluctance, oppressed in spirit, fearful of unpleasant encounters, he now experienced such a strong and irresistible attraction.

Cutting across the dark fluctuating lake of mist which submerged the square, he took the narrow road toward the Bosco Elìceo, and in a few moments was in front of the hotel. Parked along the curb on the other side of the street opposite the hotel was a row of cars. But there was no shortage of parking space, right there in front of a lateral strip of neon, already lit. As he was maneuvering into the space, Bellagamba came into his mind again. Perhaps he would be willing to take the game off his hands? In which case, parking the Aprilia there would be very convenient. Unburdening the boot of the dead birds and carrying them inside would be a cinch and the neon light would further facilitate the whole operation.

He got out of the car. As the guns were in the boot as well, he didn't bother to lock the door. He crossed to the other side of the street. He pushed open the hotel's glass door and entered, taking off his cap in the warmth and the smell.

No one was in the small office with the desk, not even the old guy with the salt-and-pepper thatch with whom he'd exchanged a few words that morning. But the confused noise of voices and crockery that issued from behind the swing doors to the right of him immediately set his heart racing. So he wasn't mistaken! In no time, when he arrived in the dining room, he would surely find if not a plate of food ready for him to devour immediately, then everything else he desired: calm, safety, a better mood, a precise and balanced sense of things. But then, during the brief wait for some real food to get his teeth into, couldn't he just begin with half a loaf of bread and with a glass of house wine? Drinking had never really been his thing. Yet today, perhaps because of the dank cold he'd endured in the hide, he felt a real desire for wine. Almost more than for food.

As soon as he'd entered the dining room, he saw it was a huge crowded space, noisy and smoky, just as he'd imagined it, true, but much darker, and so with something sad and squalid about it. Bellagamba rushed to welcome him with open arms. When he'd first come in, the man was standing gesticulating by a table of ten or so customers, far away, the farthest from the door, beneath a window on the back wall. He was laughing and making the others laugh—telling them who knows what. Until he spotted him. Then he immediately abandoned the company.

"I was convinced you'd gone straight back to the city," he said in dialect, raising his voice above the noise. "So how did it go?"

He shook his hand between both of his own while studying him solicitously with his gaze. With no jacket on, he was still wearing that rust-grey pullover, with a kind of cyclist's high collar and extending over his riding breeches.

He winked.

"Have you already had lunch?"

"No."

"What an appetite you must have by now then."

"Not too bad, but I'd like to eat."

He'd expressed himself drily, much more so than he would have liked. The fact was that he found this long preamble exasperating.

"Right away. Right away," the other stammered, intimidated, stepping aside.

He was looking round.

"Would you like to sit over there?" he finally proposed, pointing to a table in the corner, to the left of the entrance.

From a distance, he noticed the tablecloth covered with crumbs, used toothpicks and wine stains, and once more felt a shiver of disgust. But there was no other choice.

"Thanks," he said.

He walked on, reached the table and sat down.

He took a deep breath.

"What can you offer me?"

"Whatever you'd like," Bellagamba replied.

He was facing him from the other side of the table, a little bent forward, resting his hands on the back of a chair. Behind him the waiters, four or five stout country lads with dirty white jackets like hospital stretcher bearers—continually in demand, laden with plates, red in the face, their necks dripping with sweat and constantly rushing between the kitchen and dining room—went by without giving them a look.

"I still have that fine turbot," he added, winking again. "I've kept it aside specially for you."

"Good. Will it take long to cook?"

"Depends. Depends on whether you'd like it boiled or grilled. Boiled would be only twenty minutes."

He'd have to be patient. He lowered his eyelids.

"And grilled?"

"Longer. At least half an hour."

He opened his eyes and looked at his watch. Three thirty.

"I'll have it boiled then," he said. "But in the meantime, have you something already prepared? To have now."

Bellagamba revealed his small compact teeth in a nervous smile. The veins in his forehead were strangely swollen. What was wrong with him? From the depths of their sockets his blue eyes were staring at him bewildered, or so he thought: with the anxiety, for whatever reason, of an animal that senses danger.

"Would you like a fish starter?" he murmured. "Prawns, baby octopus, mantis shrimps, marinaded eel . . . there's a bit of everything."

He felt his mouth fill with a gush of saliva.

He swallowed.

"Go on, bring them," he replied.

And while the other man was already walking away toward the door that opened onto the kitchen, he added:

"Don't forget the bread. And the wine."

Soon he felt suffocated by the heat.

He stood up, took off his heavy jacket and one of the two pullovers he was wearing and threw them down in a heap with his fur cap on the seat opposite. Despite this, as soon as he sat down again he realized that wouldn't do. The skin on his forehead, his nose, his cheeks, enflamed by long exposure to the sun and the wind had begun to feel swelteringly hot. With his elbows leaning on the table and his face in his hands, he reflected that, naturally, the only thing to do would be to have a wash in some cold water straightaway. And he was about to get up to look for the ground-floor washroom when, seeing Bellagamba rushing toward him between the tables, laden with plates of antipasto and bread, and also with a bottle of wine clasped tightly under his left armpit, and with a clean tablecloth folded in four, he changed his mind. For now he might as well fill up with a bit of food. And later, if he still wanted, he could go and freshen up.

2.

BELLAGAMBA WISHED him *buon' appetito*, and before the man had turned on his heels, he had already started in on the antipasto. He was famished—what an appetite! It felt like he'd never had such an appetite in his whole life.

He filled his mouth with the sweet and sour pulp of crustaceans and swallowed, then washed it down with gulps of wine and stuffed himself with bread. Very quickly, however, he felt disgusted—with the food and with himself. What good was it all? he wondered. With his head lowered, in his corner, in that heat, in that stink, in that greasy and promiscuous half-darkness, to be chewing away, swallowing, sucking, swilling. As his stomach swelled his sense of disgust increased.

Worse than ever—that, unfortunately, was how things were.

Once again, there was nothing that didn't grate and jostle and hurt him. Between one mouthful and the next, he only had to lift his head, let his eyes rove around the dining room and each time he did so, whether his gaze fell on that long table entirely composed of hunters that when he'd entered he'd spotted Bellagamba attending to—he'd gone back to them and had immediately began talking, arguing, bawling confusedly, laughing—or else if he exchanged glances with another customer, it didn't matter which, but especially with a woman of about thirty, dark-haired, pale, stout, heavily made-up, who was sitting at a table not far from his own—without doubt a prostitute: her mouth declared it to him, the way she smoked, her nails, her dark, too-respectable trouser suit, her fur coat arranged with care, as if on a coathanger, over the back of the chair beside her, her large handbag placed in plain view beside the ashtray crammed full of butts and her eyes, mainly her eyes, black, opaque, a bit like an animal's, which roved untiringly in search of clients perhaps to take upstairs (of course with the connivance of the owner, of Signor Gino) to one of the hotel rooms...—each time he was overwhelmed by a sense of envy very like that which had tormented him all morning in the hide, when he hadn't managed to find the strength to fire off a single shot despite the double-barrelled shotgun he'd been toting in his hands. How careless and happy they were, all these others! he kept repeating to himself lowering his head to his plate once more. How clever they were to be able to enjoy life! His food, it was clear, was of a different kind, irremediably different from that of normal people who, once they've eaten and drunk, think of nothing else but digesting it all. Throwing himself at the food and drink would do him little good. When after the *antipasto* he had guzzled the rest of it, the turbot, the gorgonzola, the orange, the coffee, he would slump back into his glum ruminations about the usual things, both old and new. He felt them waiting in ambush for him, ready to leap on him as before and as ever, and all of them together.

Wherever he was, Bellagamba didn't lose sight of him for a second, that he was sure of. The birds, he thought. Why hadn't he immediately asked Bellagamba to take them? Perhaps the disquiet that continued to torment him was down to that and only that.

He raised his hand and signalled.

Passing swiftly between the tables, the other man came toward him.

"Is everything fine?" he asked with a worried air, nodding at the plate.

He swallowed and dried his lips with the napkin.

"Perfect," he replied.

He didn't know where to begin.

"Listen," he finally said. "My car boot is full of game. Would you like to have it?"

He saw that Bellagamba was smiling. It was obvious: the man thought he was proposing a deal, a business arrangement. Or perhaps a kind of small exchange in kind: some game for a lunch and later a bed.

"It's a gift," he added. "Let's be clear about that."

He downed the whole glass of wine in one swig and again wiped his mouth.

"With all the ducks and coots," he went on, "I think there might be more than forty birds. Among them all there should even be . . . even be a heron."

"Heavens!" exclaimed Bellagamba. "A heron. How did you manage to shoot that? It will be one of the white ones, I'm guessing."

"No. A red one."

He said this. And suddenly, in the dusky light, after the shots had been fired, as if the large earthy and confused face that was leaning down in front of him from the other side of the table had been whisked away, he once again saw the dog with the heron in her mouth. Utterly bled dry— among the tobacco-colored plants of the shoreline to his right, the dog had reached it when it was already dead—how much could it have weighed? Little more than its feathers did, so hardly anything . . .

He blinked.

"What a shame!" Bellagamba said, his lips twisted in disappointment. "The white ones are bigger, more beautiful, and look far better when they're stuffed . . . But the red ones are lovely big birds as well. Would you like me to organize that, to have it all sorted for your next visit? Here in the square," and saying this he lifted his arm to point to the square outside, shrouded in fog and shadow, "here in the square we have a shop where they do these things very well," adding in dialect "a sight better than you'd find in the city if you ask me. If you'd like we can go over there later and take a look. Today it's a holiday, but they keep the window lit up even on Sundays."

He shook his head emphatically.

"Heavens no."

He must have assumed an expression of disgust—the disgust that had always oppressed him at the mere thought of a taxidermist's workshop— God, what a ghastly stink there'd be, a mixture of a poulterer's, a chemist's, a lavatory and a morgue . . . On the other hand, it wasn't as if he was obliged to explain himself. Better cut things short. Let Bellagamba stand there gawping at him for as long as he liked.

He fished the car keys out of his pocket and pushed them across the table toward him

"Take them," he said. "You know my car. I've parked it out there in front."

The other stretched out his hand. Half way there, however, it came to a halt.

"Speaking of which," he said, lowering his voice, his round, catlike eyes aglint, "have you thought any more about it?"

"About what?"

"You know . . . the car!"

He took a seat facing him.

He continued in dialect, with an uncertain smile, full of embarrassed shyness: "Might we come to an arrangement, *sgnór avucàt*?"

Now it was his turn not to understand.

But then he suddenly remembered their brief discussion that morning a little before he'd left. And while he listened to everything Bellagamba was telling him, specifically that day by day managing the restaurant and hotel without a van was becoming more and more difficult—the bike and sidecar he owned, a Harley Davidson swapped for some tobacco at an

A.R.A.R. camp,[*] which because of its big engine size consumed almost more petrol than a Balilla, he could imagine how inadequate that was!— while he listened and kept on eating and drinking, increasingly, he was overwhelmed by a sense of futility. Bellagamba spared no efforts in persuading him to sell the Aprilia, expatiating in minute detail on all the uses he could put it to. These days—he was saying—it's not enough to wait for some passing hunter to deliver wild game; if, that is, someone does stop by, that's all well and good, if not, you just have to keep on hoping. To meet the ever-increasing demand of his clientele it made sense for him to acquire it directly from the "heavyweights" of the hunting world such as Commendatore Ceresa and his associates who'd be likely to bring down a hundred, a hundred and fifty kilos of game at a time. There was no other way to do it—you needed to be there in person in the valleys, at the "source" at around one o'clock in the afternoon, to buy in bulk and then be off. The same thing for fresh fish straight out of the water!—which if you hadn't the chance of leaving Codigoro really early in the morning, when it's still dark, so as to arrive at Goro, or Gorino, or Porto Tolle, or Pila, even as far away as Chioggia, just when the fishing vessels came to the shore, and chiefly to be there on four wheels, that was the only way to do it if you didn't want to come back with just a few kilos of fish. The man kept on talking, explaining, gesticulating. And he, meanwhile, his head ever heavier, could find nothing to argue with. He understood Bellagamba, he understood him and could see how sound his arguments were. The car, of course he needed it. No question about that. Instead of selling it to him, it would almost be better to give it to him. With all the birds in the boot as well.

After a while he shook himself. He looked around. His gaze alighted on the table of hunters, down there, in the smoke. So far away it was as though the whole vast Valle Nuova lay between him and them.

"Who are those people?" he asked.

---

[*] *Azienda rilievo alienazione residuati*: an organization set up at the end of the Second World War for the sale of goods that were confiscated from the enemy or abandoned by the Allies.

"It's the man I mentioned, *Commendatore* Ceresa and his friends," Bellagamba replied contritely.

They were gentlemen from Milan—he went on—more or less all of them working in industry. Since last year, as an association, they had rented a stretch of the valley from Pomposa to Vaccolino, quite close to Romea, from the Land Reclamation Offices. They usually arrived by car on Saturday evening. They dined here at his place but then prefered to sleep at the splendid deluxe "lodge" constructed entirely out of wood that they had speedily built within spitting distance of the water. "Today, though, they're about to leave, and should be back in their homes around nine this evening, that's of course if the big fog on the Via Emilia isn't to stop them."

"They're folk who fork out bigtime, that's for sure," he concluded in dialect. "Would you like me to introduce you? When I come back, I could easily do so."

Left alone, he finished eating the remains of the antipasto, then stood up. His face was flushed and hotter than ever. He had to wash it.

Swaying a bit, he passed in front of the woman in the trouser suit and, having crossed the dining room, went to shut himself in the washroom next to the kitchen.

Besides being cramped and incredibly foul-smelling, and still populous with old flies that had survived the summer, the room was far from comfortable. A small semi-circular basin of chipped porcelain with a greenish, soaked and dirty terrycloth handtowel hung on a hook on the wall next to it. On the floor was the hole of a Turkish toilet, filthy and half blocked with newspaper. Hardly any light. No mirror. Not even a scrap of soap.

He turned on the tap of running water and washed his face as best he could. He dried himself with his handkerchief. Finally, though in no great need, he turned in the opposite direction to urinate.

He only succeeded after a while. When was it—the last time he'd gone? he wondered. And just as he asked himself this, and recalled the last time had been hardly an hour ago, on the Lungari, when so as not to be seen by Gavino he had chosen to conceal himself behind the opened car door, it wasn't so much the thin colorless stream of his own urine that he was staring at but rather, with a curiosity, surprise and bitterness he'd never felt before, at the member from which the stream issued. "Huh!" he exclaimed with a grin. Grey, wretched, a mere nothing, with that sign of his circumcision, so familiar and yet so absurd . . . In the end, it was nothing but an object, a pure and simple object like so many others.

3.

"HERE'S THE key," Bellagamba said. "It's number 24 on the second floor. I'm sorry you'll have to climb so many stairs. But up there, you'll have every comfort, and there's a bath too."

They were waiting in the entrance, facing each other as they had been that morning, Bellagamba seated behind the reception desk, the lower part of his face, his square jaw and sagging cheeks in the circle of the lamp's yellowish light, and he standing with his arms laden with his jacket, pullover, fur cap, gloves. Yet they weren't alone. He heard people continually passing behind his back, the last customers on their way out. From the corner of his eye he saw them, a few at a time, reach the door that gave onto the street then disappear, hunched and swaddled shadows, into the fog and the darkness.

He rubbed his thumb between the other thumb and forefinger.

Busy replying to the fragmentary good-byes of the customers leaving, Bellagamba suddenly seemed to him distracted, inattentive. Until a moment before he was giving him his full attention, insisting in every way possible that he accept the offer to go to an upstairs room to take a "nap." Now by contrast . . . But it was clear that he didn't know how to divide his attention. He would very much have liked to accompany him upstairs personally, as he kept repeating, if only he, "Signor Avvocato" would be a little patient, in five minutes at most he would certainly be able to do so.

"Don't worry," he replied at a certain point, wearily shaking himself out of the torpor into which he'd fallen. "Let it be."

"Are you sure you know where your room is?"

"Of course."

"Number 24, second floor, the left hand corridor, third door on the right."

"Good."

"And what time would you like to be called?"

As usual the other man was observing him with the air of someone with a particular motive who pretends there isn't one. He was fairly drunk, that's true, but still alert enough to notice that.

"Now it's four o'clock," he continued. "Should we say at six?"

He tried to concentrate. If he were to wake up at six, when would he manage to leave? And then when would he get home by? Wasn't there the risk of... Once again his mind grew muddled. Better give up any attempt to reason. Better just move and flake out on a bed straightaway. Try to get some sleep.

Without replying he passed the side of the desk and moved toward the stairs.

"Have a good sleep!" Bellagamba shouted after him, adding in dialect "and be careful not to take a header down the stairs, for God's sake!"

He started to climb the stairs, his right hand gripping the rail. His jacket, pullover and so on bundled up beneath his left arm and heavy as lead, his stomach crammed with food and wine—so full and swollen that he ought to have let out his trousers by two or three notches—every step cost him an immense effort. As he went up, he stared at the feeble dusty lamp that hung high up on the ceiling of the first landing and told himself that no, he'd never be able to drag himself all the way up to the second floor. It seemed impossible, an exertion way beyond any strength he had. The porthole window a little below the light source of the lamp was completely blind. A black disc, extinguished and opaque.

He reached the landing, turned to the right, broached the second staircase, set foot on the mezzanine landing and began climbing again. At last, completely out of breath, with his heart beating madly within his ribcage and his head more giddy than ever, he found himself before the second-floor bathroom door. So he was there, motionless, still gasping, his gaze once more drawn to the small dark vertical letters of the enamelled sign on which was written BATHROOM, but he was numb, empty of all thought. Around him there was absolute silence. Even Bellagamba's voice, that loud baying that every now and then rose upstairs from the depths to vex his ears, had now gone silent. All he could hear was his own panting, the beating of his heart and the throbbing at his temples.

As soon as he was in his room, stretched out on the bed—recovered now from his breathlessness—he immediately tried to fall asleep. He ought to have undressed, or at least to have taken off his shoes and turned off the light. But no matter. If he had the patience to stay there with his eyes closed for a few minutes, forcing himself not to move and above all not to think about anything, there was not the least doubt that with all he'd drunk he would most certainly have fallen asleep.

And yet there was no way—he couldn't keep still. He had turned onto his right side, then onto his left, then again he had turned to lie on his back, and soon after he knew he'd start all over again. How odd: before he'd been stumbling every which way and now, instead, lying down, he felt as though threaded with faint, repeated electric shocks. Shifting, restless, alert, even his eyeballs seemed to be hurting. In the cavity of their orbs it seemed as though two small beasts had made their dens, so swollen with blood as to be on the verge of bursting and yet still avid to swallow more, two greedy little monsters as ready to tense and pounce as the fleeting swarms of those sparks, the glinting commas of light, that were closing in on them from all sides.

Not thinking was likewise impossible. It was like a ribbon that was unspooling of its own accord, an unstoppable, monotonous, sequential reel of images. There was Bellagamba for example. Against the dark screen of his quivering eyelids, or against the no less dark screen of thick shadows in which, if he opened his eyes, his gaze became submerged, there he was with his leathery face always thrust forward, continually twisted up into unpredictable grimaces, winks, wrinklings of the forehead, odd twitches of his eyebrows, his nose, his lips, his tongue. Then immediately afterward, other faces—the face of Nives, framed by her pillow; that of his mother with the eternal black velvet ribbon hanging loosely round her neck; then Gavino's face out of the Aprilia's side window; and even those of the hunters from Milan, one after another, *Commendatore* Ceresa and his companions about whom Bellagamba had been so loquacious: industrialists, the big shots, the sharks of the luxury chalet not far from Romea. It was obviously money—he told himself with bitterness, feeling once again offended by certain very costly articles of hunting equipment that group would be supplied with (which as it happened were not actually in sight): buckskin jackets, pigskin or chamois gloves, multicolored sweaters of Norwegian wool or cashmere, strange, distinctive footwear. Even more than that, the way they'd heaped their stuff on an extra five or six chairs, the way they spoke to each other or turned to Bellagamba (he standing respectfully, their host and servant) and yet kept him at a distance—it was money, cash, that conferred such assurance, such good health and made the one provided with more than a certain quantity appear as if of a different race, stronger, more full of life, more attractive, more likeable! Money, cash, dough: in the vicinity of those who had it, everything but *everything*—Fascism, Nazism, Communism, religion, family quarrels or affections, agricultural disputes, bank loans and so on and so forth—everything else suddenly became of no concern or importance.

Suddenly he saw before him the face of the woman in the dark trouser suit whom he'd noticed down in the dining room—her big pallid face, that of an ex-farmworker probably from the neighborhood, her large lustreless eyes which seemed focused on nothing, her fat fleshy lips, caked with lipstick. Before they'd parted Bellagamba had yelled merrily "Sleep well!" But on reflection what did Bellagamba have to be so merry about? He was joshing him of course, the way someone does who has too much need of you and of your protection, especially in the case of someone drunk. Yet mightn't it be that Bellagamba was trying in his own way, as a proficient pimp, to indicate that he should relax and not concern himself because the whore, who'd cost no more than a thousand lire, with whom he'd seen his guest exchanging glances throughout lunch, was a thing that he, Gino Bellagamba, could easily procure for him and could send upstairs to his room without delay? That was it for sure. That was what Bellagamba had been promising, now he understood, with all his winking, with all his continuous, perpetual half-saying and not saying!

He heard footsteps in the corridor. He searched gropingly behind his head for the light switch, and finding it pressed the button. It was bound to be her—he said to himself, sitting up on the bed—it could only be her. After having announced herself with all that slapping of slipper soles, in a moment she'd be knocking on the door. Or else, opening the door no further than was needed, she'd slip straight inside.

He put his feet on the floor and slowly, doing up his trousers, he walked toward the door. His heart had begun to beat madly again. He was sure he was right. A question of seconds, and then . . . the latch would be lowered, the door would begin to edge open, slowly, cautiously, inexorably, and then suddenly he would find that strange creature before him, face to face. And so? How would he react at that point? From the time when, as boys, they'd frequented brothels together, Ulderico had always been very curt and brisk with prostitutes. Not vulgar or brutal of course. Minimum chat and down to the act. While he, on the contrary—apart from the fact that for something like eight years after getting married, the idea of going with a prostitute hadn't even entered his mind—had always been shy, insecure, solicitous and on every occasion needing an interminable preamble before he got round to the infamous act . . .

From the depths of the room the tall mirror of the straw-colored wardrobe reflected an image of himself standing beside the door: a remote and sketchy image, as though about to dissolve. So how should he behave?— he asked himself in confusion. Give her something and send her away? Why not. Later, it was true, he would have to see her with Bellagamba, put up with a new series of more or less sly hints of one type or another. Important, though, not to hesitate. Let her come in, keep her there talking for a short while, and finally be rid of her, pressing two or three hundred lire into her hand. He saw no other way out of a situation like this one.

4.

As the latch was not lowered, at a certain point he wondered whether it wouldn't be better to open the door himself. Unfortunately he hadn't left the key in the lock. If he had he could have locked himself in, without standing there getting into such a state.

He opened the door and, seeing no one there, stepped out into the half-darkness of the corridor. He looked right toward the landing, then left toward the end of the corridor. No one, not a soul. How was that possible? There was no doubt, he *had* heard the sound of footsteps. He was quite sure he hadn't imagined it. Perhaps it had been an employee, perhaps the cleaning woman? On a Sunday afternoon? Why not? It wasn't that strange once he thought about it.

In the meantime, he left the door half-closed and made his way along the corridor as far as the landing. He leaned on the banister, and looked down into the dark abyss of the stairwell. From the ground floor, along with a faint gleam of light, came a vague hum of stoves, of tables being shifted, of footsteps, of far away voices. It was evident—he told himself, yawning—that they were clearing the dining room and getting it ready for the evening.

He went back into his room and locked the door. After which, hurriedly undressing, he slipped back into bed. He had kept on his woolen underclothes. But no sooner had he drawn the covers up to his nose than he was shaken with an extended shivering. The sheets were cold and damp, especially at the bottom of the bed around his feet. Still nothing like as bad as before. Without anything clinging tight about his waist he felt infinitely better. Even his stomach seemed far less heavy.

He stretched out an arm to switch off the light, turned on his right side and yawned till tears came to his eyes. And almost immediately, with the sudden permission of his whole being, he was aware that his mind had misted over, that he was falling asleep and dreaming.

He dreamed he was once again on the stairs of the Bosco Elìceo, once again climbing up them step by step, intending to reach the second floor. What he was going to do up there was not clear. He was simply ascending, effortlessly, with a mysterious lightness, even. He shook his head. A moment before, down below, Bellagamba, winking, had offered to have him carried up on a stretcher by a pair of sturdy youths he'd recruited as waiters from the neighboring countryside—he happened to have a stretcher in the entrance made of rough hemp exactly like those used in Ferrara's Sant'Anna Hospital to bear the very ill from one ward to another—as though he were weak in the legs or had a heart ailment or something worse. But the opposite was the case. Agile, calm, he went up the stairs as though borne along by a favorable wind, as though he had wings. It was neither night time nor was it early morning. Through the porthole fitted above the first set of stairs, the sky appeared a deep, sunlit blue. It was two or three o'clock on a lovely late Spring afternoon in May or June. The time just after lunch.

The hotel was full of people. Although there wasn't a living soul on the stairs, outside every facing pair of rooms along the two first floor corridors, in perfect order, some lit by the oblique rays of the sun, one could see two pairs of shoes, one male, the other female. Heavens, how many shoes! But it wasn't surprising. Even without having spotted all those shoes, it was clear that the ground floor restaurant was a cover for what was happening up here on the first as well as the second floor. Each room of the hotel, rented out by the hour, hid a couple. They came by car from everywhere, even from as far away as Milan. They talked, they chatted, they whispered, shut two by two into their cramped rooms, each with its wretched porcelain basin, brand-new but already chipped, with its metal bidet, with its wobbly, straw-colored plywood furniture, with its miserable, askew bedside rugs and its wan central light. Enough just to lend an ear to perceive the buzz, the hum, part beehive part industrial plant, that secretly ran through the entire establishment from wall to wall and floor to floor.

But at his back, the sound of a dropped, metallic object ringing out on a stair startled him and made him turn abruptly. On the landing below, that of the first floor, was the same dark-suited woman who from the moment he'd entered the dining room till a couple of minutes ago when he'd left it, had never stopped looking at him. In slippers and a dressing gown that tightened round her thighs as she crouched to pick up the key that had slipped from her hand, she was staring at him with the same insistence, turning her face three-quarters of the way toward him. She was no longer as made-up as before, in fact she was without make-up. She was smiling and staring at him, now far younger looking, much more like a girl. At last she stood up, the key in her hand. And without detaching her eyes from his, she stuck her tongue out and began to lick her upper lip.

He could only see the tip. But from the little of it that was visible he could guess that it was thick and short, bestial in its shape as much as in its color which was a wine-dark mauve. She was obviously local, perhaps a peasant—black and shining, even her eyes seemed like those of certain animals you find in the country, cows, for example, or horses— one of the many employed by Bellagamba as scullery maids, but really their main job was to entertain solitary and needy customers wanting company in the rooms upstairs. But what did she think she was doing showing him her tongue like that?—he wondered as he went on up the stairs, still observing her. Did she think it would impress him? If so, she was mistaken. Seeing her make a show of her tongue like that did nothing but disgust him.

Now, without knowing how or why, he was leaving a bathroom on the second floor and once again she was standing there, waiting for him outside the door, this time adopting a pose, leaning with her back against the landing's handrail with the dressing gown gathered around her legs to show the thickness of her thighs.

She came toward him and silently staring up at him began to touch him. He, while letting her do so and taking in the smell of roast eel that wafted from her hair, told himself that she must work here, in the Bosco Elìceo, and not even as a waitress but as a scullery maid. In a few moments, the bellowing voice of Bellagamba would sound from the depths of the staircase and order her back down to tend to the stoves or the dishes.

"Give it a rest, will you?" he tried to grumble at a certain point. "What d'you want from me?"

She continued touching him and smiled to disclose her big teeth with gaps between them.

"Me? Nothing."

"Can't you see I haven't time? Let me get on—I'm already late."

"If you'd like," she insisted, her voice no more than a whisper, "if you'd like I'll come to your room. What number is it?"

It was hard to tell from her accent where she was from. She hadn't said *vengo* for "I'll come" but *venghe*. If not from Ferrara perhaps from Emilia. But *venghe*? Perhaps she was a Southern Italian? Perhaps she'd been evacuated from Naples with her working class family after the bombardment of 1942 and ended up working as a whore in a Codigoro hotel.

"I don't have a room. I'm just passing through."

"Well then, you can come to my room. It's just upstairs, number 24. I'm good at it, you know," and again she displayed her tongue. "You'll see what a good time I'll give you."

Having said this she took his hand and hurriedly, making her slippers slap against her naked calloused heels, began to pull him behind her toward the corridor on the right.

Disconcerted, reluctant, he'd followed her. The hand pulling him on was thick and hard and seemed greasy—the hand of someone who works in the kitchen scouring pots and pans with pumice. Yet, no differently from when as a youth he'd visited brothels—and Ulderico never stopped making fun of him for what he called his "silliness"—on this occasion too more than any physical repugnance he felt hindered by fear, the fear of venereal disease. Without a condom, he could pick up the clap or even syphilis. If only he'd felt some desire to do what he was about to do! But anyway how would it be possible at a quarter to eight in the morning and with nothing in his stomach except a sip of coffee? For good or ill, he ought to get rid of her. Two hundred, three hundred lire should do the trick. He wasn't prepared to shell out any more than that.

Next thing they were in the room, she under the covers, he standing before the window from which could be seen, in the dusky light that pierced the racing clouds, the same things as from the bathroom, the chicken run with the hens, the sports field with its two battered goals facing each other, and so on, with the flat endless countryside all around the village as a backdrop.

Better you don't keep insisting—he was telling her without turning to look at her. He hadn't come to Codigoro to stay there but to go on to the valleys to hunt. It was eight o'clock. Even if he left immediately, he'd arrive almost three hours late at Volano where he'd arranged to meet someone who'd be taking him to Lungari di Rottogrande. So could he stay any longer? Clearly not.

Wouldn't you like me at least to try kissing it?"

How annoying! What a bore! All the same he turned and moved away from the window and unbuttoning his trousers drew close to her so his belly was at the level of the headboard.

"What would you be kissing? Can't you see how small it's got?"

"You're really in a bad way," she then murmured without touching him again, only looking at what he too was observing. "There's nothing there at all."

5.

HE AWOKE with a start, at first not realizing where he was. Although, even before he had stretched out his hand behind his head for the light cord, he was becoming minimally aware of his surroundings. So he'd been asleep. Asleep and dreaming. And the wake-up call? How come no one had bothered? It seemed as though hours had passed since he fell asleep. Perhaps it was already two or three in the morning.

Having switched on the light, he turned on his side to reach for his watch on the shelf of the bedside cupboard and glanced at it. Five forty-five. He rapidly understood, while at the same time registering a sudden wave of anxiety, that he'd only slept for around an hour. Tomorrow was far, far away. Between now and then gaped the immense almost unbridgeable gulf of an entire night, one of the longest nights of the year.

After ten minutes or so he went down the stairs into the ever stronger reek of rancid food.

Down in the entrance Bellagamba, as ever behind the reception desk, was trying to fix a small radio. The sports news was on, the soccer scores. He came closer. Leaning over the apparatus, noisy with static, the old Fascist seemed unaware of his presence. He could see well enough that he'd arrived at the least opportune moment. But on the other hand he had to get going right now. And before leaving, he had to pay for his meal and the use of the room.

No chance. However much he insisted, the other man would have nothing of it. Evidently—he said, his voice raised over the noise of the radio—evidently Signor Avvocato is joking. That would be a fine thing! After all the game he'd given him. So please it would be doing him a favor not to talk any more about money. Otherwise he'd be forced to return all the game or else draw up a proper account. And then it would be clear which of them was the one in debt.

He turned off the radio.

"More to the point, did you sleep well?" he enquired.

"Not badly."

"But only briefly! For how long? An hour and a half at most. You said you wanted to be called at six. I'd have preferred to leave you undisturbed for longer . . ."

He smiled with a sly air.

"I was even thinking of ringing your wife," he went on. "Just so that with this fog she shouldn't be worried."

He beat his forehead with his closed fist.

"Now I think of it. Someone telephoned from the house of the engineer Cavaglieri, and said that when you woke up would you be so kind as to call?"

He narrowed his eyes, and asked:

"Isn't he your cousin, the engineer?"

"But who was it on the telephone?" he asked without replying, and without managing to control his voice. "The engineer himself?"

"Definitely not. I don't think it was his wife either."

It must have been the housemaid, he thought, the old woman who'd answered this morning.

He stretched his hand out over the desk.

"Goodbye," he said. "It's time I left. And thanks."

"If you'd like," Bellagamba replied, shaking the hand he'd proffered with evident reluctance, "you can even call from here."

So saying, he extracted the telephone from under the desk.

"No, but thanks all the same," he said, shaking his head with an attempt at a smile.

He covered the back of the other's hand with the palm of his left hand and then, turning his back, made for the exit.

As soon as he was outside, however, he found himself of two minds as to whether to go by foot to Cafe Fetman or to take the car instead. He quickly decided on the latter. A brief walk could only do him good, he told himself, crossing the street, what with that grey, coated tongue he'd recently observed in the bathroom mirror. But it was also the case that if he walked he would then have to return and so perhaps bump into Bellagamba again. He could imagine the scene. He reentering the square, and there, waiting for him and appearing on cue behind the steamed-up glass of the entrance to Bosco Elìceo, the bony face of Bellagamba, carried away with his usual mania of spying, nosing about and digging things up. . .

Once he'd started up the car, backed out and begun moving at a walking pace toward the square—the fog still so thick it stopped him shifting even into second gear—he felt himself completely invigorated. Just as well. If the Cavaglieri family hadn't got in touch, he doubted he'd ever have had the will to phone them. Without anything else as an excuse to stay in Codigoro, all that would have been left would be to set off on his way back to Ferrara. And by now he'd already be en route, threading his way through the dense fog, always in first gear, with his eyes narrowed, for mile after mile.

He was imagining the Cavaglieri house: warm, brightly lit, and with the six girls and boys, from the oldest to the youngest, making a noisy ring around their already middle-aged mother and father, and yet somehow still youthful, still going strong. He couldn't work out why the prospect of dropping into the midst of all that inevitable din and confusion should attract rather than repel him, should so surprisingly fill him with hope and desire. Who knows, he embroidered the scene, perhaps later, after the cup of tea and the homemade *ciambella* cake and the glass of sweet Albana to be slowly sipped with the cake, they would all have pressed him to stay for supper and then, later still, at the end of the meal and the games of *tombola* that would follow, to stay the night as well, among the whole family, like an old bachelor uncle who'd become curmudgeonly and taciturn from being so long alone, in an improvised bed—perhaps in the bedroom of the youngest—Tonino or was it Tanino?—or in that of the next youngest, Andrea, the one he'd spoken to on the phone at such length and with whom therefore things would be easier, much easier than with any of the other children, to chat in the dark till his eyelids grew heavy. Perhaps indeed it would all fall out like that, he told himself. He really hoped so.

He entered the square obliquely, and to guide him through the fog he never lost sight of the small dark pinnacle of the monument for the Fallen and, only just visible, the enormous I.N.A. building with its facade full of windows without shutters from which issued a vivid white light, more that of a city than a small town, and finally arrived right in front of the Cafe Fetman. He was by now so eager to phone that, having switched off the engine and got out of the car he forgot to lock the door, as was his habit. He realized this only later when, stepping up onto the sidewalk he was about to enter the cafe. He turned round and glanced at the Aprilia. No, he decided, it wasn't worth the trouble. To phone and so on wouldn't take him more than a couple of minutes at most. And in that time, given how deserted the whole place was—the town's inhabitants were all imprisoned in their houses and the others, the visitors, had already left, were already far down the road that would take them home—no one would dream of stealing anything.

He entered.

The smoke, the steam, the noisy crowd (many of the Bosco Eliceo customers had relocated there to argue about the scores and league tables on display on a wall) and the sardonic grin with which the same grimy forty-year-old he'd encountered this morning behind the counter—all this in other circumstances would have provoked in him his usual feeling of recoil compounded with a disgust at any physical contact, an annoyance at the din, and a fear of any unpleasant encounters. But in his present state of mind he paid no heed to any of that. He asked for a telephone token. He ordered a Fernet *amaro*. And meaning to drink it after his phone call, he moved decisively toward the telephone booth at the end of the big room.

He turned the light switch. Forgetting to close the door, he dialled the number 12.

Almost immediately a woman's voice answered:
"Yes."

6.

IT WAS Cesarina, Ulderico's wife, herself.

Addressing him quite naturally with the informal *tu*, not merely as though they had known each other for years, forever, but as if they had just been speaking a few hours ago, she immediately reproached him with affectionate familiarity for having waited so long to call them. Good heavens, she was saying, instead of going to Bellagamba's to eat and to have a sleep there as well—lucky that after lunch they'd had the idea of ringing—but why, for heavens' sake, hadn't it crossed his mind to come

straight round to their place? Rico would have been more than happy.
And the children as well . . .

She had a warm, low, drawling voice, slightly querulous, and an accent
exactly like Nives's. And although the *tu* she'd addressed him with had
initially rather disconcerted him, soon enough he found it appropriate.
When, shortly, they'd meet again everything would go smoothly and it
would save them both a great deal of embarrassment.

"Just a moment," he said.

He turned to close the phone booth door.

"It was past three o'clock," he added. "And I didn't want to disturb you."

"Disturb us!" exclaimed Cesarina. "For goodness sake, you shouldn't
say that even as a joke. On Sundays and now on a holiday it was always
like Sunday, all of them got up very late so they'd usually never sit down
to lunch before two or a quarter past two. But apart from that, what
difference would it make to set an extra place? If the table were set for
nine—or ten actually including the part-time maid—it could just as well
be for eleven. And it would take nothing to prepare a bed for him for an
after-lunch snooze!"

"Thank you," he replied. "Next time I'll feel free to drop in."

"Good. That's quite right. And the hunting," she went on, "how did it
go? Did you shoot anything? Soon as Rico heard you'd come here he put
his head out of the window and said that with this weather he reckoned
you'd get nothing. But that was just envy," she added laughing. "Anyway it
seemed to me that the weather changed soon after that."

Since closing the phone booth door he could hear her much better.
She joined her phrases together with a slight whine like a hungry cat,
half nasal, half throaty. And she seemed so close now that at one point he
thought he could even hear the faint rustling of a sheet. Could she be in
bed? The speed with which she'd picked up the phone favored this notion.
It wouldn't be so outlandish that even in Codigoro a telephone extension
might be fixed up to the bedside. The phone at Bosco Eliceo must also have
had that sort of extension.

"Yes, the weather changed," he confirmed. "We took down some forty
birds in all."

He had to receive her breathless exclamations, her congratulations not, it seemed to him, without a certain air of having seen through him, as if Gavino, who might well have just called before him, had already given a very specific account of what had actually happened. On the other hand—he told himself, again registering the secret gnawing of anxiety but not yet willing to submit to it, to fall back into it—he could hardly act any differently. Gavino or no Gavino, he wouldn't want to seem the type to return from the valleys empty-handed. Even at the cost of going back to Bellagamba's to pick up a brace of ducks to bring as a gift—and God knows what that would cost him for countless reasons!—he wasn't in the least inclined to cut that kind of figure.

But, in the meantime, she'd changed the subject. She was asking him about Nives whom, she said, she hadn't seen for at least twenty years, and the fault was mainly hers, of course it was, since, lazybones that she was, she'd never wanted to set foot in Ferrara. She asked him about his girl. She asked him how they'd got through the war years, the worst ones, and if it was true—Rico had told her of it—that toward the end of the war they'd had to escape abroad. And he, while replying to each of these questions, began to wonder why she was keeping him so long on the telephone. And Ulderico? Why wasn't he speaking except by proxy? Why not pass the phone to him? If they were going to meet anyway, why not just get on with it! Why not put a lid on all the chatter!

Together with these thoughts, he could sense other, very different ones insinuating themselves into his mind. He recalled that not ten minutes earlier, on the basis of what, when speaking on the phone that morning to the aged maid and the young boy, he had imagined he'd find at the Cavaglieri household—that is, all the family gathered around, the tea and the *ciambella* cake and the big dinner table flooded with light, and after it was cleared the game of *tombola* or rummy in which he'd participate just to hold out until it was bedtime, and so on. But might he not be mistaken? he wondered. Wasn't he fooling himself? Although it would certainly be appealing to play the old misanthropic uncle whom his nephews and nieces would desperately try to cheer up and console with waves of affection and happiness, the sad fact was that this would never be anything other than a role, and a role, besides, that he would find impossible to play.

"And how's Ulderico?" he asked.

Oh, Rico's fine—Cesarina had exclaimed with a laugh. As are the children, thank God . . . It's only that Rico, bored of waiting and waiting, had got tired of staying there doing nothing and at a certain point had gone out—but he'd be back at the latest by eight o'clock. Now not even the children were home. As she'd felt like she needed a brief lie-down and the kids instead had begun in their usual fashion to kick a ball around in the living room—crash, bang—making a terrible racket, at around five she'd sent them off to the flicks with Giuseppina, the wizened old help, to be rid of them all. They wouldn't be back before seven-thirty or eight.

"And . . . where was he going?"

"Who? Rico?" and she laughed again. "Beats me," she added in dialect. "Perhaps he's off to see his mistress."

She was joking, he assumed. That, at least, was how it seemed.

"Fine thing that would be," he said, forcing himself to play along but in the meantime his throat felt constricted. "And where does he keep his mistress? Here in Codigoro?"

"Good heavens, no way," replied the other, suddenly serious.

"Perhaps he's just gone for a stroll, poor Rico," she added. "Or even ended up somewhere playing billiards or cards . . ." Only five minutes ago he rang from some bar to check if by any chance you'd called and to ask where the children were. And that almost certainly means that he'll be going to wait for them at the cinema exit to take them off to church afterward."

She emitted one of her strange sighing whines—a little longer and more marked than usual.

"But where," she went on, "where are you calling from?"

"I'm in the square at Fetman's"

"Just below the house then!" she exclaimed. "Have you checked carefully that Rico isn't by any chance there?"

He hadn't had time to look around. But if he had been there, the barman, given the sort he was, would certainly have let him know.

"I don't think he can be here," he replied.

"If that's so," Cesarina said energetically, "why not come round right away? Go on, please, and I'll get up and make you a nice cup of tea."

Before he could answer she began to explain where the house was and how to find it. It was very close to the square, she said, and more or less a hundred meters from Cafe Fetman, and more specifically in that big ten-floor building which was on the corner of Via della Resistenza. But he should take care. To reach the inner courtyard and the lift he should enter from the square since from the street, for 7, Via della Resistenza there wasn't even a proper door. The eighth floor, internal apartment no. 17, and 18 too. Ring the bell from down below and she'd let him in.

"Thanks," he said. "That's great. I'll come right now."

"D'you mean it? Then I'll put the water on for the tea. Be sure to come."

"See you soon."

He hung up, and left the phone booth.

He made his way through the crowd, looking around carefully. No, it wasn't likely he'd miss Ulderico, tall as he was—more than six foot if his memory served him. Of course he could have stowed himself away in some backroom to play billiards or cards.

"Have you seen Signor Cavaglieri, the engineer?" he asked the barman as soon as he stopped in front of him.

"No, not today."

"Thanks."

He turned round and went toward the door.

"Sir!"

Startled, he stopped and turned.

From behind the counter, through the smoke and the steam from the expresso machine, the barman was staring at him.

"The telephone token," he said. "Don't forget the token and the *Fernet*."

IV

1.

WHEN he was outside again—strange, the fog had almost completely cleared—the first thing his eyes fell on was the snout of his Aprilia. To see it from the sidewalk, a little at a tilt and with the windscreen completely dark, it seemed to him even more ancient: a kind of rusty and useless wreck. "Go to hell," he muttered to himself shrugging his shoulders. His head was once again spinning. It was that shot of *Fernet*. He should have drunk it slowly and not, as he'd done, knocked it back in one gulp.

He stepped off the sidewalk and approached the car.

After having locked the right-hand-side door, he raised his eyes to look about. From over the car's curved roof the I.N.A. building thrust itself up skyward higher than ever, massive and weighty. She'd said a hundred meters? Perhaps because the air was almost entirely fresh and clear the apartment block seemed much nearer. Through many of the small shutterless windows which dotted the facade in alternately projecting rows, half of them overlooking the square, half Via della Resistenza, he could clearly make out the interiors of the apartments, with people coming and going from room to room, men in shirtsleeves, women, children. Starting from the ground floor, he counted up to the eighth. There, on the floor that was third from the top, no light could be seen. This meant that the master bed-room looked out on the inner courtyard. Or else that Cesarina had already left the room and switched off the light to go into the kitchen.

He walked round the car and toward the block.

He thought about Cesarina. He couldn't remember what type of per-son she was when she was a girl and Ulderico had begun following her around. From her voice, though, he thought he had a good idea of the kind of woman he would be dealing with in a very short while. He'd worked that out right from the start. He only needed to hear down the receiver her drawn-out, whiny "Yees." She must be large, fat and placid, quite the oppo-site of Nives. One of those goodlooking women around forty, who always perturbed him so much that even now, at his age, every time he met one of them on the street he pretended, even to himself, not to have noticed her, not to have even seen her.

He went over their telephone call, and what she had said, together with the fact that she was alone in the house, gave him the ever more clearcut feeling of facing something decisive and unavoidable, like a kind of fork in the road. Then the more he thought back over her whole way of behav-ing toward him, apparently so candid and friendly, the more ambiguous it seemed to him. The *tu* she used with him, for example! But everything else as well, such as her point-blank introduction of the intimacies of their family life—her and Ulderico on Sundays lazing about till late in their big conjugal bed as the children did in theirs—and especially that rustle of bedclothes which had insinuated itself into his ears at a certain point, and other things too, were all equally revealing of her real intentions. And finally, what need had she to let him know, even if it were a joke, that Ulderico had gone out to visit his mistress? The fact was that with this she had wanted to repeat once more, so he should properly understand and have the idea firmly planted in his head, that she was alone in the house, quite alone, and that her husband and her kids wouldn't be back for at least a couple of hours. So there was no danger. He could come up without any worry. There was enough time, more than enough! Besides, the apartment had two doors, 17 and 18. Should the need arise, she could let him out unobserved by the tradesman's exit.

Having arrived at the foot of the block, he stepped onto the sidewalk, then went under the arches at ground floor level. His heart was beating fast and his breathing felt constricted. To calm himself down, he went toward the windows of the agricultural machinery emporium and leaned toward the roll-up security grille. In the midst of other machines of smaller dimensions he recognized through the security grille, through the thick glass pane, a large American tractor, a Caterpillar. In the dim light of the shop he could just discern that it was painted yellow. It was an enormous dark mass. Something shapeless and blind, destitute of any function.

But what a whore she is—he resumed telling himself. What an out-and-out whore!

Having lived together for years with a woman of that type, he found it no wonder that Ulderico, who held priests no less than rabbis in total scorn, had been reduced to ending his Sundays in church and receiving the benediction. By and by, who knows what a doddery old man, what a wreck, a woman like that would have made him. In a short span of time she'd furnished him with six children. But now, having sucked him dry, she was evidently busy cuckolding him at full-tilt in front of the whole town, it mattered not a whit with whom: with the barman of Cafe Fetman, barman and perhaps owner, perhaps with Bellagamba, or even—why not?—with that very Gavino Aleotti, who every now and then had worked for her husband, and no holds barred. Large, fat and placid. And most of all a whore. What was so wrong with that?—she was perhaps thinking as she awaited his arrival. If a worker like Gavino Aleotti figured in her list of men, young and robust as he undoubtedly was but nevertheless working class, why shouldn't she enroll her husband's cousin from Ferrara as well? The Ferrara cousin was no longer very young, but he was certainly quite as upper class as Rico, if not more so. And then, leaving aside their being related, hadn't the two of them been great pals, not to say inseparable when they were young, to the extent that up till the moment she became Rico's lover, the mistress he kept, they'd been in the habit of visiting girls together, even of sharing them?

7, Via della Resistenza had a door of modest proportions, located at the very far end of the block, there where the arches finished and the usual row of impoverished houses began. He saw it right away, as soon as he'd turned the corner. It had been the small vertical rectangle with the names of the occupants, fixed to the right hand door jamb and faintly lit from within, which made him recognize the door from afar.

Picking up his pace, he walked in that direction. He felt exactly like when as a boy he'd just taken his high school exams and for the first time, accompanied by Ulderico, he'd crossed the threshold of a brothel, he couldn't recall whether in Bologna or Padua. Or when, on those days around the August holiday, he and Ulderico had gone by car to climb in the mountains; when, having arived at the foot of Mount Pala or Mount Tofana, there was nothing to be done but steel himself, overcome the nausea which inevitably at that moment gripped his stomach and, after being roped together, to follow the others toward a fate which no earthly power could have forced upon him apart from the will of those who were dragging him after them.

He approached the entrance. He bent to inspect the list of surnames. He read CAVAGLIERI, ULDERICO, Engineer.

While he was close to the faint reddish light, he glanced at his watch—it was six-thirty—and calculated that the time at his disposal was quite enough to do the needful, and told himself it was true, during those long ago Sundays when he and Ulderico went out hunting, they had always ended up first with a big meal and then by going to bed with some local girl, a seamstress, a factory or farm worker, someone, in short, who was willing, whom he could carry off to La Montina himself if needs be, who could be paid off somehow, and who, perhaps after having already been passed between the cousins or between their friends, would usually, in the end, be dumped. Suddenly aware his eyes were on the little hand of his watch, the sedate, familiar, round, gold-framed face of his Vacheron-Constantin, he realized he was in a state of delirium. He'd been raving, he'd no idea for how long. From that morning, from the moment he had awoken, and then for the entire day, he'd been in this state of delirium. And still now. Codigoro. Those arches . . . With a sudden lucidity he asked himself who he was, dressed for hunting, with his fur hat on his head, at that precise moment, under those arches, who on earth was he?

He took off a glove. He touched the button of the bell, not to ring it but merely to touch it, to feel its texture. Then he stood upright. He walked out from under the arches, and keeping close to the house walls, took the lefthand side sidewalk, on the opposite side of the square toward the river port.

2.

IT WAS seven o'clock, approximately.

Perhaps it would be best to make the most of the fog having almost dispersed, he thought, and instead of wandering around Codigoro staring at the paving stones to return to the square, ring that poor woman Cesarina again to make his excuses, to get into the car and, be done with it all, and set off back to the city. Nevertheless each time such a scheme occurred to him, he dismissed it at once. So ought he to stay? With what end in view? Before the extreme loss of blood had clouded its eyes, the heron must have felt something similar: closed in on every side, without the slightest possibility of escape. With this difference, though, to his disadvantage: that he was fit, quite unimpaired, without having shed a drop of blood, and the dog . . . well, given the possibility one would go for him, he would have no other option but to face it, with his eyes wide open.

He walked hurriedly, having now reached the end of Via della Resistenza, determined not to turn his gaze toward the freight ships and barges lined up, as they were this morning, along the shore of the river port. But as soon as he became aware of the presence beside him of those motionless, mouse-colored shapes, so motionless as to seem as if rather than floating they were stuck in the muddy bed of the river, he couldn't resist the temptation to stop and observe them.

Innumerable times as a boy he'd seen boats lined up this way in the canal ports of Cesanatico, of Cervia, of Porto Corsini—in the happy, interminable holidays that they went on back then, before the war and immediately after. And yet from these low broad boats which instead of being crowned with big, bright, gaudy-colored sails, had light rigging, transparent as gauze, like lazy wisps of fog, snagged on their grim skeletal masts— from these no sense of joy, of life, or liberty could be retrieved. From the deck of a barge anchored far from the quay, almost at the center of the surrounding, mirroring water, two people were moving about, a man and a woman. The man, if his eyes weren't deceiving him, was a corpulent old guy with white hair and a black Fascist-style pullover; the woman, blonde and very young, wearing a fustian jacket and tight fitting trousers like blue jeans. They were shouting and gesticulating and running around the cabin whose small window revealed a faint light as of a lantern. Their sharp but distant cries, like those of the birds of the valley, the clacking of their clogs on the decking, their grotesque shadows, enlarged by the yellowish light from the hold . . . Unable as he was to draw closer, he felt as though he was the spectator at the edge of a vast square of a puppet show being performed for himself alone. It was all pointless. The old man, the villain, would succeed in the end in grabbing hold of the beautiful girl he was chasing, there was no doubt about it. What then? Even if, having clasped and immobilized her, he had stuck a dagger in her trembling throat, what would have happened that was so serious? You only had to observe life's events from a certain distance to conclude that all they amounted to was what they were; in other words nothing, or almost nothing.

Having passed the diagonal street which to the left led on to the cemetery and to the right to the iron bridge which became the old country road that went on to Migliaro, Migliorino and from there, the fork in the road which led to either Ferrara or Lagosanto and Comacchio, he found himself close to a solitary building. He stopped for a second time. Strange that over so many years he'd never paid it much attention. It was a large ancient manor house with a Venetian air, of the kind which was relatively common just on the other side of the River Po, in the lower Polesine district. With its fine, two-storied facade which overlooked the canal, therefore south-facing, and with ample space in front to plant trees, this would certainly, he thought, be a fine place for him to buy and live in! He crossed the street to observe the house more closely. But when he realized the decrepit state it had fallen into—the main door replaced by clumsily nailed boards, the windows without panes or shutters, the roof half stove in so that from below through the first floor window you could even see a patch of sky—he quickly dropped the idea. Disheartened, he imagined the interior, the desolation of empty rooms, fat sewer rats scurrying over the wrecked flooring, the black mouth of the big smashed fireplace on the first floor from which on stormy days terrible gusts of wind would wreak havoc from one end to the other of the big reception room, the splinters of wood—pieces flaked off the rotten shutters, off the doors that would have fallen from their hinges many years before—scattered nearly everywhere, and the dust, the cobwebs, the reek, the darkness. No. To resurrect a carcass like that would need too much strength of every kind. Perhaps not even Ulderico could have managed, the Ulderico of fifteen years ago when, still young, he had suddenly decided to leave everything behind, get married to an undistinguished woman, the nearest to hand, convert, set up house and family in the depths of the Bassa, and effectively disappear.

He walked away, but at the first crossing took a left, once more entering the thick of the inhabited zone.

He walked down one street after another—dismal little roads flanked by the small, one-story houses of the town's oldest district. He met no one. From the gaps in the closed shutters filtered the pinkish light of impoverished families. All he heard was the odd scrap of sound from radios.

At crossings he lifted his eyes to read the street signs. He knew it: just after the Liberation almost all of the street names had been changed. Narrow alleys had been dedicated to no lesser figures than Carlo Marx, Federico Engels and Giuseppe Stalin, to Antonio Gramsci and to Clelia Trotti—the famous elementary school teacher and socialist who died of consumption during the winter of 1944 here at Codigoro's local jail—to E. Curiel and so on. The pre-war ceramic signs had not been taken down, but simply covered over with plaster. And on the layer of plaster they had handwritten the new names, with a brush dipped in black paint. Reading them was not an easy task. Time and bad weather were already erasing them. He spelled out: LO MAR, ANTON GRAMSCI, E. CURIEL, USEPPE TALIN, C E IA ROTTI. He filled in the blanks of the missing letters. And didn't walk on until he'd succeeded.

In Via Antonio Labriola, which must have been just behind the square, he was stopped in his tracks by two discreetly lit ground floor windows. He drew close to the nearest one, and standing a little to one side looked inside through the glass.

In front of him was a low ceilinged, medium-sized, rectangular room—clearly some kind of eating house. The walls hung with pots and copper pans, the sooty fireplace, the two tables each occupied by four card players who wore hats or berets and had a glass of red wine inches from their elbows left him in no doubt about that. But why was it that those eight players, so silent and motionless, although they resembled in every way the customers in Bosco Elìceo and Cafe Fetman, seen here, closed in this room behind the pane of glass, should look so strange and out of reach?

He focused his attention on the four who sat at the nearest table. All of them were between thirty and forty; at least three of them looked like laborers. The one to the right, thin, bony, his cheeks dark with stubble, and a hooked nose in profile, might have been a bricklayer. The one in front, in the middle, with a big face and snub nose, with his black beret at an angle and his oil-stained hands, a mechanic. The third, to the left, crouched in the wickerwork chair, hunchbacked in his cyclist's sweater might also have been a bricklayer, or perhaps a farm worker, one of those who tends the animals. The fourth, by contrast, broad-shouldered, chunky, thick-necked, with a brown homburg at a rakish angle, was not a workman, that was for sure, but perhaps an employee of the Land Reclamation Company or of the Eridania or a small landowner. There wasn't a spare seat in the room. Everyone and everything fulfilled a precise function. He felt as though he was before a framed painting. Impossible to enter into. There was no place and no space not taken.

What should he do? Where should he go?

He lifted his arm and exposed his watch face to the light. Ten past seven.

He pulled away from the window, and spotted the dark form of Santa Maria Ausiliatrice's apse and its bell tower sited across the end of the alley-way. There it was. In church he'd surely find a pew to rest on. He could sit apart, in a corner, so as not to be seen should Ulderico and his children arrive. Crossing the threshold would be the only moment in which he'd run any risk. But was it at all likely that he'd meet the Cavaglieris as he was entering? In any case it was worth being careful.

He would never have guessed the church's interior was so vast. With a single nave and its unadorned roughcast walls, and its floor almost entirely filled by two rows of pews divided by an aisle which led to the main altar, it made him think of a cinema, an empty out-of-hours cinema where nothing was showing. There was hardly a soul. Only the priest and a novice down there by the altar, busy preparing something, and four or five old women hunched here and there in the pews.

Halfway up the sidewall opposite the entrance he noticed a chapel, the only one: a half-dark niche containing nothing but a large black crucifix carved in wood. It was there he'd find a place for himself. Should it prove necessary, he'd withdraw to the back of the chapel. On tiptoes, he made his way there.

Once he was seated, he began to scrutinize the distant, incomprehensible activities of the priest and the novice scuttling between the main altar and the sacristy. He still felt far from at ease. Having taken off his cap, his head felt cold. Besides, the proximity of the crucifix, of that blackened, nailed corpse, disturbed and intimidated him.

He yawned. How many people could the church seat?

He began to count the pews. Starting with the first row and moving back, he counted up to forty. Each row of pews would easily accommodate some twenty people. Two times four is eight. So it would seat a congregation of eight hundred.

He yawned again. A good half of the pews, especially those toward the front, closest to the main altar, bore a miniature white sign with the usual names—Callegari, Callegarini, Benazzi, Tagliati, Putinati, Pimpinati, Borgatti, Felletti, Mingozzi, Bottoni etc.—more or less the same ones you'd find among the poorest workmen and laborers in the surrounding country. And the Cavaglieris? Did they, too, have their own church pew? It was almost worth the bother of going to check.

He realized he was stepping on something, and peered down. Some paper. It looked like a newspaper.

He leaned down, picked it up and sat up again.

It wasn't a newspaper, but some Catholic propaganda print-out. On the first page there was only a thickly inked woodcut. It showed a hand tightly squeezing some ripe olives. Its rough knotty fingers with enormous nails were dripping with oil. Atop the image in spaced-out capital letters it read: TAKE NO THOUGHT FOR THE MORROW.

He opened the sheet and smoothed it out.

There was a great deal to read within. The font and point size kept on varying to keep the readers on their toes, and even the lay-out changed every now and then. Sometimes the lineation suddenly shifted to short lines centered and arranged in columns as if they were verses of a poem.

"Have you ever closely observed a mole?" he read, staring at the top of the sheet and narrowing his eyes to decipher the tiny italics of the first lines.

"Its forepaws are like spades it uses to dig the earth before it, as you might with a spoon. It uses its back legs to push its body forward. Its head is like a wedge, its nose like a pointed chisel, and both have been created so as not to be broken. Its tiny eyes are almost entirely hidden by its fur, and its ears likewise.

"Do you think it made itself that way, adapting its body to a life underground? And why have other animals that live in a similar way adapted differently? Yes, because of God. But would a God so infinitely great concern himself with such insignificant creatures?

"Don't listen to the voice of atheistic materialism! But rather observe all that surrounds you with the good, clear eye of a child of God. Then you will agree with St. Augustine who attests: 'God takes care of every creature He has made as if it were the only one in the world, and of all as if each were unique.'

"There are, however, different kinds of care.

"You take care of your shoes, of your hunting dog, of your parrot, of your potted geranium on the windowsill, of your radio, of your motorbike. And you say to your little girl 'Careful not to fall!,' 'This draft will give you a cold!,' 'Are you hungry?' 'I run to see why she's crying . . .' And you wrap her tightly in your arms to dry her tears.

"In truth, of all His creatures, God has a very special care for Man, whom he loves with a father's heart.

"After having provided for your benefit the sun, fruits, stones to build your houses, leather and wool from animals to clothe you, grass and flowers to delight you, He bends down over you to hear the beating of your heart, to calm it with the utter certainty He gives your life.

"He tells you: 'Take no thought for food or raiment. Behold the fowls of the air: for they sow not, neither do they reap, nor gather into barns; yet your heavenly Father feedeth them. Are ye not much better than they? And why take ye thought for raiment? Consider the lilies of the field, how they grow; they toil not, neither do they spin, and yet I say unto you, that even Solomon in all his glory was not arrayed like one of these . . .

"Wherefore, if God so clothe the grass of the field, which today is, and tomorrow is cast into the oven, shall He not much more think of you! He always provides for your good, be assured, even when things do not turn out as you would have wanted."

He had arrived at the bottom of the third page.

"The parrot?" he wondered. "What has the parrot to do with all this?"

He turned to the next page. Empty. There was nothing more to read.

3.

HE WENT out by the same side door he had come in by. And almost immediately, having taken a few steps in the dark down the evil-smelling little alley running alongside the church, he found himself once again in the square, beside the sacristy.

Once more he came to a halt.

Gradually widening like a chalice or a funnel the square spread itself before him in all its enormity. To the right, nearby, the shadowy mass of the former local Fascist Headquarters. To the left, no less tall but set farther back, the I.N.A. building, with its dozens of brightly lit windows. In the background, at what suddenly seemed to him a vast distance, so even the thought of crossing it on foot filled him with fatigue, with unbounded boredom, three points of light shone out: two of an equally dull yellow from the cafes opposite each other, the Fetman and the Moccia, and one of a shop window which he had only just noticed, adjacent and to the right of the low tenement block of the Trade Union Hall, and ablaze with the same bright white light of an industrial establishment in full swing as that which flooded the square from the I.N.A. building. There was no fog. During the last half hour the air had instead become crystal clear so that it allowed him to see every detail not only of the monument to the Fallen in the middle of the square but also, behind that, the miniscule bedbug-like carapace of the Aprilia's roof. He sniffed the air. The smell of urine and incense lingered in his nostrils. Mingling with these and the usual smell of the valleys, was a new odor: of burning, of roasted chestnuts. He looked around in search of the humble iron brazier replete with charcoal which must have been nearby, but without success. Who knows where it was.

He moved on.

He walked slowly, letting his legs carry him toward the center of the square, while the surrounding space and everything within it, the monument to the Fallen, the former Fascist Headquarters, the I.N.A. building, gradually assumed a different, a transformed aspect. Even the Aprilia was changing its appearance. No longer the shell it had seemed just before. One could see the double back window with its trapezoid frame. And within a moment or two, it would be possible to read, white on a black background, the numbers on the Ferrara license plate.

He headed toward Cafe Fetman. However, having covered three quarters of the distance, and noticing a group of customers leaving the premises who then stopped to chat in front of the entrance—four of them, all wearing cloaks, who seemed to be paying attention to the Aprilia, and discussing it—so as not to have to get into the car beneath their gaze, he preferred to move to the right toward the brightly lit window beside the Trade Union Hall. Some time before he'd figured out what it was—the taxidermist's workshop which Bellagamba had mentioned. It didn't matter. Without now feeling the least bit repelled by the idea, he allowed his legs to lead him, one step after another, to a yard or so from the big glass window.

He stopped there, fascinated.

Hunting rifles, belts full of cartridges, fishing rods, nets, lark mirrors, decoys for the valley, gumboots, woolen fabrics as well as fustian and velvet, and of course the stuffed animals, mainly birds, but there was also a fox, a marten, some squirrels, the odd tortoise: full to the brim with things scattered in what only seemed to be disorder, the window shone before him like a small sunny self-sufficient universe, parallel but unreachable. He was well aware that the pane of glass between him and the interior was what rendered it so. And since the pane of glass, so spotlessly clean it seemed invisible, reflected a part of his own image—barely a shadow, it's true, but still annoying—in order to be completely rid of this faint residual shadow and to pretend the glass itself wasn't there, he drew even closer, almost touching the window with his forehead, so he sensed a coldness colder than the evening air.

Beyond the window pane, silence, absolute immobility, peace.

He observed, one by one, the stuffed animals, all of them resplendent in their death, more alive than when they lived.

The fox, for example, which occupied the middle of the window display horizontally, between a pair of matching gumboots standing upright and a half-opened Browning rifle, was twisting its snout to the side, gnashing its teeth as if in the act of turning it had ended up there in that instant; and its yellow eyes, full of hatred, its bright white teeth, its flaming red maw, its thick and luminous russet-blond fur, its bushy overgrown tail all gleamed with an overbearing almost insolent health, preserved by a magic spell from any assault, both now and in the future. Even the squirrels, placed where you'd least expect to find them—there was one whose neat little head, and nothing more, peeked out of a fine leather game bag—although motionless, it still managed to express all the sly grace, the gleeful agility of its nature, like that of Walt Disney's dwarves, but with something more, something extra, perhaps related to their being there, safe, and forever separate, behind the thick glass. In the violent convergent light of the lamps their black beady eyes shone joyously, feverishly, devilishly with knowingness and irony.

It was toward the birds, however, that his gaze kept on returning.

The ducks, at least a dozen of them in a compact group, were squashed into the forestage of the little theater, so close it seemed he could have touched them, and calm at last and without fear, no longer forced to keep to the heights, suspended on their short trembling wings in the still, treacherous air. The birds of prey, by contrast, with the exception of an eagle owl perched in a central and dominant coign, were farther off, in a long row, on the shelf of a kind of partition which formed the back and sides of the window display. Reading the brass labels at the foot of the fake ebony pedestals on which each of these birds was posed upright, he recognized one by one a kestrel, a buzzard, a peregrine, an osprey, a sparrowhawk . . . These birds were also vivid and shone as if polished with a vitality which ran no risk of decay, but most of all they had become far more lovely than they'd been when they were breathing and blood ran fast in their veins— he alone, perhaps, he thought, was in a position truly to *understand* the perfection of their final, imperishable beauty, to fully appreciate it.

At one point, the better to see the green on a mallard's feathers, he had to draw back a fraction. Immediately, reflected in the pane, he once again saw the shape of his own face.

He then tried to look at himself as he had that same morning in the bathroom mirror. And while he was rediscovering beneath his fur cap the same features he awoke to every day—the receded hairline, the three horizontal furrows across his brow, the long, fleshy nose, the heavy tired-looking eyelids, the soft, almost womanish lips, the dint in his chin, the cheeks blurred with stubble—they appeared veiled, distant, as though just a few hours had been enough to sprinkle the dust of years and years over them, he felt a secret thought slowly forming within him, as yet confused but still rich with mysterious promise, a thought that would free him, and save him.

4.

IF MERELY imagining himself dead overwhelmed him with such a sudden wave of happiness, he reasoned, well then, why not actually kill himself? And why not as soon as possible? No, he should do it this same night, in his room, with the Browning or the Krupp. And he already knew exactly how.

He drove on down the road to Ferrara in the cold, clear night lit by the moon.

A little before the Eridania sugar refinery and the Land Reclamation Offices he had stopped at an A.G.I.P. petrol station to buy five hundred lire's worth of petrol and to have the windscreen cleaned, and now, back in the car, having decided what he had decided, he found it even easier to identify with the stuffed animals in the Cimini shop in Codigoro. Once in a while he shook his head. How stupid, how ridiculous and grotesque life, precious life, became once you saw it through the shop windows of a taxi-dermist! And how much better, straightaway, he felt at the mere thought of finally being done with all that tedious back-and-forth business of eating and defecating, drinking and urinating, sleeping and waking, of making trips and staying put which life consisted of! Perhaps for the first time in his life, he began to think of the dead without any fear. Only they, the dead, counted for something, only they were truly alive. It would take a couple of years to be reduced to nothing more than a skeleton—he'd read that somewhere. After which the dead experience no further change forever. Clean, hard, very beautiful, they then became like precious stones or the noble elements. Immutable, and so eternal.

The nearer he got to Ferrara, the lighter and happier, even at times friv-olous, his thoughts were. He kept on bursting out laughing.

The fleeting vision of La Montina to the left of the road, on the other side of the Volano stretch of the Po, brought Nives to mind. Immediately he began to think with amusement what would happen to La Montina in a month, or a month and a half, when Nives would establish contact for the first time in person with the property and its employees. He saw the whole scene in splendid detail: the ladylike frown of the widow and heiress, the persnickety pout of her lips in her effort to speak her most fluent Italian, the kowtowing of Benazzi, the overseer, hoping to keep his job, the caps in hand of the farm laborers and cowherds, disposed, at this stage, given the change of political climate, to wipe the slate of the recent past utterly clean, their faces a blend of the sly, the respectful and the contrite. With regard to this—here he broke into a good-natured grin—would Nives come to La Montina alone or else accompanied by the faithful Prearo in the Aprilia? That the two were in cahoots, and had been for quite some time, he alone had been blithely able to ignore, thanks to his inveterate tendency to register nothing that might put his tranquility at risk. So then, why not? Given the solemn occasion, it was likely that the excel-lent accountant should now and then double up as chauffeur, remaining for the entire duration of the managerial site inspection discreetly apart yet respectfully *à côté*. Oh, that would really be a scene to enjoy from the beginning to the end. What a shame to miss it! On the other hand, wasn't it already a satisfying enough prospect to imagine it all and, since, for good or ill, he was the husband, to arrange things so that it should actually take place?

He was so detached from himself and from the world, so relaxed and serene, that just a little way down the road, at the entry to Tresigallo, the name of the town written in big letters on a house wall at the edge of the built-up area struck him as though he had never set eyes on it before. Tresigallo. What on earth could be the source of such a name? That very evening he must remember to look it up in *Frizzi* or *Treccani*. They would surely furnish him with some information on the topic.

All the while he was slowly driving through the small town, which also looked dark and deserted. He could clearly recall, some fifteen years ago, sometime around 1930, the Fascist government had suddenly decided to transform this small farming center, one of the least significant in the province, into the site of a propaganda exercise for Ferrarese agriculture. And right on cue, as it happened, the car's headlights revealed first a vast marble-fronted barrack-like hall similar to the former Fascist HQ at Codigoro, then an endless square at the center of which stood, high above the black basalt plinth that formed its base, a statue in Lazio travertine, and beyond it a large building that resembled the new station in Florence, and constructed, as a still perfectly legible inscription above the entrance proclaimed, for the working of hemp and its derivatives. It was clear that none of this now served any purpose whatsoever. The grand hall with its imperial air, the statue of the gladiator with its naked and muscular buttocks, in all likelihood representing Fascism on the march; the building intended for the manufacture of autarchic fabrics: under the moon, they were all revealed as senseless, just pure and simple stage-settings, and the life of the town seemed more than ever, as it once had been, limited to the small circle of peasant houses huddled on one side of the parish church. He left by the opposite side to the built-up area. "Farewell and safe travels," he muttered, accelerating along the wide road bordered by trees which led straight to Ferrara. During the course of the day this was the second time he'd wished farewell to something. This morning to those poor ducks, and now to Tresigallo. Once again he broke into a laugh. But it was apt in the end. In the end, Tresigallo would have a future before it. Even with a much narrower scope, the small town would still keep going. He, by contrast—

and he thought this without a shadow of sadness, no, rather with calm good humor—where on earth was he going to in his car?

The Prospettiva Arch appeared in front of the bonnet at exactly nine twenty. Before leaving Codigoro he'd remembered to phone home. From that phone booth in Cafe Fetman he'd exchanged a few words with the cook, Elsa: just to say that he was leaving, and meant to arrive within just less than an hour and could she please tell Romeo on the entryphone to open the gates in plenty of time. He himself had made perfect time. Had Elsa carried out his instructions? Given the hour, and the supper to prepare perhaps not—she could well have forgotten. In a moment he'd find out. It was no big deal if the gates were shut. He'd just peep his horn twice.

The moon lit up the entire length of Via Montebello from the intersection with Corso Giovecca right down to the distant, massive, greyish granite arcade sited at the entrance to the Jewish Cemetery. Via Mentana, however, was almost in darkness. As soon as he'd turned the corner, he switched the headlights on full beam. The gates were wide open. In front of them, Romeo was standing, waiting calmly at the curb, with his beret, his grey woolen scarf wrapped round his neck and his hands sunk in his trouser pockets.

He slowed down, taking a quick look in the rearview mirror. He maneuvered onto the left side of the road, and signaled. He turned right. Then, again accelerating, he confidently steered through the gates and stopped in his usual spot right in front of the porch.

He left Romeo to shut the gates and waited for his old parchmenty face to appear framed in the car's side window, on the other side of the glass. How come Signor Avvocato had decided not to get out of the car? Barely concealed, his stupor was comic and, at the same time, moving.

He lowered the window half-way down.

"Would you open the inner gate for me please?" he asked quietly, gesturing to the space in front of him.

The other looked at him wide-eyed.

"Do you want to park the car in the yard?" he asked in the slow Italian he used for important occasions.

"I do," he said, smiling. "It doesn't seem that cold now."

"Would you have stuff to take in?" Romeo asked, reverting to dialect.

He gathered he was alluding to the spoils of the hunt. Though it looked like he didn't have much faith in that. His thin, violet lips had stretched into a furtive grin.

"No, far from it. I didn't shoot a thing."

Through the windscreen he saw him make his way toward the gate. It was obvious he disapproved. He could tell from the exaggerated curve of his back as he tried to open the gate. Of necessity, in a few hours time, what with one thing and another, he'd be making a fair bit of extra work for him. So he ought to treat him well, and keep him happy.

He drove the car through to the yard.

"And how is your daughter doing?" he asked after he'd got out of the car. "Did she call round this afternoon?"

Yes, she had come, Romeo confirmed. They'd both showed up, she and her husband.

He added nothing more, and made a grimace. He'd probably had to shell out some more money, he thought. But in any case what could he do about it? It wouldn't do to offer to reimburse him. Apart from the fact that he only had a few hundred lire on him, it would be too tricky a discussion to get embroiled in. And as for having a talk with the son-in-law, that William, he didn't think that was something he could promise. Making a promise he knew he couldn't keep would have been distinctly dishonest on his part. Dishonest and stupid both.

He climbed the stairs at a fair rate, with the Browning and the Krupp slung over each shoulder. But, having arrived upstairs, he stopped at the doorway. He had clearly heard the whining tones of Nives coming from the dining room. Seeing as they were already seated at the table, perhaps it would be convenient all round to show his face at once. And later, if possible, he could go to his room for a moment to wash his hands and face.

He walked across the polished, creaking parquet, half-opened the door in front of him, and peeked his head round the side.

"I'm back," he announced, while Lilla, his mother's poodle, uttered its usual little stifled woof. "Good evening."

He had taken them by surprise.

Nives and his mother were at either end of the table, Rory and Prearo, the accountant, in between, facing each other: all of them stared at him with startled looks, motionless as statues. Strange. Strange and comic.

Was it possible that Elsa, who had indeed warned Romeo of his coming, had neglected to inform Nives of his phone call? No, that couldn't be, he realized as he noticed the fact that a fifth place had been set beside Rory . . .

He came forward a step.

"My respects," murmured Prearo, half rising from his seat and jerking back his sweaty face.

"Please don't get up."

"Aren't you going to sit down?" Nives said in a complaining tone. "Go on, do, it's late."

Just at that moment, Elsa came in through the other door that opened onto the kitchen and the office. She was balancing the oval dish of boiled turkey meatloaf, and she, too, on seeing him, came to a sudden halt.

He took them all in with a single circular glance: Nives, Rory, his mother with the little black, curly-haired poodle curled up on a seat beside her, Prearo, Elsa. He felt incredibly rich, generous, disposed to be bountiful: uplifted by a kind of inebriation. Yet he knew, how well he knew it! All it would have needed was for him to decide to stay alive for one more day, for just a single day, and then that happiness, which for an hour he had carried shut tight within him like a treasure, would suddenly dissolve and he would once again feel, even toward his daughter, sitting there, staring up at him with her beautiful dark and wild blue eyes, the same old bitter sense of alienation, almost of repulsion, that had always stopped him feeling that she was his, that he loved her. That was it, he told himself, only by dying was he able to love her! And she? Would she remember him, her father, when she was grown up? What he looked like? Almost certainly not. He hoped for this on her behalf with all his heart. In his present state, this was the only gift he was able to give her.

"I'm going to my room for a moment" he said.

5.

HE, MORE than any of them, believed he was going to return in a moment. But after he'd left the dining room, and had begun to walk down the long L-shaped corridor which led from the entrance to his bedroom, he suddenly understood that he would not return, not even to announce that he'd decided to skip supper. To stay on his own, to undress, to think. To prepare himself. Nothing weighed on him, there was nothing else he desired.

He entered his room. He switched on the central light. He undid the cartridge belt and draped it on a chair. He slid the two rifles from his shoulders, and leaned them against the wall beside the glass cabinet. He took off his jacket, hanging it on the clothes-horse with wheels. He sat on the side of the bed. He bent down to unlace his boots. He straightened up. He switched on the small lamp on his bedside table. At last he stretched himself out, his hands entwined behind his neck. And he was lying thus, staring at the ill-lit ceiling, overcome by the feeling of extraordinary well-being which lying supine on the bed, on his own bed again, gave him when he heard someone knocking at the door.

"Come in," he said.

It was Elsa—he knew from her smell, a blend of cooking and soap.

"What is it?" he asked without moving, and closing his eyes.

The *riso in brodo* is getting cold, the girl replied. If Signor Avvocato didn't come down soon, then later, when it was reheated, it wouldn't taste nearly as good.

He knew where she was. Just beyond the threshold, her hand resting on the latch. He *saw* her hand: big, with swollen and grazed fingers, but appealing, not in the least unpleasant.

"No. I won't be coming down," he replied. "I'm not hungry. Would you tell the Signora that?"

He lifted his body halfway up, leaned on his elbow and gave her a smile.

"Also, I'm too tired to eat."

In the half-dark, in the lamplight that lit her healthy cheeks faintly from below, he saw her flush. Where was she from? Ah yes, from Chioggia, or rather Sottomarina di Chioggia. Blonde, rosy, sturdy, with blue eyes, just like Irma Manzoli, she was forever blushing, and he always found women who blushed easily attractive.

"Is there nothing you need?" she asked him.

He was about to say no. But an idea occurred to him. What if, by chance, there wasn't any string in the house? That would be a real disaster. To have the wherewithal to shoot himself, he absolutely needed some.

"Do you happen to have any string in the kitchen?"

"Any string?"

Poor girl. It was understandable she should stare at him like that, caught between wonder and irony.

"Before going off to sleep" he explained "I'd like to give the rifles a bit of a clean."

"I think we might have. But how long should it be?"

"A couple of meters would do."

"I'll go and see straightaway."

"Thanks," he smiled again. "Thanks a lot."

Having heard the door shut, he got to his feet, took off his wristwatch, placed it on the bedside table and walked into the bathroom.

First of all he turned on the bath taps, leaning over the bath to gauge the temperature of the water accurately. And as he gradually undressed— he knew that what he wanted was to be undressed, to wash himself completely clean, to shave, and later he might even try to empty his bowels—as he gradually took off his pullover, his flannel shirt, his string vest and then, in order, the thick wool stockings, his short socks, the corduroy trousers, the long woolen underpants, the short cotton briefs, he didn't stop thinking about how he would shoot himself, forcing himself to plot out every smallest detail of the operation.

In the countryside, he'd often been told, farmworkers generally did it this way: they propped the gun's butt on the ground and then, holding the barrel tightly in their hands, pushed the trigger down with their toe extended. He, however, intended to do it differently. He would take the string, knot one end to the trigger and the other to something solid and fixed, perhaps a bath tap. Then, having made himself quite comfortable, in a seated position, he would position the barrel. No, the string would be a decidedly clever device. Being seated, he could shoot himself in the chest, the throat, his mouth or in the middle of his forehead—wherever he chose. And in the bathroom, it hardly mattered if he made a mess of the floor.

He climbed over the edge of the bath, turned off both taps, and stretched out full-length in the lukewarm water.

All that remained to be decided—he returned to his thoughts assisted by the sudden silence—if anything did remain, was the question of which weapon to use. The Browning or the Krupp? But while he was posing the question, he already knew that the Browning would not be appropriate. He wouldn't be using that. Better the Krupp. The double barrel was far more reliable. With that gun, the risk of being left half-alive, of slowly bleeding out, was minimal. If he managed to calculate exactly the right lengths of string, one for each trigger, he would be blasted by both shots together, in the same instant. He'd not be aware of a thing.

He soaped himself from head to toe. He rinsed himself. He got out of the bath. He dried himself. He shaved. He sterilized his face with a dab of cologne. He carefully tidied his hair, using brilliantine, brush and comb. Finally, having put on his pyjamas and his beige-colored dressing gown and his slippers, he went back into his bedroom.

Elsa had brought the string. A whole ball of it. She had left it in plain sight on the middle of the bed. He took the ball in his hand and examined it. Excellent. The string wasn't too thick. Thin but sturdy, the best for the job. For tying a knot with, it would be perfect.

He leaned his elbow on the bedside table beside the Vacheron-Constantin and the Jaegar and then once more lay down in the bed, under the covers, his hands laced behind his head as before. He wouldn't leave any note. Not a single line. What would be the point? There were no debts left to pay or to collect. As for the cemetery, even there everything was in order. Prearo had always taken care of his annual contribution to the Jewish Community, with regular payments on behalf of himself and his mother. So no one could raise any objections. The president of the Community, that Cohen fellow, who ever since his marriage had stopped greeting him, never to begin again, would find himself with his hands tied.

He remained there thinking.

Toward midnight he got out of bed, went to the door, opened it and walked into the corridor.

Not every night, it's true, but quite often, he would go to visit his mother at more or less this time, especially if he'd come home just before or shortly after supper and had gone to his room to read the papers in peace, or to check some accounts. It was a very long-established habit. For that reason, it wasn't impossible that his mother, troubled not to see him come in, might take it into her head to burst in on him at two or three o'clock when he'd be most in need of being alone, of not being disturbed.

He walked down the corridor, past the entrance, the dining room, the two adjoining drawing rooms which had been left unheated for a couple of years and had now effectively been reassigned as a storage room and a larder. He moved, then, from one side of the apartment to the other, opening and shutting doors, switching lights on and off, and without worrying whether the parquet creaked. If Nives from her bedroom or Elsa in her little room next to the kitchen should hear him pass, all the better. All the better that tonight everything should seem perfectly normal to them as well, no different in any respect to every other night.

6.

THE INNER happiness he felt gave a spring to his tired legs, poise and precision to his every gesture, and calm to the beating of his heart. It was truly a treasure he was guarding within. Huge, inexhaustible, yes, and yet something to be kept secret all the same, hidden from everyone in the world. His whole joy, his whole peace derived from the certainty that he was its sole possessor.

His mother's bedroom was the last, the farthest away room in the apartment, repurposed from a small reception room which in the time of his grandfather, Eliseo, and his grandmother, Vittoria, had served exclusively for billiards. But after he had walked through the vast and chilly darkness of the second of the former drawing rooms, filled with dim presences without form, there he was at the door, lowering the latch, and opening it a crack.

"May I?" he asked as usual.

"Oh, it's you!" he heard the familiar, querulous, wavering voice exclaiming in reply.

He entered, shut the door and, in the unexpected warmth, walked to the bed which was positioned at the far side of the room, then stretched out his hand to stroke Lilla who, having delivered her ritual little harmless yelp, had immediately curled up again at her mistress's side, level with her hip. He behaved as he ever did, repeating the same acts, the same motions and preparing to say and to hear the exact same habitual phrases.

But for once he felt happy, and his mother caught his mood from the start.

Instead of beginning with her usual complaints, mainly directed at Nives, she lay there contemplating him with a satisfied air and in silence.

"How handsome you are," she said at last.

"Me handsome?" he parried. "You're joking."

"But you are. Let your mother be the judge! You should go hunting more often. Get out in the sunshine and the wind, breathe a bit of fresh air now and then as you used to and I'm sure it would do you a world of good. See what a fine color you have."

"Perhaps you're right," he replied, bowing his head. "I really ought to."

"Good boy," she said with a smile. "I saw it straightaway, you know, as soon as you came in, that your whole face looked different. But how come," she went on, still smiling and speaking in lowered tones, "you didn't want anything to eat, not even a little bowl of soup? It was very good."

"I'm sure it was. But the truth is I ate very late today so I wasn't hungry."

"What a shame. Your wife wanted to make the meatloaf herself, and I have to admit that now she's really learned how to, and so that was delicious as well . . . and where did you go to eat?"

He told her where.

"Who knows what gruesome stuff you'll have had to swallow," she exclaimed, with a grimace of disgust. "Let's hope it doesn't make you ill. But did the underwear at least keep you warm and dry enough?"

While he replied that the woolen underwear had indeed proved fortuitous, and placidly told her what he'd eaten at lunch, he was observing her closely. In bed, with two linen-covered pillows propping her up, with that graceful, loosely knitted, blue woolen shawl which covered her shoulders and breast, all so clean, the soft, cottonwool-like hair a fraction whiter than the frail parchment of her face, she too looked beautiful. Perfect.

"You're looking beautiful yourself," he said. "My compliments."

She burst out laughing. Childishly flattered, she arched back against the pillows, joined together her little, knotty hands covered with veins, and shut her eyes. How old was she? he wondered. She must be around eighty, almost double his own age. All the same her arteriosclerosis was helping to turn her into a child again—even more of a child than Rory was.

When she opened her eyes again, she wanted to know how the hunt had gone.

"I guess you won't have shot anything," she said.

She had assumed a disheartened and at the same time anxious air, as if all she wanted was to be proved wrong. Why not make her happy? She looked as though she needed to hear a fairy tale, and he was willing to tell her one. More than willing.

He replied that she was mistaken, he'd brought down more than forty ducks and coots. Only rather than carry them all back home he'd preferred to give them away. He'd given them all to Ulderico.

She was slow to catch his meaning.

"Ulderico who?" she asked.

He tilted his head toward Via Montebello, then added in a lowered tone:

"*Cavaglieri?*"

She nodded.

He waited for her to emerge from her bewilderment and reorganize her memory. Yes, him, he confirmed. As they'd recently exchanged a couple of phone calls, and he'd always been so kind, and as he was passing through Codigoro, he'd decided to pay him a visit.

Now she was on the alert, as though she'd shed twenty years.

"At his home?" she whispered.

"Yes, at his home."

"And where is his home? In the countryside?"

"No, in the town itself. Right on the main square."

"Did you see his wife as well?"

"His wife and his children too."

"His children! How many does he have?"

He showed her with his fingers.

"Six!" his mother exclaimed, clapping her hands. "Good heavens above, what a clan!"

"And his wife . . ." she continued after a pause, again in a stifled voice, wrinkling her forehead with the effort to remember, ". . . what's his wife like? Did you speak to her?"

"I certainly did. I phoned and went round. They offered me a nice cup of tea . . . they even wanted me to stay for dinner."

He saw her shake her head, give an ample sigh, then throw herself back against the pillows once more. Her eyes, always a bit too damp, had filled with tears. What was she thinking about? What had got into her? For the love of God, let it not be any sadness.

To distract her, he told her about the children. The two girls were almost grown up now. Of the four boys, all likeable good-looking lads, three of them had started playing soccer in the hallway while he was there.

"What a hullaballoo that must have been!" his mother said with a laugh, still in tears.

"It was, rather."

"And what are they called, those little ones?"

"I'm not sure. Clementina, Tonino . . . or Tanino, I didn't catch all the names. There's also one called Andrea."

Here they were interrupted by Lilla who suddenly springing up, began to bark. She had extraordinary hearing, as he'd noticed on other occasions. It was enough, say, for a truck to pass down Corso Giovecca and she would leap up in protest like a jack-in-a-box.

"Be good!" his mother told her off. "Down, you stupid thing, and go to sleep!"

When she was sure the dog had gone back to her slumbers, she seemed all of a sudden to have forgotten everything they'd been speaking of till then.

She started talking, as usual without a pause, about Lilla being so clever, that if one fine day she should start to to say "Mamma" no one who knew her would be in the least bit surprised; about Nives, fine woman, with a good head on her shoulders, an untiring worker, salt of the earth, but sometimes she could be a bit brusque, how shall we say, a bit too coarse; about Prearo, the accountant, who was saying, just this evening, at supper, that things were settling down in the political world, and that was perfectly borne out by the sense of great calm she felt around her, the same, it seemed to her, as she'd felt in the time she had spent at that convent in

Florence when the Germans were here; about Rory, poor little mite, who just today had hidden a little Christmas wish under her napkin, so well written it was, both in terms of handwriting and clear expression, and so affectionate; about a pipe for the drinking water which was leaking more every day, and how he really ought to chase Romeo so he finally attended to it; about a phone call she had received at five o'clock from her friend Carmen Scutellari, one of the Scutellaris of Via Terranuova, a call that had ended with their mutual promise to meet up in the next few days . . . It was a continuous flow of murmured words, a kind of chirping which ended, after at least twenty minutes, with an umpteenth sigh and a "Hmm!" which was happy and satisfied.

For her too everything would reach the right conclusion, he thought as he began to get to his feet. For the little that was left of her life, things would always turn out well. Regardless.

He leaned down to kiss her on the forehead.

"Bye," he said. "Goodnight."

"Yes, my dear. Goodnight to you as well."

He turned his back on her, crossed the room and reached the door.

With his hand on the latch, he turned to look at her. Surrounded by everything that was most her own and most dear to her—the little adoring dog almost touching her, then the family photographs, the heraldic arms of the House of Savoy on parchment in a silver frame, the many-colored vials of medicine, the leather spectacles case, the tiny golden parallelepiped of her Zenith alarm clock, the books on one bookcase, the last few years' issues of *Vie d'Italia* on another, the *Giornale dell'Emilia* open on the green damask quilt level with the little bundle of black fur that was Lilla and so on and on—she gave him a warm smile. White, down there, wrapped in her cocoon of light.

"Goodnight," he repeated.

"Goodnight, my dear Edgardo."

: VI :

The Smell of Hay

Two Fables

1.

ONCE upon a time, when I was a boy, there lived in Ferrara a Jewish Signorina who was not ugly, nor poor, nor stupid, nor too old—not especially desirable, if the truth be told, but not in the least deserving to be scorned—for whom, however strange it may seem, her family had not yet managed to find a husband. Strange? Well, yes. Within the confines of our community, and at that time, such a thing presented all the features of an exception. Deploying, as usual, the network of family relations and acquaintances, but also calling upon the women's section of the Italian Jewish Society, should have moved things very effectively toward the desired end. Similarly, the dance parties held during *Purim* in several locales annexed to the Temple on Via Mazzini or in the entrance hall of the Jewish kindergarten on Via Vignatagliata, parties attended by crowded, whispering rows of matrons seated along the walls and busy at their embroidery, or, in the most troublesome of cases, the letters that the Rabbi Dr. Castelfranco was implored to write to his colleagues in the neighboring Emilian or Romagnolo or Veneto cities should have done the trick: one way or another, these were the means to ensure that at the opportune moment the right person ended up presenting himself. There was never a reason to despair. When the city itself lacked sufficient resources to produce a spouse, at last a Lohengrin* would arrive from far away: to see, to be seen, and almost always to bring the matter to a fitting conclusion.

In 1934, Egle Levi-Minzi had reached the age of thirty-three. For what reason she had remained a spinster, I couldn't say with certainty. The only daughter of elderly, rather well-off parents, she still lived in their house, and, at certain precise hours of the morning and afternoon, she would always be found promenading through the streets of the center in their company—they made a nearly inseparable trio, noted by the whole city and almost proverbial. What I do know is that when they, the parents, had begun to look around in search of a possible son-in-law, the major resistance always came from her, the person most closely concerned. To keep her in this negative frame of mind, one likely component was a bit of filial and virginal mania, an excessive attachment to her old father and mother. Another, perhaps, was a secret suggestion which influenced her in the mad period of her early youth—the period, it's worth remembering, of the notorious Fascist squads of the Po Valley, so similar in many respects to our own times—some violent image of masculinity, which then, in the years that followed, had hindered her from turning toward different male types . . . However it was, the fact is that every time Egle Levi-Minzi found herself faced with a choice, this one wouldn't do, this other, likewise, that one, I ask you, that other one, you must be joking. A grimace adorned her large, melancholic mouth, already a little fallen at the corners: a slight, irritated lowering of the sparsely belashed eyelids over her sad, watery-brown, Sephardic irises: and the last suitor was added to the gradually lengthening list of rejects.

Almost halfway through 1935, I believe it was actually in June of that year, an utterly different reception awaited a suitor who had come from far further off than Bologna, or Ravenna, or Mantua, or Rovigo, or Venice. He was Russian, or rather Ukrainian. The child, he too, of parents no longer young, he was twenty-seven years old. His name was Yuri: Yuri Rotstein.

---

* The title figure of Wagner's opera *Lohengrin* (1848); a German romantic character inspired by the mysterious, damsel-rescuing Knight of the Swan in Arthurian legend.

The little family had arrived in Ferrara during the summer of the year before from Odessa. Having got off the Trieste train, they had encamped haphazardly in a small hotel in front of the station. But already before Yom Kippur they were occupying, rent-free, needless to say, a small apartment in a house on Via Vittoria which had belonged, from time immemorial, to the Jewish community. They had asked for refuge, and they had received it. The father, besides, given his perfect knowledge of all religious matters, and of written and spoken Hebrew, had been speedily given work, with duties that fluctuated between those of cantor and synagogue attendant: assigned as assistant to the rabbi, and in some cases even as his substitute, for the Sabbath morning services, for less imposing burials and for the kosher slaughter of farm animals. In brief, within a couple of months they were already well established. They expressed themselves in a slow Italian, at times with oddly harsh, Byzantine inflections; not exactly correct, one might say, but quite effectively comprehensible. The first time they presented themselves in the community's offices, the father, speaking also for the other two, had made mention of Erez, of America . . .

Father and son looked alike. Both of them tall, a good bit taller than the average height of those who went to the German School synagogue. They both had the same kind of face: long, bony and gaunt, with protruding cheekbones above which shone the same little bright-blue, slanted, *muzhik* eyes. The mother, by contrast, was short, fat and round: a servant or peasant type, with reams of white handkerchief tied round her neck.

But what most struck those present, both downstairs, in the space reserved for men, and up in the women's gallery, was the incontestible dignity of all three, the utterly unforced and moving nonchalance with which, in exchange for some modest assistance, they still behaved in the manner of guests. It was not as if they had the air of saying: "At the end of the day we're all equal, of the same religion, brothers, so this is also our house and home." Not at all. From the straightforward manner all three of them adopted at the Temple, silent, composed, without giving offence by any special Ashkenazi exhibitionism (the father still retaining his kaftan, his sparse little blondish beard, as well as the pious side locks of the same tint that curled out at his ears from under the round hat he wore; and the mother her big peasant neckerchief; though the son, by contrast, was correctly dressed in the Western style in grey flannel), they seemed troubled only about one thing: to reassure the assembly of their unwavering intent to be off again as soon as possible. They merely asked to stay for a short while, just for the time needed to get their breath back. After that, we could be sure, they'd soon enough resume their wandering through the wide world.

They weren't ever to resume their wandering through the wide world. And so their names can still be found, among those of the 183 Ferrarese Jews deported to Germany during the winter of 1943 to '44, on the great commemorative stone attached to the facade of the Jewish Temple on Via Mazzini.

However, all considered, their transmigration from the East to the West was not in vain. Egle Levi-Minzi would have a son: a male child, whom she first felt suddenly calling out to her in that very Temple, on a long-ago Saturday evening at the end of May, while she looked through the grating of the women's gallery down into the vast hall crowded with men.

It had been a question of only a few seconds.

All the men were facing toward the Chief Rabbi Castelfranco, waiting for him to intone the final solemn blessing, the *berachah*. Only one among the many, that young Ukrainian, an immigrant of but a few months, had turned round and was looking behind. He was peering up, in the direction of the women's gallery, with his magnificent blue, smiling, winking, wild eyes. So why shouldn't she have a son with that young man?—Egle Levi-Minzi had said to herself, as though awakening from a prolonged torpor. It was clear. It wasn't her that the youth was greeting, but rather the old countrywoman, his mother, who was sitting next to her. And yet, why not pretend to make a mistake, and why not respond to his smile, to his curt nod of salute, with something similar? He was poor, a foreigner. Young, younger than her by quite a few years, almost a boy. But poor. Without a house of his own. A wanderer. His parents could continue to live in the flat on Via Vittoria where the community had installed them. The young man, on the other hand . . . It was worth the effort to try. To try him out.

She had smiled. She had waved her hand.

After a moment of hesitation, the other had lifted two fingers to the brim of his hat, making a faint bow.

No, it had indeed been worth the effort. The child that Egle Levi-Minzi had was truly exceptional: a lively boy, intelligent, irrepressible, very beautiful—so much so that to the few of us who had escaped the death camps and all else, and who in 1945, no longer divided into men and women, or between one religious school and another, who found ourselves once more together at the Italian synagogue, he seemed the very personification of life that eternally ends and begins again. He was called Yuri. Yuri Rotstein. Tall, thin, bony, with those slanted eyes flashing blue above his sharp cheekbones, he still lives with his mother, alone with her forever, in their big house in Ferrara.

2.

Do you remember the Albergo Tripoli, the shady little Ferrarese hotel of the worst quality, that before the war could be found a few steps from the Estense Castle, in the vast piazza behind it—that same Albergo Tripoli I've had other occasions to mention? Well, imagine it one December night about forty years ago, and so in the darkest period of Fascism, and late at night, very late, a few minutes before they closed.

Down in the entrance hall the lights had already been turned off. When suddenly, there at the end of the hall, the door with its emerald-colored glass was swung open (a gust of humid wind swept through the empty hall and reached as far as the counter where the night receptionist sat) and, gradually emerging from the shadows, a man approached.

He walked slowly, weighed down by a big suitcase. He had the collar of his overcoat turned up, the rim of his hat tilted down to hide his eyes. Who on earth could it be? the receptionist asked himself. By the look of him, one would have thought he was a commercial traveler.

"I would like a room," said the man quietly.

"I'm afraid we won't be able to help you there," replied the receptionist.

He opened the register in front of him, hardly bothered to scan it, then made a grimace.

He lifted his head again.

"At this hour, you'll understand," he added, "the whole place is full. Besides, it being Christmas . . . "

His eyes sought out the eyes of the other, but hidden as they were beneath the Homburg's greasy rim, he failed to discern them. He could only make out the lower part of his face, its cheeks and chin unshaven.

"Don't make me go outside again, I beg you," the man said in the lowest tones, with a strong southern accent, Calabrian, or perhaps Sicilian, who knows.

"Good Lord," he sighed, doubling the "d"s percussively. "I'm dog-tired! Is there really nothing at all? Even a few hours to rest up would do me fine. I leave tomorrow morning on the nine o'clock train."

The receptionist paused. He leaned his well-combed head over the register once more.

"All I can offer you is a double room," he said, having pretended to look. "It's the only free room left. I warn you, however, that you'll have to pay the full price."

He pronounced the word "however" with distinct pleasure: the pleasure he experienced every time an opportunity arose to demonstrate how much more genteel and refined he was than Signor Müller, the owner, forever shuffling that toothpick between his gold-filled teeth, his whole behavior common. He was convinced that the traveling salesman would not insist, would turn on his heels and walk away.

But he was mistaken.

He watched him almost straightaway lift his hand, tip his hat back so as to reveal a bald forehead. He was smiling.

"Fair enough," he heard him say. "Thanks."

Then he stretched his lips as if to whistle silently, and added, winking: "My documents."

He had already slipped his right hand into the inside pocket of his coat, on the side of his heart, and had begun cautiously to rummage about in it. His kept his eyes half-closed. It was as if he was feeling pleasure.

The receptionist pressed a buzzer.

Dragging his feet, a porter, an old man, appeared. He waited while the receptionist returned the identity card to the guest and gave him the key to the double room on the third floor. After which he bent down, grasped the suitcase by its handle, and without checking he was being followed made his way toward the stairs, quietly grumbling.

"Good night, Signor Buda," said the receptionist.

The man had walked a few paces away.

"Good night," he replied.

He hadn't turned. He had done no more than lift two fingers to the rim of his hat.

"Would you like a wake up call?"

"No, that won't be necessary."

"Good night, sir."

"Good night."

The room was vast and low-ceilinged. The door was in one corner beside the radiator. Along the damp-pocked walls stood some pinewood furniture: a wardrobe, a bedside table. Near the window, curtainless, but with closed and bolted shutters, was a washbasin which sported a little mirror above it; above the mirror a square light fixture with an opaque glass cover, almost half full of detritus, from which filtered an ugly red light like that of a hospital ward. The two beds were put together. United that way, they gave the impression of an enormous double bed.

Alone, Signor Buda gave a light whistle, this time clearly audible. He looked around. The two wardrobe mirrors reflected an oblique image of the room with him in the middle, the big fiber suitcase set on the floor, close by his feet.

He passed a hand over his face.

Life is a dream, he thought.

He remained for a moment standing like that, unmoving, at the center of the room. Then he bestirred himself. He took off his overcoat and hat, went to hang them on a hook fixed to the door, then made his way to the basin. He let the water run from the tap, and finally, leaning over, began to wash his face.

Life is a dream, he thought. When on earth had he heard or read this phrase? And why had it come into his mind right at this moment?

He straightened up. He groped for and found the hand towel. He dried his face, went back to the bedside. While the icy tap water continued to flow and make its dirge-like sound, he hurriedly undressed. Finally, having taken his shaving kit from the suitcase he'd hefted onto the bed, he went to the basin a second time and began to lather his face.

He slept, Signor Buda. He dreamed. He dreamed of being asleep . . .

He dreamed that he had slept for three, at the most four hours, without dreaming.

And that finally—ding, ding, ding, ding, ding, ding—as the piazza clock had slowly struck the six hours one after the other, he had awoken.

Stretched out flat on his back, in the same position as when he'd first laid down, he gradually opened his eyes. An overpowering smell filled the room, bitter and sickly-sweet at the same time, and unmistakable! So it was time—he told himself, switching on the light above his head—he really needed to get going, to be on his way. For that reason as well. But first . . .

He sat up, threw back the covers, swung his legs down out of the bed, and so, walking barefoot on the brick floor, he moved unhesitatingly toward the wardrobe.

He opened it—and at the sight of the body, his own body, rather than being amazed, he gave a nod of assent. Good. Very good. Utterly naked, whitened gums showing, reduced to no more than the mere puppet he had to be, he was seated, leaning his long cheek, with its growth of black beard, upon his doubled-up knees.

Then, having closed the wardrobe with exaggerated slowness (only so as not to interrupt the flow of his thoughts, it was clear, for that alone), he found himself, he didn't know how, in the open air outside the hotel. The air was biting cold. Along the wide avenue that led into the city, on which a cold light had begun to dawn, there was not a living soul to be seen— from the castle to the distant Customs barrier. An equally deserted vista confronted him as he turned the corner. At the end of the straight road he had yet to cover before arriving, the railway station appeared to him grey, small, low, and yet clear in every detail.

He walked hurriedly, his gaze fixed on the station, which gradually loomed larger. And then suddenly, as soon as he had reached the square in front of it, two things entered his mind: firstly, that he had left in the bedroom at the Albergo Tripoli the big fiber suitcase with all his stuff, its top layer strewn with commercial samples and some personal effects and beneath that the banned political pamphlets; and secondly, that he hadn't paid his bill. He stopped, not really perturbed but, rather, undecided. And yet, just then hearing a few yards away, but close enough to think it right behind him, the wheeze of an invisible locomotive switching tracks inside the station, and realizing that despite all these concerns, it was too late to turn back, he continued on his way.

Anyway this was all a dream—he said to himself with a smile of bitter consolation. He knew it was, even while dreaming it: a dream within a dream.

Further News
of Bruno Lattes

1.

ENCLOSED all about by an old perimeter wall some three meters high, Ferrara's Jewish cemetery is a vast grassy expanse, so vast that the gravestones, gathered in separate and distinct groups, appear far fewer than they actually are. On the eastern side, the circling wall is in the lee of the city's walls, thickly planted even today with big trees—limes, elms, chestnuts and also some oaks—arrayed in a double row along the top of the embankment. At least along this stretch, the war has spared these beautiful, ancient plants. You can only just make out the red sixteenth-century tower that some thirty years ago served as a powder magazine, half hidden as it is behind their broad green domes.

During the summer months, the grass in our cemetery always grows with a frantic vigor. I'm not sure if that's still the case, but around 1938, at the time of the Racial Laws, the Jewish community used to entrust the cutting to an agricultural agency from the province: a firm from Quartesana, Gambulaga, Ambrogio or somewhere thereabouts. The scythers advanced slowly, in a semi-circular formation, moving their arms in synchronized rhythm. Every now and then they sent forth guttural cries, and the sentries on guard duty at the nearby powder magazine, hearing those distant voices lost in the dog days' heat haze (their sentry box standing out, white, over there at the foot of a century old black tree trunk), must have felt all the more strongly the burden of their constraint, all the more keenly their yearning to be free.

Toward five o'clock in the afternoon, the farm workers would abandon their scything. Overladen with swaying heaps of hay and drawn by a yoked pair of oxen, their carts went out one after the other into Via delle Vigne, where, at that hour, the inhabitants of the neighborhood, pensioners in shirt sleeves with a pipe or a Tuscan cigar between their teeth, old bespectacled *arzdóre** intent on darning linen or rinsing vegetables, were almost all seated out of doors, in a row in front of their little one-story dwellings. The street was narrow, little broader even in those days than a country lane. So narrow that if a funeral procession happened to be coming the other way, there would be no other option but to wait patiently, by the busy crossroads of Corso Porta Mare, for five, ten minutes, sometimes even a quarter of an hour.

As soon as the hearse had crossed the threshold of the big entrance gate, doing so with a leisurely jolt, the sharp smell of mown hay wafted across to liven up the cortège oppressed by the heat. What a relief. And what peace. Immediately there was an abrupt, simultaneous, almost joyful commotion. Some went off among the graves closest to the entrance. Others, the majority, moved away from the now stationary hearse as the gravediggers began to offload the wreaths, and together with them, the compact group of close family and other relatives who had remained in attendance by the coffin then set off at a good pace, a few at a time, toward the distant place of burial.

Only his father's insistence ("Cancer spares no one!" he'd declared with his usual pathos, and an air at once emotionally blackmailing and admonitory) had been able to induce Bruno Lattes to attend the funeral of his Uncle Celio. To avoid wasting time arguing. Even to his own surprise, he had been on his best behavior. Not only during the journey down Via Voltapaletto to the cemetery, but also afterward, mingling with the small crowd of relatives and close friends, high on whose heads the coffin had crossed the whole cemetery from west to east, he had behaved himself better than ever, polite, composed, and absolutely calm.

---

* See footnote on p. 41.

At a particular moment, though, he relapsed. While the gravediggers were doing their utmost to maneuver the coffin into the grave, his glance caught the bewildered look of his father, a look that instantly made him revert to the blind rage that had become his habitual state.

What did they have in common—he once more asked himself—he, on one side, and on the other, his father and the whole raft of kith and kin? He was tall, lean, with dark hair and complexion, while his Papa and the long line of relatives, the Camaiolos, Bonfigliolis, Hanaus, Joszs, Ottolenghis, Minerbis, Bassanis and so on, who composed the so-called "Lattes clan," were mostly short, thickset, with blue eyes, but of a washed-out blue (or if brown of a dull and lusterless tint), and bore unmistakable weak and rounded chins. And as regards character? There too no similarity could be found between him and them, thank God, not the slightest. There was nothing unstable, excitable, morbid in him, nothing that might be considered typically Jewish. His personality was much closer, at least so it seemed to him, to the strong and straightfor-ward character of his Catholic friends, and it was not for nothing that his mother, born a Catholic, as Catholic as can be, was called Marchi. And as for cancer, which ever since 1924—when his grandfather Benedetto, after two years of unspeakable suffering, had died of a stomach tumor—his father had decided that this was unquestionably the family illness (but as for Uncle Celio, no, they shouldn't talk rubbish: Uncle Celio died as a result of an attack of nephritis, a longstanding condition, and so once in a while cancer could be completely discounted . . .). Let cancer arrive, one day or another, if that's what it wanted! Please do come in, and why not take a seat! As far as he was concerned, he had already decided some time ago that in such circumstances he'd behave precisely as his mother would have behaved, always so bright and happy, poor thing, always so direct and natural. But to let cancer become a daily goad, an obsession to nurture and cradle within, between fear and delight, for years and years? How revolting! He would never capitulate to cancer in that way. Never ever.

The coffin now lay in the depths of the grave. The gravediggers had retracted their lowering ropes, and the rabbi, Dr. Castelfranco, with his nasal, singsong voice, was already reciting the prayers for the dead.

When suddenly the sound of an accordion was heard, very close by. Bruno raised his eyes.

Because of the wall separating the cemetery from the city walls, he could not make out the person playing the instrument. Up there, he could only see a soldier in front of a sentry box (no doubt guarding the powder magazine), who, tilting his sweating face forward, was nodding in time to the music.

A woman's voice was singing:

> *Love, my love*
> *Bring me roses aplenty . . .*

Someone shouted: "Silence!" Other cries of protest ensued, insults and raised fists, a volley of curses. Behind the big trees surmounting the walls, beyond the glistening, dense mass of their foliage, you could sense an open space, almost a sea breeze.

The spadefuls of earth followed each other ever more swiftly.

Bruno turned his gaze elsewhere.

And after supper—he was thinking—when on his bicycle he'd pass this stretch of the city wall, caught between the desire to let his headlight reveal the couples embracing in the grass and the fear of peering out into the cemetery's black space that lay beneath (since his childhood he'd always had a horror of will-o-the-wisps, of *ignes fatui*), he wondered if he would have the slightest chance of seeing the young soldier who'd been rooted beside his sentry box. Who knows? Bitterness and disgust: those, anyway, were the feelings he experienced in that moment.

Still, he knew it—all too well! Impatience, the almost furious agitation which tormented him now, thinking of the sentry on guard at the powder magazine—had they become friends, perhaps they'd have gone together to the cinema, and later, even though he wasn't yet eighteen, they might have stopped at a brothel . . . might have—all this turmoil wasn't merely a sudden reaction to the stupid chore that he'd had to put up with today, but surfaced from afar, way back: from a point in the lost past right at the very furthest reach of an almost infinite recession.

At his grandfather Benedetto's funeral, in August 1924, before the coffin had been lowered into the grave, the undertakers had unscrewed the lid. Then the corpse, wrapped in an embroidered linen sheet, had been strewn with quicklime, in observance of the most ancient Jewish rite. It had been Grandpa himself who had stipulated this. No sooner had he stopped breathing than someone had immediately rushed off to open the will. The will spoke clearly: the quicklime should be introduced into the coffin afterward, in the cemetery, in front of the open grave. And not earlier, that was to say, at home. Otherwise, woe betide them.

He was nine years old then. The cemetery green, on which he strode for the very first time—his memory of it remained vivid—was spanned by the first lengthening shadows of evening, along with dense swarms of mosquitoes. And these mosquitoes had seemed to him curiously akin, especially if he covered one eye with his hand, to the fighter planes that one August evening several years earlier he had seen ready to land, silently crossing the huge sky which extended in front of the breakfast-room window where Grandpa Benedetto, for the second time a widower, used to eat alone. The war was still going on. Papa was at the front. And Mamma? Where was his Mamma? Someone, perhaps his Aunt Edvige, who after the death of Grandma Esterina had taken over the running of the house, told him that his mother had left for Feltre, where she was to spend her short leave with Papa. But Feltre? Where was Feltre? And more to the point, what was Feltre? And the *rear* of which Aunt Edvige had also spoken, what was the *rear* of the battlelines? The light aircraft lazily descended out of the milky, evening sky, one after the other, without making the slightest noise. To touch them seemed easy. To touch them, he would only need to stretch his arm out from one of the two breakfast-room windows. If there hadn't, unfortunately, been his grandpa there, who was eating alone and at the same time, with glasses perched on his forehead, reading the newspaper he habitually kept propped up on a jug of water. If his grandpa, able as he was to guess everything, including his most secret thoughts, had understood what he wanted to do, he wouldn't have told him off, not at all. He would only have stared at him with those hard, piercing, blue-enamel eyes of his. And that would have been far worse.

That other August afternoon, the one in 1924 on which his Grandpa

Benedetto had been buried, the cemetery meadow seemed to have been freshly scythed: exactly as it was now. It was an invitation to run. And, in fact, having slipped his hand from the grasp of his mother, who stayed along with the others beside the grave of his grandfather that was still far from being filled, he went off to play on his own, chasing clouds of mosquitoes and moving ever farther away.

Suddenly, though, he had fallen: full-length and face down. While he was still falling, he was aware of having grazed his knee. And yet at that moment he hadn't cared about his knee. He looked round. What solitude all at once! Even though his leg was hurting him, hurting a lot, no one was paying him any attention, not even his mother. The tears on his cheeks dried, very slowly indeed.

"What have you done?" his mother had cried out when, out of breath, she finally reached his side. "If only you'd keep still for a moment! Don't you know that Grandpa Benedetto is dead?"

He paused a while before replying. At last, remembering a phrase he'd heard Papa utter that very morning at table, almost without awareness he'd repeated it exactly: word for word.

"Only the dead are happy," he'd said, sighing in the very manner of his father. And at the same time opening his eyes and peering up at his mother, he stealthily checked for a response.

After staring at him for quite a while with her beautiful brown eyes, deeply circled because of the many nights spent at the bedside of her father-in-law during the last months of his illness, though in spite of that they were more vivid and luminous than ever, his mother had placed her hand over his mouth. Then, kneeling, she'd bound his knee with her handkerchief.

2.

THE INSISTENT, furious questions that Bruno Lattes had directed at Adriana Trentini received no reply. To hell with you! Bruno finally thought, exasperated. He looked away.

He turned his gaze toward the odd, semi-circular window that gave onto the countryside in the direction of Bologna. Along the wide dock road, the Via Darsena, a stream of carts was very slowly passing. From the chimney of the Eridania sugar refinery on the right erupted thick, black, sooty smoke. How well he knew her! he went on thinking. For three years he'd done nothing else but talk. Whereas she, now he came to think of it, had always kept silent. The truth was—his insistence brought on a sudden feeling of lightness, of pure intellectual satisfaction—that even while he was wheeling out the full display of his witty, entertaining, worldly chatter, even then Adriana gave him no reason to trust her. She would, in fact, stand there listening silently, with a threatening air. Like a wall, or like a tree . . .

When he turned to look at her, he realized she hadn't moved. He looked and felt a wave of tenderness for her. With her back to the vestibule wall, Adriana fixed her gaze on a point on the floor, and every now and then, brusquely tossing her head, freed her cheeks of the hair that fell on them. But there she was again, giving him a fleeting, sidelong glance, peering up at him . . . What was she hoping to achieve, bitch that she was? Was she perhaps trying to check the time on his wristwatch?

Then he'd lost all patience.

"I'm off—I'm going now," he burst out. "Don't worry, I'm going."

He would have liked to insult her, to call her a whore, to give her a slap. But instead of that, once more he began to feel a tenderness toward her:

"Goodbye," he added, as he made his way to the door.

He felt as if he would never see her again. In the doorway he repeated: "Goodbye."

"*Ciao*," replied Adriana, without moving an inch.

That year, the fateful year 1938, winter arrived somewhat late. Only toward the end of October did the first big storms arrive, the first mists. In any case, no earlier than that, and these were the first signs. Bruno hardly ever went out. The Racial Laws had only just been issued. Besides he had told Adriana that he intended to change university to finish his thesis. He'd had enough, he declared, of the usual toing-and-froing between Ferrara and Bologna, enough of all that time wasted on trains! Within days, he meant to transfer to Florence, and stay there . . . But he'd been lying, and now feared that Adriana, when she learned the truth, would judge him as a dishonest, ridiculous little boaster.

Even at home he showed his face as little as possible: only, in effect, for meals, which anyway he often took alone, or a little earlier or later than the rest of his family. Most of the day he passed shut up in his ground-floor study, where no one ever dared set foot. He spent the hours in a state of inertia. From the high narrow window, above the green velvet armchair and the desk, a colorless light reached the room, insufficient to read by.

Daydreams continually transported him elsewhere. Sunk into the armchair, he would think of Adriana, and wonder what she would be doing just then. He envisaged her in her room: the room which, starting from last January until the first days of June, when the Trentinis had left for the seaside, for Rimini, he had so often managed to steal into at night. Stretched out on the bed, Adriana would be smoking. But who knows. Perhaps an afternoon of smoking and listening to records might have suddenly bored her. Giving way to one of her abrupt, irrational whims, maybe just out of simple curiosity, one day or another she might phone him. She might phone and he, naturally, would rush round. He'd go by bike, across the city, and there he would be, under the windows of her house, signaling by the usual whistle, their whistle. He'd run up the stairs, and find her in front of him. He was so worn-out and thin, with so much suffering in his eyes, the Racial Laws had rendered him so pitiful, that Adriana would be unable to resist—she'd throw herself into his arms without the least hesitation.

"I'd like to stay alone for a while," she'd told him just before they had separated, before she had shut herself into that frightening silence of hers. "I just want to be a child again. And besides"—she'd added, smiling cruelly—"I'm still only eighteen."

It's true, she'd said that, but what did it mean? She didn't yet have anyone else. That was certain. If she had, you could be sure some kind soul would have taken the trouble to warn him! And since she didn't have anyone else, everything still remained possible. To see her again, to speak to her: that was the essential thing. All that was needed was to find a way . . . the evening was falling slowly. With a book resting on his knees, Bruno lost himself within an infinite maze of speculation.

Later, when he went up to eat, his mother would inform him of the afternoon telephone calls. Often her memory would be vague, and she'd mix up the names.

Nothing provoked him more than this. It could make him shout or stamp his foot. Like a madman.

At least in part so as to avoid meeting his father (who, for his own reasons, intimidated by the icy expression of his son and scared of arguments about politics, had adopted the habit of never returning home before nine), after his meal, Bruno would hurriedly put on his coat and hat, and go out.

By mid November it was already bitterly cold. After an entire day spent shut indoors, in a slothful inertia, the fresh air, any movement at all, excited him. He kept away from the center and its cafes, monopolized by the hated bourgeoisie, hated and loved. He chose the back streets and by ways. Instead of Corso Giovecca, Viale Cavour, and Corso Roma, he preferred Via delle Volte, Via Coperta, Via San Romano, Via Fondo Banchetto, Via Salinguerra and so on, where he could slip into some restaurant or shady bar. Standing beside the billiards table, he watched long games played by shabby figures (not infrequently of a questionable character) . . . His arrival nearly always passed unnoticed, as did his presence, at least when he hadn't offered his services as scorer.

Sometimes, before returning home (if, that is, he hadn't ended up in a brothel), he went as far along the city walls as the section beside Porta Reno, where since summer a small, wretched fair had established itself: a carousel, two or three stalls, one of which was a shooting gallery, a little puppet theater, at that hour invariably closed with a great many boards and bolts. Why did he never tire of returning there, to such a desert, to such squalor? What kept luring him back? Not even he knew why.

It wasn't the girl in the shooting gallery, whose every movement was followed in mute contemplation by several wistful admirers, with their elbows leaned on the stall counter, no—he thought—between her and Adriana there was absolutely nothing in common. For a start, she wasn't as tall. Then, she had a straight but ungenerous profile, and blue eyes, it's true, but cold, hard, evil. Finally, there were her almost manly hands, which she used to snap open the air-rifles with a controlled and energetic gesture, reddened, swollen hands with square and deformed thumbnails. And yet he had to admit it. Those hands, those eyes, that animal body tightly sheathed in a pink sweater, her crude Tuscan accent, everything about her attracted him, fascinated him. He watched as did the others—insatiably. Every detail of her appearance spoke to him of secret vice, of mad depravity. He continuously sought her out with his gaze. If he managed to catch her eyes, he felt his heart leap. From this he extracted a bitter pleasure, a kind of vindictive joy.

He was always the last, or almost the last, to leave. Behind the stall, in the shadows, the oblong shape of a Gypsy wagon could just be seen. Three small windows adorned with curtains permitted a view of the brightly lit interior.

"Hey, beautiful," he exclaimed in a trembling, strangled voice, while the girl continued loading the rifle. "Do you have a generator?"

She didn't deign to reply.

But one night, one of the windows opened, releasing the sound of a gramophone, and some dark, curly hair, that of a man.

He wanted to laugh.

"Mon beau tzigan, mon amour . . ." he started reciting in a low voice, his eyes half closed.

The Tuscan girl hardly looked at him; then, having set down the rifle she was preparing for him, made off without haste toward the wagon. She reappeared from there some twenty minutes later. And while she resumed her place behind the counter, and handed him the rifle, she winked in the direction of the now lightless window, puffing out her thick, repainted lips.

The next night the shooting gallery and the wagon were no longer there. Gone, disappeared. Almost as if he had dreamed them, merely dreamed them.

Suddenly he understood two things: that only from that moment on could he truly know what the word "suffering" meant; and that the memory of that expression of the shooting gallery girl (an expression which the evening before had unexpectedly filled him with happiness, jealousy, and an obscure sense of wretchedness) would remain printed on him for many years to come, for who knows how long. Like a small mark, tiny but indelible.

3.

AFTER SPENDING a winter, a spring and a summer steeped in solitude, hardly finding the strength to achieve anything, reading little, studying nothing, the draft of his thesis was no more than a third done, and only going at most once a fortnight even to Bologna to meet his old university companions (all of them now graduated), toward the end of August 1939 Bruno Lattes began seriously to consider seeing Adriana Trentini one more time.

It's not as though he was nursing any excessive hopes. He understood. In the year since Adriana had left him, and with the Racial Laws which day by day became ever more rigid and oppressive (it was no joke: to be caught together would mean she would end up in the police station as a common streetwalker, and he would be sent into internal exile), in such conditions only a madman would think it conceivable they might actually get together again. And yet, wasn't it just possible that Adriana, at the seaside, far away from Ferrara, might be persuaded to make love with him one last time? She had to be! For the little it would cost her . . . This was the only way, he was now certain, that he would ever manage to break free. Having shaken the yoke of servitude off his shoulders, he might finally turn the page and begin to live again. In a few days he'd be able to finish off his thesis on Berchet,[*] and then he could graduate.

That year the Trentinis had chosen a novel resort for their holiday by the sea. Instead of renting the usual little villa in the usual Rimini, barely a hundred kilometers from Ferrara, they had ended up in Abbazia: an out of the way place, the other side of Istria, that took hours and hours to reach by train. All the better for that. In Abbazia, a slingshot from Yugoslavia, there were not likely to be any Ferraresi, apart from the engineer Trentini and his family: father, mother, the two sisters, Adriana

---

[*] Giovanni Berchet (1783–1851) was an Italian Romantic poet.

and Rosanna, and Cesare, their younger brother. Without any Ferraresi getting under their feet, he and Adriana would be able to disport themselves almost with total freedom. Should the prospect appeal to them, they could even take a stroll together ...

He left by the express train early morning on the 29th, a Tuesday, and reached Trieste around two o'clock in the afternoon. From here he chose a different mode of transport. He'd worked everything out. By local bus he could arrive at his destination at least three hours before the train, and so well before dark. And this would give him plenty of time and leisure to seek out a good room, not too expensive, but one suited to his needs.

He would need to eat as well. And yet, as soon as he'd entered the big square outside the station, and had spotted the bus parked at the sidewalk with its engine running, he immediately realized that he'd have to skip the meal. He smiled. Patience—he said to himself, quickening his pace, despite the suitcase. In Montefalcone, an hour before, he'd had a ham roll and a beer. He could easily keep going on that till the evening.

Having climbed to the top of the heights that overlooked the city, the local bus began to advance into a vast region of undulating meadowland, of scattered woods of firs and birches, and of boulders, everywhere, mounds of them, white as bones. Bruno sat next to the window. He looked at the meadows, the trees, the heaps of stones, trying to affix every last detail in his memory, noticing among other things that although the afternoon light was blinding up there, the air had become much cooler. But it was all for nothing. Curled up in his corner, with an empty stomach, soon enough his thoughts returned to their habitual groove.

Adriana and the international situation: since he had boarded the train he'd practically thought of nothing else.

After the pact between Nazi Germany and the USSR—he kept asking himself—what fate would befall Poland? Would the guarantee of France and England be enough to protect it from a German invasion? The Polish Army mainly relied on its cavalry, that same cavalry which, in 1920, performing miracles of heroism, had pushed back the Russian troops that had arrived at the gates of Warsaw. But what good would romantic cavalrymen armed with lances, sabres and pistols be against the thousands and thousands of tanks at the disposal of the Wehrmacht? It was true that Hitler had swallowed up Austria and Czechoslovakia in a couple of bites, unopposed, but was it really possible that at this point they would let him gobble Poland up as well? And Italy? And the Italian Jews? No way—this time Hitler wouldn't dare. If he dared, there would be war. And nothing would make him risk another war on two fronts, on one side Great Britain and France, on the other Poland—he had already said that and even repeated it in *Mein Kampf*.

And then Adriana again, their imminent encounter.

The Trentinis, he'd been able to check, were staying in a hotel: the Victoria, a very superior establishment. Excellent: as soon as he got off the bus, this would give him the chance to phone and ask the receptionist for her, for the Signorina Adriana. But wait—would it be better to ask for Adriana, or rather for her sister, Rosanna? He remembered clearly: when it all began, four years ago, the then twelve-year-old Rosanna had been very well-disposed and biddable. On many occasions, when, for example, there'd been the need to arrange something—this evening we'll go to the cinema, at seven we'll stop by at Zanarini's, Adriana told me to tell you that she'd booked the court for tomorrow morning at eight at the Grand Hôtel, and so on—it was usually Rosanna who would rush off on her bicycle between the two villas, to lend a helping hand and act as go-between. But now? After everything that had happened, the Racial Laws and all the rest (sisters would talk to each other, as a general rule: that for almost a year he had spent scores of nights in Adriana's bedroom was a fact Rosanna was sure to have known about), wasn't it possible that she would now say, No, that's enough, I'm no longer prepared to be the dogsbody? She must be sixteen herself now. She might well have become a different character, she could have turned sulky, moralistic. Even a hypocrite, expressing concern that her sister shouldn't waste any more time on a mad and pointless relationship, while actually only being jealous. For all of that, better not. Wiser to ask straight off for Adriana. To avoid any catastrophic and irreparable miscalculations.

With Adriana, however things fell out, supposing she would be willing to sleep with him (and as the bus drew gradually closer to Abbazia it seemed ever more likely that she would be), with Adriana he would have to act with the utmost care—with all the calm and tact he could muster. No tragic, long faces, no staring eyes, none of the gross gestures of a mad or famished beggar, no hurry. To start off, he would have to take her out for a walk exactly as they used to do in the early days, when they had returned to Ferrara after that famous summer in Rimini and would arrange to see each other at all hours of the day and in all kinds of places, including Montagnone and the Mura degli Angeli. One evening they might perhaps go to some dance hall similar to Zanarini's in Rimini, or to the Saviolo in Riccione, locales always perfect for dancing cheek-to-cheek, and even closer. Later, not perhaps the very same evening, but on a second occasion, he might persuade her to come round to his room. With this end in view, he'd need some care in the choice of a room. A hotel room, no, that wouldn't do. Preferably a room in a *pensione*. Even better would be a self-catering room of one's own. A *garçonnière*, yes, that was what was called for: to rent for two or three days, and without bothering too much about the cost. Sure, at Abbazia, something of the kind wouldn't easily be found. Beyond Abbazia, however, he could scout around nearby Fiume, a sea port and border town. And if, because of this, he were forced to put off his return home, well, he could always alert them with a telegram.

One image provoked by his fantasy, however, came back every now and then to fill him with a paralyzing sense of uncertainty, of disbelief: the great pink-and-blonde image of Adriana on the bed, naked, her skin smooth and golden, her full lips those of an American vamp, her hair so fair it seemed shot with platinum, her breasts, her belly, her thighs, her smell. Suddenly dejected, he would then say to himself:

"What chance is there?"

He phoned from the *pensione* at seven o'clock that same evening. Taken by surprise yet very calm, Adriana said that she'd be happy to meet him, but not just then: she and Rosanna had to go out to see some friends. Yes, for dinner and then a dance—she clarified, in response to his question. But why didn't he come by—she added—tomorrow morning around ten? First they could go for a swim. Then they could all eat together. Her mother would also be very pleased to see him again (her father unfortunately wasn't there: he'd had to return to Ferrara straight after the August Bank Holiday, and from that point on he'd had to bury any thought of Abbazia).

For the next two days, Wednesday the 30th and Thursday the 31st, he didn't have the chance to speak to Adriana for a minute alone: not even when they went for a swim on Wednesday morning. Rather than giving him courage, her tranquil disengagement intimidated him. She, Adriana, was large-limbed, sun-tanned, peaceful, potent. While he, nervous, pale-skinned, skeletally thin, and worse still, a terrible swimmer—how could he not cut a sorry and unprepossessing figure—someone to be rid of as soon as possible, as he hunched in the water mere yards from dry land, in the patient hope that she, the American and Aryan vamp, propelled by a few lazy strokes, way out to sea—so far out that even her graceful red rubber bathing cap was lost to sight—would finally deign to return to shore.

There had then been lunch in the fine dining room of the old Habsburg hotel, with its prospect of the breezy and bright cerulean sea, beyond a huge, stepped terrace full of multicolored parasols: a lunch almost entirely overwhelmed by the uninterrupted and daintily complaining discourse of Signora Trentini.

By then past forty, magnificent, the same hemp-hued blonde as her elder daughter, with the same blue eyes—in her case, though, a little protuberant—bovine, benign, infinitely humane and forbearing and above all glad to make a show of it. (Did she know or didn't she? It seemed, naturally, as though she didn't, but just imagine her not being fully aware of the nature of his relationship with Adriana . . .) From the start, the good woman had declared herself more than certain that the war, believed by most to be inevitable, would not break out. As with the invasion of Czechoslovakia last year, "we" would have to intervene to make peace between the opposing sides, perhaps even at the last moment. And he? Even if Adriana's mother hadn't said anything outlandish (yesterday while traveling, though torn as ever between hope and fear, hadn't he himself reached almost the same conclusions?), all the same, what scorn and agony he felt listening to her, watching her make such a show of her obtuse, egotistical, maternal and bourgeois optimism, so typically rural Emilian, and so *goy*! Yuk! He had to contradict her, maintaining that war would break out, and that "we" too would become involved in the vast and general massacre. They were a hair's breadth from a full-scale quarrel, he and Signora Trentini, even though the two of them were, it was obvious, taking care not to raise their voices too much, in consideration of those seated at neighboring tables who might overhear and perhaps intervene. In the meantime, Adriana, as much as Rosanna, hadn't risked making any comment. Separated over there, on the other side of the table, making up a couple by themselves, they had seemed to be interested in nothing other than their little brother, Cesarino. The one, big, blonde and beautiful, more beautiful than ever; the other dark-haired, still short in stature, rather insignificant: yet once more they appeared to be in agreement, like conspirators. They had literally given no quarter to their little brother at the head of the table, at the ready to stop him eating with his hands, pouring himself too much wine, and so on. During the rare moments of calm they allowed themselves, they exchanged rapid meaningful glances, wry expressions and the odd brief phrase in a completely indecipherable jargon.

Nothing else happened. As if with the swim and the family lunch on Wednesday 30th, every obligation of welcome and courtesy had been considered exhausted, from then on, at a stroke, Adriana had become unreachable. To phone was a waste of time and effort. It was Rosanna who always came to the mouthpiece, restricting herself to evasive, embarrassed scraps of information, and once it was even Cesarino who, evidently under orders, perhaps even prompted at a distance by signals, had explained that Adriana, in bed with a headache, could not be disturbed for any reason. If he should phone—she had told her brother before shutting herself in her room—he was to write down the number and she wouldn't fail to get back to him ... To return in person to the Victoria? Frankly he didn't feel up to it, he didn't dare. The outcome was that he had passed the whole of Thursday 31st without once leaving the *pensione*, stretched out on the bed with hands clasped behind his neck and eyes fixed on the ceiling. Every now and then he opened the Romancero[*] which he'd brought with him in his suitcase. Useless. Oh, he was well aware that he ought to have gone out, gone for a solitary swim, and then goodbye. But what if Adriana had called

---

[*] A collection of Spanish ballads.

him? Or had, just suppose, suddenly decided to come to his room? Within a few days, perhaps a few hours, the war would break out: now he was sure of it. And as everything, everything, would plummet into the abyss of the war, why should he hurry to deny himself this absurd hope, why shouldn't he wait just a little longer? Tomorrow, all the same, he would leave. Whatever the outcome.

He went out very late, only after he'd become aware that the light had ebbed from his room.

In a few minutes he reached the avenue on the seafront where, his hands resting on a cement balustrade raised high above the rocks, he had stood for a long while contemplating the sunset. In Abbazia the sun went down on the landward side, as at Rimini. While at Fiume, it would be the opposite. The air was tepid, the light was flustered red, the water a bolt of silk. With all its lights already on and sketching an elegant wake behind it, a fine-looking white steamboat was majestically crossing the gulf. It was heading for the open sea, to the right, having Venice as its most likely destination. When would it reach Venice? If it didn't have to call at Pola, within a few hours: five or six. Otherwise, tomorrow morning.

He then began to walk along the sidewalk amidst the crowd of holidaymakers, a crowd still numerous, still joyful, still unaware. He was about to reach the curve beyond which the view of the village of Laurana would appear, and, facing him, with a better view than he now had, the islands of Cherso and Veglia, when a "Good evening!" shouted at his back in an infantile voice (a sharp shout, followed by the hissing tear of bicycle brakes) made him jump and rapidly turn round.

It was Cesarino.

Dark, parched by the sun and the salt air, thin as a rake, in a blue-striped T-shirt, white short-trousers and clogs: after having slid forward from his saddle he remained bestriding the bike's crossbar, still gripping the handlebars. He was catching his breath and grinning. In the red-tinged, darkening light of dusk he reminded one of a Neapolitan street urchin looking for clients. Or else a demon.

"You looking for Adriana?" he had asked, running the tip of his tongue along his strangely violet-colored, almost asphyxiated lips.

"How is she?"

"Very well."

"Didn't she have a headache?"

"Sure," Cesarino had quickly replied. "But I think she had . . . her period. Even today she was vicious as a beast. But she'll be fine tomorrow. When are you going?"

"Tomorrow."

He had detached his gaze, and lowered it. From the handlebars of his bicycle, a magnificent blue Bianchi, brand new even if its mudguards were already a bit encrusted, hung something red.

Bruno had stretched out a hand to touch it. It was a little triangular-shaped pennant of rough canvas, a kind of vermillion tongue, the color of blood, one foot long. He had slowly unrolled it with his fingers, until he had seen a small, unmistakable black sign appear: a swastika.

"And that?" he had asked, raising his eyes and pointing with his chin. "Why are you flying it here?"

"Oh, no reason," was Cesarino's reply.

His smile disclosed strong, white teeth, the teeth of a young dog. Then, shrugging his angular shoulders, he'd added:

"Just 'cos it looks good."

Ravenna

MY oldest memory of Ravenna is of the period immediately after the First World War.

I must have been six years old.

In Ravenna, birthplace of Francesco Baracca,[*] an air show had been organized to honor the memory of the great aviator who died near Mount Montello on the eve of the Armistice. And my father, who only shortly before had laid aside his officer's uniform, and who was inclined to enjoy the sporting side of everything, including politics, had suddenly had the idea of a "motor excursion."

Of that drive to Ravenna I recall quite a number of details: a stop at Lavezzola to change a tire on the way there; the new, crisp grass of the airfield, the aviators with violent eyes, nearly all of them dark-haired and with mustaches like those of Baracca and his friend Ruffo di Calabria—and also like Uncle Giacomo, my mother's only brother—all of them standing rigidly to attention in front of the big motionless propellers of the machines lined up for the opening ceremony; the frightening roar of a fighter plane that later, without warning, had headed straight for the crowd, causing everyone to take to their heels . . . But there is one incident I remember with particular vividness. It was dusk, and we were on the way

---

[*] Francesco Baracca, a famous ace fighter, was born in Lugo di Romagna, about 40 kilometers from Ravenna.

back. Having passed the banks of the Reno, we were approaching Argenta. When suddenly a group of young, agricultural laborers who were taking up the left side of the road, let out a cry:

"Sharks!"

A sinewy, sunburnt arm threatened us with a scythe. Curved and shining, the blade rose high above his head. Like a flag.

"Death to the sharks!"

Papa's delicate hand, the hand of a gentleman and a surgeon, detached itself rapidly from the steering wheel, opened the glove compartment and, hey presto! withdrew a revolver. We had already gone past, the gesture had no purpose, not even as a show of force, and so the truth is that a moment later the revolver disappeared again into its hiding place. But from that moment I knew that the Romagnoli farm workers, whom we called "Bolsheviks" in our family, had a grudge against us because we owned a Fiat, a Fiat Due. Given the chance, the Bolsheviks would even be prepared to rob us of it, our beautiful car. But they wouldn't be allowed to. On our side, to defend our right of ownership, there were the fighter aces with whom we had fraternized that morning at the Ravenna airfield. And then what was the worst a scythe could do against a black revolver, a revolver that fired real bullets?

Leaving Ferrara by way of the Porta San Giorgio, after some thirty kilometers you find yourself before a kind of wall which seems to bar the way, to stop all further progress. It is the Reno, the left bank of the Reno. After that begins the region of Romagna: a plain no less flat than that of Ferrara, but cut through by big, smooth, straight and endless roads which lead to Ravenna and then to the sea.

I was ten or eleven years old. We had already begun to spend our summers at Viserba, at Rimini, at Riccione, at Cattolica, at Cesenatico and always as our means of transport we would travel in one of the other cars that we had owned after the Fiat Due (I remember an O.M., an Ansaldo, a white S.P.A.), crammed with suitcases, deckchairs and various household goods and odds and ends. Before 1930, the roads were not asphalted. It would take a whole morning to cover the hundred or so kilometers that separated Ferrara from the Romagnoli beaches.

We would arrive in the main square of Ravenna—a city of low houses, even lower than those of Ferrara, with narrow, winding streets—around midday, with the July noon sun at its height. And, especially in the first years, it was right there, in the main square, after having parked the car in the shade, next to a cafe crowded with heavy-set men, with sun-tanned faces and velvety-black feverish eyes, that we allowed ourselves a half-hour of repose. We would enter the cafe to buy something—my mother and father an espresso, the driver Dino a mortadella sandwich and a glass of Albana, and us children an ice cream, which for fear of typhoid could never be anything but lemon. Huge and shadowy, echoing with stentorian voices, with peremptory exclamations, this place was where the regional Fascist action brigades were almost permanently stationed. My father, who had begun at about this time to distance himself from Fascism somewhat—though he wouldn't break definitively with the Party until many years later in the era of the Racial Laws—would look at them with a curious expression which was a mixture of admiring pride and repugnance.

No—he would say to my mother in an undertone—compared with these stalwarts, our own Ferrara Fascists were nothing. That one there, at the back, for example—he'd continue nodding toward them with his chin—must be the Consul Braga. In 1920, perhaps even 1919, a young Socialist had thrown a hand bomb into the cafe where we were now seated. The bomb had exploded and had killed several people. And then he, Braga, although wounded in the leg, had found the strength to drag himself outside, to take a revolver from his jacket pocket, and flat on his belly and cool as can be had taken aim and bang!—he'd fired. The perpetrator was already some way off, no less than a hundred meters, but Braga's bullet went through his skull, and dropped him dead. Oh, that Ravenna brigade was famous for the little games they invented! Car races in reverse; night-time shooting contests, with the street lamps on the road to the station at Ravenna, or at Cesenatico, or else those on the promenade chosen as targets; sumptuous dinners, sometimes in dinner jackets, during which it might happen that a beautiful woman from the highest society in evening dress who was present with her husband, would at a certain point erupt in a scandalized outburst due to the fact that in the plate of risotto she'd been given, they'd mixed in who knows what hideous stuff . . .

Later on, after 1930, instead of ending up in the square, we would stop outside the city, in Sant' Apollinare in Classe.

We would go through the Porta Cesarea into a landscape suddenly changed from the torrid green one we had just passed: an immense landscape, pervaded by breezes that already had the taste of salt, bounded on one side by the uninterrupted black line of the Classe and Cervia forests and, on the other, by the blue, cloud-veiled hills of Bertinoro, Verucchio and San Marino. By then we wouldn't all be traveling together. As a rule my brother Ernesto and I would come by bicycle. We'd leave Ferrara at the first light of dawn, preceding by at least three hours the big, suffocating O.M. saloon car which, with my father always at the wheel, transported the rest of the family.

The pact we agreed on was the following. Whoever first reached Sant' Apollinare in Classe, four or five kilometers after Ravenna, would wait for the others to arrive. And between our father and us a kind of unspoken competition was always in play. Who would get there first—we relying on our legs and lungs or he driving his still brand new O.M.?

Covered in dust and drenched with sweat, sometimes we managed to cross the finishing line, which was the entrance to the basilica, ahead of them. And every time the chill of the interior, the bluish-green light that suffused it, would seem to us the very same that we'd encounter a little farther on at the seaside.

I have always been struck, in Ravenna, by the intensity of the contrasts, the possibility of a coexistence, within the borders of a single urban conglomeration, of things, of people, of feelings that are so radically different.

In Cesenatico, where we went for our holidays on eight consecutive summers, we made friends with many families from Ravenna: with the Cagnoni-Bittis, in particular, and with the Baldellis. The Cagnoni-Bittis were practicing and militant Catholics; the Baldellis anarchists and anti-clerical. The Cagnoni-Bittis were moderately anti-Fascist, the Baldellis violently so. What induced them, at the beach, to band together in the same group of boys and girls except the shared city of their birth?

Nullo Baldelli erupted at times, without apparent motive, in atrocious, elaborate oaths which his younger brother Libero would quickly echo. To hear them, Ernesto and I would be truly shocked. But the seven Cagnoli-Bitti brothers and sisters remained completely unfazed. Although they went to Mass every morning, the three girls put up with the curses of Nullo and Libero Baldelli without even batting an eyelid. It was evident that for them cursing hadn't the slightest significance. What mattered was the secret passion, the dark, rebellious, internal lava that impelled them at a certain point to boil over and explode. The angry flash which lit up on each such occasion the velvety, febrile brown eyes of Nullo and Libero was evidently of the same intensity as that which burned in the depths of the eyes of the five males of their family: the four brothers and the father, the lawyer Luigi, ex-deputy of the People's Party.[*]

In Ravenna, in 1935, I also got to know a certain Buscaroli, Vezio Buscaroli.

Although he spent his summer holidays in Cervia, I had already learned a great deal about him: first, that he lived in a fine house with a tennis court in the middle of a pine forest; secondly, that he aspired to the literary life, and had even, the year before, published a slim volume of poems; thirdly, that he enjoyed the high esteem of the original Fascist troops in Ravenna, the *pistolero* Braga foremost amongst them, ever since he'd married a magnificent girl from Massa Lombarda. At the beach I had often heard it said, by the older boys of the group, by Nullo Baldelli and Minto Cagnoni-Bitti, that the wife, a formidable big brunette, betrayed poor Buscaroli shamelessly. And right under his eyes. Who knows if this was true. Despite him having his head in the clouds, or perhaps precisely because of that, nothing would have been easier than for the Fascist Federation to give him some

---

[*] The PPI (Partito Popolare Italiano) was a Christian-Democratic party founded in 1919 in opposition to the PSI (Partito Socialista Italiano).

task or other, have him write a piece for a review or a newspaper, something of the sort. That way one of them could take his place.

One August afternoon, around three o'clock, invited by Buscaroli himself, who, though he himself never in fact played any sports at all, had landed the role of organizing a tennis match between teams representing Cesenatico and Cervia, we, the Cesenatico team, rolled up in front of his house. There were six or seven of us, all on bicycles and in tennis kit. Buscaroli was sitting in his garden, in the shade. Slumped in a deckchair, he was reading a book.

Having opened the wooden gate, we approached him. And as he said nothing, nor even got to his feet, but merely looked up at us with his bewildered, blue eyes, we felt forced to explain to him why on earth we were there. It transpired that after having organized the match, wearing everyone down with his express postcards and telephone calls, Buscaroli had forgotten the whole thing. Completely forgotten it. The evidence lay before us: there among the garden's pine trees stood the tennis court with its net in shreds and the surface utterly unfit for play.

What an idiot!—Buscaroli said of himself, tearing at his hair and without even the strength to get to his feet.—What a complete halfwit! What a ghastly impression he must have made!

Shattered, there was nothing more he could say. Then there she was, his beautiful wife, just that moment back from the beach in her Jantzen swimwear and clogs, coming toward us to take up the role of hostess and, with a candid smile flashed round the circle we made, to adroitly dispel her husband's intense discomfort . . .

We were married in August 1943, during the Badoglio period.

While, ever more numerous, the German tanks swooped down from the north and the Allied bombardments increased, we spent our honeymoon between Ravenna, Marina di Ravenna, Cervia and Rimini. It was me who chose those resorts. I wanted to show them to Val, who hardly knew them. The future was so uncertain! It was essential she saw them right now while there was still a chance.

We stayed for eight consecutive days at Marina di Ravenna, house guests of a Socialist butcher with whom, every evening, under the lamp in a small and airless breakfast-room, I engaged in long, boring political arguments. But during the day we were always by the sea. Up and down and back and forth. In a *batana** hired for a few lire, we once went to Cesenatico, and another time almost managed to get as far as Comacchio.

We would usually sail two or three kilometers from the shore, with our eyes always turned back to the pine forests that rose like dark terraces behind the white undulating profile of the sand dunes. From the open sea beyond Marina, through the narrow harbor channel, it sometimes happened that, veiled in the distance, we could make out the rooftops of Ravenna, the stocky bell towers and broad domes of its churches.

In the violet sky of evening (as the sun set behind the shoreline woods, it thrust blades of the most poignant green light between the rough ancient trunks) little silvery fighter planes made trial swoops and loops. Then, and only rising up at the last moment, they would go into a nose dive fiercely aimed at our little sailboat. And the searing roar they made, as they skimmed above our heads which ducked so close together, filled us with a childlike joy, which was mingled for me with the hidden sadness of a valediction.

---

* A sailing boat of about five meters' length, typical of the Comacchio region.

Les Neiges d'Antan

1.

T HERE was always something that stopped me becoming a friend of Marco Giori, I mean a real friend.

The Gioris weren't from Ferrara, but from Ambrogio, and so from the countryside. And since, in the low-lying lands bounded by the Po and the Reno, the city has never seen eye to eye with the country, without doubt this was a stumbling block, the first one.

A second hindrance: the age difference.

In 1930, when Marco was twenty, I was only fourteen. Which meant: I still wore short-trousers, or at best plus-fours. I went around on a standard black Bianchi bicycle from which I'd stripped the mudguards, hoping that might give it the air of a racing bike . . . I was renowned, and privately gloated over the fact, for my high marks in school . . . All in all, I was nothing but a *putìn*, a mere kiddie.

Marco Giori at that time was far from being a *putìn*, that's for sure. Furnished with a car, a cream-colored De Soto "Spider" in which, left elbow leaning out of the side window, he was wont to drive between the railway station and the Prospettiva Arch, up and down, no less than thirty times a day. By this time he was at university (having graduated from school by the old San Marino trick: he'd enrolled in Agriculture at Bologna); but above all he was tall, elegant, with ash-blond hair parted on one side of his sloping forehead à la Cary Grant, and with steel-grey eyes: there was no other youth in the city at that time who could claim to be more conspicuous or more admired than he was.

The consequence for me was that when I was riding my bike down Corso Giovecca, and in the distance spied the slender, limber form of Marco standing out at the center of a group of his contemporaries, I not only lacked the courage to stop, which anyway would have been absurd, but even to shout out a simple "*Ciao.*" They, the youth who already made love and went to brothels, some of them almost distinguished enough to enter the envied list of the city's so-called "degenerates," were often gathered in a semicircle around some foreign car parked at the curb by a party of tourists passing through. Engrossed as they were in assessing its pros and cons, I merely had to look at them to feel not only different but also inferior. It was obvious my presence counted for nothing. That I might in some way be taken into account was an aspiration futile even to think of.

But even in the years that were to follow it's not as if the relationship between me and Marco ever changed. The truth is that every now and then, when I tried to gain his confidence, I would receive a brush-off, polite but no less unwavering for that.

Just as an example: at university, when I too had got there, I enrolled in the Arts faculty in Bologna. It should be understood that Ferrara is very different from Bologna, where literary studies are very much the norm. Among us, literature students are seen somewhat as priests—undoubtedly considered with respect, even reverence, but always kept at a distance.

And afterward? Afterward I got married, left Ferrara, put down roots elsewhere, had children, wrote and published books: with all the multiplying fortunes and tribulations that entails. In any case I kept myself busy, as they say here in Rome, working, struggling, living.

And by contrast he, Marco Giori, who already at twenty-one owned a fine American car, and who, besides, in 1933, had even managed to persuade his father to buy him a blue Bugatti that could have competed in the Mille Miglia (although he very soon had a serious accident, on the Monselice highway, resulting in some fatalities: after which his *grimo*, his dad, wouldn't buy him anything else, not even an old third- or fourth-hand Balilla, and so from then on he had to undertake the commute between

Ambrogio and Ferrara in just the same way as did the old man, that is, by local bus); by contrast he—who to hear him, only aspired to get the hell out of Ambrogio, Ferrara, Italy, to go and live abroad somewhere—never left the region, and was only waiting, it seemed, for one thing: that his father should finally decide to die, and so leave him all his lands and property.

The dissimilarity between Marco and his father, Signor Amleto, had always amazed me. Between them, however, with time, something in common would emerge, as we shall see. Certainly, some thirty years ago they didn't look even remotely related.

Let's leave aside how they dressed. Marco, in the English style, seemed to have walked straight out of a men's fashion magazine, while the old man, with his cloak, with his felt hat lowered over his little round eyes of blue porcelain, with a toothpick between his thin lips, with his low, black or brown boots with nailed soles (he went around this way—they used to say in town—to strike pity into the heart of the tax collector) looked no different from the usual agricultural middlemen who on Mondays and Thursdays are still found in droves in Piazza della Cattedrale or Corso Martiri della Libertà.

But in their physiques as well, what a difference between the two of them! Squat, with short arms and legs, the skin of his face and neck intensely tanned from working in the fields—rather than skin, it looked like thick leather—one would have said that the elder Giori belonged to a different breed.

And Signora Carmen, Marco's mother? I never knew her in person.

All I know of her are two things: that she died of pernicious anaemia in 1939 and that she remained her whole life confined to Ambrogio, a huddle of poor, rustic roofs that crouched on the right bank of the Po, thirty kilometers from Ferrara, never setting foot in the city. Perhaps it was her that Marco resembled. From the Veneto, Vicenza, I think, she was said to be tall, blonde, slender and with an aristocratic air.

Until a few years ago, I had never even set eyes on Ambrogio. I happened to chance on the place late one October afternoon, returning in the company of some Roman friends from a trip to the Delta.

At a walking pace the car crossed the wide, misshapen, semi-deserted village square. It must have been around six o'clock. We were planning to have supper in Ferrara. So we had all the time in the world to stop and have something at the only bar there was.

We got out, entered the bar—to tell the truth, more of an ugly little restaurant, a kind of basement absolutely devoid of customers—and ordered in loud voices, some choosing an espresso, others a small glass of Bosco wine, still others a fizzy drink.

Taking a sip from the little coffee cup, I then returned to the entrance on my own. How sad—I said to myself, casting my gaze around. In those few minutes, the square had become even more grey and exhausted. It had turned into a huge, shapeless expanse, about to be obliterated by the oncoming darkness.

When, suddenly, at the end of the square, almost touching the squalid, stocky parish church, I saw a house. It was not a hovel like the others, but a small bourgeois villa on two floors, with the facade covered with ivy, a little balcony protruding over the entrance, a modest garden in front which was guarded right round by a robust fence of varnished iron railings.

I looked at the house, the pointed black iron spears of the main entrance gate. Without even turning to ask the sleepy-looking, little, middle-aged woman who was seated behind the bar whether that house down there, flanking the church, was actually the home of the Gioris, being sure that I wasn't mistaken, I could think of nothing but Marco's mother all the while. For years, for decades—I let my imagination run wild—old Giori had kept her locked away in the house. Never letting her go to church, just a few steps away. Never letting her visit the graveyard just beyond the village, not even on November 2, All Souls' Day. Never a trip to the city. Only allowed into the garden in summer, toward evening, to read or to embroider. It was to be supposed that he, judging her guilty of who knows what crime, had decided to make her pay in this manner, with perpetual exile in a village inhabited almost entirely by illiterate farmhands, such as Ambrogio was.

Still looking at the house, I also thought of Marco. In this last period he had returned to Ferrara far more rarely. I hadn't seen him for more than two years. It was very likely that in the meanwhile his *grimo* had died, and that

Marco, as soon as he'd laid hands on his paternal inheritance, had rushed to sell the lands, the Ambrogio house, everything. Who knows where he'd be on this very day. Perhaps in Paris like that fine figure Pelandra (if Pelandra did indeed end up in Paris), perhaps in London, perhaps New York, giving himself up without restraint to that life of pleasure and luxury of which he had always dreamed. And if one day or another I had happened to meet him in Rome? It was just as if I could see him. Bounding from the threshold of the Excelsior Hotel, he would come smiling toward me, at last, with his hand extended, and with a free and happy "*Ciao*" on his lips . . .

The gate shut, the doorway and windows perhaps bolted from within, the house seemed empty, uninhabited.

We left the bar-restaurant and walked toward the car. Wanting to stretch our cramped legs, we had parked on the opposite side of the square in front of the church. The sound of the Angelus bell sorrowfully drifted through the evening air.

In the center of the churchyard, his biretta, worn low at the back of his head, and his arms folded, a dark-haired, pale-faced, corpulent priest was conversing with two men, one young, the other old. Hearing us approach, they stopped talking and all three turned round together.

Straight away, I recognized the two men—Marco Giori and his father: the latter, a little more stooped, but as lively and sunburnt as ever, and as ever his mouth sporting the reliable toothpick.

"*Ciao*," I said, raising my arm, not without registering, even if much quietened, the quickened pulse of old.

Signor Amleto raised his hat. The priest gave a slight bow.

It seemed to me that Marco hesitated for a moment. Then he left the others and came toward me.

"What on earth brings you here?" he asked in dialect, in a calm, quiet voice, twisting his lips in his customary sardonic sneer.

Before I could reply, it was he, however, who explained his reason for being there, in Ambrogio. His father was more than eighty. It wasn't as if he was ill. Just a bit weaker, that's all, and he couldn't run the business on his own anymore.

"You can guess the delights of five hundred hectares. And then with all the problems we have nowadays . . . "

I observed him, and didn't know what to think. He was wearing an old, tobacco-colored, woolen jacket with misshapen pockets, and unsightly grey vicuña trousers, threadbare and stretched at the knees, inadmissible even for the country.

But as for his health, he looked well. He had grown stouter, more robust, as often happens at around fifty.

And while I introduced him to each of my friends, and he, in his turn, introduced them all to his father and the priest, I saw that the skin of his neck had grown deeply furrowed with age. His skin was thick, baked by the sun, almost black.

It reminded me of leather. Thick leather.

2.

AMONG THE dozen or so youths in Ferrara who, around 1937, formed the prestigious constellation of the "degenerates," it never struck me (and it's also the opinion of Uller Tumaìni, the photographer, nicknamed by his friends "al duterét," the Little Doctor, who knows these things and can judge them better than anyone), no, it never struck me that the star of Mario Spisani, called Pelandra, had ever shone with any particular brightness . . . Oh all right, Uller conceded generously, at that time even Pelandro had achieved some distinction in a life of vice and indolence. But let's be honest!—he added, immediately after—when you compare Pelandra with other eminent degenerates such as Geppe Calura or Edelweiss Fegnagnani he pales into insignificance. You can snort all the white dust you like, fuck till you slip a disc, you can even aspire to the occasional act of sodomy. But after all that? What really counts, even in such things, is that ever overlooked and undervalued attribute—sheer graft.

Uller had good judgement and to spare. Manner, tone, in a word, authority: this, Pelandra was always more than a bit short of.

From the age of twenty to twenty-five—until, I repeat, 1937—it was well known that he never said no to anything. A first-order habitué of brothels and gambling dens, distinguished consumer of cocaine, and ether in its pure state or, lacking that, whatever pigswill was on tap, Pelandra too had really excelled himself, as in their time had Geppe Calura and Edelweiss Fegnagnani and later, Eraldo Deliliers, Gigi Prendato and perhaps even Marco Giori himself. And yet where was to be found in Pelandra the sangfroid, the poise, the cool, unruffled superciliousness of the old masters and of those of his contemporaries not unworthy of the masters? His ashen face, when, at noon, he'd show up at the Caffè della Borsa in Corso Roma and it seemed that thanks to the tight shoes of lightest leather, shiny and pointed as daggers, every step took a great effort, but one that was more moral than physical; the sneer, that in a tremor of uncertainty was always stretching his bruised-looking lips, stained with nicotine and coffee grains (a humble, exhausted sneer, which at the same time was suffused with a vague presumption, as if he wanted to insinuate: "Yes I'm a wreck, as anyone can see, but what a thoroughbred wreck, don't you think?")—even at that time, when all's said and done, it was enough to look at him to be able to deduce, without much effort, that a type like him wasn't the great *maudit* he made himself out to be, and so, in the light of the fact that I will be recounting later, there's much less to wonder at.

A conscience is not something you invent. If it's there, it's there. If it isn't, one can't just make it up. The same with courage.

Toward the middle of 1938, then, unprepared spectators witnessed a surprise move which suddenly revealed that Pelandra had always had a conscience; the townsfolk learned that he, Pelandra himself, had decided quite out of the blue to get engaged—yes he, that bizarre fellow with his cappuccino snout: the friend of young Marco Giori, and that other predator, who was solely responsible for the death of poor Fadigati, the ENT doctor of Via Gorgadello who died by drowning himself in the Po, that Deliliers, who should have stayed in Porto Longone and not gone abroad to live it up with money and a car! And he got engaged in all seriousness, it should be understood: it wasn't some kind of joke! The kind of family to which his fiancée belonged, those Pasettis who lived in Via Roma (not to be confused with the ones from Via Cisterna del Follo) were, apart from their modest circumstances as proprietors of sparse agricultural lands, very respectable people, all home and church. She, Germana, a little woman who was nothing special, more plain than pretty, who, after being brought up by the nuns of Via Colombara from kindergarten until the third year of school, from the time she was fourteen had always been shut away at home; and he, in particular, from the time when he became officially engaged, no longer seemed himself, had changed from one thing to another: all this made it seem as though what was happening was something important, unprecedented, a kind of conversion.

He had changed from one thing to another, had literally become a different person.

That very passion he had formerly devoted to his excesses, an exaggerated passion, without class, and such as to provoke a sneer from those consummate operators who had always known how to pace themselves with drugs and brothels, now seemed to have been entirely rechannelled to conform to the meek pleasures of normal, respectable folk.

He'd made his peace with father and mother, two timid oldsters gone white before their time thanks to their lying, idle, prodigal son, so different from his younger brother, who at twenty was already earning a living, having assumed a post at the bank. He, Pelandra, had applied for and obtained a position as an employee in the Venice General Insurance Company, and in a short time had acquired a notable circle of business contacts. When his insurance duties obliged him to pass by the Corso Roma and he reached the Caffè della Borsa, he would never take a seat. He'd pass by in an assiduous hurry, greeting whoever greeted him, of course, but without paying attention to the scornful winks of the idlers sprawled at the little tables in their usual position—legs wide apart and their hands pressed to their crotches.

No Sunday would pass, then, without a stroll arm-in-arm with his fiancée, and behind them, they too arm-in-arm, her parents—he, very tall, gently leaning forward to let Germana clutch his coat sleeve—nor without seeing them arrive at San Carlo for the midday Mass. And if in church, at the moment of the raising of the Host, his genuflection astonished everyone, the seraphic smile which, at one o'clock, as he was leaving, suffused his chubby neophyte's face was even more of a cause for wonder. The Mass was quite delightful—his smile declared. But Sunday afternoon which, after the home-cooked soup of tagliatelline, boiled chicken and beef garnished with slices of salami and various pickled greens, baked pear and a weak black coffee, extended before him—an afternoon to pass with the hands of his fiancée clasped within his own, both of them looking out of the drawing room windows at the little garden as it gradually succumbed to dusk—wasn't that, all considered, equally delightful? No, being such a proper good person, one felt infinitely better. And one's health as well was greatly improved.

An exemplary fiancé, and following that, for ten long years, he became a no less exemplary husband and father.

At General Insurance his career was not to be a dazzling one, but nevertheless fairly impressive—immediately after the war he had been made assistant manager and then, in 1947, he was promoted to manager. Although he was not enrolled in the Christian Democratic Party, he sedulously attended the cultural debates organized by Catholic Action in the house of Count Chiozzi in Via Santo Stefano with his wife, and at those meetings, while never taking part verbally, he showed himself to be an attentive and respectful listener. In the meantime he had bestowed on his wife no fewer than four children, two boys and two girls. And the modest pride which shone forth from his whole being, from his expression to his gait, especially on those occasions when he managed to lead all of them together, walking the length of the Corso Giovecca or Viale Cavour, was very moving, to say the least. His finances had not yet permitted him to establish his own household, so that he had had to accept the hospitality of his in-laws both on his and his family's behalf. Yet very soon, however, he was to acquire a house of his own, if it was true, as it seemed to be, that in the spring of 1948 on the eve of the elections on April 18, Mario Spisani, the renowned and respected insurance broker, was already the owner of a paid off apartment, situated on the fifth floor of one of the many cheap little apartment buildings then being built in the vicinity of the aqueduct, and for the acquisition of which he had disbursed in a great wad of notes, one after the other, a round four million lire as down payment: savings which, to all appearances, had cost him a great deal of effort to accumulate.

And then as regards the amusements that from time to time the family needed, for these too he had always met the expenses. And in a manner that, all considered, was far more than merely perfunctory.

The Spisani couple went at least three times a month to the cinema, regularly choosing the opening nights and the best seats. There wasn't a single summer (necessarily excluding those of 1943, '44 and '45 spent in the small Passetti holdings in Formignana) that they didn't go on holiday in August with the children: once to Pievepelago, in the Modena Apennines, other times to the Romagnolo coast, for a while at Gatteo, then at Viserbella. Locales, these last two, where there weren't many real entertainments on offer—from this perspective how could you compare Gatteo and Viserbella with nearby Rimini and Riccione or even Cesenatico?—but where sun, air, sea, the type and quality of sand and so on are better by far than any to be found in other Italian resorts. All of this, leaving aside the great opportunity extended to a young father to turn himself, without running the least risk of ridicule, into a diligent builder of sandcastles and sand motor-racing tracks for the use and enjoyment of his offspring, and to become a zealous accompanier of the same in going for a pee or a poo behind the first convenient cabin.

Every time I return to Ferrara and pass by to say hello, it's Uller Tumaìni, the photographer, who reminds me of all this.

It has never crossed my mind to establish where the actual home of *al duturét* is, nor whether he has a wife, children, any family at all. Do these things matter? For what concerns me, it's enough to know that I can find him permanently stationed on the threshold of his "studio" in Via Garibaldi and, furthermore, unchanged, with that white doctor's smock of his unbuttoned on his slender torso, with the same cadaverous and bony face, with his black, impassive eyes, somewhat veiled, and with that small, circumflex-like mouth, twisted and withered. After so many years, wasn't it wondrous that he should have retained intact the very same air of aged youth he'd had around 1937? And isn't it right that I should be thankful to him for being, as he was, the living image of fidelity?

I like the fact that he's always the same, and as ever I like going in to have a chat with him.

The place is a cubbyhole of no more than three by four meters. Uller seated behind a small desk-table with Perspex shelves, I in front, on an arm-chair made of nickel-plate tubing. And since Uller never switches on the light except in cases of dire necessity (he doesn't care for light—neither of the electric nor the natural variety, in fact he cares so little for it that he wears dark glasses even at night), when it starts to get dark outside we have every right to be confident that no one passing by outside on the sidewalk will be able to make us out. A strange feeling, anyhow! We here, invisible, as though outside of time, as though we were dead. And there, by contrast, drawn every now and then by the dazzling neon of the shop window and the displayed photos, the ingenuous, faithful, unconscious faces of life, the passers-by, utterly exposed and leaning forward . . .

All the while Uller keeps talking to me.

Knowing what I want to hear, he has already begun to recount the decade of 1930 to 1940: the golden era which saw the flowering of one after another degenerate of the caliber of a Geppe Calura, of an "Edel" Fegnagnani, of an Eraldo Deliliers, or a Gigi Prendato. And then, however, quite suddenly, he comes to Pelandra. Certainly not to place him in a single group together with the others, the true degenerates, the great authentic debauchees of his and my own youth, but only to remind me how, for a good ten years, that is from 1938 to '48, he had done his best, "*Puvràz!*" poor thing, unquestionably his very best, to become an excellent husband, an outstanding father, the most respectable and dignified of men, and then how, on a day like any other, a Sunday afternoon exactly like an infinite number of such afternoons, he disappeared from his home, from Ferrara, from Italy, perhaps even from the world of the living, without leaving a clue or a trace behind him, nothing at all, not even a rotten corpse.

"Is that a thing to do?" pronounces *al duturét* in sage disapproval, nodding his little dark head, carefully brilliantined. "*Gnànch un strazz ad cadàver!*"*

Uller doesn't know what became of Pelandra. On this topic he always confines himself to recording the fanciful rumors he has heard doing the rounds, without adding the smallest conjecture of his own. Had Pelan-

---

* Ferrarese dialect for "*neanche uno straccio di cadavere*"—not even the trace of a corpse.

dra also drowned himself in the Po? Had he fallen in Algeria in the ranks of the Foreign Legion, or in Katanga among the throng of mercenaries, or in Vietnam? Was he still alive, under a false name in Paris, Venezuela, Australia, or in some other place? Anything is possible—Uller grants open-mindedly, shrugging. Anything at all.

Actually he was thinking of something else, and although, given his character, that may seem unbelievable, it was only and always about the human, the moral aspect. Why for heaven's sake shouldn't one—he reaches his conclusion—suddenly turn from devil to saint? Much better to sin, then repent, then go back to sinning, then once more repent. A thousand times better to lead a double, triple, even a quadruple or quintuple life rather than . . . No, no—he exclaims—there are some values, family being one of them, for which one has to be willing to swallow one's pride and to sacrifice oneself.

"Wouldn't you say?" he asks in dialect.

Perhaps I would, perhaps not. Perhaps I agree and disagree at the same time. However, it's all fine. Suddenly anxious that he gets to the point, I nod in agreement.

Maybe it didn't all happen exactly as he described, and yet the scene of the "final cutting of the cord" or rather "the final burning of the boats," that Uller, starting from this point, and maintaining a stony expression that might have done credit to the most ruthless Chicago gangster, began to recount for the umpteenth time (a joke, when one thinks of it, and hardly a new one!) always had the power to grip my heart with a strange vise, with fascination or fear, I'm not sure which.

So we're in the drawing room of the Passetti home—Uller starts off with zest—one October Sunday in 1948, between three and four in the afternoon.

The house is practically empty. A short while before the old Passetti couple had gone out with their little grandchildren and the maid, the latter pushing the pram of Alcide, the youngest. Looking out of one of the windows that had a prospect of Via Romei, Germana saw them all as one turn into Via Voltapaletto, going in the direction of Montagnone.

And now, in the drawing room, she pays attention to two things simultaneously: to the small woolen sock which her needles have almost finished knitting, and to the sleeping form of her husband, stretched out at his considerable length on that same sofa on which as fiancés they'd sat exchanging kisses. She looks up and down, up and down. Impartially giving a glance up at her Mario's back, then down to the short sock of Fabrizio, her eldest. She is a little woman, Germana, at this point around thirty years old, of a rather pleasing aspect, her figure not even too ruined by the many consecutive pregnancies.

The husband sleeps. A ray of faint autumnal sunshine falls at an angle to gild his well-nourished backside. And Germana suddenly thinks (it will be she herself who later tells this any number of times to more than half the city) that soon, it being past four o'clock, it will be time to say to her husband: "Come on, Mario, wake up." What they'd be showing at the Salvini she doesn't know, she can't remember. But it would be rather annoying to bustle in when the film had already started.

But a moment hadn't passed before the erstwhile Pelandra himself woke up under his own steam.

He assumed a seated position. He yawned.

Then he asked:

"Time is it?"

"It's past four," Germana replies, giving a glance at her wristwatch to check the fact. "You've been asleep for some time."

"It was good, that risotto with peas," he stammers.

Germana smiles.

"Really?"

"Better than good! One could tell it was cooked by you."

"Lord, I can believe it. My mother, poor thing, never adds enough butter. But this time I made sure I intervened. For risotto there's nothing like butter."

Silence.

With her face turned to the thick, almost completed sock, Germana is thinking of the new house where she, her Mario and their four children will take up residence in a fortnight, soon after All Souls' Day.

And Mario?

Mario in the meantime has risen from the sofa, and has walked across the room. Approaching the window which gives on to the garden, he now stands there, gazing out intently. What he is looking at she doesn't manage to guess. Broad and chubby as he's become, the conceited fellow, God bless him, he blocks out almost the whole view.

"I'm just going out for a moment," he announces calmly, after two or three minutes, without turning round.

"Where are you going? Into the garden?"

"The garden, my foot. I'm off to the tobacconist on the Corso Giovecca. I've a sudden yen to smoke, if you have to know . . . "

Shocked by this revelation, expressed for the most part in dialect, Germana jolts her head up.

"To smoke!" she exclaims. "Why on earth this strange new fad? You don't . . . "

"In the meantime, would you get yourself ready," he interrupts her, already on his way. "Can you do it in five minutes? Remember the program begins at a quarter to."

And he disappears through the door.

Five, ten, twenty minutes pass. Half an hour passes, an hour, an hour and a half. Two hours. The Pasetti parents, the children and the maid return from Montagnone at going on six. Apart from Alcide, who is sleeping, they are all a bit out of breath. The old folk because of the long walk. The children, who have lovely rosy cheeks, because of all their scampering across the fields. And the girl, who besides is impatient to slope off with her soldier, and seems even to be sweating because she's had to push the pram from a quarter past two until now.

The returning party finds Germana ready to go out: in a smart little suit, a hat and high heels. But she's in tears, standing there at the front door. Through her sobs, she tells how Mario went out two hours ago to buy something to smoke ("To smoke!" both her parents exclaim at once, widening their eyes), but he hasn't come back.

"What if something has happened to him?"—Germana keeps on complaining. He went out without changing, in his house jacket. Her heart tells her that something has, has indeed happened to him.

Three Apologues

1.

I T happened quite some time ago, before the opening of the big motorways. Happened? Well, it's just a manner of speech, since in reality hardly anything happened.

We had left Ferrara getting on toward four in the afternoon (it must have been May, or June), unsure as ever which route to take returning to Rome. The Flaminia or the Tiberina? By way of Rimini or of Cesena?

This time, Val seemed to have a decided preference for the Flaminia.

"In the first place," she said, as we entered Argenta, "going via Rimini the cities we have to pass through can be counted on one hand. In the second place, there's not a single mountain pass."

"There's always the Furlo," I objected.

"You surely don't mean to compare the gorge of the Furlo with the mountain pass at Coronaro!" she replied, appropriating a phrase I immediately and unhappily recognized as my own. "And then," she went on, "passes or no passes, don't you remember last year, when we came to Ferrara with the children, how pleasant it was to be able to stop at Nocera Umbra, exactly halfway? Have you already forgotten the trattoria where we had dinner? I still recall the very words you said when we set off again."

"Might I know what they were?"

"You swore that in future, every time we made this journey by car, not only would we always take the Flaminia, on the way there and on the way back, but without fail we should always stop at Nocera Umbra. We wouldn't be able to find a trattoria like that, or rather an inn with stables like those from Leopardi's era (those were your very words) in any other place."

"I might have said something of the sort," I muttered.

"Something of the sort?" Val exclaimed. "Are you seriously saying you don't remember?"

I remembered, clear as day. But the fact remained that after having left Ravenna behind us, and by then in view of Sant' Apollinare in Classe, we had come no nearer to a decision.

Val kept silent. Even I kept my mouth shut. The fork in the road, which would force the decision—to go straight on to Rimini or to curve off right to Cesena—was awaiting us less than a kilometer away.

But then, having just reached the fork and decisively steered to the right, all of a sudden my tongue was freed.

If I decided on the Tiberina—I explained to Val—I didn't do so out of caprice, but for a good reason. It was only just five o'clock now. If I put my foot down, we could get over the Mount Coronaro Pass to San Sepolcro well before dark: giving us the chance, should we be so inclined, to have a proper, an instructive look at The Resurrection by Piero della Francesca.

"And the old inn with its stables from Leopardi's era can go to hell!" I added by way of conclusion.

"So it can go to hell now," Val sighed with bitterness, as though by abandoning the Flaminia in favor of the Tiberina I had given the umpteenth guilty proof of the flightiness and inconstancy of my character, if not, by implication, also of my ever weaker attachment to her and to the family.

Having sped past the hairpin bends of the Coronaro Pass, well before dark as I'd foreseen, the San Sepolcro plain lies all before us. There's plenty of time to take a coffee and a tea (I have the coffee, Val the tea) and once again to see the Piero fresco.

Our tea and coffee drunk, we enter the old assembly room, at the end of which the rustic Christ, with his calm, terrifying gaze, invites those passing tourists in the mood to stray over the threshold and set aside, at least for a moment, their anxious frivolity. And so, about half an hour later, when we resume our journey, it's already dark.

I turn the headlights on and in a pensive, gloomy mood drive on along the big, unrutted road that leads to Città di Castello.

"What's wrong?" Val happily enquires. "Are you tired?"

"No," I reply. If I admit being tired, I can hardly object to her replacing me at the wheel till we reach Perugia, where we've decided to stop for supper.

At the foot of the hill on which Perugia lies I stop at a service station to fill up the tank.

I leave the car, walk a few steps across the huge, shadowy court, interspersed at regular intervals with pairs of petrol pumps, standing rigidly side by side like policemen, and bordered on three sides by the black countryside. My gaze is drawn up toward the bright lights of the city.

Should we eat up there in Perugia just a few minutes away? I wonder. Or wait till we get to Todi, or even Narni?

I think of Todi, of Narni, of their ill-lit alleys cut into the medieval rock hard as diamond, of their darkness, their silence. And as the idea of stopping in Perugia seems to me every moment more absurd, even loathsome, as if Perugia had not been Perugia but rather an ever-proliferating metropolis like Paris, London, New York, or especially like Rome; at the same time I dream that at Todi or else at Narni we might find a good place to eat, perhaps even to sleep. Perchance to sleep! Still—I blather on to myself—how can anyone born in a medium-sized city of the Po Valley, still in possession of their own detached house there, return to Rome without a feeling of anguish? Good God, how can people like us, in the middle of the night, cross the monstrous bridge over the Tiber, the one with the lanterns and the filthy great eagles, beyond which extends the enormous, shapeless concrete hive where we've chosen to bring up our children?

Now determined, I turn back to the car. With her head half in, half out of the window, Val is observing me closely.

"After all," she says, signaling with her chin toward a low rectangular construction which rises like an oblong box on the opposite side of the court from the road, "after all, we could just as well eat here as anywhere else."

How odd that I hadn't noticed it before. It's true. That thing is a restaurant. And suddenly, who knows why, I feel almost happy.

We sit facing each other outside on the terrace where, in front of the television, not yet switched on, a dozen or so small tables have been placed. We keep up a sort of mutual sulkiness. Though by now, it's a struggle. Even Val, it's not hard to tell, is having quite a job sustaining it.

It feels like we're on board some small, hyper-modern boat, freshly launched from the boatyard, waiting to set sail, though still moored in the port, at the edge of the breakwater. On deck everything is new. The television hoisted onto its aluminium perch; the paper tablecloths, paper that pretends to be linen; the espresso machine extraordinarily aerodynamic, gleaming in the interior through the glass walls; the wan, sidereal light emitted by the neon tubes: everything here, by its very nature, seems to speak only of the future, of those "evil days ahead," clean, functional and germless, which we'll not live to see and which will not remember us.

But then, later, drawn to the television which in the meantime had been turned on, here they are: the occupants of those invisible rustic houses round about, emerging from the unbroken, surrounding darkness to sit in silence at the stainless-steel tables, all evidently in their customary places. My beef-steak and Val's omelette confiture do not disconcert them. Once seated, they calmly order their usual: a quarter-liter of wine, a beer, a chinotto, or a fizzy lemon. So that, in the end, it's just as if we had stopped at Todi or at Narni. Or even as if, having chosen the Flaminia rather than the Tiberina, we'd found ourselves at Nocera Umbria, guests of that inn with the stables which perhaps dated back to the era of Leopardi, to which less than a year before I'd sworn eternal loyalty.

Fanned by the light breeze, and by now unconcerned about having to cross that inauspicious bridge over the Tiber at two or three in the morning, we stay on there till after eleven.

At the end of the news, I touch Val's hand.

"Should we go, then?" I propose, for once gently, fraternally.

"Yes, why not?" she immediately consents with a kindly smile.

And already, ahead of me, she's on her way to the car.

2.

I REACHED Naples toward evening. High in the air, the silver forms of the captive balloons, positioned in a semicircle to defend the port, caught the last light of day. In the alleys bustling with a happy crowd in shirtsleeves, the barbers had hoisted improbable signs in English saying "Barber Shop."

Although I had been to Naples twice before, the first visit in 1937 to compete in the *Littoriali della Cultura*, and the second the following year for the sports *Littoriali*, when the American military jeep I'd been aboard dropped me off in the Maschio Angioino neighborhood, I almost immediately realized that finding the house of C, the Finance Undersecretary, would be far from easy. After asking directions quite a few times and much slogging back and forth, I found myself around nine o'clock with my suitcase on my shoulder climbing up to the heights, which on one side overlooked Piazza dei Martiri on a steep little street zigzagging between terraces that had been turned into vegetable gardens. Every now and then I stopped: to catch my breath and to gaze at the Municipal Gardens and the Chiaia shoreline, by this hour thickly strewn with lights. I could clearly recognize both of these landmarks, but wondered if I had ever been up here before. I was almost sure I hadn't.

C's house was at the top of the hill: where, with the vegetable gardens in abeyance, the area was more densely built up. It was a small, isolated, cream colored building, on two floors, with a reserved air to it. Of light colored wood, and furnished with a pair of well polished brass handles, the front door had a no less distinctive appearance.

I pressed a small buzzer, the only one. After a few moments the door was opened by a tall, dark-haired woman, of the palest complexion, and very buxom.

She let me in and closed the door.

"How can I help you?"

I explained who I was and where I'd come from. In the meantime, while staring straight at me, she lifted a hand to adjust her hair, and in doing so disclosed a phenomenally hairy armpit.

"His Excellency hasn't come back yet"—she declared at last. Soon after lunch they had come to take him to Salerno, where that very afternoon there was to be a council meeting.

"And what time will he be back?"

She shrugged her substantial shoulders, and gave the ghost of a grimace.

"Depends. Sometimes they stay out till two, or three . . . "

She grinned.

"Till after midnight, there's little doubt," she added, with a wink.

"May I wait?"

"As you like," the woman replied.

She turned her back on me, leaving me there, in the anteroom.

I sat on a bench placed along the wall beside the entrance. The room was cool. A single, tiny, pinkish lamp which hung from the faraway height of a huge concave ceiling with vaulted panels was the only source of light. For my face and eyes, inflamed by the sun and wind and dust, I could have asked for nothing more soothing.

The woman dawdled in the adjoining room, and didn't cease her humming for a moment. I heard her subdued voice, a little hoarse; heard her cloth slippers interminably slapping the floor which I guessed to be of tile; I heard—and it seemed to be coming from the remote depths of the house—a confused din of laughter, exclamations, glasses and crockery banged down with some force.

Suddenly, after a brief pause of absolute silence, the door facing me was thrown wide open.

A man in shirtsleeves appeared.

"You're here, and without saying a word!" he exclaimed from the threshold.

He marched right up to me with his hand stretched out.

"Do come through, for heaven's sake!" he continued in the same loud voice. "Have you had supper? Come on, get up, I'll introduce you to my friends!"

He shook my hand vigorously.

"I'm P," he concluded, giving a wearied smile.

So it really was him, Giulio P, the renowned trade union organizer from Livorno who was so often spoken of in Rome, in the papers and in the Party: about his five years in prison, four in internal exile and the seven spent in France alongside Carlo Rosselli! As we walked down a long corridor in semidarkness, he in front and I behind, I gazed at him with sadness. Poor creature—I said to myself. Stooped, wearing Friulian black velvet sandals, trousers held up with braces, his shirtsleeves rolled up above his pale, angular elbows, what was wrong with him? Was he ailing perhaps, or just growing old? A moment before, in the anteroom, he had smiled at me. Parting his bloodless lips, he bared a double file of long, yellowish teeth, their gums wrecked by pyorrhoea . . .

The dining room was so exaggeratedly lit up that for a second I was dazzled. Soon enough, I began to discern six or seven persons seated around a big oval table: all men, all of them in shirtsleeves like P, but in contrast to him, with red, shining faces, glowing from the food, the wine and the joy of life. There wasn't one of them who didn't smile warmly at me. Behind, leaning on the broom handle, so tall she almost loomed over them, the beautiful maid, housekeeper, or whatever else she was, lingered at the threshold of the kitchen. She too looked at me. But with a serious, perhaps even hostile, expression.

"Have you eaten?"

I hadn't had dinner. And yet, I'm unsure why, I said I had.

"You're not just being polite, are you?"

I shook my head.

"Well, tell us about Rome."

On the table, some opened, some not, there were various tins of preserved food: American tins, naturally. I'd never seen any before. Fascinated I read their labels: Meat & Vegetables; Pork.

I took my pipe out of my pocket.

"Put it away and try some of mine," said one of them.

A hand stretched forth proffering something green, flat and shiny. What a wonder! I took the packet, and brought the opening up to my nose, and half closed my eyes.

———

In Rome, at the Party headquarters, they entertained a great many illusions about C's house. Although it had been requisitioned by the Allies, and so ought to have been one of the finest houses in Naples, it was by no means the kind of spacious military hotel they imagined! At a certain point, when a tally of the rooms was made, it soon became clear that there would be no place for me. I had to find somewhere else. And it was C in person, the very evening of my arrival, who found me a place not far from there, in Via Carlo Poerio, as the guest of his old comrade and sharer in both the political struggle and the internal exile, who was currently employed by the CIA.

Although, even there, space was all too evidently lacking. Without doubt, it was a big, even gigantic, baroque building whose facade, blackened and covered with moss, loomed over Via Poerio like an age-old Apennine rock about to crumble in a landslide. But the flat, or rather the typical straitened quarters occupied by C's friend on the piano nobile? Leaving aside the little bathroom, the kitchen that barely had space to turn round in, and a tiny entrance hall where I slept on a camp bed, it essentially consisted of only two rooms: a bedroom with a double bed and a straitened breakfast room. So fairly cramped to have to share, in whatever circumstances.

As for my host, I remember he was called Pietro. Pietro M. From Piedmont, perhaps Novara, and a former captain in the Carabinieri, he too had emigrated to France at the time of Matteotti's assassination, and from there, after the Maginot Line had been breached, he fled to the U.S. He seemed to be entirely obsessed with rations, his own private and personal rations, kept carefully locked away in the bedroom wardrobe with tall mirrors, in the breakfast room sideboard and in the kitchen cupboard.

Despotic and grumbling, he was like an *arzdóra** from the Ferrara countryside, whom he strongly resembled not only because of the mass of keys hung from his belt, but also because of the bulging contours of his belly and backside. Given which, his sudden athletic changes of mood were surprising, to say the least. On particular days when he was in a foul

———

* See footnote on p. 41.

mood he would brutally turn on me, calling me a scrounger, a "mouse in the cheese," making it clear to me that if I didn't find a way to pay him back, sooner or later he'd be forced to chuck me out—it wasn't money he was after, not at all: but as an Italian newspaper in New York was pestering him for a local-color piece on Naples, and he hadn't the time to do it, I could easily write it for him myself . . . Another day, though, he would bestow on me the most intimate confidences. Had I noticed the maid in C's house?— he wasn't beyond asking me, in low tones, with a wink. Well, yes I had. Cuckolding the good P, who for some time, though in vain, had been buzzing round her, it was he who was making love to her: and also because of that, I should try to understand, having me always about the house was hardly convenient! Little by little, however, aided by an occasional good mood, he told me many things about himself. He told me he was a member of the Masonic Lodge, that he was there in Naples employed by the CIA, it's true, but also and above all to attempt to restore to some kind of order the local Lodge which, once a flourishing concern, had gone into deep decline during the years of Fascism. He also told me he was a very important figure in the Freemasons, even more important than a general inspector of the thirty-third degree . . .

I had no reason to suppose he was exaggerating. While we were having lunch or dinner, the doorbell would continually ring. It was always he who, with a conspiratorial air, would go to open it. And while I remained in my seat and continued eating, I could hear him speaking in low tones in the small entrance hall. With whom? It was clear with whom. But had I dared to ask him when he reappeared, he would not have put up with it.

Once when M had to leave the table to rush to the bathroom (his sudden agility at such times was a wonder to behold), an unusually vigorous ringing induced me to sally forth in his place.

A tall, distinguished-looking, middle-aged man, with the authoritative presence of some high official, walked in.

"Where are you?" he asked loudly.

Without waiting for a reply, he went through to the breakfast room. But as soon as he set foot there, I saw him suddenly come to a halt.

The sight of a table laden with food and, even more than this, the sideboard fully open, had suddenly precipitated him into a state of evident confusion. He approached the sideboard, and resting one knee on the ground, leaned over, almost bent double, and knelt there, staring: with the same manner, I thought, as a literary enthusiast who suddenly finds himself in front of a shelf brimming with rare editions.

"Stew; Salmon; Corned Beef; Corn." He whispered the English names with a flawless pronunciation.

Suddenly, with his hand still adjusting his belt, M burst into the breakfast room.

The other hurriedly got to his feet.

"Greetings," he said, embarrassed.

The former policeman didn't reply. Aware that the doors of the sideboard were wide open, he threw me a sideways, furious look. He grasped his companion by the arm, and without further courtesies, dragged him almost bodily to the small entrance hall.

For a good five minutes, they stayed out there, muttering in an agitated manner. Finally the door to the stairs was slammed shut.

"How many times must I tell you," shouted Pietro M, returning to the breakfast room, "not to let anyone in? If they ring, let them ring."

I was putting on fat at a fair rate. The winter of 1943 to 1944, spent in Rome under German occupation, had reduced me to skin and bones. In the evening, before going to sleep, I dwelled on the coffee with milk, the butter, the orange marmalade that in the morning would be set before me. I'd consume them a thousand times beforehand with the help of my imagination.

I constructed that local-color piece on Naples for M. I sent various articles to the paper, entrusting them to a Communist Party car which ferried back and forth between Rome and Naples, and also wrote to Val every day. But most of my time I spent wandering about and, all considered, merely loafing.

Each morning I would take the Cumana train, as far as Lucrino. The train would stop right in front of a small seaside bathing establishment, half-wrecked by shelling and machine-gun fire.

On the beach, with my back leaned against a bathing hut, I would wait for B, an old university friend whom I'd been surprised to meet in C's house a few days after my arrival. Having returned from Russia, where, naturally, he had fought for the Axis powers, he'd taken lodgings in that area in a small villa requisitioned by the American counterespionage unit which had established a paratrooper training camp beside Lake Avernus.

Between me and B there were many things in common: university, as I've already mentioned, then the Naples Littoriali, and finally, now, we both belonged to the same Party. And yet, who knows why, if we talked it was always about something else. For my part, about general ideas: liberalism, Socialism, Communism and so forth. He, of his parachute jumps, to which he submitted, he confessed to me, only by having to overcome each and every time the protest of his whole being. He suffered from vertigo. Throwing himself out of an aeroplane was for him the worst self-inflicted punishment imaginable.

Seeing me approach, he would raise an arm.

"How do!" he'd greet me.

And then, exaggerating his broad Emilian accent:

"Today I've made another jump."

But most times, finding him asleep (fat, suntanned, his armpits reeking, and snoring loudly), I'd sit beside him on the sand, hugging my knees. Not a breath of wind would come from the bay. Heavy with diesel disgorged from a dozen landing craft stationary a hundred meters or so from the shore, the sea lifted in slow, torpid wavelets without a sound.

When my friend woke up, he always behaved in exactly the same way.

He would lift his eyelids effortfully.

"Wait a moment," he'd say, looking at me with his black, opaque, almost feverish eyes. "Have you eaten yet? *Primum edere, postea philosophari.*"

"Of course I've eaten."

He wouldn't listen. He would raise himself with a groan, then disappear inside the bathing hut, from which he'd emerge holding a rucksack brimming with all of God's blessings: a thermos of coffee and milk, meat of every kind in bags, whole roast chickens, jams and a variety of cheeses, fruit in syrup, beer in bottles and cans.

Hard to resist.

"D'you want a smoke?" B would ask a few moments later, while, obdurately continuing to gorge myself, I tried to hold back a swelling nausea.

He would be taking out from a small pocket in his bathing costume a pack of Camels.

3.

I WAS phoned by the young friend with red shoes and a ponytail, the editor of an evening newspaper. She had something new for me today: she wanted me to look over a score or so of news photographs (she'd have them sent over straight away—she said—by dispatch rider) and to tell her "within a day" which of them interested me most and why. My response would help her in the "important" enquiry that she was conducting among "writers."

"Go on, be nice," she begged on the other end of the line, flourishing the full grace of her Tuscan accent.

Not half an hour had passed before the motorcyclist was already at the door: a tall, chubby youngster in a leather jacket, a leather helmet, big gloves, goggles, and cheeks flushed with the first chill of autumn.

To varying degrees, all of the photos had something to do with crime reportage. There was the funeral of a prostitute who had been stabbed by her pimp, who then committed suicide. There was the wife of a pharmaceutical industrialist, gagged by the power of attorney exercised by the latter. Seated at the kitchen table, there was the seraphic embezzler of millions from the Catholic Church, caught in the act of raising his fat, babyish lips toward a forkful of spaghetti that a hand outside the picture was holding suspended at the level of his forehead. There was the young, muscular English actor, more renowned for his drinking sprees than for his cinematic merits, who, under the eyes of his most beautiful wife watching the scene from inside a car parked at night in Via Veneto, was vainly milling his fists in the direction of a gaggle of paparazzi in flight . . . I glanced through the entire gallery, then, at the moment of choice, came to a halt. So I have to choose. But how? Best to dismiss the dispatch rider (as I immediately did), and look at the photos one by one.

One, two, three, four. The snapshot on which I stopped, the fifth of the series, portrayed a certain Signor T, I believe it was in a room in the police station, defending himself against the accusation of boasting in public of having been awarded the Gold Medal for Valour. And I wondered how from the start an image such as this could have failed to captivate me. How could I not have immediately sympathized with a figure who, first of all, was called T, Riccardo T (the surname a truncated, somewhat risible bisyllable) who, secondly, had tried to pass himself off as a Gold Medal recipient, and who, thirdly, was dressed as he was, in a wretched striped suit, all shiny and torn, and who, finally, although the top of his skull was adorned with a plume of crow-black hair, was irremediably an old man, more than seventy if he was a day?

I looked more attentively, screwing up my eyes, as though I had before me not a real individual, but a fantasy figure. The operation I was gearing myself up for, to shuffle the true with the false or—same thing—with the imaginary, presented itself to me this time as especially arbitrary and irreverent. But what did it matter? As well as being intelligent (I deduced that from the sharp little pinhead eyes which glinted cannily behind his glasses), Signor Riccardo T was doubtless a kind and likeable person: in any case more so than many another model taken from life, which I'd necessarily had to resort to, ever since I'd begun writing short stories, novellas and novels. If he should happen to read these lines inspired by and dedicated to him, I'm convinced he will be understanding about them.

So then, we're in some nondescript office in the police station. The room is sharply divided into two parts: one lit, the other in shadow. Of those present, only Signor T, seated in front of the inspector's desk, is in the lighted part. The inspector, and the three detectives assisting the interrogation (one of these, acting as photographer, every now and then shooting with a flash) are all standing in the shadowy part, barely distinguishable shapes. They too could be anyone: southerners, of whom the police force has many. They have, however, a good-natured, courteous air, as if, beneath it all, they are having fun.

There's little to do in the police station. They're mainly just passing the time. From behind his desk, not unsympathetically, the inspector observes

Signor T. He understands. Not only is the culprit old and poor as a church mouse, he's also undernourished.

He smiles.

"Well," he begins. "And how's your health? Are you managing to survive?"

Signor T has a reply at the ready. He says that at seventy-eight he really shouldn't grumble. He has no serious infirmities (except for his teeth, by now only three or four of which remain). If anything were to worry him it would be his "economic situation."

The inspector really has got time on his hands.

"Why not try and find some work?" he asks.

"If only there were some!"—Riccardo T replies with animation. For years he's been looking. Yet, let's be clear, heavy labor is not his forte, never has been. To be a laborer or a porter requires muscles, good lungs and so on, and he, in that respect, sadly . . . besides it's worth saying that the Ts were once a "well off family" with a spacious flat on Via dell'Arancio. To sum up: he is keen, very keen, to work, but only under certain conditions. Oh to find a nice quiet little job, a bit of office drudgery, where you can sit at a desk!

"Quite right," said the inspector, with a humorous look.

Given his own work, it's not as though he's excessively sensitive. Despite that, at this point he feels embarrassed. He takes out a packet of cigarettes and offers one to Signor T, taking another for himself. The conversation has taken a strange turn—he thinks as he lights his own and the other's cigarette—strange and unwelcome. Whatever, he needs it to end. He needs to cut it short, to come to the point.

"Believe me, Inspector Sir, all we're dealing with here is a joke . . . " T starts in a low tone.

In the meantime he gives a wink, as if before judging him they should take proper account of his tortoiseshell spectacles, of the best make, of his decent enough tie, of his almost freshly laundered shirt, of his face shaven this very morning, of the biro peeking out of his jacket pocket, which attests, should there be any such need, that he's done some studying, that he knows how to write, and even of the little fingernail on his right hand, allowed to grow long, not of course from neglect, God forbid, but for ele-

gance and distinction. It's true—he told himself with a sigh—the iron-
ing of his dark suit, apparent even to himself, left quite a lot to be desired,
especially the trousers. But on the other hand, what can you do about that?
When one lives alone, without a woman in the house, whether wife or
daughter or domestic help, and when—he grins—there's really no sort of
house at all, how is one to manage? That leaves the shoes, admittedly, shoes
which unfortunately being gym shoes and therefore white, clash a bit with
the suit. And yet, when the rest, all the rest, of the outfit has a more than
dignified air, what do the shoes matter?

He winks again. He clenches his shapeless right hand, and shrugs his
scrawny shoulders.

"You must believe me, Inspector Sir," he repeats himself. "It was really
only a joke. I boasted that I had the Gold Medal just to impress them.
They'd made fun of me because of the shoes, and so I . . . But I wasn't being
serious . . . I had no desire at all to . . . "

He doesn't go on: it would obviously be imprudent.

Yet, if instead of a member of the police force, he'd had an entirely different kind of person in front of him (someone who's a writer, for example),
there's no way that he'd have stopped himself there.

One can easily, he'd say—and there'd be nothing for me to do but nod,
and encourage him with a series of minimal gestures to get it all off his
chest—one can easily reach seventy-eight years of age and, in all that time,
not have managed to come by the most modest of diplomas. One can easily
be reduced, for smokes, to scraping up fag-ends; for food, to frequenting
certain friars always willing to serve some soup; for sleep, to passing the
nights wherever you happen to be, at the station, the post office or in the
smaller parks. But for all that there's no reason why, when you meet your fellow citizens, you should entirely stop being able to hold your head up. Even
someone such as him surely had the right to a minimum of self-respect!

That is what Signor T would say if he should find himself here, in this
room, seated at the other side of my desk.

But would that be all? At this point would he really have spilled the
beans, have exhausted all he had to say?

We are seated opposite each other, and for some moments have been staring into each other's eyes.

"But do me a favor!" Signor T suddenly blurts out, pointing at me with his skeletal, nicotine-stained finger. "If you'd happened to find yourself in my situation, Professor, that evening of the gym shoes, don't you think you too might have thought up some little pretence? And wouldn't you say it, be honest, every time you needed to, including . . . including when you write . . . when"—and here he grins—"when you tell your stories? And then, why should you of all people, author of *The Gold-Rimmed Spectacles* and of *Behind the Door*, treat a poor old fellow like me with such grudging sympathy?"

On that unfortunate evening—he proceeds with a suddenly contrite air—the pretence he'd resorted to was a bit on the strong side, it's true, a fabrication that, well, he might have thought better of . . . also out of respect for the many that . . . Undoubtedly.

Yet there are so many gold medals—he adds, once again with the sneer of a fraternal washed-up, old wreck—so very many of them knocking about, with all the wars, from Libya on, that our Italy has thrown itself into! One medal more or less, let's be fair, what difference does it make?

Down There,
at the End of the Corridor

"Lida Mantovani"* had an extremely toilsome gestation. I drafted it in 1937, as a twenty-one-year old, but in the following years I refashioned it no less than four times: in 1939, in 1948, in 1953 and finally in 1955. This was the work on which I have expended my lengthiest labors. Almost twenty years.

One could fairly ask how on earth I could spend not much less than a quarter of a century in putting together a small work of hardly forty pages. What can I say? Certainly, from the beginning I have always had the greatest difficulty, I wouldn't say in *realizing*, as Cézanne uses the term, but simply in writing. No, unfortunately, the famous "gift" is something I've never possessed. Even now, writing, I stumble over every word, in the middle of every phrase I risk losing my way. I make, cross out, remake, cross out again. Ad infinitum. It's also worth taking account of another circumstance.

A third time, during the winter of 1947 to 1948, I was spurred on to rework "Deborah's Story" (as the short story was initially called: the actual

---

* "Lida Mantovani" is the title of a short story by Bassani that was formerly entitled "Storia di Debora." It was published in reworked form in 1956 in *Cinque storie ferrarese*, which itself would later be published under the title *Dentro le mura* (1973), *Within the Walls*. The other stories mentioned in this essay belong to the same collection: "La passeggiata prima di cena"; "Una lapide in via Mazzini"; "Gli ultimi anni di Clelia Trotti"; and "Una notte del '43."

title was not to be arrived at before another seven years had passed, until, as I've said, 1955), above all by Marguerite Caetani di Bassiano, the part American, part French and part Italian woman, already the animating spirit of the famous *Commerce* in Paris *entre les deux guerres*, who, having also settled in Rome, had then begun to consider founding a new international review.[*] Strange, isn't it? And yet it happened exactly like this. If, in the first issue of *Botteghe Oscure*, which came out in the spring of 1948, I appeared as a story writer (between 1942 and 1947, the years in which I'd moved from Ferrara to Rome, I had almost exclusively composed poems) it was not in obedience to some inescapable creative calling, so much as in response to an expectation, both affectionate and imperious, of a close friend. It's the unalloyed truth. And it's also true that every poem of mine, every story short or long, every novel, even every essay and, further, every passing article I ever wrote was always born, some more, some less, as "Lida Mantovani" was: painfully and with effort, and in large part by chance.

Even "The Stroll before Dinner" cost me an enormous struggle. I began to write it toward the end of 1948, and I worked over it for more than two years.

I had scribbled down a page, the opening one, then came to a halt. I felt I had in hand a strong opening, infinitely rich in promise and suggestion. But where on earth this tortuous little lane I'd taken would lead me I had no idea.

For some months the first page lay there where I'd left it. Fate disposed, though, that one fine day I showed it to Mario Soldati, with whom since the end of 1945 I'd become friends. This time it was he who spurred me on. Why not try taking it further?—he asked me. In his view the story, as an idea, was already well formed. It only needed to be *realized*, to be set on its feet. And to finish it I only had to do one thing: to stop (but not for ever, don't worry, just for a while!) gadding around Rome on my bicycle. Had I perhaps forgotten the advice given by the aged Flaubert to the young

---

[*] Marguerite Caetani (1880–1963) was a prominent literary figure who founded and directed the trilingual review *Commerce* as well as *Botteghe Oscure*.

Maupassant: "Less whoring and less rowing"? Well then, his advice to me was limited to less cycling and more desk. The bicycle might be good for writing poetry. One pedals, thinks of a verse, stops to write it down, and sets off again. But for a writer of stories, novellas, novels—obliged to draw out all that is within, but slowly—the bicycle presented a very serious and damaging risk. According to the phrase often used by Emilio Cecchi, I should: "Stop still for five minutes." The rest would happen by itself . . .

It wasn't at Rome, however, but rather at Naples, where I'd moved in the autumn of 1949 (having been appointed as a teacher at the local naval institute), and where ironically I had no bicycle at my disposal, that I managed to set about the story with the required dedication.

What a struggle, though, what a painful battle! After having spent the morning at school, and then, shut up in my little *pensione* room, having passed the whole afternoon in an attempt to write five or six lines, I would go out in the evening in search of a pizza, and make my way along the sidewalk of Via Chiatamone reeling like a drunkard. Proud of the new commitment I was putting into the work, but deeply disappointed by the results, I wondered what on earth I could expect of the future. Oh well, let's wait and see—I said to myself. In some manner the draft proceeded: I had put together various chapters. But for how long would I have to stumble on in this way, without knowing where I was going to end up? No, no. Even if one day or another it happened that I should finally bring "The Stroll before Dinner" to completion, I would never become a novelist. I would never become a Soldati, a Moravia, a Pratolini—the latter, who then lived in Naples, I saw often enough, and whenever I went to pay him a visit, in the house he occupied just below the Vomero district, he would read me long passages from his unpublished novel—all of them, lucky fellows, capable of amassing hundreds and hundreds of pages. But on the other hand—I would also say to myself, with a heart that suddenly filled again with blind pride and hope—wasn't this the very proof of my real difference? Even if, for some time, I hadn't been inclined to write any poems, wasn't I in the end a poet?

Before I completed "The Stroll" many more months would have to pass: the whole of 1950, part of 1951; and the culmination, as would prove to be the case on not a few other occasions, came upon me suddenly and unexpectedly. One morning, at school, I was giving a lesson. Abruptly, the classroom door half opened. It was the janitor with a telegram. What a joy it was to read! Marguerite Caetani had written it. She said that she liked "The Stroll," and intended to publish it in the next issue of the review.

The composition of "A Memorial Tablet on Via Mazzini" was always arduous, but set beside that of "The Stroll" it was a breeze. The struggle I'd had with "The Stroll" had been important, even decisive. It had helped me understand a great many things. I had understood, for example, that Dr. Elia Corcos, and that poor thing Gemma Brondi, his wife, were not the only characters of significance in the story. A relevant character, and by no means a minor one in the story, was also Ferrara, the city within whose bounds the events of those lives unfolded: this Ferrara, besides, rather than stepping forward to occupy the front of the stage, to show itself boldly, remained in a subordinate position behind, as a backdrop. I had, moreover, understood that a story, in order to achieve any real and poetic significance, undoubtedly had to capture the attention of the reader, but must know how to be at the same time play, pure play, an abstract geometry of volumes and spaces. "The Stroll" told the stories of Elia Corcos, Gemma Brondi, their respective and counterposed clans, Ferrara and so on. Simultaneously, however, it narrated something else: and that was the utterly private and seemingly even futile and gratuitous satisfaction derived from it by me, the writer, in creating a kind of narration which gave a sense, precisely through and by means of its structure, of an exceptionally long cinematic tracking shot. What, in fact, was "The Stroll," considered under the exclusive profile of its form, if not the mobile unravelling of an image, at first confused, barely legible, which then, with extreme slowness, almost with reluctance, was brought into focus? The past is not dead—the very structure of the story asserted—it never dies. Although it moves further away: at every passing moment. To recover the past is thus possible. What's required, however, if one really has the desire to recover it, is to travel down a kind of corridor which grows longer at every instant. Down there at the very end of the corridor—at the sunlit point where its blackened walls converge—is life, vivid and throbbing as it once was when it first took form. Eternal, then? Yes, eternal. And even if it's ever further away, ever more fugitive, it remains all the more open to new possession.

Even in "A Memorial Tablet on Via Mazzini" an absolute protagonist, another *monstre sacré*, stood out in high relief. In place of Elia Corcos, the Jewish Ferrarese doctor, revered for decades, in charge of the health of the whole town, there was Geo Josz, the Jewish Ferrarese boy, the city's sole survivor of the hell of the Nazi extermination camps. But here the city, Ferrara, was decidedly given a role of equal importance; although still a little mythical, not fully sounded out and disclosed, as it had appeared in "The Stroll." At the front of the stage, contending with the protagonist, sharing the footlights with him, there was now also the city itself. As far as the structure of the story went, this time I had considered it opportune to stress the geometry. While writing, I never ceased to picture a couple of spheres of equal size, hung in the air at the same height, and revolving slowly around their respective axes. The two spheres were identical: in volume, in their slow synchronic motions, in everything. Except that one turned in one, the other in a contrary direction. Two universes, close but separate. A harmony between them would never be possible.

"The Last Years of Clelia Trotti" and "A Night in '43" I wrote between 1953 and 1955, all considered, with far less of a struggle.

In terms of the number of characters and the context in which they are gathered together, both stories in some way repeat those in "A Memorial Tablet." On one side, the protagonist (in "The Last Years," Clelia Trotti, the old Socialist teacher who has ended up in a shabby and cruel era; in "A Night" the chemist Barilari, Pino Barilari, he too, like Geo Josz, sole surviving witness to a massacre); and, on the other, as reliable deuteragonist, the usual seething human anthill, the usual hydra with thousands upon thousands of faces of the collective conscience or unconscious. Each story always has its own structure. That of "The Last Years" had nothing to do with the converging lines of "The Stroll," or of the revolving spheres of "A Memorial Tablet." What it had were four rigid vertical elements of an opaque, translucent material, closer to paper or cloth than to stone or metal: extensive and flat, all these four elements were divided but parallel. Even if not exactly reminiscent of the sphere, however, the structure of "A Night" was once again inspired by the figure of the circle. I had imagined many circles: one inside the other. The last and smallest, so tiny as to coincide with its own absolute central point, was the prison cell, the hermit's cell, the tomb, from the window of which, in the depths of a December night, Pino Barilari, the paralysed chemist, had himself seen in a blinding flash "*ce que l'homme a cru voir.*"

Before I gathered them together in the volume entitled *Five Stories of Ferrara*—as I did in 1956—the stories were published one after the other in reviews.

Contrary to all my expectations, "The Last Years of Clelia Trotti" didn't appeal to Marguerite Caetani. She had found it inferior to the preceeding stories—"a bit boring." It's true that in the meantime I had been invited by Roberto Longhi, my art history teacher and lifelong friend, to help edit *Paragone*, a magazine that, in the end, made me feel just as welcome. But it was only the unexpected, slightly mysterious rejection of Marguerite which induced me to seek hospitality elsewhere.

However, no sooner had I finished the draft of "A Night in '43," than I began to feel I had exhausted a seam. By this stage, already, Ferrara was there. Through the act of caressing and exploring every part of her, it seemed to me that I'd succeeded in setting her upright, in gradually making her concrete, actual or, to put it another way, believable. It was some achievement, I thought. But not that big a deal. And in any case, not enough.

The full critical awareness of what I would have to do so that my five Ferrarese stories should find their successor (they'd better find it!—I had so many other things to tell, to say . . .) only arrived a year and a half later, when I began to work on *The Gold-Rimmed Spectacles*. Only then, after having finished writing the third chapter of that tale, which is not a short story, but a novel in its own right, no matter that it's short and Ferrarese, my ideas suddenly became clear: at the point at which I found myself, Ferrara, the little segregated universe I had invented, would no longer be able to reveal to me anything substantially new. If I wanted the place to come back to tell me something else, I would have to include within it also that personage who, having been excluded for many years, had persisted in setting up the theater of his own literary work within the red walls of his home town, that's to say, myself. Who in the end was I?—it was time by now that I began to ask myself precisely what, in the last lines of "A Memorial Tablet," Geo Josz had enquired of himself. A poet, fine—but what else?

Not out of detachment, but rather perhaps the better to defend myself from an excess of emotional involvement, I had practically not figured at all in *Five Stories of Ferrara*. Telling the stories of others with a heart that was almost too fraternal, too conjoined, I had always taken care to keep myself hidden behind the screen of pathos and irony which syntax and rhetoric created. But from then on, I reasoned with myself, how could I continue in this fashion, reduced in essence to a hand which writes? How could I confront anew even the moral difficulty of the kind which I found myself facing at the end of "A Night," when I had had to enter the small room of Pino Barilari, into which no one in the city besides his wife Anna had ever set foot, and had had to enter it only by means of the imagination and at the cost of many painful contortions? No—enough! Even if, following this, nothing would be more likely than that I would continue to play with geometric forms, prevalently spheres, cones, funnels, concentric circles and so on (this was a rule of art, and since I was so determined to express myself I'd better accept it!), from now on, on the stage of my little provincial theater it was myself that I would have to find a place for, one that was the right size and not of secondary importance.

The spotlights, from then on, were also on me, whether writing or not, on all of me. From then on, it was crucial that the author of "Lida Mantovani," of "The Stroll before Dinner," of "A Memorial Tablet on Via Mazzini," of "The Last Years of Clelia Trotti," of "A Night in '43," and even of the first three chapters of *The Gold-Rimmed Spectacles*, should also try to surface from his lair, if only he could describe himself, could dare finally to call himself "I."

ABOUT THE AUTHOR

G IORGIO Bassani was born in Bologna in 1916 to a Jewish family who returned to their home town Ferrara soon after the end of the First World War. He attended school, the renowned *liceo* Ariosto, in Ferrara and the Faculty of Arts at the University of Bologna where, despite the Racial Laws, he graduated in 1939. Before and after graduating he became involved in anti-Fascist activities which resulted in his imprisonment in 1943. Released after the fall of Mussolini, he married and moved to Florence, with his wife, Valeria, where they lived under assumed names. At this time, during the Salò Republic, a number of his relatives were transported to the Buchenwald death camps. Bassani settled in Rome, where his daughter, Paola, was born in 1945 and his son, Enrico, in 1949. Bassani worked as a teacher, a translator of Hemingway and Voltaire among others, and as a scriptwriter on films by Michelangelo Antonioni and Mario Soldati. He became editor of the international literary magazine *Botteghe Oscure* and later a fiction editor at Feltrinelli, where he was responsible for "discovering" and publishing Giuseppe di Lampedusa's *The Leopard* (1956). Despite this unrivalled success, he was to leave the Feltrinelli in a dispute when in 1963 he refused to publish Alberto Arbasino's novel *Fratelli d'Italia*. Concerned throughout his life with civic and political as well as cultural issues, he was vice president of RAI television network and in 1965 became president of Italia Nostra, a national heritage organization.

An extraordinarily versatile author, Bassani won numerous awards as poet, novelist, short-story writer, and essayist, including the Strega, Campiello, Bagutta, and Nelly Sachs prizes. In 1974 his fiction was collected together and published under the title *Il romanzo di Ferrara* and underwent a final revision in 1980. The four main collections of his poems have been widely acclaimed and were gathered together in 1982 as *In rima e senza*. *The Garden of the Finzi-Continis* won the Viareggio Prize and has sold more than a million copies in Italy alone. Three films have been made of his work, most notably Vittorio de Sica's adaptation of the present novel in 1970. In his last years, Bassani suffered from Alzheimer's and died in 2000. He is buried in the Jewish cemetery in Ferrara.